THE PENGUIN CLASSICS

FOUNDER EDITOR (1944–64): E. V. RIEU

FYODOR MIKHAIL DOSTOYEVSKY was born in Moscow in 1821, the second of a physician's seven children. His mother died in 1837 and his father was murdered a year later. When he left his private boarding school in Moscow he studied from 1838 to 1843 at the Military Engineering College in St Petersburg, graduating with officer's rank. His first story to be published, 'Poor Folk' (1846), had a great success. In 1849 he was arrested and sentenced to death for participating in the 'Petrashevsky circle'; he was reprieved at the last moment but sentenced to penal servitude, and until 1854 he lived in a convict prison at Omsk, Siberia. Out of this experience he wrote *Memoirs from the House of the Dead* (1861). In 1861 he began the review *Vremya* with his brother; in 1862 and 1863 he went abroad where he strengthened his anti-European outlook, met Mlle Suslova who was the model for many of his heroines, and gave way to his passion for gambling. In the following years he fell deeply into debt, but from 1867, when he married Anna Grigoryevna Snitkina, his second wife helped to rescue him from his financial morass. They lived abroad for four years, then in 1873 he was invited to edit *Grazhdanin*, to which he contributed his *Author's Diary*. From 1876 the latter was issued separately and had a great circulation. In 1880 he delivered his famous address at the unveiling of Pushkin's memorial in Moscow; he died six months later in 1881. Most of his important works were written after 1864: *Notes from the Underground* (1864), *Crime and Punishment* (1865–66), *The Gambler* (1866), *The Idiot* (1869), *The Devils* (1871), and *The Brothers Karamazov* (1880).

DAVID MAGARSHACK was born in Riga, Russia, and educated at a Russian secondary school. He came to England in 1920 and was naturalized in 1931. After graduating in English literature and language at University College, London, he worked in Fleet Street and published a number of novels. For the Penguin Classics he translated Dostoyevsky's *Crime and Punishment*, *The Idiot*, *The Devils*, and *The Brothers Karamazov*; *Dead Souls* by Gogol; *Oblomov* by Goncharov; and *Lady with Lapdog and Other Tales* by Chekhov. He also wrote biographies of Chekhov, Dostoyevsky, Gogol, Pushkin, Turgenev and Stanislavsky; and he is the author of *Chekhov the Dramatist*, a critical study of Chekhov's plays, and a study of Stanislavsky's system of acting. His last books to be published before his death were *The Real Chekhov* and a translation of Chekhov's *Four Plays*.

THE DEVILS

⟨THE POSSESSED⟩

◆

FYODOR
DOSTOYEVSKY

◆

TRANSLATED
WITH AN INTRODUCTION BY
DAVID MAGARSHACK

◆

PENGUIN BOOKS

Penguin Books Ltd, Harmondsworth, Middlesex, England
Penguin Books, 625 Madison Avenue, New York, New York 10022, U.S.A.
Penguin Books Australia Ltd, Ringwood, Victoria, Australia
Penguin Books Canada Ltd, 2801 John Street, Markham, Ontario, Canada L3R 1B4
Penguin Books (N.Z.) Ltd, 182–190 Wairau Road, Auckland 10, New Zealand

—

This translation first published 1953
Reprinted 1957, 1960, 1962, 1965, 1967, 1968, 1969
Reprinted with appendix ('Stavrogin's Confession') 1971
Reprinted 1972, 1973, 1975, 1976, 1977, 1978, 1979

—

—

Made and printed in Great Britain
by Richard Clay (The Chaucer Press) Ltd,
Bungay, Suffolk
Set in Monotype Bembo

List of Contents

DOSTOYEVSKY *began* The Devils, *or* The Possessed, *as the most con-troversial of his novels is often called in English, towards the end of 1869. He had been living abroad with his second wife Anna, the eighteen-year-old girl he had married at the age of forty-five in February 1867, for about two years, during which time he had written* The Idiot *and* The Eternal Husband. *He had left Russia in a hurry on 14 April 1867, because his creditors had threatened to put him in jail for defaulting on the payments of his debts. He would not have minded going to jail, he wrote to one of his correspondents, as it would have provided him with enough material for another* House of the Dead *and brought him in between 4,000 and 5,000 roubles, but he had a young wife to think of, and he could not expose her to such humiliation and worry. It was more probable that he preferred to try his luck at the roulette tables as an easier way of restoring his fortune. To his great surprise, how-ever, Anna stubbornly refused to pander to his passion for gambling. This he found more than annoying and, besides, so different from his ex-perience with Polina Suslova, the young girl student who had accom-panied him to Germany in July 1865. He wrote to Suslova on 23 April, soon after his arrival in Dresden with Anna, addressing her as his 'eternal friend' and discussing his literary plans with her, which he could not very well do with his young and rather simple wife. Indeed, his life with Anna in Dresden soon began to pall on him, and on 4 May he left her there and went off to Homburg, where he spent twelve days at the casino, lost all his money, pawned his watch, and had to get his fares for the return journey from Anna. He returned to Dresden in a state of moral collapse, and on 22 June left with Anna for Baden-Baden, where he began gambling again and had to go through the humiliation of crawling on his knees before his young wife before she would let him have a few gold sovereigns. He lost heavily again, went to see Turgenev, whom he still owed fifty thalers he had bor-rowed after his losses at the roulette tables in Wiesbaden two years before, quarrelled with the famous novelist, and then went to live in Geneva, where* there was no casino and where he began writing The Idiot (*in September 1867*). There his first child, his daughter Sophia, was born in February 1868, and died three months later. For almost a year – from September 1868 to August 1869 – he lived in Italy, mostly in Florence, and then returned to Dresden, where his second daughter, Lyubov, was born on 14 September.

It was in Florence that he first thought of a great novel in which he would challenge the progressive movements in Russia and proclaim his faith in the regeneration of his native land (and afterwards the whole of the world) through a return to the tenets of Christianity as held by the Greek Orthodox Church. 'I am thinking of writing a huge novel, to be called The Atheist,' he wrote from Florence to his friend the poet Maykov on 23 December 1868, 'but before I sit down to write it I shall have to read almost a whole library of atheists, catholics, and Greek Orthodox theologians. ... I have the chief character. A Russian of our set, and middle-aged, not very educated, but not uneducated, either, a man of a quite good social position, who suddenly, at his age, loses faith in God. He has spent all his life in the Civil Service, never leaving the beaten track, and without gaining any distinction, though he was already forty-five years old. ... His loss of faith in God makes a tremendous impression on him. ... He pokes his nose among the younger generation, the atheists, the pan-Slavs, the Russian fanatical sects, hermits, and priests; falls, incidentally, under the influence of a Jesuit propagandist, a Pole, and descends to the very depths by joining the sect of the flagellants – and at last comes to Christ and the Russian soil – the Russian Christ and the Russian God. (For goodness sake, don't breathe a word about it to anyone: I shall write this last novel of mine and I shall say everything to the last word, even if it is the last thing I do.)'

The final sentence about his saying everything to the last word that he thought about the destiny of Russia and the world occurs twice in his letters to Maykov and Strakhov, his journalist friend, in connexion with the first outline of The Devils, which, beginning with February 1870, was being serialized in the Moscow conservative monthly The Russian Messenger. 'I am working for The Russian Messenger now,' he wrote to Maykov from Dresden on 6 April 1870, 'because I owe them money and have put myself in an ambiguous position there. ... What I am writing now is a tendentious thing. I feel like saying everything as passionately as possible. (Let the nihilists and the Westerners scream that I am a reactionary!) To hell with them. I shall say everything to the last word.' And a day earlier he wrote to Strakhov: 'I am relying a great deal on what I am writing for The Russian

Messenger now, but from the tendentious rather than the artistic point of view. I am anxious to express certain ideas, even if it ruins my novel as a work of art, for I am entirely carried away by the things that have accumulated in my heart and mind. Let it turn out to be only a pamphlet, but I shall say everything to the last word.'

From the notes Dostoyevsky had jotted down in January 1870, it would appear that his first idea was to incorporate the main theme of his proposed novel, The Atheist, in The Devils, whose chief character, however, was not to be an ordinary civil servant but a wealthy prince, 'a most dissipated man and a supercilious aristocrat', whose life was 'storm and disorder', but who in the end 'comes to Christ'. He was to be 'a man with an idea', which absorbs him completely, though not so much intellectually as 'by becoming embodied in him and merging with his own nature, always accompanied by suffering and unrest, and having fused with his nature, it demands to be instantly put into action'. The prince is greatly influenced by a well-known Russian religious writer, who greatly influenced Dostoyevsky himself and who was to have figured in the novel. This writer's main idea Dostoyevsky defined as 'humility and self-possession, and that God and the Kingdom of Heaven are in us, and freedom, too'. But two things made Dostoyevsky give up his original idea of Nicholas Stavrogin, the main character of The Devils, who in the final draft of the novel no longer appears as a prince, though he is referred to as such in one chapter.

To begin with, his desperate financial position ('I am in a simply frightful position now,' he wrote to Maykov in his letter of 6 April, 'a real Mr Micawber. I haven't got a penny, and yet I must somehow carry on till the autumn') forced him to postpone the writing of his great novel and try to get some money by writing a merely 'tendentious' one. 'What I am writing for The Russian Messenger now,' he told Maykov in the same letter, 'I shall finish in about three months, and then, after a month's holiday, I shall sit down to my other novel. It is the same idea I wrote to you about before. It will be my last novel.' And he went on to outline the plot of what was eight years later to become known as The Brothers Karamazov.

While engaged in writing The Devils, Dostoyevsky returned again and again in his correspondence to the theme of The Brothers Karamazov, which at one stage he called The Life of a Great Sinner; and he made it quite clear that his great idea was to be left to this last novel. What was this 'great idea'? Roughly, it was the idea of the reconciliation of good and evil according to his own peculiar political and religious recipe of a State based on a docile

*peasant population and run by an autocratic Tsar, who was no longer sup-
ported by a landed aristocracy (which Dostoyevsky abominated), but who
relied entirely on the Greek Orthodox Church. Dostoyevsky, like Gogol before him, found the solution of the problem of the reconciliation of good and
evil, based on so fantastically unrealistic an idea, beyond his strength. In The
Devils, however, he was no longer concerned with so grand a design. All he
wanted to do was to settle his own personal accounts with the so-called
Westerners, that is, the Russian liberals who dreamt of converting Russia
into a constitutional monarchy on the model of a Western European country,
and the more revolutionary elements in Russia, who, like himself, refused to
have anything to do with the aristocracy or the new class of capitalists, and,
unlike himself, with the Tsar or the Church. It was here that quite an unexpected event came to his help. For it was just at this time that, following the
murder of a young student in Moscow, a revolutionary conspiracy was
discovered, which seemed to fit in with the ideas Dostoyevsky wished to
express in The Devils. The conspiracy was organized by a certain Sergey
Nechayev, who was at the time a disciple of Michael Bakunin, the author
of The Catechism of a Revolutionary and the founder of the anarchist
movement.*

*Nechayev was a Scripture master in one of the Petersburg elementary
schools (a séminariste, that is, a divinity student, as the contemporary left-
wing propagandists were nicknamed by aristocratic writers like Turgenev,
because most of them did not belong to the aristocracy and some of the more
eminent of them, like the critic Dobrolyubov, came from the priesthood class).
Since the autumn of 1868 he had also been an external student of Petersburg
University, and took a leading part in organizing the student disturbances in
1868 and 1869. In March 1869 he went abroad with a false passport to
Geneva, where he joined Bakunin and the poet Ogaryov, a close friend of
Herzen's, and from there they posted revolutionary leaflets to their friends in
Russia. He returned to Russia in August of the same year as the self-styled
representative of the World Revolutionary Movement at Geneva and organized a 'Society of National Retribution' in Moscow. Dostoyevsky embodied
all the facts relating to the organization of this society (the groups of five, etc.)
in his novel. On 21 November Nechayev (who was only twenty-two at the
time) and four members of the Moscow 'group of five' murdered the fifth
member of the group, a young student of the Moscow Agricultural College
called Ivanov, for allegedly refusing to carry out the instructions of the Geneva
committee. 'Ivanov,' the official act of indictment of Ivanov's murderers stated,*

'was enticed to the grotto in the grounds of the Moscow Agricultural College on the pretext of handing over an illegal printing press. There they at first tried to strangle him, but afterwards Nechayev seized the pistol brought by Nicolayev' (another young accomplice) 'and shot Ivanov in the head, after which Ivanov's body was weighted with stones and thrown into the pond.' Dostoyevsky's description of Shatov's murder follows closely the description of Ivanov's murder. After the murder, Nechayev, like Peter Verkhovensky in the novel, escaped first to Petersburg and then abroad. He went back to Geneva, where he rejoined Bakunin and Ogaryov and assisted them in their abortive attempt to revive Herzen's London journal The Bell. His ruthlessness in carrying out Bakunin's own principle that the end justifies the means appalled even Bakunin, who soon broke with him. Nechayev then went to London, where he began publishing his terrorist journal Village Commune, which was sharply condemned by Engels, the friend and collaborator of Karl Marx. He later returned to Switzerland, where he was arrested by the Swiss police on an extradition order as a criminal and not a political offender and handed over to the Russian police. On 8 January 1873 he was tried for murder by the Moscow District Court and sentenced to twenty years penal servitude. He was not sent to Siberia, however, but incarcerated in the Peter and Paul fortress in Petersburg, where he died one year and ten months after Dostoyevsky, in November 1882.

While Dostoyevsky was writing The Devils, Nechayev was still at large, and Dostoyevsky, who returned to Petersburg in July 1871, no doubt knew all about his revolutionary activities abroad. The sensational trial of the Nechayev followers in Russia (the police had arrested altogether 152 persons, mostly young boys and girls, of whom seventy-nine were put on trial in Petersburg in July 1871, the rest being released for lack of evidence) furnished Dostoyevsky with more material for his novel, such as, for instance, the political leaflet with the drawing of an axe and the poem 'A Noble Character' found among the leaflets confiscated by the police. An interesting fact that has only recently come to light is that Dostoyevsky even found the prototype of Kirilov in a certain Smirnov, one of the accused in the trial of the Nechayev followers. The following statement was taken by the police from Smirnov and subsequently published in the Russian Press (Smirnov had been banished to the town of Vladimir for his part in the student disturbances): 'In Vladimir I began to suffer from fits of depression and to be more and more obsessed with the idea of suicide; even now I doubt whether I shall be able to get rid of it; as I expect to remain in Vladimir till the end of my term of exile, I decided to kill myself in the Spring. This decision is connected with the kind of death I have chosen.'

The discovery of the Nechayev conspiracy, the murder of Ivanov, and the series of sensational developments which finally led to the trial of Nechayev's alleged followers in Petersburg just when Dostoyevsky himself had returned there, forced Dostoyevsky to introduce a great number of vital changes in his novel, although the first part of it had already been published in The Russian Messenger, and he only finished it in November 1871. This slipshod method of writing his 'tendentious' novel has made it into one of the most structurally untidy of Dostoyevsky's great novels. Its two chief characters – Nicholas Stavrogin and Peter Verkhovensky – are only pegs on which Dostoyevsky hung his two most violent dislikes: his dislike of the Russian aristocracy and his dislike of the revolutionaries, whom he lumped together in the person of Verkhovensky-Nechayev. Stavrogin himself remains an obscure and enigmatic figure, the mystery surrounding him being mainly due to Dostoyevsky's decision to leave him hanging in the air, as it were, rather than waste 'the great idea' he had decided to keep for his last novel on him.   The fact that the editor of The Russian Messenger refused to publish a long chapter dealing with Stavrogin's disreputable past must also to a certain extent be held responsible for the obscurity of Stavrogin's characterization. So far as Peter Verkhovensky is concerned, it is only fair to point out that Dostoyevsky himself went out of his way to emphasize the fact that he was not a Socialist, but just a 'rogue'. The other conspirators in the novel, with the exception of Kirilov – the most metaphysical character Dostoyevsky created – are quite terrifyingly alive as people, but only caricatures as 'revolutionaries'. The fact is that Dostoyevsky had only a vague idea of the revolutionary movements in Europe and was too apt to distort the ideas behind them. Indeed, his own violent political views precluded a fair and thorough appreciation of any progressive movement. To him even a mild liberal like Stepan Verkhovensky was 'a devil' who could just be 'saved' on his deathbed by a none-too-sincere recantation of his former opinions. It was only in people like Shatov – that is to say, people, who, like Dostoyevsky himself, had turned their back on their liberal past and wholeheartedly embraced a philosophy of life based on autocracy and the Church – that he saw the gleam of salvation for a tortured world. And the tragedy of Shatov was also Dostoyevsky's tragedy: both believed in Christ and both were tormented by their disbelief in God. Both were fanatical adherents of their own new creed because both were at heart uncertain whether it was the right way to the millennium. Shatov toyed with the idea of denouncing his former associates to the police in the same way as Dostoyevsky himself had actually taken steps to denounce Turgenev, the hated aristocrat and atheist, to 'posterity' long before he lampooned him as Karmazinov in The Devils.

In his letter to Maykov after his meeting with Turgenev in Baden-Baden on 28 June 1867, Dostoyevsky admitted that he never really liked the great novelist, who, he declared exultantly, had written himself out completely. But when he first met Turgenev in November 1845 he nearly 'fell in love with him', as he wrote to his elder brother Michael. No words were too extravagant to describe his admiration for the twenty-five-year-old 'poet, aristocrat, and wealthy man' who was so extraordinarily intelligent and well educated. Turgenev had just returned from Paris 'and', Dostoyevsky wrote, 'from the first moment he became so greatly attached to me that Belinsky explains it by the fact that Turgenev has fallen in love with me. ... I doubt if there is anything nature has not bestowed on him,' Dostoyevsky went on. 'And, last but not least, his character is so straightforward and has been trained in so admirable a school.' Their friendship, it is true, was not unclouded, for Turgenev liked to pull his friend's leg occasionally, and that Dostoyevsky could not stand. There was, however, no violent quarrel between them, and when, almost twenty years later, Dostoyevsky returned from Siberia and embarked with his elder brother on the publication of the political and literary periodical Time, the two resumed their interrupted relationship and seemed to be on the best of terms with one another.

Turgenev had by then become one of the leading novelists in Russia, and it was only natural that Dostoyevsky should be anxious to obtain a story from him for Time. They conducted a long correspondence, and Turgenev was very grateful to Dostoyevsky for being one of the very few men of letters who really appreciated his great novel Fathers and Sons, which raised a veritable storm of vituperation against its author, particularly among the younger progressive writers, who seemed to see in Bazarov, the hero of the novel, a libel on themselves. Dostoyevsky at last got Turgenev to promise to write a story for his journal. Indeed, Turgenev went further: he promised not to publish anything in any other Russian periodical before his story was published in Time, so as to help the circulation of the new journal on which Dostoyevsky's livelihood depended. Meanwhile, however, Time was suppressed by the authorities for an article by Strakhov on the Polish rebellion which they quite wrongly considered to be favourable to the Poles. Turgenev did not withdraw his promise, but waited for Dostoyevsky to start his periodical *Epoch* before contributing to another journal. The promised story was *Phantoms*, one of Turgenev's less successful attempts in the fantastic genre. Turgenev himself was not certain that this story was good enough to be published, but Dostoyevsky made him change his mind by writing a long letter to him in praise of it, though later on he expressed a much less favourable opinion of it in a letter to his brother. Then came Dostoyevsky's journey abroad with Suslova after the death of his brother and the financial failure of *Epoch*. He arrived in Wiesbaden in July 1865, succumbed to the lure of the roulette table, lost all his money, and, in desperation, wrote to Turgenev to ask for a loan of 100 thalers. Turgenev sent him fifty, which he repaid only eleven years later (in March 1876). It is interesting that at the time Dostoyevsky was still on very good terms with Herzen, who was in Switzerland and to whom, indeed, he had turned for help as 'one of his best friends', as he wrote to Suslova after she had left him stranded in the Wiesbaden hotel. But his break with his liberal friends was now imminent. When he left for Germany with his wife two years later, having in the meantime written *Crime and Punishment* and *The Gambler*, he had already become a bitter enemy of every progressive movement in Russia. Turgenev's novel *Smoke*, which had just been published and had roused another storm of abuse against its author, added fuel to the flames of Dostoyevsky's dislike of Turgenev and all he stood for. His dislike turned to hatred when he thought of that 'Baden-Baden bourgeois' (as Turgenev banteringly and rather unwisely described himself in a letter to Dostoyevsky) living a life of ease and comfort, while he was sitting penniless in an hotel with his young wife and had to beg her on his knees for some money to satisfy his passion for gambling. Anna left this account in her diary of the few hectic days in Baden-Baden before the meeting of the two novelists:

'June 25th. On our way home' (*from the Kursaal where Dostoyevsky lost again*) 'Fedya met Goncharov and introduced him to me. Goncharov told me that Turgenev had seen Fedya but had not gone up to him because he knew that players do not like to be disturbed. As Fedya still owes Turgenev fifty thalers, he simply has to pay a call on him, otherwise Turgenev may think that Fedya does not want to visit him because he is afraid that he would ask him for his money. That is why Fedya wants to go and see Turgenev tomorrow.

'June 26th. Fedya took fifteen thalers and went to the gaming-tables. At first he went to see Turgenev, but he was out: he is only at home till twelve o'clock. Fedya lost his fifteen thalers and returned home.

'*June 27th. This morning Fedya wanted to go and see Turgenev, but he got up so late that he put off his visit. We again had twelve gold sovereigns. Fedya took five and went to the roulette tables. When he was gone I felt awfully sad because I knew that he would be quite certain to lose again and would be terribly worried. I burst into tears and sobbed bitterly. My fears were justified: Fedya returned home in a state of terrible despair. He said that he had lost everything and began begging me to give him another two gold sovereigns, pleading that he simply had to win some money back as otherwise he could not carry on. He went down on his knees before me and implored me to give him two more gold sovereigns.*'

It was in this state of despair and complete nervous exhaustion that Dostoyevsky went to see Turgenev on 28 June with the intention of taking it all out of the man whom he hated as the calumniator of his country (practically all the Russian critics interpreted the strictures upon Russia by Potugin, one of the characters of *Smoke*, as an unpardonable libel on their country). The scene that took place at this meeting of two of the greatest Russian writers is almost unbelievable. According to Dostoyevsky, who described it in a long letter to Maykov from Geneva, he found Turgenev having an early lunch.★ Turgenev, Dostoyevsky declared, told him that he was an atheist and that he was terribly incensed by the hostile reception of his last novel. He then abused Russia and the Russians '*horribly*' and said that the Russians '*ought to crawl before the civilized Germans*'. Dostoyevsky remarked '*innocently*' that Turgenev ought to buy himself a telescope, and in reply to Turgenev's bewildered look, explained that he could then direct it towards Russia and see what was going on there, as otherwise he must really find it very hard to know anything about Russia. This transparent hint at Turgenev's preference for living abroad, with the implied suggestion that his last novel gave a distorted picture of Russia and the Russians, made Turgenev, according to Dostoyevsky, '*terribly angry*'. Dostoyevsky then went on to add insult to injury by declaring that all Germans were thieves and scoundrels and that civilization had done nothing for them. Turgenev, who had built himself a beautiful house in Baden-Baden, took this remark as a personal insult and exclaimed that '*he was more a German than a Russian himself*'. Dostoyevsky replied that although he had read *Smoke*, he never expected Turgenev to say a thing like that, and that he was therefore sorry that he had insulted

★ *It can be assumed that Dostoyevsky's description of Karmazinov in the scene with Peter Verkhovensky in Part II, Chapter VI, is a more or less accurate account of his own meeting with Turgenev, including the cutlet and the red wine and Turgenev's '*aristocratic*' habit of running to kiss his visitor, though only offering him his cheek.*

him. Still, again according to Dostoyevsky, they parted very courteously. At ten o'clock next morning, when Dostoyevsky was still in bed at his hotel, a maid brought him Turgenev's visiting-card. As Dostoyevsky had told him that he never got up before eleven, he took it to mean that Turgenev did not want to see him again, but merely returned his visit as 'a gentleman'. They did see each other again, on 13 August, at the railway station, when Dostoyevsky was leaving Baden-Baden for Switzerland, but this time they did not even exchange bows.

After giving this version of his meeting with Turgenev to Maykov, Dostoyevsky went on to deliver himself of the following characteristic remarks: 'Perhaps the spitefulness with which I described Turgenev, as well as the way in which we insulted each other, might make an unpleasant impression on you, my dear Apollon Nikolayevich. But, really, I can't help it: he has insulted me too much by his opinions. Personally, I don't care, though he is not very attractive with those aristocratic airs of his, but it is impossible to listen to such abuse of Russia from a Russian traitor.'

Turgenev was a 'traitor' because his opinions of Russia differed from those of Dostoyevsky. The frantic fury with which Dostoyevsky hated his opponents could not be better illustrated. But that was not all. A few months later Dostoyevsky, whose 'spite' was not satisfied, had the part of his letter to Maykov attacking Turgenev and calling him a traitor to his country copied out and sent to P. Bartenev, editor of Russian Archives, with an anonymous letter in which he explained that he would like it to be published in 1890 for 'posterity'. Turgenev was informed of this by a close friend of his and, quite naturally, jumped to the conclusion that Dostoyevsky wanted to get him into trouble with the Russian authorities as a follower of Nechayev. (Turgenev had already been once summoned to Petersburg to account for his association with Herzen to a special committee of the Senate.) He wrote immediately to Bartenev, declaring that Dostoyevsky's account of their meeting was a sheer travesty of the facts, and that it would never have occurred to him to express his private views to a man he considered 'non compos mentis because of his nervous fits and for other reasons. Dostoyevsky', Turgenev went on, 'spent less than an hour at my house and, after relieving his mind by fierce abuse of the Germans, of myself, and of my last book, went away; I scarcely had any time or any wish to argue with him; I repeat, I treated him like a sick man. Very likely he imagined the arguments he claims to have heard me use in his own disordered mind and wrote – his denunciation of me.'

When in 1871 Turgenev learned of Dostoyevsky's satire of him in The Devils, he wrote to a correspondent: 'I am told Dostoyevsky has "shown me up" – well, let him have his fun. He came to see me about five years ago in Baden, not to pay me back the money he had borrowed from me, but to abuse me for all I was worth – for Smoke, which, according to his ideas, should have been burnt by the public hangman. I listened in silence to his tirade, and what do I find? That I expressed all sorts of subversive opinions to him, which he hastened to retail to Bartenev. That would really have been a libel, if Dostoyevsky had not been a madman – which I do not doubt he is. Perhaps he dreamt it all.'

In Merci, Dostoyevsky's skit on Turgenev's writings in The Devils, two of Turgenev's less well known works are satirized: Phantoms, which, as Turgenev himself pointed out, Dostoyevsky had gone out of his way to praise, and Enough, a semi-philosophic essay on the destiny of man of a highly pessimistic character.

Dostoyevsky's spite and hatred not only of his opponents, but also of all imaginary 'enemies' of Russia, was perhaps entirely in harmony with his religious obsessions. In The Devils he was not able to overcome them, and this is a serious blot on a novel which, in spite of its structural and artistic blemishes, possesses a tremendous vitality, as well as moments of great tenderness. The novel is best regarded as a political melodrama (the stage at the end of it is literally strewn with corpses). It would be absurd to take Dostoyevsky's political views seriously; but it would be no less absurd to overlook his moments of great inspiration, his amazing insight into the human heart, and his shattering criticism of those aspects of man's character which profoundly affect human thought and behaviour.

D. M.

THE DEVILS

And there was there an herd of many swine feeding on the mountain: and they besought him that he would suffer them to enter into them. And he suffered them. Then went the devils out of the man, and entered into the swine: and the herd ran violently down a steep place into the lake, and were choked. When they that fed them saw what was done, they fled, and went and told it in the city and in the country. Then they went out to see what was done; and came to Jesus, and found the man out of whom the devils were departed, sitting at the feet of Jesus, clothed, and in his right mind: and they were afraid. They also which saw it told them by what means he that was possessed of the devils was healed.

Luke viii. 32–36

PART ONE

1

By way of an Introduction:
A few details from the biography of the greatly esteemed
Stepan Trofimovich Verkhovensky

I

BEFORE DESCRIBING THE EXTRAORDINARY EVENTS WHICH took place so recently in our town, hitherto not remarkable for anything in particular, I find it necessary, since I am not a skilled writer, to go back a little and begin with certain biographical details concerning our talented and greatly esteemed Stepan Trofimovich Verkhovensky. I hope these details will serve as an introduction to the social and political chronicle of our town, while the story I have in mind to relate will come later.

Let me say at once that Mr Verkhovensky had always played a rather special and, as it were, civic role amongst us and that he loved that role passionately – so much so that I cannot help feeling that he would not have been able to exist without it. Not that I have any intention of comparing him to an actor on the stage – God forbid – particularly as I have the utmost respect for him. Perhaps it was all just a matter of habit, or, better still, it may have been the result of a constant and generous desire from his earliest years of indulging in the agreeable fancy of being a famous public figure. For instance, he was very fond of his position as a 'marked' man or, as it were, an 'exile'. There is a sort of classical splendour about those two words that fascinated him and, raising him gradually in his own estimation in the course of years, finally led him to imagine himself as standing on a high pedestal, a position that was very gratifying to his vanity. In an English satirical novel of the last century a certain Gulliver, on his return from the country of the Lilliputians, where all the people were only three or four inches tall, had grown so accustomed to look upon himself as a giant that even as he walked in the streets of London he could not help shouting at the carriages and the passers-by to get out of his way and take heed he did not crush them, imagining that they were little and that he was still a giant. But that merely made everybody laugh at him and abuse him, and the uncouth coachmen even belaboured the giant with their whips. But was that fair? What does habit not do to a man! Habit had brought Mr Verkhovensky almost to the same position, though in a more innocent and inoffensive form, if one may put it that way, for he was a most excellent man.

As a matter of fact, I cannot help thinking that towards the end of his life he was completely forgotten by everybody; but, on the other hand, it would be absurd to say that he was entirely unknown. Indeed, there cannot be any doubt at all that for some time he, too, belonged to the famous galaxy of illustrious men of the last generation and that at one time – though only for the briefest moment – his name was uttered by many enthusiastic people of that day almost in the same breath as Chaadayev, Belinsky, Granovsky, and Herzen (who had only just begun his activities abroad). But Mr Verkhovensky's activities came to an end almost as soon as they began as a result of, so to speak, 'a whirlwind of concurrent events'. And what do you think? It turned out afterwards that there had been no 'whirlwind' and even no 'events', at any rate at that particular instant. It was only the other day that I discovered, to my great astonishment, from a highly reliable source, that Mr Verkhovensky had never lived in our province amongst us as an exile, as we were all led to suppose, and that he had never even been placed under police supervision. Which only goes to show how vivid one's imagination can be! For all his life he sincerely believed that he was regarded with apprehension in certain quarters, that every step of his was known and watched, and that each of our three governors, who succeeded one another during the last twenty years, brought with him, as he arrived to rule over our province, a certain preconceived idea about him that had been suggested from above and most certainly on his appointment as governor. Had anyone tried to convince our most fair-minded Mr Verkhovensky by irrefutable evidence that there was nothing he need be afraid of, he would most

certainly have been deeply offended. And yet he was undoubtedly a
highly intelligent and talented man, a man who was, as it were, even
a scholar, though so far as his scholarship was concerned ... well, he
did not really make any important contribution to scholarship, indeed
none at all, I believe. But, then, that happens again and again in Russia
with men of learning.

On his return from abroad he distinguished himself as a university
lecturer towards the very end of the forties. But he had only time to
deliver a few lectures – about the Arabs, I think. He had time, too, to
defend a brilliant thesis on the civic and Hanseatic importance of the
little German town of Hanau during the period between 1413 and
1428 and, simultaneously, on the special and rather obscure reasons
why that promise was never fulfilled. This thesis was a shrewd and
painful blow at the Slavophils of the day and at once made him innumerable and bitter enemies among them. Later on – that was after
he had lost his position at the university – he managed to publish (by
way of revenge and just to show them what a man they had lost) in a
monthly progressive periodical, which translated Dickens and propa-
gated the ideas of George Sand, the beginning of a most profound
work of research into the causes, I believe, of the extraordinary moral
nobility of certain knights of a certain epoch, or something of the
kind. Anyway, it expounded some exceedingly lofty and extraordinarily noble idea. It was rumoured afterwards that he was hastily forbidden to carry on with his research and that the progressive periodical even came to grief for having published the first part. That may
well have been so, for what did not happen in those days? But in this
particular case it is much more likely that nothing of the sort happened and that the author himself was too lazy to finish his essay. He
stopped his lectures on the Arabs because someone (probably one of
his reactionary enemies) had somehow or other intercepted a letter to
someone giving an account of certain 'circumstances' as a result of
which someone else had demanded some kind of explanation from
him. I don't know whether it is true, but it was also asserted that just
then there was discovered in Petersburg a certain vast subversive anti-
government society of thirteen members which very nearly under-
mined the foundations of the State. It was whispered that they intended to translate the works of Fourier himself. It so happened
that at that very moment the authorities in Moscow seized Mr

Verkhovensky's poetic play, written six years before in Berlin when he
was still very young, and circulated in manuscript among two literary
dilettanti and one student. That play is lying now on my table. I received it about a year ago from Mr Verkhovensky, who had only recently copied it out in his own hand. It bears his own autograph and
is bound in magnificent red morocco. I must admit that it is not without poetic merit and even some talent; it is strange, but in those days
(that is, in the thirties) people often wrote that kind of poetic drama.
I am rather at a loss to tell you what it is all about because, to be frank,
I can't make head or tail of it. It is some sort of allegory in lyrical and
dramatic form, recalling the second act of *Faust*. It opens with a chorus
of women, followed by a chorus of men, then a chorus of some spirits,
and, lastly, a chorus of souls which have never lived but which are
very anxious to live. All these choruses sing about something very indefinite, mostly about somebody's curse, but with a suggestion of the
loftiest humour. Then the scene suddenly changes and a sort of 'Festival of Life' begins in which even insects join in the singing, a tortoise
appears with certain sacramental Latin words, and, if I remember
rightly, even some mineral – that is, quite an inanimate object – also
bursts into song about something or other. In fact, they all sing incessantly, and when they speak they seem to abuse each other vaguely,
but again with a suggestion of some higher meaning. At last the scene
changes again into a blasted heath, and a cultured young man wanders
among the rocks, picking and sucking certain herbs; asked by a fairy
why he sucks those herbs, he replies that, feeling a superabundance of
life in himself, he seeks forgetfulness and finds it in the juice of those
herbs, but that his dearest wish is to lose his reason as soon as possible
(a wish that seems to be quite superfluous). Then a young man of indescribable beauty suddenly comes riding in on a black horse, followed by a vast concourse of all the nations. The young man sym-
bolizes Death, and all the nations yearn for it. And, finally, in the last
scene of all, the Tower of Babel appears and some athletes at last
finish building it with a song of new hope, and when they reach the
top, the lord (of Olympus, I suppose) runs off in a comic fashion, and
mankind, realizing the position and seizing his place, at once begin a
new life with a new insight into things. It was that sort of poetic play
that was considered dangerous in those days. Last year I proposed to
Mr Verkhovensky to publish it, since it would be regarded as utterly

innocuous nowadays, but he declined my suggestion with uncon-cealed displeasure. My view of its utter innocuousness did not please him, and I even ascribe to it a certain coldness in our relations which lasted two whole months. And what do you think? All of a sudden, and almost at the same time as I had proposed publishing it here, the play was published *there* – that is to say, abroad in one of the revolu-tionary miscellanies – and entirely without Mr Verkhovensky's know-ledge. At first he was alarmed, rushed off to see the governor, and wrote a most loyal letter in his self-defence to Petersburg, which he read to me twice but never posted, not knowing to whom to address it. In short, he was very agitated for a whole month, but I am con-vinced that deep down in his heart he was greatly flattered. He almost went to bed with the copy of the journal which someone had obtained for him, and in the day-time he kept it hidden under the mattress; he would not even permit his maidservant to make his bed, and though he daily expected the arrival of a telegram, he viewed the world at large with a scornful eye. It was just then that he made friends with me again, which is merely another proof of the extreme kindliness of his gentle and unresentful heart.

2

I don't claim for a moment that he had never suffered for his con-victions, but I am fully convinced now that he could have gone on lecturing on his Arabs as much as he liked if he had only given the necessary explanations. But at that time he allowed himself to be car-ried away by his ambition and was much too hasty in assuming once for all that his career had been completely ruined by the 'whirlwind of events'. And if the whole truth is to be told, the real cause of the change in his career was the highly delicate proposal that had been made before and renewed again by Varvara Petrovna Stavrogin, the wife of a lieutenant-general and a woman of considerable means, to undertake the education and the whole intellectual development of her only son in the capacity of a superior tutor and friend, to say noth-ing of a magnificent salary. The proposal had been made to him for the first time in Berlin, and, as a matter of fact, just at the time of the death of his first wife. His first wife was a frivolous girl from our pro-vince whom he married when he was still a rather thoughtless young man. I believe he had had a great deal of trouble with that young woman – who, by the way, was very attractive – owing to his inability to support her, and for other, partly delicate, reasons, too. She died in Paris, having been separated from him for three years before, leaving him a five-year-old son, 'the fruit of our first, joyous, and still unclouded love', as the grief-stricken Mr Verkhovensky once put it in my presence. The boy had been sent to Russia, where he was brought up by some distant aunts in some remote province. Mr Verkhovensky had declined Mrs Stavrogin's proposal on that occasion and had quickly married again before the year was out a taciturn Berlin girl, and that, too, without any particular necessity for him to do so. But apart from his marriage there were other reasons why he refused to accept the post of a tutor: he was tempted by the resounding fame of a professor who enjoyed great popularity at the time, and he, too, was eager to accept the offer of a university lectureship, for which he had been preparing himself, to try his eagle wings. And now, with singed wings, he naturally remembered the offer which even before had made him wonder whether he had been right in refusing it. The sudden death of his second wife, who did not live a year with him, settled the matter definitely. Let me be quite frank: everything was settled by the passionate sympathy, the priceless and classical friendship of Mrs Stavrogin, if indeed one may use such an expression about friendship. He flung himself into the arms of that friendship, and the whole thing was settled for twenty years. I used the expression 'flung himself into the arms', but don't let anyone jump to any rash and improper conclusions; those arms have to be understood only in the highest possible moral sense. These two remarkable beings were joined for ever in a union that was most refined and delicate.

Mr Verkhovensky also accepted the post of tutor because the property he had inherited from his first wife – a very small one – was close to Skvoreshniki, the magnificent estate of the Stavrogins within a few miles of our town. Besides, it was always possible for him to devote himself to the cause of learning and enrich Russian literature by the most profound researches in the seclusion of his study and without any interference from the enormous amount of university work. These researches did not appear; but, on the other hand, he found it possible to spend the rest of his life, more than twenty years, 'a living monument of reproach', as it were, to his country, in the words of a popular poet:

> A living monument of reproach
> ....
> Thou stoodst before thy country,
> O liberal idealist.

Perhaps the person the poet had in mind had a right to pose like that all his life, if he wanted to, however boring he may have found it. But our Mr Verkhovensky, to tell the truth, was only an imitator compared with such people, and, besides, he got very quickly tired of standing and very often preferred to lie down. But, to do him justice, even in his recumbent position he preserved the living monument of reproach – particularly as that alone was quite sufficient for our provincial public. You ought to have seen him at our club when he sat down to cards. His whole attitude seemed to say: 'Cards! Me sit down to whist with you! Is it in keeping with my position? But who is responsible for that? Who ruined my career and turned it into whist? Oh, perish Russia!' and he would majestically trump with a heart.

And to tell the truth he was very fond of a game of cards, which, especially in later years, led to frequent and unpleasant squabbles with Mrs Stavrogin, particularly as he was always losing. But of that later. I wish merely to point out that he was a man of a tender conscience (sometimes, that is), and that was why he was so often depressed. In the course of his twenty years' friendship with Mrs Stavrogin he regularly three or four times a year fell into what is known among us as a state of 'civic grief' – that is to say, into a fit of the blackest depression – but our highly esteemed Mrs Stavrogin liked that particular expression. Later on he succumbed not only to civic grief, but also to champagne; but the tactful Mrs Stavrogin protected him all his life from his trivial inclinations. And, as a matter of fact, he was in need of a nurse, for sometimes he behaved very queerly: in the midst of the most exalted grief, he would suddenly burst out laughing in a most common manner. There were moments when he would even start talking to himself in a humorous vein. And Mrs Stavrogin feared nothing so much as his humorous vein. She was a woman of the classical type, a female Maecenas, who always acted from the highest possible motives. The influence of this great lady on her poor friend for twenty years was of a most fundamental kind. I ought really to speak of her separately, which I now propose to do.

3

There are strange friendships: two friends are almost ready to kill each other, they go on like that all their lives, and yet they cannot bring themselves to part: the one who has been the first to quarrel and break up their close friendship may fall ill and even die if that should happen. I know for a fact that Mr Verkhovensky has several times jumped up from the sofa and begun beating the wall with his fists after Mrs Stavrogin's departure and even after an exchange of the most intimate confidences with her.

It all happened in good earnest. Indeed, one day he even knocked some plaster off the wall. It may be asked how I could possibly come to know so delicate a detail. Well, what if I witnessed it myself? What if Mr Verkhovensky himself has on more than one occasion sobbed on my shoulder, while describing to me in lurid colours the smallest detail of his talk with Mrs Stavrogin? (The things he told me on such occasions!) But what invariably happened after those sobs was that the very next morning he was ready to crucify himself for his ingratitude; he would send for me in a hurry or run over to see me himself just to tell me that Mrs Stavrogin was 'an angel of honour and delicacy', while he was the exact opposite. He not only came running to me, but very often described it all to her himself in the most eloquent letters and confessed to her over his full signature that no longer ago than the day before, for instance, he had told a stranger that she kept him out of vanity, that she envied him his learning and his talents, that she hated him, and was only afraid to show her hatred openly for fear that he should leave her and so damage her literary reputation; that as a consequence of that he despised himself and had made up his mind to die a violent death; and that he was waiting for her final word which would decide his fate, etc., etc., all in that vein. You can imagine after this to what a pitch of hysteria the nervous outbreaks of this most innocent of all fifty-year-old babes sometimes rose! One day I read one of these letters of his, written after some quarrel between them arising from a trivial matter, though growing venomous as it went on. I was horrified, and begged him not to send it.

'That's impossible,' he replied, almost in a fever. 'It's more honest like that. It's my duty. I'd die if I did not confess everything to her, everything!' And he did send the letter.

Mrs Stavrogin – and that was where they differed – would never have sent such a letter. It is true that he was passionately fond of writing, that he wrote to her even when they lived in the same house, and during his hysterical outbursts he would write two letters a day. I know for a fact that she always read his letters with the greatest attention, even when she received two a day, and that, having read them, she put them away in a special casket, dated and arranged in order; moreover, she treasured them in her heart. After which, keeping her friend waiting a whole day for an answer, she would meet him as if nothing were the matter, just as if nothing special had transpired the day before. Little by little she trained him so well that he did not himself dare to remind her of what had happened the day before, but merely looked hard for some time into her eyes. But she never forgot anything, while he sometimes forgot all too soon, and, encouraged by her composure, he would quite often, if friends came in, laugh and indulge in all sorts of boyish pranks over the champagne the very same day. With what venomous hatred she must have looked at him at such moments, but he did not notice anything! After a week, perhaps, or a month, or even six months, recalling by chance at some particular moment some expression in such a letter without its attendant circumstance, he would suddenly be overwhelmed with shame and be so upset that he would fall ill with one of his attacks of acute gastric catarrh. These special attacks of his were in some cases the usual result of his nervous shocks and were to a certain extent an interesting peculiarity of his physical condition.

Mrs Stavrogin, no doubt, did very often hate him; but one thing he failed to notice to the very end, namely that he had at last become her son, her creation, one might almost say her invention. He had become flesh of her flesh, and she kept and supported him not merely from 'envy of his talents'. And how offended she must have been by such a suggestion! An unbearable sort of love for him must have lain concealed in her heart in the midst of continual hatred, jealousy, and contempt. She protected him from every speck of dust, she fussed over him for twenty-two years, she would have spent sleepless nights if his reputation as a poet, a scholar, or a public man had been in danger. She had invented him, and she had been the first to believe in her own invention. He was, in a way, a sort of dream of hers. ... But in return she really demanded a great deal from him, sometimes even the obedience of a slave. And it was incredible how unforgiving she was! I may as well tell you two stories about that.

4

One day, just at the time of the first rumours about the emancipation of the serfs, when the whole of Russia suddenly rejoiced and was making preparations to be completely regenerated, a Petersburg baron, a man of the highest connexions who was closely associated with the reform, paid a call on Mrs Stavrogin while passing through our town. Mrs Stavrogin valued such visits greatly because her connexions with high society were growing weaker and weaker since the death of her husband, and in the end ceased altogether. The Baron spent an hour with her and took tea. There was no one else there, but Mrs Stavrogin did invite Stepan Verkhovensky and exhibited him. The Baron had heard something about him before, or pretended to, but he spoke very little to him at tea. Mr Verkhovensky was, naturally, anxious to make a good impression, and, besides, his manners were most exquisite. Though he was not apparently very high born, yet it happened that since his earliest childhood he had been brought up in an aristocratic house in Moscow and, consequently, decently; he spoke French like a Parisian. The Baron ought therefore to have realized at the first glance the sort of people with whom Mrs Stavrogin surrounded herself, even if she did live in the seclusion of a provincial town. But things did not turn out like that. When the Baron positively confirmed the absolute authenticity of the first rumours of the great reform which had just then been spread abroad, Mr Verkhovensky was unable to control his enthusiasm and cried 'Hurrah!', accompanying his exclamation with a gesture of the hand expressing his great delight at the news. His exclamation was not too loud and rather elegant; indeed, his enthusiasm, too, was not entirely spontaneous, and he had carefully rehearsed his gesture in front of a mirror half an hour before the tea-party; but something had apparently gone amiss, for the Baron permitted himself a faint smile, though he at once put in a polite phrase about the universal and proper way in which all

Russian hearts had been touched by the great event. He soon left, and, before leaving, did not forget to offer two fingers to Mr Verkhoven-sky. When she returned to the drawing-room, Mrs Stavrogin at first said nothing for three minutes, pretending to be looking for some-thing on the table; but suddenly she turned to Mr Verkhovensky and with a pale face and flashing eyes hissed in a whisper:

'I shall never forgive you for this!'

Next day she met her friend as though nothing had happened; she never referred to the incident again. But thirteen years later, at a tragic moment, she remembered it and reproached him with it, and she turned pale, just as she had done thirteen years before when she had reproached him for the first time. Only twice in her life had she said to him: 'I shall never forgive you for this!' The incident with the Baron was the second time; but the first incident also was so charac-teristic and, apparently, played so great a part in shaping Mr Verk-hovensky's future, that I must refer to it too.

It took place in 1855, in springtime, in the month of May, just after the news had reached Skvoreshniki that Lieutenant-General Stavro-gin, a foolish old gentleman, had died of acute indigestion on the way to the Crimea, where he was hastening to join the army on active ser-vice. Mrs Stavrogin, having been left a widow, went into mourning. It is true there was no reason why she should mourn a great deal, for she had spent the last four years in complete separation from her hus-band owing to the incompatibility of their characters, and she was giving him an allowance. (The Lieutenant-General himself only had 150 peasants and his army pay in addition to his position and his con-nexions; all the money and Skvoreshniki belonged to Mrs Stavrogin, the only daughter of a very rich Government contractor.) She was nevertheless shocked by the suddenness of the news and retired into complete seclusion. Mr Verkhovensky, needless to say, was always at her side.

It was the height of May. The evenings were extraordinarily fine. The wild cherry was in flower. The two friends met each evening in the garden and sat till nightfall in the summer-house, pouring out their hearts to one another. There were romantic moments. Under the influence of the change in her position, Mrs Stavrogin talked more than usual. She seemed to cling to her friend, and so it went on for several evenings. A strange idea suddenly occurred to Mr

Verkhovensky: 'Was the inconsolable widow counting on him by any chance to make her a proposal of marriage at the end of the year of mourning?' It was a cynical idea; but, then, the very fact that a man dwells among the stars sometimes increases his disposition to cynical thoughts, if only because his spiritual development is so many-sided. He began to consider it carefully, and came to the conclusion that it looked very much like it. He thought it over: 'It is true she has an enormous fortune, but –' And, to be sure, Mrs Stavrogin was not exactly a beauty: she was a tall, bony woman with a yellow complexion and an exceedingly long, horsy face. Mr Verkhovensky hesitated more and more; he was tortured by doubts, and even cried a few times from indecision (he wept rather frequently). In the evenings – that is to say, in the summer-house – his face involuntarily began to assume a capricious and ironical expression, a cross between something coquettish and supercilious. This happens somehow of itself and involuntarily, and indeed the more honourable the man the more noticeable it is. Goodness only knows what the truth of the matter was, but it is most likely that there was nothing stirring in Mrs Stavrogin's heart that could have fully justified Mr Verkhovensky's suspicions. And, besides, she would never have agreed to change her name of Stavrogin for his name, even if it were as renowned as hers. Quite possibly it was just a womanly desire on her part to make herself agreeable to a man, a manifestation of an unconscious feminine yearning which is so natural in certain extremely feminine circumstances. However, I won't vouch for it: the depths of a woman's heart have remained unexplored to this day! But, to continue.

I daresay she soon guessed the meaning of the strange expression on her friend's face; she was very sensitive and observant, while he was a little too innocent at times. But the evenings went on as before and their conversations were as poetic and interesting as ever. Then one day, at night-fall, they parted very amicably after a highly animated and poetical conversation, pressing each other's hands warmly at the steps of the cottage which Mr Verkhovensky occupied. Every summer he moved from the huge Skvoreshniki mansion into the little cottage which stood almost in the garden. He had only just gone in and, sunk into unhappy meditation, taken a cigar and without lighting it stopped, weary and motionless, before the open window, gazing at the little white clouds, light as fluff, gliding round the bright moon, when suddenly a faint rustle made him start and turn round. Mrs Stavrogin, whom he had left only four minutes earlier, was again standing before him. Her yellow face was almost blue, her lips were pressed tightly together and twitching at the corners. For ten full seconds she looked into his eyes in silence with a firm, implacable gaze, and then she whispered rapidly:

'I shall never forgive you for this!'

When ten years later Mr Verkhovensky told me this sad tale in a whisper, having previously locked the door, he vowed that he had been so stunned at the time that he had not heard or seen Mrs Stavrogin go. As she never once alluded to that incident again, and as everything went on as though nothing had happened, he was all his life inclined to think that it was just a hallucination before an illness, particularly as he had in fact fallen ill that night and was ill for a fortnight, which, incidentally, put an end to their meetings in the summer-house.

But in spite of his notion that it was only a hallucination, he apparently waited every day, all his life, for the continuation and, as it were, the *dénouement* of that incident. He could not believe that that was the end of it! And if so, he must have looked strangely sometimes at his friend.

5

She even designed the clothes he wore all his life herself. They were elegant and characteristic: a long, black frock-coat, buttoned almost to the top, but which fitted him beautifully; a soft hat (in summer a straw one) with a wide brim; a white cambric cravat with a large bow and hanging ends; a cane with a silver knob, and long hair to his shoulders. His hair was dark brown and it was only quite recently that it had begun to go a little grey. He was clean shaven. I am told that he was exceedingly handsome as a young man. But, in my opinion, he was unusually impressive also in his old age. And, besides, he could hardly be called old at the age of fifty-three. But because of his affected pose of a patriot he did not even try to look younger, but seemed to flaunt the solidity of his age, and in his suit, tall, spare, with his hair hanging down to his shoulders, he looked almost like a patriarch or, to be more exact, like the portrait of the playwright Kukolnik, engraved in an edition of his works published in the thirties, especially when he sat in the garden in summer, on a seat, beneath a bush of flowering lilac, leaning with both hands on his cane, an open book beside him, and sunk into a poetical reverie over the setting sun. So far as books are concerned, I should point out that in later years he seemed to avoid reading. That, however, was towards the very end of his life. The newspapers and journals, which Mrs Stavrogin ordered in great numbers, he read continually. He was always interested in the successes of Russian literature, though without losing the sense of his own dignity. At one time he was rather interested in home and foreign affairs, but soon gave it up. It also frequently happened that he would take De Tocqueville with him into the garden, while he secretly carried a Paul de Kock in his pocket. Still, this is not important.

Let me say something, too, in parenthesis about Kukolnik's portrait. Mrs Stavrogin first came across that picture as a young girl when she was still at her exclusive boarding-school in Moscow. She immediately fell in love with the portrait, as is the custom of all young girls in boarding-schools, who fall in love with anything you like and mostly with their calligraphy and drawing-masters as well. But the interesting thing is not what Mrs Stavrogin did as a little girl, but that even at the age of fifty she kept that picture among her most intimate treasures, so that it is quite likely that she designed Mr Verkhovensky's clothes in such a style that they somewhat resembled the clothes worn by the playwright in the picture. But that, too, is of course a trivial point.

During the first years or, to be more precise, the first half of the time he spent with Mrs Stavrogin, Mr Verkhovensky was still thinking of writing some book and seriously intended to start writing it every day. But during the second half he seemed to have forgotten everything he had ever known. More and more frequently he used to say to us: 'I seem to be ready to start work, I have collected all the materials, but somehow or other I cannot sit down to it! I just can't do anything!' And he would drop his head dejectedly. No doubt this was meant to increase his prestige in our eyes as a martyr to learning, but he himself was after something else. 'I've been forgotten! I'm no use to anyone!' he would exclaim more than once. This intensified despondency took hold of him especially towards the end of the fifties. Mrs Stavrogin realized at last that it was a serious matter. Besides, she could not bear the thought that her friend had been forgotten and was of no use to anyone. To distract him and at the same time to renew

his fame she took him to Moscow, where she had a number of fashionable acquaintances in the world of literature and learning; but it
seemed that Moscow, too, was unsatisfactory.

It was a peculiar time; something new was astir, something that
was quite unlike the tranquillity of the past, something that was very
strange indeed, but was felt everywhere, even in Skvoreshniki. All
sorts of rumours reached our town. The facts were generally more or
less known, but it was clear that in addition to the facts there were certain ideas that came with them, and, moreover, in great numbers. And
it was that that was so bewildering: it was quite impossible to accommodate oneself to these ideas or to find out exactly what they meant.
Mrs Stavrogin, being a woman, could not help suspecting some sort
of hidden meaning in them. She even started reading the papers and
magazines, the prohibited publications which were published abroad,
and even the revolutionary pamphlets which were just beginning to
appear at the time (she was able to obtain them all); but it merely
made her head swim. She started writing letters; but she received few
replies, and the longer it went on, the more incomprehensible it all became. Mr Verkhovensky was solemnly summoned to explain 'all
these ideas' to her once for all; but she remained decidedly dissatisfied
with his explanations.

Mr Verkhovensky's views on the general situation were extremely
supercilious; he reduced everything to the fact that he had been forgotten and was of no use to anyone. At last he, too, was mentioned,
first in the periodicals published abroad, as an exiled martyr, and immediately afterwards in Petersburg, as a former star of a famous
galaxy; he was even, for some reason, compared to Radishchev. Then
someone published a report that he was dead and promised to write
his obituary. Mr Verkhovensky immediately came to life and assumed
an air of great importance. All his disdainful views of his contempora-
ries immediately disappeared and he was overcome by a burning desire
to join the movement and show his powers. Mrs Stavrogin at once regained her old faith in everything and got terribly busy. They decided
to leave for Petersburg without delay, to find everything out on the
spot, to look into everything personally, and, if possible, to throw
themselves heart and soul into the new work. She announced, by the
way, that she was prepared to found a periodical of her own and devote her whole life to it from that very day. Seeing that it had gone so

far, Mr Verkhovensky became even more overbearing, and on the
journey to Petersburg began to treat Mrs Stavrogin almost patronizingly – which she immediately noticed and vowed to remember. She
had, as a matter of fact, another very important reason for the journey,
namely the renewal of her former connexions. She felt that she must
as far as possible remind society of her existence, or at any rate have a
good try. The official reason for the journey was to see her only son,
who was just then finishing his course of studies at the Petersburg
lycée.

6

They spent almost the whole winter season in Petersburg. By Lent,
however, everything burst like a rainbow-coloured soap bubble.
Their dreams vanished into thin air, and the confusion, far from being
cleared up, became worse confounded. To begin with, the connexions
with the higher circles failed to materialize, except on a very micro-
scopic scale and at the cost of humiliating efforts. Deeply mortified,
Mrs Stavrogin at first showed a violent interest in the 'new ideas' and
began giving evening parties. She sent out invitations to literary
people, and hundreds of them immediately turned up at her house.
Afterwards they came without being invited; and they brought their
friends with them. Never in her life had she seen such literary men.
They were incredibly vain, but made no secret of it, as though they
were so on principle. Some (though by no means all) turned up drunk,
but they seemed to regard it as some new manifestation of grace they
had discovered only the day before. They all appeared to be quite
extraordinarily proud of something. On all faces was written that they
had only just discovered some highly important secret. They abused
each other and were proud of it. It was not easy to find out exactly
what they had written, but there were critics, novelists, dramatists, sati-
rists, and exposers of abuses among them. Mr Verkhovensky wormed
his way into their highest circle, from which the movement was
directed. It was a stiff climb, but they welcomed him with open arms,
though, of course, none of them knew or had heard anything about him
except that he represented an idea. He manoeuvred so skilfully among
them that he prevailed upon them, too, to go twice to Mrs Stavrogin's
salon, in spite of their Olympian grandeur. These people were very
serious and exceedingly polite; they behaved with decorum; the others

were evidently afraid of them; but it was clear that they had no time to waste. Two or three former literary celebrities also put in an appearance. They happened to be in Petersburg at the time, and Mrs Stavrogin had long been maintaining a most refined relationship with them. But, to her surprise, these real and quite indubitable celebrities were as quiet as mice, and some of them simply hung on to this new rabble and curried favour with them shamelessly. At first Mr Verkhovensky was in luck: he was seized and exhibited at literary meetings. When he appeared for the first time on the platform at one of these public readings, he was given a great ovation which lasted for five minutes. He recalled it with tears nine years later, though more because of his artistic nature than out of gratitude. 'I swear to you, and I'm ready to have a bet on it,' he told me himself (but only to me, and in secret), 'that not a man in the audience knew anything about me – not a thing!' It was a remarkable confession: for it meant that he possessed an acute intelligence, if he could realize his position so clearly on the platform in spite of his tremendous excitement at the time; but, on the other hand, it meant, too, that he did not possess an acute intelligence if even nine years later he could not recall it without a feeling of resentment. He was made to sign two or three collective protests (he did not know himself against what); he signed them. Mrs Stavrogin, too, was made to sign a protest against some 'revolting action', and she, too, signed. However, though the majority of these 'new' men were present at Mrs Stavrogin's parties, they thought it for some reason their duty to regard her with contempt and unconcealed derision. Mr Verkhovensky used to hint to me afterwards, in his moments of bitterness, that it was from that time that she began envying him. She realized, of course, that it was not her business to associate with these people, but she received them eagerly for all that, with the hysterical impatience so characteristic of a woman and, above all, she always expected something to happen. At her evening parties she talked little, though she could talk if she wanted to, but mostly she preferred to listen. They talked about the abolition of the censorship and spelling reform, of the substitution of the Roman alphabet for the Russian one, of the exile of someone the day before, of some public disturbance in the shopping arcade, of the advisability of a federal constitution for the different nationalities in Russia, of the abolition of the army and the navy, of the restoration of Poland as far as the Dnieper, of the

agrarian reform and of the political pamphlets, of the abolition of inheritance, the family, children, and the priesthood, of the rights of
women, of Krayevsky's splendid house, for which no one seemed able
to forgive Mr Krayevsky, and so on and so forth. It was obvious that
among that rabble of 'new' men there were many impostors, but it
was no less obvious that there were also a great many good, honest
people among them, in spite of certain rather striking dissimilarities of
character. The honest ones were much more incomprehensible than
the coarse and dishonest ones; but it was impossible to tell which was
the tool of which. When Mrs Stavrogin announced her intention of
publishing a periodical, many more people flocked to her receptions,
but almost at once accusations that she was a capitalist and an exploiter
of labour were hurled against her. The familiarity of these accusations
was equalled only by their unexpectedness. The aged General Ivan
Drozdov, a former friend and fellow-officer of the late General Stavrogin, a most worthy man (in his own way, of course), a man we all
know to be extremely stubborn and irritable, who ate a lot and who
was terribly afraid of atheism, had an argument at one of Mrs Stavrogin's parties with a certain famous young man, who immediately said
to him: 'You must be a general, to talk like that,' meaning that he
could find no word of abuse worse than 'a general'. General Drozdov
flew into a great rage. 'Yes, sir,' he said, 'I am a general, and a lieutenant-general, and I've served my sovereign; and you, sir, are a puppy
and an atheist!' A most unfortunate scene followed. Next day the incident was adversely commented on in the Press, and signatures were
immediately collected for a protest against 'the outrageous conduct'
of Mrs Stavrogin for refusing to turn the General out of her house at
once. A cartoon was published in an illustrated magazine in which
Mrs Stavrogin, the General, and Mr Verkhovensky were all most
venomously caricatured as three reactionary friends; there were even
verses underneath the cartoon written by a popular poet specially for
the occasion. I may add for my part that it is quite true that many
army officers of the rank of general have an absurd habit of saying, 'I
have served my sovereign ...' as though wishing to imply that their
sovereign is not the same as the sovereign of ordinary subjects, but a
special one, one that belongs only to them.

It was impossible, of course, to remain any longer in Petersburg,
particularly as Mr Verkhovensky suffered a complete fiasco. He could

not restrain himself, and began talking about the prerogatives of art, which made people laugh at him louder than ever. At his last public reading he thought it expedient to attempt to impress his audience by patriotic eloquence, imagining that he would touch their hearts, and counting on their respect for his 'exile'. He was quite willing to admit the uselessness and absurdity of the word 'mother country'; he even declared his readiness to accept the idea of the harmfulness of religion, but firmly and loudly declared that boots were less important than Pushkin, and very much so. He was booed so mercilessly that he burst into tears there and then, on the platform, in full view of the audience. Mrs Stavrogin took him home more dead than alive. '*On m'a traité comme un vieux bonnet de coton!*' he babbled senselessly. She looked after him all night, gave him laurel and cherry drops, repeating to him till daybreak: 'You're still useful; you'll still make a public appearance; you'll be appreciated – in another place.'

Early next morning five literary gentlemen, three of whom were complete strangers, came to see Mrs Stavrogin. They told her sternly that they had looked into the question of her periodical and had come to a decision in that matter. Mrs Stavrogin had certainly never asked anybody to look into the question of her magazine or take any decision about it. Their decision was that, having founded her magazine, she should immediately hand it over to them with the capital to run it on the basis of a free co-operative association; she herself was to go back to Skvoreshniki, not forgetting to take with her Mr Verkhovensky, who was 'out of date'. Anxious to play fair, they agreed to recognize the rights of property in her case and to send her every year a sixth part of the net profits. The really touching thing about the whole proposal was that certainly four out of the five gentlemen had no selfish motives in making it, but were simply acting in the name of 'the cause'.

'We left Petersburg completely dazed,' Mr Verkhovensky used to say. 'I was completely at a loss what to make of it all and, I remember, I kept muttering some nonsense verse to the rumble of the train, goodness only knows what, all the way to Moscow. It was only in Moscow that I recovered my senses, just as though I really could find something very different there. Oh, my friends,' he sometimes cried in a moment of inspiration, 'you can't imagine the sadness and resentment that fill your soul to overflowing every time a great idea you

have long revered as sacred is taken up by some bunglers who drag it
out into the street to fools like themselves, and you suddenly come
across it in the flea-market, unrecognizable, bespattered with mud, set
up in a ridiculous fashion, at an absurd angle, without proportion,
without harmony, the plaything of stupid children! No! It was different in our time, and it wasn't that we strove for. No, no, not that at
all. I don't recognize anything any more. . . But our day will dawn
again, and again we shall put on the right path everything that is now
tottering and unsteady. Otherwise what is going to happen?'

7

Immediately on their return from Petersburg, Mrs Stavrogin sent
her friend abroad 'for a rest'; besides, it was necessary for them to part
for a time – she felt that. Mr Verkhovensky set out on his journey full
of enthusiasm. 'I shall come to life there,' he kept repeating. 'There at
last I shall set to work!' But already in his first letters from Berlin he
struck his usual note. 'My heart is broken,' he wrote to Mrs Stavrogin.
'I can't forget anything. Here in Berlin everything reminds me of my
past, my first innocent raptures, and my first agonies. Where is she?
Where are they both? Where are you, my two angels, of whom I was
never worthy? Where is my son, my beloved son? And, lastly, where
am I, my own self, my former self, strong as steel and firm as a rock
when to-day some fellow like *Andrejeff, un* Greek Orthodox clown
with a beard, *peut briser mon existence en deux*', etc., etc. As for his son,
Mr Verkhovensky had only seen him twice in his life, the first time
when he was born, and the second time quite recently in Petersburg,
where the young man was about to enter the university. All his life
the boy, as I have already mentioned, had been brought up by his aunts
(at Mrs Stavrogin's expense) in the Orenburg province about 500
miles from Skvoreshniki. As for *Andrejeff* – that is, Andreyev – he was
simply one of our local merchants, a shopkeeper, a great eccentric, a
self-taught archaeologist and a passionate collector of Russian anti-
quities, who sometimes engaged in a battle of wits with Mr Verkhovensky on some erudite subject and, particularly, on some 'progressive' idea. This worthy shopkeeper, with a grey beard and large silver
spectacles, still owed Mr Verkhovensky 400 roubles for a few acres of
timber he had bought on the latter's little estate (near Skvoreshniki).

Though Mrs Stavrogin had provided her friend liberally with funds when she sent him to Berlin, Mr Verkhovensky had specially counted on getting the 400 roubles before he left for abroad, probably for some secret purpose of his own, and he nearly burst into tears when *Andrejeff* asked him to wait another month, being, by the way, fully entitled to ask for such a postponement, for he had paid the first instalments almost six months in advance because Mr Verkhovensky was greatly in need of money at the time. Mrs Stavrogin eagerly read through this first letter and, underlining in pencil the exclamation: 'Where are you both?' put the date on it and locked it up in her casket. He was, of course, thinking of his two deceased wives. The theme of the second letter she received from Berlin was different. 'I'm working twelve hours a day ['If only he'd said seven,' muttered Mrs Stavrogin], I'm rummaging in the libraries, collating, copying, rushing about; been to see the professors. I have renewed my acquaintance with the excellent Dundasov family. What a fascinating woman Mrs Dundasov is even now! She sends you her regards. Her young husband and her three nephews are all in Berlin. I sit up talking till daybreak with the young people, and we have almost Athenian parties, but only in respect of their intellectual finesse and exquisite taste; everything is very noble: plenty of music, Spanish airs, dreams of human regeneration, ideas of eternal beauty, the Sistine Madonna, light alternating with darkness, but there are spots even on the sun! Oh, my friend, my noble and loyal friend, in my heart I am with you and I am yours; with you alone always, *en tout pays*, even *dans le pays de Makar et de ses veaux*, of whom, you remember, we so often spoke in fear and trembling, in Petersburg before our departure. I recall it with a smile. Having crossed the frontier, I felt safe at last, a strange and new sensation, for the first time after so many years' ... etc., etc.

'Well, that's all nonsense,' Mrs Stavrogin decided, folding up that letter too. 'If he has his Athenian parties till daybreak, he can't be spending twelve hours over his books. Was he drunk when he wrote it, I wonder? How dare that Dundasov woman send me her regards? However, let him have his fling. ...'

The phrase '*dans le pays de Makar et de ses veaux*' meant 'where Makar never drove his sheep' (i.e. Siberia). Mr Verkhovensky sometimes purposely translated Russian proverbs and idiomatic expressions into French in a most absurd way, no doubt being fully able to understand and translate them better; but he used to do it just for the sake of showing off, and he thought it very witty.

But his fling did not last long. He could not hold out for four months, and hurried back to Skvoreshniki. His last letters were entirely filled with outpourings of the most sentimental love for his absent friend and were literally bedewed with tears of separation. There are natures who, like lapdogs, become extremely attached to a home. The meeting of the two friends was rapturous. Two days later everything was as before and even more boring than before. 'My friend,' Mr Verkhovensky said to me a fortnight later in dead secret, 'my friend, I've discovered something that is too awful for words: *Je suis un* ordinary hanger-on *et rien de plus! Mais r-r-rien de plus!*'

8

There followed a period of dead calm which went on for almost the whole of the next nine years. Hysterical outbursts and sobbings on my shoulders, which occurred at regular intervals, did not in the least interfere with our felicity. The surprising thing is that Mr Verkhovensky did not grow fat during that time. All that happened was that his nose turned slightly red and he grew more benign. Gradually a circle of friends began to gather round him, though never a large one. Although Mrs Stavrogin had little to do with our circle, we all looked upon her as our patroness. After the lesson she had received in Petersburg, she settled down in our town for good; the winters she spent in her town residence and the summers in her country mansion in the neighbourhood. She had never before enjoyed so much influence and authority as during the last seven years in our provincial society – that is to say, up to the very time of the appointment of our present Governor. Our former Governor, the never-to-be-forgotten, good-natured Ivan Osipovich, was a near relation of hers upon whom she had at one time conferred great favours. His wife trembled at the very thought of displeasing Mrs Stavrogin, while the adulation of our provincial society almost bordered on idolatry. So Mr Verkhovensky, too, was in clover. He was a member of the club, lost grandly at cards, and was treated with respect, though many people regarded him merely as a 'scholar'. Later on, when Mrs Stavrogin permitted him to live in a separate house, we enjoyed greater freedom than ever. We met at his place twice a week; we were a very convivial gathering, especially when he was liberal with the champagne. The wine came from the shop of the same Andreyev. Every six months Mrs Stavrogin paid the bill, and on the day it was paid Mr Verkhovensky almost invariably suffered from one of his gastric upsets.

The oldest member of our circle was Liputin, a middle-aged provincial official, a great liberal who was reputed in the town to be an atheist. He had married for the second time a young and pretty girl, for whom he got a dowry, and he had, besides, three grown-up daughters. He kept his family in the fear of God and behind locked doors. He was extremely stingy, and had saved up enough from his salary to buy himself a house and put away a tidy sum, too. He was a restless sort of a person, who had not risen very high in the service. He was not greatly respected in our town and was not received in the better circles. He was, besides, a notorious scandal-monger who had been severely punished several times, once by an army officer and another time by a country gentleman, a widely respected head of a family. But we liked his keen intelligence, his inquiring mind, and his peculiar malicious cheerfulness. Mrs Stavrogin did not really like him, but, somehow, he always knew how to ingratiate himself with her.

Nor was she fond of Shatov, who only became a member of our circle during the last year. Shatov used to be a student, but he was sent down from the university after some disturbance; as a boy he was a pupil of Mr Verkhovensky's, and was born a serf of Mrs Stavrogin's, the son of her late personal valet Pavel Fedorov, and he had greatly benefited from her kindness. She disliked him for his pride and ingratitude, and she could never forgive him for not coming to her immediately after his expulsion from the university; on the contrary, he did not even reply to the urgent letter she had sent him at the time, preferring the humble position of a tutor of the children of some enlightened merchant. He went abroad with the merchant's family, more in the capacity of a nurse than a tutor; but he was very anxious to go abroad at the time. The children also had a governess, a sprightly Russian miss, who had also been engaged shortly before the family's departure abroad and who was given the job chiefly because she accepted a very small salary. Two months later the merchant turned her out for 'free thinking'. Shatov went after her, and they soon got married in Geneva. They lived together about three weeks, and then

parted as free people who recognize no obligations towards one another do, but, of course, also because of their poverty. He wandered
about Europe alone for a long time after that, eking out a precarious
existence as a bootblack in the streets and a stevedore in some port. At
last, about a year ago, he returned to his native town and went to live
with an old aunt of his, whom he buried a month later. His sister
Dasha, who had also been brought up by Mrs Stavrogin and who was
a favourite of hers whom she treated as an equal, he saw very rarely
and had little to do with her. In our company he was always sullen and
uncommunicative; but now and again when his convictions were attacked he became morbidly irritable and very unrestrained in his language. 'Shatov must be tied up before you can argue with him,' Mr
Verkhovensky sometimes joked; but he liked him. Abroad Shatov
had radically changed some of his former socialistic convictions and
gone right over to the other extreme. He was one of those idealistic
Russians who, struck by some compelling idea, immediately become
entirely obsessed by it for ever. They are quite incapable of mastering
it, but believe in it passionately, and so their whole life passes afterwards, as it were, in the last agonies under the weight of a heavy stone
which has fallen upon them and half crushed them. In appearance
Shatov entirely conformed to his convictions: he was clumsy, fair-
headed, dishevelled, short, broad-shouldered, thick-lipped, with thick,
beetling white eyebrows, a wrinkled brow, and a pair of unfriendly,
obstinately lowered eyes which seemed to be always ashamed of something. There was always a shock of hair on his head which refused to
be smoothed and stood upright. He was twenty-seven or twenty-eight
years old. 'I'm not surprised that his wife ran away from him,' Mrs
Stavrogin once said apropos of Shatov, after looking hard at him. He
did his best to dress neatly notwithstanding his abject poverty. Again,
he did not turn to Mrs Stavrogin for help, but carried on as best he
could. He did all sorts of jobs for shopkeepers, too. At one time he got
a job as a shop-assistant, at another he nearly went off on a river-
steamer with some goods as an assistant to a commercial traveller, but
fell ill before he was due to sail. It is hard to imagine the kind of poverty he endured without even thinking about it. After his illness Mrs
Stavrogin sent him 100 roubles anonymously and in secret. But he
found out the secret, thought it over, accepted the money, and went
to Mrs Stavrogin to thank her. She received him warmly, but there,

too, he shamefully disappointed her. He stayed only five minutes, without uttering a word, staring dully at the floor and smiling stupidly, and suddenly, without bothering to wait for her to finish what she had to say and at the most interesting point of her speech, he got up, made an awkward, sideways bow, was covered with confusion, and, brushing against her expensive inlaid work-table, upsetting it and smashing it to pieces, walked out nearly dead with shame. Liputin afterwards reproached him severely for not having returned with contempt the 100 roubles as coming from his former despotic mistress: he had not only accepted them, but had dragged himself off to thank her. He lived by himself on the outskirts of the town, and he did not like even one of us to go and see him. He used to come regularly to Mr Verkhovensky's parties, and borrowed newspapers and books from him.

There was another young man, a certain Virginsky, one of our local officials, who used to frequent Mr Verkhovensky's parties. He bore some resemblance to Shatov, though he was also apparently his complete opposite in every respect. But he, too, was 'a family man'. He was a pathetic and exceedingly quiet young man, and as a matter of fact in his early thirties, well educated, but chiefly self-taught. He was poor, married, had a job in the civil service, and supported an aunt and a sister-in-law. His wife, and indeed all the ladies of his family, held the most advanced views, but with them it all assumed a rather crude form; it was the case of 'an idea dragged out into the street', as Mr Verkhovensky had expressed it in a different connexion. They got everything out of books, and at the very first rumour from some of our progressive little groups in Petersburg or Moscow they were ready to throw everything overboard, if they were told to do so. Mrs Virginsky was a professional midwife in our town; as a girl she had lived a long time in Petersburg. Virginsky himself was a man of quite remarkable purity of heart, and, indeed, I rarely met a man of such honesty and passionate convictions. 'Never, never will I abandon these bright hopes,' he used to say to me, with shining eyes. Of those 'bright hopes' he always spoke quietly, with deep feeling, in half a whisper, as though in secret. He was rather tall, but extremely thin, and with narrow shoulders and extraordinarily lank hair of a reddish tint. All Mr Verkhovensky's superior gibes at some of his opinions he accepted meekly, but sometimes he answered him very seriously, and often nonplussed him. Mr Verkhovensky treated him kindly and, indeed, he treated us all like a father.

'You're all "half-baked"!' he used to remark jestingly to Virginsky, 'all who are like you; though I must say, Virginsky, that I never noticed in you that narrow-mindedness I found in Petersburg *chez ces séminaristes*, but you're "half-baked" all the same. Shatov would have dearly loved to be fully baked, but I'm afraid he, too, is only half-baked.'

'And what about me?' Liputin asked.

'You're simply the golden mean which will get on everywhere – in your own way.'

Liputin was offended.

It was said about Virginsky, and, unhappily, it was quite true, that his wife, having lived with him not even one year in lawful wedlock, suddenly informed him that he was cast off and that she preferred Lebyatkin. That Lebyatkin, who was a stranger in our town, turned out afterwards to be a highly suspicious character and not at all an army captain, as he himself claimed to be. He could only twirl his moustache, drink, and talk the most absurd nonsense that can be imagined. This man at once moved into his house in a most indecorous manner, glad to live at another man's expense, ate and slept there, and finally came to treat the master of the house with the utmost condescension. I am told that when his wife gave him his notice of dismissal, Virginsky said to her: 'My friend, till now I only loved you, but now I respect you.' But I doubt if this ancient Roman saying was ever actually uttered; on the contrary, it is said that he burst into loud sobs. One day, about a fortnight after his dismissal, all of them, the entire family, went for a picnic in the woods outside our town to have tea with their friends. Virginsky seems to have been in an excited and gay mood and took part in the dances; but suddenly and without any preliminary quarrel he seized the giant Lebyatkin, who was performing a solo can-can, by the hair, pulled him down, and began dragging him on the ground with shrieks, screams, and tears. The giant was so frightened that he did not even attempt to defend himself and he hardly uttered a word while he was being dragged along; but afterwards he resented it with all the ardour of a man of honour. Virginsky spent the whole night begging his wife on his knees to forgive him; but he obtained no forgiveness because he refused, in spite of everything, to apologize to Lebyatkin. He was, besides, taunted with having no convictions and with foolishness, the latter charge being brought against him for going down on his knees while trying to clear up some misunderstanding with a woman. The Captain soon disappeared, but he came back recently, arriving with his sister and entirely new plans; but of him later. It is not surprising that the poor 'family man' used to pour out his heart to us and was in need of our company. I don't think that he ever discussed his domestic troubles with us, though. Only once, coming back with me from Mr Verkhovensky's, did he speak of his position in a remote sort of way, but seizing me by the arm almost immediately, he cried ardently: 'That's nothing. It's only one particular case. It won't interfere with our "cause" in the least, not in the least!'

Occasional visitors used to come to our circle. A Jew, called Lyam-shin, used to turn up from time to time, as well as a certain Captain Kartuzov. An old gentleman of an inquiring mind used to come, but he died. Liputin brought an exiled Polish priest, Sloczewski, along one day, and we received him on principle for a time, but later we would have nothing to do with him.

9

At one time they used to say in the town about our circle that it was a hotbed of free-thinking, vice, and atheism; this rumour, by the way, always persisted. And yet all we did in our circle was to indulge in the most innocent, amiable, jolly typically Russian liberal chatter. 'The higher liberalism' and 'the higher liberal' – that is to say, a liberal without any aim whatever – are possible only in Russia. Mr Verkho-vensky, like any other witty person, had to have a listener, and, in addition, he had to possess the consciousness that he was fulfilling the high duty of propagating ideas. And, finally, he had to have someone to drink champagne with and exchange over a bottle of wine the well-known cheery generalities about Russia and the 'Russian spirit', about God in general and the 'Russian God' in particular; to repeat for the hundredth time the scandalous Russian anecdotes that everyone knew and everyone had been repeating over and over again. We were not averse from retailing the scandalous stories that went round our town, occasionally arriving at most severe and highly moral verdicts. We also discussed problems of general concern to mankind, talked

severely of the future fate of Europe and the human race; foretold
in a doctrinaire fashion that after the fall of the monarchy in France
that country would at once be reduced to the position of a secondary
power, and we were firmly convinced that that would happen very
easily and quite soon. We had long ago prophesied that the Pope
would assume the role of a simple archbishop in a united Italy, and
had no doubts whatever that this thousand-year-old problem was a
trifling matter in our age of humanitarian ideas, industry, and railways. But, then, 'Russian higher liberalism' always dismissed everything as airily as that. Mr Verkhovensky sometimes talked of art, and
very well, though a little abstractly. Occasionally he would recall the
friends of his youth – all names who had made their mark on the history of Russian progress – he recalled them with emotion and reverence, though not without envy either. If things got too boring, the
little Jew Lyamshin (a post-office clerk), who played the piano excellently, sat down to play, and in the intervals would give imitations
of a pig, a thunder-storm, a confinement, with the first cry of the
baby, etc., etc.; that was what he was invited for. Whenever we
over-indulged ourselves in drink – and that did happen sometimes
though not frequently – we grew excited, and on one occasion we
even sang the 'Marseillaise' in chorus to the accompaniment of
Lyamshin, though I don't know whether it went off all right. The
great day of the emancipation of the serfs on 19 February we met rapturously, and long before its arrival we began drinking toasts in its
honour. That was long ago, long before the arrival of Shatov and Virginsky, when Mr Verkhovensky was still living in Mrs Stavrogin's
house. Some time before the great day Mr Verkhovensky fell into the
regrettable habit of muttering the well-known, though somewhat
unrealistic verses, probably written by some liberal landed gentleman
of the past:

> The peasants are coming, carrying axes,
> A dreadful thing is about to occur.

Something of that kind, anyway – I don't remember the exact words.
Mrs Stavrogin overheard him muttering them one day and crying,
'Nonsense! nonsense!' left the room angrily. Liputin, who happened
to be present, observed sarcastically to Mr Verkhovensky:

'It would be a great pity if their former serfs should really do something unpleasant to our country squires in their moment of triumph.'

And he drew his forefinger round his neck.

'*Cher ami*,' Mr Verkhovensky remarked good-humouredly, 'believe me, *that* [he repeated the gesture] will be of no use whatever, either to the country squires or to any of us in general. We shan't do anything even without our heads, in spite of the fact that it is our heads that mostly interfere with our understanding.'

Let me add that many people in our town expected something extraordinary to happen on the day of the publication of the manifesto, something of the kind forecast by Liputin, all of them, by the way, so-called authorities on the peasants and the State. I believe Mr Verkhovensky, too, shared this opinion, so much so, indeed, that almost on the eve of the great day he started begging Mrs Stavrogin to let him go abroad; in short, he began to be worried. But the great day passed, and the supercilious smile reappeared on Mr Verkhovensky's face. He ventured to express a few remarkable thoughts to us about the character of the Russian in general and the Russian peasant in particular.

'Like all people in a hurry,' he concluded his series of remarkable utterances, 'we have been in too great a hurry with our dear peasants. We've made them the fashion, and a whole branch of our literature has for several years made a fuss of them, as though they were some newly discovered treasure. We crowned their lousy heads with laurel wreaths. The Russian village has for the past thousand years given us nothing but the Kamarinsky dance. A remarkable Russian poet, who was not without a sense of humour, seeing the great Rachel for the first time on the stage, cried rapturously: "I wouldn't exchange Rachel for the Russian peasant!" I'm prepared to go farther: I'd gladly give all the peasants in Russia for one Rachel. It's time we took a more sober view of things and didn't mistake our native pitch for *bouquet de l'impératrice*.'

Liputin agreed at once, but pointed out that at the time it was absolutely necessary to act against one's conscience and praise the peasants for the sake of the movement; that even high society ladies shed tears over Grigorovich's novel *Anton the Poor Wretch*, and that some of them even wrote from Paris to their estate managers in Russia that they were to treat their serfs in future as humanely as possible.

As ill-luck would have it, it happened just after the rumours about the Anton Petrov affair that a disturbance occurred in our province, too, and within only ten miles of Skvoreshniki, so that in the heat of the moment a platoon of soldiers was dispatched there. This time Mr Verkhovensky became so excited that he even frightened us. He shouted in the club that more troops should have been sent and that they ought to have been summoned by telegraph from another district; he rushed off to the Governor and assured him that he had nothing to do with it; he begged him not to involve him in the affair in any way because of his old associations, and demanded that a report of his statement should be sent at once to the proper quarters in Petersburg. It was a good thing that the whole affair soon blew over without any dire consequences, but I could not help being surprised at Mr Verkhovensky at the time.

Three years later, as is well known, people began talking of nationalism, and 'public opinion' came into being. Mr Verkhovensky had a good laugh.

'My friends,' he instructed us, 'if our nationalism has in truth been "born", as they assure us now in the papers, it is still at school, at some German *Peterschule*, sitting over a German book and repeating its everlasting German lesson, and the German master makes it go down on its knees whenever he likes. I've nothing but praise for the German teacher; but it's more likely that nothing has happened and that nothing of the kind has been born, but that everything is going on as before – that is, as God has ordered it. In my view that should be quite enough for Russia, *pour notre sainte Russie*. Besides, all these Slav movements and nationalities – all that's too old to be new. If you like, nationalism has never really existed in our country, except as some idle invention by some gentlemen at a club, a Moscow club at that. I'm not talking of the days of Prince Igor, of course. The whole thing, in fact, is the result of idleness. Everything is the result of the charming, cultured, whimsical idleness of our gentry. I've been repeating it for the last thirty thousand years. We don't know how to live by our own labour. And as for the fuss they're now making over the "birth" of some public opinion, has it all of a sudden just dropped out of the sky? Don't they realize that before we can have an opinion of our own we must first of all have work – our own work, our own initiative, our own experience! You will never get something for nothing. If we work, we shall also have an opinion of our own. And as we shall never do a stroke of work, those who have been doing our work for us, will be forming an opinion for us that is to say, the same old Europe, the same old Germans – our teachers for the last two hundred years. Besides, Russia is too big a problem for us to solve it alone, without the Germans and without work. For the last twenty years I've been sounding the tocsin and calling to work. I've given my life to that appeal, and, madman that I am, believed in it. Now I no longer believe, but I go on ringing the bell, and I shall be ringing it to the very end, to my last breath; I shall hold on to the bell-rope till they start tolling for my own requiem!'

Alas, we just nodded in agreement. We applauded our teacher, and with what ardour, too! But, gentlemen, don't we still hear to-day, and very often, too, sometimes, the same sort of 'charming', 'clever', liberal Russian nonsense?

Our teacher believed in God; 'I don't understand,' he used to say sometimes, 'why everybody here thinks I'm an atheist. I believe in God, *mais distinguons*, I believe in him as a Being who is conscious of himself in me only. You can't possibly expect me to believe as my Nastasya [his maidservant] believes, or like some gentleman who believes "just in case", or like our dear Shatov – but no. Shatov doesn't count, for Shatov believes *in spite of himself*, like a Moscow Slavophil. As for Christianity, however much I respect it, I'm not a Christian. I'm rather an ancient pagan, like the great Goethe, or like an ancient Greek. Indeed, the very fact that Christianity has failed to understand woman, which George Sand has so beautifully proved in one of her remarkable novels – is quite enough. As for the genuflexions, fastings, and the rest, I can't understand whose business it is whether I observe them or not. However busy our local informers are, I don't want to become a Jesuit. In 1847 Belinsky, who was abroad, sent his famous letter to Gogol in which he warmly reproached him for believing "in some kind of God". *Entre nous soit dit*, I can't imagine anything more comic than the moment that Gogol (the Gogol of *that* time!) read that sentence and – the whole letter! But disregarding the funny part of it, and since, as a matter of fact, I am fundamentally in agreement, I will merely point to them and say: those were men! They knew how to love their people, they knew how to suffer for them, they knew how to sacrifice everything for them, and, at the same time, they knew how to remain aloof from them and not curry favour with them in certain matters. How could you really expect a man like Belinsky to seek salvation in Lenten oil or turnips with peas!'

But at this point Shatov intervened.

'Never did those men of yours love the people; they never suffered for them, and they never sacrificed anything for them, however much they imagined it for their own comfort,' he growled sullenly, staring at the floor and turning impatiently in his chair.

'*They* didn't love the people?' Mr Verkhovensky cried in an outraged voice. 'Oh, how they loved Russia!'

'Neither Russia nor the people,' Shatov, too, cried, with flashing eyes. 'You can't love something you don't know, and they had no idea of the Russian people! All of them, and you among them, overlooked the Russian people, Belinsky especially; that becomes evident from that very letter of his to Gogol. Belinsky, exactly like the Inquisitive Man in Krylov's fable, did not notice the elephant in the museum of curiosities, but concentrated all his attention on the French socialist beetles; he never got beyond them. And yet he was, I suppose, cleverer than any of you! You've not only overlooked the people, you've treated them with horrible contempt, and that because you could not imagine any people except the French people, and even then only the people of Paris, and you were ashamed that the Russian people were not like them. And that is the naked truth! And he who has no people, has no God. You may be sure that those who cease to understand the people and lose all contact with them, at once and to that extent lose the faith of their fathers and become atheists or are indifferent. I'm speaking the truth! It is a fact that it is invariably proved to be true. That is why all of you, and all of us for that matter, are either disgusting atheists or just indifferent, dissolute trash and nothing more! You, too, Mr Verkhovensky. I'm not excluding you. In fact, it is you I had in mind when I spoke. I'd like you to know that.'

As usual, having delivered himself of such a monologue (and this happened frequently with him), Shatov grabbed his cap and made for the door, fully convinced that it was all over now and that he had broken off his friendly relations with Mr Verkhovensky for good. But the latter always managed to stop him in time.

'Hadn't we better make it up, Shatov, after this exchange of civilities?' he used to say, holding out a hand to him good-naturedly from his arm-chair.

Shatov, clumsy and bashful, disliked sentimental effusions. Outwardly he was a coarse fellow, but inwardly he was apparently a man of the most delicate feelings. Though he often went too far, he was the first to suffer for it. Muttering something under his breath in response to Mr Verkhovensky's words, and shuffling about like a bear, he would suddenly grin, put down his cap, and sit down in his old place. Wine was of course fetched, and Mr Verkhovensky proposed some suitable toast, such as the memory of some famous man of the past.

2

Prince Harry. A Marriage Proposal

I

THERE was one other person in the world to whom Mrs Stavrogin was no less attached than to Mr Verkhovensky – her only son, Nicholas Stavrogin. It was to him that Mr Verkhovensky had been invited to act as tutor. The boy was eight years old at the time, and the lackadaisical General Stavrogin, his father, was already living apart from his mother, the boy growing up entirely under her supervision. It must be said in all fairness that Mr Verkhovensky knew how to gain the devotion of his pupil. His whole secret lay in the fact that he was a child himself. I was not there at the time, and he had always been in need of a real friend. He never hesitated to make a friend of the little fellow, as soon as the child had grown older. It somehow happened naturally that there was not the slightest difference between them. He used often to wake his ten- or eleven-year-old friend at night for the sole purpose of pouring out his wounded feelings to him, or to tell him some family secret, without realizing that that was something he should not do. They flung themselves into each other's arms and cried. The boy knew that his mother was very fond of him, but he was hardly very fond of her. She did not talk to him a lot, rarely interfered with him, but, somehow, he was always morbidly aware that she was watching him. However, she had complete faith in Mr Verkhovensky so far as the education and the moral development of her son were concerned. In those days she believed in him implicitly.

I think it is true to say that the teacher was responsible for upsetting his pupil's nerves to some extent. When at the age of sixteen Nicholas was taken to the lycée, he looked sickly and pale and was strangely quiet and wistful. (Later on he was distinguished by his great physical strength.) One must also assume that if the two friends had wept and flung themselves into each other's arms, it was not always because of some domestic misunderstandings. Mr Verkhovensky succeeded in touching some of the deepest chords in his little friend's heart and in evoking in him the first and still vague sensation of that eternal and sacred longing which many a chosen spirit, having once tasted and experienced it, will never afterwards exchange for some cheap feeling of satisfaction. (There are even such lovers of sensations to whom this longing is dearer than the most complete satisfaction, if such a thing were at all possible.) Be that as it may, it was certainly a good thing that the tutor and his pupil were at last separated, though perhaps a little late.

During his first two years at the lycée the young man used to come home in the holidays. When Mrs Stavrogin and Mr Verkhovensky were in Petersburg, he was present at some of the literary parties at his mother's house, watching and listening. He spoke little and was as quiet and shy as before. He still treated Mr Verkhovensky with the same tender affection, but he was somehow more reserved; he was apparently not anxious to discuss higher things or memories of his past with him. Having finished his course of studies, he applied, at his mother's wish, for a commission in the army and soon joined one of the most famous cavalry regiments of the Horse Guards. He did not come to show himself to his mother in his army uniform and wrote only rarely to her from Petersburg. Mrs Stavrogin sent him money without stint, in spite of the fact that after the agrarian reform the income from her estate had fallen so low that at first it was less than half of what it had been before. She had, however, managed to save up a considerable sum by long years of economy. She was very interested in her son's success in the highest Petersburg society. What she could never achieve, was achieved by the wealthy young officer with expectations. He renewed acquaintances she hardly dared to dream of and was received everywhere with great pleasure. But very soon strange rumours began to reach Mrs Stavrogin: the young man suddenly gave himself up to a life of mad dissipation. Not that he gambled or drank too much; but stories were told about his life of wild rioting, about people being run over by his horses, of his brutal conduct to a lady of good society with whom he had had an affair and whom he afterwards publicly insulted. There seems to have been something very nasty about that business. It was added, besides, that he had become a regular bully, who picked quarrels with people and insulted them for the mere pleasure of insulting them. Mrs Stavrogin was upset and worried. Mr Verkhovensky assured her that those were only the first violent outbursts of a too richly endowed nature, that the storm would abate, and that all this was just like young Prince Harry, who made merry with Falstaff, Poins, and Mistress Quickly, as described by Shakespeare. This time Mrs Stavrogin did not cry, 'Nonsense, nonsense!' as she was lately all too ready to shout at Mr Verkhovensky, but, on the contrary, lent a willing ear to him, asked him to explain his words to her more precisely, took down Shakespeare's works herself, and read the immortal chronicle play with great attention. But the play did not set her mind at rest, and, besides, she did not think the resemblance very striking. She was waiting feverishly for a reply to several of her letters, and she did not have long to wait. Soon the fatal news was received that Prince Harry had fought two duels almost at the same time, that he had killed one of his opponents outright and maimed the other, and that as a consequence he was to be court-martialled. It all ended with his being reduced to the ranks with the loss of civil rights and transferred to one of the infantry line regiments, and he only escaped a heavier sentence by special favour.

In 1863 he somehow managed to distinguish himself; he was awarded a cross, raised to non-commissioned rank, and then, rather quickly, given back his commission. During that time Mrs Stavrogin despatched almost a hundred letters to Petersburg with prayers and supplications. She did not even mind humiliating herself a little in so exceptional a case. After his promotion the young man sent in his resignation, but he did not come back to Skvoreshniki again, and stopped writing to his mother altogether. They found out at last by all sorts of roundabout ways that he was back in Petersburg, but that he was no longer to be seen in society; he seemed to have gone into hiding. After some time they discovered that he was living in strange company, associating with the dregs of the Petersburg population, with some down-at-heel Civil Servants, retired army officers who had to beg for a living, and drunkards, that he visited their families, spending days and nights in slums and goodness only knows what other disreputable places, that he had sunk very low, walked about in rags, and that apparently this life was to his taste. He did not ask his mother for money; he had his own little estate, a property that once belonged to General Stavrogin, which brought him in some sort of income and which, according to rumours, he had let to a German from Saxony. At last his mother succeeded in persuading him to go back to her, and Prince Harry made his appearance in our town. It was then that I got my first opportunity of studying him closely, having never set eyes on him before.

He was a very handsome young man of about twenty-five, and I must admit I was greatly impressed by him. I expected to meet some filthy tramp enfeebled by debaucheries and reeking of vodka. He was, on the contrary, the most elegant gentleman of all those I had ever met, excellently dressed, and with the manners that only a man accustomed to the most refined society could possess. I was not the only one to be surprised: our whole town was surprised, and our town, of course, knew Mr Stavrogin's biography, and in such detail that one could hardly imagine where they could have got it from and, what was even more surprising, half of the stories about him were quite true. All our ladies were in raptures over our new visitor. They were sharply divided into two camps – in one he was adored, and in the other he was hated with a deep, abiding hatred; but both were crazy about him. Some of them were particularly fascinated because they thought that some fatal secret was probably hidden in his heart; others were most thrilled that he was a murderer. It appeared, too, that he was well educated and, indeed, that he was a man of considerable knowledge. Not much knowledge, of course, was necessary to impress us; but he could pass an opinion on highly interesting topics of the day and, what was so important, with remarkable good sense. Let me mention this as a rather strange thing: almost from the very first day we all found him to be an extremely sensible fellow. He was not very talkative, he was elegant without being over-refined, remarkably modest, and, at the same time, brave and self-confident as no one else in our town. Our dandies regarded him with envy, and were completely eclipsed in his presence. I was also struck by his face:

his hair was just a little too black, his light-coloured eyes a little too calm and clear, his complexion a little too tender and white, his colour a little too dazzling and pure, his teeth like pearls, his lips like coral – he would seem to be a paragon of beauty, yet at the same time there was something hideous about him. People said that his face reminded them of a mask; there was, by the way, a great deal of talk about his amazing physical strength. He was rather tall. Mrs Stavrogin looked at him with pride, but never for a moment without worry. He spent about six months with us – quiet, listless, and rather morose; he made his appearance in society and carried out all the rules of our provincial etiquette rigidly. He was related to our Governor on his father's side and was received at his house like a near relative. But a few months passed and the wild beast suddenly showed its claws

Let me, incidentally, add parenthetically that our dear and gentle ex-Governor, Ivan Osipovich, was a bit of an old woman, but of good family and well connected – which indeed explains the fact that he had been so many years with us without ever taking any active part in the affairs of the province. From his hospitality and general amiability he should really have been a marshal of the nobility of the good old days, and not a governor in such troublous times as ours. It was always said in our town that it was not he but Mrs Stavrogin who governed our province. Of course, it was a sarcastic saying, but I'm afraid there is not a word of truth in it. And the jokes they used to crack on this subject in our town! As a matter of fact, Mrs Stavrogin quite deliberately withdrew from all public affairs during the last few years, in spite of the great respect in which she was held by everybody who was of any consequence in our province, and voluntarily confined herself within the strict limits which she set up for herself. Instead of public affairs she suddenly turned to the management of her estate, and in two or three years raised the revenue from her property almost to what it had been in the past. Instead of her former romantic interests (her trips to Petersburg, her intentions to publish a journal, etc.), she began cutting down expenses and saving up. She kept even Mr Verkhovensky at arm's length, allowing him to take a flat in another house (which he had long been pestering her to let him do under all sorts of pretexts). Little by little Mr Verkhovensky began to refer to her as a prosaic woman or more jestingly as 'my prosaic friend'. It goes without saying that he only allowed himself to jest like that in a highly respectful manner and after carefully choosing the right occasion.

All of us who belonged to the narrow circle of Mrs Stavrogin's friends – and Mr Verkhovensky more than anyone else – saw that she regarded her son as almost a new hope, and even as a sort of new dream. Her passion for her son derived from the time of his successes in Petersburg society, and grew particularly intense from the moment she received the news that he had been reduced to the ranks. And yet she was quite plainly afraid of him, and behaved in his presence as though she were his slave. I could see that she was afraid of something vague and mysterious, something she could not put into words herself, and many times when no one was looking she would watch Nicholas intently, wondering and thinking of something – and then the wild beast showed its claws.

2

Our Prince, suddenly and for no reason at all, committed two or three shocking outrages on various persons. The striking thing about them was that they were so utterly shocking, so unlike anything anyone could have expected, not at all what usually happens, absolutely idiotic and puerile, committed goodness only knows why, without rhyme or reason. One of the most respected committee members of our club, Peter Gaganov, an elderly gentleman who was held in high esteem by everybody, had the innocent habit of adding in a passionate tone of voice to every word he uttered, 'No, sir, they won't lead me by the nose!' Well, there was no harm in that. But one day at the club when he uttered this aphorism during some heated discussion to a small number of club members who had gathered round him (all of them persons of some consequence), Nicholas Stavrogin, who was taking no part in the discussion and standing a little distance away from the group, suddenly went up to Mr Gaganov and, seizing him unexpectedly but firmly with two fingers by the nose, managed to drag him a few steps across the room. He could have no possible grudge against Mr Gaganov. One might have thought that it was merely a schoolboyish prank, however unpardonable, of course; yet it was said later that during the brief operation he looked abstracted, 'as though he were not in his right mind', but that was recalled and taken

into account long afterwards. In the heat of the moment everybody
was struck by something that happened a second later, when there
could be no doubt that he knew perfectly well what he was doing and
why, and far from looking embarrassed, smiled gaily and maliciously,
'without the slightest regret'. There was a terrific uproar; he was surrounded. Nicholas turned round and round, gazing about him, without replying to anyone and regarding the shouting people with curiosity. At last he seemed to fall into thought again, so, at any rate, I
was told, frowned, went firmly up to the affronted Peter Gaganov,
and, speaking very fast, muttered with visible annoyance:

'Frightfully sorry, sir – I honestly don't know why I should suddenly have wanted to – such a silly thing. ...'

The perfunctory manner of his apology was almost equivalent to a
fresh insult. The shouting became louder, but Nicholas just shrugged
his shoulders and went out.

All this was very silly, not to mention the gross unseemliness of the
incident, a calculated and deliberate unseemliness, as it looked at the
first glance, and therefore a deliberate and utterly impudent insult to
our entire society. That was how everybody understood it. Mr Stavrogin was immediately and unanimously expelled from the club; then
it was decided to approach the Governor in the name of all the members of the club with a written request to use 'the administrative
powers entrusted to him' immediately (without waiting for any formal court action) to restrain the mischievous ruffian, the 'society bully,
and thus protect all the decent and law-abiding citizens of our town
from humiliating attacks'. It was added with a show of innocent malice
that 'a law might perhaps be found to keep even Mr Stavrogin in his
place'. This sentence was inserted after careful consideration because
it was thought that it would annoy the Governor on account of Mrs
Stavrogin. They amplified it with relish. As it happened, the Governor was not in town at the time; he had gone to a nearby town to
stand godfather to the child of a very charming lady whose husband
had died during her pregnancy. But he was expected to return soon.
Meanwhile they gave the highly esteemed and insulted Mr Gaganov a
regular ovation; people exchanged embraces and kisses with him; the
whole town called on him. It was even planned to give a subscription
dinner in his honour, and it was only at his earnest request that they
abandoned the idea – perhaps because it had dawned on them at last

that the man had, after all, been pulled by the nose, and that there was therefore no particular reason for any celebration.

And yet how had it happened? How could it have happened? The remarkable thing is that it never occurred to anyone in our town to ascribe that wild action to madness. Which of course meant that they were inclined to expect such actions even from a sane Mr Stavrogin. For my part, I don't know to this day how to explain it, in spite of the incident which occurred soon afterwards and which apparently explained everything and, it would seem, set everybody's mind at rest. Let me also add that four years later, in answer to a discreet question from me about that incident at the club, Stavrogin said, frowning, 'Yes, I was not quite myself at the time.' But I ought not to anticipate.

The general outburst of hatred with which everyone fell upon 'the ruffian and society bully' also struck me as curious. They seemed all to be absolutely convinced that there was a premeditated desire and a calculated intention to insult our whole society by that one act. There could be no doubt that the young man had displeased everybody and, indeed, set the whole world against him – but how on earth did he manage to do it? Till the last incident he never quarrelled with anyone nor insulted anyone, but had been as courteous as a gentleman in a fashions magazine, if the latter were only able to speak. I expect he was hated for his pride. Even our ladies, who began by adoring him, were now clamouring against him more loudly than the men.

Mrs Stavrogin was terribly upset. She confessed afterwards to Mr Verkhovensky that she had been expecting it to happen long ago, every day during the last six months, and something 'of the kind', too – a most extraordinary admission from a mother. 'It's started!' she thought with a shudder. The morning after the incident at the club, she set about, carefully but firmly, obtaining an explanation from her son, but the poor woman trembled all over in spite of her firmness. She had not slept all night, and even went out early in the morning to ask Mr Verkhovensky's advice, bursting into tears in his study – a thing which had never happened to her before in front of people. All she wanted was that Nicholas should at least say something to her, that he should deign to explain himself. Nicholas, who was always extremely courteous and respectful to his mother, listened to her for some time, frowning but serious; suddenly he got up without saying a word, kissed her hand, and went out. That evening, as though on purpose, another incident occurred. Though less violent and more ordinary than the first, it increased the clamour in the town, owing to the general state of public opinion.

It was just then that our friend Liputin turned up. He came to see Stavrogin immediately after his interview with his mother, and begged him earnestly to do him the honour of coming to a party he was giving for his wife's birthday that evening. Mrs Stavrogin had long regarded with horror her son's partiality for such low company, but she dared not say anything to him about it. He had made several acquaintances beside Liputin in the third rank of our society and even among people of lower rank, but he seemed to like such friends. He had never been in Liputin's house before, though he had met him several times. He realized that Liputin had invited him because of the scandal in the club on the previous day and that as a local liberal he was very glad of it, being sincerely of the opinion that that was the way in which one had to treat members of club committees and that it was very well done. Nicholas laughed and promised to come.

There was a great number of people at the party – not much to look at, but able to stand up for themselves. Liputin, vain and envious, gave a party only twice a year, but on those occasions he spared no expense. Mr Verkhovensky, the most honoured of the guests, did not turn up because of illness. There was tea, lots of refreshments and drinks; they played cards at three tables, and the young people, while waiting for supper, danced to a piano accompaniment. Stavrogin led out Mrs Liputin – a very pretty young woman, who was terribly shy of him – took two turns round the room with her, then sat down beside her, talked to her, and made her laugh. Noticing at last how pretty she was when she laughed, he suddenly, in the presence of all, put his arm round her waist, and kissed her on the lips three times with great relish. The poor frightened woman fainted. Stavrogin took his hat and went up to the husband, who was struck dumb amid the general confusion. Looking at him, he became embarrassed himself and, muttering hurriedly, 'Don't be angry,' went out of the room. Liputin ran after him, helped him on with his fur coat, and, bowing, saw him down the stairs. But next day there followed an amusing sequel to this, comparatively speaking, innocent incident, a sequel which raised

Liputin in the general estimation ever after, and which he knew how to use to his fullest possible advantage.

About ten o'clock in the morning Liputin's maid, Agafya, a pert, cheerful, red-cheeked woman of thirty, presented herself at Stavrogin's house with a message from her master. She insisted on seeing 'the young gentleman himself'. Stavrogin had a bad headache, but he went out. Mrs Stavrogin happened to be present at the delivery of the message.

'Mr Liputin, sir,' Agafya began glibly, speaking very fast, 'told me first of all to give his best regards to you and to ask you how you were, whether you had a good night after the party, and how you felt this morning after what happened last night?'

Stavrogin grinned.

'Give my regards to your master and thank him,' he said. 'Tell him from me, Agafya, that he is the most sensible man in town.'

'And Mr Liputin, sir,' replied Agafya even more glibly, 'has asked me to say that he knows that without you telling him, and that he wished he could say as much for you.'

'Oh? But how did he know what I was going to say to you?'

'I'm sure I don't know how he knew that, sir, but after I'd left the house he came running after me, and without his cap, too. "Don't forget, Agafya, dear," he says to me, "if by any chance he should look upset and say to you, 'Tell your master that he is the most sensible fellow in town,' to say to him at once, 'The master knows that very well himself and wished he could say as much for you.'"'

3

At last the interview with the Governor took place too. Our dear, gentle Ivan Osipovich had only just returned and only just had time to hear the passionate complaint from the club. There was no doubt that something had to be done, but he felt embarrassed. Our hospitable old man seemed also to be a little afraid of his young relative. He decided, however, to persuade him to apologize to the club and to the man he had insulted, but in a satisfactory manner and, if necessary, in writing, too; then to ask him gently to leave our town and go to Italy, for example, to improve his mind or, indeed, anywhere else abroad. In the drawing-room in which this time he received Stavrogin (at other times the young man was allowed, as a relative, to wander freely all over the house), Alyosha Telyatnikov, a well-bred Civil Servant who was also a friend of the Governor's family, was opening postal packets on a table in a corner; in the next room, at the window nearest to the drawing-room door, a visitor, a stout, robust-looking colonel, a former fellow-officer of the Governor, was sitting reading the *Voice*, without of course paying any attention to what was taking place in the drawing-room; he sat with his back to the door, in fact. Ivan Osipovich began in a roundabout way, almost in a whisper, but seemed to be a little confused. Nicholas looked very unfriendly, not at all as a relative should. He was pale, sat with his eyes fixed on the floor, and listened knitting his brow as though trying to control acute pain.

'You've a kind and noble heart, Nicholas,' the dear old fellow said among other things. 'You're a man of culture, you've mixed in high society, and here, too, you've been till now a model of good behaviour, which was a great comfort to your mother, who is dear to us all. And now everything has again taken such a strange turn, which is so unfortunate for us all. I speak as a friend of your family, as an old man who loves you sincerely, and as a relative of yours whose words you cannot possibly take amiss. Tell me what makes you do such desperate things, things which are so contrary to all the accepted rules of behaviour? What is the meaning of such acts, which look as though they were committed in a state of delirium?'

Nicholas listened with impatience and annoyance. All of a sudden a cunning and mocking expression appeared for a moment in his eyes.

'I may as well tell you what made me do it,' he said morosely, and, looking round, he bent down to Ivan Osipovich's ear.

The well-bred Alyosha Telyatnikov moved away another three steps towards the window, and the Colonel cleared his throat behind the *Voice*. Poor Ivan Osipovich hastily and trustfully inclined his ear; he was exceedingly curious. And it was then that something utterly unheard of, though, on the other hand, something that in a certain sense was only to be expected, took place. The old man suddenly felt that instead of whispering some interesting secret to him, Nicholas all of a sudden seized the upper part of his ear between his teeth and bit it hard. He trembled all over, and his breath failed him.

'Nicholas, what sort of joke is this?' he moaned mechanically in a strangled voice.

Alyosha and the Colonel had scarcely time to realize what was happening; besides, they could not see what Nicholas was doing, and to the very end they thought that the Governor and the young man were whispering to each other; and yet the desperate look on the old man's face alarmed them. They stared at each other, not knowing whether to rush to his assistance as arranged, or to wait a little longer. Nicholas must have noticed that and bit the ear harder.

'Nicholas, Nicholas,' his victim moaned again. 'All right, you've had your joke – let me go now.'

Another moment and the poor man would, of course, have died of fright; but the monster spared him and let go his ear. The old man's mortal panic lasted for a full minute, and after that he had a sort of fit. But half an hour later Nicholas was arrested and taken for the time being to the guardroom, where he was locked up in a special cell with a special sentry at the door. It was a harsh decision, but our gentle Governor was so angry that he made up his mind to take the responsibility, even if he had to face Mrs Stavrogin herself. To everybody's amazement, this lady, who had hastily arrived in a state of great irritation to demand an immediate explanation from the Governor, was refused admission to the Governor's residence – thereupon she drove back home, without getting out of her carriage, hardly able to believe her senses.

And at last everything was explained! At two o'clock in the morning, the prisoner, who had hitherto been remarkably calm and even slept, suddenly raised a din, began hammering violently on the door with his fists, with unnatural strength wrenched the iron grating off the door, and broke the window, cutting his hands badly. When the officer on guard came running with a detachment of men and the keys and ordered the cell to be opened so that they might overpower and tie up the maniac, it was discovered that he was suffering from an acute form of brain-fever. He was taken home to his mother. Everything was explained immediately. All our three doctors gave it as their opinion that three days before the last incident the patient was probably in a state of delirium, though he was apparently fully conscious and possessed an extraordinary amount of cunning, that he was not in the full possession of his senses or his will, which was indeed con-

firmed by the facts. It would therefore seem that Liputin had guessed
the truth before anyone else. Ivan Osipovich, a man of delicate and
sensitive feelings, was overcome with confusion; but the interesting
fact is that he, too, must have thought Nicholas capable of any mad
action even when in the full possession of his senses. At the club the
members were ashamed, and wondered how they could have failed
to notice the most obvious thing and overlooked the only plausible explanation of all these extraordinary happenings. There were, of
course, some sceptics, but they could not maintain their position very
long.

Nicholas was in bed for over two months. A well-known specialist
was summoned from Petersburg for a consultation; the whole town
called on Mrs Stavrogin. She forgave them. When, in the spring,
Nicholas had completely recovered, and accepted without demur his
mother's proposal to go to Italy, she made him pay us all farewell
visits and as far as possible apologize where necessary. Nicholas readily
agreed to do so. It was known at the club that he had had a most delicate interview with Mr Gaganov at the latter's house, and that Mr
Gaganov was fully satisfied with the apology he had received. While
paying his visits, Nicholas looked very serious and even gloomy.
Everybody received him with apparent sympathy, but everybody
seemed for some reason to be embarrassed, and they were all glad that
he was going to Italy. Ivan Osipovich even shed tears, but did not appear anxious to embrace Nicholas even at their last meeting. As a matter of fact, there were people in our town who remained convinced
that the blackguard was merely having a good laugh at us all and that
his illness had had nothing to do with it. He also called on Liputin.

'Tell me,' he asked him, 'how could you have guessed beforehand
what I was going to say about your being a sensible chap and supply
Agafya with an answer?'

'Why,' laughed Liputin, 'simply because I, too, regard you as a
sensible fellow, and that was how I foresaw what your answer would
be.'

'All the same, it's a remarkable coincidence. However, tell me this:
you must then have thought me a sensible man, and not a madman,
when you sent Agafya?'

'A most sensible and most rational man. I merely pretended to believe that you were not in your right mind. Why, you yourself guessed

at once what I was thinking at the time and sent me a testimonial to my wit through Agafya.'

'I'm afraid there you're a little mistaken; I really was – indisposed,' murmured Nicholas, frowning. 'Good Lord,' he cried, 'do you really think that I'm capable of attacking people while in the full possession of my senses? Why should I do that?'

Liputin looked put out and did not know what to say. Nicholas grew a little pale, or so it seemed to Liputin.

'At any rate, your train of thought is certainly very amusing,' Nicholas went on. 'As for Agafya, I realize of course that you sent her to abuse me.'

'You didn't expect me to challenge you to a duel, did you?'

'Why, no! I seem to have heard that you dislike duels. ...'

'Why translate from the French?' said Liputin, again looking put out.

'You're all for keeping to your own national customs, aren't you?'

Liputin looked even more put out.

'Dear me, what's this?' cried Nicholas, noticing a volume by Considérant lying very conspicuously on the table. 'You're not a Fourierist by any chance, are you? I shouldn't be surprised if you were! Isn't that a translation from the French?' he laughed, tapping the book with his fingers.

'No, that's not a translation from the French!' Liputin cried spitefully, jumping up from his chair. 'That's a translation from the universal language of mankind, and not only from the French! From the language of the universal social republic and universal harmony – that's what it is, sir! And not only from the French!'

'Dear me,' Nicholas went on, laughing; 'but there isn't such a language, is there?'

Sometimes even a trifle attracts one's attention for a long time and to the exclusion of everything else. I shall have a great deal to say about Mr Stavrogin later on; but just now I should like to record, just as a matter of curiosity, that of all the impressions he received during the whole time he spent in our town, what stuck in his memory most was the insignificant and almost abject figure of the little provincial official, a jealous husband and coarse family tyrant, a miser and a moneylender, who locked up the remnants of meals and the candle-ends, and who at the same time was a fierce believer in goodness only knows what future 'social harmony', who at night gloated ecstatically over the fantastic visions of a future phalanstery, in the immediate realization of which in Russia and in our province he believed as firmly as in his own existence. And that in the very place where he himself had saved up enough money to buy a jerry-built little house, where he had married for the second time and taken a few hundred roubles for his wife, where perhaps for 100 miles there was not a single man, himself included, who bore any resemblance to a future member of 'the universal social republic and harmony'.

'Goodness knows where such people spring from,' wondered Nicholas, as he sometimes recalled the unlooked-for Fourierist.

4

Our Prince travelled for over three years, so that he was almost forgotten in our town. Through Mr Verkhovensky, however, we learnt that he had been all over Europe, that he had even visited Egypt, and spent some time in Jerusalem, then joined a scientific expedition to Iceland and actually visited Iceland. It was also said that he had taken a course of lectures at a German university one winter. He did not write often to his mother – once in six months or even less – but Mrs Stavrogin was neither angry nor offended. She accepted submissively and without protest the relationship which had been established once and for all between her son and herself, and incessantly pined for her Nicholas and dreamt about him. She did not communicate her dreams or complaints to anybody. She seemed even to have become less friendly with Mr Verkhovensky. She was making some plans and, it appears, became more miserly than ever, and began to economize more than ever, and was angry with Mr Verkhovensky for his losses at cards.

At last, in April of this year, she received a letter from Paris from Praskovya Drozdov, a general's widow and a friend of her childhood days. In her letter Mrs Drozdov – whom she had not seen or corresponded with for the last eight years – told her that Nicholas had become a close friend of her family and, particularly, of Lisa, her only daughter, and that he intended to accompany them to Switzerland in the summer, to Verney-Montreux, in spite of the fact that he was received like a son in the family of Count K. (a highly influential Petersburg personage), who was at present living in Paris, and spent practically all his time at his house. The letter was short and its purpose was perfectly clear, though besides the above-mentioned facts no other inferences were drawn. Mrs Stavrogin wasted no time, made up her mind at once, packed her things, and, taking her protégée Dasha (Shatov's sister) with her, went to Paris in the middle of April and afterwards to Switzerland. She came back in July alone, having left Dasha with the Drozdovs; the Drozdovs themselves, according to the news she had brought, hoped to arrive in our town at the end of August.

The Drozdovs, too, were landowners of our province, but General Drozdov's duties – he was a friend of Mrs Stavrogin's and a fellow-officer of her husband – always prevented them from visiting their magnificent estate. After the General's death, which had taken place the year before, the disconsolate widow had gone abroad with her daughter, intending, incidentally, to try out the grape cure at Verney-Montreux during the latter half of the summer. On her return to her native land, she intended to settle in our province for good. She had a large house in our town, which had stood empty and shuttered for many years. They were rich. Mrs Drozdov, known as Mrs Tushin during her first marriage, was, like her school-friend Mrs Stavrogin, the daughter of a government contractor of the old days, and she, too, received a fortune from her father for her dowry. Tushin, a retired cavalry captain, was himself a man of means as well as a man of some ability. At his death he left a considerable fortune to his only daughter, Lisa, who was then only seven years old. Now that Lisa was about twenty-two, she had at least 200,000 roubles of her own, not to mention the great fortune which she would inherit on the death of her mother, who had no children by her second marriage. Mrs Stavrogin was evidently well satisfied with her journey. In her opinion, she had come to a satisfactory arrangement with Mrs Drozdov, and she told Mr Verkhovensky all about it immediately on her return; indeed, she was extremely frank with him, which had not happened for a long time.

'Hurrah!' cried Mr Verkhovensky, snapping his fingers.

He was beside himself with joy, particularly as he had spent the whole time of his separation from his friend in a state of utter dejection. She had not even taken leave of him properly when she went abroad, and had not told anything of her plans to 'the old woman', fearing, perhaps, that he might not keep their secret. She was angry with him at the time for the considerable sum of money he had lost at cards, and which she suddenly found out. But already in Switzerland she felt that on her return she must do something for her forsaken friend, particularly as she had treated him severely for a long time past. The quick and mysterious parting from his friend had struck a chill into the timid heart of Mr Verkhovensky, and, on top of it, he was suddenly beset with other troubles. He was worried by a very serious financial liability he had incurred a long time before and which could not be settled without Mrs Stavrogin's help. Moreover, the term of office of our good and gentle Ivan Osipovich came to an end at last in May of this year; he was replaced, and his dismissal was accompanied by some unpleasantness, too. Then, during the absence of Mrs Stavrogin, the arrival of our new Governor, Andrey von Lembke, took place; simultaneously a noticeable change occurred in the attitude of our provincial society towards Mrs Stavrogin and hence also towards Mr Verkhovensky. At least, he had already made a few unpleasant though valuable observations and, I believe, felt rather apprehensive without Mrs Stavrogin. He was worried by the suspicion that the new Governor had already been told about him as a highly dangerous man. He knew positively that some of our society ladies intended to give up calling on Mrs Stavrogin. It was said about our Governor's wife (who was not expected to arrive before the autumn) that though she was rumoured to be a proud woman, she was a real aristocrat and not like 'poor old Mrs Stavrogin'. For some reason or other, everybody in our town seemed to know for a fact and in detail that our new Governor's wife and Mrs Stavrogin had once met in society and had parted enemies, so that even the mention of Mrs von Lembke was supposed to create a painful impression on Mrs Stavrogin. The jaunty and triumphant air of Mrs Stavrogin and the disdainful indifference with which she heard of the opinions of our ladies and of the excitement of our society, revived the drooping spirits of Mr Verkhovensky and cheered him up at once. He began to describe our new Governor's arrival with a kind of peculiar gloatingly obsequious humour.

'You probably know, *excellente amie*,' he said in a coquettish and affected drawl, 'what a Russian administrator means, speaking generally, and what a new Russian administrator – that is to say, a newly baked, a newly appointed one – means. ... *Ces interminables mots russes!* ... I doubt whether you know what administrative enthusiasm means in practice and what sort of thing it is.'

'Administrative enthusiasm? I have no idea.'

'I mean – *vous savez chez nous – en un mot* – appoint some miserable nonentity to sell some absurd railway tickets, and this nonentity will immediately imagine that he has the right to look down upon you as if he were a Jupiter himself, when you go to take a ticket, *pour vous montrer son pouvoir.* "You wait," he says to himself. "I'll show you my power," and in them this sort of thing reaches the point of administrative enthusiasm. *En un mot,* I've just read that some stupid verger in one of our churches abroad – *mais c'est très curieux* – drove – I mean literally drove – a highly distinguished English family, *les dames charmantes*, out of the church before the beginning of the Lenten service – *vous savez ces chants et le livre de Job* – simply on the pretext that "foreigners are not allowed to loaf about a Russian church and that they must come at the fixed times" – and he sent them into fainting fits. That verger was suffering from an attack of administrative enthusiasm *et il a montré son pouvoir. ...*'

'Cut it short, if you can, Mr Verkhovensky.'

'Mr von Lembke is making a tour of the province now. *En un mot,* this Andrey Antonovich, though he is a Russian German of the Greek Orthodox faith, and even – I'll concede him that – a remarkably handsome man in his forties –'

'What makes you think he is a handsome man? He has the eyes of a sheep.'

'Eminently. But I don't mind yielding to the opinion of our ladies –'

'Let's keep to the point, please. By the way, I see you're wearing a red tie – since when?'

'I – I've just put it on to-day –'

'And do you take your constitutional? Do you go for a five-mile walk every day, as prescribed by your doctor?'

'N-no – not always.'

'I knew it! Already in Switzerland I felt sure you didn't!' she cried irritably. 'Now you'll walk not five but eight miles a day! You've let yourself go terribly – terribly, terribly! You've not aged so much as gone to pieces – you – you gave me a shock when I saw you a few moments ago, in spite of your red tie – *quelle idée rouge!* Go on with your story about von Lembke if you've really anything to tell me about him, and please do finish it some time, I beg you. I'm tired.'

'*En un mot*, I only wanted to say that he's one of those administrators who start at forty and who before that lead obscure lives, and then suddenly become important personages by unexpectedly acquiring a wife or by some other equally desperate means. I mean, he's not in town at the moment – I mean to say that people have already dinned into his ears that I'm a corrupter of youth and a disseminator of atheism in our province. He began making inquiries at once –'

'Are you sure it's true?'

'Why, I've already taken the necessary steps, as a matter of fact. When it was reported to him that you "ruled the province", *vous savez*, he was good enough to say that "nothing of the sort is going to happen from now on".'

'He said that?'

'That "nothing of the sort is going to happen from now on", and *avec cette morgue*. ... His wife we shall have the pleasure of beholding at the end of August; she's coming straight from Petersburg.'

'From abroad. We met there.'

'*Vraiment?*'

'In Paris and in Switzerland. She's related to the Drozdovs.'

'Related? What a remarkable coincidence! I'm told she's ambitious and – and she is said to have important connexions. Is it true?'

'Nonsense! Her connexions are of no importance whatever! She was an old maid without a penny till she was forty-five, and now she's hooked that von Lembke of hers and, of course, her whole object is to make an important man of him. They're both intriguers.'

'I'm told she's two years older than he.'

'Five. Her mother wore out her skirts on my doorstep in Moscow; she used to cadge for invitations to our balls as a favour when my husband was living. And Julia used to sit all night in a corner without a dancing partner, with that turquoise butterfly on her forehead. I felt so sorry for her that I used to send her her first partner after two o'clock in the morning. She was already five-and-twenty then, and they used to take her out in short skirts like a little girl. In the end I was ashamed to invite them to my house.'

'I can see that butterfly of hers.'

'I tell you the moment I arrived I stumbled straight on an intrigue.

You read Mrs Drozdov's letter – what could be plainer? But what did I find? That fool Mrs Drozdov herself – she always was a fool – suddenly glared at me as though wondering what I came for. You can imagine how surprised I was. I looked round, and what do you think I saw? There was that von Lembke woman playing the hypocrite and with her that relation of theirs – a nephew of the late Mr Drozdov – the whole thing was as plain as a pikestaff! Of course, I put an end to all that immediately, and Praskovya is on my side again; but the intrigue, the intrigue!'

'Which you've successfully quashed. Oh, you're a Bismarck!'

'I am no Bismarck, but I am capable of seeing through hypocrisy and stupidity when I meet them. Mrs Lembke is hypocrisy and Praskovya – stupidity. I don't think I have ever met such a flabby woman in my life, *and* her legs are swollen, *and* she's good-natured. What can be more foolish than a good-natured fool?'

'An ill-natured fool, *ma bonne amie*, an ill-natured fool is still more foolish,' Mr Verkhovensky retorted nobly.

'I daresay you're right. You remember Lisa, don't you?'

'*Charmante enfant!*'

'But she's no longer an *enfant*, but a grown-up woman and a woman of character. Generous and passionate, and what I like about her so much is that she stands up to her mother, the credulous fool. We nearly had a row over that relation of theirs.'

'But, good gracious, he isn't a relation of Lisa's at all! He hasn't any designs on her, has he?'

'You see, he's a young army officer, not very talkative, and quite modest, as a matter of fact. I always want to be fair. I think he is against the intrigue himself and isn't after anything, and that it was that Lembke woman who was the chief schemer. He has a great respect for Nicholas. You see, everything depends on Lisa, but I left her on excellent terms with Nicholas, and he promised me faithfully to be back home in November. So that it's only that Lembke who is intriguing, and Praskovya is just a blind woman. Fancy her telling me suddenly that all my suspicions were unjustified; I told her to her face that she was a fool. I'm ready to endorse it on the day of judgement. And but for the fact that Nicholas had begged me to leave well alone for the time being, I wouldn't have left without exposing that hypocritical woman. She was trying to get into the good books of Count

K. through Nicholas. She was out to set a son against his mother. But Lisa, I'm glad to say, is on our side, and I came to an understanding with Praskovya. Do you know that Karmazinov is a relative of hers?'

'What? A relative of von Lembke?'

'Yes, of course. A distant one.'

'Karmazinov, the novelist?'

'Why, yes, the writer. Why are you so surprised? Of course, he thinks he is a great man. The conceited creature! She's coming with him. Now she's making an awful fuss of him over there. She intends to organize something here, some kind of literary gatherings. He's coming for a month, wants to sell his last bit of property here. I nearly met him in Switzerland – not that I wanted to in the least. However, I hope he will do me the honour of recognizing me. He used to correspond with me in the old days, been at my house. I wish you'd dress more decently, Mr Verkhovensky. You're getting more slovenly every day. ... Oh, how you torture me! What are you reading now?'

'Me? Well, I –'

'I see. Same as ever – friends, drinking, the club and cards, and the reputation of an atheist. I don't like that reputation of yours, Mr Verkhovensky. I wish they wouldn't call you an atheist, particularly now. I didn't like it before, for it's just empty talk and nothing more. It must be said at last.'

'*Mais, ma chère –*'

'Listen to me, Mr Verkhovensky. So far as learning is concerned, I am, of course, an ignoramus compared with you, but on my way back here I've been thinking a lot about you. I've come to one conclusion.'

'What conclusion?'

'I've come to the conclusion that we're not the only intelligent people in the world, but that there are people who are much more intelligent than we.'

'Witty and to the point. If there are people who are more intelligent than we are, there must also be people who are more right than we are, and that means that we, too, can make mistakes, doesn't it? *Mais, ma bonne amie,* let us suppose that I do make a mistake, but I still possess my human, eternal, supreme right of freedom of conscience, don't I? I have the right to refuse to be a bigot and a religious fanatic if I want to, for which I shall naturally be hated by all sorts of people to the end of time. *Et puis, comme on trouve toujours plus de moines que de raison*, and as I thoroughly agree with that.'

'What, what did you say?'

'I said: *on trouve toujours plus de moines que de raison*, and as I –'

'That's not yours, is it? You must have taken it from somewhere.'

'It was Pascal who said it.'

'I thought it wouldn't be – you! Why don't you ever say something short and to the point, but always go on and on and on? That's much better than what you had to say about administrative enthusiasm.'

'*Ma foi, chère* – why? Well, first of all, probably because I am not, after all, a Pascal, and, secondly, because we Russians don't know how to say anything in our own language. At least, so far we haven't said anything.'

'Well, perhaps that's not quite true. At any rate, you ought to make a note of such sayings and remember them, in case, you know, they come in useful in a conversation. Oh, my dear Mr Verkhovensky, on my way back here I did intend to have a serious, a very serious talk with you.'

'*Chère, chère amie!*'

'Now that all these Lembkes and Karmazinovs. ... Goodness, how you've let yourself go! Oh, how you torture me! I'd have liked all those people to feel a respect for you because they are not worth your little finger; but the way you carry yourself! What will they see? What am I going to show them? Instead of being a noble example, instead of keeping up the tradition of the past, you surround yourself with all sorts of riff-raff, you have acquired all sorts of horrible habits, you've grown old and feeble, you can't live without wine and cards, you read nothing but Paul de Kock, and you don't write anything, while they all write. All your time is wasted in talk. How can you possibly be friends with such a dreadful man as your inseparable Liputin?'

'Why, pray, *mine* and *inseparable*?' Mr Verkhovensky protested timidly.

'Where is he now?' Mrs Stavrogin went on sharply and sternly.

'He – he has the utmost respect for you, and he's gone to S—k to receive an inheritance which was left him by his mother.'

'He seems to do nothing but get money. How is Shatov? Still the same?'

'*Irascible, mais bon.*'

'I can't stand that Shatov of yours. He's spiteful and thinks a lot of himself.'

'How is Miss Shatov?'

'You mean Dasha? What do you want to know that for?' Mrs Stavrogin looked curiously at him. 'She's all right. I left her with the Drozdovs. I heard something about your son in Switzerland. Something bad, not good.'

'*Oh, c'est une histoire bien bête! Je vous attendais, ma bonne amie, pour vous raconter. ...*'

'I've had enough, Mr Verkhovensky; do leave me in peace. I'm worn out. We shall have plenty of time to talk things over, bad things especially. You're beginning to splutter when you laugh – that's senility or something very like it. And how strangely you seem to laugh now. Gracious me, how many bad habits you've managed to collect! Karmazinov will never call on you! And here they are glad of anything as it is. Oh, well, that's enough for the present. I'm tired! You really might spare me!'

Mr Verkhovensky 'spared' her, but he went away greatly perturbed.

5

Our friend had certainly acquired not a few bad habits, especially during recent months. He let himself run to seed visibly and rapidly, and it is quite true that he had become slovenly. He drank more, he was more easily moved to tears, and his nerves grew weaker. He had become far too sensitive to everything of artistic value. His face had acquired a strange faculty for changing extraordinarily rapidly, from the most solemn expression, for instance, to the most ridiculous and even stupid. He could not bear being left alone, and he was incessantly craving for amusement. He demanded to be told the latest bit of scandal, some local anecdote, insisting on something fresh every day. If no one came to see him for a long time, he paced the room disconsolately, walked up to the window, chewed his lips pensively, heaved deep sighs, and finished up almost by whimpering. He seemed to be full of forebodings, afraid of something unexpected and inevitable; he had become apprehensive; he began to pay great attention to his dreams.

He spent the whole of that day and evening very dejectedly, sent for me, was very excited, talked a lot, told me everything in great detail, but all rather incoherently. Mrs Stavrogin had known for a long time that he did not conceal anything from me. At last I could not help feeling that he was worried by something special, something which, perhaps, he did not clearly understand himself. As a rule, when we had met before and he had begun complaining to me, a bottle of vodka would almost invariably make its appearance after a little time and everything would become more cheerful. But this time there was no vodka, and he obviously had again and again to suppress his desire to send for it.

'And why is she so angry with me?' he kept complaining almost every minute like a child. '*Tous les hommes de génie et de progrès en Russie étaient, sont et seront toujours des* drunkards *et des* gamblers, *qui boivent* like fish – and I'm not such a drunkard and gambler as all that. … She reproaches me for not writing anything. What a curious idea! Why do I lie down? She says I ought to be "an example and a reproach". *Mais entre nous soit dit,* what else should a man who is destined to be "a reproach" do but lie down – doesn't she know that?'

And at last I saw what was the chief and particular trouble that was worrying him so persistently that evening. Many times he went up to the looking-glass and stood a long time before it. At last he turned from the looking-glass to me and said with a sort of strange despair:

' *Mon cher, je suis* a man who has let himself go to pieces!'

And, to be sure, till then, till that very day, he had always remained absolutely confident of one thing, in spite of all Mrs Stavrogin's 'new views' and all her 'changed ideas' – namely, that he was still irresistible to her feminine heart, that is to say, not only as an exile or as a famous *savant,* but as a handsome man. For twenty years he had harboured that flattering and soothing conviction, and quite possibly of all his convictions this was the most difficult to part with. Had he a foreboding that evening of the great ordeal he would have to undergo so soon?

6

Let me now describe the almost forgotten incident with which my story really begins.

At the very end of August, the Drozdovs, too, at last returned.

Their arrival, which took place shortly before that of their relative, the long-expected wife of our Governor, made a deep impression on our society. But I shall speak of all these interesting events later; now I shall merely state that Mrs Drozdov presented Mrs Stavrogin, who was expecting her so impatiently, with a most difficult problem: Nicholas had parted from them in July and, having met Count K. on the Rhine, gone with him and his family to Petersburg. (N.B. The Count's three daughters were all of a marriageable age.)

'I could get nothing out of Lisa,' Mrs Drozdov concluded. 'You know how proud and stubborn she is. But I saw with my own eyes that something had taken place between her and Nicholas. I don't know all the ins and outs, but I think that you, my dear, will have to ask your Dasha about it. If you ask me, Lisa was offended. I'm awfully glad to have brought your favourite back to you at last and handed her over to you, a good riddance.'

These venomous words were uttered with remarkable exasperation. It was obvious that the 'flabby' woman had prepared them beforehand and had been gloating over their effect long before she had uttered them. But Mrs Stavrogin was not the woman to be put out by sentimental effects and innuendoes. She sternly demanded the most precise and satisfactory explanations. Mrs Drozdov immediately lowered her tone, and even ended up by bursting into tears and plunging into avowals of the deepest friendship. This irritable but sentimental lady, like Mr Verkhovensky, was always in need of true friendship, and her chief complaint against her daughter Lisa was that she was 'no friend to her'.

But the only thing that could be gathered with any certainty from all her explanations and outpourings was that there really had been some quarrel between Lisa and Nicholas, but Mrs Drozdov evidently had no definite idea what sort of quarrel it was. As for her imputations against Dasha, she not only withdrew them completely in the end, but even asked Mrs Stavrogin particularly not to attach any importance to her words, because she had uttered them 'in irritation'. In short, everything was extremely vague, even suspicious. According to her account, the quarrel was due to Lisa's 'stubborn and sarcastic' character; Nicholas, on the other hand, though greatly in love, was too proud to put up with her sarcastic remarks, and became sarcastic himself. 'Soon afterwards,' she went on, 'we made the acquaintance of a young man, the nephew of your "professor", I believe, and indeed he has the same surname. ...'

'He's his son, not his nephew,' Mrs Stavrogin corrected her.

Mrs Drozdov never could remember the surname of Mr Verkhovensky, and she always called him the 'professor'.

'Well, his son, then; so much the better, it's all the same to me. An ordinary young man, very lively and unconventional, but nothing special about him. Well, I'm afraid Lisa herself did wrong there. She made friends with the young man to make Nicholas jealous. I can't blame her for it very much: it's the sort of thing every girl would do – something rather charming, I think. Only instead of being jealous Nicholas made friends with the young man himself, as if he did not notice anything and just as though he did not really care. That made Lisa furious. The young man soon left,(he seemed to be in a hurry to go somewhere), and Lisa began to pick quarrels with Nicholas at every favourable opportunity. She noticed that Nicholas was sometimes talking to Dasha, and that made her fly into such rages that life wasn't worth living, my dear. The doctors have forbidden me to get angry, and I got so sick of that lake that they make such a fuss about that it only gave me toothache and most awful rheumatism. Why, I've seen it stated in print that Lake Geneva gives people the toothache. It's one of its characteristics, it seems. And just then Nicholas received a letter from the Countess, and left us at once; he packed his things in one day. I must say they parted friends, and Lisa, too, was very gay and frivolous, and laughed a lot when she saw him off. Only she was pretending all the time. After he had gone she grew very wistful, and stopped mentioning him at all. Didn't let me mention him, either. And I'd advise you, too, my dear, not to mention it again to Lisa. You'll only mess things up. If you don't say anything, she will be the first to talk to you about it. You'll find out more that way. I think they'll make it up if only Nicholas carries out his promise and comes back soon.'

'I'll write to him at once. If that's all that's happened, it's just a silly quarrel; it's all nonsense! You see, I know Dasha very well. There's nothing in it.'

'I'm sorry about dear Dasha – I shouldn't have said that. They just used to talk to one another in the ordinary way – and aloud, too. But the whole thing, my dear, upset me at the time. Besides, Lisa, too, I could see treated her again with the same kindness as before.'

Mrs Stavrogin wrote to Nicholas on the same day, imploring him to come back at least one month earlier than he had intended. But there still remained something about the affair which she could not explain, something she did not know. She thought about it the whole evening and the whole night. Mrs Drozdov's opinion seemed too innocent and too sentimental to her. 'Praskovya,' she thought, 'has all her life been too sentimental, ever since she was at boarding-school. Nicholas is not the sort of man to run away because of some sarcastic remarks of a young girl. If they did quarrel, then there must have been some other reason for it. They brought that officer with them, though. Lives in their house as a relative. And about Dasha, too, Praskovya was a little too quick to apologize: I expect she must have kept something to herself, something she did not want to tell me. ...'

In the morning Mrs Stavrogin made up her mind to put an end to at least one perplexing problem, and her plan was quite remarkable for its unexpectedness. What did she really think of when she made it? It is difficult to say, and, besides, I cannot undertake to explain beforehand all its contradictions. As a chronicler, I am content to present the events exactly as they happened, and it is not my fault if they appear incredible. I must, however, put it once more on record that by the morning there was no suspicion left in her mind so far as Dasha was concerned, and, to tell the truth, she never really suspected her; she had too much confidence in her. And, besides, she thought it highly unlikely that Nicholas could fall in love with her – 'with Dasha'. Next morning, when Dasha was pouring out the tea at the breakfast table, Mrs Stavrogin observed her closely for a long time and, perhaps for the twentieth time since the day before, said to herself with utter conviction: 'It's all nonsense!'

She did notice, however, that Dasha looked tired and that she was more quiet and apathetic than usual. After breakfast both of them, according to their long-established custom, sat down to needlework. Mrs Stavrogin demanded from her a full account of her impressions abroad, especially of the countryside, the inhabitants, their towns, their customs, their arts and commerce – everything she had had time to observe. Not one question about the Drozdovs or about her life with the Drozdovs. Dasha, who sat beside her at the work-table and helped her with the embroidery, told her all about it for half an hour in her even, monotonous, but somewhat weak voice.

'Darya,' Mrs Stavrogin interrupted her suddenly, 'you have nothing special you would like to tell me, have you?'

'No, nothing,' said Dasha, after a moment's thought, looking at Mrs Stavrogin with her bright eyes.

'Nothing on your soul, on your heart, on your conscience?'

'Nothing,' Dasha repeated quietly, but with a sort of sullen firmness.

'I knew there wasn't! I want you to know, Darya, that I shall never doubt you. Now sit still and listen. Sit down on that chair, dear, opposite; I want to see you properly. That's right. Listen – do you want to be married?'

Dasha responded with a long, though not too astonished, questioning look.

'Wait, don't say anything. In the first place, there is a great difference in age – a very great difference – but you know better than anyone what nonsense that is. You're a sensible girl, and there must be no mistakes in your life. However, he is still a handsome man. … I mean, Mr Verkhovensky, whom you have always respected. Well?'

Dasha looked even more questioningly, and this time she was not only astonished, but blushed perceptibly.

'Wait, don't say anything. Don't be in a hurry. Though I have left you money in my will, what's to become of you should I die, even if you have money? You will be deceived and your money will be taken away from you – you will be ruined. But if you marry him, you'll be the wife of a famous man. Now let's consider it from his point of view: if I die now, what will become of him, though I've provided for him? But I know I can trust you to look after him. Wait, I haven't finished: he's thoughtless, irresolute, callous, egoistic, a man of low habits; but you must appreciate him if only because there are men who are much worse than he is. I do not want to get you off my hands to some blackguard, do I? Or do you think I do? But you will appreciate him mainly because I ask you to,' she broke off suddenly, irritably. 'Do you hear? What are you staring at me for?'

Dasha still listened and said nothing.

'Wait a moment – don't speak! He's an old woman – but that's all the better for you. A pathetic old woman, I admit. There is not a woman in the world whose love he deserves. But he deserves to be loved for his helplessness, and you will love him for his helplessness. You understand me, don't you? Don't you?'

Dasha nodded.

'I knew you would. I did not expect anything else from you. He will love you, because he must, he must. He *must* adore you!' Mrs Stavrogin screamed with peculiar irritation. 'Besides, he is sure to fall in love with you, even if it were not his duty to do so. I know him. And I shall always be here. You needn't worry about that: I shall always be here. He will complain about you, he will tell discreditable stories about you, he will whisper things about you to the first person he meets, he will be whining, for ever whining; he will write you letters from one room to another, two letters a day; but he won't be able to live without you all the same, and that's the main thing. Make him do as you like; if you can't make him, you'll be a fool. He'll want to hang himself. He'll threaten to do so – don't you believe it. It's just nonsense! Don't believe it, but keep your eyes open all the same, for you never can tell: he may hang himself. This sort of thing does happen with people like that: they hang themselves out of weakness and not out of strength. And that's why you must never drive him too far – that's the first rule in married life. Don't forget that he is a poet, either. Listen, Dasha: there is no greater happiness than self-sacrifice. Besides, you'll be doing me a great favour, and that's the main thing. Don't think that I've been talking nonsense. I know what I am talking about. I'm an egoist, so you be an egoist, too. I'm not forcing you to do anything; it all depends on you: whatever you say will be done. Well, what are you sitting there like that for? Say something!'

'It makes no difference to me, Mrs Stavrogin, if I really must marry someone,' Dasha said firmly.

'Must? What are you hinting at?' Mrs Stavrogin looked sternly and intently at her.

Dasha was silent, picking at the embroidery frame with her needle.

'You may be a clever girl, but you're talking nonsense. It may be true that I'm very anxious for you to marry now, but that's not because I think it's necessary. It's merely because I've set my heart on it, and only to Mr Verkhovensky. But for Mr Verkhovensky I should not have thought of marrying you now, though you are twenty. ... Well?'

'I'll do as you wish, ma'am.'

'You agree, then! Wait, don't say anything. Why are you in such a hurry? I haven't finished: I've left you fifteen thousand roubles in my will. I'm going to give them to you now, on your wedding day. You will give eight thousand to him – I mean, not to him but to me. He owes eight thousand; I'll pay his debt, but he must know that it has been paid with your money. You will be left with seven thousand, and, remember, don't give him one rouble of it. Never pay his debts. If you pay them once, you'll never see the end of it. I'll make the two of you an allowance of one thousand two hundred a year, with extras, one thousand five hundred, besides board and lodging, which I shall also pay for, just as I do for him now. Only you must have your own servants. Your yearly allowance I shall pay you in a lump sum, I shall give it to you – straight into your hands. But you, too, be kind to him, give him some money occasionally, and let his friends visit him once a week; if they come more often, turn them out. But I shall be here myself. And if I die, the allowance will go on till his death – do you hear? – till *his* death, because it is his allowance, and not yours. I'll leave you in my will besides your seven thousand – which, if you're not a fool, you will keep intact – another eight thousand. You won't get another penny from me. It's right that you should know that. Well, do you agree or not? Won't you say something at last?'

'I've told you already, Mrs Stavrogin.'

'Remember it's for you to decide. It will be just as you wish.'

'In that case, could you tell me, Mrs Stavrogin, whether Mr Verkhovensky has said anything to you about it?'

'No, he hasn't, and he doesn't know anything about it, but – he will presently!'

She got up at once and threw on her black shawl. Dasha again blushed a little and followed her with a questioning glance. Mrs Stavrogin turned suddenly to her with a face burning with anger.

'You fool!' She pounced upon her like a hawk. 'You ungrateful fool! What are you thinking about? Do you really believe that I'd compromise you in any way – however little? Why, he'll be crawling on his knees to beg you to marry him, he ought to die of happiness – that's how it shall be arranged. You know perfectly well that I will never allow anyone to hurt you. Or do you think that he'll marry you for the eight thousand and that I'm running now to sell you to him?

You're a fool, a fool! You're all ungrateful fools. Give me my umbrella!'

And she went off on foot along the wet brick pavements and wooden planks to Mr Verkhovensky.

7

It was quite true that she would not let anyone hurt Dasha; on the contrary, it was now that she considered herself to be acting as her benefactress. The most high-minded and virtuous indignation blazed up in her heart when, as she put on her shawl, she caught the embarrassed and mistrustful glance of her protégée fixed upon her. She had genuinely loved Dasha ever since she was a little girl. Mrs Drozdov was right in saying that Dasha was her favourite. Long ago Mrs Stavrogin had made up her mind once and for all that Dasha's character was not in the least like her brother's (not, that is, like the character of her brother, Ivan Shatov), that she was quiet and gentle, capable of great acts of self-sacrifice; that she was loyal, extraordinarily modest, unusually sensible, and, above all, grateful. So far Dasha evidently came up to her expectations. 'There will be no mistakes in her life,' Mrs Stavrogin said when the girl was only twelve years old, and as it was her nature to attach herself obstinately and passionately to any illusion that fascinated her, any new design, any idea that took her fancy, she decided there and then to bring up Dasha like her own daughter. She immediately set aside a sum of money for her, and engaged a governess, Miss Criggs, who lived with her till Dasha was sixteen, but who was suddenly dismissed for some unknown reason. Teachers from the grammar school came to give her lessons, among them, incidentally, a real Frenchman, who taught Dasha French. The Frenchman, too, was suddenly dismissed, almost turned out of the house. A poor lady, a widow of good family, who was a stranger in the town, taught her to play the piano. But her chief tutor was Mr Verkhovensky. It was he who really first discovered Dasha: he began teaching the quiet child before even Mrs Stavrogin thought of her. Let me repeat again: it was wonderful how children took to him! Lisa Tushin had been taught by him from the age of eight till eleven (Mr Verkhovensky, of course, taught her without any fee, which he would not have taken from the Drozdovs for anything in the world). But he grew very fond of the lovely child, and used to tell her all sorts of romantic tales about the creation of the world, the earth, and the history of mankind. His lectures about primitive man and the primitive peoples were more interesting than the Arabian tales. Lisa, who was deeply moved by these stories, used to mimic Mr Verkhovensky very amusingly at home. He got to know about it, and once took her by surprise. Lisa, thrown into confusion, flung herself into his arms and burst out crying. Mr Verkhovensky wept, too, with delight. But Lisa soon went away, and Dasha alone remained. When other teachers were engaged for Dasha, Mr Verkhovensky stopped his lessons with her and gradually lost interest in her altogether. That went on for a long time. One day, when she was already seventeen, he was suddenly amazed by her prettiness. It happened at dinner in Mrs Stavrogin's house. He began talking to the young girl, was very pleased with her answers, and ended up by proposing to give her a serious and comprehensive course of lectures on the history of Russian literature. Mrs Stavrogin was delighted, and thanked him for his excellent idea, and Dasha was very excited about it. Mr Verkhovensky prepared his lectures with special care, and at last they began. They started with the ancient period; the first lecture went off very well; Mrs Stavrogin was present. When Mr Verkhovensky had finished, and just as he was about to tell his pupil that next time he would discuss *The Lay of Igor's Army*, Mrs Stavrogin suddenly got up and declared that there would be no more lessons. Mr Verkhovensky winced, but said nothing. Dasha flushed crimson. That was the end of the matter, however. That had happened exactly three years before Mrs Stavrogin's present unexpected whim.

Poor Mr Verkhovensky was sitting alone in his room without the slightest premonition of what was about to happen. Sunk in melancholy thoughts, he had for a long time been glancing through the window to see whether any of his friends were coming. But no one would come. It was drizzling. It was getting cold. The stove would have to be heated. He sighed. Suddenly a terrible spectre appeared before his eyes: Mrs Stavrogin was coming to see him in such weather and at such an ungodly hour! And on foot! He was so startled that he forgot to put on his coat, and received her as he was: in his usual pink, wadded jacket.

'*Ma bonne amie*,' he cried weakly, rising to meet her.

'You're alone? I'm glad. I can't stand your friends. Oh, how you do smoke! Gracious, what an atmosphere! You haven't finished your tea, and it's almost twelve o'clock! Your idea of heaven is disorder. Your idea of enjoyment is dirt. What are these torn bits of paper doing on the floor? Nastasya! Nastasya! What is your Nastasya doing? Open the windows, my dear, the ventilation windows, the doors – every-thing! Open them wide, please! We'll go into the drawing-room. I've come to you on business. And, please, sweep up, my dear, for once in your life!'

'Master makes such a mess, ma'am!' Nastasya squeaked in an ex-asperated, plaintive voice.

'Well, keep on sweeping! Sweep fifteen times a day, my dear! What a horrible room!' she said when they had gone into the draw-ing-room. 'Close the door properly; I'm sure she'll be eavesdropping. You simply must get new wallpaper. I sent you the decorator with a pattern book; why didn't you choose one? Sit down and listen. Sit down, please! Where are you off to? Where are you off to? Where?'

'One moment – I –' cried Mr Verkhovensky from the other room; 'here I am!'

'Oh, you've changed your coat.' She looked him up and down quizzically. (He had put on his coat over the jacket.) 'Yes, that cer-tainly is more in tune with – with what I have to tell you. Sit down, please!'

She told him everything all at once, sharply and forcefully. She hinted at the eight thousand which he wanted so badly. She spoke at great length about the dowry. Mr Verkhovensky glared at her and trembled. He heard everything, but could not understand it properly. He tried to speak, but his voice failed him. All he knew was that every-thing would be as she said, that it was useless to argue and object, and that the question of his marriage had been irrevocably settled.

'*Mais ma bonne amie* – for the third time and at my time of life and to such a child!' he brought himself to say at last. '*Mais c'est une enfant!*'

'A child who is twenty years old, thank goodness! Don't roll your eyes, please, I beg you. You're not on the stage. You're a very clever and learned man, but you don't understand anything about life. You must always have a nurse to look after you. What's going to happen to you when I'm dead? And she'll be a good nurse to you. She's a modest, determined, sensible girl. Besides, I shall always be here, I'm not thinking of dying yet. She's a home-loving girl, an angel of gentleness. This happy thought occurred to me in Switzerland. Don't you see? I tell you she's an angel of gentleness!' she suddenly screamed furiously. 'Your place is always filthy. She'll keep it clean and orderly. Everything will shine like a mirror. Gracious, you don't think I'm going to implore you to marry such a treasure, count up all the advantages, go down on my knees before you, do you? Why, it's you who ought to go down on your knees! Oh, you vain, vain, faint-hearted man!'

'But – I'm an old man!'

'What do your fifty-three years matter? Fifty is not the end, but the middle of a man's life. You're a handsome man, and well you know it. You also know how much she respects you. If I die, what's to become of her? But married to you, she need not worry and I need not worry. You're a man of importance; you have a name, a loving heart. You receive a pension which I look upon as an obligation. You will save her, perhaps, save her! In any case, you'll be doing her an honour. You will teach her to live; you will enlarge her mind, guide her thoughts. How many people are ruined to-day because their thoughts are not properly guided. By that time you will have finished your book, and you'll at once remind people of your existence.'

'As a matter of fact,' he murmured, gratified by Mrs Stavrogin's adroit flattery – 'as a matter of fact I'm just about to start writing my *Stories from Spanish History*.'

'Well, there you are!'

'But – what about her? Did you tell her?'

'Don't worry about her; and you needn't be so curious to know, either. Of course, you must ask her yourself, beg her to do you the honour – understand? But don't worry, I'll be there. Besides, you love her, don't you?'

Mr Verkhovensky's head began to swim: the walls were going round and round. There was one terrible idea he could not grasp, try as he might.

'*Excellente amie*,' he said, his voice trembling suddenly, 'I – I could never imagine that you – you would make up your mind to – to marry me off to another woman!'

'You're not a young lady, my dear sir. Only young ladies are married off; you're getting married yourself,' Mrs Stavrogin hissed venomously.

'*Oui, j'ai pris un mot pour un autre. Mais — c'est égal.*' He stared at her, looking lost.

'I can see that it is *égal*,' she said with slow, contemptuous deliberation. 'Heavens, he's fainted! Nastasya, Nastasya! Water!'

But there was no need for water. He came to. Mrs Stavrogin picked up her umbrella.

'I see that it's no use talking to you now.'

'*Oui, oui, je suis incapable.*'

'But by to-morrow, I hope, you will have rested and thought it over. Stay at home. If anything happens, let me know, even if it's at night. Don't write me any letters, for I shan't read them. But to-morrow I shall come here again myself at the same time alone for your final answer, and I trust it will be satisfactory. See that no one is here and that everything is nice and tidy, for this is really disgusting. Nastasya, Nastasya!'

Of course, the next day he gave his consent; and he could hardly have done otherwise. There was one special circumstance here. ...

8

Mr Verkhovensky's estate, as we all knew (consisting of fifty serfs according to the old register, and adjoining Skvoreshniki), was not his at all, but belonged to his first wife, and was therefore the property of his son Peter now. Mr Verkhovensky was merely his son's trustee, and so, when his son came of age, he was put in charge of it because he had received a formal authorization from his son to manage his estate. Such an arrangement was to the advantage of the young man, for he received about 1,000 roubles a year from his father in lieu of the income from the estate, which under the new regime did not produce 500 (perhaps even less). Lord knows how such a relationship had been established. In any case, the whole of the 1,000 roubles was sent by Mrs Stavrogin, Mr Verkhovensky not contributing a rouble to it. On the contrary, he put all the money he received from the estate in his own pocket, and, besides, completely ruined it, having let it to a business man and sold, without Mrs Stavrogin's knowledge, the timber which was its only valuable asset. He had been selling the timber bit by bit. The whole of it was worth at least 8,000 roubles, but he sold it for 5,000. He sometimes lost a lot of money at the club, and was afraid to ask Mrs Stavrogin for it. She was wild with anger when at last she got to know about it. And now his beloved son wrote to say that he was coming himself to sell his property at whatever price it would fetch, and asked his father to make the necessary arrangements for its sale. It was clear that, in view of his generous and selfless nature, Mr Verkhovensky was ashamed of the way he had treated *le cher enfant* (whom he had last seen nine years ago as a student in Petersburg). Originally, the whole estate was worth 13,000 or 14,000 roubles, but at present it was doubtful whether anyone would give more than 5,000 for it. No doubt Mr Verkhovensky was fully entitled, by the terms of the trust, to sell the timber and, taking into account the 1,000 roubles his son had been receiving punctually for so many years, he could have put up a good case against any unfair demands at the final settlement. But Mr Verkhovensky was an honourable man of high principles. A marvellously beautiful idea occurred to him: when his darling Peter arrived, he would lay on the table before him 15,000 roubles – that is, the maximum amount the estate would ever have realized – without hinting at the yearly payments his son had been receiving. Instead, he would press *ce cher fils* with tears to his heart, thus putting an end to all their business accounts. He began to unfold this beautiful picture carefully and in a roundabout way to Mrs Stavrogin. He hinted that that would shed a sort of special, noble lustre on their long friendship – their 'idea'. It would also show up the fathers of the older generation and, generally, everyone who belonged to it, in a selfless and magnanimous light as compared with the younger generation of frivolous and socialistic young men.

He said a lot more, but Mrs Stavrogin made no comment. At last she told him drily that she was ready to buy their land for its maximum price – that is, for 6,000 or 7,000 roubles (while it could have been bought for four). About the remaining 8,000, which had vanished with the woods, she never uttered a word.

This had happened a month before Mrs Stavrogin proposed that he should marry Dasha. Mr Verkhovensky was shocked and began to ponder. There might in the past have been a hope that his darling son would not make an appearance at all – at least, an outsider might have expressed such a hope. Mr Verkhovensky himself, as a father, would of course have indignantly rejected the very suggestion of such a hope. However that may be, all sorts of queer rumours had till then been reaching us about darling Peter. At first, after finishing his course at the university six years before, he seemed to have loafed about Petersburg without a job. Suddenly we received the news that he had taken part in the distribution of some anonymous propaganda leaflet and was awaiting trial. Then that he had suddenly turned up abroad, in Switzerland, at Geneva – that is to say, we were afraid that he had run away.

'It all seems very queer to me,' Mr Verkhovensky used to harangue us at the time, looking greatly embarrassed. 'Dear Peter, *c'est une si pauvre tête*! He's kind, noble-minded, very sensitive, and I must say that I was very glad in Petersburg when I compared him with our modern young people, but *c'est un pauvre sire tout de même*. ... And, you know, it's all because of that half-bakedness, that sentimentality! What fascinates them is not realism, but the sentimental and idealist side of socialism; its religious aspect, as it were; its poetry – all of it second-hand, of course. And yet think what it all means to me! I have so many enemies here, and more *there*, and they are certain to ascribe it to his father's influence. Heavens, Peter a leader of the revolutionary movement! What times we live in!'

However, Peter very soon sent his full address from Switzerland for his money to be forwarded to him as usual, which meant that he was not exactly a political *émigré*. And now, after having spent four years abroad, he suddenly appeared in his own country again and sent news of his imminent arrival: which meant that he was not accused of anything. What was more, someone seemed to have taken an interest in him and become his patron. He wrote now from the south of Russia, where he was on some private business, having been entrusted with some important commission by someone. All this was admirable, but the question still remained where Mr Verkhovensky was to get the other 7,000 or 8,000 roubles to make up the 'fair' price for the estate. And what if his son should raise a clamour, and instead of that inspiring picture it should come to a lawsuit? Somehow he felt that his sensitive Peter would not give up anything that was to his interest.

'Why is it, as I have noticed,' Mr Verkhovensky whispered to me once – 'why is it that all these desperate socialists and communists are, at the same time, also such incredible misers, such acquisitive fellows, such believers in private property, and indeed, the bigger the socialist,

the more extreme he is, the stronger is his instinct for private owner-
ship – why is it? Can that, too, be merely the result of sentimentality?'

I don't know if there is any truth in this observation of Mr Verkhovensky's. All I know is that Peter had been apprised of the sale of the
timber and of everything else and that Mr Verkhovensky was aware
that he had. I also happened to read Peter's letters to his father: he wrote
very rarely – once a year or even less often. Only quite recently he had
sent two letters, almost one after the other, to tell his father of his
coming arrival. All his letters were short, dry, consisting entirely of instructions, and as father and son had since their meeting in Petersburg
been on familiar terms, according to the latest fashion, Peter's letters
reminded me forcibly of the injunctions former landowners used to
send from Moscow or Petersburg to their serfs whom they had made
their estate managers. And now all of a sudden the 8,000 roubles,
which would settle Mr Verkhovensky's financial obligations to his
son, emerged as if by magic from Mrs Stavrogin's offer. And she had
made it perfectly clear that they could not emerge from anywhere
else. So, naturally, Mr Verkhovensky consented.

As soon as she had gone, he sent for me, shutting himself up from
everybody else for the whole day. He shed tears, of course; he talked
a lot and well, frequently lost the thread of his thoughts, delivered
himself of an occasional epigram, and was mightily pleased with it.
Then he had a slight attack of gastric catarrh – in short, everything
took its usual course. After which he brought out the portrait of his
German wife, who had died twenty years before, and began addressing her plaintively: 'Will you ever forgive me?' He seemed altogether lost. To drown our sorrows, we indulged in a little drinking.
Soon, however, he fell into a sweet slumber. Next morning he tied
his cravat in a most artistic fashion, dressed with care, and went frequently to look at himself in the mirror. He sprinkled perfume on his
handkerchief – just a few drops, though – and the moment he caught
sight of Mrs Stavrogin through the window, he quickly picked up
another handkerchief and hid the scented one under a cushion.

'That's excellent!' Mrs Stavrogin expressed her approval on receiving his answer. 'In the first place, it shows fine determination on
your part, and, secondly, you've listened to the voice of reason, to
which you so seldom pay any attention in your private affairs. There
is no hurry, however,' she added, examining the knot of his white

cravat. 'For the time being say nothing, and I will say nothing. It will soon be your birthday; I'll come to see you with her. Make us some afternoon tea and, please, no wine or snacks; I'll see to it myself, though. Invite your friends – we shall make the selection together, however. If necessary, you can have a talk with her the day before, and at your party we shall not make any official announcement of your engagement, but just hint at it or make it public without any ceremonies. And then in about a fortnight there will be the wedding – a quiet wedding, if possible. In fact, it wouldn't be a bad thing if the two of you would go away for a time immediately after the wedding ceremony, to Moscow, for instance. I, too, might come with you. But the chief thing is that you shouldn't say anything about it till then.'

Mr Verkhovensky was surprised. He ventured to say that he could not possibly act like that and that it was necessary for him to talk it over with his future wife, but Mrs Stavrogin shouted at him irritably:

'What do you want to do that for? First of all, perhaps nothing will come of it –'

'What do you mean?' the future bridegroom murmured, completely stunned.

'I mean what I say. I haven't yet made up my mind. However, I'm sure everything will be as I said, so you needn't worry; I'll prepare her myself. You needn't do anything at all. Whatever is necessary will be said and done, and you have no business to see her at all. What for? What part do you expect to play? No, you'd better not come yourself nor write any letters. Not a word, I beg you. I, too, shan't say a word.'

She firmly refused to offer any explanation and went away visibly upset. It would appear that Mr Verkhovensky's excessive readiness astonished her. Alas! he simply did not realize his position, and he had not had time to consider the question from certain other points of view. On the contrary, a new tone emerged, something triumphant and flippant. He swaggered.

'I like that!' he would exclaim, stopping before me and spreading out his arms. 'Did you hear that? She wants to drive things so far that in the end I should be forced to refuse. I, too, can lose my patience and – refuse! "Sit still, what do you want to go to her for?" But why, I ask you, must I be married? Just because she gets some ridiculous idea into her head? But I am a serious man, and I'm quite capable of refusing to submit to the silly ideas of a crazy female! I have obligations towards my son and – and towards myself! I'm making a sacrifice – does she realize that? I've consented perhaps because I'm tired of life and it's all the same to me. But she can easily provoke me, and then it won't be all the same to me. She'll get my back up and I shall refuse. *Et enfin le ridicule.* … What will they say at the club? What will – what will Liputin say? "Perhaps nothing will come of it" – perfect, isn't it? That's the limit! That's – that's beyond everything! *Je suis un forçat, un Badinguet, un* man pushed to the wall….'

But at the same time a sort of capricious self-complacency, something playfully flippant could be discerned amidst all these plaintive protestations. However, in the evening we had some more drinks.

3

Another Man's Sins

I

ABOUT a week passed, and things began to be a little more involved.

Let me observe in passing that I had to put up with a great deal during that unhappy week – never leaving the side of my poor affianced friend, in the capacity of his closest confidant. He was mostly overcome with shame, though we saw nobody during that week and were entirely alone; but he was ashamed even before me, and so much so that the more he confided in me, the more vexed he was with me for it. Being very sensitive, he suspected that everyone in town already knew about it, and he was afraid to show himself not only in the club, but even among his own circle of friends. He even took his regular constitutional only well after nightfall, when it was quite dark.

A week passed and he still did not know whether he was betrothed or not, and, however much he tried, he could not find out for certain. He had not met his betrothed and, indeed, he was not sure whether she was his betrothed or not; he did not even know whether there was anything serious about the whole business. For some reason Mrs Stavrogin categorically refused to see him. In reply to one of his very first letters (and he wrote a great number of letters to her) she told him plainly not to bother her for the time being because she was very busy, and as she had a great deal of important business to communicate to him, she was purposely waiting for an opportunity when she was less busy than at the moment, and *in time* she would let him know when he could come and see her. As for his letters, she declared that she would send them back unopened, as it was 'just tomfoolery'. I read that note myself; it was he who showed it to me.

Yet those harsh and vague statements were nothing compared with his main anxiety. That anxiety tormented him greatly, incessantly; he grew thin and lost courage because of it. It was something that made him feel more ashamed than anything else, something he refused even to discuss with me. On the contrary, whenever I happened to mention it, he lied to me and dodged about like a little boy; and yet he sent for me himself every day: he could not be without me for two hours, needing me as much as air or water.

Such behaviour somewhat hurt my vanity. It goes without saying that I had long since guessed that great secret of his and seen through it. I was firmly convinced at the time that the revelation of this secret, this chief anxiety of Mr Verkhovensky's, would not have redounded to his credit, and that was why, being still young, I could not help being indignant at the coarseness of his feelings and the ugly nature of some of his suspicions. In the heat of the moment and, I must confess, perhaps feeling tired of being his confidant, I may have blamed him too much. In my callousness, I tried to make him confess everything to me himself, though I was aware that it was difficult to confess certain things. He, too, saw through me; I mean, he realized that I saw through him and that I was, indeed, angry with him, and he was angry with me for being angry with him and seeing through him. My exasperation with him was perhaps petty and stupid; but when two people spend all their time together, it makes real friendship between them rather difficult. From a certain point of view he had a true understanding of certain aspects of his position; indeed, he was very outspoken on those points which he did not think it necessary to conceal.

'Oh, she was not at all like that before,' he would sometimes admit incautiously to me about Mrs Stavrogin. 'She was not at all like that before, when we used to discuss things together. Do you know that in those days she could talk? Will you believe me when I tell you that in those days she had ideas, her own ideas? Now everything has changed! She says it is only the old, old phrases all over again. She despises our past. ... Now she is just a sort of shop-assistant, a housekeeper, a person who has a grievance against the world, and she's always cross. ...'

'But why should she be cross now that you have carried out her orders?' I objected.

He gave me a shrewd look.

'*Cher ami*, if I had not consented, she would have been angry, terribly angry! But still not as much as she is now that I have consented.'

He was very pleased with that paradox of his, and that evening we emptied a bottle between us. But that mood lasted only a short time; on the following day he was in a more dreadful state and more depressed than ever.

But I was even more vexed with him for his inability to make up his mind to pay a visit to the Drozdovs to renew their acquaintance, which he should have done on their arrival and which I understood they expected him to do, for they kept asking about him. He, too, was anxious to do it every day. He spoke of Lisa with an enthusiasm I could not understand. No doubt he remembered her as a child whom he had once been very fond of; but for some reason he imagined, besides, that in her company he would find an alleviation of his present sufferings and even a solution of his gravest doubts. He expected to find a kind of extraordinary being in Lisa. But he did not call on her for all that, though he meant to do so every day. The main thing was that I wanted desperately to be introduced to her myself just then, and Mr Verkhovensky was the only person I knew who could do that. I was greatly impressed during my frequent meetings with her – in the street, of course, when she was out riding, wearing a riding habit and mounted on a fine horse, in the company of her so-called relative, a handsome army officer, the nephew of the late General Drozdov. But my infatuation lasted only a very short time, and I soon realized the utter impossibility of my dreams myself – yet though it lasted only a very short time, it was real, and it may therefore be imagined how indignant I was with my poor friend sometimes for obstinately refusing to leave his house.

All the members of our circle had been officially informed from the beginning that Mr Verkhovensky would not be receiving any visitors for a time and that he was anxious to be left alone. He insisted that a circular to that effect should be sent out to them, though I did my best to dissuade him. As a matter of fact, it was I who went to see them all and, at his request, told everybody that Mrs Stavrogin had commissioned our 'old man' (as we all used to call Mr Verkhovensky among ourselves) to do some urgent job – namely, to arrange in order some correspondence of over several years – that he had shut himself up, and that I was helping him, etc., etc. Liputin alone I had not time to see, putting it off from day to day, but it would be truer to say that I was afraid to go to see him. I knew very well that he would not believe a word I said, that he was quite certain to jump to the conclusion that there was a secret we wanted to keep from him alone, and that the moment I left him, he would at once go all over the town to find out what it was and spread all sorts of slanderous stories about it. While I was telling myself all this, I accidentally ran across him in the street. It seemed that he had already learnt everything from our members whom I had just informed. But, strange to say, he never asked me any questions about Mr Verkhovensky and, far from being curious, interrupted me himself when I began to apologize for not having been to see him before, and immediately changed the subject. It is true he had a great deal to tell me: he was very excited and was delighted to have found someone who would listen to him. He started talking of the news of the town, the arrival of the Governor's wife with 'new topics of conversation', of the opposition which had already been organized at the club, of how everybody was shouting about the new ideas, and how ill it suited them, etc., etc. He talked for a quarter of an hour, and so amusingly that I could not tear myself away. Though I could not stand him, I must admit that he had the gift of making people listen to him, especially when he was very angry about something. This man was, in my opinion, a born spy. He knew at any given moment the latest news and all the unsavoury secrets of our town, and one could not help but be amazed how he took to heart things which sometimes did not concern him at all. It always seemed to me that the main feature of his character was envy. When I told Mr Verkhovensky the same evening of my meeting with Liputin that morning and of our conversation, the latter, to my surprise, grew very excited and put the preposterous question to me: 'Does Liputin know or not?' I tried to prove to him that it was quite impossible for him to have found out so soon and that, besides, there was no one he could have found out from, but Mr Verkhovensky would not agree with me.

'Believe it or not,' he finally concluded unexpectedly, 'but I'm convinced that he not only knows every detail of *our* position already, but that he knows something else besides which neither you nor I know anything about, and perhaps will never know, or will only know when it's too late, when there won't be any turning back!'

I said nothing, but these words suggested a great deal. We did not mention Liputin's name for the next five days after that; I could not help feeling that Mr Verkhovensky was very sorry to have revealed his suspicions to me and let the cat out of the bag.

2

One morning – that is, about seven or eight days after Mr Verkhovensky had consented to become betrothed – about eleven o'clock, when I was hurrying as usual to my sorely tried friend, an adventure befell me on the way.

I met Karmazinov, 'the great writer', as Liputin called him. I read Karmazinov as a child. His novels and stories were well known to the older and even to the younger generation. I revelled in them; they were the delight of my boyhood and youth. Later I grew a little in-different to his works; I did not care as much for his problem novels, which he wrote more recently, as for his first, his very first works, which were so full of spontaneous poetry; and his latest works I did not like at all.

Generally speaking, if I may be permitted to express my opinion, too, on so delicate a subject, all these second-rate gentlemen, who in their lifetime are usually hailed as geniuses, not only vanish almost without a trace and are erased from the memory of men as soon as they die, but are often quite forgotten and neglected after an incred-ibly short period even during their lifetime, as soon as a new genera-tion grows up and takes the place of the one in which they were active. This seems to happen in our country somehow instantaneously – just like a change of scenery in a theatre. Oh, it is not at all the same as with the Pushkins, Gogols, Molières, and Voltaires, or with all those dis-tinguished men who had something new and original to say! It is, of course, also true that these second-rate gentlemen usually write them-selves out in the most pathetic way on reaching a venerable age, with-out even being aware of it themselves. Quite often, too, a writer who has for a long time been believed to possess a great store of extra-

ordinarily profound ideas, and who is expected to exercise an extraordinary and serious influence on the progress of society, in the end
betrays such shallowness and insipidity of his fundamental idea that no
one is sorry when he succeeds in writing himself out so soon. But the
old men don't notice it, and are angry. Their vanity sometimes
assumes, especially towards the end of their careers, quite amazing
proportions. Goodness only knows who they think they are – gods at
least. People said about Karmazinov that his connexions with high
society and persons of great consequence were almost dearer to him
than his own soul. It was said about him that he would extend a cor-
dial welcome to you, flatter and charm you by his simplicity and good
humour, especially if for some reason he thought that you might be
useful to him and, of course, if you came to him with a good introduction. But that should some prince, countess, or anyone he was
afraid of happen to come in while you were there, he would consider
it his most sacred duty to ignore you in a most insulting way, just as
if you were some worthless rag or a fly, before you had time to take
your leave, and that he seriously regarded this as good form. In spite
of his perfect self-possession and excellent knowledge of good manners, his vanity, they say, reaches so hysterical a pitch that he cannot
conceal his peevishness as an author even in those society circles where
people are little interested in literature. If, on the other hand, someone
accidentally takes him by surprise by his indifference, he becomes
morbidly offended and tries to revenge himself.

About a year before, I read an article of his in a periodical written
with a most dreadful affectation of the crudest kind of poetry as well
as psychology. He described the wreck of a steamer somewhere near
the English coast, which he had witnessed himself, and how he had
watched the drowning people being saved and the dead bodies
brought ashore. The whole of this rather long and verbose article was
written solely with the object of showing what a fine fellow he was.
Between the lines one could actually read: 'Look at me, see how
bravely I behaved at those moments. What is the sea, the storm, the
cliffs, the wreckage of the steamer to you? I have described it all sufficiently with my mighty pen. Why look at that drowned woman with
the dead child in her dead arms? You'd better look at me. See how I
was unable to bear the sight, and turned away from it. Look, here I
stood with my back to it; here I was horrified, and could not bring

myself to look back; I closed my eyes – don't you think it is very interesting?' When I told Mr Verkhovensky my opinion of Karmazinov's article, he agreed with me.

When recently the news of the arrival of Mr Karmazinov reached us, I was naturally very anxious to see him and, if possible, to make his acquaintance. I knew that I could have done it through Mr Verkhovensky, for they had once been friends. And now I suddenly met him at a street crossing. I recognized him at once; he had been pointed out to me three days before when he drove past in a carriage with the Governor's wife.

He was a short, prim old man, though not over fifty-five, with a rather rubicund little face, with thick grey locks of hair straying from under his round, cylindrical hat and curling round his clean little pink ears. His clean little face was not very handsome, with its thin, long, cunningly pursed lips, with its rather fleshy nose, and with its sharp, shrewd little eyes. He was dressed somewhat shabbily, in a sort of cloak which would be worn in Switzerland or in Northern Italy at that time of the year. But, at all events, all the minor articles of his clothing – the cuff-links, collar, buttons, a tortoise-shell lorgnette on a thin, black ribbon, and his signet ring – were the same as are worn by people of irreproachable taste. I am certain that in summer he always wore coloured prunella shoes, fastening at the side with mother-of-pearl buttons. When we ran into each other, he had just stopped at the street crossing and was looking round carefully. Noticing that I was observing him with interest, he asked me in a sugary, though rather shrill, voice:

'Would you be so kind as to tell me how I am to get to Bykov Street?'

'Bykov Street?' I exclaimed in great excitement. 'Why, it's not far from here. Straight along this street and the second turning to the left.'

'Thank you very much.'

Oh, damn that minute! I believe I was shy and looked obsequious. He noticed it all in a flash and, of course, understood everything; I mean, he realized that I knew who he was, that I had read his books and worshipped him ever since I was a child, and that I was shy and regarded him obsequiously. He smiled, nodded again, and went straight along the street as I had directed him. I don't know why I turned back and followed him; I don't know why I ran for ten yards beside him. He suddenly stopped again.

'And couldn't you please tell me where the nearest cab rank is?' he cried again, addressing me.

A nasty shout; a nasty voice!

'A cab rank? The nearest cab rank is – er – by the cathedral – there are always cabs standing there,' and I nearly turned and ran for a cab.

I imagine that that was exactly what he expected me to do. Of course, I came to my senses immediately and stopped dead, but he noticed my movement and watched me with the same nasty smile. Then something happened which I shall never forget. He suddenly dropped a small bag which he was carrying in his left hand. As a matter of fact, it was not a bag at all, but a small case, or rather a sort of attaché-case, or perhaps a reticule – something like an old-fashioned lady's reticule. However, I don't know what it was; all I know is that I rushed to pick it up.

I am absolutely certain that I did not pick it up, but my first impulse to pick it up could not be denied. I certainly could not conceal it, and I blushed like a fool. The cunning fellow at once got all that could be got out of the situation.

'Don't trouble, sir; I'll pick it up myself,' he said charmingly, though not before he had realized that I would not pick up his reticule; he picked it up as if forestalling me, and, nodding again, went on his way, leaving me looking like a fool. It was just as if I had picked it up myself.

For five minutes I considered myself utterly disgraced for ever; but as I reached Mr Verkhovensky's house, I suddenly burst out laughing. The meeting struck me as so amusing that I immediately made up my mind to entertain Mr Verkhovensky with an account of it, and even to act the whole scene to him.

3

This time I found him, to my surprise, extraordinarily changed. It is true that as soon as I entered the room he rushed to meet me with a sort of extraordinary avidity, but he looked so lost that I doubt if he knew what I was talking about. But no sooner did I mention Karmazinov's name than he suddenly flew into a terrible temper.

'Don't speak of him! Don't mention his name!' he cried, almost in a frenzy. 'Here, look at this! Read! Read!'

He opened a drawer and threw on the table three small pieces of paper, written hurriedly in pencil, all from Mrs Stavrogin. The first note was written two days before, the second the day before, and the third that day, only an hour before; their contents were of no importance whatever; they were all about Karmazinov, and showed how greatly her vanity and ambition might suffer if Karmazinov should forget to call on her. Here is the first one, written the day before yesterday (there had probably been one written three days before and another four days before):

If he at last honours you with his visit to-day, please not a word about me. Not the faintest hint. Don't talk to him about me and don't remind him of me.

V.S.

Yesterday's note:

If he decides at last to pay you a visit this morning, I think the most dignified thing to do would be not to receive him at all. That's what I think about it, I don't know what you think.

V.S.

To-day's note, the last one:

I am certain that your place is filthy and full of tobacco smoke. I'm sending Maria and Foma; they'll tidy everything up in half an hour. Don't interfere with them, but stay in the kitchen while they are tidying your rooms. I'm sending you a Bokhara rug and two Chinese vases; I've long been intending to make you a present of them; and also my Teniers (for a time). You can put the vases on the window-sill, and hang the Teniers on the right under the portrait of Goethe; it's more conspicuous there, and it's always light in the morning. If he does turn up at last, receive him with the utmost courtesy, but whether you talk of trifles or of some erudite subject, behave as though you had only parted from him yesterday. Not a word about me. Perhaps I may drop in to see you in the evening.

V.S.

P.S. If he doesn't come to-day, he won't come at all.

I read the notes, and was surprised that he should be so agitated over such a trivial matter. Glancing inquiringly at him, I suddenly noticed that while I was reading he had changed the white cravat he always wore for a red one. His hat and walking-stick lay on the table. He was pale and his hands were trembling.

'I don't care a damn about her excitement!' he cried, beside himself with rage, in reply to my questioning glance. *'Je m'en fiche!* She has the cheek to be excited about Karmazinov, while not answering my letters! Here, here is one of my unopened letters she returned to me yesterday, here on the table, under that book, under *L'Homme qui rit*. What do I care if she is worried to death about her darling Nicholas? *Je m'en fiche et je proclame ma liberté. Au diable le Karmazinoff! Au diable la Lembke!* I've hidden the vases in the hall and the Teniers in the chest of drawers, and I have demanded that she should receive me at once. You hear: I've demanded it! I've sent her a note in pencil on a similar piece of paper, unsealed, by Nastasya, and I'm waiting. I want Dasha to tell me with her own lips and before the face of Heaven or, at any rate, before you. *Vous me seconderez, n'est-ce pas, comme ami et témoin.* I don't want to blush, to tell lies; I don't want secrets; I won't have any secrets in this business! Let them confess everything to me frankly, openly, honourably, and then – then I shall perhaps surprise everybody by my magnanimity! Am I a scoundrel or not, my dear sir?' he concluded suddenly, looking menacingly at me, as though it was I who considered him a scoundrel.

I begged him to have a drink of water; I had never seen him so excited before. While talking, he kept running from one corner of the room to the other, but he suddenly stopped dead before me in an extraordinary attitude.

'Do you really think, sir,' he began again, with passionate disdain, looking me up and down – 'do you really suppose that I, Stepan Verkhovensky, will not find enough moral strength in myself to pick up my bag, my pauper's bundle, and, lifting it on to my feeble shoulders, leave this house and disappear for good when honour and the great principle of independence demand it? It will not be the first time that Stepan Verkhovensky has had to ward off despotism by an act of self-denial, even if it is the despotism of a crazy woman – that is to say, the most cruel and humiliating despotism which can exist in the world, in spite of the fact that you, sir, have presumed to smile at my words. Oh, you don't believe that I can find enough moral strength in myself to end my life as a tutor in the house of some merchant or to die of hunger in a ditch! Answer me, answer me at once: do you or don't you believe it?'

But I purposely said nothing. I even pretended that I could not bring myself to offend him by a negative reply, but that I could not possibly say that I believed him. In all this exasperation of his there was something that really did offend me, and not personally, oh no! But – I shall explain myself later.

He actually turned pale.

'Perhaps I bore you, Mr G—v' (that's my name), 'and you'd prefer not to come to see me at all,' he said in the same tone of pale composure which usually precedes some uncontrollable outburst of anger.

I jumped up in alarm; at that very moment Nastasya walked into the room and silently handed him a small piece of paper, on which something was scribbled in pencil. He glanced at it and threw it to me. On the paper only three words were written in Mrs Stavrogin's hand: 'Stay at home.'

Mr Verkhovensky grabbed his hat and walking-stick in silence and quickly went out of the room; I went after him mechanically. Suddenly voices and the sound of rapid footsteps were heard in the passage. He stopped dead, as though thunderstruck.

'It's Liputin, and I'm done for,' he whispered, seizing me by the arm.

At that moment Liputin walked into the room.

4

Why he should be done for because of Liputin I did not know, and I did not really attach any significance to his words; I put everything down to his nerves. But all the same his terror was quite extraordinary, and I decided to watch him closely.

Liputin's expression as he walked into the room showed that this time he had a special right to come in, in spite of all the prohibitions. He brought with him an unknown man – a new arrival, by the look of him. In answer to Mr Verkhovensky's senseless stare, he immediately cried aloud:

'I'm bringing you a visitor, and a special one, too! I take the liberty of intruding on your solitude, sir. Mr Kirilov, a most remarkable structural engineer. And what is so important, sir, he knows your son,

Peter Verkhovensky. He's a great friend of his. He hàs a message from him, too. He's only just arrived.'

'The message is your own invention,' the visitor remarked sharply. 'There was no message at all, but it's quite true that I know Verkhovensky. I left him in the province of Kharkov ten days ago.'

Mr Verkhovensky shook hands with him mechanically and motioned him to sit down; he looked at me, he looked at Liputin, and suddenly, as though recollecting himself, he quickly sat down himself, but still keeping his hat and walking-stick in his hand without noticing it.

'Good Lord, you were just going out! And I was told that you were indisposed from too much work!'

'Yes, I'm afraid I'm not feeling well. I was just going out for a walk, I –' Mr Verkhovensky stopped short, put down his hat and walking-stick on the sofa and – reddened.

Meantime I was hurriedly examining the visitor. He was a young man – about twenty-seven – decently dressed, a well-proportioned, spare, dark-haired man, pale and with a somewhat muddy complexion and black, lustreless eyes. He looked a little pensive and absent-minded, he spoke abruptly and not altogether grammatically, transposing the words rather queerly and getting muddled if he had to use a sentence that was too long. Liputin noticed Mr Verkhovensky's great alarm, and was obviously gratified. He sat down in a wicker chair, which he dragged almost into the middle of the room, so as to be at the same distance from both the host and his visitor, who had installed themselves on sofas at opposite sides of the room. His sharp eyes darted about curiously, all over the room.

'I haven't – er – seen Peter for a long, long time,' Mr Verkhovensky brought himself to murmur to his visitor. 'You met him abroad?'

'Here and abroad.'

'Mr Kirilov,' Liputin put in quickly, 'has only just arrived from abroad himself, after an absence of four years. He went there to perfect himself in his profession, and arrived here in the hope of obtaining a job on the construction of our railway bridge. He's at present waiting for a reply. He knows the Drozdovs and Lisa through Peter.'

The engineer sat rather stiffly and listened with awkward impatience. I couldn't help feeling that he was angry about something.

'He knows Mr Stavrogin, too.'

'You know Mr Stavrogin, too?' Mr Verkhovensky inquired.

'Yes, sir; I know him too.'

'I – I haven't seen Peter for a very long time and – and so I have hardly the right to – er – call myself his father – *c'est le mot*. I – er – how was he when you left him?'

'Well, I just left him – he's coming himself.' Mr Kirilov again hastened to extricate himself from the necessity of going into details. He certainly was angry.

'He's coming! At last I – You see, I haven't seen Peter for such a long time!' Mr Verkhovensky got entangled in his sentence. 'I'm now waiting for my poor boy, before whom – oh, before whom I'm so guilty! That is, what I really meant to say was that when I left him in Petersburg, I – I mean, I didn't think – er – there was much in him – *quelque chose de ce genre*. A very nervous boy, you know, very emotional and – er – timid. When he went to bed he said his prayers, bowed down to the ground and made the sign of the cross on his pillow for fear of dying in the night – *je m'en souviens. Enfin*, no artistic feeling of any kind, I mean no feeling for higher things, for something fundamental, no germ of any future great idea – *c'était comme un petit idiot*. But I'm afraid I've become a little muddled. I'm sorry, I – er – you've found me –'

'Are you serious about his crossing his pillow?' the engineer suddenly inquired, with a kind of special curiosity.

'Yes, he did.'

'All right; just wanted to know – go on.'

Mr Verkhovensky looked questioningly at Liputin.

'I'm very glad you came to see me, but I'm afraid I'm not in a position at present to – er – where, incidentally, are you staying?'

'Bogoyavlenskaya Street, at Filippov's house.'

'Oh,' I observed involuntarily, 'that's where Shatov lives.'

'Yes, in the very same house,' Liputin cried. 'Shatov lives in the attic upstairs, and Mr Kirilov has taken a room downstairs in Captain Lebyatkin's flat. He knows Shatov, and he knows Shatov's wife, too. He was a close friend of hers abroad.'

'*Comment!* Do you really know something about that unhappy marriage *de ce pauvre ami* and that woman?' cried Mr Verkhovensky, suddenly carried away by emotion. 'You're the first man I've met who has known her personally; and if only –'

'What nonsense!' the engineer cut him short, flushing all over. 'How you exaggerate everything, Liputin! I haven't seen Shatov's wife at all – perhaps once only from a distance, and not at all near to. I know Shatov. Why do you invent all sorts of things?'

He turned sharply on the sofa, snatched up his hat, put it back again, and, settling down once more as before, glared challengingly with his flashing black eyes at Mr Verkhovensky. I could not for the life of me understand such strange irritability.

'Excuse me,' Mr Verkhovensky observed importantly, 'I realize that it can be a most delicate matter –'

'No question of any delicate matter here at all, and it's really shameful, but I didn't shout "Nonsense" at you, sir, but at Liputin, because he always exaggerates. I'm sorry if you thought I was referring to you. I know Shatov, but I don't know his wife at all – not at all!'

'I quite understand, I understand. And if I insisted, it's only because I'm very fond of our poor friend, *notre irascible ami*, and have always taken an interest in him ... I can't help thinking that he changed his former, perhaps too youthful, but quite sound ideas a little too abruptly. And he is now clamouring so much about *notre sainte Russie* that I have for some considerable time been inclined to ascribe this sudden organic change – I can't call it anything else – to some violent shock in his family life, to wit, to his unhappy marriage. I, who know my poor Russia like the palm of my hand and who have given my whole life to the Russian people, and what's more –'

'I don't know the Russian people either and – I've no time to study them,' the engineer once more snapped out and again turned sharply on the sofa.

Mr Verkhovensky stopped short in the middle of his speech.

'He is – he is studying them,' Liputin broke in. 'He has already begun his study, and is writing a most interesting article on the causes of the increasing number of suicides in Russia and, generally, on the causes which lead to the increase or decrease of suicides in society. He has reached amazing conclusions.'

The engineer became terribly excited.

'You've no right at all,' he muttered angrily. 'It isn't an article at all – I never – such silly things – I asked you confidentially, just by chance. It's not an article at all; I'm not publishing and you have no right to –'

Liputin was obviously enjoying himself.

'Sorry; perhaps I've made a mistake in calling your literary work an article. Mr Kirilov is only collecting observations, and not dealing with the essence of the problem or, as it were, its moral aspect. Indeed, he rejects morality as such and is in favour of the latest principle of general destruction for the sake of the ultimate good. He already demands more than a hundred million heads for the establishment of common sense in Europe – many more than they demanded at the last Peace Congress. In this sense Mr Kirilov goes further than anybody else.'

The engineer listened with a faint, contemptuous smile. For half a minute they were all silent.

'All this is stupid, Liputin,' Mr Kirilov said at last with some dignity. 'If I by chance pointed out something to you and you got hold of it, I can't help it. But you've no right, because I never talk to anyone. I scorn to talk. If I've convictions, then it's clear to me; but you – you've acted stupidly. I don't discuss things if everything's done with. I hate discussions. I never want to discuss –'

'Well, perhaps you're quite right,' Mr Verkhovensky could not resist interposing.

'I'm sorry, but I'm not angry with anyone here,' the visitor went on warmly, talking very fast. 'For four years I've seen few people. ... For four years I spoke very little, and have done my best not to meet anyone, for reasons of my own, which is nobody's concern – for four years. Liputin discovered it and laughs. I understand and don't mind. I don't take offence – just annoyed at his liberty. And if I don't expound my ideas to you,' he concluded unexpectedly, glancing round at us all with a resolute look, 'it's not because I'm afraid that you will inform the Government against me. That's not it. Please, don't imagine any nonsense of that kind. ...'

No one made any reply to these words. We merely exchanged glances. Even Liputin forgot to snigger.

'I'm awfully sorry, gentlemen.' Mr Verkhovensky got up from the sofa determinedly – 'but I'm not feeling too well and I'm rather upset. You'll have to excuse me.'

'Oh, you want us to go,' Mr Kirilov started, snatching up his cap. 'Glad you said so; I'm so forgetful, you know.'

He rose and went up good-humouredly to Mr Verkhovensky with an outstretched hand.

'I'm sorry you're not well, and I came.'

'I wish you every success among us,' replied Mr Verkhovensky, shaking his hand benevolently and without hurry. 'I quite understand that if, as you say, you have spent so many years abroad and avoid people for reasons of your own and forgot Russia, you must look with surprise upon us who are born and bred Russians, as indeed we must look on you likewise. *Mais cela passera.* One thing, though, does puzzle me: you want to build our bridge, and yet you say you're in favour of the principle of general destruction. They won't let you build our bridge!'

'What? What did you say? Oh, hang it all!' cried the astonished Kirilov, and suddenly burst into a merry and good-humoured laugh. For a moment his face assumed a most child-like expression which I thought suited him very much. Liputin rubbed his hands with delight at Mr Verkhovensky's happy remark. But I couldn't help wondering all the time why Mr Verkhovensky was so frightened of Liputin and why he had cried, 'I'm done for,' when he heard him coming.

5

We were all standing in the doorway. It was the moment when hosts and visitors exchange their last hurried and most courteous words, and then part in the best of humour.

'Mr Kirilov is so upset to-day,' Liputin suddenly put in as he was going out of the room, as it were casually, 'because he's had a row with Captain Lebyatkin over his sister. Captain Lebyatkin thrashes that fair, crack-brained sister of his with a whip – a real Cossack whip – every morning and evening. Mr Kirilov has taken the little cottage in the yard so as not to have anything to do with it. Well, good-bye.'

'His sister? A sick one? With a whip?' Mr Verkhovensky cried as though somebody had suddenly hit him with a whip. 'What sister? What Lebyatkin?'

His former terror came back all at once.

'Lebyatkin? He's a retired captain. He used to call himself a first lieutenant before.'

'What do I care about his rank? What sister? Good Lord! You say Lebyatkin? But there used to be a Lebyatkin here –'

'It's the same fellow – *our* Lebyatkin – you remember at Virginsky's?'

'But that one was caught with forged notes, wasn't he?'

'Well, he's come back now. Been here for almost three weeks, and under the most singular circumstances.'

'But he's a scoundrel!'

'Is there any reason why we shouldn't have a scoundrel among us?' Liputin grinned suddenly, feeling Mr Verkhovensky all over with his furtive eyes.

'Good Lord! I didn't mean that at all – though, as a matter of fact, I quite agree with you about the scoundrel, with you particularly. But go on, go on; tell me more. What did you mean by that? I'm quite certain you meant something by that!'

'Oh, it's all a lot of nonsense, sir. I mean, it seems the Captain didn't go away from us because of any forged notes, but merely because he wanted to find his sister, who had apparently been hiding from him somewhere. Well, now he has brought her; that's all there is to it. Why do you look frightened, sir? Anyway, I'm merely repeating what he told me when he was drunk. When he's sober he doesn't say a word about it. He's a highly irritable fellow, and, if you know what I mean, a military aesthete, but in very bad taste. And his sister is lame as well as mad. She seems to have been seduced by someone, and Mr Lebyatkin, it appears, has for many years been receiving a yearly allowance from her seducer as a sort of compensation for his wounded honour. That's what can be gathered from his talk, at any rate; though if you ask me, it's only drunken talk. He's just boasting. And, besides, that sort of thing is usually settled much more cheaply. Still, there can be no doubt that he has large sums of money in his possession; about a fortnight ago he was walking about barefoot, but now I've seen hundreds of roubles in his hands. His sister has some sort of fit every day. She screams, and he "keeps her in order" with his whip. A woman, he says, must be inspired with respect. What I can't understand is how Shatov can live in the same house with him. Mr Kirilov has only been able to stay three days there. He knows him from Petersburg, and now he's taken the cottage so as not to be disturbed.'

'Is that true?' Mr Verkhovensky addressed the engineer.

'You talk, Liputin,' Kirilov muttered angrily.

'Mysteries, secrets,' Mr Verkhovensky exclaimed, unable to restrain himself. 'Where have we suddenly got so many mysteries and secrets from?'

The engineer frowned, blushed, shrugged his shoulders, and walked out of the room.

'Mr Kirilov even snatched the whip away from him,' added Liputin. 'He broke it, threw it out of the window, and they had a violent quarrel.'

'Why do you blab, Liputin?' Kirilov quickly turned round again. 'It's silly. Why do you do it?'

'But why out of modesty conceal the most generous impulses of one's heart? Your heart, I mean, not mine.'

'How silly and quite unnecessary. ... Lebyatkin's stupid and quite worthless – useless for the cause and utterly pernicious. Why do you babble all sorts of things? I'm going.'

'Oh, what a pity!' cried Liputin, with a bright smile. 'I'd have liked to amuse you, Mr Verkhovensky, with another little anecdote. As a matter of fact, I came here with the intention of telling you it, though I expect you must have heard about it yourself. Another time, then. Mr Kirilov is in such a hurry. Good-bye, sir. The anecdote concerns Mrs Stavrogin. She greatly diverted me the other day. Sent for me specially. It's too funny for words. Good-bye, sir.'

But here Mr Verkhovensky simply pounced upon him: he seized him by the shoulders, dragged him back into the room, and made him sit down on a chair. Liputin looked scared.

'Why, yes,' he began, watching Mr Verkhovensky warily from his chair, 'she sent for me suddenly and asked me to tell her "confidentially" what I honestly thought about Mr Stavrogin: was he mad or not? Don't you think it's amazing?'

'You're crazy!' Mr Verkhovensky murmured, and all of a sudden completely lost control of himself. 'Liputin, you know very well that you only came here to tell me a vile story of this sort and – something worse!'

In a flash I remembered his suggestion that Liputin knew not only more than we did about our affair, but also something we should never know.

'Really, Mr Verkhovensky,' Liputin murmured as though he were frightened, 'really –'

'Shut up and begin! I'd like to ask you very much, Mr Kirilov, to come back, too, and be present. Please do. Sit down. And you, Liputin, tell us all about it frankly, simply, and without humming and hawing!'

'Had I known, sir, that you'd be so shocked I wouldn't have begun at all. And I thought that you knew all about it from Mrs Stavrogin herself!'

'You didn't think anything of the kind! Begin, begin, I tell you.'

'Oh, very well, but do me the favour of sitting down. I don't feel like sitting down and having you standing over me when you're so excited. Shan't be able to tell it to you coherently.'

Mr Verkhovensky restrained himself and sank impressively into an arm-chair. The engineer stared gloomily at the floor. Liputin gazed at them with tremendous enjoyment.

'Well, how shall I begin? You've put me off –'

<h2 style="text-align:center">6</h2>

'The day before yesterday she suddenly sent one of her servants to ask me to call on her at twelve o'clock the next morning. Can you imagine that? I didn't go to my office, and punctually at twelve o'clock yesterday I was ringing the bell. I was shown into a drawing-room, and a minute later she came in, asked me to take a seat, and sat down herself opposite. I sat there unable to believe my senses: you know yourself, sir, how she has always treated me! She went straight to the heart of the matter without beating about the bush, as is her custom. "You remember", she said, "that four years ago, when Mr Stavrogin was ill, he was responsible for some strange actions which puzzled the whole town till everything was explained. One of these actions concerned you personally. When Mr Stavrogin recovered, he went, at my request, to call on you. I know that he talked to you before, too. Tell me openly and frankly how did you" – here she became a little confused – "find Mr Stavrogin then? What was your opinion of him in general? What sort of opinion did you form of him, and – what do you think of him now?"

'At this point she was completely confused, so that for a whole minute she sat waiting, and then she suddenly flushed. I got scared. She began again in a tone of voice that was not exactly moving – that wouldn't have been at all what you would expect from her – but very impressive.

'"I want you", she said, "to listen to me very carefully. I sent for you now because I regard you as a perspicacious and clever person who is capable of forming an unbiased opinion" (What compliments!) "You will, of course," she said, "also realize that it's a mother who's talking to you. Mr Stavrogin has suffered many misfortunes in his life and passed through many vicissitudes. All that," she said, "might have affected the state of his mind. I don't mean madness, of course," she said; "that's unthinkable!" She said that proudly and firmly. "But there might be something strange, something peculiar, a certain trend of thought, a tendency to take certain unconventional views." (Those were her exact words, sir, and I couldn't help being astonished at the preciseness with which Mrs Stavrogin is able to express herself. A lady of great intellect!) "At least," she said, "I myself have noticed a certain restlessness in him and a tendency to peculiar moods. But I'm his mother and you're a stranger, and therefore capable, with your intelligence, of forming an independent opinion. I implore you, finally" (she actually used that expression: "I implore you") "to tell me the whole truth, without any prevarication. And if you will give me your word never to forget that I have spoken to you in confidence, you can expect me always to be ready and willing to show you my gratitude in future at every opportunity." Well, sir, what do you think of it?'

'You – you've so shocked me,' Mr Verkhovensky murmured feebly, 'that I don't believe you.'

'No, no, please observe,' Liputin cried, as though he had not heard Mr Verkhovensky, 'please observe how upset and worried a woman of her high social standing must have been to put such a question to a man like me, and even condescend to ask me to keep it a secret. What can it mean? She hasn't received some unexpected piece of news from Mr Stavrogin, has she?'

'I don't know – I don't think there has been any news – I haven't seen her for some days, but – but let me tell you, sir,' Mr Verkhovensky murmured, evidently hardly able to think clearly – 'but let me tell you, Liputin, that if she told you all that in confidence and you're now discussing it in the presence of all of us –'

'Absolutely in confidence! May the Lord strike me dead if I – But as for talking about it here – well, what about it? We're not strangers, are we? Take Mr Kirilov – he isn't exactly a stranger either, is he?'

'I'm afraid I can't agree with you. No doubt we shall keep the secret – the three of us here, I mean – but I'm afraid you, Liputin, won't, and I don't trust you in anything.'

'What do you mean, sir? Why, I'm more interested than anybody else, for wasn't I promised eternal gratitude? As a matter of fact, I wanted to draw your attention in this connexion to a very strange incident, psychological rather than simply strange. Last night, under the influence of my conversation with Mrs Stavrogin (you can imagine yourself what an impression it made on me), I put a rather discreet question to Mr Kirilov: "You knew Mr Stavrogin, both in Petersburg and abroad," I said. "What is your opinion of the state of his mind and his abilities?" He replied in his usual laconic manner that he was a man of fine intellect and sound judgement. "And have you ever noticed in the course of years," I further asked, "any, as it were, aberration of ideas or any peculiar turn of thought or any – how shall I put it? – signs of madness?" In short, I repeated Mrs Stavrogin's own question. Well, what do you think? Mr Kirilov suddenly grew thoughtful and frowned, just as he is doing now. "Yes," he said, "I have sometimes thought there was something strange." And, mind you, if Mr Kirilov could have thought there was something strange, something must really be the matter with him, mustn't it?'

'Is it true?' Mr Verkhovensky asked, turning to Kirilov.

'I'd rather not talk about it,' Kirilov replied, suddenly raising his head and looking at him with flashing eyes. 'I'd like to contest your right, Liputin. You have no right in this case to mention me. I did not give you the whole of my opinion at all. I may have known him in Petersburg, but that was ages ago, and though I've met him recently, I know Mr Stavrogin very little. Please leave me out, and – and all this looks like gossip.'

Liputin threw up his hands with an air of wronged innocence.

'So I'm a gossip, am I? Are you sure I'm not a spy as well? It's all right for you to criticize, Kirilov, if you insist on being left out of it all. You wouldn't believe it, Mr Verkhovensky – I mean, Captain Lebyatkin, sir, does seem to be a stupid fellow – that is, he is as stupid as – well, I'm ashamed to say how stupid he is – there's a Russian comparison signifying the degree of it; but he, too, considers himself injured by Mr Stavrogin, though he has a high opinion of his cleverness. "I'm amazed at that man," he says. "He is a wise serpent" (his own words, sir). Well, I asked him (still under the influence of yesterday's interview and after my talk with Mr Kirilov), "Captain," I said, "what do you think: is your wise serpent mad or not?" Well, believe me, it was just as if I had whipped him from behind, without his permission. He simply leapt to his feet. "Yes," he said, "yes, but that can't influence —" but what it could not influence he did not say; and he fell to thinking so sadly, so deeply, that he seemed to have grown sober all of a sudden. We were sitting in Filippov's public-house at the time. Half an hour later he suddenly banged the table with his fist. "Aye," he said, "perhaps he is mad; but that cannot influence —" and again he did not say what it could not influence. Of course, I'm only giving you the gist of our conversation, but the idea is clear enough: ask whom you like, they are all struck by one thought, though it never occurred to them before. "Aye," they all say, "he's mad; he is very clever, but maybe he's mad too."'

Mr Verkhovensky sat, looking pensive and thinking hard.

'And how does Lebyatkin know?'

'You'd better ask Mr Kirilov, who has just called me a spy. I'm a spy and I don't know, but Mr Kirilov knows everything there is to know about it, but he keeps mum.'

'I don't know anything, or very little,' the engineer replied with the same exasperation. 'You made Lebyatkin drunk to find out. You brought me here to find out and make me talk. You must be a spy, then!'

'I haven't made him drunk yet! He isn't worth the money, with all his secrets. That's what they are worth to me; I don't know what they are to you. It is he who flings money about. Twelve days ago he came to ask me to lend him fifteen copecks; now it's he who treats me to champagne, and not I him. But you've given me an idea, and I daresay, when I think it necessary, I'll make him drunk just to find out what it's all about, and perhaps I shall find out – all your little secrets,' Liputin snapped back spitefully.

Mr Verkhovensky looked in bewilderment at the two disputants. Both were giving themselves away, and they did not seem to care about it. I couldn't help thinking that Liputin had brought that fellow

Kirilov to us with the sole purpose of drawing him into a conversation through a third person for reasons of his own – his favourite trick.

'Mr Kirilov knows Mr Stavrogin very well,' he went on irritably; 'only he conceals it. As for your question about Lebyatkin, he got to know him in Petersburg before any of us, five or six years ago, during that little known, if I may put it that way, period of Mr Stavrogin's life before he ever dreamed of gladdening our hearts by coming here. Our Prince, I can only presume, gathered a very curious set of people round him in Petersburg in those days. It was at that time, I believe, that he made his acquaintance with Mr Kirilov.'

'Take care, Liputin! I warn you Stavrogin means to come soon, and he knows how to stand up for himself.'

'Why warn me? I'm the first to shout from the house-tops that he's a man of the finest and most discriminating intellect, and I entirely re-assured Mrs Stavrogin yesterday on that score. "The only thing I can't vouch for," I told her, "is his character." Lebyatkin, too, kept repeating yesterday: "He's the victim of his own character." Yes, in-deed, Mr Verkhovensky, it's all very well for you to shout about slan-ders and spying, and, mind, only after you've wormed everything out of me, and with such extraordinary curiosity, too. Now, Mrs Stavro-gin – she went straight to the point yesterday. "You were personally interested in that affair," she said to me, "and that's why," she said, "I appeal to you." And I should think so, too! What motive could I possibly have when I've swallowed a personal insult from his lordship in public! I should have thought I had excellent reasons to be inter-ested, and not only for the sake of gossip. He shakes hands with you one day, and next day he slaps your face for no earthly reason in return for your hospitality and in the presence of your best friends, just be-cause the fancy takes him. Too well off, if you ask me! And the fair sex means everything to these butterflies and brave cock-sparrows. Coun-try squires with tiny wings like the ancient cupids. Romantic lady-killers! It's all very well for you, sir, a confirmed bachelor, to talk, and to accuse me of talking scandal about his lordship. Now, if you'd only marry a young and pretty girl – for you're still a very handsome man – you, too, would lock and bolt the door against our Prince, and put up barricades in your own house! Why, if only Miss Lebyatkin, who's whipped every day, were not mad and lame, I most certainly would have thought that she was the victim of the passions of his lordship and that it was from him Captain Lebyatkin had suffered "in his family dignity", as he expressed it himself. Only perhaps that's inconsistent with his refined taste, though even that wouldn't have stopped him. Every pretty face has its attractions for him so long as he's in the right mood for it. You're talking about scandalous stories I'm supposed to be spreading, but am I spreading them, when the whole town is talking about it? I'm just listening and nodding in agreement. There's no law against nodding, is there?'

'The town's talking? What's the town talking about?'

'I mean, it's Captain Lebyatkin who screams for all the town to hear when he's drunk, and isn't that the same thing as if the whole market-place were ringing with it? Is it my fault? I'm only interested in it as among friends, and I'm among friends here, am I not?' he asked, looking at us with an innocent air. 'Now, take the following case, for instance: it would appear that his lordship had sent Captain Lebyatkin three hundred roubles from Switzerland by a most honourable young lady, a very modest person, as it were, an orphan, whom I have the honour of knowing. But a little later Lebyatkin received most precise information from someone whose name I need not mention, except that he, too, is a most honourable, and hence a most trustworthy person, to the effect that he'd been sent not three hundred but one thousand roubles! Which means, Lebyatkin keeps clamouring, that the "young lady has robbed me of seven hundred", and he vows to get his money, even if he has to send for the police, at least he threatens to, and he goes on shouting for the whole town to hear.'

'It's vile, vile of you!' cried the engineer, jumping up suddenly from his chair.

'But it's you who are the honourable person who assured Lebyatkin in Mr Stavrogin's name that he'd been sent one thousand roubles, not three hundred. Why, the Captain told me so himself when he was drunk.'

'It's an – an unfortunate misunderstanding. Someone's made a mistake and – it's nonsense, and you, sir, you – it's vile!'

'But I'd like to believe that it's nonsense, and I'm very sorry to have to listen to all that talk, for, say what you will, a girl of a most sterling character is implicated, first, in the matter of the seven hundred roubles, and secondly, in undeniable intimate relations with Mr Stavrogin. For his lordship would certainly not hesitate to disgrace a girl of good character or to bring dishonour upon a married woman, as indeed that incident in my house proves. If he happened to come across a great-hearted man, he'd force him to cover up another man's sins with his honourable name. That is the sort of thing I had to put up with – I'm speaking of myself, sir. ...'

'Take care, Liputin!' Mr Verkhovensky said, half rising from his arm-chair and turning pale.

'Don't believe him – don't believe him,' the engineer kept exclaiming in great agitation. 'Someone's made a mistake and Lebyatkin's drunk – everything will be explained – I can't stand it any more – I – I think it's mean and – enough – enough!'

He ran out of the room.

'What on earth are you doing? Wait, I'm coming with you!' Liputin cried in alarm. He jumped up from his chair and rushed out after Kirilov.

7

Mr Verkhovensky stood pondering for a moment, looked at me out of the corner of his eye, picked up his hat and stick, and walked quietly out of the room. I went after him again as before.

'Oh, yes, you can be a witness – *de l'accident*,' he said, as he went out of the gates, noticing that I was following him. '*Vous m'accompagnerez, n'est-ce pas?*'

'You're not going there again, are you, sir? Have you considered what might happen?'

'But I can't possibly marry to cover up "another man's sins", can I?' he whispered to me, stopping for a moment, with a pathetic and uneasy smile – a smile of shame and utter despair and, at the same time, of a strange kind of exaltation.

I was just waiting for those words. At last those unmentionable words, so carefully concealed from me, were out, after a whole week of evasion and pretence. I was absolutely mad with fury.

'How could such a dirty, such a base idea occur to you, sir, to you with your lucid mind, your kind heart, and – even before Liputin!'

He looked at me, made no answer, and walked on. I did not want to lag behind. I wanted to tell Mrs Stavrogin what I thought of it all. I could have forgiven him if, coward that he was, he had only learnt it from Liputin, but it was perfectly plain now that he had thought of it long before Liputin, and that Liputin had merely confirmed his suspicions and added fuel to the flames. He had not hesitated to cast suspicion upon the girl from the very first day, even before he had any grounds for it, even those that had occurred to Liputin. Mrs Stavrogin's tyrannical actions he explained by her desperate desire to cover up the aristocratic misdeeds of her precious Nicholas by a marriage to an honourable man! I dearly wished he should be punished for it.

'O! Dieu, qui est si grand et bon! Oh, who can comfort me?' he cried, stopping dead suddenly after walking another hundred paces.

'Please, let's go back at once and I'll explain everything to you!' I exclaimed, turning him by force towards home.

'Look who's here!' A fresh, cheerful young voice rang out near us like music. 'Mr Verkhovensky, is it you? You?'

We had not seen anything, and yet a young girl on horseback, Lisa Tushin, with her inseparable escort, suddenly made her appearance beside us. She pulled up her horse.

'Come here, come here, quickly!' she called out gaily in a loud voice. 'I haven't seen him for twelve years, and I recognized him at once, while he – Do you really not recognize me?'

Mr Verkhovensky seized the hand held out to him and kissed it reverently. He gazed at her as though he were lost in prayer and could not utter a word.

'He knows me and is pleased! Maurice, he is delighted to see me! Why haven't you been to see us this fortnight? Auntie tried to persuade me that you were ill and mustn't be disturbed, but I knew Auntie was lying. I kept stamping my feet and swearing at you, but I was absolutely, absolutely determined that you should call on us first, and that's why I never sent for you. Goodness, he hasn't changed a bit!' She scrutinized him, bending down from the saddle. 'He's quite ridiculously unchanged! Oh yes, he has. He has wrinkles, lots of wrinkles round his eyes and on his cheeks, and some grey hair, too; but his eyes are the same! And have I changed? Have I? Why don't you say something?'

I remembered at that moment the story that she had been ill when she was taken away to Petersburg at the age of eleven; and that during her illness she had cried and asked for Mr Verkhovensky.

'You – I –' he murmured in a voice breaking with joy. 'I was just exclaiming, "Who will comfort me?" and then I heard your voice. I think it's a miracle *et je commence à croire.*'

'*En Dieu! En Dieu qui est là-haut et qui est si grand et si bon?* You see, I remember all your lessons by heart. Maurice, if only you knew what faith he preached to me at that time *en Dieu, qui est si grand et si bon!* And do you remember your stories about how Columbus discovered America and how all of them cried: "Land! land!"? My nanny Alyona says that after that lesson I was feverish all night and cried: "Land! land!" And do you remember how you told me the story of Prince Hamlet? And do you remember how you described to me how the poor emigrants were transported from Europe to America? And it wasn't true at all: I found out later how they were transported. But how well he lied to me, Maurice! It was almost better than the truth. Why do you look at Mr Drozdov like that? He's the best and most faithful man in the whole world, and you simply must love him as you love me! *Il fait tout ce que je veux.* But, darling Mr Verkhovensky, you must be unhappy again, or you wouldn't shout in the middle of the street asking who was going to comfort you. You're unhappy, aren't you? Aren't you?'

'Now I am happy!'

'Is Auntie treating you badly?' she went on, without listening. 'The same wicked, unjust, dear old Auntie who is so precious to us all! And do you remember how you used to throw yourself into my arms in the garden and how I used to comfort you and cry – but don't be afraid of Mr Drozdov. He knows all, all about you. He's known everything a long time. You can cry on his shoulder as much as you like and he'll stand there as long as you like! Raise your hat, take it off for a minute, stand on tiptoe, and I'll kiss you on the forehead as I kissed you the last time when we parted. Do you see how that young girl is watching us out of the window? But come closer, closer! Heavens, how grey he is!'

And, bending over in the saddle, she kissed his forehead.

'Now let's all go back to your home! I know where you live. I shall be there directly, in a minute. I'll make you the first visit, you obstinate man, and then I'll drag you home for a whole day. Go, please, and get ready to welcome me.'

And she galloped off with her young man. We went back. Mr Verkhovensky sat down on the sofa and burst into tears.

'*Dieu! Dieu!*' he cried, '*enfin une minute de bonheur!*'

In less than ten minutes she arrived as promised, accompanied by Mr Drozdov.

'*Vous et le bonheur, vous arrivez en même temps!*' he said, rising to meet her.

'Here are some flowers for you; I've just been at Madame Chevalier's; she has flowers all the winter for birthday gifts. Here's Mr Drozdov; let me introduce him to you. I wanted to bring you a pasty instead of flowers, but Mr Drozdov assures me that it's not in the Russian spirit.'

Maurice Drozdov was an artillery captain, a tall and handsome man of about thirty-three, of an irreproachably correct appearance, with an impressive and at first sight even stern countenance, in spite of his remarkable and most delicate kindness which one could not fail to perceive almost at the first moment of making his acquaintance. He was taciturn, however, appeared to be self-sufficient, and was not keen on making friends. Many in our town said later that he was not very intelligent: but that was not altogether fair.

I won't attempt to describe how beautiful Lisa was. The whole town was already talking about her beauty, though some of our ladies and young girls indignantly disagreed with those who were impressed by it. There were some among them who already hated her, chiefly for her pride: the Drozdovs had scarcely begun paying visits, which offended many people, though the real reason for the delay was Mrs Drozdov's indisposition. She was also hated because she was a relative of the Governor's wife and because she went out riding every morning. Hitherto we had never had any horsewomen; it was natural, therefore, that the appearance of Lisa on horseback in the streets before she had had time to pay calls should have offended our society. Yet everybody knew that she went out riding on doctor's orders, and that gave rise to all sorts of sarcastic remarks about her delicate health. The first thing one noticed about her was her morbid, nervous, incessant restlessness. Alas! the poor girl was very unhappy, and everything was explained later. Now, as I recall the past, I could not say that she was as beautiful as she seemed to me then. Perhaps she was not beautiful at all. Tall, slender, but supple and strong, one could not help being struck by the irregularities of her features. Her eyes seemed to slant Kalmuk-fashion; she was pale, she had high cheekbones, a dark complexion, and a thin face; but there was something attractive and irresistibly engaging in that face. There was tremendous power in the burning look of her dark eyes; she came 'conquering and to conquer'. She seemed proud and occasionally even arrogant; I don't know if she ever succeeded in being kind, but I do know that she badly wanted to and that she went through agonies to force herself to be a little kind. There were, of course, many fine impulses and most commendable initiative in her nature; but everything in her seemed to be perpetually seeking its equilibrium and not finding it; everything was in chaos, in a state of agitation and restlessness. Perhaps the demands she made upon herself were too severe and she was unable to find in herself the necessary strength to satisfy them.

She sat down on the sofa and looked round the room.

'Why do I always feel sad at such moments? Can you answer that one, you learned man? All my life I thought that I'd be awfully pleased when I saw you and remembered everything, and now I don't seem to be pleased at all, though I do love you. ... Good heavens, look, there's my portrait! Let me see it. Oh, yes, I remember it, I remember!'

The excellent miniature of twelve-year-old Lisa in water-colours had been sent nine years before by the Drozdovs from Petersburg to Mr Verkhovensky. Since then it had always hung on the wall in his study.

'Was I really such a pretty child? Can that really have been my face?'

She got up, and with her portrait in her hand looked at herself in the mirror.

'Take it away quickly!' she cried, giving back the portrait. 'Don't hang it up now, please. Do it later. I don't want to look at it again!' She resumed her seat on the sofa. 'One life is over, another has begun and gone, then a third one begins, and so it goes on and on. All the ends seem to be cut off, as though with a pair of scissors. You see what old tales I'm telling you, and yet there's a lot of truth in them.'

She looked at me and smiled; she had glanced at me several times already, but in his agitation Mr Verkhovensky forgot that he had promised to introduce me.

'And why does my portrait hang under those daggers in your room? And why have you such a large collection of daggers and swords?'

He had, as a matter of fact, hanging crossways on the wall, two curved daggers, I don't know why, and one real Circassian sword. As she asked this question she looked so directly at me that I wanted to say something, but I stopped short. Mr Verkhovensky realized what was wrong at last and introduced me.

'I know, I know,' she said; 'I'm very pleased to meet you. Mother, too, has heard a lot about you. Let me introduce you to Mr Drozdov – he's a splendid person. I had already formed an amusing idea about you: you're Mr Verkhovensky's confidant, aren't you?'

I blushed.

'Oh, I'm awfully sorry; I haven't used the right word at all – not at all amusing, but just –' (She flushed and was overwhelmed with confusion.) 'However, why be ashamed of the fact that you're a splendid person? Well, it's time we were going, Maurice. I shall expect you in half an hour, Mr Verkhovensky. Goodness, what a lot we shall have to talk about! Now I'm your confidante, and we shall talk about everything – about *everything*, you understand?'

Mr Verkhovensky was alarmed at once.

'Oh, Mr Drozdov knows everything! Don't mind him!'

'What does he know?'

'What do you mean?' she cried in astonishment. 'Why, so it's true that they're concealing it! I refused to believe it. They're hiding Dasha, too. Auntie would not let me see Dasha this morning. She says Dasha's got a headache.'

'But – but how did you find out?'

'Goodness gracious, like everyone else. Really!'

'But does everyone know?'

'Why, of course! Mother, it is true, got to know about it first through Nanny, who was told by your Nastasya. You told Nastasya, didn't you? She says you told her yourself.'

'I – I did say something to her once,' Mr Verkhovensky murmured feebly, blushing all over, 'but I – I just hinted – *j'étais si nerveux et malade et puis –*'

She burst out laughing.

'Your confidant was not at hand, and Nastasya happened to be there – well, that was quite enough! And all the gossips in town are her best friends! Oh, never mind, it doesn't matter; let them all know, it's better that way. Please, don't be late: we dine early. Oh, I forgot,' she sat down again. 'Listen, what is Shatov like?'

'Shatov? He's Miss Shatov's brother.'

'I know he is her brother,' she interrupted him impatiently. 'What a funny person you are, really! I want to know what he is like, what sort of person?'

'*C'est un pense-creux d'ici. C'est le meilleur et le plus irascible homme du monde.*'

'I've heard that he's a very queer person. However, that wasn't what I meant. I understand he knows three languages, English, too, and can do literary work. In that case I've lots of work for him; I want an assistant, and the sooner the better. Do you think he'll take the work or not? He's been recommended to me.'

'Oh, I'm sure he will, *et vous ferez un bienfait.*'

'I'm not doing it for the sake of a *bienfait*; I really want an assistant.'

'I know Shatov pretty well,' I said, 'and if you authorize me to give him your message I'll go at once.'

'Tell him to come to-morrow morning at twelve o'clock. Splendid! Thank you. Are you ready, Maurice?'

They went away. I, of course, ran off at once to see Shatov.

'*Mon ami,*' Mr Verkhovensky said, overtaking me on the front steps, 'I simply must see you at ten or eleven o'clock when I come back. Oh, I feel very, very guilty before you and – and before everyone.'

8

Shatov was not at home. I ran round two hours later – again he was out. At last, at eight o'clock, I went to his place again, hoping to find him in or else to leave a note; again he was out. I thought of going to see Captain Lebyatkin downstairs to ask him about Shatov; but everything was locked up there, and everything quiet and dark inside as though the place had been deserted. Remembering the stories I had heard so recently, I passed by the door of Lebyatkin's flat with some curiosity. In the end I decided to call again early next morning. To tell the truth, I did not think much of my idea of leaving a note. Shatov might have ignored it – he was such a shy and stubborn fellow. Cursing my bad luck, I was on the point of going out at the gate when I suddenly ran into Mr Kirilov; he was just going into the house and recognized me first. As he himself began questioning me, I told him everything in general terms, and that I had a note for Shatov.

'Come along,' he said, 'I'll arrange everything.'

I remembered Liputin telling us that he had taken the wooden cottage in the yard that very morning. A deaf old peasant woman, who waited on him, lived in the same cottage, which was too large for him. The owner lived in a new house in another street, where he kept a public-house, and the old woman, who was apparently a relation of his, stayed behind to keep an eye on his old house. The rooms in the cottage were fairly clean, but the wallpaper was dirty. In the room we entered the furniture was of all sorts and sizes and utterly worthless: two card-tables, a chest of drawers made of alder, a large deal table from some peasant cottage or kitchen, chairs and a sofa with a wicker work back and hard leather cushions. In one corner was an ancient icon, in front of which the old woman had lit a lamp before we came in, and on the walls hung two large dark oil-portraits, one of the late Emperor Nicholas I, painted, to judge by the look of it, in the twenties, and the other of some bishop.

On entering the room, Mr Kirilov lighted a candle and took out of his trunk which stood, still unpacked, in a corner, an envelope, sealing-wax, and a glass seal.

'Seal your note and address the envelope.'

I tried to explain that I did not think that was necessary, but he insisted. Having addressed the envelope, I picked up my cap.

'I thought you might like a cup of tea,' he said. 'I have bought some tea. Will you have some?'

I did not refuse. The old woman soon brought in the tea – that is, a huge teapot of boiling water, a little teapot full of strong tea, two large earthenware, coarsely decorated cups, a loaf of white bread, and a whole soup-plate of lump sugar.

'I like tea,' he said, 'at night; I walk about a lot and drink; till daybreak. Abroad tea at night is inconvenient.'

'Do you go to bed at daybreak?'

'Always; for ages. Don't eat a lot; always tea. Liputin's cunning, but impatient.'

I was surprised that he should want to talk; I made up my mind to take advantage of the opportunity.

'I'm afraid we had some unpleasant misunderstandings this morning,' I observed.

He scowled.

'Damn nonsense; silly! It's all damn nonsense, because Lebyatkin's drunk. I said nothing to Liputin, but just explained a few things because he got it all wrong. Liputin lets his imagination run away with him. Made a mountain out of a molehill. I trusted Liputin yesterday.'

'And me to-day?' I said, laughing.

'Well, you know everything, don't you? This morning Liputin was weak, or impatient, or unreliable, or – envious.'

The last word surprised me.

'I'm afraid you've used so many adjectives that it would be strange if one of them did not apply to him.'

'Or all of them together.'

'Well, that's what Liputin really is. He is – chaos! Tell me, he was lying this morning when he said that you wished to write something, wasn't he?'

'Why should he?' he said, frowning again and staring at the floor.

I apologized and tried to assure him that I was not attempting to pry into his private affairs. He blushed.

'He spoke the truth – I am writing. Only it makes no difference.'

We were silent for a minute. He suddenly smiled his childlike smile I had noticed that morning.

'He invented that about the heads himself out of a book. He told me first himself. Understands it badly. All I'm looking for are the reasons why people dare not kill themselves. That's all. And all that makes no difference, either.'

'How do you mean they don't dare? Are there so few suicides?'

'Very few.'

'Do you really think so?'

He did not reply, got up and began pacing the room lost in thought.

'What deters people from committing suicide in your opinion?' I asked.

He looked at me absent-mindedly, as though trying to remember what we were talking about.

'I–I'm afraid I don't know much yet. Two prejudices deter them, two things. Two only. One a very little one, and the other a very big one. But the little one is also big.'

'What's the little one?'

'Pain.'

'Pain? Do you really think that's so important in – in a case like that?'

'Most important. There are two kinds: those who kill themselves from great sorrow or from spite, and those who are mad or whatever it is – those do it suddenly. They think little about the pain, but do it suddenly. But those who do it from reason – they think a lot.'

'But are there people who do it from reason?'

'Lots. But for prejudice there would be more; many more; all.'

'Not all, surely?'

He said nothing.

'But aren't there ways of dying painlessly?'

'Imagine,' he said, stopping before me, 'imagine a stone as big as a large house; it's suspended and you are under it; if it fell on you – on your head – would you feel any pain?'

'A stone as big as a house? Of course, I'd be frightened.'

'I'm not talking of fear. Would it hurt?'

'A stone as big as a mountain weighing millions of pounds? Of course, it wouldn't hurt.'

'But if you stood under it while it was hanging over you, you'd be terrified of the pain. Everybody would be terrified – the greatest scientist – the greatest doctor. Everyone will know it won't hurt, and everyone will be afraid that it will hurt.'

'Well, and what is the second reason, the big one?'

'The next world!'

'You mean punishment?'

'Makes no difference. The next world – just the next world.'

'But aren't there atheists who do not believe in the next world at all?'

Again he said nothing.

'Perhaps you judge from yourself?'

'Everyone must judge from himself,' he said, reddening. 'Full freedom will come only when it makes no difference whether to live or not to live. That's the goal for everybody.'

'The goal? But perhaps no one will want to live then.'

'No one,' he said emphatically.

'Man's afraid of death because he loves life,' I remarked. 'That's how I see it, and that's how nature has ordered it.'

'That's despicable and that's where the whole deception lies.' His eyes flashed. 'Life is pain, life is fear, and man is unhappy. Now all is pain and fear. Now man loves life. And that's how they've done it. You're given life now for pain and fear, and that's where the whole deception lies. Now man is not yet what he will be. A new man will come, happy and proud. To whom it won't matter whether he lives or not. He'll be the new man! He who conquers pain and fear will himself be a god. And that other God will not be.'

'So, according to you, the other God does exist, after all?'

'He doesn't exist, but He is. There's no pain in a stone, but there's pain in the fear of a stone. He who conquers pain and fear will himself become a god. Then there will be a new life, a new man, everything will be new. Then history will be divided into two parts: from the gorilla to the annihilation of God, and from the annihilation of God to –'

'To the gorilla?'

'... to the physical transformation of the earth and man. Man will be god. He'll be physically transformed. And the world, too, will be transformed, and things will be transformed, and thoughts and all feelings. What do you think? Will man be physically transformed then?'

'If it is all the same whether to live or not to live, everyone will kill himself and that's perhaps the only change that will come about.'

'It makes no difference. Deception will be killed. Everyone who desires supreme freedom must dare to kill himself. He who dares to kill himself has learnt the secret of the deception. Beyond that there is no freedom; that's all, and beyond it there is nothing. He who dares to kill himself is a god. Now every one can make it so that there shall be no God and there shall be nothing. But no one has done so yet.'

'There have been millions of suicides.'

'But none of them for that reason. All of them did it from fear, and not for that. He who kills himself only to kill fear will at once become a god.'

'Perhaps he won't have time,' I observed.

'That makes no difference,' he replied quietly, with calm pride, almost with contempt. 'I'm sorry you seem to be laughing,' he added half a minute later.

'I find it strange that you should have been so irritable this morning and are now so calm, though you speak with warmth.'

'This morning? It was funny this morning,' he replied with a smile. 'I don't like abusing people, and I never laugh,' he added sadly.

'Well, you don't seem to spend your nights very cheerfully over your tea.'

I got up and took my cap.

'You think so?' He smiled with some surprise. 'Why not? No, I – I don't know.' He suddenly grew confused. 'I don't know about the others, but I feel that I can't do the same as everybody. Everybody thinks and then at once thinks of something else. I can't think of something else. All my life I think of one thing. God has tormented me all my life,' he concluded suddenly with amazing frankness.

'Would you mind telling me why you don't speak our language correctly? Have you forgotten how to speak after five years abroad?'

'Don't I speak correctly? I don't know. No, it's not because of living abroad. I've spoken like that all my life. Makes no difference to me.'

'Another more delicate question: I quite believe you that you don't like meeting people and talk very little with people. Why have you talked so much with me now?'

'With you? You sat so quietly this morning and you – but, it makes no difference – you're very like my brother, very, extremely,' he said, blushing. 'He died seven years ago. He was older – very, very much.'

'I expect he must have had a great influence on your way of thinking.'

'N-no, he spoke little – never said anything. I shall give your note to Shatov.'

He saw me to the gate with a lantern, to lock it after me. 'He's mad as a hatter, of course,' I decided.

At the gate I had another encounter.

9

No sooner did I lift my foot over the high beam at the bottom of the gate than I was suddenly seized by the chest by a strong hand.

'Who's that?' roared a voice. 'Friend or foe? Own up!'

'He's one of us, one of us!' Liputin squeaked in his thin voice nearby. 'It's Mr G—v, a young gentleman of classical education and in close touch with the highest society.'

'I like a chap who belongs to society, classi- – that means high-ly ed-duc-cated. Retired Captain Ignatius Lebyatkin, sir, at the service of the world and friends – if they're true friends, if they're true friends, the scoundrels!'

Captain Lebyatkin, a stout and fleshy man over six feet in height, with curly hair and a red face, stood before me. He was so drunk that he could scarcely stand on his feet and he articulated his words with difficulty. I had seen him before, as a matter of fact, from a distance.

'Oh, and that one, too,' he roared again, noticing Kirilov, who was still standing there with his lantern. He raised his fist, but put it down at once. 'I forgive you for your l-learning! Ignatius L-lebyatkin – high-ly ed-duc-cated –

> A blazing cannon-ball exploded
> In Ignatius' breast with love corroded.
> And, armless, in an agony of pain,
> For Sebastopol he wept again.

Though I was never at Sebastopol, and though I never lost an arm; but what rhymes, sir, what rhymes!' he shouted, thrusting his drunken face forward.

'He is in a hurry, he's going home,' Liputin tried to persuade him. 'He'll tell Miss Lisa about it to-morrow.'

'Lisa!' he roared again. 'Stop! Don't go! Another version:

> A star goes riding graciously
> In a throng of amazons wild;
> And from her horse she smiles at me
> The aris-tocra-tic child.

Why, it's a paean! It's a paean, you stupid ass, to a Star-Amazon! The loafers, they don't understand! Stop!'

He grabbed hold of my overcoat, though I was trying with all my might to escape through the gate.

'Tell her that I'm the soul of honour, and as for that hussy Dasha – I'll break her in two. A damned serf girl, and she dare not –'

At this point he fell down, for I had torn myself out of his hands by force and fled down the street. Liputin followed on my heels.

'Kirilov will pick him up,' he chattered away, in great excitement. 'Do you know what I've just found out from him? Did you hear his verses? He's sealed those very verses to the "Star-Amazon" in an envelope and is going to send them to Miss Tushin to-morrow. He signed them with his full name! What a fellow!'

'I bet you suggested it to him yourself.'

'You'll lose your bet,' Liputin broke into a loud laugh. 'He's in love, in love like a cat, and, you know, it all began with hatred. At first he hated Miss Tushin so much for riding on horseback that he almost swore at her in the street. He did swear at her, in fact! Only the day before yesterday he swore at her as she rode past. Luckily, she did not hear. And to-day he wrote her a poem! Do you know that he even intends to take the risk of proposing to her? Seriously! Seriously!'

'I'm surprised at you, Liputin,' I said furiously; 'you're always to be found in the company of some villainous rogue, and you always lead him on.'

'You're going a bit too far, Mr G—v! You don't feel just a little bit afraid of a rival by any chance, do you?'

'Wha-at?' I cried, stopping in my tracks.

'Very well, as a punishment I shan't tell you anything more! And you would like to know, wouldn't you? For instance, that that silly fool isn't an ordinary captain now, but a landowner of our province, and a substantial one at that, for Mr Stavrogin has just sold him his estate, formerly of two hundred serfs, and God's my witness, I'm not lying. I've only just found it out myself, but from a most trustworthy source. And now find the rest out for yourself. Shan't say another word. Good-bye!'

10

Mr Verkhovensky was expecting me with hysterical impatience. He had been back an hour. He gave me the impression of being drunk; indeed, for the first five minutes I thought he was drunk. Alas! his visit to the Drozdovs had completely unsettled him.

'*Mon ami*, I've completely lost the thread of my thoughts. Lisa – I adore that angel and I think as much of her as ever; but I couldn't help feeling that they both wanted to see me solely in order to find something out from me – that is, simply worm it out of me, and then good-bye! Yes, I'm afraid, that's what it was.'

'You ought to be ashamed of yourself to talk like that!' I exclaimed, unable to control myself.

'My dear friend, I'm utterly alone now. *Enfin c'est ridicule*. There, too, you know, the whole thing's full of mystery. They simply flung themselves upon me about those noses and ears and about some sort of Petersburg secrets. You see, it's only now that they have found out about those incidents with Nicholas four years ago. "You were here, you saw it; is it true that he is insane?" And where they got the idea from I don't know. Why is Mrs Drozdov so anxious that Nicholas should be mad? The woman wants it. She wants it, I tell you. *Ce Maurice*, or what's his name? – that Drozdov fellow, *brave homme tout de même*, it can't be for his sake, surely; and after she was the first to write from Paris to *cette pauvre amie*. ... *Enfin*, this Praskovya, as *cette chère amie* calls her; she's a real type, she's Gogol's Korobochka; only she's a spiteful Mrs Box, a provocative Mrs Box, of immortal memory, and in a greatly magnified form.'

'Why, that'll make her into a big trunk! Are you sure she's a magnified version of Gogol's character?'

'Well, a reduced form, then. What does it matter? Only don't interrupt me, for the whole thing just keeps going round and round in my head. They seemed to have finally fallen out there. Except Lisa; She still keeps on with her "Auntie, Auntie", but Lisa's sly, and there's something there I can't make out. Secrets. But she's fallen out with the old woman. *Cette pauvre* Auntie, it is true, tyrannizes over everyone – and now she has to deal with the Governor's wife, the disrespect of society, and Karmazinov's "disrespect". Then she suddenly gets that idea about her son's madness, *ce Lipoutine, ce que je ne comprends pas*, and – and I'm told she's been dabbing her forehead with vinegar, and here are we with our complaints and letters. Oh, how I have tortured her; and at such a time, too! *Je suis un ingrat!* Just think, on my return I found a letter from her. Read it, read it! Oh, how beastly it was of me!'

He gave me the letter he had just received from Mrs Stavrogin. She seemed to be sorry for this morning's 'stay at home'. Her letter was polite, but brief and emphatic for all that. She asked Mr Verkhovensky to go to see her the day after to-morrow – on Sunday – at twelve o'clock, and advised him to bring one of his friends (she mentioned my name in brackets) with him. For her part, she promised to invite Shatov as the brother of Dasha. 'You will be able to get your final answer from her: will that satisfy you? Is this the formality you were so anxious about?'

'Note that exasperated phrase about the formality at the end of her letter. Poor, poor woman, my lifelong friend! I confess, this *sudden* decision on which my whole future depends came as a great blow to me. I must say I still had hopes, but now *tout est dit*, I know now that all is over; *c'est terrible*. Oh, that that Sunday would never come and everything would be as before: you'd be coming to see me, and I'd be here. ...'

'You're distraught by all those nasty things Liputin said. All those innuendoes.'

'My friend, you've laid your well-meaning finger on another sore spot. These well-meaning fingers are pitiless, as a rule, and sometimes blundering. I'm sorry, but, you know, I'd almost forgotten all about it. I mean, about those nasty innuendoes, that is. I hadn't really forgotten about them; but, in my folly, tried all the time I was with Lisa to be happy, and persuaded myself I was happy. But now – oh, now I'm thinking of that generous and kind-hearted woman, so tolerant of my despicable shortcomings – that is to say, she may not be so tolerant as all that; but think what I'm like, with my worthless, rotten character! Why, I'm just a spoilt child, with all the egoism and none of the innocence of a child. For twenty years she has been looking after me like a nurse, *cette pauvre* Auntie, as Lisa so delightfully calls her. And suddenly, after twenty years, the child has got it into its head to get married – sending her one letter after another, and she has vinegar compresses on her head and – and, well, I've got what I wanted now, and on Sunday I shall be a married man – of all things! And why on earth did I insist on it myself? Why did I write those letters? Oh, yes, I forgot to tell you: Lisa worships Dasha. At least, she says so. "*C'est un ange*," she says about her, "only a rather secretive one." They both advised me to marry her – even Praskovya – well, no, not Praskovya. She didn't advise me. Oh, how much venom there is locked up in that little "box"! As a matter of fact, Lisa didn't advise me, either. "What do you want to get married for?" she said to me. "Your intellectual pleasures ought to be enough for you!" She laughed. I forgave her her laughter, for she's so unhappy herself. But, they told me, you certainly cannot get on without a woman. The infirmities of age are coming upon you, and she'll tuck you in, or whatever it is. ... *Ma foi*, while I've been sitting with you here, I kept on saying to myself that Providence was sending her to me at the close of my stormy days, and that she would tuck me in, or whatever it is ... *enfin*, she'll be useful to keep house for me. Everything is in such a frightful mess here. Look at all that rubbish! I told Nastasya this morning to tidy up, and that book is still on the floor. *La pauvre amie* is always cross with me for the untidiness of my rooms. Oh, now I shall no longer hear her voice! *Vingt ans!* And – and I believe they've been getting anonymous letters, too. Think of it! Nicholas is said to have sold his estate to Lebyatkin. *C'est un monstre! et enfin* who's that Lebyatkin? Lisa listens, listens – oh, how she listens! I forgave her her laughter, for I saw her face as she listened, and *ce Maurice* – I shouldn't like to be in his shoes now, *brave homme tout de même*, but rather shy; but never mind him. ...'

He fell silent; he was tired and confused, and sat with his head drooping, gazing motionless at the floor with weary eyes. I took advantage of the lull in our conversation to tell him about my visit to Filippov's house, and curtly and dryly expressed the opinion that Lebyatkin's sister (whom I had never seen) might really at one time have been one of Nicholas's victims during the mysterious period of his life, as Liputin had put it, and that it was very probable indeed that Lebyatkin was receiving money for some reason from Nicholas. But that was all. As for the slanderous stories about Dasha, I was sure that it was all nonsense – innuendoes spread by Liputin – and that this, at any rate, was what Kirilov, whom there was no reason to disbelieve, warmly maintained. Mr Verkhovensky listened to my assurances with a distracted air, as though they had nothing to do with him. I mentioned, by the way, my conversation with Kirilov, adding that Kirilov was probably mad.

'He's not mad,' Mr Verkhovensky muttered listlessly, as though against his will, 'but he's one of those people who have little minds. *Ces gens-là supposent la nature et la société humaine autres que Dieu ne les a faites et qu'elles ne sont réellement.* People make advances to them, but not Stepan Verkhovensky, at any rate. I saw them that time in Petersburg, *avec cette chère amie* (oh, how I used to humiliate her then!), and I wasn't afraid of their insults or their praise. I shan't be afraid now, either, *mais parlons d'autre chose.* I think I've done something dreadful – you see, I sent Dasha a letter yesterday and – oh, how I curse myself for it!'

'What did you write to her about?'

'Oh, my friend, believe me, it was so honourably meant. I told her

that I had written to Nicholas five days before, and with the most
honourable intentions.'

'I understand now!' I cried warmly. 'And what right had you to
couple their names like that?'

'But, *mon cher*, please don't crush me completely, don't shout at
me! I am as it is utterly squashed, like – like a cockroach, and, after
all, I still think that it was all so honourable. Suppose there really
was something – *en Suisse* – or – or that something was just starting.
Oughtn't I to consult their hearts first, so as not to – *enfin*, so as not to
interfere with their hearts and be an obstacle in their paths? ... My
motives were absolutely honourable. ...'

'Oh, dear, what a stupid thing you've done!' I cried involuntarily.

'It was stupid,' he echoed eagerly; 'you've never said anything
more intelligent, *c'était bête, mais que faire, tout est dit*. For I shall marry
her just the same, even if it is only to cover up another man's sins. So
what did I have to write those letters for? Isn't that so?'

'You're starting all over again!'

'Oh, now you won't frighten me with your shouts. You see quite
a different Stepan Verkhovensky before you now. The other one has
been buried; *enfin, tout est dit*. And why do you shout? Only because
you're not getting married yourself and you won't have to carry the
notorious ornament on your head. Do you wince again? My poor
friend, you don't know women, whereas I've spent all my life studying them. "If you want to conquer the whole world, conquer yourself," that is the only good thing that other romantic like you, my
future bride's brother, Shatov, ever said. I gladly appropriate that saying from him. Well, I, too, am ready to conquer myself, and I'll be
getting married; but what is it that I'll be conquering instead of the
whole world? Oh, my friend, marriage is the moral death of every
proud soul, of all independence. Married life will corrupt me, will rob
me of my strength, my courage to serve our cause. There will be children; not mine, either, I daresay – I mean certainly not mine: a wise
man is not afraid to look truth in the face. This morning Liputin advised me to put up barricades against Nicholas; he is stupid, Liputin
is. A woman will deceive the all-seeing eye itself. In creating woman
le bon Dieu knew, of course, the risk he was running, but I'm sure that
it was she who interfered with him and forced him to create her that
way and – with such attributes; who would otherwise have incurred

so much trouble for nothing? Nastasya, I know, might be angry with me for such free-thinking, but – *enfin, tout est dit.*'

He wouldn't have been himself if he had dispensed with the cheap, quibbling sort of free-thinking which flourished in his day. Now, at any rate, he comforted himself with his little quibble, but not for long.

'Oh, if only there wouldn't be any day-after-to-morrow, any Sunday!' he cried suddenly, but in utter despair this time. 'Why shouldn't there be one week without a Sunday – *si le miracle existe*? What would it really have cost Providence to blot out one Sunday from the calendar? Just to prove His power to the atheist *et que tout soit dit*! Oh, how I have loved her! Twenty years, all these twenty years, and she has never understood me!'

'But who are you talking about?' I asked in surprise. 'I don't understand you, either!'

'*Vingt ans!* And not once has she understood me – oh, that is cruel! And does she really think that I'm getting married because I'm afraid or because I'm poor? Oh, the disgrace of it! Auntie, Auntie, I'm doing it for you! Oh, let her know that, auntie, that she was the only woman I have adored for twenty years! She must know that, for otherwise there won't be any wedding, otherwise they'll have to drag me by force to *ce qu'on appelle le* altar!'

It was the first time I had heard this confession, made with such energy, too. I won't conceal the fact that I was terribly tempted to laugh. But I was wrong.

'He's the only one left to me now, the only one, my only hope,' he cried suddenly in great agitation, as though struck all at once by a new thought. 'Now only he, my poor boy, can save me and – oh, why doesn't he come? Oh, my son, oh, my dear Peter – and though I don't deserve to be called father, but rather a tiger, still – *laissez-moi, mon ami*, I'll lie down a little to collect my thoughts. I'm so tired, so tired, and I expect it's time you went to bed too. *Voyez vous*, it's twelve o'clock. …'

4

The Cripple

I

SHATOV made no difficulties and, as I had suggested in my note, called at midday on Lisa. We arrived almost at the same time; I, too, was paying my first call. All of them – that is, Lisa, her mother, and Mr Drozdov – were sitting in the large drawing-room and having an argument. The mother was asking Lisa to play some waltz on the piano – and when Lisa began to play the waltz asked for, her mother declared that it was not the right one. Mr Drozdov, in the simplicity of his heart, took Lisa's part and tried to convince the old lady that it was the right waltz; but Mrs Drozdov lost her temper and began to cry. She was ill, and even walked with difficulty. Her legs were swollen, and for the last few days she had done nothing but make scenes and find fault with everyone, though she was rather afraid of Lisa. They were pleased to see us. Lisa flushed with pleasure, and after saying 'Merci' to me for bringing Shatov, of course, went up to him, regarding him with curiosity.

Shatov stopped awkwardly in the doorway. Having thanked him for coming, she led him up to her mother.

'This is the Mr Shatov I told you about, and this is Mr G—v, a great friend of mine and Mr Verkhovensky's. Maurice also made his acquaintance yesterday.'

'And which is the professor?'

'There's no professor at all, Mother.'

'I'm sure there is. You said yourself that there'd be a professor – I suppose it's that one.' She indicated Shatov disdainfully.

'I never said anything to you about expecting a professor. Mr G—v is in the civil service and Mr Shatov is a former student.'

'Student or professor – they're all from a university. You only want to argue. But the Swiss one had a moustache and a little beard.'

'Mother always calls Mr Verkhovensky's son a professor,' Lisa said, and she took Shatov away to the sofa at the other end of the drawing-room.

'I'm awfully sorry,' she whispered to Shatov, 'but when her legs are swollen she's always like that. I'm afraid she's ill,' she added and went on scrutinizing him with great curiosity, especially his shock of hair.

'Are you in the army, sir?' asked the old woman to whom Lisa had so mercilessly abandoned me.

'No, ma'am, I'm in the Civil Service.'

'Mr G—v is a great friend of Mr Verkhovensky's,' Lisa immediately called out.

'Do you serve under Mr Verkhovensky? He, too, is a professor, isn't he?'

'Goodness, Mother, you must be seeing professors in your dreams, too,' Lisa cried with annoyance.

'There are too many of them about in real life. You're always contradicting your mother, darling. Were you here four years ago, when Mr Stavrogin was staying with his mother?'

I replied that I was.

'And wasn't there some Englishman with you, too?'

'No, ma'am, there wasn't.'

Lisa laughed.

'Well, you see, there was no Englishman. It must be a lie, then. Mrs Stavrogin and Mr Verkhovensky are lying. Everybody is lying.'

'It was Auntie and Mr Verkhovensky yesterday who thought there was some resemblance between Mr Stavrogin and Prince Harry in Shakespeare's *Henry IV*, and that's why Mother thinks there ought to be an Englishman,' Lisa explained to us.

'If Harry wasn't there, there was no Englishman there, either. It was Nicholas alone who was playing the fool.'

'Mother is saying that on purpose, I assure you,' Lisa found it necessary to explain to Shatov. 'She knows all about Shakespeare. I read her the first act of *Othello* myself, but she's in great pain now. Mother, it's striking twelve – it's time you took your medicine.'

'The doctor is here, ma'am,' a maid announced at the door.

The old lady got up and started calling her dog: 'Zemirka, Zemirka, you'll come with me, at any rate, won't you?'

Zemirka, a repulsive old lap-dog, refused to obey her mistress and crawled under the sofa where Lisa was sitting.

'So you don't want to! Very well, I don't want you, either. Goodbye, sir; I'm sorry I don't know your name,' she addressed me.

'Anton Lavrentyevich –'

'Never mind, sir; with me it goes in at one ear and out at the other. Don't you come with me, Maurice; it was Zemirka I called. Thank God, I can still walk about by myself, and to-morrow I'll go for a drive.'

She walked out of the room in a temper.

'Please,' said Lisa to me, 'talk to Mr Drozdov. I'm sure you will both profit from getting to know one another better.'

She smiled nicely at Mr Drozdov, who beamed all over with delight. I had, willy-nilly, to talk to Mr Drozdov.

2

To my surprise, Lisa's business with Shatov was really concerned only with literature. I don't know why, but I imagined that she wanted to see him on quite a different matter. We – that is, Mr Drozdov and myself – seeing that they were not trying to hide anything from us and were talking aloud, began to listen to their conversation. Presently we, too, were invited to join in. It was all about an idea Lisa had had for some time of publishing what she considered would be a useful book; but, being quite inexperienced, she wanted someone to help her with it. The seriousness with which she began to explain her plan to Shatov quite surprised me. 'Must be one of the new women,' I thought. 'She's not been to Switzerland for nothing.' Shatov listened to her attentively, his eyes fixed on the floor, and showed no surprise whatever that a frivolous society girl should take up such a seemingly unsuitable job.

Her literary plan was as follows. Hundreds of papers and journals are published in Russia, both in the capital cities and in the provinces, and every day innumerable events are reported in them. The year passes, the papers are everywhere put away in cupboards or torn up and thrown away, or are used for making bags, or all sorts of things. Many of the facts published in them make an impression and are remembered by the public, but are eventually forgotten. Many people would like to look them up, but what a labour it is to try to find what they want in that sea of paper, when they often do not know either the day or the place or even the year in which the incident occurred. And yet if all the facts for a whole year were to be carefully classified and published in one book, according to a definite plan and with a definite object in view, under their appropriate headings, with cross-references, and arranged according to months and days, such a reference book might provide a useful outline of the characteristics of Russian life for the whole year, even though the actual number of published facts would be very small compared with the events of the year.

'Instead of a large number of sheets of paper, you would get a few bulky volumes – that's all,' observed Shatov.

But Lisa spoke warmly in defence of her idea, though, because of her inexperience, she found it difficult to express herself clearly. She maintained that there need be no more than one book, and that even that need not be too bulky. But even if it were bulky it would be easy to consult, for everything depended on the plan and the way the facts were presented. Naturally, not everything would be collected and re-published. Official decrees, Government Acts, local regulations, laws – all such facts, however important, might be entirely omitted from the proposed publication. Quite a lot could be omitted, only those events being selected for publication which were more or less typical of the moral life of the people, the personal character of the Russian people at any given moment. Anything, of course, might be included: odd incidents, fires, public subscriptions, good or bad actions, all sorts of pronouncements and speeches, perhaps even reports of floods, perhaps even some Government decrees; but whatever was selected must be characteristic of the period; everything published would express a certain point of view, a certain well-defined intention, an idea that would throw a light on the whole mass of events. And, finally, the book would also be of interest to the general reader, apart from its usefulness as a reference book. It would have to give, as it were, a picture of the spiritual, moral, and inner life of Russia for a whole year.

'We want everyone to buy it,' Lisa insisted. 'We want it to be found in every house. I realize, of course, that everything depends on the plan, and that's why I apply to you,' she concluded.

She talked very excitedly, and though her explanations were rather obscure and incomplete, Shatov began to understand.

'You want something with a tendency, a selection of facts with a well-defined tendency,' he muttered, still not looking up.

'Not at all. There's no question of selecting anything of a tendentious nature. We don't want any bias. Complete impartiality – that must be our only tendency.'

'There's nothing wrong about a tendency,' said Shatov, stirring. 'Besides, it will be impossible to avoid it if there is going to be any selection at all. The selection of the facts will show the way they are to be interpreted. Your idea isn't bad.'

'So you think that it is possible to publish such a book?' Lisa cried happily.

'It will have to be carefully looked into. It's a big thing. It's impossible to plan it all at once. You must have experience. And even when we come to publish the book, I doubt whether we shall know how to do it. After many trials, perhaps. But the idea is certainly worth considering. It's a useful idea.'

He raised his eyes at last, and they were beaming with pleasure – so interested was he.

'Did you think of it yourself?' he asked Lisa tenderly and as though shyly.

'The snag is how to carry it out, not the idea itself,' Lisa replied, smiling. 'I'm not very clever, I'm afraid. I understand very little and I can follow only what's clear to myself.'

'Follow?'

'It isn't the right word, is it?' Lisa inquired quickly.

'Oh, you can use that word if you like. I don't mind.'

'I thought when I was abroad that I, too, could be of some use. I have money of my own and I am not doing anything with it. Why shouldn't I, too, do something for the common cause? Besides, the idea came to me suddenly, as though of itself. I didn't invent it at all, and I was delighted with it. But I realized at once that I wouldn't be able to carry it out without someone to assist me, because I can't do anything by myself. My collaborator would of course become the co-editor of the book. We'd go halves: the plan and the work will be your contribution, and the original idea and the means for carrying it out mine. Don't you think such a book will pay its expenses?'

'If we plan it properly, it will sell.'

'I warn you I'm not doing it for profit, but I would like the book to sell, and I'd be proud if we did make a profit.'

'I see; but what have I got to do with it?'

'Why, I want you to be my collaborator – we'll go halves. You'll work out the plan.'

'But how do you know that I shall be able to work out the plan?'

'I was told about you and – and here, too, I've heard – I know that you're very clever and – and – are doing useful work – and – think a lot; Peter Verkhovensky spoke of you to me in Switzerland,' she added hurriedly. 'He's a very clever man, isn't he?'

Shatov glanced at her quickly, but at once lowered his eyes.

'Mr Stavrogin, too, told me a lot about you.'

Shatov suddenly reddened.

'Here – here are the newspapers.' Lisa hastily picked up from a chair a bundle of tied-up newspapers she had previously prepared. 'I've tried to mark the facts for selection, to sort them out, and I've numbered them – you'll see.'

Shatov took the bundle.

'Take it home with you and have a look. Where do you live?'

'In Bogoyavlenskaya Street, Filippov's house.'

'I know. I'm told a certain captain lives in the same house as you, a Mr Lebyatkin,' Lisa went on, speaking rapidly as before.

Shatov sat for a whole minute without replying, staring at the floor and holding the bundle in his outstretched hand.

'You'd better look for someone else for that kind of job,' he said at last almost in a whisper, dropping his voice in a very strange way. 'I won't be of any use to you at all.'

Lisa flushed. 'What job are you talking about? Maurice,' she cried, 'please let me have the letter I received yesterday.'

I also went after Mr Drozdov to the table.

'Have a look at this,' she addressed me suddenly, unfolding the letter in great agitation. 'Have you seen anything like it? Read it, please. Read it aloud. I want Mr Shatov to hear it too.'

With no little astonishment I read aloud the following missive:

> To the paragon of Ladies, Miss Tushin.
>
> Madam,
>
> Oh, what grace
> In Miss Tushin's face,
> When with her cousin on side-saddle forth she sallies,
> And playful zephyr with her tresses dallies,
> Or when with her mother in church she bows low,
> And on devout faces a red flush doth show!
> Then for the joys of lawful wedlock I yearn
> And after her, with her mother, never a tear I spurn.
> Composed by an untutored man during an argument.

Madam,

I pity myself most of all that I have not lost an arm at Sebastopol for the glory of our country, not having been there at all, but having served throughout the campaign as a supplier of low victuals which I consider a scurvy business. You are a goddess of antiquity and I am nothing, and have caught a vision of immortality. Look on these as verses and nothing more, for verses are after all nonsense and justify what would have been considered rank insolence in prose. Can the sun be angry with an amoeba if the latter should write a poem to it from the drop of water where there are millions of them if you look through a microscope? Even the club for the protection of larger animals in the best Petersburg society, which quite rightly shows compassion to the dog and the horse, despises the tiny amoeba, not mentioning it at all on account of its not being big enough. I am not big enough either. The idea of marriage may seem absurd; but I shall soon be the owner of a property which in the old days would have been worth two hundred serfs through the good offices of a hater of mankind whom you should despise. I could tell a lot and I can produce documents which may even mean Siberia. Don't despise my offer. For the letter from the amoeba see the poem.

> Captain Lebyatkin, your most humble servant who is ever
> at your command.

'That was written by a man who was drunk, a scoundrel!' I cried indignantly. 'I know him.'

'I received the letter yesterday,' Lisa began to explain, blushing and speaking hurriedly. 'I at once realized, of course, that it was from some fool, and I haven't yet shown it to Mother because I don't want to upset her more. But if he means to go on like that, I don't know what to do. Mr Drozdov wants to go to see him and forbid him to pester me any more. But as I have already looked on you as my collaborator,' she addressed Shatov, 'and as you live in the same house, I wanted to question you, to get an idea what more to expect from him.'

'He's a drunkard and a blackguard,' Shatov muttered with some reluctance.

'But is he always as stupid as that?'

'Good Lord, no! He isn't stupid at all when he's sober.'

'I knew a general who used to write verses exactly like that,' I observed, laughing.

'Even this letter shows that he knows very well what he is up to,' the taciturn Mr Drozdov remarked unexpectedly.

'I'm told he lives with some sister – does he?' asked Lisa.

'Yes, he does.'

'I'm told he bullies her. Is that true?'

Shatov glanced at Lisa again, scowled, and muttering, 'What do I care?' moved towards the door.

'Wait, please,' Lisa cried in alarm. 'Where are you going? We've still so many things to discuss.'

'What is there to discuss? I'll let you know to-morrow.'

'Why, the most important thing of all – the printers! Please believe me, I'm not treating it as a joke. I'm quite serious about it,' Lisa assured him with growing alarm. 'If we decide to publish it, where are we going to have it printed? That's the most important question, for we shan't go to Moscow for it, and such a publication cannot be entrusted to any of our local printers. I made up my mind long ago to get a printing-press of my own, in your name, if necessary, and I know Mother will let me do so, provided it is in your name.'

'How do you know that I could be a printer?' Shatov asked sullenly.

'Why, Peter Verkhovensky told me in Switzerland that you're just the right person to manage a printing-press and that you are familiar with that sort of business. He even wanted to give me a note to you, but I forgot to ask him for it.'

Shatov, as I now recall, changed colour. He stood still for a few seconds more, and then suddenly walked out of the room.

Lisa got angry.

'Does he always go away like that?' she asked, turning to me.

I was about to shrug my shoulders when Shatov suddenly returned, went straight up to the table, and put down the bundle of newspapers he had taken with him.

'I shan't be your collaborator; I can't spare the time.'

'But why not? Why not? You're not angry, are you?' Lisa asked in a grieved and beseeching voice.

The sound of her voice seemed to surprise him; for a few seconds he looked intently at her, as though wishing to penetrate into her very soul.

'Makes no difference,' he muttered, 'I don't want to. ...'

And he left the house. Lisa was completely taken aback, quite unreasonably so – at least so it seemed to me.

'What an extraordinarily queer chap!' Mr Drozdov remarked in a loud voice.

3

No doubt he was 'queer', but there was a great deal that was not clear to me in all that. There was some hidden meaning in it. I simply could not believe in this publication; then there was that stupid letter, in which a suggestion was quite clearly made to give some information and 'produce documents', which they all seemed to have ignored, talking about something quite different; lastly that printing-press and Shatov's sudden departure just because they spoke of a printing-press. All this led me to believe that something had happened before my arrival, something I knew nothing about, and that, consequently, I was not wanted and that it was none of my business. Besides, it was time I left. I had been there long enough for a first visit. I went up to say good-bye to Lisa.

She seemed to have forgotten that I was in the room. She was still standing in the same place by the table, with her head bowed and her eyes fixed on one spot on the carpet.

'Oh, I'm sorry,' she murmured in an ordinary polite tone of voice. 'You're going, too. Well, good-bye. Give my regards to Mr Verkho-vensky, and do ask him to come to see me as soon as possible. Maurice, Mr G—v is going. I'm sorry Mother can't come out to say good-bye to you.'

I went out, and had reached the bottom of the stairs when a footman overtook me at the front door.

'Mistress wants you to come back, sir. ...'

'Your mistress or Miss Lisa?'

'Miss Lisa, sir.'

I found Lisa not in the large drawing-room, where we had been sitting, but in the reception-room next to it. The door leading to the drawing-room, where Maurice was left alone, was closed.

Lisa smiled at me, but she looked pale. She was standing in the middle of the room, evidently unable to make up her mind and strug-gling with herself. But she suddenly took me by the hand, and with-out uttering a word, led me quickly to the window.

'I must see *her* at once,' she whispered, gazing at me with burn-ing, determined, impatient eyes, which did not brook the slightest contradiction. 'I must see *her* with my own eyes, and I'm asking you to help me.'

She was completely beside herself and in despair.

'Who do you want to see, Miss Lisa?' I asked in alarm.

'That Miss Lebyatkin, that cripple. ... Is it true that she is lame?'

I was amazed.

'I have never seen her, but I've heard that she is lame,' I murmured with hurried readiness and also in a whisper. 'I heard it yesterday.'

'I must see her. I simply must. Could you arrange it for to-day?'

I felt awfully sorry for her.

'I'm afraid it's impossible, and, besides, I should not know how to arrange it,' I tried to persuade her. 'I'll go and see Shatov –'

'If you won't arrange it for to-morrow, I shall go to her myself, alone, because Mr Drozdov refuses to come with me. You're my only hope, for I have no one else I can turn to. I'm afraid I spoke stupidly to Shatov. ... I'm sure you're a very honest person and, perhaps, devoted to me. Please arrange it.'

I was overcome by a passionate desire to help her in every way.

'This is what I'll do,' I said, after thinking it over for a moment. 'I'll go there myself, and I'll see her to-day for certain, *for certain*. I'll arrange it so that I'll see her. I give you my word. Only, please let me take Shatov into my confidence.'

'Tell him that I want to see her and that I can't wait any longer, but that I wasn't deceiving him just now. Perhaps he went away because he's very honest and didn't like to think that I was deceiving him. I wasn't deceiving him. I really want to publish the book and found a printing business.'

'He is honest,' I affirmed warmly.

'However, if you can't arrange it for to-morrow, I shall go there myself, whatever happens, and even if everyone were to find out.'

'I'm afraid I shan't be able to see you before three o'clock to-morrow,' I observed, recovering my senses a little.

'Very well, at three o'clock, then. So I was right in thinking at Mr Verkhovensky's yesterday that you're a little – devoted to me, wasn't I?' she said, smiling as she pressed my hand to say good-bye and hurried off to rejoin Drozdov.

I left the house, feeling uneasy about my promise, and scarcely realizing what had happened. I had seen a woman in real despair, who was not afraid to compromise herself by confiding in a man she hardly knew. Her sweet smile at so difficult a moment in her life and her hint that she had already noticed my feelings yesterday stabbed me to the heart. But I was sorry for her, I was sorry for her – that was all! Her secrets suddenly became something sacred to me, and even if anyone had tried to reveal them to me now, I believe I would have stopped my ears and refused to listen to anything more. I had a curious premonition of something. ... Besides, I had no idea how I could possibly do anything. What's more, I did not know what exactly I was supposed to arrange – an interview, but what sort of an interview? And how was I to bring them together? My only hope was Shatov, though I should have known beforehand that he would not help me in any way. But I rushed off to see him all the same.

4

It was after seven o'clock in the evening that I found him at home. To my surprise, he had visitors – Mr Kirilov and another man I knew only slightly, a certain Shigalyov, Mr Virginsky's brother-in-law.

This Shigalyov had apparently been staying in our town for the last two months; I don't know where he came from; all I heard about him was that he had published some sort of article in a Petersburg progressive journal. Virginsky had introduced him to me casually in the street. Never in my life have I seen such dejection, gloom, and despondency on the face of a man. He looked as though he were expecting the end of the world not at some indefinite time, according to prophecies which might never come true, but with absolute definiteness – say, the day after to-morrow, at exactly twenty-five minutes past ten. We hardly said a word to one another on that occasion, but merely shook hands like two conspirators. I was particularly struck by his ears, which were of unnatural size, long, broad, and thick, sticking out in a most peculiar way. His movements were awkward and slow. If Liputin did sometimes dream of the phalanstery being established in our province, Shigalyov most certainly knew the day and the hour when it would come to pass. He made an ominous impression on me; I was the more surprised at meeting him at Shatov's, as Shatov was not particularly fond of visitors.

From the stairs I could hear them talking very loudly, the three of them together, and apparently having an argument; but the moment I entered the room they fell silent. They were arguing standing up, but now they all suddenly sat down, so that I, too, had to sit down. The stupid silence lasted for fully three minutes. Though Shigalyov recognized me, he pretended not to know me, not because of any unfriendly feelings towards me, but for no particular reason. Kirilov and I exchanged bows, but in silence and for some reason we did not shake hands. At last Shigalyov began looking at me sternly and frowningly, with the most naïve assurance that I should suddenly get up and go away. Finally, Shatov got up from his chair and all of them, too, suddenly jumped to their feet. They went out without saying good-bye, Shigalyov alone saying in the doorway to Shatov, who was seeing them off:

'Remember that you are obliged to submit a full account of your action.'

'To hell with your accounts, and I'm hanged if I am under any obligation to anybody,' Shatov said, seeing him out and fastening the door on the latch.

'The dirty twisters!' he said, glancing at me and smiling somewhat wryly.

He looked angry, and it seemed strange to me that he should have spoken first. Whenever I had gone to see him before (which was not often) he would invariably sit scowling in a corner, answer sullenly, and it was only after a long time that he grew animated and began talking with pleasure. Even then he always scowled when saying good-bye, and opened the door for you as though he were getting rid of a personal enemy.

'I had tea yesterday with that Kirilov,' I observed. 'He seems to have gone mad on atheism.'

'Russian atheism has never gone farther than a pun,' Shatov muttered, putting in a new candle in place of the burnt-out end.

'No, that man did not give me the impression of a punster. I don't think he knows how to talk, let alone make puns.'

'They're men made of paper,' Shatov observed calmly, sitting down on a chair in a corner and leaning with both hands on his knees. 'It's all because of their servile thoughts. There's also hatred there,' he went on after a minute's silence. 'They would be the first to be dreadfully unhappy if Russia were suddenly to be reorganized even according to their own ideas and if, somehow or other, she were suddenly to become an immeasurably prosperous and happy country. They would have no one to hate then; no one to despise; no one to laugh at. It's just an everlasting animal hatred of Russia which has corroded their organism. And there's no question here of any tears through smiles, tears hidden from the world. Never has an untruer word been said in Russia than that about the hidden tears,' he shouted, almost ferociously.

'Good Lord, what are you saying!' I said, laughing.

'You're of course a "moderate liberal",' Shatov said, smiling, too. 'You know,' he went on suddenly, 'I may have been talking nonsense about "servility of thoughts"; I expect you will tell me at once, "It's you who are the son of a flunkey, but I'm not a flunkey".'

'I certainly did not want to say anything of the kind – good Lord!'

'Don't apologize. I'm not afraid of you. Once I was only the son of a flunkey, but now I've become a flunkey myself. Same as you. Our Russian liberal is a flunkey before everything else. He's only waiting for the opportunity of polishing someone's boots.'

'What boots? What sort of allegory is this?'

'Dear me, it's not an allegory at all! I see, you are laughing. Mr Verkhovensky was right when he said that I lay under a stone, squashed, though not crushed to death, but only wriggling; it was a good image.'

'Mr Verkhovensky assures everybody that you're mad on the subject of the Germans,' I laughed. 'But we've picked up something from them, all the same.'

'We took twenty copecks from them and gave them a hundred roubles.'

We were silent for a minute.

'He got that sore lying in America.'

'Who? What sore?'

'I'm talking of Kirilov. I spent four months with him there lying on the floor of a hut.'

'Why, have you been to America?' I asked, surprised. 'You never mentioned it before.'

'There was nothing to tell. Two years ago we spent our last penny, three of us, to go to the United States in an emigrant steamer "to find out for ourselves what the life of the American worker was like and in this way to check by *personal* experience the state of a man living under the worst possible social conditions". That was why we went there.'

'Good Lord!' I laughed. 'If you wanted to find that out "by personal experience" you should have gone to some place in our province at harvest time, and not rushed off to America!'

'We hired ourselves out as workers to an exploiter of labour there. There were six of us Russians working for him – students, landowners who had left their estates, army officers – and all with the same noble object. Well, so we worked, got drenched, were worn out, and at last Kirilov and I left. We fell ill. We couldn't stand it any longer. When he paid us off, our employer, the exploiter, cheated us, and instead of thirty dollars as agreed, he paid me eight and him fifteen; we were also beaten there more than once. So after that Kirilov and I, unable to obtain employment, lay on the floor of a hut side by side for four months in that filthy little town; he thought of one thing and I of another.'

'Did your employer really beat you? In America? I can imagine the names you must have called him!'

'Not a bit of it. On the contrary, Kirilov and I at once decided that, compared to the Americans, we Russians were like little children, and that one had to be born in America, or at least get thoroughly acclimatized there, before one could hope to be on the same level with them. Why, even when they asked us a dollar for something that wasn't worth a penny, we paid it with pleasure, nay, with enthusiasm. We praised everything: spiritualism, lynch law, six-shooters, hoboes. One day when we were travelling a chap put his hand into my pocket, took out my hairbrush, and began brushing his hair with it; Kirilov and I just glanced at each other and made up our minds that it was quite all right and that we liked it very much.'

'It's funny how we not only think of such things, but actually do them,' I observed.

'Men made of paper,' Shatov repeated.

'Still, to cross the ocean in an emigrant ship to an unknown country, even if it is only to "find out by personal experience", etc. – well, there's something fine about it, something that requires a lot of guts. But how did you get out of it?'

'I wrote to a man in Europe, and he sent me a hundred roubles.'

While talking, Shatov, as usual, kept his eyes fixed steadily on the floor, even when he was excited. But now he suddenly raised his head.

'Do you want to know the name of that man?'

'Who was it?'

'Nicholas Stavrogin.'

He got up suddenly, turned to his limewood writing-desk, and began rummaging in it. There was a vague, though well-authenticated, rumour in our town that about two years ago his wife had been Stavrogin's mistress in Paris. That was at the time Shatov was in America, and, it is true, long after she had left him in Geneva. 'If that is so,' I thought, 'then what made him mention Stavrogin's name now, and why be so emphatic about it?'

'I haven't repaid him the money yet,' he said, turning suddenly to me again, and, looking hard at me, resumed his seat in the corner and asked abruptly in quite a different tone of voice: 'I presume you've come for something. What is it?'

I at once told him everything, in its exact chronological order, adding that though I had had time to collect my thoughts after the first excitement was over, I felt more confused than ever: I realized that it was of great importance to Lisa, I wanted very much to help her, but the trouble was that I did not know how to keep my promise, and that I could not even tell what exactly I had promised her. Then I told him firmly once again that she never meant to deceive him, that there had been some misunderstanding, and that she was very upset by the extraordinary way in which he had gone off that morning.

He listened very attentively.

'Perhaps I did do a stupid thing this morning. I'm afraid I often do. Anyway, if she did not know herself why I went away like that, then so much the better for her.'

He got up, went to the door, opened it a little, and began to listen for any noise on the stairs.

'Do you want to see that person yourself?'

'Yes, that's exactly what I do want; but how is it to be done?' I said, jumping up from my chair, greatly pleased.

'Well, all we have to do is to go down while she is alone. When he comes back he'll beat her black and blue if he finds out that we've been there. I often go there without his knowledge. I had a fight with him the other day when he started beating her again.'

'Good Lord!'

'Oh, yes. I dragged him away from her by the hair. He tried to thrash me, but I frightened him. That was the end of it. I'm afraid he'll come back drunk and remember it – he'll give her a bad beating for that.'

We went downstairs at once.

5

The door of Lebyatkin's flat was closed but not locked, and we had no difficulty in getting in. The whole flat consisted of two dismal little rooms with grimy walls on which the filthy wallpaper literally hung in shreds. That part of the house had been used for some years as a public-house, till its landlord Filippov moved it to his new house. The other rooms of the former public-house were locked up, and these two were let to Lebyatkin. The furniture consisted of ordinary benches and deal tables, with the exception of an old easy-chair with one arm missing. In the second room, in a corner, was a bed covered with a cotton counterpane, which belonged to Miss Lebyatkin; as for the Captain himself, he slept on the floor, often without bothering to undress. Crumbs, dirt, wet puddles were everywhere; a large, soaking-wet floor-cloth lay in the middle of the first room, together with an old, worn-out shoe in the same puddle. One could see that no one bothered to do any housework here: the stoves were not heated, food was not cooked; they did not even have a *samovar*, as Shatov later told me. The Captain had arrived penniless, with his sister, and, as Liputin said, at first had really gone begging from house to house. Having unexpectedly got money, he had at once started drinking and gone crazy with drink, so that he was incapable of looking after the house.

Miss Lebyatkin, whom I was so anxious to meet, was sitting as quiet as a mouse on a bench at a deal kitchen table in a corner of the second room. She did not call out to us when we opened the door; she did not even stir from her place. Shatov told me that they never locked their front door and that on one occasion it was left wide open all night. By the dim light of a thin candle in an iron candlestick I caught a glimpse of a woman of about thirty, thin and pale, wearing an old dark cotton dress, with a long, uncovered neck, and scanty, dark hair twisted into a knot on the nape of her neck as big as the fist of a two-year-old child. She looked at us rather gaily; besides the candlestick, she had on the table in front of her a little peasant looking-glass, an old pack of cards, a tattered song-book, and a white roll of German bread from which one or two bites had been taken. It was obvious that Miss Lebyatkin used powder and rouge and painted her lips. She also blackened her eyebrows, which were long, thin, and dark anyhow. Three long wrinkles stood out rather sharply on her high, narrow forehead in spite of the powder. I already knew that she was lame, but during our visit she did not get up and walk about. Her emaciated face might have been quite good-looking a long time ago when she was still a young girl; but her soft, tender grey eyes were remarkable even now; there was something dreamy and sincere in the gentle, almost joyful look she gave us. This gentle and unruffled joy, which also came out in her smile, surprised me, after all I had heard about the Cossack whip and the other brutalities of her precious brother. It was strange that instead of the uncomfortable feeling of revulsion and even dread one usually experiences in the presence of these God-afflicted creatures, I almost took pleasure in looking at her from the very first moment, and it was pity rather than revulsion that I felt afterwards.

'This is how she sits literally for days on end, all alone, without moving, telling her own fortune by cards or looking at herself in the glass,' Shatov said, pointing her out to me from the doorway. 'He doesn't even get any food for her. The woman from the cottage sometimes brings her something out of the goodness of her heart. It beats me how they can leave her all alone with a candle!'

To my surprise, Shatov spoke in a loud voice, as though she were not in the room.

'Good evening, my dear,' Miss Lebyatkin said affably.

'I've brought you a visitor, Miss Lebyatkin,' said Shatov.

'I'm glad to see him,' she said, looking intently at me from behind the candle. 'I don't know who it is you've brought. I don't remember seeing him before.'

She at once turned again to Shatov, without paying any attention to me during the whole of the ensuing conversation, just as if I were not in the room at all.

'You must have got tired walking up and down alone in your little

room in the attic, I suppose?' she said, laughing and showing two rows
of excellent teeth.

'Yes, I got tired of it, and I wanted to pay you a visit, too.'

Shatov moved a bench up to the table, sat down on it, and made
me sit down beside him.

'I'm always glad to have a talk, my dear; only you're a funny man,
all the same – just like a hermit. When did you comb your hair last?
Come on, let me comb it for you again,' she said, producing a little
comb from her pocket. 'I expect you've never touched it since I
combed it last.'

'Why, I don't believe I have a comb,' Shatov said, laughing, too.

'Haven't you really? Then I'll give you mine, not this one – another one – only don't forget to remind me.'

She began combing his hair with a most serious air, and even parted
it on one side. Then she drew back a little to have a good look whether
it was all right, and put the comb back into her pocket.

'Do you know, my dear,' she said, shaking her head, 'you may be
a sensible man, but you're bored. I find it strange to look at you all. I
can't understand how people can be bored. Heartache is not boredom.
I'm happy.'

'Are you happy with that brother of yours, too?'

'Do you mean Lebyatkin? He's my footman. And I don't care a bit
whether he's here or not. I tell him: Lebyatkin, fetch me some water,
Lebyatkin, fetch me my shoes, and he runs to fetch them. Sometimes
you just can't help laughing at him.'

'And that's exactly how it is,' Shatov addressed me again unceremoniously in a loud voice. 'She treats him just like a footman. I've
heard her myself shouting to him: "Lebyatkin, fetch me some water!"
Only, you see, he doesn't run to fetch her the water, but beats her for
ordering him about like that. But she isn't in the least afraid of him.
She has some sort of nervous fit almost every day, accompanied by
loss of memory, so that afterwards she doesn't remember anything of
what has happened. And she's always confused about time. Do you
think she remembers when we came in? Well, perhaps she does, but
I'm sure she's already changed everything to suit her own fancy and
takes us now for some other people, though she may remember that
I'm her darling Shatov. It makes no difference whether I speak in a
loud voice or not. She never listens to you. Becomes engrossed in

her own day-dreams at once. Yes, becomes engrossed in them. Quite an extraordinary dreamer. She'll sit in the same place for eight hours, for a whole day even. Look at that roll: she's probably had one bite of it this morning, and she'll finish it to-morrow. Now she's started telling her fortune by cards.'

'I'm doing my best to tell my fortune, my dear, but it doesn't come out right, somehow,' Miss Lebyatkin interposed, catching the last word, and she put out her left hand without looking for the roll (she must have also heard Shatov mention the roll). She got hold of it at last, but after keeping it for some time in her left hand, she became so engrossed in what she was saying that she put it back on the table again without being conscious of it and without having taken a bite of it.

'It always comes out the same: a journey, a wicked man, somebody's treachery, a death-bed, a letter from somewhere, unexpected news. I think it's all lies. What do you think, my dear? If people tell lies, why shouldn't cards tell lies?' She suddenly mixed up the cards. 'I told Mother Praskovya – such a nice old woman – the same thing. She used to come to my cell to ask me to tell her fortune on the cards, without letting the Mother Superior know about it. And she wasn't the only one who came. "Oh dear, oh dear," they all kept crying excitedly, shaking their heads and talking nineteen to the dozen, but I just laughed. "How can you expect to get a letter, Mother Praskovya," I said to her, "when you haven't had one for twelve years?" Her daughter had been taken to some place in Turkey by her husband, and for twelve years she had had no news of her. Well, so next evening I was having tea with the Mother Superior (a princess by birth she was), and there was some lady visitor there, too – ever such a romantic lady she was – and also a little monk from Athos monastery happened to be there at the time; such a funny man, I thought. And what do you think, my dear? That same little monk had brought Mother Praskovya a letter from her daughter in Turkey that very morning – so much for the knave of diamonds – unexpected news, you see! Well, so we are having our tea, and the little monk from Athos says to the Mother Superior, "And most of all, reverend Mother Superior," he says, "the Lord will bless your convent for having such a great treasure hidden in it." "What treasure is that?" asks the Mother Superior. "Why," says the monk, "Mother Lisaveta the Blessed." And that saintly Lisaveta, she lived in a cage seven feet long and five feet high that was let into the wall of our nunnery, and she had been sitting there behind the iron bars for seventeen years, come summer, come winter, in nothing but a hempen shift, and all the time she kept poking at the hempen cloth with a straw or a twig that she would pick up, and she never uttered a word, never combed her hair or washed for seventeen years. In winter they would push a sheepskin through the bars to her, and every day a crust of bread and a mug of water. The pilgrims gazed, marvelled, sighed, and put down some money. "Some treasure!" the Mother Superior replied (she was angry, for she disliked Lisaveta very much). "Lisaveta only sits there out of sheer spite, out of sheer obstinacy, and the whole thing is nothing but hypocrisy." I must say I did not like that; for, you see, in those days I was thinking of shutting myself up too. "If you don't mind my saying so," I says, "God and nature are one and the same thing." They all cried in one voice: "Well, I never!" The Mother Superior laughed, started whispering something to the lady visitor, asked me to come up to her and was ever so nice to me, and the lady visitor gave me a pink ribbon for a present. Would you like me to show it to you? Well, and the little monk at once began to lecture me, and he talked ever so kindly and humbly, and I daresay he knew what he was talking about, too. I sat and listened. "Do you understand?" he asked. "No," I said, "I don't understand a word, and," I said, "leave me alone, will you?" And since then they've left me in peace, my dear. Meanwhile one of our lay sisters, who lived in our convent as a penance for uttering prophecies, whispered to me as we were coming out of church: "What is the Mother of God, do you think?" "She's the great Mother," I said, "the hope of the human race." "Yes," she said, "the Mother of God is great mother earth, and therein lies a great joy for men. And every earthly sorrow and every earthly tear is a joy for us; and when you have filled the earth under you with your tears a foot deep, you will rejoice at everything at once. And there will be nothing, nothing left of your sorrow; for such," she said, "is the prophecy." Those words sank into my mind at the time. Since then, when saying my prayers and bowing down to the ground, I kiss the earth every time. I kiss it and weep. And let me tell you this, my dear: there is nothing wrong about those tears; and though you may not grieve at all, your tears will flow all the same from joy. They will flow of themselves; that's the truth. Sometimes I would go off to the shore of the lake: on one side was our convent and on the other our hill with its pointed top – they called it the Peak. I would go up that hill, turn my face to the east, fall down to the ground, and weep and weep, and I don't know how long I wept, and I didn't remember anything then, and I don't know anything. Then I'd get up and go back. The sun would be setting – oh, so big, so glorious, so lovely – do you like looking at the sun, my dear? It's ever so nice, but ever so sad, too! I would turn to the east again, and the shadow, oh, the shadow from our hill was flying like an arrow far, far away over the lake – so narrow and so long, almost a mile long – as far as the island on the lake, and it would cut that rocky island right in two, and as it cut it in two, the sun would set altogether and suddenly everything would grow dark. Then I would feel so miserable and my memory would suddenly come back. I'm afraid of the dark, my dear. But it was my little baby I wept for most ...'

'Why, did you have a baby?' Shatov, who had been listening very attentively all the time, nudged me with his elbow.

'Of course I had a baby: a little, rosy baby with such tiny little nails, and I was so miserable because I couldn't remember whether it was a boy or a girl. Sometimes I thought it was a boy and sometimes a girl. As soon as it was born, I wrapped it in cambric and lace, tied it round with pink ribbons, strewed it with flowers, got it ready, said a prayer over it, and carried it away, unbaptised as it was, carried it through a wood; and I was afraid of the wood, and was frightened; and what I wept for most was that I had a baby but couldn't remember whether I had a husband or not.'

'You may have had one, mayn't you?' Shatov asked cautiously.

'You're so funny, my dear. The way you talk! I may have had one, but what's the use of it if it's the same as if I hadn't had one? There's an easy riddle for you – guess it if you can!' she laughed.

'Where did you take your baby?'

'I took it to the pond,' she sighed.

Shatov nudged me with his elbow again.

'But what if you never had a baby at all and you just imagined it all – eh?'

'You ask me a hard question, my dear,' she replied pensively, without being in the least surprised at such a question. 'I can't tell you anything about it. Perhaps I hadn't. But I daresay it's just your curiosity.

I'll never stop crying for him, in any case. I couldn't possibly have dreamt about it, could I?' And big tears glistened in her eyes. 'Oh, my dear, is it true that your wife has run away from you?' she asked, suddenly putting both hands on his shoulders and gazing at him pity-ingly. 'Don't be angry; I feel miserable myself. Do you know what kind of dream I had, my dear? He came to me again, beckoned to me, and said: "My little pussy, little pussy, come to me!" It was his calling me his "little pussy" that pleased me so much; he loves me, I thought.'

'Maybe he really will come,' Shatov muttered in an undertone.

'No, my dear, that's just a dream – he will never come. Do you know the song –

> Not for me thy new tall house,
> Mine alone this little cell.
> Here I'll dwell to save my soul,
> Here I'll pray to God for thee.

Oh, my dear, my dear, why don't you ever ask me anything?'

'Because you won't tell – that's why I don't ask.'

'I shan't tell you, I shan't, I shan't; even if you kill me, I shan't tell you,' she said quickly. 'Burn me, if you like, but I shan't tell you. And however much I suffered, I shan't tell anything. People will never know!'

'There, you see, everyone has his own troubles,' Shatov said more softly, lowering his head more and more.

'But if you'd asked me, I might have told you – I might have told you!' she repeated rapturously. 'Why don't you ask? Ask, ask me properly, and perhaps I will tell you. Beg me, my dear, so that I should agree. ... Oh, my dear, my dear!'

But Shatov said nothing; the silence lasted about a minute. Tears streamed softly down her powdered cheeks; she sat leaning with both her hands on Shatov's shoulders, but no longer looking at him.

'Oh, what do I care about you?' Shatov said, suddenly getting up from the bench. 'Besides, it's not my business to pry into your affairs. Come on, get up!' He angrily pulled the bench from under me and, picking it up, put it back where it stood before.

'If he comes, he must not know that we've been here. It's time we were off.'

'Oh, still talking about that flunkey of mine, are you?' Mary Leb-yatkin laughed suddenly. 'You're afraid! Well, good-bye, dear visitors.

One minute, though; I've something to tell you. That Kirilov and our landlord, Filippov, the man with the big red beard, came here this morning, just as my brother flew at me. Our landlord caught hold of him and flung him across the room, and he shouted, "It's not my fault, sir; I'm suffering for another man's iniquity!" So, would you believe it, we nearly split our sides with laughter ...'

'Oh, my dear woman, it was I, and not the red-beard. It was I who dragged him away from you by the hair; your landlord was here the day before yesterday. He came to have it out with you, and you've got all mixed up.'

'Wait; I think that I have got mixed up. Perhaps it was you. But why argue about silly things like that? It makes no difference to him who drags him off, does it?' She laughed.

'Let's go,' Shatov suddenly gave me a pull. 'The gate's creaking. If he finds us here, he'll beat her black and blue.'

But we had scarcely time to run out on the stairs when we heard a drunken shout at the gate, followed by a string of oaths. Shatov let me into his room and locked the door.

'You'll have to stay here for a minute if you don't want to be involved in a row. Listen to him squealing like a little pig. He must have stumbled over the gate again. Every time he falls flat over it.'

We did not get off without a row, however.

6

Shatov stood listening at the locked door of his room. Suddenly he sprang back.

'He's coming here; I knew it!' he whispered furiously. 'I'm afraid we shan't get rid of him till midnight.'

There followed several heavy knocks on the door with a fist.

'Shatov, Shatov, open up!' the Captain yelled. 'Shatov, my dear friend!

> I've come to bid thee, friend, good morrow,
> To tell thee that the sun doth r-rise,
> That with its light it hath banished sorrow,
> Filled the for-ests – with wild surmise,
> To tell thee I'm awake – curse thee! –
> Wide-awake 'neath a birch.

'Reminds me of the birch, ha, ha!

> Every little bird – from thirst expires –
>   I'm going to have a drink. ...
> A drink – don't know what drink –

Oh, to hell with stupid curiosity! Shatov, do you realize how good it is to be alive?'

'Don't answer,' Shatov whispered to me again.

'Open up! Do you realize, I say, that there is something higher than a brawl – among men? There are moments of an hon–our–able person. ... Shatov, I'm a good chap; I'll forgive you ... Shatov, to hell with political leaflets, eh?'

Silence.

'Don't you realize, you silly ass, that I'm in love? I've bought myself a frock-coat. Look, the frock-coat of love. Paid fifteen roubles for it. A captain's love calls for good manners. ... Open up!' he roared savagely all of a sudden and again began knocking furiously on the door with his fists.

'Go to blazes!' Shatov, too, suddenly roared.

'You s-slave! You bondslave! And your sister, too, is a slave, a bondswoman – a th-thief!'

'And you sold your sister.'

'That's a lie! I put up with this libellous accusation, but with one word I could – can you guess who she is?'

'Who?' Shatov, unable to suppress his curiosity, suddenly went up to the door.

'Can you guess, I ask you?'

'Don't you worry; I shall guess. Tell me who?'

'I'm not afraid to say! I'm never afraid to say anything in public!'

'I question it,' Shatov taunted him, nodding to me to listen.

'No?'

'I don't think so.'

'You don't think so?'

'Well, say it, if you're not afraid of being birched by your master. You're a coward, aren't you? A captain, indeed!'

'I – I – she – she is –' the Captain stammered in a voice trembling with excitement.

'Well?' Shatov put his ear to the door.

A silence ensued for at least half a minute.

'Dirty rotter!' the Captain said at last, and he beat a hasty retreat downstairs, puffing like a *samovar*, and stumbling noisily on every step.

'He's a cunning devil,' Shatov said, coming back from the door. 'He won't give himself away even when he's drunk.'

'What is it all about?' I asked.

Shatov dismissed my question with a wave of the hand, opened the door, and again began listening for any noise on the stairs. He listened a long time, and even quietly descended a few steps to make sure. At last he came back.

'Can't hear anything, which means that he isn't thrashing her. Must have dropped off at once. It's time you were gone.'

'Look here, Shatov; what am I to make of it all now?'

'Oh, anything you like!' he replied in a weary and disgusted voice, sitting down at his writing-desk.

I went away. A highly improbable idea was getting a stronger and stronger hold of me. The thought of the next day made my heart sink.

7

That 'next day' – that is, the Sunday on which Mr Verkhovensky's fate was to be irrevocably decided – was one of the most momentous days in my chronicle. It was a day of surprises, a day on which events of the past came to a head and events of the future had their beginning, a day of harsh explanations and even greater confusion. In the morning, as the reader knows already, I had to accompany my friend to Mrs Stavrogin's, while at three o'clock in the afternoon I had to see Lisa to tell her – I did not know what – and to assist her – I did not myself know how. And yet it all ended in a way nobody could have expected. In a word, it was a day of most extraordinary coincidences.

To begin with, when Mr Verkhovensky and I arrived at Mrs Stavrogin's at precisely twelve o'clock – the time she had fixed – we did not find her at home: she had not yet returned from church. My poor friend's composure, or rather discomposure, was such that this circumstance at once bowled him over. He sank into an arm-chair in the drawing-room almost in a state of collapse. I offered him a glass of water; but in spite of his pallor and shaking hands he refused it with dignity. By the way, his rig-out on that occasion was remarkable for its unusual smartness: he had got himself up almost as if he were going to a ball, in an embroidered lawn shirt, a white cravat, a new hat in his hand, new straw-coloured gloves, and even a faint odour of scent. No sooner did we sit down than Shatov arrived, ushered in by the butler, which clearly showed that he, too, came by official invitation. Mr Verkhovensky was about to get up to shake hands with him, but Shatov, after glancing at us attentively, walked off to the opposite corner of the room, where he sat down without even nodding to us. Mr Verkhovensky again looked at me in dismay.

We sat like that for a few minutes in utter silence. Mr Verkhovensky began whispering something to me very rapidly, but I did not catch his words. He stopped abruptly, being too excited to finish what he was going to say. The butler came in again, ostensibly to put something right on the table, but more probably to have a look at us. Shatov suddenly addressed him with a loud question.

'Do you happen to know, Alexey,' he said in a loud voice, 'if Miss Shatov has left with Mrs Stavrogin?'

'Mrs Stavrogin, sir,' the butler explained decorously and edifyingly, 'has gone to the cathedral alone, and Miss Shatov was pleased to remain in her room upstairs, as she isn't feeling quite well.'

My poor friend again exchanged a rapid and alarmed glance with me, so that in the end I even began to turn away from him. Suddenly a carriage drove up to the entrance of the house with a loud clatter, and a certain distant commotion announced the return of Mrs Stavrogin to us. We all jumped up from our chairs, but another surprise awaited us: we heard the approach of many footsteps, which meant that Mrs Stavrogin did not return alone, and that really was rather odd, because she herself had asked us to come at that particular time. At last we heard someone come in very rapidly, as though running, and Mrs Stavrogin certainly could not have come in like that. Suddenly she almost flew into the room, out of breath and in a state of great agitation. She was followed at some distance and at a slower pace by Lisa, and arm in arm with her – Miss Mary Lebyatkin! If I had seen it in a dream I would not have believed it!

To explain this utterly unexpected development, I must go back an hour and describe in greater detail the extraordinary adventure that had befallen Mrs Stavrogin at the cathedral.

To begin with, almost our whole town – that is, of course, all the upper strata of our society – was present at the morning service. It was known that the Governor's wife would attend the cathedral for the first time since her arrival in our town. Let me observe that it was already rumoured that she was a free-thinker and an adherent of 'the new principles'. All our ladies knew, besides, that she would be most exquisitely and elegantly dressed, and that was why the dresses of our ladies were this time quite unusually smart and gorgeous. Mrs Stavrogin alone was, as always, modestly dressed in black; she had invariably dressed like that for the past four years. On her arrival at the cathedral she took up her usual place in the first row on the left, and a liveried footman placed a velvet cushion for kneeling on before her – in short, everything was just as usual. But it was also noticed that all through the service she prayed with quite unwonted zeal; afterwards, when people recalled the events of that day, it was said that she had even had tears in her eyes. At last the morning service was over and our chief priest, Father Pavel, came out to deliver a solemn sermon. His sermons were popular and were highly thought of in our town; people even tried to persuade him to publish them, but he never could make up his mind to. This time the sermon happened to be quite unusually long.

And it was during the sermon that a lady drove up to the cathedral in an old-fashioned cab – that is, a cab in which ladies could only sit sideways, holding on to the cabman's belt and swaying at every jolt of the carriage, like a blade of grass in the wind. Such cabs still ply their trade in our town. Stopping at the corner of the cathedral – for there were a great number of carriages and even mounted police at the gates – the lady jumped out of the cab and offered the cabby four copecks in silver.

'You don't want more, do you, cabby?' she cried, seeing him pull a face. 'I'm afraid it's all I have,' she added in a plaintive voice.

'Oh, well, never mind, lady; I expect it's my own fault for not telling you the right fare,' the cabby said, with a hopeless wave of the hand, looking at her as though he had wanted to add, 'And it would be a sin to take advantage of the likes of you, anyway'; then, thrusting the leather purse into his coat, he started his horse and drove off, followed by the jeers of the cabbies who were standing by. Jeers and exclamations of surprise also followed the young woman as she made

her way to the cathedral gates between the carriages and the footmen
who were waiting for their masters to come out soon. And, indeed,
there was something strange and unexpected in the sudden appearance
of such a person among the people in the street. She looked haggard
and pale, and she walked with a limp; her face was thickly covered
with powder and rouge, her long neck was quite bare, for she wore
neither kerchief nor pelisse, but only an old dark dress, in spite of the
cold and windy, though bright, September day. Her head was bare,
too, and her hair was gathered in a tiny bun at the nape of the neck,
with an artificial rose stuck on the right side of it, the kind of rose that
was sold together with a palm and a little cherub in the market during
Holy Week. I had noticed such a palm and cherub in the wreath of
paper roses under the icons in the corner of the room when I visited
Miss Lebyatkin the day before. And as a finishing touch, the young
woman, though walking modestly and with downcast eyes, was smiling slyly and gaily. If she had lingered a moment longer, she would
probably not have been admitted to the cathedral. But she managed
to slip in and, on entering the church, pushed her way imperceptibly
to the front.

Though the sermon was only half over, and though the entire congregation listened to it with complete and hushed attention, a few
eyes glanced with curiosity and amazement at the new arrival. She
knelt down on the dais in front of the high altar, her powdered face
touching the floor. She lay there a long time, and was apparently
weeping. But on raising her head again and getting up from her knees,
she very soon recovered her high spirits. Gaily and with obviously intense enjoyment, she let her eyes roam over the faces of the congregation and over the walls of the cathedral; she gazed with special interest at some of the ladies, even standing on tiptoe to have a better look
at them, and she even laughed once or twice, her laughter ending in a
strange sort of giggle. But the sermon came to an end and the cross
was brought out. The Governor's wife was the first to go up to the
cross, but she stopped two paces in front of it, evidently with the intention of letting Mrs Stavrogin go up to it first; Mrs Stavrogin, for
her part, was walking straight up to it, as though she did not notice
anyone in front of her. The unusual courtesy of the Governor's wife
no doubt implied an unmistakable and, in a way, clever snub; so
everybody in the cathedral interpreted it. Mrs Stavrogin, too, no

doubt interpreted it that way; but she walked on as before without noticing anyone and, having kissed the cross with an unshaken air of dignity, she immediately turned and walked to the entrance. A liveried footman cleared a path for her, though everyone made room for her anyhow. But at the very door, before she had time to reach the front steps, a small crowd of people blocked her way for a moment. Mrs Stavrogin stopped, and suddenly a strange, extraordinary creature, a woman with a paper rose in her hair, pushed through the crowd and went down on her knees before her. Mrs Stavrogin, who was not easily put out, especially in public, looked at her sternly and gravely.

I hasten to point out here, as briefly as possible, that though Mrs Stavrogin had in recent years become, it was said, a little too careful, and even somewhat stingy, she did not mind giving money occasionally to some charity. She was a member of a benevolent society in Petersburg. In the last year of famine she sent 500 roubles to the central committee of the fund in aid of the sufferers, and this was talked of in our town. Finally, quite recently, before the appointment of the new Governor, she was planning to found a local ladies' committee to raise a fund in aid of the poorest expectant mothers of our town and province. In our town she was accused of being ambitious; but the well-known impetuosity of her character, as well as her persistence, nearly triumphed over the difficulties; the committee was on the point of being founded, and the original idea assumed greater and greater dimensions in the entranced mind of the foundress: she was already dreaming of the foundation of a similar committee in Moscow and of the gradual expansion of its activities throughout all the other provinces. And now, with the sudden appointment of a new Governor, everything had come to a standstill; the wife of the new Governor, it was said, had already delivered herself in public of a few biting and, above all, shrewd and sensible remarks about the supposed impracticability of the fundamental idea of such a committee, which, needless to say, had been passed on, suitably embellished, to Mrs Stavrogin. The Lord only knows what is hidden in men's hearts, but I expect Mrs Stavrogin now stopped at the very gates of the cathedral with a certain feeling of pleasure, knowing that the wife of the Governor, followed by the entire congregation, would have to pass by any moment, and thinking to herself: 'Let her see for herself that I don't care what she may think of me or what clever remarks she may make about the vanity of my charitable works. I don't care a fig for all of you!'

'What's the matter, my dear? What do you want?' Mrs Stavrogin said, looking more attentively at the kneeling young woman.

Mary Lebyatkin stared at her with an awfully timid, shamefaced, but almost reverent expression. Suddenly she gave the same strange giggle.

'What does she want? Who is she?' Mrs Stavrogin asked, looking imperiously and inquiringly at the crowd. 'Are you unhappy? Are you in need of assistance?'

'Yes, ma'am, I'm in need – I've come –' the 'unhappy' woman murmured in a voice that shook with emotion. 'I've come only to kiss your hand –' And again she giggled.

With the childish expression with which little children make up to someone in order to get something, she bent forward to grasp Mrs Stavrogin's hand, but suddenly, as though frightened, she drew her hands back.

'Was that all you came for?' Mrs Stavrogin said, smiling compassionately, but at once took her mother-of-pearl purse out of her pocket, and producing a ten-rouble note, gave it to the stranger. She took it. Mrs Stavrogin was very interested, and evidently did not consider the strange woman a common beggar.

'Fancy giving her ten roubles!' someone cried in the crowd.

'Please, ma'am, let me kiss your hand,' the 'unhappy' woman murmured, holding on tightly with the fingers of her left hand to a corner of the ten-rouble note, which fluttered in the wind.

Mrs Stavrogin for some reason frowned slightly and held out her hand with a grave, almost stern, expression; the young woman kissed it reverently. Her grateful eyes glowed with emotion. It was just at that moment that the Governor's wife came up, followed by a whole crowd of our ladies and high officials. The Governor's wife was forced to stop for a moment in the crush; many other people also stopped.

'You are shivering. Are you cold?' Mrs Stavrogin said suddenly and, slipping off her cloak, caught by her footman in mid-air, she removed from her shoulders her black (and not by any means cheap) shawl and with her own hands wrapped it round the bare neck of the young woman who was still kneeling before her.

'Please get up; get up from your knees, I beg you!'

The woman got up.

'Where do you live? Doesn't anyone know where she lives?' Mrs Stavrogin asked, looking round impatiently again.

But it was no longer the same crowd: all she could see were the familiar faces of fashionable men and women, observing the scene, some with disapproval and surprise, some with sly curiosity and, at the same time, with an innocent but keen desire for some scene, while some went so far as to grin.

'I think it's Lebyatkin's sister,' some good-natured fellow at last volunteered an answer to Mrs Stavrogin's question.

It was our worthy merchant Andreyev, a man who was generally respected, in spectacles, a grey beard, wearing a Russian coat and a round, cylindrical hat, which he was now holding in his hand. 'She lives at Filippov's house in Bogoyavlenskaya Street,' he added.

'Lebyatkin? Filippov's house? Yes, I've heard something about it. Thank you, Mr Andreyev. But who's this Lebyatkin?'

'He calls himself a captain, ma'am. A man who is not too mindful of what he does or says, I'm afraid. She's his sister all right. I expect she must have escaped from the house,' Mr Andreyev added, lowering his voice and giving Mrs Stavrogin a significant look.

'I see. Thank you, Mr Andreyev. Are you Miss Lebyatkin, my dear?'

'No, ma'am, I'm not Miss Lebyatkin.'

'Then perhaps your brother is Lebyatkin?'

'Yes, ma'am, Lebyatkin is my brother.'

'Now, this is what I'm going to do, my dear. You'll come with me, and I'll see that you're taken to your home from my house. Would you like to come with me?'

'Oh, yes, I'd love to!' Miss Lebyatkin clapped her hands with excitement.

'Auntie, take me with you, too, please!' Lisa cried.

Lisa, I ought perhaps to explain, arrived at the service with the Governor's wife, while her mother had, by the doctor's orders, gone for a drive in her carriage, taking Mr Drozdov with her to keep her company.

'My dear, you know I'm always glad to have you, but what will your mother say?' Mrs Stavrogin began, with a grand air, but became suddenly confused, noticing Lisa's unusual excitement.

'Please, Auntie, you simply must take me with you,' Lisa implored, kissing Mrs Stavrogin.

'*Mais qu'avez vous donc, Lise!*' the Governor's wife said with distinct surprise.

'Oh, I'm awfully sorry, darling; but I have to go to Auntie's,' Lisa turned quickly to her unpleasantly surprised *chère cousine* and kissed her twice.

'And please tell *maman* to come to fetch me at once at Auntie's,' Lisa rattled on. '*Maman* was awfully anxious to call on you. She told me so herself this morning. I forgot to mention it to you. I'm sorry. Please, don't be angry, *Julie, chère ... cousine.* Auntie, I'm ready!'

'If you won't take me with you, Auntie,' she whispered rapidly and desperately in Mrs Stavrogin's ear, 'I'll run screaming after your carriage.'

It was a good thing no one heard her. Mrs Stavrogin even recoiled a step and glared at the mad girl. That look decided everything: she made up her mind there and then to take Lisa with her.

'We must put an end to this!' she cried involuntarily. 'Very well, I'll be glad to take you, Lisa,' she said at once in a loud voice, 'if Mrs Lembke will let you come, of course,' she added, turning with a frank look and a dignified air to the Governor's wife.

'I most certainly don't want to deprive her of that pleasure, particularly as' – Mrs Lembke suddenly murmured with surprising courtesy – 'I know myself what a fantastically despotic little head she carries on her shoulders.' Mrs Lembke smiled charmingly.

'Thank you very much indeed,' Mrs Stavrogin thanked her with a courteous and stately bow.

'And I am all the more pleased to do it,' Mrs Lembke went on murmuring rapturously, even flushing all over with agreeable excitement, 'because I'm sure Lisa is not only delighted to be with you, but also carried away by such a beautiful – such – if I may say so – such a lofty feeling of – of compassion –' She glanced at the 'unhappy' woman, 'and – and on the very steps of the cathedral, too!'

'Such feeling does you honour, madam,' Mrs Stavrogin expressed her approval magnificently.

Mrs Lembke held out her hand impulsively, and Mrs Stavrogin hastened to touch it with her fingers. The general effect was excellent, the faces of some of those present beamed with pleasure, while others smiled sweetly and ingratiatingly.

In a word, it now became perfectly clear to everybody that it was not Mrs Lembke who had till now been slighting Mrs Stavrogin by refusing to pay a call on her, but, on the contrary, Mrs Stavrogin herself had kept Mrs Lembke 'at arm's length', while the Governor's wife would have run to pay a call on her if she were sure that Mrs Stavrogin would not turn her out of her house. Mrs Stavrogin's standing rose incredibly high.

'Do get in, my dear,' Mrs Stavrogin motioned Miss Lebyatkin into the carriage which had just then driven up.

The 'unhappy' woman rushed joyfully to the carriage door, where the footman helped her in.

'Gracious me, are you lame?' cried Mrs Stavrogin, as though she were really terrified, and she turned pale. (Everyone noticed it at the time, but did not understand what it meant.)

The carriage rolled away. Mrs Stavrogin's house was very near the cathedral. Lisa told me afterwards that Miss Lebyatkin laughed hysterically during the three minutes of the drive, while Mrs Stavrogin sat 'as though in a trance' – that was Lisa's own expression.

5

The Wise Serpent

I

MRS STAVROGIN rang the bell and flung herself into an arm-chair by the window.

'Sit down here, my dear.' She motioned Miss Lebyatkin to a chair by a large round table in the middle of the room. 'Mr Verkhovensky, what do you think this means? Here, have a look at that woman – what does it mean?'

'I – I,' murmured Mr Verkhovensky.

But a footman came in.

'A cup of coffee at once, please! As quickly as possible! Let the carriage wait!'

'Mais, chère et excellente amie, dans quelle inquiétude –' Mr Verkhovensky cried in an expiring voice.

'Oh, French, French! You can see at once that it's high society!'
Miss Lebyatkin cried, clapping her hands and preparing to listen
ecstatically to a conversation in French.

Mrs Stavrogin stared at her almost in terror.

We were all silent, waiting to see what the end of it would be.
Shatov did not raise his head, and Mr Verkhovensky looked dismayed,
as if he were to blame for everything. Beads of perspiration broke out
at his temples. I glanced at Lisa (she was sitting in a corner, almost next
to Shatov). Her eyes darted piercingly from Mrs Stavrogin to the
lame woman and back again; her lips were distended in a smile, but
it was not a nice smile. Mrs Stavrogin saw that smile. In the meantime Miss Lebyatkin looked completely entranced: she studied Mrs
Stavrogin's beautiful drawing-room with delight and without the
least sign of confusion – the furniture, the rugs, the pictures on the
walls, the painted rococo ceiling, the big bronze crucifix in the corner,
the porcelain lamp, the albums, the bric-à-brac on the table.

'So you're here, too, my dear!' she cried suddenly, addressing
Shatov. 'Just fancy, I saw you ages ago, but I thought to myself, "It
can't be him! How could he have come here?"' and she laughed gaily.

'You know this woman?' Mrs Stavrogin turned to him at once.

'Yes, ma'am,' Shatov muttered, about to move from his chair, but
he remained sitting.

'What do you know? Please tell me quickly!'

'Why,' he faltered, grinning without any reason. 'You can see for
yourself ...'

'What can I see? Come on, say something!'

'Well, she lives in the same house as I – with her brother, an army
officer.'

'Well?'

Shatov again hesitated.

'Oh, it's hardly worth talking about,' he grunted and fell silent determinedly. He even went red in the face with determination.

'To be sure, I could hardly have expected anything more from
you!' Mrs Stavrogin cut him short indignantly.

She saw clearly now that everybody in the room knew something,
and yet they were all afraid of something and evaded her questions,
anxious to conceal something from her.

The footman entered carrying a small silver tray and handed her the cup of coffee she had specially ordered, but at a sign from her went immediately over to Miss Lebyatkin with it.

'Drink it, dear, and get warm. You must have got frozen outside the church.'

'*Merci*,' said Miss Lebyatkin, taking the cup and suddenly bursting out laughing at having said *merci* to the footman. But, catching Mrs Stavrogin's stern look, she flushed and put the cup on the table.

'You're not angry, Auntie,' she murmured with a kind of flippant playfulness.

'Wha-a-at?' Mrs Stavrogin sat up in her chair with a start. 'I am no aunt of yours, am I? What did you mean by that?'

Miss Lebyatkin, not expecting such an outburst of anger, trembled all over convulsively and fell back in her chair.

'I. I thought that's how I should address you,' she murmured, staring wide-eyed at Mrs Stavrogin. 'Lisa called you that.'

'Which Lisa are you talking about?'

'That young lady there.' Miss Lebyatkin pointed to Lisa with a finger.

'Since when has she become Lisa to you?'

'Why, you called her that yourself ten minutes ago,' Miss Lebyatkin said, recovering her spirits a little. 'And I saw a beautiful girl like her in my dream.' She smiled as though unintentionally.

Mrs Stavrogin reflected and calmed down a little; she even smiled faintly at Miss Lebyatkin's last words. The young woman, having caught sight of her smile, got up and, limping, walked shyly up to her.

'Please take it back,' she said suddenly, taking off the black shawl Mrs Stavrogin had put round her shoulders earlier. 'I forgot to return it to you. Don't be angry with me for being so rude.'

'Put it on at once and keep it. Go and sit down and have your coffee, and please don't be afraid of me, my dear. Calm yourself. I'm beginning to understand you.'

'*Chère amie* –' Mr Verkhovensky ventured again.

'Heavens, Mr Verkhovensky, I scarcely know where I am without you – You might at least spare me. Please ring the bell beside you – the maids' room.'

No one spoke. Her eyes darted suspiciously and irritably over all our faces. Agasha, her favourite parlour-maid, came in.

'Bring me the check shawl I bought in Geneva, please. What's Miss Shatov doing?'

'She isn't very well, ma'am.'

'Will you go and ask her to come here, please? Tell her that I'd be greatly obliged if she came here, even if she does not feel well.'

At that moment there was again an unusual noise of footsteps and voices in the adjoining rooms and, suddenly, the panting and 'distraught' Praskovya Drozdov, leaning on the arm of Maurice Drozdov, appeared in the doorway.

'Oh, dear, I could scarcely drag myself here. Lisa, you mad thing, what are you doing to your mother?' she screamed, putting, as all weak and irritable women often do, all her accumulated irritation into that scream. 'My dear Mrs Stavrogin, I've come to you for my daughter!'

Mrs Stavrogin glanced at her frowningly, half rose to meet her, and, making little attempt to conceal her vexation, said:

'Good afternoon, Praskovya. Do me a favour and take a seat. I had an idea you would come.'

2

Mrs Drozdov could not possibly have been surprised by such a reception. Mrs Stavrogin had always, indeed from the time they were children, treated her former school friend despotically and, under the guise of friendship, almost with contempt. But this was quite an exceptional occasion. During the last few days the two households had almost reached the point of a complete rupture, a fact I have already mentioned briefly. The reasons for the incipient rupture were still a mystery to Mrs Stavrogin, and that made them all the more offensive; but what especially aroused Mrs Stavrogin's anger was that Mrs Drozdov had begun treating her of late with quite extraordinary disdain. Mrs Stavrogin, of course, felt deeply hurt, and in the meantime certain rumours had begun to reach her which also irritated her exceedingly, particularly because of their vagueness. Mrs Stavrogin was of a most straightforward and frankly proud disposition, with, if I may put it that way, a propensity for taking things by direct assault. And she always showed a preference for open warfare. However that may be, the fact remains that the two ladies had not met for the last five days. The last visit had been made by Mrs Stavrogin, who had left 'that Drozdov creature' feeling offended and perplexed. I think I am justified in stating that Mrs Drozdov had come with the naïve conviction that Mrs Stavrogin had some reason to be afraid of her. That could be plainly discerned from the way she looked. But it would seem that Mrs Stavrogin was possessed by the demon of the most arrogant pride every time there was the least suspicion that she was for some reason supposed to have been humiliated. Like many women of weak character who allow themselves to be insulted for a long time without protest, Mrs Drozdov, for her part, showed quite an extraordinary enthusiasm for launching an attack at the first favourable opportunity. It is true she was ill just then, but it was during her bouts of illness that she always was more irritable than usual. I may add, finally, that if a quarrel had broken out between the two old childhood friends, none of us in the drawing-room would have embarrassed them in any way, for we were looked upon as old friends and almost as underlings. I realized this not without a certain feeling of alarm at the time. Mr Verkhovensky, who had not sat down since the arrival of Mrs Stavrogin, sank exhausted into a chair the moment he heard Mrs Drozdov's scream, and tried desperately to catch my eye. Shatov turned sharply in his chair and even grunted something under his breath. I had the impression that he wanted to get up and go away. Lisa was on the point of getting up, but she resumed her seat immediately without paying the slightest attention to her mother's scream, not because of her 'contrariness', but because she was apparently entirely obsessed by some other powerful emotion. Her eyes were fixed almost abstractedly on some invisible point in the air, and she even stopped taking any notice of Miss Lebyatkin.

3

'Oh dear, here, is it?' Mrs Drozdov exclaimed, pointing to the armchair near the table and sinking down in it heavily with the help of Mr Drozdov. 'I wouldn't have sat down in your house, my dear, if it weren't for my poor legs!' she added in a strained voice.

Mrs Stavrogin raised her head slightly and pressed the fingers of her right hand gingerly to her right temple, evidently feeling an acute twinge of pain there (*tic douloureux*).

'Good gracious, Praskovya, why shouldn't you sit down in my house? Your husband has treated me as a good friend all his life, and you and I used to play at school together as little girls.'

Mrs Drozdov waved her hands in annoyance.

'I knew it! You always start talking about our school when you want to be nasty to me – it's a well-known trick of yours! But if you ask me, it's only fine talk. I can't stand that boarding-school of yours!'

'I can see that you're in a particularly bad temper to-day. How are your legs? Here, they're bringing you some coffee. Have it, please, and don't be cross – there's a dear!'

'You always talk to me as if I were a little girl. I don't want your coffee – so there!'

And she waved her hand querulously at the servant who was offering her the coffee. (The others, too, by the way, refused coffee, except Mr Drozdov and myself. Mr Verkhovensky accepted it, but put it down on the table. Though Miss Lebyatkin wanted another cup badly and, indeed, had already put out her hand for it, she changed her mind and declined it decorously, quite obviously pleased with herself for doing so.)

Mrs Stavrogin smiled wryly.

'I expect you're again imagining something, my dear Praskovya, and that's why you've come here. All your life you've only lived by imagining things. You got cross with me just now because I mentioned our boarding-school. But do you remember how you came one day and told the whole class that the Hussar officer Shablykin had proposed to you and how Mme Lefebure proved that you were telling a lie. But you did not tell a lie – oh, no – you just imagined it all to amuse yourself. Well, come, tell me what's wrong now? What are you imagining now? What are you so dissatisfied with now?'

'And you fell in love with the priest at our school, our scripture master. There's something for you to remember, since you're so spiteful! Ha, ha, ha!'

She laughed maliciously, and then went off into a fit of coughing.

'Oh, so you haven't forgotten the priest, have you?' Mrs Stavrogin gave her a baleful look.

Her face turned green. Mrs Drozdov suddenly sat up with a dignified air.

'I'm afraid, my dear, I'm not in a laughing mood now. Why did you involve my daughter in your family scandal before the whole town? That's what I've come here to find out.'

'In my family scandal?' Mrs Stavrogin asked, drawing herself up menacingly.

'Mother, I, too, would like to ask you very much to moderate your language,' Lisa said suddenly.

'What did you say?' Her mother was about to start screaming again, but controlled herself suddenly as she caught sight of her daughter's flashing eyes.

'How could you talk about a family scandal, Mother?' Lisa cried, flushing. 'I came here of my own free will, with Mrs Lembke's permission, because I wanted to find out this poor woman's story and be of some use to her.'

'The poor woman's story!' Mrs Drozdov repeated slowly, with a spiteful laugh. 'Is it your business to get yourself mixed up in such "stories"? We've had enough of your bullying, my dear,' she turned furiously to Mrs Stavrogin. 'I don't know whether it's true or not, but I've heard it said that you've got everybody in the town dancing to your tune. Well, it seems your turn has come, too.'

Mrs Stavrogin sat straight as an arrow on the point of being shot from the bow. For ten seconds she looked sternly and fixedly at Mrs Drozdov.

'Well, Praskovya,' she said at last with ominous calm, 'thank God that there are no strangers here. You've said a lot you'll be sorry for.'

'I'm not so frightened of public opinion as some people I could mention are, my dear. It's you who, because of your pride, are terrified of public opinion. As for there being no strangers here, I daresay that's certainly something you ought to be pleased about.'

'You've grown wiser this last week, have you?'

'It's not I who've grown wiser this week. It's just that truth has this week come out at last.'

'Which truth has come out this week? Listen, Praskovya; don't you try to exasperate me. Explain yourself this very minute. I ask you frankly: what truth has come out and what exactly do you mean by that?'

'Why, the whole truth is sitting there!' Mrs Drozdov suddenly pointed a finger at Miss Lebyatkin with that desperate determination which no longer cares for any consequences so long as it can crush an opponent.

Miss Lebyatkin, who had watched her all the time with gay curiosity, burst out laughing joyfully at the sight of the angry visitor's finger pointing at her and shifted excitedly in her chair.

'Dear Lord, have they all gone off their heads?' Mrs Stavrogin cried, and, turning pale, she threw herself against the back of her chair.

She turned so pale that it even caused a commotion in the room. Mr Verkhovensky was the first to rush up to her; I, too, drew near; even Lisa got up, though she remained standing by her chair; but the most frightened person of all was Mrs Drozdov herself: she uttered a cry, raised herself in her chair as much as she could and almost wailed in a mournful voice:

'My dear, please forgive me for my wicked foolishness! Water! Give her some water, somebody!'

'Don't whimper, I beg you, Praskovya; and go back to your places, gentlemen, please. I don't want any water!' Mrs Stavrogin said firmly, though not in a loud voice, with pale lips.

'Oh, my dear,' Mrs Drozdov went on, having composed herself a little, 'my dear friend, I may be guilty of having said something I shouldn't, but it's those anonymous letters some horrible people have been bombarding me with that have exasperated me beyond all endurance. I wish they'd send them to you, since it's you they are writing about! After all, my dear, I have a daughter!'

Mrs Stavrogin gazed at her in silence with wide-open eyes, listening with astonishment. At that moment a side-door in the corner was opened noiselessly and Dasha Shatov walked into the room. She stopped and looked round. She was struck by our dismay. Quite possibly she did not at once notice Miss Lebyatkin, of whose presence no one had warned her. Mr Verkhovensky caught sight of her first. He made a quick movement, went red in the face, and for some unknown reason announced in a loud voice: 'Miss Shatov!' so that all eyes at once turned on her.

'So that's Dasha!' Miss Lebyatkin cried. 'Well, Shatov, darling, your sister is not at all like you! How dare my brother call such a beautiful girl the serf-girl Dashka!'

Meanwhile Dasha had gone up to Mrs Stavrogin; but, struck by

Miss Lebyatkin's exclamation, she turned round quickly and stopped dead before her chair, staring fixedly at the half-witted woman.

'Sit down, Dasha,' Mrs Stavrogin said with terrifying composure. 'Nearer; that's right. You can see this woman from your seat. Do you know her?'

'I've never seen her,' Dasha replied quietly and, after a short pause, added: 'I suppose it's the sick sister of a Mr Lebyatkin.'

'And I, too, my dear, see you for the first time now, though I've long ago wanted to meet you because in every gesture of yours I can see an educated lady,' Miss Lebyatkin cried with enthusiasm. 'As for that flunkey of mine calling you names, is it really possible that a charming and educated young lady like yourself should have taken his money? For you are a dear, a dear, a dear; you can take it from me!' she concluded rapturously, waving her hand in front of her own face.

'Do you understand anything?' Mrs Stavrogin asked with proud dignity.

'I understand everything, ma'am.'

'You've heard about the money?'

'I suppose it must be the money which in Switzerland I undertook to hand over to Mr Lebyatkin, her brother, at the request of Mr Stavrogin.'

For a moment there was silence.

'Did Nicholas himself ask you to hand it over?'

'He was very anxious to send that money – three hundred roubles in all – to Mr Lebyatkin. He did not know his address, but only knew that he would be in our town. He asked me to give it to Mr Lebyatkin if he arrived.'

'But what money was – lost? What was that woman talking about just now?'

'That I don't know, ma'am. I, too, have heard that Mr Lebyatkin is saying about me in the hearing of other people that I didn't give him all the money, but I don't know what he means. I was given three hundred roubles, and I sent him three hundred roubles.'

Miss Shatov had almost regained her composure completely. And let me add here that it was difficult to astonish this girl and disconcert her for long – whatever her real feelings might be. She now gave all her answers without hurrying, replying to each question with precision, quietly, smoothly, without a trace of her first sudden agitation and without the least embarrassment which might have implied a consciousness of any sort of guilt. Mrs Stavrogin kept her eyes fixed on her all the time she was speaking. For a minute Mrs Stavrogin thought it over.

'If,' she said at last firmly, and obviously addressing herself to the spectators in the room, though she looked only at Dasha, 'if Nicholas addressed his request not to me but asked you, he must have had his own reasons for doing so. I have no right to pry into them if he thought it necessary to keep it a secret from me. But the very fact that you took part in this business is sufficient to put my mind at rest about those reasons of his. I want you to know that, Dasha. You above all. But you see, my dear, you, who are ignorant of the ways of the world, could commit an indiscretion with a clear conscience; and you did so when you undertook to have dealings with some rascal. The rumours spread by this rascal merely prove your mistake. But I shall find out about him, and, since it is my duty to protect your interests, I shall know how to take your part. Now we have to put an end to all this.'

'The best thing to do when he comes to see you,' Miss Lebyatkin suddenly interposed, leaning forward in her chair, 'is to send him to the servants' quarters. Let him play cards on a chest with the servants, while we sit here and have coffee. I daresay you might send him a cup of coffee, but I have nothing but contempt for him.'

And she tossed her head expressively.

'We must put an end to this,' Mrs Stavrogin repeated, after having listened attentively to Miss Lebyatkin. 'Please ring the bell, Mr Verkhovensky.'

Mr Verkhovensky rang and suddenly stepped forward in great agitation.

'If – if I –' he murmured excitedly, getting red in the face, faltering and stammering – 'if I, too, have heard a most disgusting story, or rather slander, then – it was with the utmost indignation – *enfin c'est un homme perdu et quelque chose comme un forçat evadé.* ...'

He broke off and did not finish; Mrs Stavrogin screwed up her eyes and examined him from top to toe. The deferential butler came in.

'The carriage,' Mrs Stavrogin ordered. 'And you, Alexey, get ready to take Miss Lebyatkin home. She'll tell you where herself.'

'Mr Lebyatkin, ma'am, has been waiting for her for some time downstairs and has asked me to announce him.'

'That's impossible, madam.' Maurice Drozdov, who had sat all the time without uttering a word, suddenly stepped forward agitatedly. 'If you don't mind my saying so, madam, he is not the sort of person who can be admitted into a drawing-room. He – he – he's an impossible fellow, madam.'

'Let him wait,' Mrs Stavrogin said to the butler, who disappeared.

'*C'est un homme malhonnête et je crois même que c'est un forçat evadé, ou quelque chose dans ce genre*,' Mr Verkhovensky muttered again, and again he reddened and again stopped abruptly.

'Lisa, it's time we were going,' Mrs Drozdov declared with a touch of contempt in her voice, getting up from her seat.

She was apparently sorry for having, in her alarm, called herself a fool a few minutes ago. When Dasha was speaking, she had listened with her lips pursed superciliously. But what struck me most was the way Lisa looked from the moment Dasha had come in: her eyes flashed with hatred and contempt which she did not trouble to conceal.

'Wait a moment, Praskovya, I beg you,' Mrs Stavrogin stopped the old lady with the same unnatural placidity. 'Will you please sit down? I want to say all I have to say, and your poor legs must be hurting you. That's right. Thank you. A short while ago I lost my temper and spoke rather impatiently to you. I am sorry, and I beg you to forgive me. I behaved foolishly, and I'm the first to regret it, for above all I like to be fair in everything. Now you, too, lost your temper, of course, and you mentioned certain anonymous letters. Every anonymous communication must be treated with contempt, if only because it is not signed. If you're not of that opinion, I don't envy you. In any case, if I were in your place I shouldn't have mentioned it at all; I shouldn't have soiled my hands with it. But you did. However, as you have started it, I can tell you that six days ago I, too, received a ludicrous anonymous letter. The rascal who wrote it informs me that Nicholas has lost his reason and that I ought to beware of some lame woman who "will play an important part in my life". I remember the exact phrase he used. Knowing that Nicholas has very many enemies, I immediately sent for a certain person here, one of the most secret, most vindictive, and most despicable of his enemies, and after talking to him I realized at once what the contemptible source of the anonymous letter was. If you, too, my poor Praskovya, have *because of me* been troubled by similar despicable letters and, as you put it, were *bombarded* with them, I am of course the first to be sorry to have been the innocent cause of it. That's all I wanted to say to you by way of explanation. I'm sorry to see that you're so tired and so worried now. Moreover, I have definitely made up my mind to *admit* the suspicious character whom Mr Drozdov has just inaccurately described as a person you could not *receive*. Lisa, in particular, has no business to be here. Come, Lisa, my dear, and let me kiss you again.'

Lisa crossed the room and stopped silently before Mrs Stavrogin, who kissed her, took her hands, and, holding her at a little distance from herself, looked at her with feeling, made the sign of the cross over her, and then kissed her again.

'Well, good-bye, Lisa,' she said (there were almost suppressed tears in her voice). 'Believe me when I tell you that I shall never give up loving you, whatever may be in store for me now. God bless you. I have always done his holy will. ...'

She was about to say something more, but restrained herself and fell silent. Lisa went back to her seat, still without uttering a word and as though deep in thought, but she suddenly stopped before her mother.

'I shan't go yet, Mother,' she said in a quiet voice; 'I shall stay with Auntie a little longer.'

There was a note of iron determination in those quiet words of hers.

'Goodness me! what's this I hear?' Mrs Drozdov cried, throwing up her hands helplessly.

But Lisa did not reply. She did not seem to hear her. She returned to her seat in the corner of the room and again fixed her gaze on some invisible spot in the air.

A triumphant and proud expression came into Mrs Stavrogin's face.

'Mr Drozdov,' she said, 'I have a great favour to ask of you. Will you be so good as to go and have a look at that man downstairs, and if there is the slightest possibility of his being *admitted*, bring him up here.'

Mr Drozdov bowed and went out. A minute later he brought in Mr Lebyatkin.

4

I have, I believe, already described the appearance of that gentleman: a tall, curly-headed, thick-set fellow of about forty, with a purple, rather bloated and flabby face, with cheeks that shook with every movement of his head, with tiny, bloodshot, sometimes cunning eyes, with a moustache and side-whiskers, and a repulsive-looking Adam's apple which was beginning to be covered with a layer of fat. But the most striking thing about him was that he appeared wearing a frock-coat and clean linen. 'There are people who look indecent in clean linen,' as Liputin had once said to Mr Verkhovensky, who had reproached him jestingly for being untidy. The Captain even had a pair of black gloves, the right one of which he held in his hand, and the left, tightly stretched and unbuttoned, covered only half his fleshy left paw, in which he held a brand-new glossy top hat which he must have worn for the first time that day. It seemed, therefore, that the 'frock-coat of love', about which he had shouted to Shatov the day before, did actually exist. All this – that is, the frock-coat and the clean linen – had been procured (as I found out later) on the advice of Liputin for some mysterious purpose. There could be no doubt that his arrival now (in a hackney carriage) was most certainly at the instigation and with the connivance of some other person; alone it would never have occurred to him, nor would he have been able to dress, get ready, and make up his mind in three-quarters of a hour at most, even if it could be assumed that he had learnt of the scene outside the cathedral immediately. He was not drunk, but was in the heavy, dull, hazy condition of a man who had suddenly come to after many days of drinking. It seemed to me that one had only to tap him on the shoulder once or twice and he would be drunk again.

He was about to rush into the drawing-room, but suddenly tripped over the rug near the doorway. Miss Lebyatkin nearly died with laughter. He gave her a fierce look and suddenly took a few rapid steps towards Mrs Stavrogin.

'I have come, madam,' he roared out in a thunderous voice.

'Be so good, sir, as to sit down there, on that chair,' Mrs Stavrogin said, drawing herself up. 'I shall hear you from there as well, and I shall be able to see you better from here.'

The Captain stopped short, looking vacantly before him, but he turned and sat down where he was told on the chair close to the door. His face betrayed a great lack of self-confidence and, at the same time, arrogance and a sort of incessant exasperation. He was in a state of panic, that was clear enough; but his vanity, too, was hurt; and it was

easy to see that his exacerbated vanity might, on occasion, tempt him
to do something rash, in spite of his cowardice. He was apparently
afraid of every movement of his clumsy body. It is a well-known fact
that such gentlemen, finding themselves by some miracle in society,
are driven into a state of horrible misery by their own hands and their
inability to find a place for them. The Captain sat motionless in his
chair, with his hat and gloves in his hands, glaring stupidly at Mrs
Stavrogin's stern face. He would, no doubt, have liked to have a good
look round the room, but for the time being he could not summon
enough courage to do so. Miss Lebyatkin, finding his figure again terribly funny, went off into another peal of laughter, but he did not stir.
Mrs Stavrogin kept him in that position pitilessly for a long time – a
whole minute – scrutinizing him relentlessly.

'Will you first of all, sir, be so kind as to give me your name yourself?' she said in a measured and expressive tone of voice.

'Captain Lebyatkin, ma'am,' the Captain roared. 'I've come,
ma'am –' He stirred in his chair again.

'Allow me!' Mrs Stavrogin stopped him again. 'Is this pathetic
creature who has aroused my interest so much really your sister?'

'Yes, ma'am, she is my sister who has escaped from my supervision,
for she is in such a condition –'

He suddenly faltered and turned purple.

'Don't misunderstand me, madam,' he said, growing terribly confused. 'Her own brother will not soil the – I mean, in such a condition
does not mean in such a condition – in the sense that is derogatory to
her – her reputation – lately –'

He stopped short suddenly.

'Sir!' Mrs Stavrogin raised her head.

'I mean in this condition!' he suddenly concluded, tapping the
middle of his forehead with his finger.

There was a short pause.

'And has she suffered from this illness long?' Mrs Stavrogin asked
with some hesitation.

'Madam, I've come to thank you for your generosity at the church
in a Russian, a brotherly way –'

'A brotherly?'

'I mean, not a brotherly, but merely in the sense that I'm my sister's
brother, madam, and believe me, madam,' he went on, speaking

rapidly and again turning purple in the face, 'I am not so uneducated as might appear at first sight in your drawing-room. My sister and I, madam, look very small in the luxurious surroundings here. And, besides, madam, I'm afraid I have many enemies who are only too glad to spread all sorts of disreputable stories about me. But I care nothing for reputation. Lebyatkin, madam, is proud, and – and I – I've come to thank you – here's the money, madam!'

And so saying, he snatched a wallet out of his pocket, pulled a bundle of banknotes out of it, and began counting them with shaking fingers in a fierce fit of impatience. It was plain that he was anxious to explain something as quickly as possible and, in fact, an explanation was badly needed; but probably realizing that his preoccupation with the money made him look even more silly, he entirely lost control of himself: he just could not manage to count the money, his fingers got in each other's way, and, to complete his humiliation, a green note slipped out of his wallet and fell zigzagging to the carpet.

'Twenty roubles, madam,' he cried suddenly, jumping up with the bundle of notes in his hand and his face covered with perspiration from his agony of mind; noticing the note which had dropped on the floor, he bent down to pick it up, but, feeling ashamed for some reason, he gave it up with a wave of the hand.

'For your servants, madam – for the footman who picks it up – let him remember Miss Lebyatkin!'

'I'm afraid I can't possibly permit that,' Mrs Stavrogin said hurriedly and with some alarm.

'In that case –'

He bent down, picked it up, went purple in the face, and suddenly walking up to Mrs Stavrogin, held out the money he had counted.

'What's the meaning of this, sir?' she cried, apparently alarmed in good earnest and recoiling in her chair.

Mr Drozdov, Mr Verkhovensky, and myself stepped forward.

'Don't be afraid, don't be afraid; I'm not mad, indeed I'm not mad,' the Captain assured everybody excitedly.

'Yes, sir, you are mad!'

'Madam, it's not at all what you think! Of course, I'm just an insignificant link – your mansions, madam, are richly furnished, but not those of Mary the Unknown, those of my sister, madam, my sister, née Lebyatkin, but whom we shall for the time being call Mary the

Unknown, for the time being, madam, *for the time being*, mind you; for God himself will not allow it for ever! Madam, you gave her ten roubles, and she took them, but only because it was from *you*, madam! Do you hear that, madam? This Unknown Mary would not take it from anyone in the world, for if she did her grandfather, the officer who was killed in the Caucasus before the very eyes of General Yermolov, would turn in his grave; but from you, madam, from you she will take anything. But with one hand she will take it and with the other she will hold out to you twenty – yes, madam, twenty – roubles as a subscription to one of the charitable societies in Petersburg of which you, madam, are a member, for you yourself, madam, published an announcement in the *Moscow Gazette* that you have in your possession a subscription list of a charitable society to which everyone may subscribe. ...'

The Captain suddenly stopped short; he was breathing heavily, as though after some difficult feat. All that about the charitable society he had probably prepared beforehand, perhaps even with Liputin's direct assistance. He perspired more than ever: beads of perspiration literally stood out on his temples. Mrs Stavrogin watched him closely.

'The subscription list,' she said severely, 'can always be had from my doorkeeper downstairs and, if you want to, you can enter your subscription there. I must therefore ask you to put your money away and not wave it in the air. Thank you. I must also ask you to resume your seat. Thank you. I'm very sorry, sir, to have been mistaken about your sister and given her some money because I thought she was poor, whereas she is so rich. One thing, though, I cannot understand, sir. Why can she take money only from me, and not from anyone else? You were so insistent on this point that I must ask you to give me a most precise explanation of it.'

'Madam, that is a secret which can be buried only in the grave!' replied the Captain.

'But why?' Mrs Stavrogin asked, but, somehow, no longer so firmly.

'Madam, madam!'

He fell silent gloomily, his eyes fixed on the ground and his right hand pressed to his heart. Mrs Stavrogin waited without taking her eyes off him.

'Madam,' he roared suddenly, 'will you permit me to ask you one question? Only one, but frankly, openly, in the Russian fashion, from the heart?'

'Please do.'

'Have you ever suffered in your life, madam?'

'I suppose what you want to say is that you have suffered or that you are still suffering because of someone.'

'Madam, madam' – he suddenly jumped to his feet again, perhaps not even noticing it and beating his breast – 'so much has accumulated here, in this heart of mine, so much, madam, that God himself will be surprised when it all comes out on the Day of Judgement!'

'You put it rather strongly, didn't you?'

'Madam, I may be speaking irritably –'

'Don't let it worry you, sir. I shall know when to stop you.'

'May I ask you one more question, madam?'

'By all means.'

'Can one die just out of the nobility of one's soul?'

'I'm afraid I don't know. I've never asked myself that question.'

'You don't know! You never asked yourself that question!' he cried with pathetic irony. 'Well, if that is so then

Be still, despairing heart!'

and he smote his breast fiercely.

He was again pacing the room. It is characteristic of these people that they are completely incapable of controlling their desires; on the contrary, they are overcome by an irresistible urge to reveal them in all their squalidness the moment they arise. Finding himself in a strange environment, such a man usually starts timidly, but if you give in to him by a hair's breadth, he will immediately begin treating you with arrogance. The Captain was already excited. He walked about the room, waving his arms, not listening to questions, talking about himself very rapidly, so that his tongue would sometimes refuse to obey him, and without finishing one sentence, began another. It is true, he could not possibly have been absolutely sober. Lisa, too, was in the room – Lisa, whose presence seemed to have gone to his head, though he never glanced at her once. However, this is merely my theory. Anyway, there must have been some reason which induced Mrs Stavrogin to overcome her repugnance for that man and listen to him. Mrs Drozdov was simply shaking with terror without, apparently, realizing what it was all about. Mr Verkhovensky, too, trembled, but that, on the contrary, was because he was always inclined to see too much in everything. Mr Drozdov stood in the attitude of a man who was ready to rush to everybody's defence. Lisa was very pale. She watched the wild Captain steadily with wide-open eyes. Shatov sat without stirring; but the strangest thing of all was that Miss Lebyatkin had not only ceased laughing, but had grown terribly sad. She leaned against the table with her right arm and followed her brother's harangues with a long, melancholy gaze. Dasha alone seemed to me to be perfectly composed.

'All this is just absurd nonsense,' Mrs Stavrogin said, getting angry at last. 'You haven't answered my question – why? I'm waiting for an answer.'

'I haven't answered – why? You're waiting for my answer – why?' the Captain repeated with a wink. 'This little word "why" has covered the whole universe like a flood ever since the first day of creation, madam, and every minute all nature cries to its Creator: "Why?" And for seven thousand years it has received no answer. Do you really expect Captain Lebyatkin alone to answer it? Would that be fair, madam?'

'That's all nonsense, and it isn't at all what I mean,' Mrs Stavrogin fumed, losing her patience. 'It's an allegory. And, besides, sir, you're using a much too florid style, and I consider that to be a piece of impertinence on your part.'

'Madam,' the Captain went on, without listening to her, 'I might have liked to be called Ernest, and yet I'm forced to go through life with the vulgar name of Ignatius – why is that, do you think? I should have liked to be called Prince de Monbart, and yet I'm only Lebyatkin, a name derived from the Russian word for swan – "*lebed*". Now, why's that? I am a poet, madam, a poet at heart, and I could have had a thousand roubles from a publisher, and yet I'm forced to live in a pigsty – why? why? Madam, in my opinion Russia is nothing but a freak of nature – nothing else!'

'You absolutely refuse to say anything more definite?'

'I can read you my poem *The Cockroach*, madam.'

'Wha-a-at?'

'Madam, I'm not mad! I shall go mad one day, I shall most certainly go mad one day, but I'm not mad yet. Madam, a friend of mine,

a most hon-nourable man, has written a Krylov fable under the title
of *The Cockroach* – may I read it?'

'You want to read some Krylov fable?'

'No, madam, I don't want to read a Krylov fable; but my fable, my
own fable, my own work! Please, madam, believe me – and I mean no
offence to you – that I'm not so corrupt and uneducated as not to
know that Russia possesses a great fable-writer, Krylov, to whom the
Minister of Education has raised a monument in the Summer Gardens
for the diversion of young children. You'll find my answer is at the
bottom of that fable, in letters of fire!'

'Very well, read your fable.'

> 'In a wood a cockroach lived,
> A cockroach old and wise,
> Into a glass one day he dived,
> Full of cannibal flies.'

'Goodness gracious, what is it all about?' cried Mrs Stavrogin.

'What I mean is,' the Captain hastened to explain, waving his arms
about frantically with the exasperated irritation of an author who is
interrupted in his reading, 'that when flies crawl into a glass in summer, they turn into cannibal-flies; any fool can understand that. Please,
madam, don't interrupt. Don't interrupt. You will see, you will
see ...' he went on, still waving his arms about:

> 'Room enough the cockroach needs,
> The flies all murmur and rage –
> Too full our glass! Our deeds,
> O Jove, deserve a better stage.
> But while they clamour and rail
> Nikifor nears the place,
> Old and wise and bent and pale –

'I'm afraid I haven't quite finished it, but, never mind, I'll explain it
in a few words,' the Captain rattled on. 'Nikifor takes the glass and,
without taking any notice of the shouting, empties the whole thing into
a pigsty, flies, cockroach and all, which he should have done long ago.
But, mind you, madam, the cockroach does not raise a murmur! That
is the answer to your question: "Why?"' he cried triumphantly. 'The
cockroach does not murmur! As for Nikifor, he represents nature,' he
added, speaking rapidly and pacing the room self-complacently.

Mrs Stavrogin became terribly angry.

'And may I ask you, sir, what about the money which you claim to have received from Mr Stavrogin and which you dare to accuse a member of my household of not having given you?'

'A libel!' Lebyatkin roared, raising his right hand tragically.

'No, sir, it is not a libel!'

'Madam, there are circumstances which compel a man to put up with family disgrace rather than to proclaim the truth aloud. Lebyatkin, madam, will never say anything he shouldn't!'

He seemed to have gone blind; he was inspired; he felt his importance; something of the kind he must certainly have dreamed about. He felt already like insulting somebody, playing some dirty trick on someone, showing his power.

'Ring the bell, please, Mr Verkhovensky,' said Mrs Stavrogin.

'Lebyatkin is cunning, madam!' he said, winking, with an evil smile. 'He is cunning; but he, too, has an Achilles' heel. He has his portals to passion! And these portals, madam, are the old, battle-scarred bottle, in whose praise Denis Davydov has sung. And, madam, it is while he finds himself in those portals that he sends off a letter in verse, a most wonderful letter, which, however, he would have dearly wished to take back afterwards with the tears of his whole life, for the feeling of the beautiful is destroyed. But the bird has flown, and you won't catch it by the tail! It was in those portals, madam, that Lebyatkin might have said something about an honourable young lady, driven by the honourable indignation of his soul chafing under the injuries inflicted upon it, and his enemies have made use of it. But, madam, Lebyatkin is cunning. And in vain does the sinister wolf watch over him every minute, filling his glass and waiting for the end: Lebyatkin will never say anything he shouldn't, and instead of the expected revelation, all he finds at the bottom of the bottle is – Lebyatkin's cunning! But enough – oh, enough! Madam, your splendid mansions might belong to the most honourable of men, but the cockroach does not murmur! Make a note of that, madam; make a note of the fact that he does not murmur, and recognize his great spirit!'

At that moment a bell rang downstairs in the porter's room, and almost immediately the butler, who had been rather late in answering Mr Verkhovensky's ring, came in. The sedate old servant was quite extraordinarily excited.

'Mr Stavrogin has just arrived and is coming here,' he announced in answer to Mrs Stavrogin's inquiring look.

I particularly remember her at that moment: at first she went pale, but suddenly her eyes flashed. She drew herself up in her chair with a look of extraordinary determination. Everyone, in fact, was startled. The completely unforeseen arrival of Stavrogin, who was only expected to arrive in a month's time, was not only strange because of its unexpectedness, but because of its fateful coincidence with the present moment. Even the Captain stood still like a post in the middle of the room, with his mouth open, looking at the door with a terribly stupid expression.

And presently we heard footsteps in the next room, a very long and narrow room, little hurried footsteps, which were approaching rapidly. Someone seemed to be running, and suddenly there rushed into the drawing-room – not Mr Stavrogin, but a young man nobody seemed to know.

5

I think I'd better pause here a little and describe, in however cursory a way, the person who had made so sudden an appearance among us.

He was a young man of about twenty-seven, slightly above medium height, with rather long, thin fair hair and with a wispy, barely discernible, moustache and beard. He was dressed decently, even fashionably, but not smartly; at the first glance he looked a little round-shouldered and awkward, though in fact he was not round-shouldered at all, and rather free-and-easy in his manners. He seemed to be a sort of eccentric, and yet afterwards we all found his manners extremely agreeable and his conversation always to the point.

No one could say that he was not good-looking, but no one liked his face. His head was elongated at the back and somewhat flattened at the sides, so that his face looked rather sharp. His forehead was high and narrow, but his features rather small; his eyes were sharp, his nose small and pointed, his lips long and thin. He looked a little ill, but it only seemed so. He had wrinkles on each cheek and near his cheek-bones, which made him look like a man who had just recovered from a serious illness. And yet he was perfectly well and strong, and he had never been ill.

He walked and moved about very hurriedly, but he was in no hurry to go anywhere. It seemed as though nothing could embarrass him; he remained the same in any situation and in any society. He possessed a great deal of self-complacency, but he was completely unaware of it himself.

He talked rapidly and hurriedly; but at the same time self-confidently, and he was never at a loss for a word. His thoughts were unruffled, for all his hurried appearance, precise and final – and that was particularly noticeable. His articulation was amazingly clear; his words fell from his lips like large, smooth grains, always carefully chosen and always at your service. At first you could not help liking it, but later on you hated it, and just because of his too clear enunciation, of this string of ever-ready words. You somehow could not help feeling that he must have a sort of peculiarly shaped tongue in his head, a sort of unusually long and thin one, very red and with an exceedingly sharp and incessantly and uncontrollably active tip.

Well, this was the young man who now flew into the drawing-room, and, honestly, I still believe that he began talking in the next room and that he came in talking. He was at Mrs Stavrogin's side in a flash.

'... Just imagine, my dear Mrs Stavrogin,' he rattled away, 'I came in thinking that he'd been here for at least a quarter of an hour – he arrived an hour and a half ago – I met him at Kirilov's – he went straight there half an hour ago. Told me to be here, too, in a quarter of an hour –'

'But who told you to come here? Who?' Mrs Stavrogin asked.

'Why, Mr Stavrogin, of course! Good Lord! you don't mean to say that you've only heard of it this minute? But his luggage at any rate should have arrived here long ago! Do you mean to say they never told you? Well, then, I'm the first to bring the news. We could, of course, send someone to look for him, though I expect he's sure to be here himself any moment and, I daresay, at the moment which suits him best and, unless I am much mistaken, fits in with his plans.' Here he glanced round the room, his eyes resting with particular attention on the Captain. 'Why, my dear Miss Drozdov, how nice to meet you first! How do you do?' And he rushed up to shake hands with Lisa, who smiled gaily at him. 'And I can see that dear Mrs Drozdov hasn't forgotten her "professor", either, and I don't think she is as angry with him as she used to be in Switzerland, is she? But how are your poor legs, my dear Mrs Drozdov? And were your Swiss doctors right in prescribing the climate of your native country for them? I beg your pardon? Fomentations? Yes, I expect that must be very good for them. But, my dear Mrs Stavrogin' – he quickly turned round again – 'you can't imagine how sorry I was to have missed you abroad and to have been unable to pay my respects to you personally. I had, besides, so much to tell you … I did write to my old man here, but I expect that, as usual, he –'

'Peter!' Mr Verkhovensky cried, recovering from his stupor in a flash, throwing up his hands in surprise, and rushing up to his son. 'Pierre, mon enfant, I never recognized you!' And he hugged him in his arms, tears streaming out of his eyes.

'Now, now, don't be naughty, don't be naughty! No noble gestures, please. That will do, that will do. Please, please,' Peter murmured hurriedly, trying to free himself from his father's embrace.

'I never was a good father to you – never!'

'All right, that'll do. We'll discuss it later. I knew you'd be a naughty boy. Come now, calm yourself, please.'

'But I haven't seen you for ten years!'

'All the more reason why there shouldn't be any emotional scenes.'

'Mon enfant!'

'All right, I know you love me, Pater. I believe you. Please take your arms away. Don't you see how embarrassing it is for all the people here? Ah, here at last is Stavrogin! Now, look here, Pater, do behave yourself!'

Nicholas Stavrogin was, indeed, already in the room. He entered very quietly, and stopped for a moment at the door, imperturbably scrutinizing the company.

I was struck by his appearance the moment I looked at him, just as I had been four years before, when I saw him for the first time. I had not forgotten him a bit, but there seem to be faces which every time they appear bring something new with them, something you have not noticed before, though you may have seen them a hundred times. He was apparently the same as he had been four years before: just as elegant, as impressive-looking, and almost as young, and he walked into a room as statelily as ever. His faint smile was just as officially amiable and just as complacent; his expression just as stern, thoughtful, and rather absent-minded. In short, it seemed as though we had parted only the day before. But one thing did strike me: though he had been considered very handsome before, his face really was 'like a mask', as some sharp-tongued ladies of our society had expressed it. But now – now, I don't know why, he looked to me at the first glance as quite incontestably handsome, so much so that it was impossible to say that his face was like a mask. Was it because he was just a little paler than before and had apparently gone thinner? Or was it perhaps because some new idea was now reflected in his eyes?

'Nicholas,' cried Mrs Stavrogin, sitting up erect in her chair and stopping him with an imperious gesture, 'stop a moment!'

But to explain the terrible question which immediately followed that gesture and exclamation – a question I could never have imagined even Mrs Stavrogin would have had the courage to utter – I must ask the reader to remember what Mrs Stavrogin's character had been all through her life and its extraordinary impulsiveness at some moments of crisis. I must also ask him to take into account the fact that in spite of the unusual determination of her spirit and the considerable amount of common-sense and, as it were, practical and even business-like tact she possessed, there were moments in her life during which she surrendered herself entirely and, if one may put it that way, completely without restraint. I should finally like to ask him to take into account the fact that the present moment could really have been for her one of those moments in which the whole essence of her life was focused – the whole of her past, present, and perhaps future. May I also remind him, in passing, of the anonymous letter she had received and the secret of which she had let out so irritably to Mrs Drozdov a short while ago, having, I believe, omitted to mention the contents of that letter; and it was perhaps in that letter that the explanation of the terrible question which she put to her son must be sought.

'Nicholas,' she repeated, rolling out each word clearly in a firm voice, in which a menacing challenge could be heard, 'I beg you to tell me at once, without moving from your place, whether it is true that this unfortunate cripple – there she is – there – look at her! – is it true that she is – your lawful wife?'

I remember that moment very well: he did not bat an eyelid, but looked steadily at his mother; the expression of his face did not change in the slightest. At length he smiled slowly, a kind of condescending smile, and, without uttering a word in reply, went up quietly to his mother, took her hand, raised it respectfully to his lips, and kissed it. And so strong was his invariable and irresistible influence on his mother, that even at that moment she dared not snatch her hand away. She just looked at him, all of her transformed into a question, and her whole appearance showed that she would not be able to stand the uncertainty another moment.

But he still did not speak. Having kissed her hand, he once more looked round the room and, unhurriedly as before, went straight to Miss Lebyatkin. It is very difficult to describe people's faces at certain moments. I remember, for instance, that Miss Lebyatkin, frozen with panic, rose to meet him and folded her hands in front of her, as though beseeching him; at the same time I can distinctly remember the rapture in her eyes, a sort of wild rapture, which almost distorted her features – a rapture people find it difficult to bear. Perhaps both were there, both the terror and the rapture; but I remember moving quickly towards her (I was standing almost beside her), for I thought that she was going to faint immediately.

'You shouldn't be here,' Stavrogin said to her in a gentle, melodious voice, and his eyes were filled with an extraordinary tenderness.

He stood before her in a most respectful attitude, and every move-ment of his showed his sincere respect for her.

The poor woman murmured breathlessly and in an impulsive half-whisper:

'But may I – now – go down on my knees before you?'

'No, you can't possibly do that,' he replied, giving her a brilliant smile, so that she, too, all at once laughed happily.

'You must remember,' he went on gravely in the same melodious voice, talking tenderly to her, as though she were a child, 'that you are a girl, and that though I'm your most devoted friend, I'm a stran-ger to you, not your husband, nor your father, nor your fiancé. Give me your arm and let us go; I'll escort you to the carriage and, if you will let me, I shall take you home.'

She listened to him attentively and lowered her eyes, as though wondering what to do.

'Let's go,' she said with a sigh, giving him her hand.

But just then she had a slight accident. She must have turned a little carelessly and stepped on her lame leg, which was shorter than the other, and she fell sideways into the arm-chair, and but for that she would have fallen on the floor. He caught hold of her at once and supported her. Then he took her firmly by the arm, looking greatly concerned for her, and led her carefully to the door. She was obviously upset by her fall, for she was overcome with confusion, blushed and felt terribly ashamed. Her eyes fixed silently on the floor and limping painfully, she hobbled after him, almost suspended on his arm. They went out of the room like that. Lisa, I observed, suddenly jumped up from her chair and for some reason as they were going out of the room followed them with a motionless stare to the very door. Then she sat down again in silence, but her face seemed to twitch spasmodically, as though she had touched some horrible snake.

While the scene between Stavrogin and Mary Lebyatkin was going on, everybody in the room was speechless with amazement; you could have heard a pin drop; but the moment they left, everybody suddenly burst into speech.

6

They said little, though: they mostly uttered astonished cries. I am afraid I can't very well remember the exact order in which it all happened at the time, for everything was in confusion. Mr Verkhovensky was shouting something in French and throwing up his hands in amazement, but Mrs Stavrogin was too preoccupied with her own thoughts to take any notice of him. Even Mr Drozdov muttered something abruptly and rapidly. But Peter Verkhovensky was more excited than anyone; he was trying desperately to convince Mrs Stavrogin about something, gesticulating wildly, but for a long time I could not make out what he was talking about. He also addressed Mrs Drozdov and Lisa, and even shouted something in passing to his father in his excitement – in a word, he kept rushing about the room. Mrs Stavrogin, all flushed, jumped up from her chair and shouted to Mrs Drozdov, 'Did you hear? Did you hear what he said to her just now?' But Mrs Drozdov was not in a condition to reply. She just muttered something with a wave of the hand. The poor woman had her own worries: she kept turning her head every minute towards Lisa and looking at her in panic, not daring even to think of getting up and leaving before her daughter had got up. In the meantime the Captain was only too anxious to slip away. That I noticed very well. He had undoubtedly been in a state of great terror ever since Nicholas

Stavrogin had appeared; but Peter seized him by the arm and would not let him go.

'That's absolutely necessary; it's absolutely necessary,' he rattled away, still trying to convince Mrs Stavrogin.

He stood before her, while she was sitting down again and, I remember it distinctly, was listening eagerly to him; he succeeded in the end in getting her attention.

'It's necessary. You can see for yourself, madam, that there is a misunderstanding here. It looks very strange, I admit; but, actually, the whole thing is as clear as daylight and as plain as a pikestaff. I realize very well that I haven't been authorized by anyone to tell you about it, and I daresay I cut rather a funny figure trying to thrust myself upon you. But, to begin with, Mr Stavrogin himself does not attach any importance to this business and, finally, you must admit yourself, madam, that there are cases in which a man finds it very difficult to offer a personal explanation. It is therefore absolutely necessary that a third person should undertake to do it for him, particularly as he finds it so much easier to discuss certain matters of a rather delicate nature. Believe me, madam, Mr Stavrogin cannot be blamed for refusing to answer your question at once by offering a completely satisfactory explanation, in spite of the fact that the whole thing is of no importance whatever. I have known him in Petersburg. Besides, the whole incident really redounds to his honour, if one must use that vague word "honour"...'

'Do you mean to say that you were the witness of a certain incident which gave rise to – to this misunderstanding?' asked Mrs Stavrogin.

'I not only witnessed it, I took part in it,' Peter replied quickly. 'If you'll give me your word that this won't offend Mr Stavrogin, who has always been most nice and considerate to me and who conceals nothing, absolutely nothing, from me, and if you're quite sure that by doing so you'll give him pleasure –'

'Why, of course it'll please him; for I consider it myself a highly pleasant duty on my part. I'm convinced that he would have asked me to do it himself.'

The obtrusive desire of this gentleman, who seemed to have dropped from the sky, to relate incidents from another man's private life was rather strange, and contrary to all the accepted rules of conduct. But, having found her weakest spot, he succeeded in deceiving her. At the time I had no idea of the man's true character, let alone of his designs.

'Go on; I'm listening,' Mrs Stavrogin declared cautiously and with reserve, somewhat piqued by her own condescension.

'There's nothing much to tell really and, as a matter of fact, it cannot even be said to have been an incident,' he rattled on, 'though I daresay a novelist who had nothing else to do might make a novel of it. It's a rather interesting little affair, Mrs Drozdov, and I'm sure that Miss Lisa will be interested to hear it, for there's a lot here which, though not particularly odd, is certainly rather fantastic. Five years ago Mr Stavrogin met this man in Petersburg – I mean, this Mr Lebyatkin who stands gaping here and who, I believe, was trying to give us the slip. I beg your pardon, Mrs Stavrogin. I shouldn't advise you to run off, though, my dear retired official of the commissariat department (you see, I remember you very well). Mr Stavrogin and I know all about your little escapades here, for which, don't forget, you'll be called to account. I beg your pardon again, Mrs Stavrogin. In those days Mr Stavrogin used to call this gentleman his Falstaff; that,' he suddenly explained, 'must be some old burlesque character, at whom everybody laughs and who lets everybody laugh at him provided he's paid for it. In those days Mr Stavrogin led a rather – shall I say? – burlesque sort of life in Petersburg – I'm afraid I can't describe it by any other word, because he's not the sort of man to give in to despair, and he wasn't keen on doing anything in particular at the time. I'm only speaking of that time, Mrs Stavrogin. Lebyatkin had a sister, the woman who has been sitting here just now. The brother and sister had no place of their own, but just lived wherever they could. He used to roam about under the arches of the arcade, always in his old uniform, stopping the more decently dressed passers-by, and spending whatever money he got on drinks. His sister subsisted like a bird of the air. She helped with the charring in the furnished rooms and lived on the few pennies she earned as a servant. It was a frightful life. I won't attempt to describe the life in those slum tenements, a life to which Mr Stavrogin had taken in those days out of sheer eccentricity. I'm only talking about that particular time, Mrs Stavrogin; as for "eccentricity", that's his own expression. He does not conceal much from me. Miss Lebyatkin, who for a time happened to meet Mr Stavrogin rather frequently, was greatly struck by his appearance. He was, as it were, a diamond on the filthy background of her life. I'm not very good at describing feelings, and that's why I'd rather say nothing about them; but the rabble there immediately made fun of her, and she became depressed. They always laughed at her there, but she had not noticed it before. Even then she was not quite right in her head, though she was not as bad as now. I have reason to believe that as a child she had received some sort of education through a rich lady who was interested in her. Mr Stavrogin had never paid any attention to her, and spent his time mostly in playing preference with a greasy old pack of cards for farthing stakes with some Government clerks. But on one occasion when she was being treated badly he (without so much as a by your leave) caught a Government clerk by the scruff of his neck and threw him out of a first-floor window. It was not a question of any chivalrous indignation at injured innocence: the whole operation was performed amid roars of laughter, and Mr Stavrogin laughed more than anybody! Everything, however, ended happily, and they made friends again and started drinking punch. But the injured innocence herself never forgot it. In the end, of course, she lost her reason completely. I repeat, I'm not very good at describing feelings, but in her case it was all a matter of a delusion. And, as though on purpose, Mr Stavrogin aggravated her condition; instead of laughing at her, he suddenly began treating Miss Lebyatkin with unwonted respect. Kirilov, who happened to be there (a highly original fellow, Mrs Stavrogin, and an exceedingly abrupt man; you'll meet him perhaps one day, he lives here now) – well, so this Kirilov, who as a rule never opens his mouth, suddenly got excited and, I remember, told Mr Stavrogin that by treating that woman like a marquise, he was wrecking her life completely. I may add that Mr Stavrogin had a certain respect for Kirilov. Well, what do you think he said to him? "You, Mr Kirilov," he said, "think that I'm laughing at her, but you're wrong. I do indeed respect her because she is better than any of us." And, you know, he said it in such a serious tone of voice, too. And yet during those two or three months he never really said a word to her, except *good morning* and *good-bye*. I, who was there, remember very well that in the end she went so far as to look on him almost as her fiancé who dared not "elope" with her because he had many enemies and all sorts of family troubles, or something of the sort. There was a lot of laughter about it, I can tell you! The end of it was that when Mr Stavrogin had to leave for home, he had made some provision for her upkeep, settling on her a considerable yearly allowance of, I believe, three hundred roubles, if not more. Anyway, let's say it was a silly idea of his, the whim of a prematurely tired man, or even, as Kirilov maintained, a new experiment of a man who was weary of life and who was anxious to find out to what a pass a mad cripple could be brought. "You've purposely chosen one of the most wretched human beings," Kirilov said, "a cripple, a woman doomed to suffer disgrace and blows all her life, knowing, too, that this poor woman was dying of comic love for you, and you're trying to spoof her on purpose just to find out what will come of it." But, after all, why should a man be blamed for the delusions of a crazy woman with whom, mind you, he had scarcely exchanged two sentences all the time? There are things, Mrs Stavrogin, which it is not only impossible to discuss intelligently, but which it is not even intelligent to discuss. All right, let's say it was a piece of eccentricity, but there's nothing worse one can say about it, is there? And yet they've made a whole story out of it. You see, Mrs Stavrogin, I'm not entirely unaware of what's been going on here.'

The speaker suddenly broke off, and was about to turn to Lebyatkin, but Mrs Stavrogin stopped him. She was in a state of tremendous exaltation.

'Have you finished?' she asked.

'Not yet. To complete my story I should like, if you don't object, to ask this gentleman a few questions about a certain matter. You'll see what it is in a minute, Mrs Stavrogin.'

'Not now; leave it till later, please. Just wait a moment, I beg you. Oh, how right I was to have let you speak!'

'And please consider this, Mrs Stavrogin,' Peter said with a start. 'Could Mr Stavrogin possibly have explained it all himself in answer to your question, which was perhaps a bit too categoric?'

'Oh, it was!'

'And wasn't I right in saying that in certain cases it is much easier for a third person to explain things than for the man who is interested in the affair himself?'

'Yes, yes. ... But you're mistaken about one thing, and I'm sorry to say you are still mistaken. ...'

'Oh? What is it?'

'You see – but won't you sit down, Mr Verkhovensky?'

'Oh, just as you like. I'm feeling rather tired. Thank you.'

He quickly pulled out an easy-chair, turned it so that he was sitting between Mrs Stavrogin, on one side, Mrs Drozdov at the table, on the other, while facing Mr Lebyatkin, from whom he did not take his eyes for a moment.

'You are mistaken in calling this an "eccentricity" ...'

'Oh, well, if that's all. ...'

'No, no, no; wait, please,' Mrs Stavrogin stopped him, evidently preparing herself for a long and ecstatic talk.

No sooner did Peter Verkhovensky notice that than he was all attention.

'No, that was something higher than eccentricity and, I assure you, something sacred even! A proud man, a man who has suffered humiliation early in life, a man who has reached the stage of "mockery" to which you have so aptly referred – in short, a Prince Harry, as your father so splendidly called him at the time, which would have described him perfectly if he did not resemble Hamlet even more, in my opinion, at any rate.'

'*Et vous avez raison*,' Mr Verkhovensky senior remarked impressively and with feeling.

'Thank you, my dear Mr Verkhovensky. I thank you, too, especially for your undeviating faith in Nicholas and in the greatness of his soul and calling. This faith you even strengthened in me when I was losing heart.'

'*Chère, chère* ...' Mr Verkhovensky was about to step forward, but checked himself in time, having realized that it was dangerous to interrupt.

'And if there had always been near Nicholas,' Mrs Stavrogin was almost intoning now, 'some gentle Horatio, great in his humility – another beautiful expression of yours, my dear Mr Verkhovensky – he might have long ago been saved from the sad and sudden "demon of irony" who has tormented him all his life. (The Demon of Irony is another wonderful expression of yours, my dear Mr Verkhovensky.) But Nicholas has never had a Horatio, or an Ophelia. He only had a mother, and what can a mother do alone and in such circumstances, too? Do you know, Mr Verkhovensky' – she turned to Peter – 'I can quite well understand how a man like Nicholas could frequent even such filthy slums as those you have told us about. I can see so clearly now that "mockery" of life (what a wonderfully apt expression of yours!), that insatiable desire for contrast, that gloomy background of the picture against which he appears like a diamond, according to your comparison, Mr Verkhovensky. And then one day he meets there a human being who is ill-treated by everybody, a cripple, half insane, but at the same time one who is perhaps filled with the most noble sentiments! ...'

'Well, yes, I suppose so. ...'

'And after that don't you understand that he is not laughing at her like the rest. Oh, you people! You can't understand that he is protecting her against those who might do her wrong, that he is treating her with respect like a "marquise" (this Kirilov probably has a deep understanding of people, though he did not understand Nicholas!). If you like, it was probably just this contrast that caused the trouble; if the unfortunate woman had been in a different environment she'd probably never have been brought to such a state of frenzied delusion. A woman, only a woman can understand it, my dear Peter Verkhovensky, and what a pity it is that you – I mean, not that you are not a woman, but, at any rate, that you are not one for once to understand!'

'What you mean is that the worse things are, the better it is – I quite understand, I quite understand, Mrs Stavrogin. It's the sort of thing we find in religion: the harder a man finds life, or the more downtrodden and the poorer the people are, the more stubbornly they dream of their heavenly rewards, and if a hundred thousand priests also invoke the same thing, inflaming their dream and building on it, then – oh, I understand you, Mrs Stavrogin, don't you worry.'

'Well, it's not exactly what I meant; but tell me, should Nicholas have laughed to dispel that delusion in that unhappy organism ...' (Why Mrs Stavrogin used the word organism, I could not understand) '... should he have laughed at her and treated her as the other clerks? Do you really not see the lofty feeling of compassion, the noble thrill of the whole organism with which Nicholas sternly answered Kirilov: "I do not laugh at her." Oh, what a lofty, what a sacred answer!'

'*Sublime*,' Mr Verkhovensky senior murmured.

'And please note that he's not at all so rich as you think. It is I who am rich, and not he, and he took practically nothing from me at that time.'

'I understand, I understand it all, Mrs Stavrogin,' said Peter Verkhovensky, with rather an impatient movement.

'Oh, it's my character! I recognize myself in Nicholas. I recognize that youthfulness, that tendency towards dark and stormy impulses. And if we ever get to know one another better, Mr Verkhovensky – and for my part I sincerely wish it, particularly as I am already so much indebted to you – you will then perhaps understand. ...'

'Oh, believe me, I wish it, too, madam,' Peter Verkhovensky muttered abruptly.

'You will understand then the impulse which, because of the blindness of your unselfish feelings, makes you take up a man who may be unworthy of you in every respect, a man who does not in the least understand you, who is ready to torture you at every opportunity; and in spite of everything make him all of a sudden into a sort of ideal, into your dream. To concentrate all your hopes on him, worship him, love him all your life absolutely without knowing why – perhaps just because he is unworthy of it. ... Oh, how I've suffered all my life, my dear Peter Verkhovensky!'

Mr Verkhovensky senior, with a pained look on his face, tried to catch my eye, but I avoided him in time.

'... And only recently, quite recently – oh, how unfair I've been to Nicholas! You won't believe me, but they have been worrying me on all sides, all of them, all – my enemies, my friends, all sorts of stupid, loathsome people; my friends perhaps more than my enemies. When they sent me the first contemptible anonymous letter, you won't believe it, Mr Peter Verkhovensky, but I hadn't contempt enough left in me to answer all that wickedness. Never, never shall I forgive myself for my lack of spirit!'

'I've heard something about the anonymous letters here,' said Peter Verkhovensky, coming suddenly to life, 'and I shall find those who wrote them, don't you worry!'

'But you can't imagine the sort of intrigues that have been started here! They have driven even our poor Mrs Drozdov to distraction – and what has she to do with it? Perhaps, my dear Praskovya, I was rather unfair to you to-day,' she added in a generous outburst of tender emotion, though not without a certain triumphant irony.

'Oh, I shouldn't worry about that, my dear,' Mrs Drozdov murmured reluctantly. 'If you ask me, we ought to put an end to all this. ... There's been too much talk about it. ...' And again she glanced timidly at Lisa, but Lisa was looking at Peter Verkhovensky.

'And that poor, that unfortunate creature, that insane woman, who had lost everything but only kept her heart, I am now determined to adopt,' Mrs Stavrogin suddenly cried. 'It is a sacred duty that I intend to fulfil. From this day I shall take her under my protection!'

'And that would be even a very good thing in a certain sense,' Peter cried, coming entirely to life. 'I'm sorry, but I haven't finished yet. It is the question of her protection I want to discuss. You see, after Mr Stavrogin had gone at the time (I'm beginning from where I left off, Mrs Stavrogin), this gentleman here, this same Mr Lebyatkin, immediately took it into his head that he had the right to do anything he liked with the allowance provided for his sister, with the whole of it; and he did. I don't know exactly how it had been arranged at the time by Mr Stavrogin, but a year later, when he was abroad, he got to know what was happening, and was forced to make other arrangements. Again I don't know the details, but I do know that the charming young lady was placed in some remote convent, in very comfortable surroundings, but under friendly supervision. You see what I mean, don't you? Well, what do you think Mr Lebyatkin decided to do? First of all he did his utmost to find out where his source of income – that is, his sister – had been hidden. Only a short time ago he attained his object, took her away from the convent, having asserted some sort of right over her, and brought her straight to this town. Here he does not feed her; he beats her, bullies her, and after getting a considerable sum of money from Mr Stavrogin in some way, he at once takes to drink and, instead of showing his gratitude, finishes up by sending an arrogant challenge to Mr Stavrogin, making all sorts of absurd demands and threatening to issue a summons against him if he does not pay the allowance directly to him. In this way he takes Mr Stavrogin's voluntary gift for an enforced tribute – how do you like that? Mr Lebyatkin, is *everything* I've said just now true?'

The Captain, who had been standing silently and with lowered eyes, took two quick steps forward and turned purple.

'You have treated me cruelly, sir,' he exclaimed with abrupt emphasis.

'How do you mean – cruelly, and why? But, if you don't mind, we shall talk of cruelty or kindness later; now I must ask you just to answer my first question: is *everything* I've said true or not? If you find that it isn't true, you'd better let us hear your statement at once.'

'I – you know yourself, sir –' the Captain muttered, but he broke off and fell silent.

I ought to explain that Peter Verkhovensky was sitting in an armchair with his legs crossed, while the Captain was standing before him in a most respectful pose.

Mr Lebyatkin's hesitations did not apparently please Peter Verkhovensky: his face was distorted for a moment by a spasm of anger.

'You're not by any chance about to make some statement, are you?' he said, looking meaningfully at the Captain. 'In that case please do – we're waiting.'

'You know yourself, sir, that I can't make any statement.'

'I don't know it. In fact, it's the first I've heard of it. Why can't you make any statement?'

The Captain was silent, his eyes fixed on the ground.

'Permit me to go, sir,' he said firmly.

'But not before you give us some answer to my first question: is *everything* I've said true?'

'It's true, sir,' Lebyatkin said in a dull voice, raising his eyes to his tormentor. Beads of perspiration broke out on his forehead.

'Is *all* of it true?'

'Yes, sir, it's all true.'

'Have you nothing to say or add? If you feel that we've been unjust, say so: protest, speak up if you're dissatisfied.'

'No, sir, there's nothing.'

'Have you been threatening Mr Stavrogin lately?'

'That – that – that was more drink than anything, sir.' He suddenly raised his head. 'Sir, if family honour and unmerited disgrace cry out among men, is then – is then a man to blame?' he roared again, suddenly forgetting himself.

'And are you sober now, Mr Lebyatkin?' Peter Verkhovensky looked piercingly at him.

'Yes, sir, I'm – sober.'

'What do you mean by family honour and unmerited disgrace, sir?'

'I wasn't talking about anybody, I didn't have anybody in mind – I was merely talking to myself,' the Captain said, breaking down again.

'It seems you were very offended by the expressions I used about you and your conduct, weren't you? You're very touchy, Mr Lebyatkin. But, mind, I haven't even begun to discuss your conduct in its real sense. I shall begin discussing it, that may very well happen, but I haven't begun yet – not in its *real* sense.'

Lebyatkin gave a start and stared wildly at Peter Verkhovensky.

'Sir, I'm only just beginning to wake up.'

'I see! And was it I who woke you up?'

'Yes, sir, it was you who woke me up. I have been asleep for four years under a lowering sky. May I go now, sir?'

'You may now, unless Mrs Stavrogin finds it necessary –'

But Mrs Stavrogin waved her hands, dismissing him.

The Captain bowed, took two steps towards the door, stopped suddenly, put his hand to his heart, tried to say something, did not say it, and rushed hurriedly out of the room. But in the doorway he knocked against Stavrogin, who quickly stepped aside. The Captain somehow suddenly cowered before him and stopped dead in his tracks without taking his eyes off him, like a rabbit in front of a boa-constrictor. After a moment's pause, Stavrogin pushed him gently aside with his hand and walked into the drawing-room.

7

He looked cheerful and composed. Perhaps something very nice had just happened to him, something we still knew nothing about. He seemed, indeed, to be particularly pleased with something.

'Will you forgive me, Nicholas?' Mrs Stavrogin could not forbear asking as she got up hastily to meet him.

But Nicholas just laughed.

'Just as I thought!' he cried good-humouredly and jokingly. 'I see that you know everything already. After I had gone out of this room I could not help wondering in the carriage whether I shouldn't really have told you my little adventure, for my going off like that was certainly strange. But when I remembered that I had left Peter with you I stopped worrying.'

As he spoke, he threw a quick glance round the room.

'Mr Verkhovensky told us an old Petersburg interlude from the life of a whimsical fellow,' Mrs Stavrogin interposed ecstatically. 'A mad, wayward fellow, but one whose feelings were always lofty, one who was always chivalrous and noble ...'

'Chivalrous? Good Lord, have you really got as far as that?' Nicholas said, laughing. 'However, I'm very grateful to Peter for being in such haste this time.' (He exchanged a quick glance with Peter.) 'You ought to know, Mother, that Peter is a universal peacemaker. That's his role in life, his hobby, his illness, and I should like to recommend him to you especially as such. I can imagine the sort of tale he dashed off to you here. He always, as it were, scribbles away when telling you something: there's a regular Record Office in his head. And, please, remember that being a realist he cannot tell a lie and that he puts truth far above his own interests.' (As he said this, he was still looking round the room.) 'You can, therefore, clearly see, Mother, that it is not you who should ask me for forgiveness, and if there is a streak of madness in this affair, it is I who am responsible for it, which, of course, means that, when all is said and done, it is I who am mad – for after all I must keep up my reputation here.'

At this point he embraced his mother tenderly.

'At all events, you have heard everything now and the whole business is over and done with, so that there's no need to discuss it any more,' he added, and a sort of firm, dry note crept into his voice.

Mrs Stavrogin understood that note, but her exaltation did not pass away; quite the contrary, in fact.

'I didn't expect you for another month, Nicholas!'

'I'll explain everything to you, of course, Mother, but now –'

And he went across to Mrs Drozdov.

But that lady scarcely turned her head to him, in spite of the fact that she had been stunned by his sudden appearance half an hour ago. She had fresh worries now: from the very moment the Captain had walked out of the room and collided with Stavrogin in the doorway, Lisa had suddenly started laughing, at first quietly and intermittently, then her laughter grew more uncontrollable, louder and more audible. She became red in the face. The contrast with her recent gloomy expression was quite striking. While Stavrogin was talking to his mother, she motioned twice to Mr Drozdov to come up to her, as though wishing to whisper something to him; but the moment he bent over her, she burst out laughing. It looked as though she were laughing at poor Mr Drozdov. She did, however, try to control herself, and put her handkerchief to her lips. Stavrogin turned to greet her with a most innocent and good-humoured air.

'Please, excuse me,' she replied, speaking very rapidly, 'you – you have, of course, met Mr Drozdov. Goodness, how inexcusably tall you are, Maurice!'

And again laughter. Mr Drozdov was tall, but not at all inexcusably so.

'Have you – been here long?' she murmured, again restraining herself and even looking embarrassed, but with flashing eyes.

'Oh, over two hours,' replied Nicholas, scrutinizing her intently.

I must explain that he was unusually reserved and courteous, but apart from his courtesy he looked absolutely indifferent, even bored.

'And where are you going to stay?'

'Here.'

Mrs Stavrogin was also observing Lisa, but she was suddenly struck by an idea.

'But where have you been all this time, Nicholas, for over the last two hours?' she asked, going up to him. 'The train arrives at ten o'clock.'

'I first took Peter to see Kirilov. I met Peter at Matveyeva' (three stations before our town) 'and we travelled together in the same compartment.'

'I had been waiting for the train at Matveyeva since daybreak,' Peter Verkhovensky interposed. 'Our back carriages were derailed during the night. I nearly broke my legs.'

'Broke your legs!' Lisa cried. 'Mummy, and we wanted to go to Matveyeva last week, so we, too, might have broken our legs!'

'Merciful heavens!' Mrs Drozdov cried, crossing herself.

'Mummy, Mummy, darling Mummy, you mustn't be frightened if I really break both legs. It may really happen to me. You say yourself that I gallop like mad every day. Will you take me out for walks when I'm lame, Maurice?' She burst out laughing again. 'If that should happen, I won't allow anyone to take me out except you. You need have no doubt about that. But, suppose I break only one leg. Do be a darling and say that you'll consider it a great pleasure.'

'A pleasure to have only one leg?' Mr Drozdov said, frowning gravely.

'But you'll be able to take me out, only you and no one else!'

'You'll be taking me out even then, Lisa,' Mr Drozdov growled even more gravely.

'Goodness, do you realize that he has just been trying to make a joke?' Lisa cried almost in a panic. 'Don't you ever dare do anything of the kind, Maurice! But, really, what an awful egoist you are! I do think that, to your credit, you're slandering yourself. I know that, on the contrary, you'll be telling me from morning till night that without a leg I've become much more fascinating There's one thing, though, that can't be helped, I'm afraid: you're so awfully tall, and without a leg I shall be ever so small: how will you manage to take me on your arm, I wonder. No, we shall certainly be no match then!'

And she went off into a nervous fit of laughing. Her jokes and conjectures fell flat, but she was obviously not after glory.

'Hysterics!' Peter whispered to me. 'We'll have to get a glass of water quick!'

He was right. A minute later everybody was fussing round her and a glass of water was brought. Lisa kept embracing her darling mummy, kissing her warmly, weeping on her shoulder, and almost at the same moment throwing back her head and gazing intently at her face, she burst out laughing again. Mrs Stavrogin quickly took both of them off to her rooms, going out by the same door by which Dasha had come in earlier. But they were not away long, not more than four minutes …

I'm trying now to remember every detail of those last few moments of that memorable morning. I remember that when we were left without the ladies (except only Dasha, who had not stirred from her seat), Stavrogin went up to every one of us and exchanged greetings with each one except Shatov, who remained sitting in his corner, his head lowered more than ever. Mr Verkhovensky began making some rather witty remarks to Stavrogin, but the latter quickly went up to Dasha. On the way, however, he was intercepted by Peter Verkhovensky, who dragged him off almost by force to the window, where he began whispering something very rapidly to him, evidently something very important, to judge by the expression on his face and the gestures which accompanied his whispering. But Stavrogin listened to him very languidly and absent-mindedly, with his official smile, and in the end even impatiently, and all the time he seemed to be trying to get away. He left the window just as our ladies returned. Mrs Stavrogin made Lisa sit down in her old place, telling her that they must wait and rest for at least another ten minutes and that fresh air would scarcely be good for her strained nerves. She certainly was putting herself out a little too much in looking after Lisa, and she sat down beside her herself. Peter, who was now free, immediately rushed up to them and started a rapid and gay conversation. It was then that Stavrogin at last went up to Dasha with his unhurried step. Dasha was all in a quiver at his approach and jumped up quickly with unconcealed embarrassment and blushing all over.

'I believe I ought to congratulate you – or not yet?' he said, with a rather peculiar expression on his face.

Dasha said something in reply, but I could not catch her words.

'I'm sorry if I'm being indiscreet,' he said, raising his voice, 'but you know that I was expressly informed about it. Did you know?'

'Yes, I know that you were expressly informed.'

'I hope I haven't dropped a brick by my congratulations,' he laughed, 'and if Mr Verkhovensky –'

'What on? What have you to be congratulated on?' Peter suddenly rushed up to them. 'What have we to congratulate you on, Miss Shatov? Why, not on that, surely? Your blushes tell me that I've guessed right. And, indeed, what else does one congratulate our fair and virtuous maidens on? And what congratulations mostly bring a blush to their cheeks? Well, accept my congratulations, too, if I'm right in my guess, that is. And pay up! You remember we had a bet in Switzerland that you would never get married, don't you? Good heavens, talking of Switzerland – what am I thinking of? You know that's really what I came for, and I almost forgot. Tell me,' he turned quickly to his father, 'when are you going to Switzerland?'

'I – to Switzerland?' Mr Verkhovensky asked, looking astonished and confused.

'Why? Aren't you going? But you are getting married, aren't you? Didn't you write?'

'*Pierre!*' cried Mr Verkhovensky.

'What do you mean – Pierre? You see, I don't mind telling you, if it'll please you, that I've come flying here to let you know that I'm not at all against it, since you insisted on having my opinion as soon as possible. But if,' he rattled on, 'you have to be "saved", as you wrote and implored me in the same letter, then I am of course at your service again. Is it true that he is getting married, Mrs Stavrogin?' He quickly turned to that lady. 'I hope I'm not being indiscreet. He wrote me himself that the whole town knew about it and that all are congratulating him, so that to avoid them he only goes out at night. I have his letter in my pocket. But would you believe it, Mrs Stavrogin, I simply can't make head or tail of it! Just tell me one thing, sir' – he turned to his father – 'have I to congratulate you or to "save" you? I know it sounds incredible, but in one line he writes that he is the happiest man in the world, and in the next that he is plunged in the most profound despair. To begin with, he asks me to forgive him. Well, I suppose he's true to type there, but all the same I must say this: just imagine, the man has only seen me twice in his life, and that, too, by the sheerest accident, and now that he is getting married for the third time, he suddenly takes it into his head that by his marriage he is violating some sort of parental obligations towards me, he implores me a thousand miles away not to be angry with him and to grant him my permission! Now, please don't be offended, sir. I dare say it's typical of your age. I'm broad-minded and I don't blame you, and let us even assume that it does you honour, etc., etc. But, again, the trouble is, you see, that I can't understand what the chief trouble is about. There is something here about some "sins in Switzerland". I'm getting married, he writes, because of some sort of sins or because of another man's sins, or whatever it is – in short, "sins". The girl, he says, is a real treasure, but, of course, he is "unworthy" of her – that's his style, I suppose. But apparently because of those sins or circumstances, he is forced to lead her to the altar and go to Switzerland. Therefore, leave everything and come at once to save me. Can you make anything of it? However – however, I can see from the expression on your faces,' he went on, turning round with the letter in his hand and scrutinizing every face in the room with an innocent smile – 'I can see that, as usual, I've dropped a brick – at least, I believe I have – as a result of my foolish frankness or, as Mr Stavrogin says, by being too precipitate. You see, sir' – he turned to his father again – 'I thought that I was among friends here, among your friends, sir, your friends. For I'm really a stranger in this company, and I see – I see that all of you know something and that I'm the only one who does not know that something.'

He still went on looking round the room.

'So Mr Verkhovensky wrote to you that he was getting married for the sins another man had committed in Switzerland and that you were to fly here to "save" him – in those very words?' Mrs Stavrogin said, going up to him, yellow with rage, with her face distorted and her lips twitching.

'I mean to say, you see, if there is something here I haven't understood,' Peter said, looking as though he were alarmed and talking more rapidly than ever, 'then, of course, it's entirely his fault for writing like that. Here's his letter. You see, Mrs Stavrogin, there was simply an endless and uninterrupted succession of letters, and during the last two or three months one letter followed another, and I must admit that in the end I sometimes did not read through them. You must forgive me, old boy, for my stupid admission; but come, be frank, admit that though addressing them to me, you wrote them more for posterity, so that it really doesn't make any difference to you. Please, please, don't be offended. After all, we are blood relations, you know! But this letter, Mrs Stavrogin, this letter I did read through. These "sins", madam, these "sins of another man" – must be some little sins of our own, and I bet anything you like most innocent ones at that, though they made us suddenly start this mare's nest with its undercurrent of self-sacrificing zeal – it was, indeed, this self-sacrificing zeal that made us start it. For, you see, our financial position is not quite as it should be, and we can't very well keep it a secret any longer. We have, you know, a weakness for cards – but, I'm sorry, perhaps I ought not to have said it – that's quite beside the point – I'm afraid I talk too much. But I do assure you, Mrs Stavrogin, he did frighten me and I was really half ready to "save" him. After all, I feel rather ashamed myself. Why should I be holding a knife to his throat? I'm not such a heartless creditor, am I? He writes something here of a dowry – but, look here, old boy, you're not really getting married, are you? That's just like you – talk nineteen to the dozen, but more for the sake of hearing yourself talk. ... Oh dear, I'm sure, Mrs Stavrogin, you're probably blaming me now and quite certainly for the way I talk. ...'

'On the contrary,' Mrs Stavrogin interposed maliciously, 'I can see that you've reached the end of your patience and, I daresay, for a very good reason.'

She had listened with malicious glee to all the 'truthful' outpourings of Peter Verkhovensky, who was quite obviously playing a part (what kind of a part I did not know at the time, but that he was playing a part was all too plain, and he played it rather clumsily, too).

'On the contrary,' she went on, 'I'm only too grateful to you for speaking. Without you I should never have found it out. For the first time in twenty years my eyes have been opened. Nicholas, you said just now that you, too, had been expressly informed. Was it Mr Verkhovensky who wrote to you to the same effect?'

'I did get a most innocent and – and very honourable letter from him.'

'I see that you are embarrassed and are trying to find the right words – that's enough! Mr Verkhovensky, I'd like you to do me a great favour,' she suddenly addressed him with flashing eyes. 'Be so good as to leave us at once and don't ever darken my door again!'

I must ask the reader to remember her recent 'exaltation' which had not yet passed. It is true Mr Verkhovensky, too, was not free from blame. But what really amazed me at the time was the extraordinary dignity with which he had heard Peter's 'exposures', which he had never thought of interrupting, and Mrs Stavrogin's 'excommunication'. Where did he get so much spirit from? One thing only was clear to me; namely, that he was undoubtedly deeply grieved at his first meeting with his darling Peter – that is, by the way his son had repaid him for his embraces. That was a deep and *real* grief to his heart and in his eyes, at least. There was something else that hurt him badly at that moment; namely, his own poignant realization that he had acted despicably. He admitted this to me himself afterwards very frankly. And surely a *real* genuine grief is sometimes capable of transforming even a phenomenally irresponsible person into a resolute and determined one, for a short time, at all events; and what's more, genuine grief sometimes turns even fools into wise men, also for a time, of course; that is the characteristic of such grief. And if so, what might not happen with a man like Stepan Verkhovensky? A revolution, in fact – also for a time, of course.

He bowed with dignity to Mrs Stavrogin without uttering a word (it is true, there was nothing he could do). He had meant to leave the house like that, but he could not restrain himself, and went up to Dasha. She seemed to have anticipated it, for she began speaking at once herself, almost in a panic, as though hastening to forestall him:

'Please, Mr Verkhovensky, don't say anything, for goodness sake,' she began, speaking rapidly and excitedly, with a drawn face and hastily holding out her hand to him. 'Rest assured that I still respect you as much as ever and – and that I think just as highly of you, and – and please think well of me too – Mr Verkhovensky, and I shall appreciate it very, very much.'

Mr Verkhovensky bowed very low to her.

'It's your business, Dasha,' Mrs Stavrogin said. 'You're absolutely free to do as you like. You've been so before, you are so now, and you will be so in future,' she concluded impressively.

'Good Lord, I see it all now!' Peter Verkhovensky cried, slapping himself on the forehead. 'But – but what an awful position to be in, after all this! My dear Miss Shatov, I'm frightfully sorry! Do you realize what you let me in for, old boy, eh?' he addressed his father.

'Pierre, you might speak differently to me, mightn't you, my friend?' Mr Verkhovensky said very quietly.

'Don't shout, please,' Pierre said, with a wave of his hands. 'Believe me, it's all your sick old nerves, and it won't do you a bit of good to shout. You'd better tell me why you didn't warn me, for you must have realized that I'd be the first to start talking!'

Mr Verkhovensky gave him a penetrating look.

'Pierre, do you really mean to say that you, who know so much of what is going on here, knew nothing about this business, and heard nothing about it?'

'Good Lord! What extraordinary people! So it isn't enough that you are an old baby, you must be a spiteful baby as well? Mrs Stavrogin, did you hear what he said?'

A hubbub of voices arose; but suddenly an extraordinary incident occurred which no one could have anticipated.

8

Let me first of all mention the fact that during the last two or three minutes a new sort of mood came over Lisa: she was whispering something very rapidly to her mother and to Mr Drozdov, who was bending over her. She looked worried, but at the same time determined. At last she got up from her place, evidently anxious to leave at once, and she hurried her mother, who was assisted out of the armchair by Mr Drozdov. But it seemed they were not destined to leave without seeing everything to the end.

Shatov, who had been completely forgotten by everyone in his corner (not far from Lisa) and who in all likelihood did not know himself why he was sitting there and not going away, suddenly got up from his chair and walked unhurriedly, but with resolute steps, across the room to Stavrogin, looking him straight in the face. Stavrogin noticed him approaching at a distance and smiled faintly; but when Shatov came up close to him he stopped smiling.

When Shatov stopped silently before him without taking his eyes off his face, everybody in the room suddenly became aware of it and fell silent, Peter Verkhovensky last of all; Lisa and her mother stopped in the middle of the room. So passed five seconds; the look of insolent perplexity on Stavrogin's face suddenly changed to that of anger, he knit his brows and suddenly –

And suddenly Shatov swung his long, heavy arm and, with all his might, struck him a blow in the face. Stavrogin staggered violently.

Shatov hit him in a rather special sort of way, not at all as one would expect a man to slap another man's face (if one may use such an expression), not with the palm of his hand, but with his clenched fist, and his fist was big, heavy, and bony, with red hairs and freckles. If the blow had fallen across the nose, it would have broken it. But it fell across the cheek, brushing against the left corner of the lip and the upper teeth, from which blood streamed at once.

I believe this was immediately followed by a cry, perhaps it was Mrs Stavrogin who cried out – that I can't remember because again everything in the room was plunged into dead silence. However, the whole scene did not last more than about ten seconds.

Still, a great deal happened in those ten seconds.

Let me again remind the reader that Stavrogin was one of those men who knew not the meaning of fear. At a duel he could coolly face his opponent's pistol, take aim himself, and kill with calm brutality. If anyone had slapped his face he would, I believe, not have challenged him to a duel, but killed him on the spot; he most certainly belonged to those men who would do that, and he would have killed his man knowing perfectly well what he was doing and not at all in a fit of anger. I can't help feeling, indeed, that he never knew those outbursts of blazing anger during which it is impossible to think rationally. Even during the fits of blind rage which sometimes overcame him, he was always able to retain full control of himself, and therefore to realize that he would certainly be sentenced to penal servitude for murdering a man not in a duel; nevertheless, he would certainly have killed anyone who insulted him, and without the slightest hesitation, either.

I have been carefully studying Stavrogin during the last year and, because of special circumstances, I know a great number of facts about him when writing this. I should compare him perhaps with certain gentlemen long since dead, about whom some legendary stories have been preserved in our midst. It was said, for instance, about the member of the Decembrist insurrection L—n that he knowingly looked for danger all his life, that he revelled in the sensation of it and made it into a physical necessity; that as a young man he would fight a duel for no reason at all; that in Siberia he would go hunting bears armed only with a knife, that in the Siberian forests he liked to meet escaped convicts, who, I may observe in passing, are more terrible than bears. There can be no doubt that these legendary gentlemen were capable of experiencing, and that to the highest degree, the sensation of fear, otherwise they would have led much quieter lives and the feeling of danger would not have become a physical necessity to them. What fascinated them so much was, of course, the conquest of fear. What appealed to them was the continual flush of victory and the consciousness that no one in the world could conquer them. L—n had long before his exile to Siberia struggled with hunger and laboured hard to earn a bare subsistence rather than accept his rich father's demands, which he considered unjust. His conception of struggle was therefore many-sided; and he did not esteem his steadfastness and strength of character so highly only in bear-hunts and duels.

But, nevertheless, many years have passed since then, and the nervous, tortured, and dichotomous nature of the people of our time is quite incompatible with the craving for those direct and unmixed sensations which were so sought after by some restlessly active gentlemen of the good old days. Stavrogin would perhaps have looked down on L—n, and he might even have called him a bragging bully and a coward, though it is true, he would not have said it aloud. He

would have shot his opponent dead in a duel and would have gone
hunting bears, if necessary, and would have defended himself against
a robber in a forest as successfully and as fearlessly as L—n, though
without any sensation of enjoyment, but simply from unpleasant
necessity, languidly, listlessly, and even with a feeling of boredom. So
far as malice is concerned, there has undoubtedly been an advance as
compared with L—n or even Lermontov. There was perhaps more
malice in Stavrogin than in those two put together, but his malice was
cold, calm, and, if one may put it that way, *rational*, which means that
it was the most abominable and most terrible kind of malice. I repeat
again: I thought him at the time and I still think him (now that everything is over) the sort of man who, if he received a blow in the face or
a similar insult, would have killed his adversary on the spot and without challenging him to a duel.

And yet in the present case what occurred was something quite
different and amazing.

No sooner had he regained his balance after having been almost
knocked down in so humiliating a way, and the horrible and, as it
were, wet thud of the blow in the face had scarcely died away in the
room, than he seized Shatov by the shoulders with both hands, but at
once, almost at the same moment, he snatched his hands away and
folded them behind his back. He did not utter a word, but looked at
Shatov and turned as white as a sheet. But, strangely enough, the light
in his eyes seemed to go out. Ten seconds later his eyes looked cold
and – I'm sure I'm not lying – calm. Only he was terribly pale. Of
course I don't know what was going on inside him, I merely saw him
from the outside. I can't help feeling, though, that if such a man existed who, to test his fortitude, would, for instance, seize a red-hot iron
bar and clench it in his hand, and for the next ten seconds try to overcome the unbearable pain and end up by overcoming it, then that
man, so it seems to me, would have gone through an experience similar to what Stavrogin had gone through during those ten seconds.

Shatov was the first to lower his eyes, and evidently because he was
forced to lower them. Then he turned slowly and walked out, but not
at all in the same way as he had walked up to Stavrogin. He went out
of the room quietly and, somehow, awkwardly, with his shoulders
hunched up, his head hanging, and as though he were debating something with himself. I think he was whispering something. He walked

up to the door carefully, without brushing against anything or upsetting anything; he opened the door just enough to squeeze through
it almost sideways. As he was going out, the tuft of hair standing on
end at the back of his head was particularly noticeable.

Then, before anybody had time to cry out, one fearful scream was
heard. I saw Lisa seize her mother by the shoulder and Mr Drozdov
by the arm and pull them violently two or three times in an attempt
to drag them out of the room. But she suddenly uttered a scream and
fell full length on the floor in a faint. I can still heard the thud of her
fall as her head hit the carpet.

PART TWO

1

Night

I

EIGHT DAYS PASSED. NOW THAT IT IS ALL OVER AND I AM writing this chronicle, we know what it was all about; but at the time we did not know anything, and it is only natural that all sorts of things seemed strange to us. Mr Verkhovensky and I, at any rate, at first shut ourselves up and looked on with apprehension from a distance. I did go out occasionally and, as before, brought him various pieces of news, without which he could not rest.

Needless to say, all sorts of rumours spread throughout the town, that is, about the slap in the face, Lisa's fainting fit, and the other events of that Sunday. But what we could not make out was who was responsible for divulging so quickly and so accurately all that had happened. None of those present, it seemed to us, would have thought it to their advantage or, indeed, necessary to give away the secret of what had taken place. There were no servants in the room; Lebyatkin alone might have told something, not so much out of malice, for he had left in a state of extreme fear (and fear of an enemy destroys one's malice against him), but simply out of sheer inability to keep anything to himself. But Lebyatkin and his sister had disappeared without a trace next day; he was no longer at Filippov's house, he had moved no one knew where and seemed to have vanished into thin air. Shatov, from whom I wanted to find out about Miss Lebyatkin, shut himself up in his room and, I believe, remained there during the whole of those eight days, even discontinuing his work in the town. He refused to see me. I went to see him on Tuesday and knocked at his door. I received no answer, but being convinced by unmistakable evidence that he was at home, I knocked again. Then, apparently jumping off his bed, he strode to the door and shouted to me at the top of his voice: 'Shatov is out.' With that I went away.

Mr Verkhovensky and I, not without apprehension about the boldness of our theory, but encouraging each other, at last came to the conclusion that only Peter Verkhovensky could have been responsible for spreading these rumours, though shortly afterwards he told his father himself that he was surprised to hear everybody discussing the story, especially at the club, and that the Governor and his wife seemed to know every detail of it. Another remarkable thing was that already on Monday evening I met Liputin and he knew everything to the last word, so that he certainly must have been one of the first to find out.

Many of the ladies (and some from the highest circles) showed an unusual interest in the 'mysterious cripple', as they called Mary Lebyatkin. Some of them were even anxious to see her and make her acquaintance, which shows that the people who were in such haste to hide the Lebyatkins had apparently been well advised to do so. But what everybody was particularly interested in was Lisa's fainting fit, and all 'society' showed the utmost curiosity about it, if only because it directly concerned our Governor's wife as Lisa's relative and patroness. And the things they said! The air of mystery that surrounded the affair naturally intensified the gossip: both houses were shut up; Lisa, it was said, was in bed with a high temperature; the same thing was asserted of Stavrogin, all sorts of disgusting details being added about a knocked-out tooth and a swollen cheek. It was even whispered here and there that there would soon be a murder in our town, that Stavrogin was not the sort of man to put up with an insult, but that he would kill Shatov, though in mysterious circumstances reminiscent of a Corsican vendetta. The idea was found to be rather attractive; but the majority of the young people belonging to the higher strata of our society listened to these stories with contempt and with an air of most contemptuous indifference, which was certainly not genuine. In general, the old hostility of our society to Stavrogin became strikingly evident. Even serious-minded people were eager to accuse him, though they did not know themselves of what. It was whispered that he had ruined Lisa's reputation and that they had had an affair in Switzerland. Cautious people, of course, restrained themselves, but everybody listened with relish. Other things were occasionally said, though not in public, but in private, and almost behind closed doors – strange things which I mention here merely as a warning to my readers and solely with a view to the further developments of my story. Some people, knitting their brows, said, goodness only knows on what ground, that Stavrogin had some special business in our province, that through Count K. he had entered in Petersburg into relations with some highly placed persons, that it was quite likely that he had some important Government job and had perhaps even been entrusted with some mission by someone. When sober-minded and sedate people smiled at this rumour, observing, reasonably enough, that a man who existed on public scandals and who started his public life in our town with a swollen face did not look like a Government official, they were informed in a whisper that his job was not official but rather confidential, and that in such cases the very nature of the job demanded that the man carrying it out should be as little like a Government official as possible. Such a remark produced an effect: it was a well-known fact that our rural self-governing boards were watched rather carefully in Petersburg. I repeat, these rumours lasted only a short time and disappeared without a trace, for the time being at any rate, when Stavrogin made his first public appearance; but I may add that many of these rumours were to a certain extent due to a few brief but spiteful remarks dropped, abruptly and vaguely, in the club by Artemy Gaganov, a retired captain in the Guards, who had recently returned from Petersburg. Gaganov was a very big land-owner of our province and district, a man of high Petersburg society, and the son of the late Pavel Gaganov, the greatly respected commit-tee member of our club, who over four years before had been assaulted in so extraordinarily sudden and coarse a manner, a fact I have men-tioned earlier at the beginning of my story.

It immediately became known to everyone that Mrs Lembke had made a special call on Mrs Stavrogin and that at the door she was in-formed that Mrs Stavrogin was very sorry she could not receive her because she was not well. It was also known that two days later Mrs Lembke sent to inquire after Mrs Stavrogin's health. Finally, that she began 'defending' Mrs Stavrogin everywhere, of course only in the highest sense; that is, in the vaguest possible way. She listened coldly and sternly to the hurried insinuations first made about the Sunday incident, so that in the following days they were no longer made in her presence. It was in this way that the idea generally gained ground everywhere that Mrs Lembke knew not only all about that mysterious affair, but also all its mysterious significance to the smallest detail, and she knew it not as a third person, but as one who had taken part in it. Let me add in passing that gradually she was already beginning to acquire that great influence among us which she undoubtedly craved to possess and that she was already beginning to see herself as 'surrounded' by a circle of devotees. A section of our society recognized her practical ability and tact – but of that later. Peter Verkhovensky's rapid social success, which surprised his father very much at the time, can also partly be explained as due to Mrs Lembke's patronage.

Perhaps Mr Verkhovensky and I exaggerated it a little. To begin with, Peter Verkhovensky became acquainted almost instantly with the whole town, within the first four days of his arrival. He arrived on Sunday, and on Tuesday I already saw him in a carriage with Artemy Gaganov, who, in spite of his exquisite manners, was a proud, irritable, and haughty man, and with whom, because of his character, it was very difficult to get on. Peter was also well received at the Governor's house – so much so, indeed, that he at once occupied the position of a young man who was an intimate friend of the family whose presence was always welcome. He dined there almost every day. He had first met Mrs Lembke in Switzerland, but there was really something curious about the rapidity of his success in the Governor's house. For, after all, at one time he was reputed to be a revolutionary *emigré* and, whether true or not, he did contribute to some revolutionary publications abroad and take part in congresses, which could be proved from newspaper reports, as I was one day maliciously informed by Alyosha Telyatnikov, now, alas, a retired low-grade civil servant, who had also been treated as a friend of the family in the house of our late Governor. But one fact was quite undeniable: the former revolutionary, far from being prevented from returning to his beloved country, seemed almost to have been encouraged to do so, so perhaps there was nothing in it. Liputin had whispered to me once that there were rumours that Peter Verkhovensky had fully accounted for his actions and had been pardoned on mentioning a number of names of other revolutionaries and in that way, perhaps, expiated his own transgressions, promising to be useful to his country in future. I repeated this malicious story to Mr Verkhovensky, who, though he was hardly able to think clearly, fell into deep thought. It became known later that Peter Verkhovensky had arrived in our town with excellent letters of introduction, at least he brought one to the Governor's wife from an important old lady whose husband was one of the most influential old gentlemen in Petersburg. This old lady, Mrs Lembke's godmother, mentioned in her letter that Count K. knew Peter Verkhovensky very well through Stavrogin, that he had treated him with the utmost kindness, and that he found him 'a most worthy young man in spite of his former errors.' Mrs Lembke set great store on her meagre connexions with 'society', which she kept up with so much difficulty, and was naturally pleased to receive the letter from the influential old lady; but all the same there was something rather peculiar there. She put her husband on an almost familiar footing with Peter, so that Mr Lembke even found it necessary to complain about it – but of that, too, later. I may also mention, just as a matter of interest, that Karmazinov, too, was favourably disposed to Peter and immediately invited him to go and see him. Such promptitude, coming from a man who had so high an opinion of himself, hurt Mr Verkhovensky's feelings most of all. But I interpreted it differently: in asking the nihilist to call on him, Mr Karmazinov no doubt had in view his relations with the progressive young people in Moscow and Petersburg. The great writer was most painfully afraid of the advanced Russian revolutionary youth, and imagining, in his ignorance, that the keys to Russia's future were in their hands, he ingratiated himself with them in a most humiliating way, mainly because they paid no attention to him whatever.

2

Peter Verkhovensky dropped in to see his father twice, but unfortunately I was not there at the time. He visited him for the first time on Wednesday; that is, four days after their first meeting, and that, too, on business. By the way, they had settled their difficulties over the estate somehow without anyone being aware of it. Mrs Stavrogin took it all on herself and paid everything, taking possession of the land, of course, and merely informed Mr Verkhovensky that everything had been settled, and her butler, Alexey Yegorovich, brought him some papers to sign, which he did in silence and with the utmost dignity. I may add in connexion with his dignity that I hardly recognized the old man during those days. He carried himself as he had never done before, became extraordinarily taciturn, and had not written one letter to Mrs Stavrogin since that Sunday, which seemed a miracle to me. And, what was more surprising, he had become very quiet and composed. He seemed to have come to some final and irrevocable conclusion which made him face the world with complete calm. That was clear. He had hit upon this idea, sat still and waited for something. At first, though, he was indisposed, especially on Monday; he had an attack of his gastric catarrh. Nor could he remain without any news all that time; but whenever, leaving the facts alone, I began to discuss the main point of the affair and advance some theories, he at once waved his hands at me, demanding that I should stop. But both his interviews with his darling son left a painful impression on him for all that, though they did not shake him. On the two days after those interviews he lay on the sofa, his head wrapped round in a towel soaked in vinegar; but at heart he remained absolutely calm.

Occasionally, however, he did not wave his hands at me. Sometimes, too, I could not help feeling that the mysterious determination he had acquired seemed to be failing him and that he had begun struggling with some new and tempting trend of thought. That lasted only a few moments, but I put them on record. I suspected that he dearly wished to assert himself again, to leave his seclusion, to challenge them to a fight, to unsheathe his sword for the last time.

'*Cher*, I'd have crushed them!' he cried suddenly on Thursday evening, after his second interview with his son, as he lay stretched out on the sofa with his head wrapped in a towel.

Up to that moment he had not uttered a word to me all day.

'"*Fils, fils cher*" and so on, I agree that all these phrases are nonsense, the sort of language cooks would use, but, never mind, I can see it now myself. I didn't do anything for him, I sent him off from Berlin to his aunt in Russia, a baby in arms, by post, and so on – I admit it. ... "You," he said to me, "did nothing for me; you sent me off by parcel post, and you've robbed me here." "But, you wretch," I shouted to him, "hasn't my heart been bleeding for you all my life, though I did send you away by parcel post?" *Il rit*. But I admit it, I admit it – all right, so I did send him off by parcel post,' he concluded almost in delirium.

'*Passons*,' he resumed once more five minutes later. 'I don't understand Turgenev. His Bazarov is a sort of fictitious character, it does not exist at all; they themselves were the first to repudiate him as bearing no resemblance to anyone. That Bazarov is a sort of vague mixture of Nozdryov and Byron, *c'est le mot*! Have a good look at them: they cut capers and squeal with joy like puppies in the sun. They are happy, they are the victors! What sort of Byron is that? And, besides, how trivial! What a vulgar, what an itching vanity, what a mean craving for *faire du bruit autour de son nom*, without noticing that *son nom* – Oh, what a caricature! "Good Lord!" I cried to him, "do you really mean to offer yourself to the people just as you are in the place of Christ?" *Il rit. Il rit beaucoup, il rit trop*. He has a strange sort of smile. His mother did not have a smile like that. *Il rit toujours*.'

Again there was silence.

'They're cunning; they had arranged it all beforehand on Sunday,' he suddenly blurted out.

'Oh, without a doubt,' I cried, pricking up my ears. 'It was all a conspiracy, and they didn't even bother to keep it dark, and it was so badly acted.'

'I'm not talking about that. Do you realize that they did not bother to keep it dark on purpose so that those – those whom it concerned – should notice it. Do you see that?'

'No, I don't.'

'*Tant mieux. Passons*. I'm very irritable to-day.'

'But why argue with him, sir?' I said reproachfully.

'*Je voulais convertir*. You can laugh, if you like. *Cette pauvre* auntie, *elle entendra de belles choses*. Oh, my dear fellow, would you believe it that I felt like a patriot the other day? But, then, I always knew I was a Russian – and a real Russian must always be like you and me. *Il y a là-dedans quelquechose d'aveugle et de louche*.'

'Absolutely,' I replied.

'My dear friend, the real truth always sounds improbable, do you know that? To make truth sound probable you must always mix a lie with it. People have always done so. Perhaps there's something we don't understand in that triumphant squeal? I wish there was. I wish there was.'

I said nothing. He, too, was silent for a long time.

'They say French intellect —' he suddenly babbled incoherently, as though in a fever; 'that's a lie; it has always been like that. Why libel French intellect? It's simply Russian laziness, our humiliating inability to produce an idea, our disgusting parasitism among the nations. *Ils sont simplement des paresseux*, and it has nothing to do with French intellect! Oh, the Russians ought to have been extirpated for the good of humanity, like noxious parasites! It wasn't that — it is not that at all we've been striving for. I don't understand anything. I've given up trying to understand! "But do you realize, do you realize," I cried to him, "that if you put the guillotine in the forefront, and with such enthusiasm, too, it is only because chopping off heads is the easiest thing in the world and having an idea the most difficult!" *Vous êtes des paresseux! Votre drapeau est une guénille, une impuissance.* Those carts, or how does it go there: "the rumble of the carts carrying bread to humanity", are more useful than the Sistine Madonna, or how do they put it there — *une bêtise dans ce genre.* "But do you realize," I cried to him — "do you realize that unhappiness is just as necessary to man as happiness — just as necessary!" *Il rit.* "You are delivering yourself of *bons mots*," he said, "while lying comfortably (he used a much coarser expression) on a velvet sofa." And, observe, too: our custom of a son addressing his father in familiar terms is all very well so long as both of them are good friends, but what if they keep abusing each other?'

We were again silent for a minute.

'*Cher*,' he suddenly concluded, raising himself quickly, 'do you know that this will most certainly end in something?'

'I'm quite sure it will,' I said.

'*Vous ne comprenez pas. Passons.* But — as a rule, in our world things come to nothing, but here it will end in something. I'm sure of it. I'm sure of it.'

He got up, paced the room in violent agitation, and, walking up to the sofa again, sank down on it exhausted.

On Friday morning Peter left for some place in our district and stayed there till Monday. I learned of his departure from Liputin, and it was just then, too, that it came out in the course of our conversation that the Lebyatkins, brother and sister, were living somewhere in the Gorschechnaya suburb on the other side of the river. 'I took them there myself,' added Liputin and, leaving the Lebyatkins, he suddenly informed me that Lisa was getting married to Mr Drozdov and that, though no public announcement of the engagement had been made, the engagement had taken place and the whole thing was settled. Next day I met Lisa out riding in the company of Drozdov, her first ride after her illness. She beamed at me from a distance, laughed and nodded to me in a very friendly way. I told Mr Verkhovensky about it, but he seemed only interested in the news about the Lebyatkins.

And now, having described our enigmatic situation during the eight days we knew nothing, I shall go on to describe the subsequent events of my chronicle, writing, as it were, with full knowledge and describing everything as it became known afterwards and has now been explained. I shall start with the eighth day after that Sunday; that is, with the Monday evening, for it was as a matter of fact with that evening that 'the new troubles' began.

3

It was seven o'clock in the evening. Stavrogin was sitting alone in his study, the room he had always liked, lofty, covered with rugs, and with somewhat heavy, old-fashioned furniture. He was sitting in a corner on the sofa, dressed for going out, but he did not seem to be in a hurry to go anywhere. On the table in front of him stood a lamp with a shade. The walls and corners of the large room remained in darkness. He looked pensive and absorbed, not altogether calm; his face looked tired and a little haggard. One of his cheeks was really swollen; but the rumour about a knocked-out tooth was an exaggeration. The tooth had only been loosened, but now it had grown firm again. He had also had a cut inside his upper lip; but that, too, had healed. His swelling, however, had lasted a whole week merely because he refused to see a doctor and have it lanced in time, preferring to wait till the ulcer burst of itself. He not only refused to see a doctor, but would not even allow his mother to see him, except for a moment once a day and that, too, at dusk, when it was getting dark and the lamps had not been lighted yet. He did not receive Peter Verkhovensky, either, though Peter ran over to see Mrs Stavrogin two or three times a day while he was in town. At last on Monday, returning in the morning after his three days' absence, rushing all over the town and having dinner at Mrs Lembke's, he came in the evening to see Mrs Stavrogin, who had been expecting him impatiently. The veto had been removed: Stavrogin was receiving visitors. Mrs Stavrogin herself saw Peter to the door of the study; she had long been anxious for them to meet, and Peter promised to see her after his interview with Nicholas and tell her all about it. She knocked timidly at the door of Stavrogin's study and, receiving no answer, ventured to open the door a couple of inches.

'Nicholas, may I show Peter Verkhovensky into your room?' she asked quietly and restrainedly, trying to catch sight of Stavrogin behind the lamp.

'Of course, of course we may!' Peter himself cried in a loud and cheerful voice and, opening the door with his hand, he went in.

Stavrogin had not heard the knock on the door; he only heard his mother's timid question, but had no time to answer it. Before him at that moment lay a letter he had just read and over which he was pondering deeply. He gave a start on hearing Peter's sudden exclamation and covered up the letter quickly with a paper-weight he happened to lay his hand on; but he did not entirely succeed in hiding it: a corner of the letter and almost the whole of the envelope could be clearly seen.

'I purposely shouted at the top of my voice to give you time to prepare yourself,' Peter whispered hastily, with quite remarkable ingenuousness, rushing up to the table and at once staring at the paperweight and the corner of the letter.

'And I suppose you were just in time to see me hiding the letter I had just received under the paper-weight,' Stavrogin said calmly, without stirring from his place.

'A letter? Good heavens! what do I care about your letter?' the visitor cried. 'But – the main thing is,' he whispered, turning to the door, which was already closed and nodding his head towards it.

'She never eavesdrops,' Stavrogin remarked coldly.

'I wouldn't mind if she did,' Peter immediately interposed, raising his voice cheerfully and sitting down in an easy chair. 'I have nothing against it; only I've just dropped in to have a talk with you alone. Well, at last I've succeeded in getting to see you! First of all, how are you? I can see you're all right. I suppose you'll be able to come to-morrow, won't you?'

'Perhaps.'

'Set their minds at rest at last – set mine at rest!' He gesticulated furiously with a jocose and pleasant air. 'If only you knew what a lot of nonsense I've had to tell them. But I expect you know.'

He laughed.

'I don't know everything. I've only heard from my mother that you've been rather – busy.'

'I mean I didn't tell them anything definite,' Peter suddenly bridled up, as if defending himself against a violent attack. 'You know, I put Shatov's wife into circulation; that is, the rumours about your affair with her in Paris, which of course explained the incident on Sunday – you're not angry, are you?'

'I'm sure you've done your best.'

'Well, that's exactly what I was afraid of. But, anyhow, what does "done your best" mean? It's a reproach, isn't it? However, you go straight to the point. What I feared most when coming here was that you would refuse to come straight to the point.'

'I haven't the least intention of coming straight to anything,' Stavrogin said with some irritation, but he laughed at once.

'I didn't mean that, no, no, don't misunderstand me, I didn't mean that at all!' Peter cried, waving his arms, pouring forth his words like so many peas, and immediately feeling pleased that Stavrogin was irritated. 'I shan't bother you with *our* business, especially in your present condition. I've only come to discuss Sunday's affair, and that, too, only with a view to taking the most necessary steps, for we can't go on like this. I've come with the frankest explanations, which I need more than you – I said that as a sop to your vanity, but at the same time it's quite true. I've got to be frank with you from now on.'

'Am I to assume, then, that you haven't been frank before?'

'You know that yourself. I've foxed you many times. You smile. Well, I'm glad you do, for I can use your smile as an excuse for an explanation; I purposely provoked that smile by using the word "foxed", so that you should get angry with me for daring to think that I might fox you, and that would give me the opportunity of explaining myself at once. You see, you see how frank I've become now. Well, are you going to listen?'

Stavrogin, who listened to Peter with a contemptuously calm and even ironical expression notwithstanding the latter's obvious desire to exasperate him by the insolence of his premeditated and intentionally crude naïveties, at last betrayed a certain uneasy curiosity.

'Now, please listen.' Peter began wriggling more than ever. 'When I was coming here – I mean here in general – to this town ten days ago, I made up my mind, of course, to play a certain part. I daresay it would have been best without any part at all, my own character, wouldn't it? There's nothing more cunning than my own character, for no one will believe it. To be frank, I had meant to play the part of a little fool, for a little fool is much easier than one's own character. But as a fool is after all something extreme, and as anything extreme arouses curiosity, I finally decided to be my own self. Well, sir, what is my own character like? The golden mean: neither wise nor foolish, not very gifted, and dropped from the moon, as wiseacres here say, isn't it?'

'Well, I don't know; perhaps it is,' Stavrogin said with a faint smile.

'Oh, so you agree – I'm very glad. I knew all along that that was exactly what you thought. Don't worry, don't worry; I'm not angry and I haven't at all defined my character in that way to fish for compliments: oh, no, no! You're a very gifted fellow, a very clever fellow indeed! Aha, you're smiling again! So I've slipped up again, have I? You wouldn't have said: you're a clever fellow. All right, then, I believe you: let's take it for granted. *Passons*, as my dear pater says, and, let me add parenthetically, don't be angry with me for my verbosity. By the way, there's a curious thing for you: I always talk a lot; I mean, I use a great many words and talk very fast, and yet I never somehow hit the mark. And why do I use a great many words and can't hit the mark? Well, because I don't know how to speak. Those who know how to speak well, speak briefly. So, that proves – doesn't it? – that I am not gifted. But as this gift of not being gifted is natural to me, why shouldn't I make an unnatural use of it? And, in fact, I do. It is true that on my way here I thought at first of keeping silent. But, you know, to be silent requires a great deal of talent, and therefore it doesn't suit me at all. Secondly, say what you like, but to be silent is dangerous. And so I finally decided that it would be best to talk, but just as it behoves a man without talent; that is, to talk, talk and talk, to be in a devilish hurry to prove my point and, in the end, become muddled in my proofs, so that the man listening to me should go away without knowing what exactly I was trying to prove, leave me with a shrug, or, better still, with a smile of contempt. As a result you've convinced them of your simplicity, you've bored them to tears, and you've been utterly incomprehensible – three advantages all at once! Who, I ask you, would suspect me of harbouring mysterious designs after that? Why, every man-jack of them would consider himself personally offended if anyone were to suggest that I had some mysterious designs. And, besides, I sometimes amuse them – and that's absolutely invaluable. Why, they're already quite willing to forgive me everything now because the clever fellow who had been publishing revolutionary pamphlets out there had turned out to be stupider than themselves. It is so, isn't it? I can see from your smile that you approve.'

As a matter of fact, Stavrogin did not smile at all; on the contrary, he was listening with a frown and with some impatience.

'I beg your pardon? What was it you said? Makes no difference?' Peter rattled on (Stavrogin had not said anything at all). 'Of course, you may rest assured that I'm not here at all in order to compromise you by my association with you. But I'm afraid you're terribly touchy to-day. I came running to you with a cheerful and open heart, and you seem to be making a mental note of every word I utter in order to bring it in evidence against me. I assure you I'm not going to touch on any delicate subject to-day. I give you my word, and I agree to all your conditions beforehand.'

Stavrogin was obstinately silent.

'I beg your pardon? What was it? Did you say anything? I see, I see, I seem to have made another blunder. You have never offered me any conditions, and you're not going to. I believe you. All right, don't worry. I know very well myself that it isn't worth while offering them to me. I'm right, am I not? I'm taking the words out of your mouth, and of course it's just because I'm not gifted. Not a trace of talent. You're laughing? I beg your pardon? What did you say?'

'Nothing,' Stavrogin laughed at last. 'I just remembered that I really called you a man without talent once, but you were not there at the time, so you must have been told about it. I wish you'd hurry up and get to the point.'

'But I am at the point! I'm talking about Sunday!' Peter rattled away. 'Well, what was I on Sunday? What was I on Sunday? What do you think? Why, a man too much in a hurry, a mediocrity, and I took possession of the conversation by force in the most heavy-handed fashion. But they forgave me everything, first because I dropped from the moon – that, I believe, they are all agreed on now – and, secondly because I told them a nice little story and got you all out of a mess. Isn't that so? Isn't that so?'

'That is, what you did was to tell your story in such a way as to leave a doubt in their minds and suggest some previous understanding and conspiracy, while there was no such understanding between us and I had never asked you to do anything.'

'That's right, that's right!' Peter cried as though he were really delighted. 'I did that just because I wanted you to see what was at the back of my mind. I was playing the fool chiefly because I was trying to catch you, to compromise you. What I really wanted to find out was how much you were afraid.'

'What I'd like to know is why you are so frank now?'

'Don't be angry! Don't be angry! Don't glare at me! But you're not glaring at me at all, are you? You want to know why I am so frank? Why, just because everything is different now, everything is finished and done with, covered up in sand. I've suddenly changed my ideas of you. We've come to the end of the old road; now I shall never compromise you in the old way; I shall do it in a new way now.'

'Changed your tactics, have you?'

'There are no tactics. Now you're entirely at liberty to do as you like; that is to say, if you want to you can say *yes*, and if you want to you can say *no*. There's my new tactic for you. And I shan't breathe a word about *our* business until you tell me to yourself. You are laughing? Go on, laugh. I'm laughing myself. But I'm serious now, serious, serious, though it is true – isn't it? – that a man who is in such a hurry isn't gifted at all. All right, I may not be gifted; but I'm in earnest, I'm in earnest.'

He was in fact speaking seriously, in quite a different tone of voice and in a peculiar state of excitement, so that Stavrogin gazed curiously at him.

'You say that you've changed your ideas about me?' he asked.

'I changed my ideas about you the moment you withdrew your

hands after Shatov had hit you, and please, that's enough, that's enough! No more questions. I shan't say anything more now.'

He jumped to his feet, waving his arms about, as though waving away any questions he might be asked; but as there were no questions and there was no need for him to go, he sank back into his arm-chair, a little reassured.

'Incidentally, parenthetically,' he rattled on immediately, 'some people here are saying that you're going to kill him and even taking bets about it, so that Lembke even thought of instructing the police to keep you under observation, but his wife forbade it. But enough about that – enough. I just mentioned it to let you know. By the way, one more thing: I moved the Lebyatkins to the other side of the river on the same day, you know. Did you get my note with their address?'

'I got it that day.'

'I didn't do that out of "mediocrity". I did it in all sincerity, because I wanted to be of use to you. If it showed any lack of talent, it was sincere, at any rate.'

'Oh, it's all right, I suppose. Perhaps it was the only thing to do,' Stavrogin said thoughtfully. 'Only, please, don't write any more notes to me.'

'I couldn't help it. It was only one.'

'So Liputin knows?'

'I couldn't help that, either. But Liputin, you know yourself, dare not – incidentally, it wouldn't be a bad idea to go to see our chaps, I mean, the chaps and not *ours*, or you'll think I'm to blame again. But don't worry, not immediately, but sometime. It's raining just now. I'll let them know; they'll get together and we'll go there in the evening. They're waiting with gaping mouths, like young rooks in a nest, to see what present we shall bring them. A hot-headed lot. They've got their note-books out, they're all ready for a debate. Virginsky – a cosmopolitan, Liputin a fourierist with a strong leaning towards police work; an indispensable man, let me tell you, in one resepct, but demanding strict treatment in all others; and, last but not least, the fellow with the long ears; he'll read a paper on his own system. And, you know, they are hurt that I'm treating them casually and throwing cold water over them – ha, ha! We must certainly go and see them.'

'Have you presented me to them as a sort of chief?' Stavrogin said as carelessly as possible.

Peter glanced at him quickly.

'By the way,' he said, as though he had not heard Stavrogin's question, to change the subject, 'I have been here two or three times to see your mother and have been obliged to say a great deal to her.'

'I can imagine it.'

'No, don't imagine anything. I've merely told her that you won't kill anybody and all sorts of other sweet things. And do you know? She found out the very next day that I had moved Miss Lebyatkin to the other side of the river. Did you tell her that?'

'I never thought of it.'

'I knew it wasn't you. But who except you could have told her? It would be interesting to find out.'

'Liputin, of course.'

'N-no, not Liputin,' Peter murmured, frowning. 'I shall find out who. It looks to me like Shatov. However, it's of no importance. Let's drop the subject. By the way, I was waiting all the time for your mother to ask me the main question. ... Well, yes, at first she was terribly morose, but when I arrived to-day she was beaming all over. What does that mean?'

'That was because I've given her my word to propose to Lisa within five days,' Stavrogin suddenly said with unexpected frankness.

'Oh, well – of course,' Peter murmured, as though embarrassed. 'There are rumours about her engagement, do you know? It's true, though. But you're right; she'd come running from the altar; you have only to call her. You're not angry at my saying that?'

'No, I'm not.'

'I notice that it's awfully difficult to make you angry to-day, and I'm beginning to be afraid of you. I'm terribly curious to know how you will appear to-morrow. I expect you've got lots of things ready. You're not angry with me for my saying that?'

Stavrogin said nothing at all, which completely exasperated Peter Verkhovensky.

'By the way, did you answer your mother seriously about Lisa?' he asked.

Stavrogin gave him a cold, penetrating look.

'Oh, I see; just to set her mind at rest, of course.'

'And what if I meant it?' Stavrogin asked firmly.

'Well, may the Lord bless your union, as they say in such cases. It won't harm the cause (you see, I didn't say *our* cause; you don't like the word *our*), and as for me, well, I – I'm of course at your service. You know that.'

'You think so?'

'I – I think nothing, nothing,' Peter said hurriedly, laughing, 'because I know that, so far as your private affairs are concerned, you've considered everything carefully beforehand and that whatever you do is carefully thought out. I was merely saying that I am seriously at your service, always and everywhere and in any contingency, I mean in *any* – you understand, don't you?'

Stavrogin yawned.

'I'm boring you,' Peter said, suddenly jumping to his feet, snatching his brand-new round hat, as though he were about to go.

But he remained and went on talking incessantly, though he stood up, occasionally pacing the room, slapping his knee with his hat at the exciting parts of the conversation.

'I also meant to amuse you by telling you about the Lembkes,' he cried gaily.

'No, thank you. Later, perhaps. How is Mrs Lembke, by the way?'

'What fine manners you all have, though! You care no more about how she is than about how a grey cat is, and yet you ask. Mind you, I'm all for it. She's all right, and she has an almost superstitious respect for you. She expects a lot from you, too, almost superstitiously. She doesn't say a word about the Sunday affair, and she's certain that you will come out of it with flying colours just by appearing in society. I assure you she imagines you can do anything. However, you're an enigmatic and romantic figure now, more than ever before – an extremely advantageous position. They're all agog to meet you. They were pretty warm when I went away, but now more than ever. By the way, thank you again for the letter. They're all afraid of Count K. You know, I believe they think you're a Government spy. I don't deny it – you don't mind?'

'No.'

'That's nothing. It will come in useful in the future. They have their own way of doing things here. I encourage it, of course. Mrs Lembke at the head, Gaganov too. . . . You're laughing? It's all tactics on my part; I talk nonsense and then all of a sudden I make an intelligent

remark, just when they are all looking for it. They crowd round
me and I start talking nonsense again. They have all given me up by
now. "He's a capable fellow," they say, "but he has dropped from
the moon." Lembke invites me to join the civil service to put me on
the right path. You know, I'm treating him terribly; that is, I'm compromising him, and he just glares at me. Mrs Lembke encourages it.
And, by the way, Gaganov is awfully angry with you. He said all
sorts of nasty things about you yesterday at Dukhovo. I told him the
whole truth at once; I mean, not the whole truth, of course. I spent a
whole day with him at his Dukhovo estate. A lovely estate, and an
excellent country house.'

'He isn't at Dukhovo now, is he?' Stavrogin asked suddenly, almost
jumping to his feet and leaning forward.

'No, he drove me back to town this morning; we returned together,' said Peter, as though he had never noticed Stavrogin's sudden
excitement. 'Sorry, I seem to have dropped a book.' He bent down to
pick up an expensive book of drawings he had knocked down. '*The
Women of Balzac* with illustrations.' He opened it suddenly. 'Haven't
read it. Lembke, too, writes novels.'

'Does he?' Stavrogin asked, as though he were interested.

'In Russian. In secret, of course. Mrs Lembke knows and allows it.
He's a dolt, though he has his own methods; they have it all worked
out. Such strict form, such self-restraint! I wish we had something of
the kind.'

'You're not praising the administration, are you?'

'Why, of course! It's the only thing in Russia that is natural and
that's been successful – but I won't, I won't,' he cried suddenly. 'I'm
not talking about that; not a word on so delicate a subject. However,
good-bye. You look rather green.'

'I'm feverish.'

'I can believe it. You'd better lie down. By the way, we have members of the sect of castrates in our district – an interesting people. However, about that later. Incidentally, here's another anecdote for you. On
Friday evening I was drinking with some army officers. We have three
friends among them, *vous comprenez*? They were discussing atheism,
and I need hardly say they gave short shrift to God. Squealing with
joy. By the way, Shatov maintains that the only way to start a revolution in Russia is to start with atheism. It may be true. One grey-

haired fool of a captain sat there a long time without uttering a word, then he suddenly stood up in the middle of the room and, you know, said aloud as if speaking to himself, "If there is no God, then what sort of captain am I after that?", picked up his cap, threw up his arms, and went out.'

'He expressed quite a sensible idea,' Stavrogin said, yawning for the third time.

'Did he? I didn't understand it. I meant to ask you about it. Well, what else is there? The Spigulin factory is quite interesting. They employ, as you know, five hundred workers. It's a hotbed of cholera. It hasn't been cleaned for fifteen years, and the factory hands are never paid their proper wages. The owners are millionaires. I assure you that there are a number of workers there who have quite a good idea about the *Internationale*. You're smiling, are you? You will see. Only give me just a little time! I've asked you to fix the time already, and now I ask you again, and then – but sorry, sorry; I won't, I won't. I'm not going to talk about it; don't frown. Well, good-bye. Good Lord,' he cried, coming back, 'I forgot the most important thing: I was told just now that our box had arrived from Petersburg.'

'You mean?' Stavrogin looked at him, not understanding.

'I mean your box – your things, coats, trousers, underwear, linen, have come. Is it true?'

'Yes, I was told something about it this morning.'

'I see, so can't I get it now at once?'

'Ask Alexey.'

'All right, to-morrow then – to-morrow. My new jacket, my dress-coat, and three pairs of trousers are with your things. From Charmer's, by your recommendation, you remember?'

'I hear that you are acting the gentleman here,' said Stavrogin, with a smile. 'Is it true that you're going to take riding lessons from the riding-master here?'

Peter smiled wrily.

'Look here,' he said, speaking very rapidly in a trembling and choking voice, 'look here, we'd better leave personalities out of it once and for all. You can, of course, despise me as much as you like, if it amuses you so much, but all the same I suggest it will be much better if we leave personalities out of it for a time, don't you think so?'

'Very well; I shan't do it again,' said Stavrogin.

Peter grinned, slapped his knee with his hat, shifted from one leg to the other, and assumed his former expression.

'Some people here,' he said with a laugh, 'even consider me as your rival with Lisa, so I must take care of my appearance, mustn't I? But who is supplying you with this information? Good Lord, eight o'clock exactly. I must be off. I promised to go and see your mother, but I don't think I will this time. You go to bed and you'll feel much better to-morrow. It's dark and raining outside, but I've a cab waiting for me, for it isn't quite safe at night in the streets. ... Oh, by the way, there's an escaped convict from Siberia roaming about the town and the neighbourhood, a fellow called Fedka. Used to be a serf of mine, but Father sent him to the army fifteen years ago and took money for him. Quite a remarkable personality.'

'Have you – er – talked to him?' Stavrogin asked, raising his eyes at him.

'I have. He doesn't hide from me. He's ready for anything – anything; for money, of course; but he's got convictions, too, of a sort, to be sure. Oh, yes, again by the way: if you were serious about that plan of yours – you remember, about Lisa – then let me assure you again that I, too, am ready for anything. Whatever you say, I'm entirely at your service. Why, what's the matter? What are you reaching for your stick for? Good Lord, what am I talking about? It isn't the stick at all. You know, for a moment I thought you were looking for your stick!'

Stavrogin was not looking for anything and was not saying anything either, but he got up rather suddenly, with a strange look on his face.

'If you want me to do something about Mr Gaganov,' Peter blurted out suddenly, this time quite openly indicating the paper-weight with his head, 'then you can rely on me to make all the necessary arrangements, and I'm sure you won't be able to do without my help.'

He went out suddenly without waiting for an answer, but thrust his head through the door once more.

'I'm saying this,' he cried, speaking rapidly, 'because Shatov had not the right, either, to risk his life last Sunday when he assaulted you, had he? I'd like you to make a note of that.'

He disappeared again without waiting for an answer.

4

Perhaps he thought as he disappeared behind the door that, left alone, Stavrogin would start banging on the wall with his fists, and no doubt he would have been glad to have seen it if that had been possible. But he would have been greatly mistaken: Stavrogin remained entirely composed. For about two minutes he remained standing at the table in the same attitude, apparently pondering deeply; but soon a cold, languid smile appeared on his lips. He sat down slowly in his old seat on the sofa and closed his eyes as though he were feeling exhausted. The corner of the letter was still peeping out from under the paper-weight, but he made no attempt to put it right.

Soon he was completely lost to his surroundings. Mrs Stavrogin, who had been terribly worried during the last few days, could not restrain herself and, as soon as Peter Verkhovensky, who had promised to see her but had not kept his promise, left the house, she took the risk of going to see Nicholas herself, though it was not her usual time. She was still hoping against hope that he would tell her something definite at last. She knocked quietly as before and, again receiving no answer, opened the door herself. Seeing that Nicholas was sitting unusually motionless, she cautiously walked up to the sofa with a beating heart. She seemed to be surprised that he had fallen asleep so quickly and that he could sleep while sitting so upright and motionless, so that his breathing could scarcely be perceived. His face was pale and stern, but it looked completely frozen and immobile; his brows were slightly drawn together and frowning; he certainly looked like a lifeless wax figure. She stood over him for about three minutes, hardly daring to breathe, and suddenly she was seized with panic; she tiptoed out of the room, stopped for a moment at the doorway, hurriedly made the sign of the cross over him, and went away unobserved, with a new heavy feeling and with a new anguish.

He slept a long time – over an hour – and all in that state of stupor: not one muscle on his face stirred, not the slightest movement could be observed in his whole body; his brows were knit as sternly as before. If Mrs Stavrogin had stayed in the room for another three minutes, she would most certainly not have been able to bear the overpowering sensation that lethargic immobility gave her and would have wakened him. But he suddenly opened his eyes himself, and remaining absolutely still as before, seemed to be staring inquisitively and persistently at some object in the corner of the room, though there was nothing special or new there.

At last the quiet, low chime of the large clock on the wall, striking the half-hour, resounded through the room. He turned his head to glance at it rather uneasily, but almost at the same moment the other door at the back of the room opened and the butler, Alexey Yegorovich, came in. He carried in one hand a winter overcoat, a scarf, and a hat, and in his other a silver salver with a note on it.

'Half-past nine,' he announced in a soft voice, and putting down the clothes on a chair in the corner, he held out the tray with the note, a small piece of paper which was not sealed and which had only two lines written on it in pencil.

After reading it, Stavrogin picked up a pencil from the table, scribbled a couple of words at the end of the note, and put it back on the tray.

'Take it back as soon as I leave the house, and now help me to dress,' he said, getting up from the sofa.

Noticing that he was wearing a light velvet jacket, he thought for a moment, and then told the butler to fetch him the coat he wore on more ceremonious evening visits. Having at last finished dressing and put on his hat, he locked the door through which his mother had come in, took the concealed letter from under the paper-weight, and, without uttering a word, went out into the corridor, followed by the butler. From the corridor they reached the narrow, stone back-stairs and went down to the passage which led straight into the garden. A small lantern and a big umbrella, specially placed there for the occasion, stood in the corner of the passage.

'This perpetual rain, sir, has made the streets very muddy,' the butler announced in the faint hope of deterring his master for the last time from his trip.

But Stavrogin opened his umbrella and, without a word, went into the damp and wet old garden, which was dark as a cellar. The wind howled and tossed the almost denuded tops of the trees, and the little, sand-covered paths were soggy and slippery. The butler walked along as he was, bareheaded and in his frock-coat, lighting the way three paces ahead with the lantern.

'Won't we be seen?' Stavrogin asked suddenly.

'Not from the windows, sir,' the butler replied softly and in measured tones. 'Besides, I have taken care of everything.'

'Is Mother asleep?'

'She retired to her room at exactly nine o'clock, sir, as she has been doing regularly during the last few days, and I don't think she could find out anything now. At what time shall I expect you back, sir?' he added, plucking up courage to ask the question.

'At one o'clock or half-past. Not later than two.'

'Very good, sir.'

After crossing the garden by the winding paths both of them knew so well, they came to the stone wall and there, in the farthest corner, they found a little gate, which led out into a narrow and deserted lane. The gate was almost always locked, but the old butler had the key in his hands now.

'Won't the gate creak?' Stavrogin asked again.

But the butler told him that it had been oiled the day before, 'and to-day too.' He was soaked to the skin by now. Unlocking the gate, he handed the key to Stavrogin.

'If you're going a long way, sir,' he could not resist warning his master for a second time, 'I should like to remind you to beware of the local roughs, especially in the deserted lanes, and most of all on the other side of the river.'

He was an old servant, who had looked after Stavrogin as a child, who had dandled him in his arms, a serious-minded and stern man, who was fond of reading or listening to devout works.

'Don't worry, Alexey.'

'May the Lord's blessing be upon you, sir; but only if what you do is just and righteous.'

'What did you say?' Stavrogin stopped as he was about to step into the lane.

The butler repeated his words firmly; he had never before ventured to express himself in such words to his master.

Stavrogin locked the gate, put the key in his pocket, and walked along the lane, sinking five inches into the mud with every step he took. He came out at last into a long, deserted street. He knew the town like the palm of his hand; but it was a long way to Bogoyavlenskaya Street. It was past ten o'clock when he stopped before the locked gates of Filippov's dingy house. The ground floor had been

empty since the departure of the Lebyatkins, and its windows were
shuttered, but there was a light in Shatov's attic. As there was no bell,
he began pounding on the gates with his hand. A little window was
opened, and Shatov looked out into the street; it was terribly dark and
it was difficult to make anything out; Shatov peered for some time –
over a minute.

'Is it you?' he asked suddenly.

'It's me,' replied the uninvited guest.

Shatov slammed the window, went downstairs, and opened the
gate. Stavrogin stepped over the high plank at the bottom of the gate
and, without uttering a word, passed by him straight into Kirilov's
cottage.

5

All the doors there were unlocked and not even closed. The passage
and the first two rooms were dark, but there was a light burning in
the last room where Kirilov lived and had his tea. Laughter and some
very curious cries could be heard coming from it. Stavrogin went
straight towards the lighted room, but stopped in the doorway without going in. There was tea on the table. In the middle of the room
stood the old woman, the landlord's relative, bareheaded and wearing
only a petticoat, a pair of shoes on bare feet, and a hare-skin jacket. In
her arms she held an eighteen-months-old baby with nothing on but a
shirt, its little legs bare, its cheeks flushed, and its white hair ruffled. It
had apparently just been taken out of its cradle, for there were still tears
in its eyes; but at that moment it was stretching out its little arms, clapping its hands, and laughing, as children do, with a sob in its voice.
Kirilov was bouncing a red india-rubber ball on the floor before it;
the ball bounced up to the ceiling and back again, the baby crying,
'Baw! baw!', Kirilov catching the 'baw' and giving it to the baby,
who threw it clumsily with its little hands, and Kirilov ran to pick it
up again. At last the 'baw' rolled under the cupboard. 'Baw, baw!'
shrieked the child. Kirilov lay flat on the floor and tried to reach the
'baw' with his hand from under the cupboard. Stavrogin went into
the room; the child, catching sight of him, clung to the old woman
and went off into a prolonged childish cry; the woman at once carried
it out of the room.

'Stavrogin?' said Kirilov, raising himself from the floor with the ball in his hands and not in the least surprised at the unexpected visit. 'Want any tea?'

He got up from the floor.

'Thank you, I won't refuse it, if it's hot,' said Stavrogin. 'I'm soaked to the skin.'

'Yes, it's hot – very hot, in fact,' Kirilov declared, looking pleased. 'Sit down. You're covered with mud, but it doesn't matter; I'll go over the floor with a wet floor-cloth later.'

Stavrogin made himself comfortable in a chair and drank his cup of tea almost at a gulp.

'Another cup?' asked Kirilov.

'No, thank you.'

Kirilov, who had not sat down till then, at once took a seat opposite him.

'What brought you here?' he asked.

'Business. Read this letter. It's from Gaganov. Remember I told you about it in Petersburg.'

Kirilov took the letter, read it, put it on the table, and looked expectantly at Stavrogin.

'I met this Gaganov for the first time in my life, as you know,' Stavrogin began to explain, 'a month ago in Petersburg. We came across each other two or three times in the presence of other people. Without trying to make my acquaintance and without speaking to me, he still found an opportunity of being very insolent to me. I told you about it at the time. But what you don't know is that before leaving Petersburg he sent me a letter, which, though not like this one, was extremely impertinent, and the strange thing about it was that it contained no explanation of the reason why it was written. I replied to him at once, also by letter, and told him quite frankly that he was probably angry with me for the incident with his father four years ago in the club here and that I, for my part, was quite prepared to make him every possible apology on the ground that my action was unintentional and was caused by my illness. I asked him to take this into account and accept my apologies. He did not reply and went away, and now I find him here absolutely mad with fury. Several things he has said about me in public have been repeated to me. They were extremely abusive and contained most extraordinary charges. Then to-day I received this letter, a letter the like of which I don't think anybody ever received before, full of abuse and such expressions as "your slapped face". I came here hoping that you wouldn't refuse to be my second.'

'You said a letter the like of which no one has ever received,' Kirilov observed. 'It's possible to send one in a rage; lots write 'em. Pushkin wrote to Hekern. All right, I'll come. Tell me how.'

Stavrogin explained that he wanted to settle it the next day and that he was most anxious that Kirilov should start again with offering an apology, and even with the promise of another letter of apology, but on condition that Gaganov, too, promised not to write any more letters. As for the letter he had received, he would consider it as though it had never been written.

'Too many concessions,' said Kirilov. 'He won't agree.'

'My chief idea in coming here was to find out whether you would agree to convey such terms to him.'

'I will. It's your affair. But he won't agree.'

'I know he won't agree.'

'He wants to fight. Tell me how you intend to fight.'

'You see the point is that I'd like to have it all over by to-morrow. You'll be at his place at about nine o'clock in the morning. He'll listen and won't agree, but he'll arrange a meeting between you and his seconds, let us say at eleven o'clock. You will arrange all the details with them, and about one or two o'clock we shall all meet at the appointed place. Please do your best to arrange it so. The weapons, of course, are to be pistols, and I ask you specially to arrange to fix the barriers at ten paces apart; you will then put us ten paces from the barriers, and at a given signal we start walking towards one another. Each of us must walk up to the barrier, but we have a right to fire earlier if we like, while walking. That's all, I think.'

'Ten paces between the barriers is too near,' Kirilov remarked.

'Well, make it twelve, but not more. You realize that he wants to fight in earnest, don't you? Do you know how to load a pistol?'

'I do. I've got pistols. I'll pledge my word that you've never used them. His second will do likewise about his. Two pairs of pistols, and we'll toss up, his or ours.'

'Fine.'

'Would you like to see the pistols?'

'By all means.'

Kirilov squatted down on his haunches before his trunk in the corner. It had not been unpacked, but he took out the things he wanted from it when required. He pulled out from the bottom a palm-wood box lined with red velvet and produced a pair of beautiful and very expensive pistols from it.

'I've got everything: powder, bullets, cartridges. I've also got a revolver. Wait a minute.'

He went back to his trunk and pulled out another box with a six-chambered American revolver inside it.

'You've got lots of firearms, and expensive ones, too.'

'Yes. Very.'

Kirilov, who was poor and almost destitute, though he never noticed his poverty, was displaying his precious weapons, which he must have acquired at a great sacrifice to himself, with evident pride.

'You haven't changed your mind, have you?' asked Stavrogin rather cautiously after a minute's pause.

'No,' Kirilov replied curtly, having guessed at once from Stavrogin's tone of voice what his question was about.

'When?' Stavrogin asked, more cautiously still, after a short pause.

Meanwhile Kirilov had replaced the two boxes in the trunk and resumed his seat.

'That doesn't depend on me, as you know – when they tell me to,' he muttered, as though a little troubled by the question, but at the same time with evident readiness to answer any other question.

He did not take his black, lustreless eyes off Stavrogin, looking very calmly, but also kindly and affably, at him.

'I can understand a fellow wanting to shoot himself,' Stavrogin began, frowning a little, after a long and thoughtful silence that lasted three minutes. 'I've thought of it myself sometimes, and then always some new idea occurred to me; if one were to commit some crime, I mean, something shameful, that is, something really disgraceful, something very mean and – ridiculous, so that people would remember it for a thousand years and remember it with disgust for a thousand years, and suddenly the thought came: "One blow in the temple and there would be nothing more." What would I care for people then or that they would remember it with disgust for a thousand years? Isn't that so?'

'You call that a new idea?' said Kirilov, after a moment's reflection.

'I – I don't say that – but when the idea occurred to me I felt it as quite a new idea.'

'Felt an idea?' said Kirilov. 'That's good. There are many ideas which are always there and which suddenly become new. That's true. I see a great deal now as though for the first time.'

'Let us suppose that you had lived on the moon,' Stavrogin interrupted, without listening and continuing to develop his idea. 'Let us suppose that you committed all those ridiculous and abominable crimes there. You know from here that they will laugh at you there and think of your name with disgust for a thousand years, for ever, for as long as the moon lasts. But now you are here and you're looking at the moon from here: what do you care what you've done there and that the people there will think with disgust of you for a thousand years? It's true, isn't it?'

'Don't know,' replied Kirilov. 'I've not been on the moon,' he added without any irony, but merely as a statement of fact.

'Whose child was it just now?'

'The old woman's mother-in-law came on a visit – no, her daughter-in-law – it's all the same. Three days. Lying ill with the baby. It howls at night – awful – it's the stomach. Mother's asleep; the old woman brings it here. I amuse it with the ball. The ball's from Hamburg. I bought it in Hamburg – to throw up and catch it. Strengthens the back. It's a girl.'

'Do you love children?'

'I do,' Kirilov replied, rather indifferently, however.

'In that case you must love life, too, mustn't you?'

'Yes, I love life. Why?'

'But you've made up your mind to shoot yourself.'

'What about it? Why put the two together? Life's one thing, and that's another. Life exists, but death doesn't exist at all.'

'Do you believe in a future everlasting life?'

'No, not in a future everlasting but in an everlasting life here. There are moments, you reach moments, and time comes to a sudden stop, and it will become eternal.'

'You hope to reach such a moment?'

'Yes.'

'That's hardly possible in our time,' Stavrogin said, also without the slightest irony, slowly and as though pensively. 'In the Revelation the angel swears that there will be no more time.'

'I know. That's very true. Clear and precise. When all mankind achieves happiness, there will be no more time, for there won't be any need for it. A very true thought.'

'Where will it be hidden?'

'It will not be hidden anywhere. Time is not an object, but an idea. It will be extinguished in the mind.'

'Old philosophic clichés, the same from the beginning of time,' Stavrogin muttered with an expression of mingled pity and contempt.

'The same! The same from the beginning of time and never any others!' Kirilov cried with glittering eyes, as though that idea contained a triumphant proof of all he stood for.

'I believe you're happy, aren't you, Kirilov?'

'Yes, very happy,' Kirilov replied, as though making the most ordinary reply.

'But weren't you distressed so recently? Weren't you angry with Liputin?'

'Well – I don't feel like abusing anyone now. I didn't know then that I was happy. Ever seen a leaf, a leaf from a tree?'

'I have.'

'I saw one recently, a yellow one, a little green, wilted at the edges. Blown by the wind. When I was a boy of ten I used to shut my eyes deliberately in winter and imagine a green leaf, bright green with veins on it, and the sun shining. I used to open my eyes and couldn't believe it because it was so beautiful, and I used to shut them again.'

'What's that? An allegory?'

'N–no – why? Not an allegory, just a leaf, one leaf. A leaf's good. All's good.'

'All?'

'All. Man's unhappy because he doesn't know that he's happy. Only because of that. That's all – that's all! He who finds out will become happy at once – that very minute. That mother-in-law will die, but the little girl will remain – all's good. I discovered it suddenly.'

'But what about the man who dies of hunger or the man who insults and rapes the little girl – is that good too?'

'Yes, it is. And he who blows his brains out for the child, that's good too. And he who doesn't blow his brains out, that's good too. All's good – all. It's good for all those who know that all's good. If they knew that it was good for them, then it would be good for them, and as long as they don't know that it is good for them, it will not be good for them. That's my idea in a nutshell – all of it – there isn't any other!'

'When did you find out that you were so happy?'

'Last week, on Tuesday – no, on Wednesday, because it was already Wednesday – during the night.'

'In what connexion?'

'Don't remember. It just happened. Was walking about the room – makes no difference. I stopped the clock. It was twenty-three minutes to three.'

'As a symbol of the fact that time must stop?'

Kirilov said nothing.

'They are not good,' he resumed suddenly, 'because they don't know that they are good. When they find out, they won't rape a little girl. They have to find out that they are good, for then they will all at once become good, every one of them.'

'Well, you've found that out, so I suppose you are good?'

'I am good.'

'As a matter of fact, I agree with you,' Stavrogin muttered, frowning.

'He who teaches that all are good will bring about the end of the world.'

'He who taught it was crucified.'

'He will come, and his name will be the man-god.'

'The god-man?'

'The man-god; there is a difference there.'

'It wasn't you who lighted the lamp before the icon, was it?'

'Yes, I lit it.'

'You believe in God, then?'

'The old woman likes the lamp to be lit – and she was too busy to-day,' Kirilov muttered.

'But you don't yet say prayers yourself, do you?'

'I pray to everything. Look there: a spider crawling on the wall – I look at it and I am grateful to it for crawling.'

His eyes glowed again. He kept looking steadily at Stavrogin all the time, and his look was firm and implacable. Stavrogin watched him, frowning and with a feeling that amounted to disgust, but there was no sneer in his expression.

'I hope that when I come next time you will be believing in God, too,' he said, getting up and picking up his hat.

'Why?' said Kirilov, getting up too.

'If you found out that you believed in God, you would believe in Him, but as you don't know that you believe in God, you don't believe in Him,' Stavrogin said with a laugh.

'That's not it,' said Kirilov, after thinking it over. 'You've distorted my idea. A smoking-room joke. Remember what you've meant in my life, Stavrogin.'

'Good-bye, Kirilov.'

'Come at night. When?'

'You haven't forgotten about to-morrow, have you?'

'Oh dear, I had. But don't worry, I shan't over-sleep. At nine o'clock. I know how to get up when I want to. I go to bed and say to myself: "At seven o'clock", and I wake up at seven o'clock; "At ten o'clock" – and I wake up at ten o'clock.'

'You've quite remarkable powers,' Stavrogin said, looking at his pale face.

'I'll come along and open the gate.'

'Don't trouble, Shatov will open it for me.'

'Oh, Shatov. All right, good-bye.'

6

The front door of the empty house in which Shatov lived was not locked; but having got into the passage, Stavrogin found himself in complete darkness and began groping with his hand for the stairs to the attic. Suddenly a door opened on the top landing and a light appeared. Shatov did not come out himself, but only opened his door. When Stavrogin stopped in the doorway, he saw him standing expectantly at the table in the corner.

'You will receive me on business?' he asked from the doorway.

'Come in and sit down,' replied Shatov. 'Lock the door. Wait, I'll do it myself.'

He locked the door, returned to the table, and sat down opposite

Stavrogin. He had grown thinner during this week and was now, it seemed, running a high temperature.

'You've made me ill,' he said in a soft undertone, lowering his eyes. 'Why didn't you come?'

'Were you so sure I'd come?'

'Yes. Wait a moment – I was delirious, perhaps I still am – wait a moment.'

He got up and took down something from the top of the three shelves near the wall. It was a revolver.

'One night, in delirium, I imagined that you were coming to kill me, and early next morning I spent my last penny on buying a revolver from that rogue Lyamshin; I was not going to let you get me. Then I recovered my senses. I have no ammunition. Since then it has been lying there on the shelf. One moment –'

He got up, and was about to open the ventilation window.

'Don't throw it out.' Stavrogin stopped him. 'What for? It costs money, and to-morrow people will be saying that there are revolvers lying about under Shatov's window. Put it back. So. And now sit down. Tell me, why do you seem to apologize to me for thinking that I might come to kill you? I haven't come to make peace with you now, but to discuss some important business. First of all, tell me this: am I right in thinking that you didn't strike me because of my affair with your wife?'

'So you know yourself that I didn't?' Shatov said, lowering his eyes again.

'Nor because you believed the silly story about your sister.'

'No, no, of course not! It is silly! My sister told me from the very first,' Shatov said harshly and impatiently, stamping his foot slightly.

'So that I was right and you, too, were right,' Stavrogin went on in a calm tone of voice. 'You are right: Mary Lebyatkin is my lawful wife, whom I married in Petersburg four and a half years ago. You struck me because of her, didn't you?'

Shatov, entirely taken aback, listened and said nothing.

'Yes, I guessed it, but I didn't believe it,' he muttered at last, looking strangely at Stavrogin.

'And you struck me?'

'I did it because of your fall,' Shatov muttered almost incoherently, flushing, '– because of your lie. I didn't go up to you to punish you:

when I went up to you I didn't know that I was going to hit you. I did it because you meant so much in my life. I –'

'I understand, I understand. Spare your words. I'm sorry you are feverish. My business is most important.'

'I have been waiting too long for you,' Shatov said, almost trembling all over, and got up from his chair. 'Tell me what's your business – I'll tell you too – later –'

He sat down.

'The business I've come about is of quite a different kind,' Stavrogin began, scrutinizing him with curiosity. 'Owing to certain circumstances I was compelled to choose this hour to-day to warn you that they might kill you.'

Shatov looked wildly at him.

'I know that my life may be in danger,' he said slowly, 'but how could you know about it?'

'Because I'm also one of them, like you. I'm a member of their society, just as you are.'

'You – you, too, are a member of the society?'

'I can see from your eyes that you expected everything from me except that,' Stavrogin said, smiling faintly. 'But please tell me, did you know already that an attempt was going to be made on your life?'

'The idea never occurred to me. And I don't think so even now, in spite of what you've said, though – though no one can possibly say what those fools may do!' he cried suddenly in a fury, banging the table with his fist. 'I'm not afraid of them! I've broken with them. That fellow came four times to tell me that it was possible – but,' he looked at Stavrogin, 'what exactly do you know about it?'

'Don't be alarmed; I'm not deceiving you,' Stavrogin went on rather coldly, with the expression of a man who was only doing his duty. 'You ask me what I know. I know that you became a member of the society abroad, two years ago, and at the time of the old organization, immediately before your departure for America and, it would appear, just after our last conversation, about which you wrote such a lot to me in your letter from America. By the way, I'm sorry for not having answered you by letter, but confined myself –'

'– to sending money. Wait.' Shatov stopped him, hurriedly pulling out a drawer and taking out a rainbow-coloured banknote from under the papers. 'Here, take it. It's the hundred roubles you sent me. I should have perished there without you. You would have had to wait a long time for it if it had not been for your mother: she gave me these hundred roubles nine months ago because I was so poor after my illness. But go on, please.'

He was breathless.

'In America you changed your views, and on returning to Switzerland you wanted to resign. They said nothing to you, ordered you to take over a printing-press here in Russia from someone and to keep it until you handed it over to someone who would come to you from them. I don't know all the details, but I believe that it's true on the whole, isn't it? You undertook to carry out their instructions in the hope or on condition that it would be their last demand on you and after that they would release you entirely. Whether true or not, I found it out not from them, but by chance. But what you don't seem to know even now is that those gentlemen have no intention of parting with you.'

'That's absurd!' Shatov cried at the top of his voice. 'I've told them honestly that I disagreed with them about everything! I've a right to do that, the right of conscience and thought. … I won't put up with it! There's no power on earth which could –'

'Look here, you'd better not shout,' Stavrogin said earnestly, interrupting him. 'That Verkhovensky is such a mean fellow that it wouldn't surprise me if he or a confederate of his was eavesdropping outside in your passage. Even that drunkard Lebyatkin has probably been instructed to keep an eye on you and, perhaps, you on him – am I right? You'd better tell me whether Verkhovensky has agreed to accept your arguments now or not.'

'He has. He said it was quite in order and that I had the right to –'

'Well, in that case he's deceiving you. I know that even Kirilov, who scarcely belongs to them at all, has been supplying them with information about you; and they have many agents, some of whom don't even know that they are in the service of the society. You've always been kept under observation. Peter Verkhovensky, by the way, came to settle your business once for all, and he has been fully authorized to do so – namely, to liquidate you at the first favourable opportunity as one who knows too much and who might inform the authorities. I tell you again that this is certain. And let me add that they are for some reason convinced that you are a police spy and that if you haven't informed against them as yet, you are sure to do so. Is that true?'

Shatov made a wry face at hearing such a question, uttered in such a matter-of-fact tone of voice.

'Even if I were a spy, against whom am I supposed to inform?' he said angrily, without giving a direct answer. 'No, leave me alone; to hell with me!' he cried, grasping at his original idea which, according to all the signs, seemed to agitate him more powerfully than the news of his own dangerous position. 'You, you, Stavrogin, how could you get yourself involved in such a shameful and stupid, third-rate absurdity? You are a member of their society! Is that Nicholas Stavrogin's great heroic feat?' he cried almost in despair.

He even clasped his hands, as though he could make no more bitter and melancholy discovery than that.

'I'm sorry,' Stavrogin said, looking really surprised, 'but you seem to regard me as a sort of a sun and yourself as a sort of insignificant insect compared with me. I noticed it even from the letter you sent me from America.'

'You – you know – oh, don't let's discuss me,' Shatov broke off suddenly. 'If you can explain anything about yourself, then you'd better explain it. Answer my question!' he repeated heatedly.

'With pleasure. You asked me how I could have got into such a thieves' kitchen? After what I've told you I think I owe you a little frankness in this matter. You see, strictly speaking, I don't really belong to the society at all and have never belonged to it, and I am more entitled than you are to leave them because I never joined them. On the contrary, from the very beginning I told them that I was not one of them, and if I did occasionally help them, I did it merely by accident, having nothing else to do. I took a certain part in the reorganization of the society according to the new plan, but that was all. But they have changed their minds now, and have decided that it would be dangerous to let me go, and I believe that I, too, have been sentenced.'

'Oh, it's always a death sentence with them, and it's all done on official documents, on papers with seals, signed by three men and a half. And do you really believe that they are capable of carrying it out?'

'As regards that particular point,' Stavrogin went on, looking as indifferent as ever, and speaking rather languidly, 'you're partly right and partly not. There can be no doubt that, as always in such cases, there's a lot that's fantastic about it: a handful of people exaggerates its own size and importance. I'll even go so far as to say that, in my opinion, the whole society consists only of Peter Verkhovensky, and it's merely his great modesty that makes him consider himself to be only an agent of his own society. However, the fundamental idea of it is no more silly than others of the same kind. They have connexions with the *Internationale*; they have succeeded in getting their agents in Russia, they even hit on a highly original method – but, of course, only theoretically. As for their intentions here, you must not forget that the development of our Russian organization is so obscure, and indeed almost always so unexpected that they really might try anything in this country. Verkhovensky, remember, is an obstinate fellow.'

'He's a louse, an ignoramus, an idiot who doesn't understand a thing about Russia!' Shatov shouted fiercely.

'You don't know him well enough. It's true that all of them know very little about Russia, but only a little less than you and me. And, besides, Verkhovensky is an enthusiast.'

'Verkhovensky an enthusiast?'

'Yes, indeed. There is a point where he stops being a clown and is transformed into – a madman. Let me remind you of one of your own sayings: "Do you realize how powerful one man can be?" Please don't laugh. He is quite capable of pulling a trigger. They are convinced that I, too, am a spy. All of them, inexperienced as they are in their own business, are terribly fond of accusing people of being spies.'

'But you're not afraid, are you?'

'N-no. I'm not very much afraid. But your case is quite different. I warned you so that you should bear it in mind. To my way of thinking, you needn't take it amiss that you are threatened with danger by fools. It's not a question of whether they are intelligent or not. They've raised their hands against much better men than you or me. Oh, well, it's a quarter past eleven' – he looked at his watch and got up from his chair. 'I should like to ask you another question, a question that has nothing to do with what we've been discussing.'

'For God's sake!' cried Shatov, leaping to his feet.

'You mean?' Stavrogin looked inquiringly at him.

'Do, do ask your question, for God's sake,' Shatov repeated in inexpressible agitation, 'but on condition that I ask you a question too. Please, let me – I can't – ask your question!'

Stavrogin waited a little and began.

'I understand that you've had a certain influence on Mary and that she likes to see you and listen to you. Is that so?'

'Yes – she did listen –' Shatov said, looking a little embarrassed.

'I intend to make a public announcement of my marriage to her in a short time here in town.'

'But is that possible?' Shatov whispered, almost with horror.

'How do you mean? There's no difficulty about it. The witnesses to the marriage are here. It all took place in a perfectly legal and orderly manner, and if it has not been made public till now it is only because the only two witnesses of the marriage, Kirilov and Peter Verkhovensky, and, finally, Lebyatkin himself (whom I have the pleasure of considering one of my relations now), gave their word to say nothing about it.'

'I didn't mean that. You talk so calmly about it – but go on! Listen. You were not forced into that marriage, were you?'

'No, nobody forced me into it,' said Stavrogin, smiling at Shatov's challenging haste.

'And what's all this about her baby she keeps talking about?' Shatov kept asking feverishly and disconnectedly.

'Keeps talking about her baby? Good Lord, I knew nothing about it. It's the first time I've heard of it. She never had a baby. She could not have had one: she is a virgin.'

'I see! I thought so. Listen!'

'What's the matter with you, Shatov?'

Shatov hid his face in his hands, turned away, but suddenly gripped Stavrogin by the shoulder.

'Do you know,' he cried, 'do you know at least, why you did all that and why you've made up your mind to accept such punishment now?'

'Your question is intelligent and malicious, but I'm going to surprise you, too: yes, I almost know why I got married then and why I've made up my mind to accept such a punishment, as you call it, now.'

'Let's leave it – we'll discuss it later. Let's talk about the main thing, the main thing: I waited two years for you.'

'Did you?'

'I've waited too long for you, I've been thinking of you incessantly. You're the only man who could have – I wrote to you about it from America.'

'I remember your long letter very well.'

'Too long to be read through? I agree. Six sheets of note-paper. Don't speak – don't speak! Tell me, can you spare me another ten minutes, but now, immediately? I've waited too long for you!'

'By all means, I can spare you half an hour, but no more, if that's all right.'

'But,' Shatov interposed furiously, 'on condition that you change your tone. Do you hear? I demand it, when I should really beg you. ... Do you understand what it means to demand when one should beg?'

'I understand that in this way you exalt yourself over everything that is ordinary for the sake of higher things,' Stavrogin said with a faint smile. 'I'm also sorry to say that I can't help noticing that you're feverish.'

'I ask to be treated with respect – I demand it!' shouted Shatov. 'Not respect for my personality – to hell with it! – but for something else, just for this once, just for a few words. We are two human beings and we've met in infinity – for the last time in this world. Drop your tone and speak like a human being! Speak for once in your life with a human voice. I'm not asking it for myself, but for you. Do you realize that you must forgive me for that blow in the face, if only because I presented you with the opportunity of learning how powerful you were. Again you smile your superior, disdainful smile. Oh, when will you understand me? Away with the gentleman! Please understand that I demand it – I demand it, otherwise I won't speak. I shan't for anything in the world!'

His frenzy was bordering on delirium. Stavrogin frowned and seemed to be more on his guard.

'Since I have agreed to stay for half an hour,' he said earnestly and impressively, 'when time is so precious to me, you may be sure that I mean to listen to you, at least with interest and – and I'm sure I shall hear a lot that's new from you.'

He sat down on a chair.

'Sit down!' cried Shatov and, somehow all at once, he sat down himself.

'But let me remind you,' Stavrogin once more put in, 'that I was about to ask you a great favour regarding Mary, a favour which is very important to her, at any rate.'

'Well?' Shatov frowned suddenly, like a man who has been interrupted in the most important place and who, though still looking at you, has had no time to grasp your question.

'And you did not let me finish,' Stavrogin concluded with a smile.

'Oh, that's nonsense – later, later!' Shatov waved his hand impatiently, having at last realized Stavrogin's grievance, and turned straight to his main subject.

7

'Do you know,' he began almost menacingly, leaning forward in his chair with flashing eyes and raising the fore-finger of his right hand before him (evidently without being aware of it himself) – 'do you know who are now the only "god-bearing" people on earth, destined to regenerate and save the world in the name of a new god and to whom alone the keys of life and of the new word have been vouch-safed – do you know which is that people and what is its name?'

'To judge by your manner I must needs conclude and, I suppose, without delay that it is the Russian people.'

'And you are already laughing – oh, what a tribe!' Shatov again nearly leapt to his feet.

'Calm yourself, I beg you. On the contrary, I was, as a matter of fact, expecting something of the kind.'

'Expecting something of the kind? And don't you know those words yourself?'

'I know them very well. I can see perfectly well what you are driving at. The whole of your phrase, and even the expression the "god-bearing" people is merely the sequel of the talk we had abroad over two years ago shortly before your departure for America. At least, as far as I can remember now.'

'It is entirely your phrase, and not mine. Your own, and not just the sequel of our conversation. "Our" conversation didn't take place at all; there was a teacher, uttering big words, and a pupil, who had arisen from the dead. I was that pupil and you were the teacher.'

'But, if you remember, it was after those words of mine that you joined the society, and only then left for America.'

'That's right, and I wrote to you from America about that. I wrote to you about everything. It is quite true that I could not tear myself away all at once from what I had grown so closely attached to since my childhood, on which I had lavished all the raptures of my hopes and all the tears of my hatred. It is difficult to change gods. I did not believe you then because I did not want to believe and for the last time I pinned all my hopes on that cesspool. But the seed remained and grew. Seriously, tell me seriously, did you read my letter from America to the end? Perhaps you didn't read it at all?'

'I read three pages of it: the first two pages and the last page and glanced through the middle. However, I always meant to –'

'Oh, it makes no difference! Forget it! To hell with it!' Shatov dismissed it with a wave of the hand. 'If you have gone back on those words of yours about the people, how could you have brought yourself to utter them at that time? That's what I find so unbearable now.'

'I wasn't joking with you then, either. By trying to convince you, I was perhaps more concerned about myself than about you,' Stavrogin said enigmatically.

'You were not joking! In America I lay three months on straw beside a wretched fellow, and I learnt from him that at the very time you were planting the idea of God and country in my heart, that at that very time, perhaps during those very days, you had been envenoming the heart of that poor fellow, of that maniac Kirilov. You filled him with lies and slanders and brought him to the verge of insanity. Go, look at him now – he's your creation. But you have seen him, haven't you?'

'Let me first of all point out to you that Kirilov himself has just told me that he is happy and that he is very good. Your assumption that it all happened at the same time is almost true; but what of it? I repeat, I was not deceiving either of you.'

'Are you an atheist? Are you an atheist now?'

'Yes.'

'And then?'

'Just as then.'

'When I began the conversation it was not myself I asked you to respect. A man of your intelligence ought to have understood it,' Shatov muttered indignantly.

'I did not get up at your first word, I didn't close the conversation, I did not go away from you, I still am sitting here and answering your questions and – your shouts quietly, which means that I haven't yet lost my respect for you.'

Shatov interrupted with a wave of the hand:

'Do you remember your expression that "An atheist can't be a Russian," that "An atheist at once ceases to be a Russian"? Do you remember it?'

'Oh?' Stavrogin asked, as though questioning him in turn.

'Do you ask? Have you forgotten? And yet that is one of the most precise formulations of one of the chief characteristics of the Russian spirit that you have divined. You can't have forgotten it! Let me remind you of something else you said at the same time: "A man who does not belong to the Greek Orthodox faith cannot be a Russian."'

'I expect that's a Slavophil idea.'

'No, our present-day Slavophils will have nothing to do with it. But you went even further: you believed that Roman Catholicism is not Christianity; you maintained that Rome proclaimed a Christ who yielded to the third temptation of the devil, and that, having proclaimed to the whole world that Christ could not hold out on earth without an earthly kingdom, Catholicism had thereby proclaimed the antichrist and ruined the whole Western world. It was you who pointed out that if France was in agonies, it was solely the fault of the Catholic Church, for she had rejected the stinking Roman god, but had not found another one. That was what you could say then! I remember our talks.'

'If I were a believer I should, without a doubt, repeat it even now. I did not lie, speaking as a believer,' Stavrogin said very seriously. 'But I assure you that this repetition of my old ideas makes an extremely unpleasant impression on me. Won't you stop?'

'If you were a believer?' Shatov cried, without paying the slightest attention to Stavrogin's request. 'But didn't you tell me that if it were mathematically proved to you that truth was outside Christ, you would rather remain with Christ than with truth? Did you say that? Did you?'

'But let me ask you a question too.' Stavrogin raised his voice. 'What is the object of this impatient and – ill-natured examination?'

'This examination will be over for ever and you will never be reminded of it again.'

'You still insist that we are beyond space and time.'

'Shut up!' Shatov suddenly shouted. 'I'm stupid and clumsy, but let my name perish in ridicule! Will you allow me to repeat your principal idea of that time? Oh, only a dozen lines, just the conclusion.'

'Repeat it if it is only the conclusion.'

Stavrogin was about to look at his watch, but he controlled himself and did not look.

Shatov again leaned forward in his chair, and for a fraction of a second even raised his finger again.

'Not one people,' he began, as though reading it line by line and at the same time continuing to look menacingly at Stavrogin – 'not one people has yet ordered its life in accordance with the principles of science and reason. There has never been an instance of it, except only for a moment, out of folly. Socialism is by its very nature bound to be atheistic because it has proclaimed from the very first that it is an atheistic institution and that it intends to organize itself exclusively on the principles of science and reason. Reason and science have always, to-day and from the very beginning of time, played a secondary and a subordinate part; and so they will to the end of time. Peoples are formed and moved by quite a different force, a force that dominates and exercises its authority over them, the origin of which, however, is unknown and inexplicable. That force is the force of an unquenchable desire to go on to the end and, at the same time, to deny the existence of an end. It is the force of an incessant and persistent affirmation of its existence and a denial of death. It is the spirit of life, as the Scripture says, "rivers of living water", the running dry of which is threatened in Revelation. It is the aesthetic principle, as the philosophers call it, an ethical principle, with which they identify it, the "seeking of God", as I call it much more simply. The purpose of the whole evolution of a nation, in every people and at every period of its existence, is solely the pursuit of God, their God, their very own God, and faith in Him as in the only true one. God is the synthetic personality of the whole people, taken from its beginning to its end. It has never happened that all or many peoples should have one common God, but every people has always had its own special one. The first sign of the decay of nations is when they begin to have common gods. When gods begin to be common gods, the gods die as well as the faith in them, together with the peoples themselves. The more powerful a nation, the more individual its god. There has never yet been a nation without a religion, that is to say, without the conception of good and evil. Every people has its own conception of good and evil and its own good and evil. When the conceptions of good and evil become general among many nations, then these nations begin to die out, and the very distinction between good and evil begins to get blurred and to vanish. Reason has never been able to define good and evil, or even to separate good from evil, not even approximately; on the contrary, it had always mixed them up in a most pitiful and disgraceful fashion; as for science, its solutions have always been based on brute force. This was particularly true of that half-science, that most terrible scourge of mankind, worse than pestilence, famine, or war, and quite unknown till our present century. Half-science is a despot such as has never been known before. A despot that has its own priests and slaves, a despot before whom everybody prostrates himself with love and superstitious dread, such as has been quite inconceivable till now, before whom science itself trembles and surrenders in a shameful way. These are your own words, Stavrogin, except only what I have said about half-science; that is mine, because I represent only half-science, and that's why I hate it particularly. As for your own ideas and even your own words, I haven't changed anything, not a single word.'

'I don't think so,' Stavrogin remarked cautiously. 'You accepted them ardently and you modified them ardently without being aware of it. The very fact that you reduce God to a simple attribute of nationality –'

He suddenly began watching Shatov with intensified and special attention, intent not so much on his words as on Shatov himself.

'I reduce God to the attribute of nationality?' Shatov cried. 'On the contrary, I raise the people to God. And indeed has it ever been otherwise? The people is the body of God. Every people is a people only so long as it has its own particular god and excludes all other gods in the world without any attempt at reconciliation; so long as it believes that by its own god it will conquer and banish all the other gods from the world. So all believed from the very beginning of time – all the great nations, at any rate, all who have been in any way marked out, all who have played a leading part in the affairs of mankind. It is impossible to go against the facts. The Jews lived only to await the coming of the true God, and they left the true God to the world. The Greeks deified nature and bequeathed the world their religion – that is, philosophy and art. Rome deified the people in the State and bequeathed the State to the nations. France throughout her long history was merely the embodiment and development of the idea of the Roman god, and if she at last flung her Roman god into the abyss and gave herself up to atheism, which for the time being they call socialism, it is only because atheism is still healthier than Roman Catholicism. If a great people does not believe that truth resides in it alone (in itself alone and in it exclusively), if it does not believe that it alone is able and has been chosen to raise up and save everybody by its own truth, it is at once transformed into ethnographical material, and not into a great people. A truly great people can never reconcile itself to playing second fiddle in the affairs of humanity, not even to playing an important part, but always and exclusively the chief part. If it loses that faith, it is no longer a nation. But there is only one truth, and therefore there is only one nation among all the nations that can have the true God, even though other nations may have their own particular great gods. And the only "god-bearing" people is the Russian people and – and – and do you, Stavrogin, really think me such a fool,' he suddenly shouted furiously, 'as not to be able to distinguish whether my words at this moment are silly old platitudes that have been ground in all the Moscow Slavophil mills, or an entirely new word, the last word, the only word of regeneration and resurrection and – and what do I care whether you laugh at me or not at this moment? What do I care about your complete failure to understand me, not a word, not a sound? Oh, how I despise your supercilious laughter and your expression at this minute!'

He jumped up from his place; he was positively foaming at the mouth.

'On the contrary, Shatov, on the contrary,' Stavrogin said, looking extraordinarily serious and self-possessed, without rising from his seat, 'on the contrary, your passionate words have brought back many extremely powerful recollections to my mind. In your words I recognize my own mood two years ago, and now I shall not say, as I did a short while ago, that you have exaggerated the ideas I had then. It seems to me, indeed, that they were even more exceptional and more absolute, and let me assure you for the third time that I'd very much like to confirm what you have said just now, even to the last syllable, but –'

'But you a hare?'

'Wha-at?'

'Your own disgusting expression,' Shatov said, laughing spitefully and sitting down again. '"To cook a hare – you must first catch it, to believe in God – you must have God", that, I'm told, was one of your favourite sayings in Petersburg, like Nozdryov, who tried to catch a hare by its hind legs.'

'No, what he did was to boast that he had caught it. I hope you won't mind if I, too, trouble you with a question, particularly as I am, it seems to me, fully entitled to ask it now. Tell me, have you caught your hare, or is it still running about?'

'Don't dare to ask me in such words! Use others, others!' Shatov suddenly began trembling all over.

'By all means I shall put it differently,' Stavrogin said, looking sternly at him. 'All I wanted to know is whether you believe in God yourself.'

'I believe in Russia. I believe in the Greek Orthodox Church. I – I believe in the body of Christ – I believe that the second coming will take place in Russia – I believe –' Shatov murmured in a frenzy.

'But in God? In God?'

'I – I shall believe in God.'

Not a muscle moved in Stavrogin's face. Shatov looked defiantly at him with blazing eyes, as though he wished to reduce him to ashes with his look.

'You see, I haven't told you that I don't believe at all!' he cried at last. 'I merely want to let you know that I am an unfortunate, dull book and nothing more so far, so far. ... But to hell with me! It is you, not I, who matters. I'm a man without talent, and I can only give my blood, and nothing more, like every man without talent. But to hell with my blood, too! I'm talking about you. I've been waiting here two years for you. I've been dancing naked before you for the past half-hour. You, you alone could have raised the banner!'

He did not finish what he wanted to say, and leaned, as though in despair, with his elbows against the table, his head propped up on his hands.

'Since you mention it,' Stavrogin interrupted suddenly, 'I'd like to draw your attention to something rather odd: why, do you think, is everybody so anxious to thrust a banner in my hand? Peter Verkhovensky, too, is convinced that I could have "raised their banner" – at least, that's what I'm told he said. He's got the idea that I could play the part of a Stenka Razin for them because of my "unusual aptitude for crime" – those were his very words.'

'What did you say?' asked Shatov. 'Because of your "unusual aptitude for crime"?'

'Exactly.'

'I see. And is it true,' he said, with a malicious grin, 'is it true that in Petersburg you belonged to a secret society given up to a bestial sensuality? Is it true that the Marquis de Sade could have taken lessons from you? Is it true that you enticed and debauched children? Speak, don't dare to lie!' he cried, beside himself. 'Nicholas Stavrogin cannot lie before Shatov who slapped his face! Tell me everything, and if it's true I'll kill you at once, right here, on the spot!'

'I did say it, but I didn't molest children,' said Stavrogin, but only after a pause that lasted much too long. He went pale in the face and his eyes flashed.

'But you did say it!' Shatov went on imperiously, without taking his gleaming eyes off him. 'Is it true that you maintained that you saw no distinction in beauty between some voluptuous and brutish act and any heroic exploit, even the sacrifice of life for the good of humanity? Is it true that you found the same sort of beauty and equal enjoyment in both extremes?'

'It's impossible to answer like this – I refuse to answer,' muttered Stavrogin, who could have got up and gone away if he liked, but who did not get up and go away.

'I don't know why evil is bad and good is beautiful either,' Shatov, who was still trembling all over, persisted, 'but I do know why the feeling for the distinction between them becomes blurred and is lost in such gentlemen as the Stavrogins. Do you know why you got married to that woman in so infamous and despicable a fashion? Just because the infamy and absurdity of such a marriage reached the pitch of genius! Oh, you never walk at the edge of the abyss, but precipitate yourself over it boldly, head downwards. You got married because of your passion for cruelty, because of your passion for remorse, because of your moral turpitude. It was a case of morbid hysteria. The challenge to common sense was too tempting to be resisted! Stavrogin and a wretched, mentally deficient, destitute cripple! Did you feel a sensuous thrill when you bit the Governor's ear? Did you? You idle, loafing son of a nobleman, did you?'

'You're a psychologist,' said Stavrogin, growing paler and paler, 'though you're partly mistaken about the reasons for my marriage. I wonder who could have supplied you with all this information,' he asked, smiling constrainedly. 'Not Kirilov? But he took no part in it.'

'You're turning pale, aren't you?'

'But what do you want?' Stavrogin asked, raising his voice at last. 'I've been sitting for half an hour under your lash, and the least you can do is to let me go civilly, if – if you really have no reasonable motive for treating me like that.'

'A reasonable motive?'

'Certainly. It is your duty at least to let me know your motive I've been waiting for you to do so, but all I got was frenzied spite. I must ask you to be so good as to open the gate for me.'

He got up from his chair. Shatov rushed after him furiously.

'Kiss the earth, drench it with your tears, ask forgiveness!' he cried, seizing him by the shoulder.

'But I didn't kill you – that morning, did I? I drew back my hands, didn't I?' Stavrogin said, almost with anguish, lowering his eyes.

'Come on, tell me everything! You came to warn me of danger – you've let me speak – to-morrow you intend to make a public announcement of your marriage! Do you suppose I don't see from your face that some new menacing idea has taken hold of you? Stavrogin, why am I condemned to believe in you for ever? Could I have spoken like this to anyone else? I have modesty, but I was not ashamed of my nakedness because I was speaking to Stavrogin. I was not afraid of caricaturing a great idea by my touch because Stavrogin was listening to me. ... Don't you know that I shall kiss your footprints after you have gone? I can't tear you out of my heart, Nicholas Stavrogin!'

'I'm sorry I cannot bring myself to like you, Shatov,' said Stavrogin coldly.

'I know you cannot. I know you're not lying. Listen. I can put everything right: I'll catch the hare for you.'

Stavrogin was silent.

'You're an atheist because you're a spoilt son of a gentleman, the last son of a gentleman. You've lost the distinction between good and evil because you no longer know your own people, and you won't know it at all, neither you, nor the Verkhovenskys, father and son – nor I, for I, too, am a gentleman – I, the son of your serf and footman Pashka. ... Listen, find God through work; everything is in that, or you'll vanish like rotten mildew; find God through work.'

'God through work? What kind of work?'

'Peasants' work. Go, give up your riches. Ah, you're laughing! You're afraid it might turn out to be a trick?'

But Stavrogin was not laughing.

'You think that it is possible to find God through work, and by peasants' work?' he repeated, after thinking it over, as though he'd really come across something new and serious which was worth considering. 'By the way,' he changed the subject, 'you just reminded me: do you know that I'm not rich at all, so that I haven't anything to throw away? Indeed, I'm scarcely in a position even to provide for Mary's future. And another thing: I came to ask you if you can possibly manage to see Mary in future, too, because you're the only person who can exert some influence on her poor brain. I'm saying this just in case anything should happen.'

'All right, you want me to see Mary,' Shatov said, waving one hand while he held a candle in the other. 'All right, afterwards, of course. ... Listen, go and see Tikhon.'

'Whom?'

'Tikhon. Tikhon, who used to be a bishop, but retired because of illness. He lives here in the town, on the outskirts, in the Efimevsky Borogorodsky monastery.'

'What is it all about?'

'Nothing. Lots of people go and see him. You go and see him, too. Why shouldn't you? Why not?'

'It's the first time I've heard of him and – and I've never met that sort of man. Thank you, I'll go and see him.'

'This way,' Shatov said, lighting him down the stairs. 'Here you are,' he said, flinging open the gate into the street.

'I shan't come to see you again, Shatov,' Stavrogin said quietly as he stepped through the gateway.

It was still as dark as ever and pouring with rain.

2

Night (continued)

I

HE walked all along Bogoyavlenskaya Street; at last it was downhill all the way, his feet slithered in the mud, and suddenly a wide, misty, and apparently empty expanse opened up before him – it was the river. Instead of houses there were hovels, and the street was lost in a large number of irregular lanes. For a long time Stavrogin made his way alongside the fences without going too far away from the river, but he never lost his way and scarcely thought of it. He was pre-occupied with something else and, on coming out of a deep reverie, he looked round with surprise when he found himself almost in the middle of our long, wet pontoon bridge. There was not a soul about, so that he could not help feeling strange when he suddenly heard, almost at his elbow, a familiarly obsequious but rather pleasant voice with that sweetly drawling intonation affected by our over-civilized tradesmen or the young, curly-headed shop-assistants from the shopping arcade.

'Excuse me, sir, but would you mind very much if I got under your umbrella?'

And, sure enough, a figure crept, or merely pretended to creep, under his umbrella. The tramp walked beside him, almost 'shoulder to shoulder', as soldiers put it. Slowing down, Stavrogin bent over to examine him more closely as far as it was possible in the darkness: he was a short man, looking like a tipsy artisan, and wearing rough and shabby clothes. A soaked cloth cap with its brim half torn off was perched precariously on his shaggy, curly head. He seemed a strong, spare, swarthy man with very dark hair and large eyes, which were certainly black, with a hard glitter and a yellow-ing tinge in them, like a gipsy's; that could be divined even in the pitch darkness. He was probably about forty, and he was not drunk.

'Do you know me?' asked Stavrogin.

'You're Mr Stavrogin, sir. You was pointed out to me at the railway station just as the train stopped last Sunday. Besides, I've heard a lot about you, sir, before.'

'From Mr Verkhovensky? You – you're not Fedka the Convict, are you?'

'I was baptised Fyodor, sir. I still got my mother living in these here parts. She's a very old woman now, sir, and she gets more and more bent every day; offering up prayers for me day and night, she is, sir, so that she don't waste her time, seeing as how she is so old, lying about doing nothing on the stove.'

'You're an escaped prisoner, aren't you?'

'Yes, sir, changed my occupation, I have. Gave up my books, bells, and church work because I got a life sentence and I'd have had to wait a long time to serve my sentence, sir.'

'What are you doing here?'

'Well, sir, I gets along as best I can. My uncle died in the prison here last week – been serving a sentence for counterfeiting, he has – so by way of holding a wake I threw two dozen stones at the dogs – that's all I been doing so far, sir. Besides, Mr Verkhovensky, sir, promises to get me a passport, a merchant's one, too, that'll give me the opportunity of travelling all over Russia. So, you see, sir, I've to wait till he's good enough to get it for me. He's doing me a kindness, he is, because, you see, sir, he says to me: "My dad," he says, "lost you at cards at the English club, and I," he says, "consider it an unjust act of inhumanity," he says. Won't you give me three roubles, sir, for something to warm myself?'

'So you've been waiting for me here, have you? I don't like that. By whose orders?'

'I ain't received no orders from nobody, sir. I done it just because I knows how kind-hearted you are, sir, and everybody knows that, sir. I'm on my beam end, honest I am, as you can see for yourself, sir. Last Friday I stuffed my belly full of meat pasty. Since then I ate nothing one day, fasted another, and hadn't a bite on the third. There's plenty of water in the river, to be sure, but I've drunk so much of it, sir, that there's a regular tiddler's pond in my belly. So won't you

spare something for a poor devil like me, sir? I have a lady friend waiting for me not far from here, but I daren't show her my face without
a couple of roubles in my pocket.'

'What did Mr Verkhovensky promise you from me?'

'He didn't promise nothing, sir, but only said in so many words
that I might be of some use to you, sir, if an occasion should arise. But
he didn't rightly explain what it was exactly he had in mind, for Mr
Verkhovensky, sir, seems very anxious to see whether I have the
patience of a Cossack, and he won't trust me an inch, he won't.'

'Oh? Why not?'

'Mr Verkhovensky, sir, is an astrologer and there ain't a planet he
don't know, but he, too, can make a slip like the rest of us. It's gospel
truth I'm telling you, sir, as afore God because I've heard so much
about you. Mr Verkhovensky, sir, is one thing, and you, I daresay, is
another. Once he says a man's a scoundrel, nothing will make him
change his mind: a scoundrel he'll remain. Or if he calls a man a fool,
he won't know nothing more of that man except that he's a fool. But
me, sir, I may be a fool Tuesdays and Wednesdays, but a much cleverer
man than him on Thursdays. So, you see, sir, what he knows very
well about me is that I'm in a hell of a fix about getting myself a passport – for without proper documents it ain't possible to live in Russia –
and that's why he thinks he has me in the hollow of his hand. I tell
you, sir, Mr Verkhovensky finds life very easy¹ – very easy, indeed, sir
– for once he's got a certain opinion of a man, he sticks to it. And, besides, he's a terrible miser, he is. He thinks that without his knowing
about it I shan't dare to trouble you, but I'm standing afore you just as
afore God – been waiting for you on this here bridge, sir, for three
nights, I have, in the belief that I can find my own way, quiet-like,
without him. Much better, I thinks to myself, bow to a boot than to
a bast-shoe.'

'And who told you that I was going to cross the bridge at night?'

'Well, sir, to tell the truth, I got to know about it by chance, most
through the stupidity of Captain Lebyatkin, for he can't keep his
mouth shut, he can't. So that your three roubles, sir, will just pay me
for the boring time I've had these three days and nights. As for my
clothes what got soaked, I shan't say nothing about it – I'll just grin
and bear it, sir.'

'I'm going to the left, you to the right. Here's the end of the bridge.

Listen, Fyodor, I like people to understand what I say once for all: I won't give you a penny. Don't let me see you again on the bridge or anywhere else. I have no use for you now or in future, and if you won't obey, I'll tie your hands behind your back and take you to the police. Be off!'

'Ah, well, you could have let me have something for my company, sir. Made you feel more cheerful like, I have, by walking alongside of you.'

'Away with you!'

'But do you know your way, sir? There are hundreds of turnings here – I could show you which to take, for this here town, sir, is just as if the devil himself had carried it in his basket and strewn it all over the blooming place.'

'I'll tie you up!' Stavrogin turned round to him menacingly.

'Perhaps you'll change your mind, sir. It doesn't take much to do an injury to a poor bloke like me.'

'I see you're sure of yourself!'

'I'm sure of you, sir, and not very much of myself.'

'I don't need you at all. I've told you so already.'

'But I need you, sir, that's the trouble! Well, it can't be helped. I'll wait for you on your way back, sir.'

'I give you my word of honour if I meet you I'll tie you up.'

'In that case, sir, I'd better get a belt ready for you. Good-bye, sir, and thank you for sheltering me under your umbrella. I shall be grateful to you for it to my dying day.'

He fell behind. Stavrogin reached his destination, feeling worried. This man who had dropped out of the blue was absolutely convinced that he was indispensable to him and could not wait to tell him so. People, in fact, treated him unceremoniously all round. But it was also possible that the tramp had not been altogether lying and that it was not at Peter Verkhovensky's instigation, but on his own initiative, that he hoped to obtain some employment from him; and if that was so, it certainly was most interesting.

2

The house which Stavrogin had reached stood in a deserted lane between fences, behind which kitchen gardens stretched literally to the very end of the town. It was an entirely secluded little wooden house, which had just been built and not yet lined with thin planks. The shutters of one of the windows were left open on purpose and a lighted candle was placed on the window-sill – evidently as a signal to the late visitor who was expected that night. Thirty paces away from the house Stavrogin made out on the front steps the figure of a tall man, probably the master of the house, who had come out impatiently to scan the road. He soon heard his voice which sounded impatient and rather timid.

'Is that you, sir? You, sir?'

'It's me,' Stavrogin replied, but not before he had reached the front steps, closing his umbrella.

'At last!' Captain Lebyatkin – for it was he – began stamping and fussing round him. 'Please let me take your umbrella, sir. It's very wet, sir. I'll open it and let it drip here on the floor in the corner. Come in, sir, come in.'

The door, leading from the passage into a room which was lighted by two candles, was wide open.

'If you hadn't promised to come for certain, I'd have given up waiting for you.'

'A quarter to one,' Stavrogin said, looking at his watch as he entered the room.

'And it's pouring with rain and such a prodigious distance. I'm afraid I've no watch, and all I can see from the windows are kitchen gardens, so that – er – one lags behind the times – but – er – I'm not complaining, because I haven't a right to complain, sir. I'm merely saying this because I've been eaten up with impatience all the week to – er – have it all settled at last.'

'What do you mean?'

'I mean to hear my fate, sir. Sit down, please.'

He inclined his head, pointing to a chair by a table in front of the sofa.

Stavrogin looked round; the room was tiny with a low ceiling; the furniture consisted only of the most essential things, wooden chairs and a sofa, all new, without covering or cushions, two limewood tables, one by the sofa and the other in a corner, covered with a table-cloth and laid with all sorts of things over which a spotlessly clean napkin was spread. Indeed, the whole room was apparently kept spotlessly clean. Captain Lebyatkin had not been drunk for the last eight days; his face looked bloated and yellow; his eyes darted about uneasily, curiously, and evidently puzzled. It was all too obvious that he did not know himself in what tone to speak and what line it would be most advantageous for him to take.

'As you see' – he waved his hand round the room – 'I live like the holy man Zossima. Sobriety, solitude, and poverty – the vow of the knights of old.'

'You think the knights of old took such vows?'

'Perhaps I'm mistaken. Alas, I haven't had a proper education! I've ruined everything! Believe me, sir, it was only here that I first recovered from my shameful weakness – not a glass, not a drop, sir! I have my little home, and for six whole days I've experienced the bliss of a clear conscience. Even the walls smell of resin and remind me of mother nature. And what sort of man have I been? What was I?

> At night homeless I wander,
> My tongue hanging out by day,

as the poet so felicitously puts it. But – you're soaked to the skin – won't you have some tea?'

'No, thank you.'

'The samovar has been boiling since eight o'clock, but I'm afraid it's – er – gone out now – like everything in this world. The sun, too, they say, will go out one day. However, I'll get it going again, if necessary. Agafya isn't asleep yet.'

'Tell me, Mary –'

'Is here, is here,' Lebyatkin assured him quickly in a whisper. 'Would you like to have a look at her?' he asked, pointing to the closed door of the adjoining room.

'She is not asleep?'

'No, no, good heavens, no! How could she be? On the contrary, she's been expecting you all the evening, and the moment she heard of your coming, she at once dolled herself up,' he concluded, twisting his face into an amused smile, but instantly checking himself.

'How is she in general?' Stavrogin asked, frowning.

'In general? You know that yourself, sir,' he said with a pitying shrug. 'But at the moment – at the moment, sir, she's telling her fortune by cards.'

'All right, later. First I have to settle with you.'

Stavrogin sat down on a chair.

The Captain did not dare to sit down on the sofa, but immediately pulled up another chair and bent forward, in tremulous expectation, to listen.

'What have you got there under the napkin in the corner?' Stavrogin asked, suddenly noticing it.

'That, sir?' Lebyatkin, too, turned to look. 'That's also part of your generous gifts, sir, by way of a house-warming, as it were, and taking into consideration the great distance you had to walk and your natural fatigue,' he sniggered complaisantly.

He got up from his chair and, tiptoeing to the little table in the corner, reverently and carefully lifted the napkin. Beneath it was a cold meal: ham, veal, sardines, cheese, a small green decanter, and a tall bottle of Bordeaux; everything had been laid neatly, expertly, and almost swaggeringly.

'Was it you who took the trouble to prepare it?'

'Me, sir. I got it all ready yesterday. Everything to the best of my ability. Mary, as you know, isn't very interested in these things. But the main thing is that it's all part of your own generous gifts, it's all your own, for you're the master here, and not I. I am, as it were, only your agent; for in spirit, sir, in spirit I am independent of all that. You will never rob me of this my last possession!' he concluded touchingly.

'I see. Well, won't you resume your seat?'

'I'm grateful, sir, grateful and independent!' he cried, sitting down. 'Oh, sir, so much has accumulated in my heart, that I could hardly wait for you to come. Now you've to decide my fate and the fate of that – that unfortunate woman, and then – then I shall, as in the old days, four years ago, pour out my heart to you. You did me the honour to listen to me in those days, you read my stanzas. What does it matter if they did call me your Falstaff from Shakespeare? What does that matter, I say, if you meant so much in my life! But now, sir, I'm in a state of great apprehension, and it is from you alone that I look for advice and light. Mr Verkhovensky is treating me abominably!'

Stavrogin listened with interest and scrutinized him closely. It was plain that though Captain Lebyatkin had given up drinking, his state of mind was still far from harmonious. Such confirmed drunkards always end up by becoming permanently incoherent, dazed, and, as it were, a little touched in the head and crazy, though, given the right opportunity, they will go on cheating, bluffing, and swindling almost as well as anybody else.

'I can see that you haven't changed a bit in these four years and more, Captain,' Stavrogin said in what sounded a more affable tone of voice. 'It seems it is true that the second half of a man's life is usually only made up of the habits he has amassed during the first half.'

'Grand words, sir! You solve the riddle of life!' the Captain cried, half bluffing and half really in undisguised admiration, for he was a great lover of aphorisms. 'Of all your sayings, sir, I've memorized one especially, one I heard you say in Petersburg: "One must really be a great man to be able to hold out even against common sense." Yes, sir!'

'And a fool as well.'

'Quite right, sir, and a fool as well, but you've been delivering yourself of such witty sayings all your life, while they – why, let Liputin, let Verkhovensky try to say anything of the kind! Oh, how cruelly I've been treated by Mr Verkhovensky, sir!'

'But what about yourself, Captain? How did you behave?'

'I was drunk, sir; and, besides, I have hundreds of enemies! But now, now I've turned over a new leaf and I shall renew myself like a serpent. Do you know, sir, that I'm making my will and that, in fact, I've made it already?'

'That's interesting. What are you leaving and to whom?'

'To my country, to humanity, and to the students, sir. I read in the papers the biography of an American. He left his huge fortune to factories and to the applied sciences, his skeleton to the students of the academy there, and his skin to be made into a drum with the proviso that the American national anthem might be beaten on it day and night. Alas, we are pigmies compared with the soaring thoughts of the United States of America. Russia is a freak of nature, but not of intellect. If I were to try to bequeath my skin for a drum to, let us say, the Akmolinsky infantry regiment, in which I had the honour of starting my service, with the proviso that the Russian national anthem might be beaten on it every day in front of the drawn-up regiment, they would consider it a liberal idea and forbid my skin to be used for that purpose, and therefore I confine myself to the students. I want to bequeath my skeleton to the Academy of Sciences, but only on one condition – namely that a label should be stuck on its forehead for ever with the inscription: "A Repentant Freethinker". Yes, sir!'

The Captain spoke warmly, and there could be no doubt that he believed in the grandeur of the American's will, but that he was also a rogue who was very anxious to amuse Stavrogin, whose jester he had been for a very long time before. The latter did not even smile, but, on the contrary, asked in a rather suspicious tone of voice:

'So you intend to publish your will in your lifetime and receive a reward for it?'

'Well, what if I do, sir, what if I do?' Lebyatkin said, observing him closely. 'Think of the sort of life I have had! Why, I've even given up writing poetry, and yet there was a time, sir, when even you found my verses very amusing over a bottle! Don't you remember? But my writing days are over. I've written only one poem, like Gogol his *Last Story*. Do you remember he proclaimed to Russia that it came "in a burst of song" out of his heart? Well, so I, too, have sung my last song and it's all over now!'

'What poem is that?'

'"If She A Leg Should Break!"'

'Wha-at?'

That was what the Captain was waiting for. He had an unbounded admiration and respect for his poems, but owing to a certain duplicity of his nature, he was also pleased that in the past Stavrogin had been vastly amused and sometimes even convulsed with laughter by his verses. In this way he killed two birds with one stone: his vanity as a poet was satisfied and he kept his job as Stavrogin's jester; but now he had a third very special and ticklish object in view: by bringing his verses on the scene, the Captain intended to justify himself in one point about which he always felt for some reason most apprehensive and most guilty.

'"If She A Leg Should Break," that is, if she should have a fall from her horse. It's a fantasy, sir, a mad dream, but the dream of a poet. I was struck one day when I saw a lady on horseback and I asked myself the important question: "What would happen then?" I mean, in case of an accident. Well, it's obvious: all her admirers would beat a hasty retreat, all her suitors would disappear, nothing doing, my pretty lass –

only the poet would remain true to her with his heart crushed in his breast. And, mind you, sir, even a louse may be in love and there is no law against it. And yet the young lady was offended by my letter and my verses. I'm told that even you were angry. Were you? That's a pity. I wouldn't believe it. But who could I harm with my imagination alone? Besides, I swear on my honour, Liputin kept egging me on: "Send it, send it! Every man has a right to send a letter!" So I sent it.'

'I believe you sought her hand in marriage, didn't you?'

'Enemies, enemies, enemies!'

'Read me your verses!' Stavrogin interrupted him sternly.

'Ravings, ravings, just ravings.'

However, he drew himself up, stretched forth his hand and began:

> The fairest of all has broken a leg,
> And now she is fairer than ever before,
> And far more I love her, my sweet, and I beg
> Her remember how I loved her of yore.

'That'll do,' Stavrogin said with a wave of the hand.

'I'm dreaming of Petersburg,' Lebyatkin quickly changed the subject, as though he had never written the verses, 'I'm dreaming of regeneration. ... Sir, you who've done so much for me, could I count on you not to refuse me the money for the journey? I've been waiting for you all the week, as if you were the sun.'

'I'm sorry. I have hardly any money left and, besides, why should I give you money?'

Stavrogin seemed suddenly angry. Drily and briefly he enumerated all the Captain's misdeeds: drunkenness, lying, squandering the money intended for Mary, taking her from the convent, his insolent letters threatening to make public the secret, the way he had behaved about Dasha, etc., etc. The Captain rocked to and fro in his chair, gesticulated, began to reply, but every time Stavrogin stopped him peremptorily.

'And another thing,' he said at last, 'you keep on writing about your "family disgrace". Why do you consider your sister's marriage to Stavrogin a disgrace?'

'But her marriage is kept a secret, sir! Her marriage is kept a secret, a fatal secret. I receive money from you and then I'm suddenly asked:

what is that money for? But my lips are sealed. I can't answer, for my answer would do harm to my sister and to my family honour.'

The Captain raised his voice: it was his favourite subject and he considered it to be his trump card. Poor man! he never suspected what a blow was in store for him. Calmly and precisely, as though it were a matter of a most ordinary family arrangement, Stavrogin told him that in a few days, perhaps even the next day or the day after, he intended to make his marriage known everywhere, 'to the police as well as to the public at large', so that the question of family honour would be settled by itself as well as the question of subsidies. The Captain glared at him: at first he didn't even understand what he was talking about; it had to be explained to him.

'But – but she's a half-wit!'

'I'll make the necessary arrangements.'

'But – but what about your mother?'

'Well, she can do as she likes.'

'But will you take your wife to your house?'

'Perhaps I will. However, that's not your business. It has nothing at all to do with you.'

'What do you mean – it's nothing to do with me?' the Captain cried. 'But what's going to happen to me?'

'Well, you will certainly not be admitted to my house.'

'But I'm a relation.'

'People run from such relations. Why should I go on giving you money then? Tell me if you can.'

'But, sir, that's impossible! You'll reconsider it, I'm sure. Why, you don't want to commit suicide, do you? And what will people think? What will the world say?'

'I don't care a damn for your world! I married your sister when I wanted to, after a drunken dinner, for a bet, for a bottle of wine, and now I shall announce it publicly. Why shouldn't I, if it amuses me?'

He said it with a special sort of irritability, so that Lebyatkin began with horror to believe him.

'But what about me? What about me? It's me who matters most! You're not pulling my leg, are you?'

'No, I'm not.'

'Well, say what you will, sir, but I don't believe you. If you do that, I'll summons you.'

'You're a damned fool, Captain.'

'I don't care. What else is there left for me to do?' the Captain said, utterly at a loss. 'Before at least I got free lodgings for the housework she did in those furnished rooms, but what's going to happen to me now if you abandon me to my fate?'

'But you want to go to Petersburg to get a new job, don't you? By the way, is it true what I hear about your intention of going to Petersburg to lay information with the authorities in the hope of obtaining a pardon by turning King's evidence?'

The Captain glared with a gaping mouth and did not reply.

'Listen, Captain,' Stavrogin suddenly said, speaking very seriously and bending down to the table. Till then he had been talking a little ambiguously, so that Lebyatkin, who had got used to his role as a jester, was up to the last moment a little uncertain whether Stavrogin was angry in good earnest or whether he was only pulling his leg, whether he really had the wild notion of announcing his marriage or whether he was only fooling. But now Stavrogin's stern expression was so convincing that a shiver ran down the Captain's spine. 'Listen and speak the truth, Lebyatkin. Did you inform the authorities about anything or didn't you? Did you really manage to do anything or not? Have you out of sheer stupidity sent a letter to someone?'

'No, sir, I haven't and – and I never thought of doing it,' the Captain said, staring blankly at Stavrogin.

'You're lying. You did think of it. That's what you want to go to Petersburg for. If you haven't written, have you by any chance said something to somebody here? Tell me the truth. I've heard something.'

'I told Liputin when I was in my cups. Liputin's a traitor. I opened my heart to him,' whispered the poor Captain.

'Never mind your heart, you mustn't be a damned fool. If you thought of it, you should have kept it to yourself: intelligent people hold their tongues nowadays and don't talk.'

'But,' the Captain said, trembling, 'you've taken no part in anything, sir. It's not you I –'

'I daresay you wouldn't have informed against your milch-cow, would you?'

'Judge for yourself, sir!' And, in despair and with tears, the Captain began hurriedly to tell the story of his life for the last four years.

It was the most stupid story of a fool who had got himself involved in
some business that did not concern him and the importance of which
he did not grasp up to the last moment because of his drunkenness and
debauchery. He told how already in Petersburg he had allowed himself to be drawn in at first simply through friendship, like a true student, though he was not a student, and without knowing anything
and without being guilty of anything, he had scattered all sorts of leaflets on staircases, leaving them by the dozen at doors, putting them
through letter-boxes instead of newspapers, taking them to theatres,
throwing them into people's hats, and slipping them into pockets.
Later on he began taking money from them, for 'I was so hard up,
sir, I was so hard up!' He had distributed 'all sorts of rubbish' in different districts of two provinces. 'What got my goat most of all, sir,' he
cried, 'was that it was against all civil and still more patriotic laws!
One day they suddenly printed that peasants should go out with pitch-
forks and that they should know that those who went out poor in the
morning would go home rich at night – think of it, sir! It made me
shudder, but I went on distributing them. Or suddenly five or six lines
addressed to the whole of Russia and without rhyme or reason:
"Hurry up and close down your churches, abolish your God, break
your marriage vows, do away with the rights of inheritance, arm
yourselves with knives," and goodness only knows what else. It was
with that bit of paper – the one with the five lines – that I was nearly
caught, but the officers in the regiment, bless their hearts, gave me a
thrashing and let me go. And last year I was nearly caught when I
was passing off French counterfeit notes for fifty roubles on Korovayev, but, thank goodness, Korovayev fell into a pond when he was
drunk and they did not succeed in showing me up. Here at Virginsky's
I proclaimed the freedom of the socialist wife. Last June I was again
distributing illegal leaflets in one of our districts here. I'm told I'll
have to do it again. Mr Verkhovensky suddenly gave me to understand that I have to carry out his orders; he's been threatening me
for some time. Look how he treated me on Sunday! I'm a slave,
sir, I'm a worm and not a God, and that's where I differ from our poet
Derzhavin. But, sir, think how hard up I am!'

Stavrogin listened to it all with interest.

'A great deal of what you tell me I didn't know at all,' he said. 'But,
of course, anything could have happened to you. Listen,' he said, after

a moment's reflection, 'if you like, you can tell them – you know whom – that Liputin told a lie and that you merely wanted to scare me by threatening to inform against me, believing that I, too, was compromised and that you might get more money from me that way. Do you understand?'

'But do you really think, sir, that I'm in such great danger? I was only waiting for you to come to ask you.'

Stavrogin laughed.

'They wouldn't of course let you go to Petersburg even if I were to give you the money for the journey – but it's time I went to see Mary.' And he got up from his chair.

'But what about Mary, sir?'

'Why, I told you.'

'But did you mean that, too?'

'You still don't believe it, do you?'

'Will you really cast me off like an old worn-out boot?'

'I'll see,' laughed Stavrogin. 'All right, let me go now.'

'Would you like me to wait on the front steps so that – er – I shouldn't by chance overhear something, for – er – the rooms here are so small, sir.'

'That's a good idea. Wait on the steps. Take my umbrella.'

'Your umbrella? But, sir, am I worth it?' the Captain said ingratiatingly.

'Every man has a right to an umbrella.'

'You've defined the minimum of human rights in one short sentence, sir.'

But already he was muttering mechanically; he was too much crushed by the news and was completely at a loss what to make of it. And yet no sooner had he gone out on the front steps and had put up the umbrella than the usual comforting idea that he was being deceived and lied to began to take shape in his foolish and knavish head, and if that was so he had nothing to be afraid of, for they were afraid of him.

'If they lie and cheat, then what is it all about?' the thought stirred uneasily in his head. The announcement of the marriage seemed an absolute absurdity to him. 'It is true anything may come to pass with a wonder-worker like that; he lives to do harm to people. But what if he is afraid himself after the insult he received on Sunday, and afraid as he has never been before? So, fearing lest I should announce it myself, he comes running here to tell me that he will do it. Don't slip up, Lebyatkin! And why does he come sneaking here at night if he means everybody to know it himself? And if he is afraid, then it is right now he is afraid, for the last few days. Look out, Lebyatkin, don't make a mess of things!

'Trying to frighten me with Verkhovensky. Hell, I'm in a mess! I'm in a frightful mess! Shouldn't have said anything to Liputin! The devil knows what those fiends are up to. Never could make them out. Getting busy again as they were five years ago. And to whom could I have given the information? "You haven't written to anyone out of sheer stupidity?" I see! So it's possible to write to someone as though out of stupidity? Is he perhaps advising me to do it? "You're going to Petersburg for that purpose." The rogue! I was just toying with the idea, and he guessed it! Just as if he were suggesting to me to go himself. It's one of two things: either he is really afraid himself because he's done something he shouldn't or – or he isn't afraid of anything, but is merely egging me on to inform against them all! Oh, dear, what a mess you're in, Lebyatkin, old fellow! Oh, I hope to goodness I don't make a mistake!'

He was so absorbed in thought that he was even forgetting to eavesdrop. However, eavesdropping was not so easy; the door was a thick one, made of one piece of wood, and they were talking in very low voices; all he could hear was some indistinct sounds. The Captain even spat with annoyance and went out again, lost in thought, to whistle on the front steps.

3

Mary's room was twice as big as that occupied by the Captain, and its furniture was also of the same rough-and-ready kind; but the table in front of the sofa was covered with a gay-coloured cloth, and a lamp was burning on it; the bed was screened off by a green curtain which ran the whole length of the room, and, in addition, there was a big, soft arm-chair beside the table in which, however, Mary never sat. In the corner of the room, as in her old room, there was an icon with a little lighted lamp in front of it. On the table the same indispensable things were laid out: a pack of cards, a small hand mirror, a song-book, and even a fancy loaf. There were, besides, two books with coloured pictures, one – extracts from a popular travel book, adapted for boys and girls in their teens, and the other – a collection of light, edifying stories, mostly about the age of chivalry, specially written for Christmas presents and schools. There was also an album with various photographs. Mary was, of course, expecting the visitor, as the Captain had warned him; but when Stavrogin entered her room she was asleep, half reclining on the sofa, her head lying on a wool-embroidered cushion. The visitor closed the door noiselessly behind him and, without moving from his place, began scrutinizing the sleeping young woman.

The Captain had told a little lie when he said that she had dolled herself up. She was wearing the same dark dress as on Sunday at Mrs Stavrogin's. Her hair, too, was done up in the same small bun at the nape of her neck; her long, lean neck was uncovered in the same way. The black shawl, which Mrs Stavrogin had given her as a present, lay carefully folded on the sofa. Her face was crudely rouged and powdered as before. Stavrogin had been standing for scarcely a minute when she suddenly woke up, as though she had felt him looking at her, opened her eyes, and quickly sat up. But something strange must have happened to her visitor, for he remained standing in the same place at the door, his motionless and piercing glance fixed steadily and silently upon her face. Perhaps his glance was unnecessarily stern. Perhaps it showed disgust and even a malignant enjoyment of her fright – or perhaps Mary had imagined it all at the moment she had awakened from her sleep; but suddenly, after waiting for almost a minute, the face of the poor woman became positively distorted with terror: it twitched convulsively, she raised her trembling hands and suddenly burst into tears, exactly like a frightened child; in another moment she would have begun to scream. But the visitor recollected himself; his face changed in a flash, and he walked up to the table with the most affable and kindly smile.

'I'm sorry I frightened you, Mary, by coming in so unexpectedly when you were asleep,' he said, holding out his hand to her.

His words, spoken in so kindly a voice, produced their effect. Her panic was gone, though she was still looking at him with dread, evidently trying to grasp something. She held out her hand, too, fearfully. At last a smile appeared timidly on her lips.

'Hullo, Prince,' she whispered, looking rather strangely at him.

'I expect you had a bad dream, didn't you?' he went on, with a still more friendly and amiable smile.

'And how did you know that I was dreaming about *that*?'

And suddenly she began trembling again, recoiling from him, and raising her hand as though in self-defence, she was again about to burst into tears.

'Come, pull yourself together,' Stavrogin tried to argue with her. 'What is there to be afraid of? Don't you recognize me?'

But for a long time his words had no effect on her. She gazed at him in silence with the same agonizing perplexity, with a distressful thought in her poor head, trying painfully to grasp something. One moment she lowered her eyes and another she shot a quick, all-embracing glance at him. At last, though she did not quieten down, she seemed to make up her mind.

'Sit down beside me, please, so that I can have a good look at you afterwards,' she said in quite a firm voice, clearly with some new object in mind. 'And don't worry now, please, for I shan't look at you, but will keep my eyes fixed on the ground. And don't look at me, either, until I ask you to. Sit down,' she added impatiently.

A new feeling was apparently taking possession of her more and more.

Stavrogin sat down and waited; they were silent for rather a long time.

'I must say,' she murmured suddenly almost with a feeling of repugnance, 'it all seems so strange to me. It is true I had bad dreams, but why should I have dreamt of you looking like that?'

'Oh, let's leave your dreams alone,' he said impatiently, turning to her, in spite of her request, and, perhaps, the same expression came back for a moment into his eyes. He saw that she would have liked to look at him, very much, perhaps, but that she restrained herself stubbornly and kept her eyes fixed on the ground.

'Listen, Prince' – she suddenly raised her voice, 'listen, Prince –'

'Why did you turn away?' he cried, unable to control himself. 'Why don't you look at me? What is the meaning of this comedy?'

But she did not seem to hear him at all.

'Listen, Prince,' she repeated for the third time in a firm voice, with an unpleasant, troubled expression, 'when you told me the other day in the carriage that our marriage was to be announced, I felt frightened because I thought that that would be the end of our secret. But now I don't know. I've been thinking it over, and I'm afraid I'm not good enough for it at all. I daresay I could dress and perhaps receive visitors, too: it's easy enough to invite someone for a cup of tea, especially if you have servants. But, all the same, what will people say? I had a good look round that house that Sunday morning. That pretty girl never took her eyes off me, especially when you came in. It was you who came in, wasn't it? Her mother is just a silly old society woman. My Lebyatkin excelled himself too. I kept looking at the ceiling not to burst out laughing – the ceiling there is beautifully painted. *His* mother should have been an abbess. I'm afraid of her, though she gave me her black shawl. No doubt, they must all have formed quite a strange idea of me; I wasn't angry, only I sat there thinking: what kind of a relation am I to them? Of course, all people expect from a coun- tess are spiritual qualities, for she has plenty of servants for her domes- tic ones – and I suppose some kind of refined coquetry, to be able to receive foreign travellers. But all the same that Sunday they looked on me as hopeless, I'm afraid. Dasha alone is an angel. I'm awfully afraid that they may hurt *his* feelings by some careless remark about me.'

'Don't be afraid and don't worry,' Stavrogin said, making a wry face.

'However, it won't matter much to me if he does feel a little ashamed of me, for there will always be more pity than shame, though of course it does depend on the man. You see, he knows that I ought to pity them more than they me.'

'I suppose you were rather offended with them, Mary, weren't you?'

'Who, me? No,' she laughed good-naturedly. 'I wasn't offended at all. I had a good look at you all then: you were all angry, you had all quarrelled with one another; you meet and you don't know how to have a good laugh together. So rich and so little gaiety – it seems all so revolting to me. But I don't pity anybody now, except myself.'

'I've heard that you found it hard to live with your brother without me. Did you?'

'Who told you that? It's nonsense. It's much worse now. I'm hav- ing bad dreams now, and my dreams are bad because you've come. What have you come for, I'd like to know?'

'Would you like to go back to the convent?'

'Well, I knew they would suggest that I should go back there! Good heavens, do you think I don't know what your convent is like? And why should I go back to it? What am I to go there with? I'm all alone in the world now! It's late for me to start a third life.'

'You seem to be very angry. You're not afraid that I'm no longer in love with you, are you?'

'Oh, I don't care a pin about you! I'm afraid that I might completely fall out of love with someone.'

She gave a disdainful laugh.

'I suppose I must have done something very wrong to *him*,' she suddenly added, as though speaking to herself. 'Only I don't know what it is. Oh, the consciousness of that will haunt me all my life. Always – always – all these five years – day and night – I was afraid that I'd done something wrong to him. I've prayed and prayed, thinking all the time how greatly I've wronged him. And now it turns out to be only too true.'

'What turned out?'

'What worries me is whether there isn't something on *his* part,' she went on without answering his question, indeed even without hearing it. 'And then again how could he associate with such worthless people? The Countess would have been glad to devour me, though she made me sit in the same carriage with her. They're all in the plot – could he be in it too? Could he have betrayed me too?' Her chin and lips were twitching. 'Listen, have you read about Grishka Otrepyev, the Pretender to the Russian throne, who has been damned in seven cathedrals?'

Stavrogin did not reply.

'Well, I think I'm going to turn round now and look at you,' she said, apparently making up her mind suddenly. 'Turn to me, too, and look at me, only more closely, please. I want to make sure for the last time.'

'I have been looking at you for a long time.'

'Fancy that!' said Mary, looking intently at him, 'you've grown very fat.'

She was about to say something else, but suddenly her face became distorted, for the third time, with terror and again she recoiled from him, raising her hand before her.

'What on earth is the matter with you?' cried Stavrogin, almost in a fury.

But her terror lasted only a moment; her face was distorted by a strange smile, suspicious and unpleasant.

'Please, Prince, get up and come in,' she said suddenly in a firm and insistent voice.

'Come in? Where am I to come in from?'

'For five years I've kept imagining how *he* would come in. Get up and go out of the door into that room. I'll sit as though I were not expecting anything, and pick up a book, and then you'll suddenly come in after travelling abroad for five years. I want to see what it will be like.'

Stavrogin gnashed his teeth inwardly and muttered something to himself.

'That's enough,' he said, striking the table with his hand. 'Please listen to me, Mary. Do me a favour and attend to me carefully, if you can. You're not completely mad, are you?' he blurted out impatiently. 'To-morrow I shall announce our marriage. You will never live in a big mansion. You can get that idea right out of your head. Do you want to live with me for the rest of your life, but only far, far away from here? I mean in the mountains, in Switzerland; there's a place there I know. And don't be afraid; I shall never leave you and I shan't put you in a lunatic asylum, either. I shall have enough money to live without having to ask for help. You'll have a maid; you won't have to do any work at all. Everything you want that it is possible to have, you shall have. You will say your prayers, go anywhere you like and do what you like. I won't touch you. I won't ever leave that place, either. If you like I won't speak to you all my life; or if you like you can tell me your stories every evening as you used to do in those furnished rooms in the Petersburg tenements. I'll read books to you, if you want me to. But on one condition: that we stay in that place – and it is a very gloomy place – all our lives. Would you like to? Do you agree? You won't regret it, torment me with tears and curses, will you?'

She listened to him with great interest, and for a long time she said nothing, thinking it over.

'The whole thing seems incredible to me,' she said at last ironically and sulkily. 'I might have to live for forty years in those mountains.'

She laughed.

'All right, so we shall live forty years there,' Stavrogin said, frowning.

'I see. No, I won't go there for anything in the world.'

'Not even with me?'

'Why, what are you that I should go with you? Sit on top of a mountain with you for forty years – what an idea! And, really, how patient people have become nowadays! No, it's impossible for a falcon to be an owl. My prince isn't like that at all!' She raised her head proudly and solemnly.

It suddenly dawned on him:

'Why do you call me Prince?' he asked quickly. 'And who do you take me for?'

'Why, aren't you a prince?'

'I never have been a prince.'

'So you admit it yourself – you tell it to my face yourself that you're not a prince?'

'I tell you I have never been one.'

'Merciful heavens!' she cried, clapping her hands together in astonishment. 'I expected everything from *his* enemies, but such insolence – never! Is he alive?' she shrieked, beside herself, turning on Stavrogin. 'Have you killed him or not? Confess!'

'Who do you take me for?' he cried, jumping to his feet with a distorted face.

But it was difficult to frighten her now. She was triumphant.

'Who knows who you are and where you've sprung from? Only in my heart, deep down in my heart, have I felt all this intrigue! And I've been sitting here wondering what blind owl has been trying to humour me. No, my dear, you're a poor actor, even worse than Lebyatkin. Give my regards to the Countess and tell her to send a better man than you. Has she hired you? Tell me! Has she given you a job in her kitchen out of the kindness of her heart? I can see through your tricks. I understand you all, every one of you!'

He seized her firmly by the arm above the elbow, but she laughed in his face.

'You certainly are very like him, perhaps you're a relation of his – what a clever lot! Only my man is a bright falcon and a prince, and you're an owl and a shopkeeper! My man will bow down to God or won't bow down to Him – just as he pleases, and – why, Shatov (oh, the darling!) slapped you on the cheek, my Lebyatkin told me. And what were you so afraid of when you came into the room that Sunday? Who had frightened you? As soon as I saw your mean face when I fell and you picked me up – it was as if a worm had crawled into my heart: it's not *he*, I thought to myself, not *he*! My falcon would never have been ashamed of me in front of a young society lady! Oh, dear Lord, the only thing that kept me happy all these five years was the thought that my falcon was living somewhere beyond the mountains, flying there and looking at the sun. ... Tell me, you pretender, how much money did they pay you? Did they have to pay you a lot of money before you gave your consent? I wouldn't have given you a penny. Ha, ha, ha! Ha, ha, ha!'

'Oh, you idiot!' Stavrogin snarled, grinding his teeth and still holding her firmly by the arm.

'Away, pretender!' she cried imperiously. 'I'm the wife of my Prince! I'm not afraid of your knife!'

'Knife!'

'Yes, knife! You've a knife in your pocket! You thought I was asleep, but I saw it: the moment you entered the room, you took out your knife!'

'What did you say, you unhappy wretch? What dreams do you dream?' he cried, pushing her away from him with all his might so that she knocked her shoulders and head painfully against the back of the sofa.

He bolted from the room. But she jumped up immediately and ran after him, hopping and limping, and, though kept back by the frightened Lebyatkin with all the force he could muster, she shouted after him in the darkness, shrieking and laughing:

'Grishka Otrepyev – anathema!'

4

'A knife! A knife!' he repeated in unquenchable rage, striding along through the mud and the puddles without picking his way. It is true that there were moments when he badly wanted to laugh, loudly and furiously; but for some reason he controlled himself and restrained his laughter. He came to his senses only on the bridge, on the very spot

where he had met Fedka a few hours ago. Fedka was indeed waiting
for him there. Seeing Stavrogin, he took off his cap, bared his teeth in
a gay grin, and at once began chattering briskly and merrily about
something. At first Stavrogin went past him without stopping, and
for some time he did not even bother to listen to the tramp who
trailed behind him. Suddenly he was struck by the thought that he
had completely forgotten him, forgotten him just when he was himself muttering under his breath: 'A knife! A knife!' He grabbed the
tramp by the scruff of the neck and gave vent to the pent-up rage
within him by flinging him violently against the bridge. For a moment Fedka thought of showing fight, but realizing almost immediately that in the hands of his adversary, who had, besides, taken him
by surprise, he was like a wisp of straw, he quieted down and fell
silent and did not even think of offering any resistance. Pinned to the
ground on his knees and with his elbows twisted behind his back, the
cunning tramp calmly waited for what was going to happen next,
without, it seems, the slightest apprehension of danger.

He was not mistaken. Stavrogin had already taken off his woollen
scarf with his left hand in order to bind his prisoner's arms, but suddenly he released him for some reason and pushed him away. The
tramp jumped to his feet at once, turned round, and a short, broad
cobbler's knife, which seemed to have appeared out of nowhere in a
flash, gleamed in his hand.

'Away with that knife! Put it away, put it away at once!' Stavrogin
ordered with an impatient gesture, and the knife vanished as instantaneously as it had appeared.

Stavrogin went on his way without uttering a word and without
turning round; but the pertinacious villain kept pace with him in
spite of everything, though he was no longer chattering and even kept
his distance respectfully, trailing a yard behind. They both crossed the
bridge like that and came out on the bank of the river, turning this
time to the left, again into a long, deserted lane, which led to the centre
of the town by a shorter way than through Bogoyavlenskaya Street.

'Is it true what I hear, that you robbed a church in our district the
other day?' asked Stavrogin suddenly.

'Well, you see, sir, I went to the church with the idea of saying my
prayers,' the tramp answered sedately and courteously, as if nothing
special had happened; not only sedately, but even with dignity. There

was no trace of his former 'friendly' familiarity. The man who was talking now was quite obviously a serious, business-like man, one, it is true, who had been gratuitously insulted, but who was capable of overlooking an insult.

'And when the good Lord brought me here,' he went on, 'I thought to myself – oh, what heavenly bliss! The whole thing, sir, happened because I was destitute, and the likes of us, sir, can't carry on without some help. As God is my witness, sir, it was a sheer loss to me – the good Lord has truly punished me for my sins: I got only twelve roubles for the censer, the pyx, and the deacon's strap. I got next to nothing for the chin setting of St Nicholas of pure silver; they said it was plated.'

'Murdered the watchman, didn't you?'

'You see, sir, it was together with the watchman that I robbed the church, and it was only later, at daybreak, by the river, that we had an argument about who should carry the sack. Afraid, sir, I didn't ought to have done it, but I did make it a little easier for him.'

'Go on killing, go on stealing – go on!'

'Well, sir, Mr Verkhovensky says the same to me – just like you – the same advice, word for word, because, sir, he's uncommonly mean and hard-hearted about helping a fellow creature. And, besides, he don't believe one bit in the Heavenly Father what has created us out of a little earthly clay. He says that it was nature what done everything even to the last beast. He don't understand, besides, that a chap like me can't do nothing without someone stretching out a helping hand to him 'cause that's the way it is with the likes of us. If you starts telling him, he just stares at you like a sheep at the water. You can't help marvelling at him. Now take Captain Lebyatkin, sir, him you've just been visiting. When he was living at Filippov's house before you came, he left his door standing wide open all night, himself lying asleep on the floor dead drunk and his money dropping all over the floor from his pockets. Seen it with my own eyes, I have, sir, 'cause for the likes of us it ain't possible to get along without somebody holding out a helping hand.'

'Did you say you saw it with your own eyes? Why, you didn't go there at night, did you?'

'Maybe I did, sir; only no one knows nothing about it.'

'Why didn't you kill him?'

'Well, sir, I thought it over – see? – and I resisted the temptation, in a manner of speaking. For, you see, sir, having found out for certain that I can always count on picking up a hundred and fifty roubles, why should I do a thing like that if by biding my time I could help myself to a thousand and five hundred? For Captain Lebyatkin, sir, and I've heard him with my own ears, greatly relied on your generosity when drunk, and there ain't an inn in this here town, sir, not even the lowest pub, where he hasn't shouted about it every time he was drunk good and proper. So that, having had it repeated by hundreds of people, I, too, sir, began to put all my hopes on your lordship. I'm telling you this, sir, like you was my own father or my own brother, for Mr Verkhovensky will never hear about it from me, and not a soul in the world, neither. So won't your lordship let me have three roubles now? You'd set my mind at rest, sir, I mean by letting me know what's on your mind, for the likes of us can't get along without somebody holding out a helping hand, sir.'

Stavrogin burst out laughing and, taking out his purse, in which he had about fifty pounds in small notes, he threw him one note out of the bundle, then another, a third, and a fourth. Fedka caught them in the air, rushing after the notes which dropped in the mud, snatching them up and shouting, 'Oh, oh, oh!' Stavrogin ended up by throwing the whole bundle at him and, still laughing, walked on along the street, this time alone. The tramp stayed behind to pick up the money, crawling on his knees in the mud after the scattering notes, which were blown about on the wind and fell into puddles, and for a whole hour his fitful cries, 'Oh! oh!', could be heard in the darkness.

3

The Duel

I

THE duel took place on the following day, at two o'clock in the afternoon, as arranged. Artemy Gaganov's determination to fight at all costs helped to bring about a quick decision. He did not understand his opponent's conduct and was in a state of blazing fury. For a whole month he had been insulting him with impunity and was unable to make him lose his temper. He had to receive a challenge from Stavrogin, for he himself had no real excuse for issuing a challenge. And he was ashamed to acknowledge his secret motive for the fight, namely his morbid hatred of Stavrogin for the insult to his family four years before. Besides, he considered such an excuse impossible himself, particularly in view of the humble apologies Stavrogin had offered him twice already. He decided that Stavrogin was a shameless coward; he just could not understand how Stavrogin could have put up with the public insult he had received from Shatov. That was why he had made up his mind at last to send that extraordinarily rude letter, which finally forced Stavrogin to propose a meeting. Having dispatched the letter the day before, he was awaiting Stavrogin's challenge with impatience, calculating morbidly the chances of its being issued, one moment full of hope and another full of despair. In any case, he took steps to provide himself with a second the evening before, namely Maurice Drozdov, an old friend of his, a former schoolmate, and a man he greatly respected. So that when Kirilov came with his message at nine o'clock next morning, he found the ground already prepared. All Stavrogin's apologies and quite unheard-of concessions were at once rejected, at the first word, and with quite unwonted passion. Drozdov, who had only learnt of the turn the affair had taken the evening before, opened his mouth with surprise at such incredible proposals and was about to insist on a reconciliation, but observing that Gaganov, who had divined his intentions, was almost trembling in his seat, he held his peace and said nothing. But for the word he had given his old schoolfellow, he would have gone away at once; he only remained in the hope of being of some help at the crucial moment of the affair. Kirilov passed on the challenge; all the conditions of the encounter proposed by Stavrogin were at once accepted without the slightest objection. Only one addition, and a ferocious one at that, was made. If after the first shots nothing decisive happened, they were to have another encounter, and if that, too, was inconclusive, a third one. Kirilov frowned, objected to the third encounter, but, having got nothing for his pains, agreed on one condition, namely: 'Three times – yes, but a fourth time – no!'

This was conceded. At two o'clock in the afternoon the meeting therefore took place at Brykov, that is, in the small copse on the outskirts of the town between Skvoreshniki and Spigulin's factory. The rain of the previous night was over, but it was wet, damp, and windy.

Low, ragged, sooty clouds scudded across the cold sky; the tree-tops rustled intermittently in the gusts of wind and creaked on their roots; it was a melancholy morning.

Drozdov and Gaganov arrived at the spot in a smart open carriage and pair, driven by the latter; they were accompanied by a groom. Stavrogin and Kirilov arrived almost at the same moment, not in a carriage but on horseback, and they, too, were accompanied by a groom. Kirilov, who had never mounted a horse before, sat bolt upright in the saddle, grasping in his right hand the heavy box of pistols which he would not entrust to the groom, while with his left hand he was, in his inexperience, continually tugging at the reins, which made his horse toss its head and show an inclination to rear; this, however, did not alarm the rider in the least. Touchy and quick to take offence, Gaganov considered the arrival of the horsemen a fresh insult directed at himself, since his enemies seemed to be too sure of success if they did not think it necessary to bring a carriage with them in case Stavrogin was wounded and had to be driven back home. He alighted from his carriage yellow with rage, feeling that his hands were trembling, a fact which he communicated to Drozdov. He ignored Stavrogin's bow completely and turned away. The seconds cast lots: it fell on Kirilov's pistols. They measured out the barriers, the opponents were put in their proper places, and the carriage and horses were sent off with the grooms at a distance of three hundred yards. The pistols were loaded and handed to the combatants.

It is a pity I have to get on with the story and can't spare any time for descriptions, but I shall have to make a few comments for all that. Drozdov looked upset and worried. Kirilov, on the other hand, was completely composed and unconcerned, very precise about the smallest details of the duties he had undertaken, but without the slightest fuss and almost without any curiosity as to the fatal issue of the affair which was so close. Stavrogin looked paler than usual. He was rather lightly dressed in an overcoat and a white goatskin hat. He seemed very tired, frowning from time to time and not caring to disguise his low spirits. But Gaganov was at that moment the most remarkable figure of them all, so that I simply must say a few words about him in particular.

2

So far I have had no opportunity of describing his appearance. He was a very tall man of about thirty-three, with a fair complexion, well fed, as the common people say, almost fat, with rather handsome features. He had retired from the army with the rank of colonel, and if he had served long enough to become a general, he would have cut an even more impressive figure and would quite likely have made a good fighting general.

It is important for the proper characterization of the man to mention the fact that the chief reason for his retirement from the army was the thought of the family disgrace which had haunted him so long and so painfully after the indignity Stavrogin inflicted upon his father in the club four years before. He honestly believed that it was dishonourable to remain in the service and was quite certain in his mind that he was discrediting his regiment and his fellow-officers, though none of them knew of the incident. It is true that he had wished to resign his commission on a former occasion, long before the insult to his father and for quite a different reason, but he could not make up his mind. Strange as it may sound, his original desire, or rather motive for his retirement, was the manifesto of 19 February about the liberation of the peasants. Gaganov, who was one of the richest landowners of our province, whose material losses after the manifesto had not been so great, either, and who, moreover, was quite capable of convincing himself of the humanity of the measure and almost understanding the economic advantages of the reform, suddenly thought himself personally insulted after the publication of the manifesto. It was something unconscious, something in the nature of a feeling, but the more unaccountable it was, the stronger it grew. Until the death of his father, however, he could not make up his mind to take any drastic steps; but in Petersburg he became known for the 'honourable' trend of his thoughts among many important personages with whom he zealously kept up his connexions. He was a self-centred man, a man who shut himself up from the rest of the world. Another characteristic: he belonged to those strange, but still surviving, types of noblemen in Russia who are exceedingly proud of the purity of their ancient lineage and take it too seriously. At the same time he could not bear Russian history and, generally, regarded Russian customs as more or less brutish. Even in his childhood, in the special military school for the children of the wealthier and more distinguished families in which he had the privilege of being educated, certain romantic notions struck deep roots in his mind: he loved castles, medieval life, all the operatic part of it, chivalry; even in those days he almost wept with shame that in the days of the Moscow Kingdom the Tsar could inflict corporal punishment on a Russian nobleman, and blushed when he compared it with his present position. This stiff, extremely stern man, who had such an excellent knowledge of the army and who carried out all his duties, was a dreamer at heart. It was said of him that he could have addressed meetings and that he had the gift of language; but he had never opened his mouth during the thirty-three years of his life. He held himself haughtily aloof even in the distinguished Petersburg circles in which he had moved of late. His meeting in Petersburg with Stavrogin, who had just returned from abroad, nearly drove him out of his mind. At this moment, standing at the barrier, he was in a state of terrific excitement. He kept imagining that the duel would somehow not come off, and the slightest delay threw him into a panic. He looked pained when Kirilov, instead of giving the signal for the duel to begin, suddenly addressed the combatants, just for the sake of form, it is true, as he himself explained in a loud voice.

'I am only saying it as a matter of form. Now that the pistols are in your hands and it is time to utter the word of command, I must ask you for the last time whether you would like to make it up. It's the duty of a second '

As though on purpose, Drozdov, who had not uttered a word till then, but who had been reproaching himself ever since the day before for his compliance and connivance, suddenly welcomed Kirilov's suggestion.

'I'm entirely in agreement with what Mr Kirilov has said,' he declared. 'The idea that it is impossible to become reconciled at the barrier is a superstition which is only suitable for Frenchmen. Besides, I honestly can't see what the offence is supposed to be – I – er – I've been wanting to say so for a long time because – because all sorts of apologies have been offered, haven't they?'

He flushed all over. He had rarely had an opportunity of speaking so much and with such excitement.

'I'd like to repeat again that I'm ready to make every possible apology,' Stavrogin put in quickly.

'Such a thing is impossible,' Gaganov shouted furiously, addressing Drozdov and stamping with rage. 'If you are my second and not my enemy, sir, you will explain to that man' – he pointed with his pistol at Stavrogin – 'that such concessions only add insult to injury! He doesn't think it's possible to be insulted by me! He doesn't consider it disgraceful to run away at the barrier from me! Who does he take me for after that, do you think? And you – you're my second, sir! You're only irritating me so that I should miss him.' He stamped again, his lips covered with foam.

'Negotiations are at an end,' Kirilov shouted at the top of his voice. 'Please, listen to the words of command. One, two, three!'

At the word *three*, the combatants began walking towards each other. Gaganov at once raised his pistol and fired at the fifth or sixth step. He stopped for a second and, having made sure that he had missed his opponent, quickly walked up to the barrier. Stavrogin, too, walked up to it, raised his pistol, but, holding it rather high, fired without taking aim at all. Then he took out his handkerchief and wrapped it round the little finger of his right hand. It was only then that they noticed that Gaganov had not missed him altogether, but that the bullet had only grazed the fleshy part of his finger without touching the bone; it was only a slight scratch. Kirilov at once declared that, if the opponents were not satisfied, the duel would go on.

'I declare,' Gaganov croaked (his throat was parched), addressing himself again to Drozdov, 'that this man' – he pointed again at Stavrogin – 'fired in the air on purpose – deliberately. That's another insult! He wants to make the duel impossible!'

'I have the right to fire as I like so long as I keep to the rules,' Stavrogin declared firmly.

'No, he hasn't!' Gaganov shouted. 'Explain it to him, please!'

'I'm entirely of the same opinion as Mr Stavrogin,' Kirilov announced.

'Why does he spare me?' Gaganov raged, without listening. 'I despise his clemency! I refuse to accept it – I –'

'I give you my word that I had no intention of insulting you,' Stavrogin declared impatiently. 'I fired in the air because I don't want to kill any more people, either you or anyone else. It's nothing to do with you personally. It's true, I don't consider myself offended, and I'm sorry that makes you angry. But I shall not permit anyone to interfere with my rights.'

'If he is so afraid of the sight of blood, then ask him why he challenged me,' Gaganov roared, still addressing Drozdov.

'How could he help challenging you?' Kirilov interposed. 'You wouldn't listen to anything. How was he to get rid of you?'

'Let me say this,' Drozdov, who was considering the position painfully and with an effort, declared. 'If an opponent declares beforehand that he intends to fire in the air, the duel cannot possibly go on for – er – delicate and – er – obvious reasons.'

'I never said that I intended to fire in the air every time,' Stavrogin cried, losing patience. 'You can't possibly know what I have in mind and how I'm going to fire next time. I'm not interfering with the duel at all.'

'If that is so, then the encounter can go on,' said Drozdov to Gaganov.

'Gentlemen, take your places!' Kirilov commanded.

Again they walked towards each other, again Gaganov missed, and again Stavrogin fired into the air. It is true that he could have denied firing in the air: he could have claimed to have aimed properly, if he had not admitted that he had missed deliberately. He did not aim straight at the sky or at a tree, but seemed to aim at his opponent, though he pointed his pistol several feet above his hat. The second time his aim was indeed much lower and much more plausible. But it was quite impossible to convince Gaganov now.

'Again!' he cried, grinding his teeth. 'Never mind! I have been challenged and I'm going to make use of my rights! I shall fire a third time – I insist!'

'You're fully entitled to do so!' Kirilov rapped out.

Drozdov said nothing. They were placed a third time; the signal to fire was given. This time Gaganov walked right up to the barrier and began taking aim from there at a distance of twelve paces. His hands were trembling too much to take good aim. Stavrogin stood with his pistol lowered awaiting his shot without moving.

'Too long! You're taking aim too long,' Kirilov shouted impetuously. 'Fire! Fi-i-re!'

But the shot rang out, and this time Stavrogin's white fur hat flew off. The aim had been fairly good; the crown of the hat was pierced very low down; a quarter of an inch lower and everything would have been at an end. Kirilov picked up the hat and handed it to Stavrogin.

'Fire, don't keep your opponent waiting!' Drozdov shouted in great excitement, seeing that Stavrogin seemed to have forgotten to fire as he was examining his hat with Kirilov.

Stavrogin gave a start, glanced at Gaganov, turned away and without caring this time for his opponent's feelings, fired into the copse. The duel was over. Gaganov stood as though he had been crushed. Drozdov went up to him and started saying something, but he did not seem to understand. As he was going away, Kirilov took off his hat and nodded to Drozdov; but Stavrogin forgot his former politeness; after firing into the copse, he didn't even turn towards the barrier. He handed his pistol to Kirilov and walked quickly towards the horses. He looked angry; he did not speak. Kirilov, too, was silent. They mounted their horses and set off at a gallop.

3

'Why don't you speak?' he called impatiently to Kirilov when they were not far from home.

'What do you want?' Kirilov replied, almost slipping off his horse which reared up.

Stavrogin controlled himself.

'I didn't want to offend that – fool, but I have offended him again,' he said softly.

'Yes, you have offended him again,' Kirilov snapped. 'And, besides, he isn't a fool.'

'Still, I did what I could.'

'No, you didn't.'

'What should I have done, then?'

'You shouldn't have challenged him.'

'And have my face slapped again?'

'Yes, have it slapped again.'

'I can't understand it!' Stavrogin said angrily. 'Why does everybody expect something from me that is not expected from anybody else? Why should I put up with things no one else puts up with? Why should I agree to burdens no one else can bear?'

'I thought you were looking for a burden yourself.'

'Me looking for a burden?'

'Yes.'

'You – you realized that?'

'Yes.'

'Is it so noticeable?'

'Yes.'

They were silent for a minute. Stavrogin looked very troubled. He was almost stunned.

'I did not shoot at him because I didn't want to kill anyone. I assure you there was nothing else,' he said quickly and uneasily, as though justifying himself.

'You shouldn't have offended him.'

'But what else should I have done?'

'You should have killed him.'

'Are you sorry I didn't kill him?'

'I'm not sorry for anything. I thought you really meant to kill him. You don't know what you're looking for.'

'I'm looking for a burden,' Stavrogin laughed.

'If you didn't want bloodshed yourself, why did you give him a chance to kill you?'

'If I hadn't challenged him, he would have killed me anyhow without a duel.'

'That's not your business. Perhaps he wouldn't have killed you.'

'But just given me a beating?'

'That's not your business. Bear your burden. There is no merit otherwise.'

'To hell with your merit. I'm not looking for anyone's approval.'

'I thought you were,' Kirilov concluded very coolly.

They rode into the courtyard of Stavrogin's house.

'Won't you come in?' Stavrogin asked.

'No, thanks. I'm going home. Good-bye.'

He dismounted and put his box under his arm.

'You're not angry with me, are you?' Stavrogin said, holding out his hand to him.

'Not at all!' Kirilov said, coming back to shake hands with him. 'If

I find my burden light because I'm made that way, then perhaps yours is heavier because that's how you're made. There's not much to be ashamed of, just a little.'

'I know that I'm a worthless character, but I'm not trying to pretend to be a strong one.'

'Don't try. You're not a strong man. Come and have tea with me.'

Stavrogin entered his room greatly perturbed.

4

He found out at once from the butler that Mrs Stavrogin, very pleased that her son had gone out for a ride for the first time after the eight days of his illness, had ordered her carriage and had driven out alone for a breath of fresh air, as she used to do regularly before, for, the butler added, during the last eight days she had forgotten what it meant to have a breath of fresh air.

'Has she gone alone or with Miss Shatov?' Stavrogin interrupted the butler with a quick question, and he frowned when he heard that Dasha felt too unwell to accompany his mother and was at present in her rooms.

'Listen, old man,' he said as though suddenly making up his mind, 'keep an eye on her all day to-day, and if you see her coming to me, stop her at once, and tell her that for the next few days, at any rate, I cannot see her – that I ask her not to come and that – when the time comes – I shall send for her myself – do you hear?'

'I shall tell her, sir,' said the butler in a distressed voice, dropping his eyes.

'But not before you're quite sure that she's coming to me herself.'

'Don't worry, sir, there won't be any mistake. It was through me that your meetings were arranged till now. Miss Shatov always turned to me for help.'

'I know. But don't say anything before she comes herself. Let me have some tea, please, as soon as possible.'

As soon as the old man went out, however, the door opened and Dasha appeared in the doorway. She looked composed, but her face was pale.

'Where have you come from?' Stavrogin cried.

'I was standing outside and waited for him to leave the room before

I went in. I heard what you said to him, and when he came out just now I hid behind the wall round the corner, on the right, and he did not notice me.'

'I have long been thinking of breaking off with you, Dasha, for a while – for the present. I couldn't see you last night in spite of your note. I meant to write to you myself, but I'm not good at writing,' he added with annoyance and as though with disgust, too.

'I thought myself that we'd better break it off. Mrs Stavrogin is very suspicious about our relations.'

'Well, let her be.'

'She mustn't be worried. So now it's the end?'

'You're always expecting the end, aren't you?'

'Yes, but I'm sure of it.'

'Nothing comes to an end in this world.'

'But here it will be the end. When you call me, I'll come. Good-bye now.'

'And what sort of end will it be?' Stavrogin asked with a grin.

'You're not wounded and you haven't – shed any blood?' she asked without answering his question about the end.

'The whole thing was silly. I didn't kill anyone, don't worry. However, you'll hear everything to-day from everyone. I'm a little out of sorts.'

'I'm going. There won't be any announcement of your marriage to-day, will there?' she added irresolutely.

'Not to-day, nor to-morrow. I don't know about the day after to-morrow. Perhaps we shall all be dead then, and so much the better. Leave me, please. Leave me.'

'You won't ruin the other woman – the mad one – will you?'

'I shan't ruin the mad ones, either the one or the other, but I believe I shall ruin the sane one: I'm so mean and wicked, Dasha, that I shouldn't be surprised if I really did call you "at the very end", as you say, and you'll come in spite of your sanity. Why are you ruining yourself?'

'I know that at the end I shall remain alone with you and – I'm waiting for that.'

'But what if I do not call for you at the end? What if I run away from you?'

'That will never happen. You will call for me.'

'There's a great deal of contempt for me in the way you said that.'

'You know that it's not contempt only.'

'So you admit that there is some contempt?'

'Sorry, I didn't express myself properly. God's my witness that it is my dearest wish that you should never need me.'

'One sentence deserves another. I, too, should have wished not to ruin you.'

'You can never ruin me, whatever you do, and you know it better than anyone,' Dasha said quickly and firmly. 'If I can't come to you, I'll be a hospital nurse or a district nurse, or I shall go about selling the Bible. That's what I have decided to do. I can't be anyone's wife. I can't go on living in such a house as this. I don't want that. You know it all, don't you?'

'No, I never could make out what you wanted. I can't help feeling that you are interested in me just as some elderly nurses are for some reason interested in one particular patient as compared with other patients, or rather as some pious old ladies, who never miss a funeral, find some corpses more fascinating than others. Why do you look so strangely at me?'

'Are you very ill?' she asked sympathetically, scrutinizing him in a rather peculiar way. 'Heavens, and this man thinks he can do without me!'

'Listen, Dasha, I seem to be always seeing phantoms now. One little devil proposed to me on the bridge yesterday to murder Mary and Lebyatkin so as to put an end to my marriage without anybody suspecting anything. He asked me for three roubles on account, but made it quite clear that the whole transaction would cost no less than fifteen hundred. There's a calculating devil for you! A book-keeper! Ha, ha!'

'But are you quite sure it was just a phantom?'

'Oh, no, it wasn't a phantom at all! It was Fedka the convict, an escaped prisoner. But that's not important. What do you think I did? I gave him all the money from my purse, and he is now absolutely convinced that I've given him that on account!'

'You met him last night and he made you such a proposal? But can't you see that they've entangled you completely in their net?'

'Oh, let them! But,' he added with a malicious and irritable smile, 'I can see by the way you look at me that there's a question on the tip of your tongue you're dying to ask me.'

Dasha looked frightened.

'I've no question to ask you and I've no doubts at all,' she cried in alarm, as though wishing to get rid of the question. 'You'd better say nothing!'

'You mean you're quite sure that I won't go to Fedka's shop?'

'Oh God!' she cried, clasping her hands in despair, 'why do you torture me like this?'

'I'm sorry; forgive my silly joke. I expect I must be picking up bad manners from them. Since last night, you know, I feel awfully like laughing – laughing all the time, without stopping, for hours and hours. I seem to be infected with laughter. Listen – Mother has just arrived. I recognize her carriage by the noise it makes when it stops at the front steps.'

Dasha seized his hand.

'May the Lord protect you from your demon and – call me, call me as soon as possible!'

'Oh, what sort of a demon is it? It's simply a nasty, scrofulous little devil with a cold in his head, one of the failures. But I can see, Dasha, that there's something you again don't dare to say, isn't there?'

She looked at him with pain and reproach and turned to go.

'Listen,' he called after her with a malicious, twisted smile, 'if – well, I mean if – you see, if I were to go to that shop and then called for you afterwards – would you come after that?'

She went out without turning or replying, her face buried in her hands.

'She'll come even after I've been to the shop!' he whispered after a moment's thought, and a look of disdainful contempt came into his face. 'A hospital nurse! Well ... But perhaps that's really what I want.'

4

All Agog

I

THE impression created on our entire society by the story of the duel, which spread quickly all over the town, was particularly remarkable for the unanimity with which everyone hastened to take Mr Stavrogin's part. Many of his former enemies now resolutely declared themselves to be his friends. Such an unexpected change in public opinion was mainly due to a certain person, who till then had expressed no opinion on the matter, but who now uttered a few very pointed words that at once lent a significance to the event which was exciting the curiosity of the great majority of our citizens. It happened like this: on the very next day after the duel the whole town gathered at the house of our marshal of nobility, whose wife's name-day it was. Julia Lembke was present, or, rather, presided over the festivities. She arrived with Lisa, radiant with beauty and looking particularly gay, which at once seemed rather suspicious to many of our ladies at this time. By the way, there could no longer be any doubt about her engagement to Maurice Drozdov. In reply to a playful question of a retired, but highly important, general, of whom more will be said later, she said openly that evening that she was betrothed. And what do you think? Not one of our ladies would believe in her engagement. All of them went on stubbornly to assume some romance, some fatal family mystery, which had taken place in Switzerland, and for some reason Mrs Lembke was supposed to have had a hand in it. It is difficult to say why these rumours or, as it were, fancies had gained so firm a hold and why it was so resolutely maintained that Mrs Lembke was involved in it. As soon as she came in, all turned to her with strange looks, all agog. I may add that because the duel had happened so recently and because of the certain circumstances attending it, it was discussed with a certain circumspection at the party, and in whispers. Besides, nothing was yet known about the steps the authorities intended to take. The two duellists, so far as was known, were not troubled by the police. It was common knowledge, for instance, that Mr Gaganov had returned to his Dukhovo estate early in the morning without any interference. Meanwhile everybody, of course, was eager for somebody else to be the first to broach the subject and thus open the door to the impatience of everybody. They pinned their hopes on the above-mentioned general, and they were not disappointed.

This general was one of the most pompous members of our club. He was not a very wealthy landowner, but a man of a most fascinating turn of mind, an old-fashioned lady-killer, by the way, who was very fond, in large assemblies, of talking aloud, with all the weighty authority of a general, about the very subjects everyone spoke of in discreet whispers. That was, so to speak, his special role in our society. On such occasions he usually spoke in a drawl, enunciating each word with particular relish. He most probably acquired this habit from the Russians travelling abroad or from those wealthy Russian landowners who had incurred the largest financial losses from the peasant reform. Mr Verkhovensky even remarked on one occasion that the greater a landowner's losses, the more genteel was his speech and the more he drawled his words. He himself, incidentally, spoke in a most genteel and drawling manner, but never noticed it in himself.

The General began speaking like a man who was competent to express an opinion. For he was not only a distant relation of Gaganov's and, indeed, had engaged in a law-suit with him, but had fought two duels himself in the old days, and had even been reduced to the ranks and exiled to the Caucasus for one of them. Someone mentioned that Mrs Stavrogin had been seen driving out after her indisposition that day and the day before. As a matter of fact, he did not even mention her by name but merely referred to the most excellent matching of her four grey horses from the Stavrogins' stud. The General suddenly observed that he had met 'the young Stavrogin' that very day on horseback. Everyone at once fell silent. The General munched his lips and all of a sudden announced, twisting his presentation gold snuff-box between his fingers:

'I'm sorry I wasn't here a few years ago – I mean, that I was in Carlsbad at the time. H'm! I'm very interested in that young man about whom so many stories reached me at the time. H'm! Is it true that he's mad? Someone told me so then. A few days ago I'm suddenly told that a student has insulted him in the presence of his cousins and that he crawled under the table to hide himself from him. And yesterday I heard from Stepan Vysotsky that Stavrogin had just fought a duel with that – er – that Gaganov fellow. Just with the gallant idea of putting himself up as a target to an infuriated man. To get rid of him. H'm! That's the sort of thing a Guards officer would have done in the twenties. Does he visit anyone here?'

The General paused as though in expectation of an answer. The door of public impatience had been flung wide open.

'Why, what can be simpler?' Mrs Lembke suddenly cried in a loud voice, irritated by the way everyone in the room suddenly turned their eyes on her as though by word of command. 'Is there anything surprising in the fact that Stavrogin fought a duel with Gaganov but took no notice of the student? He couldn't possibly challenge one of his former serfs to a duel, could he?'

Significant words! A clear and simple idea which seemed, however, never to have occurred to anyone till then. Words which had quite extraordinary consequences. All scandal and gossip, all the petty small talk was at once pushed to the background. Those words put an entirely new complexion on the affair. A new character appeared on the scene, a person everyone had misjudged, a person with an almost ideal severity of social standards. Mortally insulted by a student, that is to say, an educated man and no longer a serf, he ignored the insult because the man who had attacked him was a former serf of his. Society had gossiped and slandered him; frivolous society had looked with contempt upon a man who had had his face slapped; but he had scorned public opinion which had failed to rise to an understanding of the real standards of social conduct and yet discussed them.

'And in the meantime you and I, sir, sit and discuss the correct standards of conduct,' one old club member said to another, moved by a vehement and generous feeling of self-reproach.

'Yes, sir, yes,' the other agreed with pleasure; 'you never can tell with the younger generation, can you?'

'It's not a question of the younger generation, sir,' a third one, who happened to be standing near them, observed; 'it's not a question of the younger generation. The man we're talking about is a star, sir, and not just one of our younger set. That's the way to look at it.'

'It's just the man we need. We haven't enough people of his sort.'

The main point about it was that the 'new man' had not only revealed himself as 'a genuine nobleman', but was also one of the wealthiest landowners in the province, and therefore could be counted on being one of the leading personages in our town who could be of great assistance in public affairs. I believe I have already briefly referred to the attitude of our landowners.

They even got excited about it.

'He not only refused to challenge the student, but also took his hands off him – mark that specially, sir,' one club member pointed out, addressing the General.

'Nor did he drag him through our new courts,' added another.

'In spite of the fact that for a personal insult to a born gentleman he would have got fifteen roubles damages – ha, ha, ha!'

'No, let me tell you the secret of our new courts,' a third one cried, working himself up into a frenzy. 'If a man is caught red-handed stealing or embezzling money, he had better run home quickly while there is still time and murder his mother. He'll then at once be acquitted of everything, and the ladies will wave their lawn hankies at him from the public gallery. It's the truth I'm telling you!'

'It's the truth! It's the truth!'

The inevitable anecdotes were trotted out. Stavrogin's connexions with Count K. were mentioned. Count K.'s severe and private views on the latest reforms were well known, as well as his remarkable public activities, that had a little slackened off lately. Suddenly everyone became convinced that Stavrogin was engaged to one of Count K.'s daughters, though there seemed to be no ground whatever for such a rumour. As for his marvellous adventures in Switzerland and his affair with Lisa, even our ladies no longer mentioned them. Let me, incidentally, add that the Drozdovs had by this time managed to pay all the visits they had omitted at first. They all found Lisa to be a most ordinary girl who 'flaunted' her delicate nerves. Her fainting on the day of Stavrogin's arrival, it was now explained, was simply due to her terror caused by the student's outrageous behaviour. They all did their best to emphasize the prosaic nature of the events which they had before tried to put in so fantastic a light. As for the lame woman, they forgot all about her now and were even ashamed to talk of her. 'Why, even if there had been hundreds of lame women – who hasn't been young once!' Stavrogin's respectful treatment of his mother was harped upon, various virtues were discovered in him, and the learning he had acquired during the four years he had spent at the German universities was good-naturedly commented on. Gaganov's conduct was declared to be absolutely unpardonable. Mrs Lembke was finally acknowledged to be a woman of remarkable insight.

When, therefore, Stavrogin himself at last made his appearance in society, he was received by everyone with the most naïve gravity. In all the eyes fixed upon him the most impatient expectations could be read. Stavrogin at once lapsed into most stern silence, which, of course, satisfied everybody much more than if he had talked his head off. In a word, he was successful in whatever he did; he became the fashion. Anyone who once appears in provincial society, cannot possibly hide himself away again. Stavrogin began to carry out his social

duties as punctiliously as before. People did not find him very cheerful
company: 'The man has been through a great deal; he is not like other
people; he has something to be sad about.' Even his pride and that
fastidious unapproachability, for which he was so hated in our town
four years before, were now liked and respected.

Mrs Stavrogin exulted more than anyone. I cannot say whether she
was really sorry about her shattered dream of her son's marriage to
Lisa. Here, of course, her family pride, too, came to her assistance. One
thing was strange, though: Mrs Stavrogin suddenly became most
firmly convinced that her Nicholas had 'made his choice' at Count
K.'s, but, which was even stranger than that, what convinced her were
the idle rumours which reached her as they did everybody else. She
was afraid to ask Stavrogin a direct question. Once or twice, however,
she could not refrain from reproaching him good-humouredly and in
a rather roundabout way for not being frank with her. Stavrogin smiled
and remained silent. The silence was taken as a sign of assent. And yet,
for all that, she never forgot the cripple. The thought of her lay like a
heavy stone on her heart, like a nightmare. It tortured her with
strange phantoms and conjectures, and all this side by side with her
dreams of the daughters of Count K. But of that later. It goes without
saying that the attitude of society towards Mrs Stavrogin was again
marked by extreme courtesy and respect, but she took little advantage
of it and very seldom drove out on visits.

She did, however, pay an official visit to the Governor's wife. No
one, of course, was more enchanted and charmed by Mrs Lembke's
words at the name-day party of the Marshal's wife than she. They removed a great deal of worry from her mind and explained much of
what had been troubling her since that luckless Sunday. 'I did not
understand that woman!' she said solemnly and, with the impulsiveness characteristic of her, she frankly told Mrs Lembke that she had
come to *thank* her. Mrs Lembke was flattered, but remained as independent as ever. She was beginning at this time to be aware of her
own importance, perhaps a little too much so. For instance, she declared in the course of her conversation with Mrs Stavrogin that she had
never heard of Mr Verkhovensky either as a public figure or as a scholar.

'I am, of course, only too glad to receive young Verkhovensky. He
is rather absurd, but he's young, though he certainly is a highly educated man. He is not some retired old-fashioned critic like his father.'

Mrs Stavrogin at once hastened to observe that Mr Verkhovensky had never been a critic, but had, on the contrary, spent all his life in her house. He became famous for the circumstances that attended his early career, circumstances which were 'well known to the whole world', and more recently for his work on Spanish history. He also planned to write about the position of modern German universities and, she believed, something else on the Dresden Madonna. In a word, Mrs Stavrogin was determined not to surrender Mr Verkhovensky to the tender mercies of Mrs Lembke.

'The Dresden Madonna? You mean the Sistine Madonna? My dear Mrs Stavrogin, I sat for two hours before that picture and came away completely disillusioned. I couldn't make it out at all and was quite astonished. Karmazinov, too, says that it is difficult to understand. No one finds anything remarkable in it now, neither Russians nor the English. It's the old men who made such a fuss of it.'

'It's the new fashion, then, I suppose?'

'Well, you know, I believe that we mustn't treat our younger generation with disrespect. People shout that they are communists, but in my opinion we must treat them with understanding, and not underestimate them. I read everything now – all the papers, the communes, natural sciences – I get everything, for after all one must know where one's living and with whom one has to deal. One can't spend all one's life in the world of one's imagination. I've come to the conclusion and made it my rule to be as nice as possible to the young people and in this way keep them from going over the brink. Believe me, my dear Mrs Stavrogin, that only we who belong to the best society can by our good influence and, above all, by our kindness keep them from the abyss into which the intolerance of these stupid old men pushes them. However, I am glad to learn from you about Mr Verkhovensky. You've given me an idea: he may be useful at our literary reading. I'm arranging a fête, you know, a subscription entertainment in aid of the poor governesses of our province. They are scattered all over Russia; there are six of them in our district alone; in addition there are two telegraphist girls, two academy students, and the rest would like to be trained for some job, but they haven't the means. The lot of the Russian woman is terrible, Mrs Stavrogin! This has now been made into a university question and there has even been a meeting of the State Council about it. In this strange Russia of ours one can do anything one likes. And that again is why I believe that only by the kindness and the warm sympathy of all our best people can this great common cause be put on the right path. Dear me, haven't we plenty of people of irreproachable character among us? To be sure we have, but they are all scattered. Let us close our ranks and we shall be stronger. In a word, I am thinking of arranging a literary matinée, then a light luncheon, then an intermission, and in the evening of the same day a ball. We thought of starting the evening with *tableaux vivants*, but that apparently would be too expensive, and so there will be for the public one or two quadrilles in masks and fancy dress representing well-known literary movements. It was Mr Karmazinov who suggested this amusing idea. He has been helping me a lot. You know, he's going to read us his last work, which no one knows yet. He is laying down his pen and isn't going to write anything any more; this last thing of his is his farewell to the public. It's a delightful little thing, called *Merci*. The title is in French, but he finds it even more amusing and subtle because of that. I do, too, and as a matter of fact I advised him to choose this title. I think Mr Verkhovensky, too, might read us something, if it isn't too long and – not too learned. I think Peter Verkhovensky and someone else will also read something. Peter will be round at your place and tell you the programme. Or perhaps I'd better bring it to you myself.'

'You won't mind if I add my name to your subscription list, will you? I'll tell Mr Verkhovensky and ask him myself.'

Mrs Stavrogin returned home completely enchanted. She had been won over to Mrs Lembke's side and was, for some reason, very angry with Mr Verkhovensky, who, poor man, sat at home and knew nothing about it.

'I'm charmed with her and I can't understand how I could have been so mistaken about that woman,' she said to Stavrogin and to Peter Verkhovensky, who had dropped in to see them in the evening.

'But you must make peace with the old boy, all the same,' Peter urged. 'He's in despair. You've cut him completely. Yesterday he saw you in your carriage and bowed, and you turned away. You know, we can give him a leg up. I'm counting on him to do something for me and I think he can still be useful.'

'Oh, he'll read something.'

'It wasn't that I had in mind. I meant to go and see him to-day. Shall I tell him about it?'

'If you like. I don't know, though, how you're going to arrange it,' she said irresolutely. 'I intended to have it out with him myself and wanted to fix the time and place.'

She frowned:

'Oh, it's not worth while fixing a time. I'll simply tell him.'

'Very well, tell him. However, you may as well add that I shall most certainly fix a time to see him. Do tell him that.'

Peter ran off, grinning. As far as I can remember, he was particularly spiteful all the time, and even allowed himself to be extremely rude and abrupt with almost everyone. It was curious how everyone somehow forgave him. Everyone seemed to take the view that he had to be regarded in a special sort of way. I may add that his attitude to Stavrogin's duel was particularly malicious. It took him by surprise; he even turned green when he was told about it. But perhaps his vanity was hurt: he learnt about it only on the following day when everyone knew of it.

'But you had no right to fight a duel,' he whispered to Stavrogin five days later, meeting him by chance at the club.

It is certainly remarkable that they had not met anywhere during those five days, though Peter had called on Mrs Stavrogin almost every day.

Stavrogin gave him a silent, absent-minded look, as though not understanding what he was talking about, and went on his way without stopping. He was just then passing through the large ballroom on his way to the bar.

'You've been to see Shatov, too. ... You intend to make it known about Mary,' he whispered, running after him and, as it were absent-mindedly, catching hold of his shoulder.

Stavrogin shook off his hand and quickly turned to him, with a menacing frown. Peter looked at him with his lips distended in a strange smile. Stavrogin walked on.

2

He went to see the 'old man' straight from Mrs Stavrogin's, and if he was in such haste, it was simply out of spite, because he had made up his mind to get his own back for an insult of which I had no idea at the time. What happened was that during their last interview – namely, on Thursday of the previous week – Mr Verkhovensky, who, as a matter of fact, himself started the quarrel, had ended by driving his son out of his house with a stick. He concealed the fact from me at the time; but now, no sooner did Peter rush into the room with his usual grin, which was so grossly arrogant, and his unpleasantly inquisitive eyes darting all over the place, than Mr Verkhovensky made a secret signal to me not to leave the room. This was how their real relations were revealed to me, for this time I heard their whole conversation.

Mr Verkhovensky was sitting stretched out on the sofa. Since that Thursday he had grown thin and sallow. Peter sat down beside him with a most familiar air, tucking his legs up unceremoniously and taking up much more room on the sofa than his respect for his father warranted. Mr Verkhovensky made room for him in silence and with a dignified air.

An open book was on the table. It was Chernyshevsky's novel *What's To Be Done?* I'm afraid I must reveal one strange weakness in my friend: the fantastic idea that he must leave his seclusion and fight a last battle took more and more possession of his sick fancy. I realized that he had got hold of the novel and was *studying* it with the sole purpose of knowing their arguments and methods beforehand from their 'catechism' so that when the inevitable conflict with the 'shriekers' came he would be ready to refute them triumphantly before *her* eyes. Oh, how that book tortured him! He sometimes threw it down in despair and, jumping up from his seat, walked up and down the room almost in a frenzy.

'I agree that the author's fundamental idea is right,' he said to me feverishly, 'but that makes it more awful! It's just our idea – yes, ours! We were the first to plant it, to nurture it, to get it ready – and what new thing could they say after us? But, good Lord, how they have expressed it all, distorted, mutilated it!' he cried, rapping on the book with his fingers. 'Were those the conclusions we wanted to draw? Who can recognize the original idea here?'

'Enlarging your mind?' Peter said with a grin, picking up the book from the table and reading the title. 'You should have done it long ago. I'll bring you much better books, if you like.'

Mr Verkhovensky again ignored his son's remark with dignity. I was sitting on a sofa in the corner of the room.

Peter quickly explained the purpose of his visit. Mr Verkhovensky was of course greatly taken aback and listened in alarm which was mixed with extreme indignation.

'And that Mrs Lembke really thinks that I'd go to read at her house?'

'But, don't you see, they don't need you at all. What they want is to be nice to you so as to get into Mrs Stavrogin's good books. And I don't think you will dare to refuse. Besides,' he added with a grin, 'I expect you're dying to do it. All you old fogies are hellishly conceited. But take my advice, old man, don't be too boring. What have you got there? Spanish history? You'd better let me have a look at it three days before the reading, or I'm sure you'll send them all to sleep.'

The hurried and all-too-obvious rudeness of these stinging remarks was quite obviously deliberate. He was apparently trying to pretend that it was quite impossible to talk to Mr Verkhovensky in a more refined and intelligent manner. Mr Verkhovensky continued resolutely to ignore his son's insults. But the news brought by his son produced a more and more overwhelming impression on him.

'And she herself, she *herself*, sir, asked *you* to tell me this?' he asked, turning pale.

'Well, you see, as a matter of fact she is going to let you know when and where she'd like to see you so that you can come to a mutual understanding – that, I suppose, is all that's left over from that romantic love affair of yours. You've been flirting with her for twenty years and you've certainly managed to teach her some droll methods. But don't worry, it's quite different now. She herself keeps repeating every minute that she is only just beginning "to see things in their true light". I told her in so many words that all this friendship of yours is nothing but a mutual outpouring of slops. She told me a lot of things, old man. Dear me, you have been a regular flunkey all this time, haven't you? I just couldn't help blushing for you.'

'I've been a regular flunkey?' cried Mr Verkhovensky, no longer able to restrain himself.

'Worse, you were a hanger-on; that is, a flunkey of your own free will. Too lazy to do a job of work, and we've quite a passion for money, haven't we? She, too, can see it all now – at least, she's been telling me some horrible things about you. Why, old man, I simply roared with laughter over your letters to her. I felt ashamed and disgusted. But, then, you're so depraved, so depraved! There's always something fundamentally depraving in charity – you're the best example of that!'

'She showed you my letters!'

'All of them. But of course I couldn't possibly read them all – could I? Good Lord, the reams and reams of paper you've covered! There must be more than two thousand letters there, I should think. But you know, old man, it's my belief that there was one moment when she'd have been ready to marry you. Wasn't there? You missed your chance in the stupidest way! I'm speaking from your point of view, of course, but you would certainly have been better off than now when you've almost been married off to cover up "another man's sins". Married off like a clown to make people laugh – for money.'

'For money! Did she say it was for money?' Mr Verkhovensky cried, deeply hurt.

'What else? But don't worry, I stood up for you. It's the only way you have of justifying your actions. She realized herself that you needed money like everybody else, and that from that point of view you were probably right. I proved it to her as clearly as I could that such an arrangement had been to the advantage of both of you. She was the capitalist and you were her sentimental clown. Still, I don't think she's angry about the money, though you did milk her like a nanny-goat. What she is so furious about is that she should have believed in you for twenty years, that you should have taken her in with that high-falutin talk of yours and made her go on lying for so long. That she was lying herself – that she will never admit, but that's why she'll jolly well make you suffer for it. What I can't understand is how it never occurred to you that you'd have to pay for it one day. You couldn't have been as stupid as that. I advised her yesterday to send you to the workhouse – now, keep your temper, please. I meant a decent workhouse, of course – nothing to hurt your feelings. I believe she'll do it, too. Do you remember your last letter to me three weeks ago?'

'You didn't show it to her, did you?' Mr Verkhovensky cried, jumping up with horror.

'Rather! Showed it to her first thing. The very same letter in which you told me that she was exploiting you, that she was jealous of your talent, and – well – that business about the other man's "sins". But, incidentally, old boy, you are devilishly conceited, you know. I simply roared with laughter. Your letters are damned boring, though. Your style is just horrible. I often didn't bother to read them at all. As a matter of fact, I've still got a letter of yours I've never opened. I'll send it back to you to-morrow. But that last letter of yours is a real masterpiece! How I laughed. Lord, how I laughed!'

'Monster! Monster!' cried Mr Verkhovensky.

'Damn it, one can't talk to you. Look here, you're not getting offended, as you were last Thursday, are you?'

Mr Verkhovensky drew himself up menacingly.

'How dare you talk to me like that?'

'Like what? Am I not making myself plain?'

'Tell me, you monster, are you my son or not?'

'You ought to know that better than I. But, of course, every father is inclined to be blind in such a case –'

'Shut up! Shut up!' Mr Verkhovensky cried, trembling all over.

'Now, look here, you go on screaming and swearing as you did last Thursday when you tried to threaten me with your stick, but I found that document, you know. I found it on that very day. Turned my trunk inside out just from curiosity. It's true there's nothing definite – you can take as much comfort as you like from that. It's only a note from my mother to that Polish gentleman. But if we take her character into account.'

'Another word and I'll box your ears!'

'What a man!' said Peter, suddenly addressing himself to me. 'You see, this has been going on between us since last Thursday. I'm glad you're here to-day, at any rate. You can judge between us. To begin with, a fact: he reproaches me for talking like this about my mother, but wasn't he the first to suggest it to me? In Petersburg, when I was still at school, didn't he wake me twice in the night, embrace me, and cry like an old woman; and what do you think he told me during those nights? Why, the same indecent stories about my mother. It was from him I first heard about it.'

'Oh, I did it from the highest motives in the world! Oh, you didn't understand me. You understood nothing, nothing!'

'But all the same your action was meaner than mine – it was meaner, you must admit. For, you see, it makes no difference to me

really. So far as I'm concerned, you needn't worry: I'm not blaming
my mother. Whether it was you or that Pole, it's all the same to me.
It's not my fault that you made such a stupid mess of things in Berlin.
I could hardly have expected you to have managed it more intelligently. But aren't you a funny man after all that? And what difference does it make to you whether I am your son or not? Listen,' he
said, turning to me again, 'he's never spent a rouble on me all his life.
Till I was sixteen he didn't know me at all, then he robbed me here,
and now he shouts that his heart has been bleeding for me all his life
and struts about like an actor before me. Good heavens! man, I'm not
Mrs Stavrogin, am I?'

He got up and picked up his hat.

'Henceforth a father's curse be upon you!' Mr Verkhovensky
stretched forth his hand over him, looking as white as a sheet.

'The idiotic things the man will say!' Peter exclaimed with genuine
surprise. 'Well, good-bye, old boy. I shan't be coming to see you
again. Don't forget to let me have your stuff in good time, and do try
not to write some nonsense: facts, facts, and facts, and, above all, keep
it short. Good-bye.'

3

However, there were other reasons there. Peter Verkhovensky really
had certain designs on his father. As I see it, he meant to drive the old
man to despair, and thus involve him in a public scandal of a certain
kind. He needed that for some other, independent, reasons, which I
shall discuss later. A great multitude of such plans and designs had
accumulated in his brain at that time – all of them, needless to say,
fantastic. He had another victim, besides Mr Verkhovensky, in mind.
In general, he had quite a number of victims, as became apparent afterwards; but on this one he counted especially, and it was none other
than Mr von Lembke himself.

Andrey Antonovich von Lembke belonged to that favoured (by
nature) tribe, of which there are several hundred thousand in Russia,
according to the official census, and which perhaps does not realize itself that, taken as a whole, it forms a closely organized union. A union
that has, of course, not been deliberately organized, but that exists as
an independent tribal unit, without any verbal or written agreement,
by dint of some moral compulsion, and which can always count on

the mutual support of its members everywhere and in any circumstances. Von Lembke had the honour to be educated in one of those Russian educational establishments to which the young people of the wealthier and better connected families are sent. Almost immediately after the completion of their studies, the pupils of this establishment are appointed to rather important positions in one of the Government departments. One of von Lembke's uncles was a lieutenant-colonel of the Engineering Corps, and another a baker. But he managed to get into this select public school, where he met not a few of his fellow tribesmen. He was a good sport and not a particularly brilliant scholar, and everybody liked him. And when many of the boys in the higher forms, mostly Russians, had already learnt to discuss important social problems and in a way, too, that seemed to suggest that they were only waiting to leave school to solve them all, von Lembke still indulged in the most innocent schoolboy pranks. He amused them all, it is true, by these not particularly clever pranks, which were cynical at best, but that was exactly what he had set out to do. Sometimes when his teacher asked him some question during a lesson, he would blow his nose in a remarkable sort of way which would make his schoolmates and the teacher laugh; another time, in the dormitory, he would act some obscene living picture amid general applause, or, again, he would play the overture from 'Fra Diavolo' with his nose (and very cleverly, too). He was also remarkable for his deliberately untidy appearance, finding it for some reason very witty. In his last year at school he began writing Russian verses. His own tribal language he spoke rather ungrammatically, like many others of his tribe in Russia. This bent for versification led him to strike up a friendship with a gloomy classmate, who seemed to be depressed by something, the son of a poor Russian general, who was considered in school as one of the great future luminaries of Russian literature. The boy took a patronizing interest in von Lembke. But it happened that three years after leaving school, this gloomy schoolboy, who had given up his job in order to devote himself to Russian literature and was as a result going about in torn boots, his teeth chattering with cold, wearing a summer overcoat in the late autumn, one day accidentally met his former protégé 'Lembke', as everybody, incidentally, called him at school, on the Anichkin bridge. And what do you think? He did not even recognize him at first and stopped dead with surprise. Before him stood an irreproachably dressed young man, with wonderfully trimmed side-whiskers of a reddish tint, wearing pince-nez and patent-leather boots, gloves of the freshest hue, and a wide Charmère overcoat, and with a brief-case under his arm. Lembke was very nice to his old school-friend, gave him his address, and asked him to call on him some evening. It also appeared that he was no longer 'Lembke' but von Lembke. His school-friend did call on him, however, though perhaps just out of spite. On the staircase, which was far from beautiful and certainly not the main entrance of the house, but which was covered with red felt, he was stopped by the porter, who asked him what his business was. A bell rang loudly on the top floor. But instead of the riches which the visitor expected to find, he discovered his 'Lembke' in a very small sideroom, which looked dark and dilapidated, divided into two by a large, dark-green curtain, and furnished with upholstered though old furniture, with dark-green curtains at high, narrow windows. Von Lembke lived in the house of a very distant relative, a general who had taken him under his wing. He welcomed his visitor cordially, was serious and gracefully courteous. They talked of literature, too, but strictly within the bounds of decorum. A footman in a white tie brought them some weak tea and little dry, round cakes. His friend, out of spite, asked for some soda-water. It was brought, but after some delay, Lembke looking rather embarrassed as he summoned the foot-man a second time and gave him the order. However, he asked his visitor himself whether he would like something to eat, and was evidently relieved when the latter declined his offer and, at last, went away. Lembke was simply embarking on his career just then and merely sponged on his fellow-tribesman, the important General.

He was at that time sighing for the General's fifth daughter, and his feeling was apparently reciprocated. But Amalia was nevertheless married in due course to an elderly German factory owner, an old friend of the General's. Lembke did not shed many tears and set about making a cardboard theatre. The curtain went up, the actors came out and gesticulated with their hands; the audience sat in the boxes, the orchestra moved their bows across the fiddles by some mechanical device, the conductor waved his baton, and in the stalls the young gentlemen and the officers clapped their hands. It was all made out of cardboard, and it was all devised and executed by von Lembke himself. He spent six months on his theatre. The General arranged an intimate party on purpose; the theatre was exhibited; all the General's five daughters with the newly-wed Amalia, her factory owner, and many young married ladies with their German escorts examined and admired the theatre; then there was dancing. Lembke was very satisfied and was soon consoled.

Years passed and his career was made. He always secured important jobs in Government departments, and always under chiefs of his own tribe, and he was promoted at last to a rather high rank for a man of his age. He had wished to get married for a long time and he had long since been looking out for the right sort of girl. He had sent a novel to a magazine without telling his superiors about it, but it had not been accepted. On the other hand, he made a cardboard model of a railway train, and again the result was most successful: the passengers with their children and dogs, carrying trunks and bags, came out on the platform and got into the carriages. The guards and the porters walked about, the bell was rung, the signal given, and the train moved out of the station. He spent more than a year over that clever toy. But still he had to get married. His circle of acquaintances was fairly large, mostly in the world of his German fellow-countrymen. But he also mixed in Russian society, chiefly as part of his duties, of course. At last, when he was in his thirty-ninth year, he came in for a legacy. His uncle the baker died, leaving him thirty-seven thousand in his will. All he needed now was an important post. In spite of his rather high official standing, Mr von Lembke was a very modest man. He would have been perfectly satisfied with some independent little official post, giving him the right to superintend the purchase of firewood for Government departments, or something nice and comfortable of that kind, and he would have been glad to keep such a job all his life. But just then, instead of the Minna or Ernestine he had expected, Julia suddenly appeared on the scene. His career at once rose a rung higher. The modest and precise von Lembke felt that he, too, could be ambitious.

By the old way of reckoning, Julia owned two hundred serfs, and she had besides a great number of friends in high places. On the other hand, von Lembke was a handsome man and she was already over forty. The interesting thing is that he gradually fell in love with her in good earnest, as he became more and more used to the idea that he was her fiancé. On the morning of their wedding day he sent her a poem. She liked it all very much, even the verses: to be forty is no joke. Very soon a certain rank and a certain decoration were bestowed on him and then he was appointed governor of our province.

Before her arrival in our town, Julia Lembke put in a good deal of work on her husband. In her view, he was not without abilities, he knew how to enter a room and to show off to advantage, he knew how to listen to a person and keep silent with a thoughtful air, he had acquired a few highly decorous poses, he could even make a speech, had indeed some odds and ends of ideas, and he had assumed the necessary gloss of the latest 'liberal' idea. But she was still worried that he was somehow very unsusceptible to new ideas and that, after his long and arduous pursuit of a career, was quite undeniably beginning to feel the need of a rest. She tried to inspire him with her ambition, and he suddenly started making a Lutheran church: the pastor came out to preach the sermon, the congregation listened with piously folded hands, one lady was drying her tears with a tiny handkerchief, an old gentleman was blowing his nose; in the end a little organ, specially ordered and dispatched from Switzerland at no small expense, played a tune. As soon as she got wind of his new toy, Julia became really alarmed, carried it all off, and locked it up in a box in her room: to make up for it she let him write a novel, but on condition that it was kept secret. Since then she had decided to depend only on herself. Unfortunately, there was a great deal of frivolity and very little method in her plans. Destiny had kept her an old maid too long. One idea after another flashed through her ambitious and somewhat exasperated mind. She nourished grandiose schemes, she resolutely made up her mind to rule the province, she dreamed of immediately surrounding herself with loyal followers, she adopted a definite policy. Von Lembke even got a little alarmed, though, with his Civil Service tact, he soon realized that there was actually nothing he need be afraid of so far as his position of governor was concerned. The first two or three months passed very satisfactorily indeed. But then Peter Verkhovensky turned up and rather queer things began to happen.

The trouble was that from the very first young Verkhovensky had shown a most flagrant disrespect for von Lembke and had assumed some strange rights over him, while Julia, always so jealous of her husband's position, refused to notice it at all; at least, she did not think it important. The young man became her favourite; he ate, drank, and

almost slept in the house. Von Lembke tried to defend himself, called
him 'young man' before strangers, patted him patronizingly on the
shoulder, but he made no impression: Peter Verkhovensky still seemed to be laughing in his face, even while conducting an apparently
serious conversation, and he would say the most outrageous things to
him before people. One day, on his return home, he found the young
man asleep in his study without permission. Peter explained that he
had come in, and not finding him at home, 'had a nap'. Von Lembke
was offended and again complained to his wife; after making fun of
his irritability, she pointedly remarked that he did not apparently
know how to make people treat him with respect. At least 'that boy'
never permitted himself any undue familiarity with her, and, besides,
he was 'naïve and fresh, though perhaps a little unconventional'. Von
Lembke sulked. This time she made peace between them. Peter did
not, it is true, apologize, but dismissed the whole matter with a crude
joke, which might at another time have been taken for a new insult,
but was taken in the present circumstances as a sign of repentance. The
weak spot in their relationship was that von Lembke had from the
very beginning made the mistake of telling Peter about his novel.
Imagining him to be an ardent young man of a romantic disposition
and having long been dreaming of a listener, he had one evening during the first days of their acquaintance read him two chapters from his
novel. Peter listened without concealing his boredom, yawning discourteously, and without saying one word in its praise; as he was
leaving, he asked for the manuscript so as to be able to form an opinion of it at home at his leisure, and von Lembke gave it him. He had
not returned the manuscript since that evening, though he called every
day and replied to all inquiries with a laugh. In the end he said that he
had lost it in the street. When she heard of it, Julia was terribly angry
with her husband.

'You didn't tell him anything about your cardboard church, did
you?' she asked him almost in dismay.

Von Lembke began to brood, and brooding was bad for his health
and had been forbidden by his doctors. Apart from the fact that there
was apparently a great deal of trouble in the province, of which we
shall speak later, he had special reasons – his feelings were hurt, let
alone his vanity as a governor. When contracting his marriage,
von Lembke had never entertained the possibility of any domestic

disagreements and conflicts. That was what he had imagined all his life when dreaming of his Minna or Ernestine. He felt that he was not able to stand domestic storms. At last Julia had a frank talk with him.

'You can't possibly be angry with him for that,' she said, 'if only because you're three times more sensible than he and because your social position is infinitely higher than his. The boy still has a great deal of his old freethinking habits. In my opinion, it is simply naughtiness. But nothing can be done in a hurry. It must all be done gradually. We must not under-estimate our young people. My policy is to be kind to them and in this way hold them back from going over the brink.'

'But he says such awful things,' von Lembke replied. 'I can't treat him tolerantly when he asserts in public and in my presence that the Government deliberately makes the common people drunk on vodka in order to brutalize them and prevent them from rising against it. Imagine my position when I'm forced to listen to that kind of talk in the presence of all sorts of people.'

As he said this, von Lembke recalled a conversation he had had with Peter Verkhovensky a few days before. With the innocent purpose of disarming him by his liberal ideas, he had shown him his own private collection of all sorts of political leaflets, printed in Russia and abroad, which he had been carefully collecting since 1859, not so much as a hobby, but out of commendable curiosity. Realizing what he was after, Peter said rudely that there was more sense in one line of some of those leaflets than in a whole Government office, 'perhaps not excepting your own '.

Lembke winced.

'But in our country this is premature, much too premature,' he said almost beseechingly, pointing to the leaflets.

'No, it isn't. You see, you're afraid, and that means that it isn't premature.'

'But, look here, in this one, for instance, they call for the demolition of churches.'

'Why not? You're an intelligent man, and I think I'm right in saying that while you're not a believer yourself, you realize very well that religion is necessary in order to brutalize the people. Truth is more honest than lies.'

'I agree, I agree, I agree with you entirely, but I still maintain that it is premature in this country, much too premature,' von Lembke said, pulling a face.

'Well, in that case what sort of Government servant are you if you agree to the demolition of the churches and marching on Petersburg with staves and make it merely a question of time?'

Caught out so crudely, Lembke was greatly shocked.

'It isn't that, it isn't that at all,' he went on, carried away and becoming more and more exasperated in his vanity. 'You're a young man and you don't know our aims, and that is why you are mistaken. You see, my dear fellow, you call us Government officials, don't you? All right. Independent officials? All right. But what do we do, do you think? We bear the responsibility and, as a result, we serve the common cause just as you do. We merely hold together what you are pulling apart and which without us would fall apart. We're not your enemies. Not by any means. We say to you: go on, progress, and you may even undermine certain things – I mean, of course, everything that's old and has to be completely reorganized. But, if need be, we shall keep you within the necessary limits, and by doing so save you from yourselves, for without us you would only set Russia rocking and rob her of her decent appearance, while it is our task to take care of her decent appearance. Please, realize that we need each other. In England the Whigs and the Tories also need each other. Well, then: we are the Tories and you are the Whigs. That's how I see it.'

Von Lembke grew positively excited. He had been fond of talking in a clever and liberal vein even in Petersburg, and, besides, no one was eavesdropping on him here. Peter did not speak and, contrary to his custom, looked grave. That excited the orator more than ever.

'Do you know that I, the "master of the province",' he went on, pacing his office – 'do you know that just because I've so many duties, I cannot carry out a single one of them, and, on the other hand, I can say just as truly that there's nothing for me to do here. The whole secret lies in the fact that everything here depends on the views of the Government. Let's suppose that for political reasons or for the sake of allaying popular passions the Government decided to found a republic and, simultaneously, strengthen the powers of the governors. If that should happen, we, the governors, will accept a republic. But why only a republic? We'll swallow anything you like. At least, I feel that I'm ready. In a word, let the Government instruct me by telegraph to carry out an *activité dévorante*, I shall give them an *activité dévorante*. I told them straight: "Gentlemen, one thing only is needed to maintain the equilibrium and assure the well-being of all provincial institutions – the strengthening of the Governor's powers." You see, it is absolutely necessary that all these institutions, whether agricultural or legal, should lead as it were a dual sort of existence – that is, on the one hand, it is necessary (and I agree that it *is* necessary) that they should exist; but, on the other hand, it is necessary that they should not exist – all in accordance with the views of the Government. If the Government should take it into their heads to declare that the institutions had suddenly become necessary, I should immediately see to it that they were there. Should the need for them pass, no one would be able to find them in my province. That's how I understand *activité dévorante*, and you can't have it without strengthening the Governor's powers. I'm telling you this as man to man. I've already told them in Petersburg, you know, that I must have a special sentry at the entrance to the Governor's house. I'm waiting for an answer.'

'You must have two,' said Peter.

'Why two?' von Lembke asked, stopping short before him.

'I think one isn't enough to make people respect you. You must have two.'

Lembke made a wry face.

'You – you do permit yourself goodness only knows what, sir. You take advantage of my good nature and you make all sorts of insulting insinuations and play the part of some *bourru bienfaisant*.'

'Well, that's as may be,' Peter muttered, 'but all the same you're paving the way for us and preparing for our success.'

'But who is "us", pray, and what success?' von Lembke said, staring at him in surprise, but he got no answer.

After listening to this account of their conversation, Julia was greatly displeased.

'But,' von Lembke defended himself, 'I can't possibly treat your favourite as if I were his superior, especially when we're alone in the room. I – I admit I might have said something I shouldn't just – just out of the goodness of my heart.'

'From too much goodness. I didn't know you had a collection of political leaflets. Can I see it?'

'But – but he asked me if he could borrow it for one day.'

'And again you gave it to him?' Julia cried angrily. 'How indiscreet!'

'I'll send someone round to him at once to bring it back.'

'He won't give it back.'

'I shall demand it!' von Lembke cried, flying into a rage, and he even jumped up from his seat. 'Who is he, pray, that I should be so much afraid of him, and who am I that I should not dare to do anything?'

'Sit down and calm yourself,' said Julia, restraining him. 'I'll answer your first question: he came to me with most excellent letters of introduction. He has ability and occasionally he says very clever things. Karmazinov assured me that he had connexions almost everywhere and that his influence on the young people in Petersburg and Moscow was very great. And if through him I succeed in winning them all over and grouping them all round me, I shall save them from ruin by providing a new outlet for their ambitions. He is devoted to me with all his heart and he obeys me implicitly.'

'But while you're being nice to them, they might do – goodness only knows what. Of course, it's an idea,' von Lembke defended himself vaguely, 'but – but I've just heard that similar political leaflets have appeared in one of our districts.'

'But there was such a rumour in the summer – leaflets, counterfeit notes, all sorts of things, and yet so far not one of those has been found. Who told you?'

'I heard it from von Blum.'

'Oh, save me from your von Blum and please don't ever mention him to me again!'

Julia was so furious that for a minute she could not utter a word. Von Blum was a clerk in the office of the Governor whom she particularly detested. Of that later.

'Please don't worry about Verkhovensky,' she said in conclusion. 'If he had taken part in any pranks he would not talk as he does to you and to everyone else here. People who are fond of using fine phrases are not dangerous. Even I might talk like that. And if anything did happen, I should be the first to find out from him. He is fanatically, fanatically devoted to me.'

I may add here, anticipating events, that were it not for Julia Lembke's self-conceit and ambition, probably nothing of what those wretched people succeeded in perpetrating among us would have happened. She was undoubtedly responsible for a great deal.

5

Before the Fête

I

THE day of the fête, which Julia Lembke organized in aid of the governesses of our province, had been several times fixed and put off. She was always surrounded by Peter Verkhovensky and the little Civil Servant Lyamshin, who ran errands for her. Lyamshin used to visit Stepan Verkhovensky at one time, but he suddenly found favour in the Governor's house because he played the piano. Liputin, too, whom Julia Lembke planned to appoint the editor of a future independent provincial newspaper, was often in her company. There were also several married and unmarried ladies and, finally, even Karmazinov, who, though he was not dancing attendance on the Governor's wife, had declared aloud and with a complacent air that he had a pleasant surprise for everybody when the literary quadrille began. There was a great number of subscribers and donors, all of them belonging to the most select provincial society; but even the most unselect were admitted provided they came with money. Julia Lembke observed that an intermingling of the different classes of the population ought sometimes to be permitted, for 'otherwise who will enlighten them?' A private domestic committee was organized at which it was decided that the fête would be of a democratic character. The large number of subscriptions tempted them to indulge in a vast expenditure of money; they wanted to do something marvellous – that was why the fête was postponed. They could still not make up their minds where to hold the ball: whether at the huge house of the wife of the marshal of nobility, which she put at their disposal for that day, or at Mrs Stavrogin's country mansion in Skvoreshniki. Skvoreshniki was a little too far, but many members of the committee insisted that it would be 'freer' there. Mrs Stavrogin herself would have very much liked the festivities to take place in her house. It is difficult to say why this proud woman almost fawned on Julia Lembke. She probably liked to see how Mrs Lembke, in her turn, almost humbled herself before Nicholas Stavrogin, and was nicer to him than to anyone. I repeat again: Peter Verkhovensky constantly impressed upon everyone in the Governor's house in whispers the idea – an idea he had already expressed earlier – that Stavrogin was a man who had most mysterious connexions with most mysterious circles and that he had certainly been entrusted with some secret mission.

The people of our town were in a strange state of mind at the time. Among the ladies, especially, a sort of frivolous attitude was to be observed, and it cannot be said that it all happened gradually. A number of extremely free-and-easy notions seemed to be in the air. A mood of levity and frivolity set in, and I can't say that it was always pleasant. A certain moral laxity was in fashion. Afterwards, when it was all over, the blame was put on Julia Lembke, her circle and her influence; but I doubt if it was Julia alone who was the cause of it. On the contrary, at first many people fell over themselves in praising our new Governor's wife for her ability to unite society, as well as for the fact that things became much more cheerful. Several rather scandalous incidents occurred for which Mrs Lembke could not be blamed at all, but at the time everybody laughed and was highly amused, and there was no one who could put a stop to it. It is true that a rather large number of people kept away, having their own particular views on the course of events; but even they did not grumble at the time; indeed, they even smiled.

I remember a rather large circle of people sprang into being at the time whose centre was perhaps really to be found in Mrs Lembke's drawing-room. In that intimate circle, which always surrounded her – among the young people, of course – all sorts of mischievous pranks, sometimes of a rather free-and-easy nature, were allowed, and even became the rule. This circle even included several very charming ladies. The young people arranged picnics, parties, sometimes rode through the streets in a regular cavalcade, in carriages and on horseback. They looked for adventures, even deliberately organized and invented them themselves, solely for the sake of having an amusing story to tell. They treated our town as if it were the town of Folly from Shchedrin's famous satire. They were called buffoons or scoffers, because there was nothing much that they would not do. It so happened, for instance, that the wife of one of the army lieutenants stationed in our town, a very young and pretty brunette, though she looked worn out from her husband's ill-treatment, thoughtlessly sat down to play whist for high stakes at a party in the hope of winning enough money to buy herself a cloak, but instead of winning, lost fifteen roubles. Afraid of her husband, and having no money of her own, she remembered what a spirited girl she had been before her marriage and decided to ask the son of our mayor, a young blade worn out with dissipation, though he was still young, who was also at the party, to lend her some money. He not only turned down her request, but went, laughing at the top of his voice, to tell her husband. The lieutenant, who found it hard to make ends meet on his scanty army pay, took his wife home and there proceeded to get his own back on her to his heart's content in spite of her wails, shrieks, and entreaties on her knees to forgive her. This outrageous incident excited nothing but laughter in our town, and though the poor wife of the lieutenant did not belong to Mrs Lembke's circle, one of the ladies of the 'cavalcade', an eccentric and dashing young woman, who happened to know her, went to see her and took her away to stay at her house. Here our madcaps at once got hold of her, made much of her, loaded her with presents, and kept her for four days without returning her to her husband. She lived with the adventurous lady, and spent her days driving about with her and with the rest of the frolicsome company in their trips round the town and taking part in their gay parties and dances. They were all the time trying to make her summons her husband and start a lawsuit. They assured her that they would stand by her and would appear as witnesses in court. The husband kept quiet, not daring to assert his rights. The poor girl realized at last that she had got herself into a mess and, nearly dead with fear, ran away in the evening of the fourth day from her protectors to her lieutenant. Exactly what happened between her and her husband is not known; but two shutters of the little wooden bungalow in which the lieutenant lived were not opened for two weeks. When Mrs Lembke heard of what had happened, she was very angry with the mischief-makers and greatly displeased with the conduct of the dashing lady, though the latter had introduced the lieutenant's wife to her on the first day of her abduction. However, the whole incident was soon forgotten.

Another time, a young Government clerk from another district married the daughter of a Government clerk of our town, a beautiful girl of seventeen, known to everybody in our town. But suddenly the news leaked out that the young husband treated the beautiful girl very discourteously on the wedding night in revenge for his insulted honour. Lyamshin, who was almost a witness of the affair, because he had got drunk at the wedding and stayed the night in the house, rushed round the town in the early morning to spread the glad tidings. At once a party of about a dozen men was made up, all of them on horseback, some on hired Cossack horses – for instance, Peter Verkhovensky and Liputin, who in spite of his grey hair took part in almost all the scandalous adventures of our flighty youth. When the young couple appeared in the street in a carriage and pair on their way to pay visits, according to the generally observed custom on the day after a wedding, in spite of anything that might have happened, the whole cavalcade surrounded the carriage, laughing merrily and accompanying them all over the town the whole morning. It is true, they did not follow them into the houses, but waited on their horses by the gates; they also refrained from any special insults to the groom or the bride, but still they caused a public scandal. The whole town talked about it. Everybody, of course, laughed. But this time von Lembke got angry and again had a lively scene with his wife. Mrs Lembke, too, was exceedingly angry, and even made up her mind to close the door of her house to the reprobates. But on the following day she forgave everybody as a result of Peter Verkhovensky's exhortations and of a few words from Karmazinov. The latter thought the 'joke' rather amusing.

'It is in accordance with the local customs,' he said. 'At any rate, it's characteristic and – daring. And, look, everybody is laughing; you alone are outraged.'

But there were pranks which were quite intolerable and which betrayed a certain unmistakable tendency.

A certain respectable woman, though of the artisan class, appeared in our town, selling gospels. People started talking about her, because of the interesting reports about such sellers of gospels which had recently appeared in the Moscow and Petersburg newspapers. Again the same rogue Lyamshin, assisted by an unemployed divinity student who hoped to get a job at a school, quietly secreted into the woman's bag, while pretending to buy books from her, a whole bundle of indecent and obscene photographs from abroad, donated specially for that purpose by a highly respectable old gentleman, whose name I shall not mention, but who wore a high decoration round his neck and who, as he put it, loved 'a healthy laugh and a merry jest'. When the poor woman began taking out the sacred books in our shopping arcade, the photographs, too, were scattered all over the place. There was loud laughter and murmurs of indignation. A crowd surrounded the woman and started abusing her, and she would certainly have been attacked if the police had not arrived in the nick of time. The woman was locked up in a cell at the police station, and it was only in the evening, thanks to the efforts of Maurice Drozdov, who had learnt with indignation the full details of this horrible story, that she was set free and escorted out of town. Mrs Lembke would now most certainly have turned Lyamshin out of her house, but the young people had brought him to her that very evening with the news that he had composed a new piece for the piano and persuaded her to hear it. The little piece, which, in fact, was rather entertaining, bore the comic title: 'Franco-Prussian War'. It began with the menacing strains of the Marseillaise:

> Qu'un sang impur abreuve nos sillons!

A flamboyant challenge was heard, the flush of future victories. But suddenly, mingling with the masterly variations on the national anthem – somewhere on one side, from below, from some corner, but very close, came the trivial strains of Mein lieber Augustin. The Marseillaise ignored them; the Marseillaise reached the climax of intoxication with its own grandeur; but Augustin was gaining strength, it was getting more and more insolent, and suddenly the strains of Augustin began to blend with the strains of the Marseillaise. The latter was apparently getting angry; unable to ignore Augustin any longer, it tried to shake it off, to brush it off, like some obtrusive, insignificant fly, but Mein lieber Augustin was hanging on firmly; he was gay and self-confident, he was full of joy and arrogance, and the Marseillaise suddenly somehow became terribly stupid: it could no longer conceal its resentment and exasperation; it was a wail of indignation, tears, and oaths with arms outstretched to Providence:

> Pas un pouce de notre terrain, pas une de nos fortresses.

But already it was forced to sing in time with Mein lieber Augustin. Its melody passed in a most stupid way into that of Augustin, it drooped and died. Only from time to time could a snatch of the original tune be heard: *qu'un sang impur* ... but immediately they passed most mortifyingly into the horrible waltz. Finally, it was utterly subdued: it was Jules Favre sobbing on Bismarck's bosom and giving away everything, everything. ... But now it was Augustin's turn to assert himself: hoarse sounds were heard, one had a feeling of countless barrels of beer, the frenzy of self-glorification, demands for milliards, expensive cigars, champagne and hostages; *Augustin* passed into a wild roar. ... The Franco-Prussian war was at an end. Our young people applauded. Mrs Lembke smiled and said, 'Well, how can one turn him out?' Peace was made. The blackguard really had a sort of talent. Mr Verkhovensky assured me one day that men of the highest artistic talent could be the most awful blackguards and that one thing had nothing to do with the other. There was a rumour afterwards that Lyamshin had stolen that piece from a talented and modest young fellow he knew, who happened to be passing through our town and whose name remained unknown, but that is by the way. This scoundrel, who had been following Mr Verkhovensky about for several years, mimicking at his parties, when requested, all sorts of Jews, the confession of a deaf peasant woman or the birth of a child, now sometimes caricatured Mr Verkhovensky himself in a most diverting manner at Mrs Lembke's parties under the title of 'A Liberal of the Forties'. Everybody was convulsed with laughter, so that in the end it was quite impossible to turn him out: he had become too indispensable. Besides, he fawned slavishly on Peter Verkhovensky, who by that time had obtained quite an unusually powerful influence over Mrs Lembke.

I shouldn't have talked about this blackguard, and he would not have been worth discussing, but for an outrageous incident in which he, too, was said to have taken part, and that incident I cannot possibly omit from my chronicle.

One morning the news of an infamous and outrageous sacrilege spread like wildfire through the town. At the entrance to our huge market-place stands the ancient church of Our Lady's Nativity, which is one of the most remarkable ancient monuments of our old town. At the gates of the enclosure surrounding the church, a large icon of the Blessed Virgin had for many years been displayed behind a grating in the wall. One night this icon had been robbed, the glass of the icon-case broken, the grating smashed, and a few stones and pearls (I don't know whether they were worth anything) removed from the crown and the setting. But the chief thing was that besides the robbery a senseless and mocking sacrilege had been perpetrated: behind the broken glass of the icon a live mouse was said to have been found. Now, four months later, it was positively established that the crime was committed by Fedka the convict, but, for some reason, Lyamshin is said to have been involved in it. At the time no one mentioned Lyamshin and he was not suspected at all, but now everyone is saying that it was he who put the mouse there. I remember that our authorities were rather at a loss. A crowd had gathered round the place of the crime since early morning. There was always a crowd there, though perhaps not such a big one – about a hundred people all told. Some came, others went. Those who came, crossed themselves and kissed the icon; people began contributing to a collection, a church plate made its appearance, and a monk was stationed near it, and it was only at three o'clock in the afternoon that the authorities realized that the people should be told not to stand there in a crowd, but move on after they had prayed, kissed the icon, and contributed to the collection. This unfortunate incident produced a most gloomy impression on von Lembke. Mrs Lembke, as I was told, said afterwards that since that ill-omened morning she began to notice in her husband that strange dejection which persisted up to the time, two months ago, when he left our town on account of illness and which apparently afflicts him even now in Switzerland, where he continues to rest after his brief term of office in our province.

I remember I went into the square at one o'clock in the afternoon; the crowds were silent and their faces grave and gloomy. A merchant drove up in a hackney carriage. He was fat and sallow-faced. He alighted, bowed to the ground, kissed the icon, put a rouble in the collection plate, got back, sighing, into the carriage, and drove off again. Then a carriage drove up with two of our ladies accompanied by two of our madcaps. The young men (one of whom was not so young, either) also got out and made their way to the icon, pushing people aside rather unceremoniously. Neither of them took off his hat, and one of them put his pince-nez on his nose. The crowd began to murmur – in low voices, it is true, but far from amiably. The chap with the pince-nez took out of his purse, which was crammed with banknotes, a copper coin and flung it on the plate; both of them, laughing and talking loudly, went back to their carriage. At that moment Lisa suddenly rode up, accompanied by Maurice Drozdov. She jumped off her horse, threw the reins to her escort, whom she told to stay on his horse, and went up to the icon just when the copper coin had been flung on the collection plate. Her cheeks coloured with indignation; she took off her round hat and gloves, fell on her knees before the icon on the muddy pavement, and reverently prostrated herself three times. Then she took out her purse, but as there were only a few silver coins in it, she at once took off her diamond ear-rings and put them on the plate.

'May I? May I? As an ornament for the setting?' she asked the monk in great excitement.

'You may,' the monk replied. 'Every contribution is a blessing.'

The people were silent, neither approving nor disapproving. Lisa mounted her horse in her muddy dress and galloped away.

2

Two days after the incident I have just described I met her among a large company of people who were setting out to go somewhere in three carriages surrounded by men on horseback. She signalled to me with her hand, stopped her carriage, and insisted that I should join their company. There was room for me in the carriage, and she introduced me laughingly to her companions, smartly dressed ladies, explaining to me that they were off on a highly interesting expedition. She went on laughing loudly, and seemed a little too happy. Just recently she had become rather playfully gay. The expedition was indeed an eccentric one: they were all going across the river to the house of the merchant Sevostyanov, where our saintly half-wit and prophet Semyon Yakovlevich, famous not only in our town but also in the surrounding provinces as well as in Moscow and Petersburg, had been living for the past ten years in a cottage in the courtyard, in seclusion, contentment, and comfort. Everyone went to see him, especially visitors from all parts of the country, in an attempt to get some saintly message from him, paying homage and bringing offerings. The offerings, sometimes considerable ones, were piously sent to some church, mostly to the monastery of Our Lady, unless Semyon Yakovlevich disposed of them himself; for that purpose a monk from the monastery was always on duty in Semyon Yakovlevich's room. They were all expecting to get a great deal of amusement from their visit. No one of the company had ever seen Semyon Yakovlevich. Only Lyamshin had been there before, and he was telling everybody that the saint had ordered him to be driven out with a broom and had thrown two large boiled potatoes after him with his own hand. I noticed Peter Verkhovensky among the horsemen, again on a hired Cossack horse, which he rode rather clumsily, as well as Stavrogin, also on horseback. Stavrogin occasionally joined these diverting excursions, in which case he assumed a correspondingly gay demeanour, though, as usual, he spoke little and seldom. When, after crossing the bridge, the cavalcade was passing our local inn, someone suddenly announced that a man had just been found shot in one of the rooms of the inn and that the police had been sent for. It was at once proposed that the company should have a look at the suicide. The proposal found general support: our ladies had never seen a suicide. I remember one of them said in a loud voice that she felt so bored with everything that she did not think they need worry their heads about the kind of entertainment they might get, provided it was interesting. Only a few of them remained outside the inn; the rest entered the dirty corridor in a body and among them, to my surprise, I also noticed Lisa. The door of the room of the man who had shot himself was open and they did not, of course, dare to prevent us from going in. The suicide was quite a young fellow of about nineteen, no more, who must have been very good-looking. He had thick fair hair, a regular oval face, and a beautiful, noble forehead. Rigor mortis had already set in, and his small white face looked as if it had been carved out of marble. On the table lay a note in his own hand, asking the police not to blame anyone for his death and explaining that he had shot himself because he had 'squandered' 400 roubles. The word 'squandered' was actually used in the note: there were three grammatical mistakes in the four lines of the note. A fat landowner, who was evidently a neighbour of his and who had been staying at the inn on some business of his own, seemed to be particularly distressed. It appeared from his words that the boy had been sent by his family, his widowed mother, sisters, and aunts, from the country to the town to make all sorts of purchases under the supervision of a woman relative in our town, for the trousseau of his eldest sister, who was going to be married, and bring them home. He

was entrusted with the 400 roubles, saved up in the course of many
years, his relatives sighing with apprehension and sending him off
with endless exhortations, prayers, and signs of the cross. Till then the
boy had been modest and reliable. On his arrival in town three days
before he had not gone to his relation, but had stopped at the inn and
gone straight to the club in the hope of finding in some back room a
travelling croupier or, at least, some card game at high stakes. But
there was no card game that evening, nor any croupier. On his return
to his hotel room about midnight, he asked for champagne, havana
cigars, and ordered a supper of six or seven courses. But the champagne made him drunk and the cigars made him sick, so that he did
not even touch the food they had brought, and he went to bed almost
unconscious. On awakening next morning as fresh as a daisy, he at
once went to a gipsy camp in the suburb on the other side of the river
about which he had been told at the club the day before, and he did
not come back to the inn for two days. At last at five o'clock in the
afternoon of the previous day he had arrived drunk, gone to bed at
once, and had slept till ten o'clock in the evening. When he woke up,
he ordered a cutlet, a bottle of Château d'Yquem, and some grapes,
paper, ink, and his bill. No one noticed anything peculiar about him;
he was calm, gentle, and amiable. He must have shot himself at about
midnight, though it was strange that no one had heard the shot, and
they only discovered it that day at one o'clock in the afternoon when,
failing to get an answer to their knocks, they broke down the door.
The bottle of Château d'Yquem was half empty, and there was half a
plateful of grapes left over. He had shot himself through the heart
with a small, double-barrelled revolver. There was very little blood;
the revolver had fallen out of his hand on to the carpet. The boy himself was half-reclining on a sofa in the corner of the room. Death must
have been instantaneous; there was no sign of any death agony on the
face; he looked very serene, almost happy, as though he had no worry
in the world. Our entire company stared at him with eager curiosity.
Generally speaking, there is always something diverting for a stranger
in every calamity that befalls one of his fellow-men – whoever he may
be. Our ladies looked at the dead boy in silence, while their companions excelled themselves by their witty remarks and their cool presence of mind. One of them remarked that it was the best solution and
that the boy could not have done anything more sensible; another one

concluded that he had had a good time, short though it was. A third
one suddenly blurted out the question why people had started hanging
and shooting themselves so frequently among us, as though they had
become uprooted or as though the floor had suddenly given way under their feet. The people in the room looked at the philosopher askance. Then Lyamshin, who prided himself on his role as a clown,
filched a bunch of grapes from the plate, another one, laughing, did
the same, and a third one stretched out his hand for the Château
d'Yquem, but was stopped by the arrival of the police commissioner,
who even told them to 'clear out of the room'. As all of them had already seen all they wanted, they left the room at once without any
argument, though Lyamshin began pestering the police commissioner about something. The general merriment, laughter and playful talk
were almost twice as lively during the second half of the journey.

We arrived at Semyon Yakovlevich's exactly at one o'clock in the
afternoon. The gate of the merchant's rather large house was wide
open and everyone was free to enter the cottage. We learnt at once
that Semyon Yakovlevich was having his lunch, but that he was receiving. The whole crowd of us went in together. The room in which
the saintly half-wit received his visitors and had his meals was fairly
large. It had three windows and was divided into two equal parts by
a wooden lattice-work partition right across the room from one wall
to the other which was about four feet high. The ordinary visitors remained outside the partition, and the lucky ones, at a signal from the
saint, were admitted through a little door in the partition into his
half of the room where, if he felt like it, he asked them to sit down on
the sofa or on old leather chairs. He himself invariably presided in an
old-fashioned, shabby Voltaire chair. He was a rather big, bloated,
sallow-faced man of about fifty-five, fair and bald, clean-shaven, with
a swollen right cheek and a somewhat twisted mouth. He had a large
wart on the left side of his nose, narrow eyes, and a calm, stolid, sleepy
face. He was dressed German fashion in a black frock-coat, but without waistcoat or tie. A rather coarse, but white shirt peeped out from
under his frock-coat; his feet (there was apparently something wrong
with them) he kept in a pair of slippers. I have heard that he had been a
Civil Servant and had received some rank. He had just finished his fish
soup and was starting on his second course – potatoes in their jackets

with salt. He never ate anything else, but he drank a lot of tea, of which he was very fond. Three servants, provided by the merchant, were continuously scurrying round him, one of them wearing a frock-coat, another one looking like a labourer, and a third like a verger. There was also a very high-spirited boy of sixteen. Besides the servants there was present a venerable-looking, grey-haired monk with a collection mug, who was a little too fat. On one of the tables a huge samovar was boiling, and there was also a tray on it with almost two dozen glasses. On another table opposite the gifts brought by the visitors had been placed: some loaves and some pounds of sugar, about two pounds of tea, a pair of embroidered slippers, a silk handkerchief, a length of cloth, a piece of linen, etc. Practically all the gifts of money went into the monk's mug. The room was full of people – about a dozen visitors alone; two of whom sat in Semyon Yakovlevich's part of the room: a grey-headed old man – a pilgrim of 'the common people' – and a little, dried-up monk, who seemed to have come a long way and who was sitting demurely with his eyes cast down. The other visitors all stood on the other side of the partition, most of them also peasants, with the exception of a fat merchant, who had come from the county town, a man with a large beard, dressed in the traditional Russian garb, who was known to be worth 100,000 roubles; there were, besides, a poor, elderly gentlewoman and a landowner. They were all waiting for their lucky turn, not daring to be the first to speak. Four people were kneeling, but the man who attracted most attention was the landowner, a corpulent man of about forty-five, who knelt close to the partition, most conspicuous of all, and waited reverently for a friendly look or word from Semyon Yakovlevich. He had been kneeling there for about an hour, but the saint still took no notice of him.

Our ladies crowded close to the partition, whispering gaily and giggling. They pushed aside or got in front of the other visitors, even those who knelt on the floor, except the landowner, who remained stubbornly in full view of everybody, even holding on to the partition by his hands. They looked gaily and with eager curiosity at Semyon Yakovlevich, through lorgnettes, pince-nez, and even opera-glasses; Lyamshin, at any rate, gazed at him through a pair of opera-glasses. Semyon Yakovlevich glanced calmly and lazily at them with his little eyes.

'Good-lookers! Good-lookers!' he was good enough to say in his hoarse bass and with a light exclamatory note in his voice.

Everyone in our party laughed: 'What is the meaning of good-lookers?' But Semyon Yakovlevich relapsed into silence and finished eating his potatoes. At length he wiped his mouth with a napkin and they gave him his tea.

He did not usually have his tea alone, but invited some of his visitors to have it with him, as a rule, pointing himself to the lucky ones. Ig-noring the rich and the highly placed, he sometimes ordered tea to be given to some peasant or to some decrepit old woman; another time he would ignore the beggars and treat some fat, wealthy merchant. The tea, too, was served in different ways, some getting lumps of sugar to suck, some having their tea sweetened with sugar, while some got it without sugar altogether. This time he favoured the little monk with a glass of sweetened tea, and the old pilgrim, who was given tea without sugar. The fat monk with the collection mug from the mon-astery was for some reason not given any tea at all, though hitherto he had been given his glass every day.

'Semyon Yakovlevich, do say something to me; I've been dying to meet you for ages,' the gorgeously attired lady from our carriage, who had observed that one ought not to stand on ceremony with amuse-ments so long as they were diverting, sang out with a smile, screwing up her eyes.

Semyon Yakovlevich did not even look at her. The landowner, who was kneeling, heaved a loud and deep sigh, which sounded as though it had come out of a huge pair of bellows.

'A glass of sweet tea!' Semyon Yakovlevich suddenly pointed to the merchant who was worth 100,000.

The merchant came forward and stood next to the landowner.

'Put more sugar in his tea!' Semyon Yakovlevich ordered after the glass of tea had been poured out, and more sugar was added to it. 'More, more!' and they put in more sugar a third time, and then a fourth.

The merchant began drinking his syrup without a murmur.

'Lord!' whispered the people and began crossing themselves.

The landowner heaved another loud and deep sigh.

'Father! Semyon Yakovlevich!' the poverty-stricken lady, whom our company had pushed to the wall, cried in an anguished voice, which was so strident that everybody in the room looked up at her in surprise. 'I've been waiting for a blessing for a whole hour, dear father. Tell me what to do; advise me, poor wretched woman that I am!'

'Ask her,' Semyon Yakovlevich ordered the verger.

The verger went up to the partition. 'Have you done what Semyon Yakovlevich told you last time?' he asked the widow in a quiet, steady voice.

'How could I, Father?' the widow wailed. 'How could I do it? I can't do anything with them. They're cannibals; they've issued a writ against me. They threaten to drag me to the Supreme Court. Their own mother, too!'

'Give it her!' Semyon Yakovlevich pointed to a sugar-loaf.

The boy rushed up to the table, grabbed the sugar-loaf and took it to the widow.

'Thank you, Father; you're very good to me, I'm sure. And what am I to do with it all?' the widow wailed.

'More, more!' Semyon Yakovlevich heaped his gifts upon her.

They dragged another sugar-loaf to her. 'More, more!' the saintly half-wit ordered, and she was given a third and, then, a fourth.

The monk from the monastery sighed: as on previous occasions, all that could have gone to the monastery that very day.

'But what am I to do with it all?' the poor widow moaned humbly. 'Can't keep it all myself, can I? It'll only make me sick. It isn't some sort of prophecy, is it, Father?'

'Aye, aye,' someone said in the crowd. 'It is a prophecy!'

'Another pound for her, another!' Semyon Yakovlevich persisted.

There was a whole sugar-loaf left on the table, but Semyon Yakovlevich pointed to the pound of sugar, and the widow was given the pound.

'Lord, Lord!' the peasants sighed and crossed themselves. 'It's a prophecy for sure!'

'First sweeten your heart with mercy and loving-kindness, and then come here to complain against your own children, the flesh of your flesh – that's, I daresay, the meaning of this emblem,' the fat monk from the monastery, who had not been favoured with a glass of tea, said quietly but self-complacently, having taken upon himself to act as an interpreter in a fit of wounded vanity.

'How can you say such a thing, Father?' the little widow suddenly burst out angrily. 'Why, they dragged me into the flames by a rope when Vershinin's house caught fire. They put a dead cat in my trunk. They're up to all sorts of wickedness.'

'Kick her out!' Semyon Yakovlevich suddenly waved his arms. 'Kick her out!'

The verger and the boy rushed behind the partition. The verger took the widow by the arm, and, calming down, she shuffled off to the door, looking back at the sugar-loaves which the boy was dragging behind her.

'Take one back!' Semyon Yakovlevich ordered the labourer who had stayed behind.

The servant rushed after them, and the three servants came back after a short time, carrying the sugar-loaf which had been given the widow and then taken away from her. She carried off three, however.

'Semyon Yakovlevich,' someone cried at the back of the crowd by the door, 'I saw a bird in my dream – a jackdaw. It flew out of water and into the fire. What does the dream mean?'

'Frost,' said Semyon Yakovlevich.

'Semyon Yakovlevich, why don't you answer me?' the lady in our party began again. 'I've been interested in you for such a long time.'

'Ask him,' said Semyon Yakovlevich, pointing to the landowner who knelt on the floor without listening to her.

The monk from the monastery, to whom the order was addressed, walked gravely up to the landowner.

'What sin have you committed? And have you been ordered to do something?'

'Not to fight, not to give rein to my hands,' the landowner replied hoarsely.

'Have you done it?' asked the monk.

'Can't do it. My own strength gets the better of me.'

'Kick him out! Kick him out! Use the broom! The broom!' cried Semyon Yakovlevich, waving his hands.

Without waiting for the punishment to be meted out, the landowner jumped up from the floor and rushed out of the room.

'He's left a gold coin behind,' the monk announced, picking up a half imperial from the floor.

'Give it him,' Semyon Yakovlevich thrust a finger at the rich merchant, who took the gold piece, not daring to refuse it.

'Gold unto gold,' said the monk from the monastery, unable to restrain himself.

'And give this one tea with sugar,' Semyon Yakovlevich suddenly pointed to Maurice Drozdov.

The servant poured out the tea, and was about to offer it by mistake to the dandy with the pince-nez.

'The long one, the long one,' Semyon Yakovlevich corrected him.

Maurice took the glass, made a military half bow, and began drinking it. I don't know why, but everybody in our company was convulsed with laughter.

'I say,' Lisa suddenly addressed herself to Maurice Drozdov, 'won't you kneel down where the gentleman who has just left was kneeling?'

Drozdov looked bewildered at her.

'Please, you'll do me a great favour. Look here, Maurice,' she burst out suddenly, speaking rapidly, persistently, stubbornly, and passionately, 'you must kneel down. I must see you on your knees. If you won't, I shall never see you again. I want you to – I want you to!'

I don't know what she had in mind, but she demanded it with relentless persistence, as though she were hysterical. Drozdov, as we shall see later, attributed these capricious impulses of hers, which had recently become particularly frequent, to outbursts of blind hatred for him, and not to spite, for, on the contrary, she thought very highly of him, she was fond of him and respected him, and he knew that himself – but to some peculiar unconscious hatred she was at times quite unable to suppress.

He silently handed his glass to an old woman who was standing behind him, opened the door of the partition, and, without being invited, stepped into Semyon Yakovlevich's private half of the room, and knelt down in the middle of the floor in the sight of all. I can't help thinking that his simple and delicate soul was deeply shocked by Lisa's crude and scoffing whim before the whole company. Perhaps he thought that she would be ashamed of herself when she saw his humiliation on which she had so insisted. Of course no one but he would have dreamt of changing a woman's character by so naïve and risky a method. He remained kneeling looking grave and imperturbable, tall, ungainly, ridiculous. But no one of our party laughed; the unexpectedness of his action produced a painful effect. Everybody looked at Lisa.

'Anoint! Anoint!' Semyon Yakovlevich muttered.

Lisa went suddenly pale, cried out, and rushed behind the partition. A rapid, hysterical scene took place: she tried with all her might to raise Drozdov from his knees, tugging at his elbow with both hands.

'Get up, get up!' she screamed, beside herself. 'Get up at once! At once! How dare you kneel!'

Drozdov got up from his knees. She squeezed his arms above the elbows and looked intently into his face. There was terror in her eyes.

'Good-lookers! Good-lookers!' Semyon Yakovlevich repeated again.

She dragged Drozdov back behind the partition at last; an agitated stir passed through our whole company. The lady from our carriage, probably wishing to relieve the tension, asked Semyon Yakovlevich for the third time in a loud and strident voice, with her affected smile:

'Well, Semyon Yakovlevich, won't you "pronounce" something to me too? And I did count a lot on you, I must say.'

'Kick her in the —, in the —!' Semyon Yakovlevich addressed himself to her with an extremely indecent word.

The words were uttered fiercely and with terrifying clarity. Our ladies shrieked and ran headlong out of the place and the gentlemen burst into homeric laughter. That was the end of our visit to Semyon Yakovlevich.

And it was at this point that another extremely enigmatic incident is said to have occurred and, to be quite frank, it is because of it that I have described this visit in such detail.

I am told that when they all rushed in a crowd out of the room, Lisa, supported by Drozdov, suddenly found herself face to face with Stavrogin in the doorway. I may add that since that Sunday morning when she fainted they had not approached each other or spoken to each other, though they had met frequently. I saw them meeting in the doorway: it seemed to me that both of them stood still for a moment and looked rather strangely at one another. But I may not have seen them properly for the crowd. I am assured, on the contrary, and very seriously, too, that after having looked at Stavrogin, Lisa quickly raised her hand to the level of his face and would certainly have struck him if he had not managed to draw back in time. Perhaps she objected to the way he had looked at her or perhaps to the way he grinned, especially after such an episode with Drozdov. I admit I did not see it myself, but everyone assured me that they had, though all of them could not possibly have seen it in that confusion, but perhaps some of them might. Only I did not believe it at the time. I do remember, though, that Stavrogin was rather pale all the way back to town.

3

Almost at the same time – that is to say, on the same day – the interview between Mr Verkhovensky and Mrs Stavrogin took place at last. Mrs Stavrogin had long been thinking about it, and had informed her former friend about it, but for some reason she kept putting it off. It took place at Skvoreshniki. Mrs Stavrogin arrived at her country house, full of bustling activity: the day before it was finally decided that the fête would be given at the house of the marshal's wife. But Mrs Stavrogin, with her quick brain, at once realized that there was nothing to prevent her afterwards from holding her own fête in Skvoreshniki to which the whole town would again be invited. Then everyone would be able to see for themselves whose house was best and where people could count on a better reception and where a ball was given with better taste. In general, it was impossible to recognize her. She looked quite a different woman and seemed to have been transformed from an unapproachable 'high society lady' (Mr Verkhovensky's expression) to a most ordinary, feather-brained society woman. However, that may have only seemed so.

Having arrived at her empty country house, she went through all the rooms in the company of her faithful old butler, Alexey Yegorych, and Foma, a man of wide experience of affairs and a specialist in interior decorations. They started discussing plans: what furniture to bring from the town house; what things and what pictures; where to put them; how best to arrange the flowers and which flowers to get from the hot-houses; where to hang the curtains, where to have the buffet, and should they have one or two buffets, etc., etc. And it was while thus busily engaged that she suddenly took it into her head to send a carriage for Mr Verkhovensky.

Mr Verkhovensky had long before been warned about his coming visit and was ready, expecting to receive such a sudden invitation any day. As he got into the carriage, he crossed himself; his fate was being decided. He found his friend in the big drawing-room, sitting on a small sofa in the recess in front of a small marble table, a paper and pencil in her hands; Foma was measuring the height of the gallery and the windows, while Mrs Stavrogin herself was putting down the figures and making notes on the margin. She nodded to Mr Verkhovensky, without interrupting her work, and when the latter murmured a greeting, she gave him her hand hurriedly and, without looking, motioned him to a seat beside her.

'I sat there waiting for five minutes, "suppressing my feelings",' he told me afterwards. 'The woman I saw was not the woman I had known for twenty years. The utter conviction that everything was at an end lent me a strength that surprised even her. I swear to you she was astonished by my steadfastness in that last hour.'

Mrs Stavrogin suddenly put down her pencil on the table and turned quickly to Mr Verkhovensky.

'Mr Verkhovensky, we have to discuss business. I'm sure you've prepared all your high-sounding words and all sorts of fine phrases, but we'd better go straight to the point. Don't you think so?'

He was shocked. She was in a hurry to show her hand. What might be her next move?

'Wait. Don't say anything. Let me speak first, and then you can say what you like, though I really don't know what you could say to me,' she went on, talking very rapidly. 'The twelve hundred roubles of your allowance I consider it my sacred duty to continue to the end of your life. Well, perhaps not my sacred duty, but simply an agreement. That's much more realistic, isn't it? If you like, we can have it in writing. I have made special arrangements in case of my death. But you will get from me at present a flat and servants and your maintenance in addition. Put into cash, it would make another fifteen hundred roubles, wouldn't it? I'll add an extra three hundred roubles, making a total of three thousand. That should suffice you for a year, shouldn't it? It's not too little, is it? In special emergencies I shall of course let you have more. And so, take your money, let me have my servants back and live just by yourself where you like – in Petersburg, in Moscow, abroad or in our town, but not with me. Do you hear?'

'Not so long ago I was presented with quite different demands from the same lips and with the same suddenness and the same insistence,'

Mr Verkhovensky said slowly and with melancholy distinctness. 'I humbled myself and danced the *gopak* to please you. *Oui, la comparaison peut être permise. C'était comme un petit cosak du Don, qui sautait sur sa propre tombe.* Now –'

'Stop, sir. You talk an awful lot. You did not dance, but you came to see me in a new cravat, new linen and gloves, oiled and scented. I assure you, you were very anxious to get married yourself; it was written on your face and, believe me, it was a most inelegant expression. If I did not tell you about it at the time, it was only out of delicacy. But you were anxious to get married in spite of the disgusting things you wrote privately about me and your betrothed. Now it's quite different. And why drag in the *cosak du Don*, and what grave have you in mind? I don't understand your comparison at all. I don't want you to die. Live as long as you like. I shall be delighted.'

'In a workhouse?'

'A workhouse? One doesn't go into a workhouse with an income of three thousand a year. Oh, I see,' she said with a laugh. 'Peter did make a joke about a workhouse one day. Gracious me! there really is a special workhouse which it is worth keeping in mind. It's for most respectable people. There are colonels there, and a general is very anxious to go there too. If you went there with all your money you'd find peace, contentment, and servants, too. You'd be able to devote yourself to your studies there and you could always make up a party for a game of preference.'

'*Passons.*'

'*Passons?*' Mrs Stavrogin winced. 'Well, in that case, that's all I have to say. From now on we shall live separately.'

'Is that all? Is that all that remains after twenty years? Our last farewell?'

'You're awfully fond of pathetic exclamations, Mr Verkhovensky. It's no longer the fashion. People to-day talk rudely but plainly. And you would harp on our twenty years! Twenty years of mutual self-admiration and nothing more. Every letter you wrote to me was not written for me but for posterity. You're a stylist and not a friend. Friendship is merely a glorified expression. In reality it is nothing but a reciprocal outpouring of slops.'

'Heavens, how many words you've picked up from others! Lessons learnt by heart! And they've already put their uniform on you! You, too, are rejoicing! You, too, are basking in the sun! *Chère, chère,* for what a mess of pottage have you sold them your freedom!'

'I'm not a parrot to repeat other people's words,' Mrs Stavrogin said, boiling with rage. 'Don't worry, I have saved up plenty of words of my own. What have you done for me during those twenty years? You wouldn't even let me look at the books which I ordered for you, and which but for the bookbinder would have remained uncut. What did you give me to read when I asked you during those first years to be my guide? Always Kapfig. Nothing but Kapfig. You were even afraid that I might become an educated woman, and you took appropriate measures. And yet it is at you that people are laughing. I must confess I always considered you only as a critic and nothing more. When on our way to Petersburg I told you that I intended to publish a periodical and dedicate my life to it, you at once looked at me ironically and became horribly supercilious.'

'You're quite wrong, quite wrong. At the time we were afraid of persecution.'

'I'm not wrong at all, and you had no reason to be afraid of persecution in Petersburg. Do you remember how afterwards in February, when the news of the liberation of the serfs came, you suddenly came running to me in a panic and began demanding that I should at once give you a written statement that the proposed periodical had nothing to do with you and that the young people had been coming to see me and not you, and that you were only a tutor who lived in my house because he had not been paid his fees? Isn't that so? Do you remember it? You most certainly have been overdoing things all your life, Mr Verkhovensky.'

'That was only a moment of weakness, a moment while we were alone,' he cried sorrowfully. 'But are we really to break off everything because of such unimportant impressions? Is there nothing more left between us after all those long years?'

'You're horribly calculating. You always want me to be in your debt. When you returned from abroad, you looked down on me and you wouldn't let me utter a word. But when I went abroad myself and spoke to you afterwards about my impressions of the Madonna, you wouldn't listen to me and you smiled in a superior way into your cravat, as though I was incapable of the same feelings as you.'

'It wasn't that at all – it probably wasn't that at all – *J'ai oublié.*'

'It was that all right. And, besides, what was there to be so superior about, because it was all nonsense and just one of your inventions. Now no one, no one gets excited over the Madonna. No one wastes time over it, except some old-fashioned old men. That's been proved.'

'It's been proved, has it?'

'It's of no use whatever. This jug is useful because one can pour water into it; this pencil is useful because you can write anything with it, but that Madonna is just a woman's face which is inferior to any face in nature. Try drawing an apple and put a real apple beside it – which would you take? You wouldn't hesitate, would you? That's what all our theories boil down to now that the first light of free investigation has fallen on them.'

'I see, I see.'

'You laugh ironically. And what, for instance, did you tell me about charity? And yet the enjoyment you get from charity is a supercilious and immoral enjoyment, the enjoyment a rich man gets from his wealth, his power, and his importance when he compares it with the importance of a poor man. Charity corrupts both giver and receiver and, besides, does not achieve its aim because it merely increases poverty. Loafers who are too lazy to work crowd round those who give away money like gamblers round a gaming-table, hoping to win. But the miserable coppers which are thrown to them are not enough to satisfy one man out of a hundred. How much have you given away in your life? Not more than a few pennies, I'm sure. Try to remember when last you gave something away. Two years ago? More likely four. You're just raising a clamour and hindering progress. Charity ought to be forbidden by law, even in the present state of our society. Under the new régime there won't be any poor at all.'

'Oh, what a cataract of borrowed phrases! So it's come to the new régime, has it? Unhappy woman, may the Lord help you!'

'Yes, sir, it has come to that. You were very careful to conceal all these new ideas from me, with which everyone is already familiar, and you did it solely out of jealousy, so as to wield your power over me. Even that Julia creature is a hundred miles ahead of me. But I, too, am beginning to see things clearly now. I've defended you, sir, as much as I could. Everybody without exception thinks that it is your fault.'

'That'll do!' he said, rising from his seat; 'that'll do. And what else shall I wish you? Not repentance, surely?'

'Sit down for a minute, sir. I have something else I'd like to ask you. You've received an invitation to read at the literary matinée. I was responsible for it. Tell me, what are you going to read.'

'I'm going to read about that queen of queens, that ideal of humanity, the Sistine Madonna, who in your opinion is not worth a glass or a pencil.'

'Not something from history?' said Mrs Stavrogin in mournful surprise. 'But they won't listen to you. You would think of that Madonna! What's the use of talking about her if you'll only send them all to sleep? I assure you, Mr Verkhovensky, that what I'm saying is entirely in your own interest. Don't you think it would be much wiser if you took some short but entertaining medieval Court incident from Spanish history, or, better still, some anecdote which you could enlarge with some anecdotes and witty sayings of your own? They had such gorgeous courts in those days, such fine ladies, poisonings. Karmazinov says it would be strange indeed if you couldn't find something entertaining to read from Spanish history.'

'Karmazinov, that fool who's written himself out, looking for a subject for me!'

'Karmazinov, that almost statesman-like intellect! You're very free with your language, sir!'

'Your Karmazinov is a silly old woman, spiteful and worthless. Chère, chère, since when have you become so enslaved by them? Oh, dear God!'

'I can't stand him even now for the airs he gives himself, but I must do justice to his great intellect. I repeat I've defended you as far as I could and to the best of my ability. And why must you be so dull and ridiculous? Couldn't you instead walk on to the platform with a nice smile as the representative of a past age, and just tell them two or three anecdotes in your inimitable way as you alone can sometimes tell them? Even though you're an old man, though you belong to an age that has passed, and though you have dropped behind them, there's nothing to prevent you from admitting it with a smile, in your foreword, and everybody will realize that you're a nice, good-natured, witty old fossil. In a word, a man of the old school, but so far advanced that he is able to appreciate the absurdity of certain ideas which he has hitherto followed at their true value. Do me a favour, I beg you.'

'Chère, enough! Don't ask me. I can't. I'll talk to them about the

Madonna, but I shall raise a storm which will either crush them all or strike me down alone!'

'It's sure to strike you down alone, Mr Verkhovensky.'

'Such is my fate. I shall tell them about that vile slave, that stinking and depraved flunkey who will first mount the ladder with a pair of scissors in his hands and slash the divine countenance of the great ideal in the name of equality, envy, and – and digestion. Let my curse thunder out and then, then –'

'To a lunatic asylum?'

'Maybe. But in any case, whether I'm defeated or whether I'm victorious, I shall take up my bag that very evening, my pauper's bag, leave all my belongings behind me, all your gifts, all your allowances and promises of future blessings, and go away on foot to end my life as a tutor in some merchant's house or die of hunger in some ditch. I have spoken. *Alea jacta est!*'

He rose again.

'I've been convinced,' Mrs Stavrogin said, getting up with flashing eyes – 'I've been convinced for years that all you live for is to put me and my house to shame by some disgraceful story like that! What do you mean by your tutorship in a merchant's house or by your dying in a ditch? It's just spite, calumny, and nothing else!'

'You've always despised me, but I shall end up like a true knight who remains faithful to his lady, for your opinion of me has always been dearer to me than anything in the world. From now on I shall accept nothing, but shall revere you disinterestedly.'

'How silly!'

'You've never respected me. I may have had thousands of weaknesses. Yes, I have sponged on you; I speak the language of nihilism; but sponging has never been the guiding principle of my actions. It has just happened like that, of itself; I don't know how. I always thought that there was something higher than food between us and – I've never, never been a scoundrel! And so I go on my way to make amends! I'm setting out late in the year, in the late autumn, a mist lies over the fields, the road before me is covered with the hoar frost of old age, and the wind howls about the grave towards which I walk. ... But forward, forward on my way, on my new way –

> Full of the purest love,
> True to his own sweet dream. ...

Oh, farewell, my dreams. Twenty years! *Alea jacta est!*'

His face was wet with tears that suddenly gushed out of his eyes; he picked up his hat.

'I don't understand Latin,' said Mrs Stavrogin, trying hard to control herself.

Who knows, perhaps she too felt like crying, but indignation and caprice got the better of her once more.

'I know only one thing: that all this is just a silly whim. You'll never be able to carry out your threats, which are full of egoism. You won't go anywhere. You won't go to any merchant. You'll end your days quite simply on my hands, getting your pension and having your dreadful friends come to see you on Tuesdays. Good-bye, sir.'

'*Alea jacta est!*' he said, bowing low to her, and came back home more dead than alive with excitement.

6

Peter Verkhovensky is Busy

I

THE day of the fête was finally fixed, and von Lembke was looking more and more melancholy and pensive. He was full of strange and ominous forebodings, and this worried Mrs Lembke greatly. It is true everything was not quite right. Our former easy-going Governor had left the administration of the province not altogether in good working order; at the moment a cholera epidemic was approaching; there were serious outbreaks of plague among the cattle in some country districts; all that summer fires raged in towns and villages, and among the common people the foolish rumours of incendiarism gained more and more ground. Cases of robbery were twice as numerous as usual. But all this, of course, would have been perfectly normal had there not been other weighty reasons which disturbed the composure of the hitherto happy von Lembke.

What worried Mrs Lembke most of all was that he was becoming more uncommunicative every day and, strange to say, more secretive. And what indeed did he have to hide? It is true he rarely answered her back and mostly obeyed her implicitly. At her insistence, for instance, two or three measures were passed of a very risky and almost illegal character with the idea of increasing the Governor's powers. A number of rather sinister actions were connived at with the same aim in view; for instance, people who should have been put on trial and sent to Siberia were, at her insistence, recommended for promotion. It was also decided systematically to ignore certain complaints and inquiries. All this came to light afterwards. Lembke not only signed everything, but did not even discuss the question of his wife's share in the execution of his duties. On the other hand, he would at times start a row over 'absolute trifles', to Mrs Lembke's great surprise. No doubt he felt the need of recompensing himself by a few moments of mutiny for the days of obedience. Unfortunately, Mrs Lembke, for all her insight, could not grasp the noble finesse of her husband's noble character. Alas, she had other worries, and that was the source of many misunderstandings.

It ill becomes me to dwell on certain things and, besides, I don't think I am able to. Neither is it my business to discuss administrative mistakes, and that is why I shall completely leave out the administrative aspect of the whole affair. When I began my chronicle, I had quite other tasks in mind. Besides, the Commission of Inquiry which has just been set up in our province will no doubt bring to light a great many things; it is only a matter of waiting a little. However, it is impossible to avoid certain explanations.

But to return to Mrs Lembke. The poor lady (I feel very sorry for her) could have achieved everything that attracted and allured her so much (glory and so on) without any of the violent and eccentric efforts she resolved to make from the very start. But whether it was from an excess of romantic feelings or from the long and sad failures she had suffered as a young girl, she felt suddenly, with the change in her fortunes, that she had been somehow specially chosen, almost anointed, that over her 'a tongue, like as of fire' had burst, and it was that tongue of fire that was the cause of all the trouble: for, say what you will, it is not like a chignon which will fit any woman's head. But it is the hardest thing in the world to convince a woman of this truth; on the contrary, anybody who has a mind to agree with her, will be sure of success, and they vied with each other in agreeing with her. The poor woman suddenly found herself the sport of the most conflicting influences while imagining that she was highly original. Many clever people feathered their nests and took advantage of her simplicity during the short period of her rule. And what a hopeless tangle she got herself into under the pretence of independence! She was in favour of big agricultural estates, the aristocratic element, and the increase of the Governor's prerogatives and, at the same time, of the democratic element, the new institutions, law and order, free-thinking, and social reforms; the strict etiquette of an aristocratic *salon* and the free-and-easy, almost public-house manners of the young people who surrounded her. She dreamed of *giving happiness* and reconciling the irreconcilable, or, what was more likely, of the union of everything and everybody in the adoration of her own person. She had special favourites; she was very fond of Peter Verkhovensky, who, incidentally, got his way with her by the grossest flattery. But she liked him for another reason, too, a reason that is most remarkable and most characteristic of the poor lady: she was always hoping that he would disclose to her a conspiracy against the Government! However hard it may be to imagine it, that was so. For some obscure reason she believed that it was in our province that a plot against the Government was being hatched. By his silence on certain occasions and his hints on others, Peter helped to confirm her in that strange idea. She, on the other hand, imagined that he had connexions with every revolutionary movement in Russia and, at the same time, was loyal to her to the point of adoration. The discovery of the plot, gratitude from Petersburg, a brilliant career in front of her, the exercise of an influence on the younger generation by 'kindness' so as to keep it from going over the brink – all this lived happily side by side in that fantastic head of hers. For she had saved and mastered Peter Verkhovensky (for some reason she was absolutely convinced of this) and she would save the others, too. None of them would perish. She would save them all. She would sort them out, she would send in the right report about them, she would act in the highest interests of justice, and history and the entire Russian liberal movement would possibly bless her name. But the conspiracy would be discovered, all the same. All the advantages at one blow.

Still, it was absolutely necessary that Mr Lembke should be more cheerful, at least before the fête. He simply had to be cheered up and reassured. With that aim in view, she sent Peter to him in the hope that he might relieve his depression by some sedative known only to him. Perhaps even by conveying some information to him, as it were, from the horse's mouth. She had implicit faith in his adroitness. Peter had not been in von Lembke's office for some time. He rushed in there at the very moment when the patient was in a most difficult mood.

2

A contingency had arisen with which Mr von Lembke was utterly unable to deal. In the district in which Peter Verkhovensky had been having a great time recently a second lieutenant had been reprimanded by his superior officer in front of the whole company. The second lieutenant was a young man who had recently arrived from Petersburg. He was taciturn and morose, of a dignified appearance, though rather small, stout, and ruddy-cheeked. He resented the reprimand and suddenly flung himself upon his superior officer with a sort of unnatural scream that astonished the whole company; his head bent down savagely, he struck the officer and bit him on the shoulder with all his might, and it was with some difficulty that he was dragged off. There could be no doubt that he had gone mad. At least it was found that during recent weeks his behaviour had been very peculiar. For instance, he had thrown two icons belonging to his landlady out of his room, having chopped up one of them with an axe; in his room he had placed on three stands, in the form of three lecterns, the works of Vogt, Moleschott, and Buechner, and before each lectern he burned a wax church candle. From the large number of books found in his room it could be gathered that he was a well-read man. If he had had fifty thousand francs he might have sailed to the Marquesas Islands like the 'cadet' to whom Mr Herzen refers with such gay humour in one of his works. When he was arrested, a whole bundle of the most desperate political leaflets was found in his pockets and in his lodgings.

Political leaflets are by themselves a trivial affair and, in my opinion, not worth worrying about. We've seen lots of them. Besides, those leaflets were not new: exactly the same were, as I was told later, not so long ago scattered in another province, and Liputin, who had visited that district and the neighbouring province six weeks earlier, assured me that he had seen similar leaflets there. But what struck von Lembke was that the manager of Spigulin's factory had brought the police just at the same time two or three bundles of exactly the same leaflets as those found in the second lieutenant's room. They had been left at the factory during the night and had not yet been opened, so that none of the workmen had had time to read any of them. The whole thing was silly, but it made Lembke ponder deeply. The affair appeared to him in an unpleasantly complicated light.

This happened just at the beginning of the 'Spigulin incident' at the factory. The incident had caused a great deal of excited talk in our town and had created a stir in the Petersburg and Moscow papers, which published all sorts of versions of it. About three weeks earlier one of the workmen there had fallen ill and died of Asiatic cholera. A few more people fell ill of it later. The townspeople were in a panic because the cholera epidemic was approaching from the neighbouring province. I may add that, so far as possible, all the necessary sanitary precautions had been taken to meet the uninvited guest. But the factory of the Spigulins, who were millionaires and people with influential connexions, had somehow been overlooked. And then everybody started clamouring that the factory was the breeding-place of the infection and that the factory itself, and especially the workmen's quarters, were so filthy that, if there had been no cholera epidemic at all, it would have started there. Precautionary measures were, of course, taken immediately, and Mr Lembke vigorously insisted on their being carried out without delay. The factory was thoroughly cleaned up in three weeks, but the Spigulins, for some unknown reason, closed it. One of the Spigulin brothers resided permanently in Petersburg and the other left for Moscow after the authorities had ordered his factory to be cleaned up. The manager began to pay off the workers and, as it now appears, swindled them right and left. The workers began to protest, demanding to be paid fairly, and rather foolishly went to the police, but without raising a great clamour and without getting very much excited over it. It was just then that the revolutionary leaflets were handed to Lembke from the manager.

Peter Verkhovensky flew into the Governor's study without sending in his name, just like an old friend of the family, and, besides, he had a message from Mrs Lembke. Seeing him, von Lembke scowled and stood still at his desk with an unfriendly look on his face. Till then he had been walking up and down his study, discussing some private business with an official of his office by the name of Blum, a very awkward and morose German whom he had brought with him from Petersburg in spite of his wife's strong opposition. At the entrance of

Peter Verkhovensky, Blum retired to the door, but he did not leave the room. Peter even imagined that he had exchanged a significant glance with his superior.

'Aha, so I've caught you, you secretive ruler of the town,' Peter cried, laughing and covering up the leaflet which lay on the table with his hand. 'That will add to your collection, won't it?'

Von Lembke flushed. His face seemed suddenly to twitch.

'Leave it alone at once!' he shouted, wincing with anger. 'And don't you dare, sir –'

'What's the matter with you? I believe you're angry.'

'Let me tell you, sir, that I do not intend to put up with your *sans façon* any more and I'd like you to remember –'

'Good gracious, he really is angry!'

'Shut up! Shut up!' von Lembke cried, stamping on the carpet. 'And don't dare –'

Goodness only knows what might have happened. There was, indeed, another thing, besides, which neither Peter nor Mrs Lembke knew anything about. The unhappy Lembke had been so upset during the last few days that he had even begun to be secretly jealous of his wife and Peter Verkhovensky. In solitude, especially at night, he spent some very disagreeable moments.

'And I thought that if a man reads you his novel in private for two days running till after midnight and wants to know your opinion of it, he has at least given up these official relations. Mrs Lembke treats me as a friend – what on earth is one to make of you?' Peter said with rather a dignified air. 'Here's your novel, by the way,' he said, putting on the table a large, heavy, rolled-up manuscript, wrapped in blue paper.

Lembke blushed and looked embarrassed.

'Where did you find it?' he asked cautiously, with a rush of joy he was unable to control, but which he did his best to conceal.

'Well, just imagine it, wrapped up as it is, it had rolled under the chest of drawers. I must have thrown it down rather carelessly on the chest of drawers as I came in. My charwoman found it the day before yesterday when she was scrubbing the floor. Dear me, you certainly gave me some work!'

Lembke dropped his eyes sternly.

'Haven't slept for two nights running, thanks to you. It was found the day before yesterday, but I kept it – been reading it ever since. Too busy in the daytime, so I read it at night. Well, sir, I can't say that I liked it. It's not my kettle of fish. But what does that matter? I've never claimed to be a critic, and the important thing is, my dear chap, that I simply couldn't tear myself away from it, though I didn't like it. The fourth and fifth chapters are – are damned good! Damned good! And what a lot of humour you've shoved into it – I roared with laughter. But how wonderfully you can make fun of things *sans que cela paraisse*! Well, the ninth and tenth chapters are all about love – not my kettle of fish, I'm afraid, but it certainly is effective. Nearly burst into tears when I read Igrenev's letter, though you've certainly shown him up cleverly. You know, it's moving all right, but at the same time you tried, as it were, to exhibit his false side. Am I right? Have I guessed it or not? But the ending, you know – oh, well, I really felt like giving you a good beating for it. For what idea are you trying to develop? Why, it's the same old deification of domestic happiness, multiplying of children and money – and they lived happily ever after – good Lord! You'll enchant your readers, for even I couldn't tear myself away from the book, but that makes it all the worse! The reader is as big a fool as ever, but that's why intelligent people ought to shake him up, while you – but there, that's enough. Good-bye. Don't be angry another time. I've come because I had something to tell you, but you're such a funny fellow –'

Meanwhile Lembke took his novel and locked it up in an oak bookcase, having managed incidentally to give Blum a wink to make himself scarce. Blum disappeared with a long, mournful face.

'I'm not such a funny fellow, but I'm simply – it's all these unpleasantnesses,' he muttered, frowning, but without anger and sitting down at the table. 'Sit down, please, and tell me what you have to say. I haven't seen you for a long time, Mr Verkhovensky, only, please, don't rush in again with that manner of yours – when one's busy it sometimes is – er –'

'My manner is always the same.'

'I know, my dear fellow, and I believe you don't mean anything by it, but sometimes one is worried – please take a seat.'

Peter sprawled on the sofa and at once tucked up his legs under him.

3

'What are you so worried about – not about that silly nonsense, surely?' he nodded towards the leaflet. 'I can bring you as many of these leaflets as you like. I've already made their acquaintance in the Kh—v province.'

'You mean when you were staying there?'

'Why, of course; it was not in my absence. There was one with a vignette – an axe printed at the top of it. Allow me.' He picked up the leaflet. 'Ah, yes, there's an axe on this one, too. It's the same one – an exact replica of it.'

'Yes, an axe. You see, an axe.'

'Why, you're not frightened of the axe, are you?'

'I'm not referring to the axe, sir, and – er – I'm not frightened. But this business, I mean, it's such an awful business – there are circumstances here.'

'Which? You mean that they should have brought it from the factory? Ha, ha! Do you know that in that factory of yours the workers will soon be composing such leaflets themselves.'

'What do you mean?' von Lembke glared at him sternly.

'I mean what I say. You'd better look after them carefully. You're much too mild a man, Mr Lembke. You write novels. You want the good old-fashioned methods here.'

'What old-fashioned methods? What are you talking about? The factory has been cleaned. I gave the order and it was cleaned up.'

'But there's mutiny among the workers. You should have them flogged, every man-jack of them, and the whole thing would be settled.'

'Mutiny? Nonsense! I gave the order, and it was cleaned up.'

'Good Lord! Mr Lembke, you're too mild a man.'

'First of all, I'm not so mild as you think, and, secondly –' von Lembke felt hurt again. He spoke to the young man with an effort, out of curiosity, wondering whether he would tell him anything new.

'Ah-h, another old friend!' Peter interrupted him, swooping down on another piece of paper lying under a paper-weight, some kind of political leaflet, but obviously printed abroad, and in verse. 'Well, this one I know by heart: *A Noble Character!* Let's see. Yes, it is *A Noble Character.* I met this character when I was abroad. Where did you dig it up?'

'You say you met him abroad?' von Lembke said with a start.

'I should think so. Four months ago, or five even.'

'You seem to have seen quite a great deal abroad,' von Lembke said, giving him a sharp look.

Peter unfolded the piece of paper without listening to him, and read the poem aloud:

A Noble Character

Not for him the pride of place,
Champion of the Human Race,
Victim of the tyrant's spite,
And the nobles' rancorous might,
The life he chose was one of seeking
Torture, misery, death, and beating –
With this intent to teach the people
That all are brothers, free and equal.
Leader of a rebel band,
He sought, at last, a foreign strand,
Fleeing from the Tsar's dark dungeons,
Thong and rack and hangman's bludgeons.
But the people, resolved to smash
The tyrant's chains and flee the lash,
From Smolensk to far Tashkent,
Chafing, waited for the student.
They waited for him all to rise
'Gainst tyrant Tsar and nobles' prize,
To claim their right to own the land
And forever more for truth to stand,
Against the bonds so triple twined,
Dark deceivers of the human mind,
Marriage, church, and family ties,
That filled the old world with tricks and lies.

'I expect you got it from that officer, didn't you?' Peter asked.

'Do you know the officer, too?'

'I should think so. I went on the spree with him for two days. I'm afraid he certainly deserved to go off his head.'

'Perhaps he didn't go off his head at all.'

'Oh? You mean because he started biting people?'

'But, look here, if you saw that poem abroad and then it's found here in that officer's room –'

'What? Rather mysterious, don't you think? You're not by any chance cross-examining me, are you? You see,' he began suddenly in a tone of unusual gravity, 'on my return from abroad I explained to certain people what I saw there, and my explanations were found to be satisfactory, otherwise I should not have rejoiced this town with my presence. I think that so far as that goes the affair is at an end and that I owe no more explanations to anyone. And, mind you, it is not at an end because I was an informer, but because I couldn't help doing otherwise. The people who wrote to Mrs Lembke knew the position, and wrote about me as an honest man. But, damn it, all that is over and done with. I've come to discuss a serious matter with you, and I'm glad you've told that chimney-sweep to clear out. It's something of the utmost importance to me, Mr Lembke. I have something special to ask you.'

'Oh? Well, go on. I'm waiting and, I must confess, I am very curious to hear what you have to say. And may I add, sir, that you rather surprise me.'

Von Lembke was a little agitated. Peter crossed his legs.

'In Petersburg,' he began, 'I talked frankly of many things, but certain other things – this, for instance,' he tapped *A Noble Character* with his finger, 'I passed over in silence, first, because it wasn't worth talking about and, secondly, because I only told them what they wanted to know. In things of this kind I hate to put myself out too much. That's the difference, as I see it, between a scoundrel and an honest man who is the victim of circumstances. Anyway, let's forget it. Well, sir, but now – now when these fools – I mean now when it has all come out and is already in your hands and I can see that it's impossible to hide anything from you, for you are a man who has eyes in his head and it is impossible to say what's in your mind, I – I – er – in short, I've come to ask you to save one man, another fool, possibly even a madman, for the sake of his youth, his misfortunes, and also because of your humanitarian principles. ... For I suppose it's not only in those novels of yours that you are so humane!' He suddenly cut short his speech with impatience and coarse sarcasm.

In a word, one could see that he was a straightforward man, though awkward and not very shrewd, from an excess of humanitarian feelings and, perhaps, also of delicacy – above all, a little on the stupid side, as von Lembke at once summed him up with great acuteness. He had indeed long suspected it, especially when, during the last week, particularly at night, he had cursed him inwardly for his inexplicable successes with Mrs Lembke.

'Who is the man you are asking a favour for and what is it all about?' he inquired majestically, doing his best to conceal his curiosity.

'It's – it's – damn it, I can't be blamed for trusting you, can I? It's not my fault if I respect you as a man of honour and, above all, as a sensible fellow who's capable of understanding – oh, damn it. ...'

The poor fellow evidently could not pull himself together.

'You must realize, of course,' he went on, 'that by giving you his name I'm betraying him. I am betraying him, am I not? Am I not?'

'But how do you expect me to guess his name if you can't make up your mind to tell it me?'

'Well, of course, that's the trouble. You always knock a fellow down with that logic of yours – damn it – well, damn it, that "noble character", that "student" is – Shatov – that's all I have to tell you.'

'Shatov? How do you mean Shatov?'

'Shatov is the "student" who is mentioned in that poem. He lives here. A former serf, the fellow who slapped –'

'Oh, yes, I know, I know!' Lembke cried, screwing up his eyes. 'But, look here, what exactly is he accused of and, what's more important, what do you want me to do?'

'Why, don't you see? I want you to save him! I used to know him eight years ago, I – well, I might almost be said to have been his friend,' Peter Verkhovensky said, getting more and more agitated. 'Well, but I am under no obligation to give you an account of my past life,' he declared, dismissing it with a wave of the hand. 'All this is of no importance. Just a matter of three and a half persons, and if you add those abroad, there won't be even a dozen of them. The main thing is that I put my trust in your humanitarian feelings and your intelligence. I'm sure you'll understand and you'll put the matter in its true perspective and not as goodness knows what: just as the foolish fancy of a crazy chap, as the result of misfortunes – misfortunes, mind you, that go back for many years, and not as some sort of unheard of conspiracy against the Government!'

He was almost breathless.

'Yes, I see. It's he who's responsible for the revolutionary leaflets with the picture of the axe,' von Lembke concluded almost majestically. 'But, look here, if he alone is involved, then how could he have distributed them here and in the provinces and even in the Kh—v province and, finally and most important of all, where did he get them?'

'But I'm telling you that there are only about five of them, or a dozen at most – how should I know?'

'You don't know?'

'But, damn it all, why should I know?'

'But you knew that Shatov was one of the conspirators, didn't you?'

'Oh, well!' Peter Verkhovensky gave it up with a wave of the hand, as though defending himself against the overwhelming perspicacity of his questioner. 'Well, listen. I'll tell you the whole truth. I don't know a thing about the revolutionary leaflets, I mean, not a damn thing – nothing at all, do you understand what that means? Well, of course, the second lieutenant, and someone else, and again someone else here, and – well, perhaps Shatov, too, and someone else – well, that's the lot – flotsam and jetsam all of them. But it's for Shatov I've come to intercede. He must be saved because this poem is his, his own composition, and it was through him it was published abroad. That I know for certain. As for those leaflets, I know nothing about them.'

'If the poem is his, then the leaflets are quite certainly his too. But what makes you suspect Mr Shatov?'

With the air of a man who had completely lost his patience, Peter Verkhovensky snatched his wallet from his pocket and took a note out of it.

'Here is the evidence you want!' he cried, flinging it on the table.

Lembke unfolded it. The note was written apparently about six months before from our town to some place abroad. It was very short, only a few words.

I can't print *A Noble Character* here. Can't do anything. Print it abroad.
IV. SHATOV.

Lembke gazed intently at Peter. Mrs Stavrogin was right in saying that he had a somewhat sheep-like look, at times especially.

'What I mean is this,' Peter said quickly. 'He wrote this poem here six months ago, but he could not get it printed – I mean, on a secret printing press, and that is why he asks that it should be printed abroad. … That's clear, isn't it?'

'Yes, sir, that's clear; but whom is he asking? That's what's not so clear,' Lembke observed with sly irony.

'Why, Kirilov of course. The note was written to Kirilov, who was abroad at the time. You didn't know it, did you? Though what really annoys me is that you're probably only pretending not to know, and that actually you knew about this poem and everything else long ago. How else did it come to be on your desk? Just happened to get there? Why are you tormenting me if that is so?'

He mopped his brow agitatedly with his handkerchief.

'Perhaps I do know something,' Lembke parried cleverly. 'But who is this Kirilov?'

'Well, he's an engineer who arrived in our town a few weeks ago. He was Stavrogin's second. A maniac. A madman. Your second lieutenant might indeed be suffering only from delirium tremens, but that one is stark raving mad – I guarantee you that. Oh, sir, if the Government only knew what sort of people they all are, they wouldn't bother to raise a hand against them. Every one of them ought to be locked up in a lunatic asylum. I had a good look at them in Switzerland and at their congresses.'

'You mean from where they direct the movement in this country?'

'But who directs it? Three men and a half? Why, one gets bored to tears looking at them. And what movement in this country do you mean? The leaflets? And what new members have they got? Second lieutenants who suffer from delirium tremens and two or three students! You're an intelligent man; let me put this question to you: why don't they get more important people to join their movement? Why are they always students and two or three hobbledehoys of twenty-two? I daresay a million sleuth-hounds are after them, and how many have they found? And have they got so many members? Seven people. I tell you, it's too boring for words.'

Lembke listened to him attentively, but with an expression which said: 'Don't you tell me such stories!'

'But, look here. You just said that this note was sent to some address abroad, but there is no address on it. How, then, do you come to know that the note was addressed to Mr Kirilov and, besides, that it was sent to some address abroad and – and that it really was written by Mr Shatov?'

'Well, all you have to do is to get a specimen of Shatov's hand-writing and compare it. You must have some signature of his in your office. As for Kirilov, he showed it to me himself at the time.'

'So you were yourself –'

'Of course I was myself. They showed me all sorts of things there. As for this poem, it seems that the late Herzen wrote it for Shatov when Shatov was still wandering abroad, in memory of their meet-ing, it seems, as an expression of his admiration or as a letter of recom-mendation – damn it – and Shatov circulates it among the young people. This is what Herzen thinks of me, as it were.'

'I see!' Lembke saw the point at last. 'No wonder I couldn't make it out: a political leaflet – well, that's easy to understand, but why a poem?'

'I knew you'd see it. And why the hell did I have to tell you about it? Look here, let me have Shatov; as for the rest, to hell with all of them; and that goes for Kirilov, too, who has shut himself up in Filip-pov's house, where Shatov lives too. He is hiding there. They don't like me because I've gone back – but promise to let me have Shatov, and I'll deliver you the rest on a plate. You'll find me useful, sir! The whole wretched lot of them, I think, numbers only nine or ten people. I'm keeping an eye on them myself. For reasons of my own, sir. Three of them are already known to us: Shatov, Kirilov, and the second lieutenant. The rest I'm just keeping an eye on – I'm not very short-sighted, though. It's the same as in the Kh—v province: two students, one schoolboy, two twenty-year-old noblemen, one teacher, and one retired major of about sixty, who has gone silly with drink, have been caught there. That was all. And you can take my word for it that that was all. The authorities were surprised to find that there were no more. But you must give me six days. I've got it all worked out: six days and no more. If you want some sort of result, don't touch them for another six days, and I shall tie them all up in a bundle for you. If you stir, the birds will fly away. But let me have Shatov. I'm for Shatov. The best thing would be to summon him in secret and in a friendly way to your office and cross-examine him, having first let him see that you know everything. But I expect he'll throw himself at your feet and burst into tears! He's a neurotic fellow. Very unhappy. His wife is Stavrogin's mistress. Be nice to him and he'll tell you every-thing, but you must give me my six days first. And above all – above all: not a word to Mrs Lembke. It's a secret. Can you keep a secret?'

'What do you mean?' Lembke cried, staring at him in surprise. 'Haven't you told Mrs Lembke – anything at all?'

'Told her? Good Lord, no. Oh, my dear Mr Lembke, really! You see, I value her friendship too much and I have too great a respect for her – and so on and so forth – but you won't catch me slipping up like that. I do not contradict her because, as you know yourself, it is dan-gerous to contradict her. I may have dropped a hint to her, because she loves it; but, good heavens, I'd never dream of betraying any names to her or anything of that sort, as I have to you just now. For why have I turned to you now? Because after all you're a man, a serious man, a man of long and dependable experience in the Service. You've had experience of life, too. I suppose you know every step in such a matter by heart from your experience in Petersburg. Why, if I were to tell her those two names, for instance, she'd raise such a storm ... For, you know, she'd like to astonish Petersburg. No, sir, she's too hot-headed – that's the trouble.'

'Yes, there's something of that *fougue* in her,' Lembke murmured, not without pleasure, though feeling sorry at the same time that the boor had had the impudence to express himself rather freely about Mrs Lembke.

But Peter probably thought that what he said was not enough, and that he had to exert himself a little more to flatter 'that Lembke fel-low' and get him completely in his power.

'Yes, you're quite right: a *fougue* it is,' he said. 'She may be a woman of genius, a literary lady, but – she's sure to frighten away the birds. She wouldn't be able to keep the secret for six hours, let alone six days. Oh, my dear Mr Lembke, never rely on a woman to keep any-thing for six days! You do admit that I've had some experience in such matters, don't you? I do know something about it, don't I? And I think that you, too, know that I'm in a position to know something about it. I am not asking you to wait for six days just for fun, but be-cause I have a good reason for it.'

'I've heard,' Lembke said hesitatingly, afraid to reveal his thoughts, 'I've heard that on your return from abroad you expressed – er –

as it were – your repentance to – er – the proper quarters – didn't you?'

'Well, whatever happened there is nobody's business.'

'Well, of course, I – er – don't want to pry into – er – but I couldn't help feeling that you've talked in quite a different vein till now: about the Christian faith, for instance, about social institutions and, last but not least, about the Government.'

'I may have said all sorts of things. I'm saying them still, but these ideas ought not to be applied as those fools do it – that's the point. For what's the use of biting a man's shoulder? Why, you agreed with me yourself, only you said that it was premature.'

'It wasn't that I agreed about or said that it was premature.'

'You certainly weigh every word you say, don't you? Ha, ha! A careful man!' Peter suddenly remarked gaily. 'Listen, my dear sir, I had to get to know you better, and that's why I spoke in that vein. You're not the only one I get to know like that. There are lots of other people I treat in the same way. I may have wanted to find out what sort of a man you were.'

'What did you want to know that for?'

'Oh, I don't know,' he said, laughing again. 'You see, my dear and highly esteemed sir, you're very clever; but it hasn't yet come to *that*, and it won't come to it, either. You see what I mean? Perhaps you do. Though I did give certain explanations to the proper quarters on my return from abroad, and I really don't know why a man of certain convictions should not be able to act for the success of his sincere convictions, but – er – no one *there* asked me to send in a report about your character, and I've not accepted any such orders from *there*. Consider: I need not have divulged those two names to you. I could have sent them off straight *there*, that is, where I made my first explanations. And if I'd been acting for the sake of my financial or some personal advantage, it would have paid me better not to have told you, for now they will be grateful to you, and not to me. I've done it solely for Shatov,' Peter added nobly, 'for Shatov alone because of our old friendship. Well, of course, when you take up your pen to write *there*, I shouldn't mind at all if you said something in my favour, if you like – I shouldn't dream of stopping you, ha, ha! Good-bye, sir. I'm afraid I've stayed too long as it is and,' he added pleasantly as he got up, 'I shouldn't really have talked so much!'

'On the contrary, I'm very glad that the affair is, so to speak, being cleared up,' von Lembke said, getting up and looking very amiable, too, evidently under the impression of Peter's last words. 'I accept your services gratefully, and you may be sure that so far as I'm concerned I shall do my best to put in a good word about your zeal. ...'

'Six days, that's the chief thing. I must have six days, and you must not do anything during that time.'

'All right.'

'Of course, I don't tie your hands, and I shouldn't dare to do anything of the sort. You naturally have to keep an eye on them, but please don't shoo them off before the right time – that's where I rely on your intelligence and experience. I suppose you've got lots of bloodhounds hidden away somewhere as well as sleuth-hounds – ha, ha!' Peter blurted out gaily and thoughtlessly (like a young man).

'Oh, it isn't at all like that,' von Lembke declined a direct answer pleasantly. 'That is the sort of thing young people are apt to think – I mean, that the authorities have lots of things up their sleeves. But, by the way, there is something I'd like to ask you about: if that Kirilov was Stavrogin's second, then Mr Stavrogin, too, is in that case –'

'What about Stavrogin?'

'I mean, if they're such friends –' ·

'Oh, no, no, no! You're wrong there, clever as you are. You surprise me! I thought that you were not without some information about it. You see, Stavrogin is quite the opposite; I mean, absolutely. *Avis au lecteur!*'

'Really? Are you quite sure?' Lembke asked mistrustfully. 'Mrs Lembke told me that according to the information she had received from Petersburg, he is a man with certain, as it were, instructions –'

'I don't know anything, nothing at all – good-bye, good-bye – *avis au lecteur!*' Peter suddenly and openly declined to discuss it.

He rushed to the door.

'Please, please, Mr Verkhovensky,' Lembke cried, 'I have one more little thing to discuss with you, and I won't detain you long.'

He took an envelope out of the drawer of his desk.

'Here's another specimen of the same kind, and you may take it as proof that I trust you implicitly. Here, have a look. What do you make of it?'

There was a letter in the envelope, a strange, anonymous letter addressed to Lembke which he had only received the day before. Peter, to his intense annoyance, read as follows:

Your Excellency,

For that you are according to your rank. I declare herewith an attempt on the life of gentlemen of the rank of general and on our motherland. For everything points to that. Have been distributing hundreds for many years myself. Also godlessness. A mutiny is being organized, and several thousands of revolutionary leaflets, and after each of them a hundred people will be running, with their tongues hanging out, if the authorities do not first confiscate them; great rewards have been promised them, and the common people is stupid, and there's vodka too. The common people, looking for the guilty ones, ruin both guilty and innocent, afraid of the one and the other. I repent of what I have not done, for such are my circumstances. If you'd like me to inform the authorities for the salvation of our country, and also of the churches and the icons, I am the only man who can do it. But on condition that I get a pardon from the secret police by telegraph at once, for me alone, and let the rest answer for it. Put a candle at seven o'clock each evening in the porter's window for a signal. When I see it, I shall believe and come to kiss the merciful hand from the capital city, but on condition that I get a pension, for else how am I to live? But you won't be sorry, for you'll get a star. It must be done in secret, or they'll wring my neck.

Your Excellency's desperate servant.

Falls to your feet

repentant freethinker *Incognito*.

Von Lembke explained that the letter was left the day before in the porter's room when there was no one there.

'Well, what do you think?' Peter asked almost rudely.

'In my opinion it's an anonymous squib, by the way of a joke.'

'Most likely it is. One can't fool you.'

'I think so chiefly because it's so stupid.'

'And have you received any other squibs here?'

'Yes, twice; anonymous letters.'

'Well, of course, they wouldn't sign it. In a different style? By different hands?'

'Yes, in a different style and by different hands.'

'Facetious ones, like this one?'

'Yes, facetious and, you know, very disgusting.'

'Well, if there were others, then this one must certainly be the same.'

'And, above all, because it's so stupid. For those fellows are educated, and they would never write like that.'

'Yes, yes, of course.'

'But what if this one really wants to inform the authorities?'

'Not likely,' Peter snapped drily. 'What does he mean by the telegram from the secret police and the pension? It's obviously a squib.'

'Yes, yes,' Lembke said shamefacedly.

'Do you know what? Leave it with me. I promise to find out who
wrote it. I'll find it out before the others.'

'Take it,' Lembke agreed, though with some hesitation.

'Have you shown it to anyone?'

'No, of course not. I showed it to no one.'

'I mean, to Mrs Lembke?'

'Good Lord, no! And for goodness sake don't show it to her yourself!' Lembke cried in alarm. 'She'll be so shocked and – she'll be
awfully angry with me.'

'Yes, I daresay you'd be the first to catch it. She'd say it was your
own fault if people write such letters to you. I know what female logic
is like. Well, good-bye. I may even present you with the author of
this letter in a couple of days. Above all, remember our agreement!'

4

Peter Verkhovensky may have been far from stupid, but Fedka the
convict was right when he said that he would invent a man himself
and live with him. He left Lembke fully convinced that he had put his
mind at rest for six days at least, and he wanted those six days very
badly indeed. But he was wrong, his idea being merely based on the
fact that from the very start he had invented for himself once and for
all a Lembke who was a complete simpleton.

Like any other morbidly mistrustful person, Lembke was always
exceedingly and joyfully trustful the moment he left uncertainty behind him. The new turn of events appeared to him at first in a most
favourable light, in spite of certain new and troublesome complications. At any rate, his old doubts entirely vanished. Besides, he had
been so tired during the last few days, he had felt so worn out and so
helpless that his soul longed for a rest. But, alas, he was troubled again.
His long life in Petersburg had left ineradicable traces on his mind.

The official and even the secret history of the 'new generation' were fairly familiar to him – he was a curious man and he used to collect revolutionary leaflets – but he could never understand a word of it. And now he felt like a man lost in a forest: he felt instinctively that there was something incongruous and utterly absurd and anomalous in Peter Verkhovensky's words – 'Though,' he said to himself, feeling entirely at a loss, 'goodness only knows what may not happen with this "new generation" and what they may be up to!'

And as though on purpose, Blum again poked his head in through the door. He had been waiting not far off all during Peter's visit. This Blum was a distant relation of Lembke, though he had carefully and timidly concealed this fact all his life. I must ask the reader's indulgence if I devote just a few words to this insignificant person. Blum belonged to the strange category of 'unlucky' Germans, not at all because he had no ability, but for no reason whatsoever. 'Unlucky' Germans are not a myth, but really do exist even in Russia, and form a class of their own. Lembke had a most touching sympathy for him all his life, and he got him some subordinate job under him wherever he could and as much as his own successes in the Service would allow. But he had no luck anywhere. Either his job was temporarily abolished, or a new man was appointed as the head of his department; and once he was nearly put on trial with some other officials. He was extremely conscientious, but gloomy without reason and to his own detriment: red-haired, tall, stooping, dismal, even sentimental and, though very humble, obstinate and pertinacious like an ox, but always at the wrong moment. He, as well as his wife and his numerous children, had been deeply attached to Lembke for many years. With the exception of Lembke, nobody ever liked him. Mrs Lembke at once demanded his dismissal, but she could not overcome her husband's obstinacy. That was the cause of their first quarrel. It happened immediately after their marriage, during the first days of their honeymoon, when Blum, who had till then been carefully concealed from her, suddenly materialized with the humiliating secret of his relationship. Lembke besought her with folded hands, told her pathetically all the story of Blum and their friendship since the days of their childhood, but Mrs Lembke considered herself disgraced for ever, and even resorted to fainting. Von Lembke, however, would not budge an inch, declaring that he would not give up Blum for anything in the world, or let him go, so that in the end she was astonished and was obliged to let Blum stay. It was decided, however, that their relationship to Blum should be concealed even more carefully than before, if that were possible, and that even Blum's Christian name and patronymic should be changed, because for some reason he, too, had the same name and patronymic as Mr Lembke. In our town Blum did not know anybody except the German chemist; he paid no visits to anyone and led, as was his wont, a solitary and parsimonious existence. He had known of Mr Lembke's reprehensible literary efforts for a long time. He was for the most part called in to listen to secret readings of the novel, and he would sit there like a post for six hours on end; he perspired, made superhuman efforts to keep awake and to smile; on returning home he groaned and moaned together with his long-legged and scraggy wife about their benefactor's unhappy weakness for Russian literature.

Lembke gave Blum an anguished look.

'I beg you, Blum, to leave me alone,' he began, speaking rapidly and agitatedly, evidently anxious to prevent the resumption of their talk, which had been interrupted by the arrival of Peter Verkhovensky.

'But, sir, it could all be arranged in the most delicate manner and without any publicity, for you possess all the necessary powers,' Blum insisted respectfully but doggedly on something, stooping as he came nearer and nearer by small steps to Lembke.

'Blum, you're so loyal and devoted to me that I'm always in a panic when I look at you.'

'You always say witty things and you're so delighted with what you say that it never interferes with your sleep. But that's how you do yourself harm.'

'Blum, I've just come to the conclusion that we're wrong, absolutely wrong.'

'Not from what that false and vicious young man whom you suspect yourself has been telling you, sir? He got the better of you by his flattery and praise of your literary talent.'

'Blum, you don't understand a thing. Your plan is absurd, I tell you. We shan't find anything, and there's sure to be a terrible to-do, then laughter, and then Mrs Lembke –'

'We shall most certainly find what we're looking for, sir,' Blum said, stepping up to him firmly and placing his right hand on his heart. 'We shall search his place suddenly early in the morning, showing the

utmost courtesy to the gentleman himself and acting strictly in accordance with the letter of the law. The young men, Lyamshin and
Telyatnikov, are quite certain that we shall find all we want. They've
been there many times. No one is well disposed to Mr Verkhovensky.
Mrs Stavrogin has openly refused to do anything for him any more,
and every honest man, if there is such a man to be found in this un-
civilized town, is convinced that the source of disbelief in God and
socialist doctrine has always been concealed there. He keeps all the
prohibited books, Ryleyev's *Reflections* and all Herzen's works. I have,
in any case, got a rough catalogue of his books.'

'Good heavens, everyone has those books. How simple-minded
you are, my poor Blum!'

'And many political leaflets,' Blum went on, without listening to
his superior's remarks. 'We shall end by getting on the track of the
leaflets which are printed here. That young Verkhovensky looks very
suspicious to me, sir.'

'But you are mixing up the father and the son. They don't get on
together. The son openly laughs at his father.'

'That's only a mask, sir.'

'Blum, you've sworn to worry me to death. Just think! He's, after
all, a person of consequence here. He's been a professor, he's a well-
known man. He'll raise a clamour, and everybody in town will at
once start making jokes at our expense, and, well, we'll make a mess
of everything and – and think, man, what will Mrs Lembke say. ...'

Blum pressed on and did not listen.

'He was only a lecturer, sir. Only a lecturer, and just a collegiate
assessor by rank when he retired.' He smote his chest. 'He hasn't any
marks of distinction and he was dismissed on suspicion of plotting
against the Government. He's been under police supervision and I'm
sure he still is. And in view of the disorders, which have come to light
now, it is most certainly your duty, sir. It's you, sir, who are missing
the chance of obtaining a distinction by your tacit support of the real
criminal.'

'Mrs Lembke! Get out, Blum!' von Lembke cried suddenly on
hearing his wife's voice in the next room.

Blum started, but he did not give in.

'Please, sir, please give me your permission,' he persisted, pressing
both his hands more firmly to his chest.

'Get out!' von Lembke cried, grinding his teeth. 'Do what you like – afterwards – Oh, Lord!'

The curtain was parted and Mrs Lembke came in. She stopped majestically at the sight of Blum, giving him a haughty and offensive look, as though the very presence of that man was an affront to her. Blum made her a deep bow, silently and respectfully, and, doubled up with respect, tiptoed to the door, with his hands held a little apart.

Whether he really took Lembke's last hysterical cry as a direct permission to carry out his request, or whether he acted against his conscience for the direct advantage of his patron, being quite certain that all would turn out well in the end, the result of this talk between the Governor and his subordinate was, as we shall presently see, most unexpected. It amused a great many people; it received the greatest possible publicity; it made Mrs Lembke furious with anger, utterly disconcerting Mr Lembke and throwing him at the most critical time into a state of the most lamentable indecision.

5

It was a very busy day for Peter Verkhovensky. From von Lembke he hurried off to Bogoyavlenskaya Street, but while walking along Bykov Street, past the house where Karmazinov was staying, he suddenly stopped, grinned, and went into the house. He was told by the servant that he was expected, which interested him greatly, for he had not warned Karmazinov of his coming visit.

But the great writer really had been expecting him, and not only that day but the day before and the day before that. Three days earlier he had given him his manuscript of *Merci* (which he had intended to read at the literary matinée on the day of Mrs Lembke's fête). He had done it out of kindness, for he was certain that he would agreeably flatter the young man's vanity by letting him read the great work beforehand. Peter had long noticed that this vain, pampered gentleman, who was so offensively unapproachable to anyone but the elect, this almost 'statesmanlike' writer, was simply trying to ingratiate himself with him, and that with quite unwonted eagerness. I can't help thinking that the young man realized at last that Karmazinov, even if he did not consider him to be the ringleader of all the secret revolutionary organizations in Russia, at least considered him one of the few men who were initiated into all the secrets of the Russian revolution and who had an incontestable influence upon the younger generation. The state of mind of the 'cleverest man in Russia' interested Peter, but for certain reasons he had so far tried to avoid entering into any explanations with him.

The great writer was staying at his sister's house. His sister was the wife of a Court chamberlain who owned land in our district. Both of them, husband and wife, worshipped their famous relative, but to their great regret they were in Moscow during his present visit, so that the honour of welcoming him fell to an old lady, a very distant and poor relation of the Court chamberlain's, who lived with the family and had long been in charge of the housekeeping. Since Mr Karmazinov's arrival the whole household walked about on tiptoe. The old lady wrote to Moscow almost every day, how he had slept and what he had for his dinner, and once she even sent a telegram with the news that after a dinner at the Mayor's he had to take a spoonful of a certain medicine. It was only on rare occasions that she dared to enter his room, though he treated her courteously, but drily, and spoke to her only when he wanted something.

When Peter came in, he was having his morning cutlet with half a glass of red wine. Peter had been to see him before, and every time he found him having his morning cutlet, which he ate in front of him, but he never asked the young man to join him in the meal. After the cutlet, a small cup of coffee was brought in. The footman, who served the food, wore a frock-coat, soft, noiseless boots and gloves.

'Ah-h!' Karmazinov got up from the sofa, wiping his mouth with a napkin and with an expression of the purest joy came up to exchange kisses with Peter – a characteristic habit of Russians, if they are very famous indeed.

But Peter knew from experience that while Karmazinov seemed eager to exchange kisses, he merely held up his cheek, and so he did the same this time; both their cheeks touched. Karmazinov, without showing that he had noticed it, sat down on the sofa and very pleasantly pointed to an arm-chair opposite in which Peter sprawled.

'I don't suppose you – er – would like any lunch, would you?' Karmazinov asked, this time contrary to his custom, but of course with an air which implied that he expected a polite refusal.

Peter, however, at once expressed a desire to have lunch. A shadow of offended surprise passed over the face of the host, but only for a fraction of a second. He rang nervously for the servant, and in spite of his breeding, raised his voice fastidiously as he gave orders for a second lunch to be served.

'What will you have: a cutlet or coffee?' he asked once more.

'A cutlet and coffee, please, and tell him to bring some more wine; I'm famished,' replied Peter calmly, scrutinizing his host's clothes.

Mr Karmazinov was wearing a kind of indoor wadded jacket with little mother-of-pearl buttons, but it was very short, which was not becoming to his rather prominent belly and his firmly rounded thighs; but tastes differ. A woollen checkered rug covered his knees and trailed to the floor, though it was warm in the room.

'You're not ill, are you?' Peter observed.

'No, I'm not ill, but I'm afraid of falling ill in this climate,' the writer answered in his shrill voice, scanning every word very tenderly, however, and with his agreeable, aristocratic lisp. 'I've been expecting you since yesterday.'

'But why? I didn't promise to come.'

'That's true, but you have my manuscript. Have you – er – read it?'

'Manuscript? What manuscript?'

Karmazinov looked terribly surprised.

'But you've brought it with you, haven't you?' he cried, becoming suddenly so alarmed that he even stopped eating and looked panic-stricken at Peter.

'Oh, you mean your *Bonjour*, do you?'

'*Merci*.'

'Very well, *Merci*. I've forgotten all about it. Afraid I haven't read it. I've had no time. I really don't know – it's not in my pockets – must have left it on my desk. Don't worry, it'll turn up.'

'No, I think I'd better send somebody to your place at once. It might get lost and, besides, it might be stolen.'

'Oh, who'd want it? And why are you so afraid? Mrs Lembke told me that you always have several copies made – one abroad at your notary's, another in Petersburg, a third in Moscow, and the fourth you send to your bank, I believe.'

'But, my dear fellow, Moscow might burn down and my manuscript with it. No, I think I'd better send for it at once.'

'Wait, here it is!' Peter said, producing a bundle of notepaper from his back pocket. 'Got a little crumpled, I'm afraid. Would you believe it? It's been lying in my pocket with my handkerchief ever since I took it from you. Forgot all about it.'

Karmazinov seized his manuscript eagerly and, for the time being, put it respectfully on a special table near him, but so that he could keep it in sight every moment.

'I don't suppose you read very much, do you?' he hissed, unable to restrain himself.

'No, not very much.'

'And nothing at all in the way of Russian literature?'

'In the way of Russian literature? One moment, though, I believe I have read something. *On the Way, By the Way*, or *At the Parting of the Ways*, or something of the kind. Can't remember. Read it a long time ago, five years ago. I've no time.'

A short pause ensued.

'As soon as I arrived I assured everyone that you're a very intelligent man and now, I believe, they're all raving about you.'

'Thank you,' Peter answered calmly.

Luncheon was brought in. Peter applied himself to his cutlet with extraordinary appetite, dispatched it at once, drank his wine and gulped down his coffee.

'This boor,' Karmazinov thought, looking askance at him as he finished eating his cutlet and draining his wine to the last gulp, 'this boor probably grasped at once the biting irony of my words – and I'm sure he's read my manuscript with avidity. He's just lying for some good reason of his own. But quite likely he isn't lying at all, but really is genuinely stupid. I like a man of genius to be a little stupid. Isn't he a sort of genius among them? To hell with him, though.'

He got up from the sofa and began pacing the room from one corner to another, by way of a constitutional, which he did every day after lunch.

'You're leaving soon?' asked Peter from his arm-chair, lighting a cigarette.

'I really came to sell my estate, and I'm entirely in the hands of my manager.'

'But didn't you come here because they expected an epidemic there after the war?'

'N-no, not entirely for that reason,' Mr Karmazinov continued, scanning his sentences good-naturedly, and each time he turned from one corner to the other he threw out his little right foot jerkily, though only a little. 'I really do intend to live as long as possible.' He laughed, not without venom. 'There's something in our landed gentry that makes them wear out very quickly, in every respect. But I mean to wear out as late as possible, and now I am going abroad for good; there the climate is better and the houses are of stone and everything much stronger. Europe will last my time, I think. What do you think?'

'How should I know?'

'Well, if the Babylon there really does fall and if its fall be great (and I agree with you entirely about that, though I think that it will last my time), there's nothing that can fall here in Russia, comparatively speaking. We have no stones to crash upon us, and I suppose everything will dissolve in mud. Holy Russia is least of all capable of offering resistance to anything. The peasants still carry on somehow with the help of their Russian God, but, according to the latest information, the Russian God is very unreliable and scarcely held out against the peasant reform. It shook him up a bit, anyway. And what with the railways, and what with you. ... I'm afraid I don't believe in the Russian God at all.'

'And in the European one?'

'I don't believe in any. I've been slandered to the Russian youth. I've always sympathized with every one of its movements. I was shown the revolutionary leaflets you have here. People are puzzled by them because they are afraid of their form, but they are all convinced of their power, though they may not realize it. Everyone has long ago been going downhill and everyone has known for a long time that there's nothing they can hold on to. What makes me absolutely convinced of the success of this mysterious propaganda is that Russia today is pre-eminently the only place in the world where anything you like may happen without the slightest opposition. I know perfectly well why well-to-do Russians all rush abroad and why more and more of them go abroad every year. It's simply instinct. The rats are first to leave a sinking ship. Holy Russia is a country of wood, of poverty. A dangerous country, a country of vainglorious paupers in the highest strata of society, while the overwhelming majority of the people live in tumbledown shacks. She'll be glad of any solution. All you have to do is to explain it to her. The Government alone still tries to resist, but it just waves its cudgel about in the dark and hits its own supporters. Everything here is doomed and sentenced to death. Russia, as she is now, has no future. I've become a German and I'm proud of it.'

'But you began about the leaflets. Tell me everything: what do you think of them?'

'Everyone is afraid of them, so that they must be powerful. They openly expose deceit and prove that there's nothing we can get a firm grip on in our country, nothing to lean on. They speak aloud, while all are silent. What is so irresistible about them (in spite of their form) is their hitherto unheard-of boldness in looking the truth straight in the face. This ability to look the truth straight in the face is characteristic only of the Russians of this generation. No, in Europe they are not so brave: theirs is a kingdom of stone, they still have something to lean on there. As far as I can see and as far as I can judge, the whole essence of the Russian revolutionary idea consists of the negation of honour. I like its being so boldly and fearlessly expressed. No, in Europe they won't understand it yet, but that's just what we shall so eagerly embrace here. For a Russian honour is just an unnecessary burden. And it always has been a burden, throughout the whole of our history. He can be attracted much more by the open "right to dishonour". I belong to the older generation and, I confess, I'm still in favour of honour, but that's just a matter of habit. I'm still fond of the old forms, let us say, out of cowardice. I must somehow carry on for the few more years that are left to me.'

He suddenly stopped short.

'Good Lord!' he thought to himself, 'I go on talking, and he's watching me in silence. He wants me to ask him a straight question. That's what he's come for. And, by Jove, I will.'

'Mrs Lembke asked me to find out from you by some subterfuge what sort of surprise you are preparing for the ball the day after tomorrow,' Peter Verkhovensky asked suddenly.

'Yes,' Karmazinov said with a dignified air, 'there most certainly will be a surprise, and I shall certainly make them all sit up, but I shan't tell you my secret.'

Peter did not insist.

'Doesn't a certain Shatov live here?' the great writer asked. 'Just think of it, and I haven't seen him yet.'

'A very nice chap. What about it?'

'Oh, nothing. He seems to be saying all sorts of things. It was he who slapped Stavrogin's face, wasn't it?'

'Yes.'

'And what's your opinion of Stavrogin?'

'Don't know. A lady-killer, I believe.'

Karmazinov hated Stavrogin because the latter had taken it into his head to ignore him completely.

'I daresay,' he said, with a titter, 'the lady-killer will be the first to be strung up on a tree, if what they say in those revolutionary leaflets comes to pass.'

'Perhaps even sooner than that,' Peter said suddenly.

'Serve him right, too,' Karmazinov assented, no longer laughing, but apparently in good earnest.

'You said so once before and, you know, I told him about it.'

'Did you really?' Karmazinov laughed again.

'He said if he were to be hanged, it would be quite enough if you were flogged, and not just as a matter of form, but so that it hurts, just as peasants are flogged.'

Peter took his hat and got up. Karmazinov held out both hands to him at parting.

'And what,' he suddenly squeaked in his honeyed voice and with a sort of special intonation, still keeping Peter's hands in his, 'and what if what you're planning were actually to happen – when, do you think, is it to be?'

'How should I know?' Peter answered rather rudely.

Both looked intently into each other's eyes.

'Just roughly? Approximately?' Karmazinov squeaked still more sweetly.

'You'll have time to sell your estate and to clear out, too,' Peter muttered still more rudely.

Both looked at each other even more intently. There was a minute's silence.

'It'll start at the beginning of May and will be over by the first of October,' Peter said suddenly.

'Thank you, thank you very much,' Karmazinov said in a fervent voice, pressing Peter's hands.

'A rat like you will have plenty of time to leave the ship!' Peter thought as he went out into the street. 'But if that almost statesman-like mind so confidently inquires about the exact time and thanks me so respectfully for the information I've given him, then we no longer need have any doubts about ourselves,' he added, grinning. 'Well – well. He isn't such a fool, after all, and – he's only an emigrating rat. A man like him will never tell the police!'

He ran off to Filippov's house in Bogoyavlenskaya Street.

6

Peter first of all called on Kirilov. The latter was, as usual, alone, and this time he was doing some physical exercises, that is to say, he was standing with his legs apart and waving his arms above his head in some special sort of way. A ball lay on the floor. His breakfast had gone cold on the table and had not been cleared away. Peter stood for a minute on the threshold.

'I can see you're taking great care of your health,' he said in a loud and cheerful voice as he entered the room. 'What a lovely ball, though; bounces beautifully, too. Is it also for your exercises?'

Kirilov put on his coat.

'Yes, that, too, is for my health,' he muttered drily. 'Sit down.'

'I've only come in for a minute. However, I will sit down. Your health is all very well, but I've come to remind you of our agreement. The time's approaching in – a certain sense,' he concluded with an awkward twist of his body.

'What agreement?'

'What do you mean – what agreement?' Peter asked with a sudden start. He even looked alarmed.

'It's not an agreement nor an obligation. Haven't bound myself to do anything. Your mistake.'

'Look here, what on earth do you mean?' Peter jumped up.

'Just as I like.'

'Meaning?'

'Just as ever.'

'How am I to understand that? Does it mean that you're still of the same mind?'

'It does. Only there's no question of any agreement. I haven't bound myself to do anything. I promised of my own free will, and now, too, it's of my own free will.'

Kirilov offered his explanations in a sharp and scornful voice.

'All right, all right, so it is of your own free will, so long as you don't change your mind,' Peter said, sitting down again with a satisfied air. 'You're losing your temper over a word. You've become very irritable of late. That's why I've avoided calling on you. Still, I was absolutely sure that you wouldn't betray us.'

'I can't say that I like you very much, but you can be absolutely sure. Though I don't recognize betrayal or non-betrayal.'

'Still, you know,' Peter said, looking alarmed again, 'we must get everything settled so that we know where we are. The whole thing demands the utmost precision, and you keep on administering shocks to me. May I talk it over with you?'

'Go on,' Kirilov snapped, without looking at him.

'You decided long ago to commit suicide – I mean you had such an idea in your mind. Am I expressing myself properly? There's no mistake, is there?'

'I've still got the same idea.'

'Very well. And don't forget that no one has forced you to it.'

'I should think not. What silly nonsense you talk!'

'All right. I'm sorry I expressed myself so stupidly. No doubt it would have been very foolish to force you. To continue: you were a member of the society during its old organization and disclosed it to one of its members.'

'I didn't disclose it to anybody. I simply told him.'

'All right. It would have been absurd to "disclose it", anyway. What sort of disclosure is it? You simply told it. Very well.'

'It isn't very well, because you go on jabbering. I don't owe you any explanation, and you will never understand my ideas. I want to commit suicide because I've got such an idea, because I don't like the fear of death, because – because it's not your business to know. What do you want? Some tea? It's cold. Let me get you another glass.'

Peter had really got hold of the tea-pot and was looking for an empty glass. Kirilov went to the cupboard and brought a clean glass.

'I've just had lunch at Karmazinov's,' the visitor observed. 'Then I listened to him talking and was covered with perspiration. I ran all the way to your place and also got covered with perspiration. I'm dying for something to drink.'

'Drink it. Cold tea's good.'

Kirilov resumed his seat and once more stared at the opposite corner of the room.

'The idea has occurred to the society,' he went on, 'that I could be useful to them by committing suicide, and that when you get yourself in a mess here and the police are looking for those responsible for it, I should suddenly shoot myself, leaving a letter in which I'd take the blame for everything, so that they wouldn't suspect you for a whole year.'

'For a couple of days, anyway. Even one day can be precious.'

'All right. So I was told that if I had nothing against it I should wait. I told them I'd wait until the society let me know the time, because it makes no difference to me.'

'Yes, but remember that you undertook to write your last letter with my help and that, on your arrival in Russia, you'd be at my – well, in a word, at my disposal; I mean, for that occasion only, of course. You're quite free to do what you like otherwise,' Peter added almost amiably.

'I didn't undertake it. I agreed to it, because it makes no difference to me.'

'All right, all right. I haven't the least intention of hurting your feelings, but –'

'It's not a question of my feelings.'

'But don't forget that they collected one hundred and twenty thalers for your fares, which means that you've taken money.'

'Not at all.' Kirilov flushed. 'The money wasn't for that. One doesn't take money for that.'

'One sometimes does.'

'You're lying. I made a statement in a letter which I sent from Petersburg, and I repaid you one hundred and twenty thalers in Petersburg; I repaid you personally – and it was sent off from there unless you kept it for yourself.'

'All right, all right, I don't want to argue about it. It was sent off. The important thing is that you're still of the same mind as before.'

'I am. When you come and say: "It's time!" I'll carry it all out. Well, is it to be soon?'

'Not very many days now. But remember we compose the letter together on that very night.'

'I don't mind if it's the same day. You told me I'd have to take the responsibility for the leaflets, didn't you?'

'And something else.'

'I shan't take the responsibility for everything.'

'What won't you be responsible for?' Peter asked, looking startled again.

'What I don't choose. That's enough. I don't want to talk about it any more.'

Peter controlled himself and changed the subject.

'I've something else I want to talk to you about,' he said. 'Will you spend this evening with us? It's Virginsky's birthday, and we'll all meet there on this pretext.'

'Don't want to.'

'Please do come. It's important. We must create an impression by our numbers and – and our faces. You've a face – I mean, you have a fateful face.'

'You think so?' Kirilov laughed. 'All right, I'll come, but not because of my face. When?'

'Oh, as early as possible. About half-past six. And, you know, you can go in, sit down and not speak to anyone, however many there may be there. Only please don't forget to bring a pencil and a piece of paper with you.'

'What's that for?'

'What difference does it make to you? It's my special request. You'll sit there without speaking to anyone, listen, and just pretend to take a few notes from time to time. You can draw something, if you like.'

'What nonsense! What for?'

'But what difference does it make to you? You keep saying that it's all one to you.'

'No – what for?'

'I'll tell you. Because one member of our society, the inspector, has stayed behind in Moscow, and I told someone here that the inspector might pay us a visit. They'll think that you are the inspector, and as you've already been here three weeks, they'll be even more surprised.'

'Hocus-pocus. There's no inspector in Moscow.'

'All right, so there isn't. To hell with him! But what business is that of yours, and what sort of trouble will it be to you? You are a member of the society, aren't you?'

'Tell them that I'm the inspector. I'll sit there without uttering a word. But I don't want pencil and paper.'

'But why not?'

'Don't want them.'

Peter got very angry; he even went green in the face, but again he controlled himself. He got up and took his hat.

'Is *he* here?' he asked suddenly in an undertone.

'Yes.'

'That's good. I'll soon get him out of here. Don't worry.'

'I'm not worrying. He only spends the night here. The old woman is in the hospital. Her daughter-in-law is dead. I've been here alone for two days. I've shown him the place in the fence where a board can be taken out. He crawls through. No one sees.'

'I shall take him away soon.'

'He told me he had many places where he could spend a night.'

'He is lying. The police are after him, and here it's safe so far. You don't discuss things with him, do you?'

'I do. All night. He calls you awful names. I've been reading Revelation to him at night. We have tea, too. He listened. Yes, he was interested, very interested, the whole night.'

'Damn it, you'll convert him to Christianity!'

'But he is a Christian. Don't worry. He'll kill them. Why do you want to kill?'

'No, I don't want him for that. I've other plans for him. Does Shatov know about Fedka?'

'I don't talk to Shatov. Don't see him.'

'He isn't angry, is he?'

'No, we're not angry, but just avoid each other. Spent too much time in America together.'

'I'm going to call on him now.'

'As you like.'

'Stavrogin and I may come and see you after the meeting, about ten.'

'Do.'

'I have some important matter to discuss with him. Look here,

make me a present of your ball. You don't want it any more now, do
you? I may use it for my exercises. I can pay you for it, if you wish.'

'Take it. I don't want your money.'

Peter put the ball in the back pocket of his coat.

'But I'll give you nothing against Stavrogin,' he muttered as he saw
his visitor out.

Peter glanced at him in surprise, but did not reply.

Kirilov's last words disconcerted Peter greatly; he had scarcely time
to make up his mind what they could mean, but as he was walking up
the stairs to Shatov's room he did his best not to look displeased but
was as amiable as he could. Shatov was at home and a little indisposed.
He was lying on his bed, but was fully dressed.

'What awful luck!' Peter cried from the doorway. 'Are you seriously ill?'

The amiable expression suddenly vanished from his face; his eyes
flashed with hatred.

'Not at all,' Shatov replied, jumping up nervously. 'I'm not ill at
all; just a little headache. . . .'

He looked a little lost. The sudden appearance of such a visitor
alarmed him.

'I've come to you on a business which does not allow for any illness,' Peter began quickly and in a rather imperious tone. 'May I sit
down?' He sat down. 'Please sit down on your bed again. So. On the
pretext of Virginsky's birthday some of our members will hold a
meeting at his place. However, there's not going to be anything more
– we've taken all the necessary measures. I shall come with Nicholas
Stavrogin. I shouldn't, of course, have dragged you there, for I know
your present frame of mind – I mean, we don't want to make you feel
uncomfortable – not that we're afraid you'd inform the police. But,
as things have turned out, you'll have to come. You'll meet there the
people with whom we shall have finally to decide how you are to
leave the society and to whom you are to hand over what you've got.
We shall arrange it very quietly. I'll take you into some corner.
There'll be lots of people there, and there's no reason why they should
all know. I must say I had to do a bit of talking on your behalf, but
now I think that they, too, will agree on condition that you hand over
the printing press and all the papers. After that you can go where you
like.'

Shatov listened, frowning and resentful. The nervous fear he had felt a moment earlier had left him completely.

'I don't recognize any obligation on my part to give an account to anyone you damn well may appoint,' he declared categorically. 'No one has a right to set me at liberty.'

'I'm afraid that's not quite so. A lot of things have been entrusted to you. You had no right to break with us just like that. And, finally, you made no clear statement about it, so that you put them in an ambiguous position.'

'I stated my position clearly in writing as soon as I arrived here.'

'No, it wasn't clear at all,' Peter objected calmly. 'For instance, I sent you *A Noble Character* to print here and keep the copies in your place until called for. Also two leaflets. You returned it all with your ambiguous letter which did not mean anything.'

'I refused point blank to print them.'

'Yes, you refused, but not point blank. You wrote that you couldn't, but you didn't explain why. "I can't" isn't the same as "I don't want to". One might have thought that you couldn't print them for financial reasons. That's how it was understood, and they thought that you were still willing to continue your connexion with the society, and hence they could have entrusted you with some other job and, as a result, have compromised themselves. Here they maintain that you simply wanted to deceive them so that you might inform the police when you received some important communication. I defended you as much as I could and showed them your brief note of a couple of lines as evidence in your favour. But, having re-read it now, I had to admit that your two lines are far from clear and are liable to be misleading.'

'So you very carefully preserved my letter, did you?'

'The fact that I kept it means nothing; I've got it still.'

'Well, to hell with it!' Shatov cried furiously. 'Let your fools think that I've informed the police. What do I care? I'd like to see what you can do to me!'

'You'd be put on a black list and hanged at the first success of the revolution.'

'That's when you seize power and conquer Russia?'

'You needn't laugh. I repeat, I did my best to defend you. But whatever your attitude, I'd still advise you to come to the meeting to-night. Why all these meaningless words from false pride? Wouldn't it be much better to part friends? In any case, you'll have to hand over the printing press, the type, and the old papers. We could discuss that.'

'I'll come,' Shatov muttered, looking down thoughtfully.

Peter kept casting sidelong glances at him from his chair.

'Will Stavrogin be there?' Shatov asked suddenly, raising his head.

'Most certainly.'

'Ha, ha!'

Again they were silent for a minute. Shatov was grinning scornfully and irritably.

'And what about that rotten *Noble Character* of yours which I refused to print? Has it been published?'

'It has.'

'You're making schoolboys believe that Herzen himself wrote it in your album, aren't you?'

'Yes, Herzen himself.'

Again they were silent for about three minutes. At length Shatov got up from the bed.

'Get out of here! I don't want to be in the same room with you!'

'I'm going,' Peter replied rather cheerfully, getting up at once. 'Just one more thing: Kirilov is all by himself in his cottage without a maidservant, isn't he?'

'Yes, he's all by himself there. Go, please; I can't stand being in the same room with you!'

'Well, you're a fine fellow now,' Peter thought to himself gaily as he went out into the street. 'You'll be a fine fellow in the evening, too, and that's just how I want you to be. I couldn't wish for anything better! The God of the Russians himself seems to be helping me!'

7

He must have been very busy that day running about from one place to another; and apparently successfully – to judge from the self-satisfied expression on his face when, exactly at six o'clock that evening, he called on Stavrogin. But he was not at once admitted to Stavrogin's room; Maurice Drozdov was having an interview with Stavrogin behind the locked door of the latter's study. This piece of news immediately disturbed him. He sat down close to the door of the study to wait for the visitor to go away. He could hear the conversation, but could not make out the words. The visit did not last long; soon he heard a noise, the sound of a loud and sharp voice, then the door opened and Drozdov came out, looking as white as a sheet. He did not notice Peter, and walked away quickly. Peter at once rushed into the study.

I cannot omit a detailed account of the very brief interview of the two 'rivals' – an interview which seemed impossible in the circumstances, but which had nevertheless taken place.

It happened like this. Stavrogin was taking an after-dinner nap on the sofa in his study when the butler announced the arrival of the unexpected visitor. When he heard his name, Stavrogin jumped up, unable to believe it. But presently a smile appeared on his lips – a smile of haughty triumph and, at the same time, of blank, incredulous astonishment. As he came in, Drozdov was apparently struck by this curious smile; at least, he suddenly stopped in the middle of the room, as though undecided whether to go any farther or retrace his steps. His host, however, at once assumed a different expression, and with a look of grave perplexity took a step towards him. Drozdov did not accept the hand Stavrogin held out to him, pulled up a chair awkwardly, and, without uttering a word, sat down before his host, without waiting to be asked. Stavrogin sat down on the sofa facing him obliquely and waited, gazing in silence at Drozdov.

'Marry Miss Lisa, if you can,' Drozdov suddenly said, making him a present of the girl, and the curious part of it was that from the tone of his voice it was impossible to say whether it was a request, a piece of advice, a concession, or an order.

Stavrogin still remained silent, but his visitor had apparently said all he had come to say, and he kept looking straight at Stavrogin, expecting a reply.

'If I am not mistaken, and I'm informed that it is indeed so, Lisa is already engaged to you,' Stavrogin said at last.

'She is,' Drozdov confirmed in a clear and firm voice.

'You haven't quarrelled, have you? You – you must forgive me for mentioning it, Mr Drozdov.'

'No, she "loves and respects" me – those are her words. Her words are most precious to me, sir.'

'I don't doubt it.'

'But you ought to know that even if she were standing at the altar and you were to call her, she'd leave me and everyone else and go to you.'

'From the altar?'

'Even after the wedding ceremony.'

'Aren't you mistaken?'

'No, I'm not mistaken. Out of her intense hatred of you, a hatred that is absolutely sincere, there come every moment flashes of love and – infatuation – the most sincere and immeasurable love and – infatuation! On the other hand, out of the love that she feels for me, a love that is also sincere, there come every moment flashes of hatred – oh, the most intense hatred! I could never have imagined such – such metamorphoses.'

'But I'm surprised that you should have taken upon yourself to come here to dispose of Lisa's hand. Have you any right to do so? Has she authorized you?'

Drozdov frowned and lowered his head for a minute.

'That's all words on your part,' he said suddenly, 'revengeful and triumphant words. I'm sure you can read between the lines, and do you really think this is the time for petty vanity? Aren't you satisfied yet? Must I go into it in detail and dot my i's and cross my t's? All right, I will do so, if you are so anxious to witness my humiliation: I have no right whatever, and there can be no question of any authorization. Lisa knows nothing about it, but her fiancé is off his head and should be locked up in a lunatic asylum, and, to crown all, has come to tell you about it himself. You're the only man in the whole world who can make her happy, and I'm the only one to make her unhappy. You are after her, you are pursuing her, but – I don't know why – you won't marry her. If it is a lovers' quarrel that you had abroad and if, to make it good, you have to sacrifice me – do so. She is too unhappy, and I cannot bear it. My words are not an order or a permission, and there is therefore no reason why your vanity should be hurt. If you had wished to take my place at the altar, you could have done it without any permission on my part, and I should not, of course, have had to come with my mad proposals, particularly as now there can no longer be any question of our marriage. I can't lead her to the altar when I feel that I've acted like a blackguard, can I? For what I'm doing now and the fact that I'm giving her to you, her worst enemy, is in my opinion so discreditable a thing that I shall never get over it.'

'Are you going to shoot yourself on our wedding day?'

'No, much later. Why stain her bridal dress with my blood? Quite possibly I shall not shoot myself at all, either now or later.'

'I take it that by saying that you merely wish to set my mind at rest – or do you?'

'Your mind? What can a few more drops of blood mean to you?'

He turned pale and his eyes glittered. For a minute they were silent.

'I'm sorry I've asked you those questions,' Stavrogin began once more. 'Some of them I had no right to ask you, but one question I have the right to ask you: tell me, what facts have led you to form a conclusion as to my feelings for Lisa? I mean your assumption of the strength of my feelings which you seem to be so sure about that you came here and – took the risk of such a proposal.'

'What do you mean?' Drozdov cried with a start. 'Haven't you been trying to get her? Aren't you still trying to get her, and don't you want her any more?'

'I must say that, generally speaking, I dislike discussing my feelings for any woman with anyone, no matter whom, except the woman herself. I'm sorry, but I'm afraid that's the sort of queer person I am. But instead I shall tell you the whole truth about myself: I am married, and it's quite impossible for me either to marry or to try to "get" anyone.'

Drozdov was so taken aback by these words that he fell back in his chair and for some time stared speechlessly at Stavrogin.

'You know, I never thought of that,' he muttered. 'You said that morning that you were not married and – and I believed you were not married.'

He turned terribly pale; suddenly he banged his fist on the table with all his might.

'If after this admission you won't leave Lisa alone, and if you make her unhappy, I'll knock your brains out with a stick like a dog in a ditch!'

He jumped to his feet and walked quickly out of the room.

When Peter ran into the room he found Stavrogin in a most unexpected frame of mind.

'Oh, it's you!' Stavrogin burst out laughing at the top of his voice, and he seemed to be laughing at Peter, who had rushed into the room looking so curious.

'So you've been listening at the keyhole, have you? Wait a minute. Now what have you come for? I believe I promised you something. Oh, yes, I remember: "our" meeting! Let's go. I'm very glad, and you couldn't have thought of anything more appropriate at this moment.'

He grabbed his hat, and both of them at once left the house.

'Are you laughing in anticipation of meeting "our" crowd?' Peter cried gaily in an ingratiating voice, sometimes trying to walk beside Stavrogin on the narrow brick pavement, and sometimes running down into the mud of the road; for his companion was completely unaware that he was walking in the middle of the pavement and leaving no room for anyone else.

'I'm not laughing at all,' Stavrogin replied in a loud and cheerful voice. 'On the contrary, I'm sure that they are all extremely serious people.'

'"Dismal blockheads", as you were good enough to call them on one occasion.'

'There can be nothing more amusing than a dismal blockhead.'

'Oh, you mean Drozdov, don't you? I'm sure he came to give up his fiancée to you. Didn't he? It was I who asked him indirectly – believe it or not. And if he won't give her up, we'll take her away from him ourselves, won't we?'

Peter, of course, realized the risk he was running in venturing on such dangerous ground, but when he was excited he preferred to risk anything rather than remain in ignorance. Stavrogin just laughed.

'And you still hope to help me?' he asked.

'If you ask me to. But do you know there is a better way?'

'I know your way.'

'No, no. That is a secret so far. Only remember that a secret costs money.'

'I know what it costs,' Stavrogin muttered under his breath, but he controlled himself and was silent.

'How much? What did you say?' Peter gave a start.

'I said: to hell with you and your secret! You'd better tell me who you have got there. I know that we're going to a birthday party, but who is going to be there?'

'Oh, the whole damn crowd. Even Kirilov.'

'Are all of them members of circles?'

'You're in the devil of a hurry, aren't you? We haven't formed even one group here so far.'

'How, then, did you distribute so many political leaflets?'

'Where we are going now there are only four members of the group. The rest, in expectation of being admitted, keep spying on one another and come running to me with their reports. A reliable lot. All of it material that we have to organize before we clear out. However, you wrote the rules yourself, so there is no need to explain.'

'Well, do you find it hard going? Any hitch?'

'Hard going? Couldn't be better. I'll tell you something really funny: the first thing that creates a tremendous impression is a uniform. There's nothing more powerful than a uniform. I purposely invent titles and appointments: I have secretaries, secret emissaries, treasurers, chairmen, registrars and their assistants – they lap it all up, they love it. The next powerful force is, of course, sentimentality. You know, socialism among us spreads chiefly because of sentimentality. The only trouble is the second lieutenants who bite people. However careful you are, you're sure to get into trouble. Then come the downright swindlers, though I must say that they aren't perhaps such a bad lot; sometimes, indeed, they are very useful, but one has to spend a great deal of time on them: they must be kept under constant observation. And, well, finally, the main force – the cement that holds everything together – is their being ashamed of possessing an opinion of their own. Yes, indeed, that is a most wonderful force! And who has worked so much, who is the "dear man" who has laboured so hard that not a single idea of their own has been left in their heads! They think it's a disgraceful thing!'

'But if so, why are you so worried?'

'Why, if a chap is just lying about gaping at everybody, you can't help grabbing him. Don't you seriously believe in the possibility of success? I see, you have faith, but the will is wanting. It's just with people like this that success is possible. I tell you they'll go through fire for me. All I have to do is to raise my voice and tell them that they are not sufficiently "liberal". The fools reproach me for having deceived them about the central committee and its "innumerable branches". You once blamed me for it yourself, but what sort of deceit is it? You and I are the central committee. As for the branches, there will be as many of them as you like.'

'What a rabble!'

'Good material. They, too, will come in useful.'

'And you're still counting on me?'

'You're the boss. You're a force. I shall only be at your side, your secretary. We, you know, will get into our bark, our oars of maple, our sails of silk, the fair maiden Lisa at the helm – or how the hell does that ballad go –'

'Got stuck,' Stavrogin burst out laughing. 'No, my dear fellow, let me add a little introduction to your fairy-tale. Can you count on your fingers the people who can be accepted as members of your circles? All this is just bureaucracy and sentimentality – all this is just so much cement, but there's one thing that is much better: persuade four members of the circle to murder a fifth on the excuse that he is an informer and you'll at once tie them all up in one knot by the blood they've shed. They'll be your slaves. They won't dare to rebel and call you to account. Ha, ha, ha!'

'Well, well,' thought Peter to himself, 'you'll pay dearly for those words, my dear chap, and this very evening, too. You go a little too far.'

So, or almost so, Peter must have thought to himself. However, they were already approaching Virginsky's house.

'I suppose you must have told them that I'm a member from abroad who is in touch with the Internationale – a sort of inspector?' Stavrogin asked suddenly.

'No, not an inspector. You won't be the inspector. But you are one of the founder-members from abroad, who knows the most important secrets – that's the part you have to play. You will, of course, make a speech, won't you?'

'What gave you that idea?'

'You simply must make a speech now.'

Stavrogin was so surprised that he stopped dead in the middle of the street not far from a street lamp. Peter met his stare calmly and arrogantly. Stavrogin spat and walked on.

'And are you going to make a speech?' he suddenly asked Peter.

'No, I'd rather listen to you.'

'Confound you, you give me an idea!'

'What idea?' Peter rasped out.

'Perhaps I shall make a speech, but I shall give you a thrashing afterwards – a jolly good thrashing, you know.'

'By the way, I told Karmazinov this morning that you said he ought to be thrashed, and not only as a matter of form but as they flog peasants, till it hurts.'

'But I never said anything of the kind, ha, ha!'

'Never mind. Se non è vero.'

'Well, thanks – thanks a lot.'

'Do you know what Karmazinov said? That our creed is in essence a negation of honour and that the easiest way in which a Russian could be won over is by telling him frankly that he has a right to be dishonourable.'

'Excellently put! Golden words!' Stavrogin cried. 'A bull's eye! The right to be dishonourable – why, this ought to make everybody come running to us. No one will be left behind! But, look here, Verkhovensky, you're not by any chance a member of the secret police, are you?'

'If you really thought so, you wouldn't have said it aloud.'

'I understand, but we're by ourselves.'

'No, for the time being I'm not a member of the secret police. All right, here we are. Assume the right expression, Stavrogin. I always do when I go in. Try to look as grim as possible. That's all you need. It's very simple really.'

7

At Virginsky's

I

VIRGINSKY lived in his own house, or rather in his wife's house in Muravyinaya Street. It was a wooden bungalow, and there were no lodgers in it. On the pretext of Virginsky's birthday party, about fifteen people had gathered there; but the party was not at all like an ordinary provincial birthday party. From the very beginning of their married life, the Virginskys had decided once and for all that it was silly to invite people to a birthday party and that there was 'nothing to be so glad about'. In a few years they had somehow managed to withdraw from all society. Though a man of ability and far from poor, people for some reason regarded him as an eccentric fellow who was fond of seclusion and who, in addition, talked 'disdainfully'. Mrs Virginsky herself, a professional midwife, was for that very reason considered to occupy the lowest rung of the social ladder, lower even than the priest's wife, in spite of the fact that her husband had been an army officer. But there was no trace of the humility proper to her social station about her. And after her most stupid and inexcusably candid affair on principle with a scoundrel like Captain Lebyatkin, even the most indulgent of our ladies turned away from her with singular contempt. But Mrs Virginsky took it all as though it were just what she needed. It was re-markable that the very same high-and-mighty ladies always sought the professional services of Mrs Virginsky, if they happened to find themselves in an interesting condition, completely ignoring the other three midwives of our town. She was sent for even by the country families of our district – so great was everybody's faith in her know-ledge, luck, and skill in emergency cases. In the end she confined her practice entirely to the wealthiest houses; for she had quite an in-ordinate love of money. Fully aware of her power, she made no at-tempt to curb her character. She would, perhaps on purpose, frighten her nervous patients in the best houses by some incredible nihilist dis-regard of the decencies of social behaviour or by jeering at everything 'holy' just when the 'holy' might have come in most useful. Our town doctor Rozanov, who was also an obstetrician, positively as-serted that on one occasion, when a patient in labour was screaming and calling on the name of the Almighty, Mrs Virginsky's atheistic remarks, which came unexpectedly like 'a pistol shot', so scared the patient that it helped to bring about a quick delivery. But though a nihilist, Mrs Virginsky, when necessary, did not disdain social or old-fashioned prejudices, provided they could be of advantage to her. She would, for instance, never miss a christening of a baby she had brought into the world, and she always arrived wearing a green silk dress with a train, and always made up the hair at the back of her head into curls and ringlets, though at any other time she seemed to take a special delight in her untidy appearance. And though during the christening ceremony she always preserved 'a most insolent air', to the great em-barrassment of the officiating clergy, when it was over she invariably handed round the champagne herself (it was for that reason that she came and dressed up), and woe betide any guest who, having taken the glass, forgot to put some money on the tray for her 'tip'.

The guests who gathered that evening at Virginsky's (most of them were men) had a sort of casual and special look. There were neither refreshments nor cards. Two tables were drawn together in the middle of the large drawing-room, which was papered with rather old blue wallpaper. The tables were covered with a large and not very clean table-cloth, and two samovars were boiling on them. A huge tray with twenty-five glasses and a basket with white French bread, cut into a great number of small pieces, just as in a high-class boarding-school for boys and girls, stood at one end of the table. The tea was poured out by Mrs Virginsky's sister, an unmarried woman of thirty, a taciturn and venomous creature, with hair that was almost colourless and no eyebrows, a staunch upholder of the 'new' ideas, of whom Virginsky was mortally afraid in his domestic life. There were only three ladies in the room: Mrs Virginsky herself, her browless sister, and Virginsky's sister, a young girl who had just arrived from Petersburg. Mrs Virginsky, a lady of a very imposing appearance, good-looking but rather dishevelled, wearing an everyday greenish woollen dress, was sitting and gazing at her guests with bold eyes as though she were in haste to say with her look: 'You see, I'm not a bit afraid of anything.' The newly arrived Miss Virginsky, a student and a nihilist, who was also rather good-looking, red-cheeked, short, plump, and round as a little ball, was sitting beside Mrs Virginsky, almost in her travelling clothes. She held a roll of paper in her hand and gazed at the guests with impatient, dancing eyes. Virginsky himself felt a little indisposed that evening, but he came out and sat in an arm-chair by the table. The guests were also all sitting down, and there was the feeling of an official meeting in the staid manner in which they all occupied their seats round the table. They were all evidently expecting something, and in the meantime carried on a loud and irrelevant conversation. When Stavrogin and Verkhovensky appeared, a sudden hush fell on the room.

But I think I ought to give a few explanations to make the position clear.

I can't help thinking that these people had assembled that evening at Virginsky's house in the agreeable hope of hearing something specially interesting, and that they had been told beforehand what to expect. They represented the flower of the reddest 'liberalism' of our ancient town, and had been very carefully selected by Virginsky for this 'meeting'. I may add that some of them (not very many, though) had never visited him before. No doubt, most of the guests had no clear idea what exactly they were to expect. It is true that they all looked upon Verkhovensky at the time as an emissary from abroad who was armed with plenary powers. That notion had somehow been generally accepted at once, and naturally appealed to them. And yet among the small number of citizens who had met under the pretext of celebrating a birthday there were a few who had received definite proposals. Peter Verkhovensky had succeeded in forming a 'group of five' in our town just like the one he had formed in Moscow and the one which, as it now appears, he had formed among the army officers of our district. I am told that he had another one in the Kh—v province. These five chosen ones were sitting now at the general table, and very skilfully assumed the air of ordinary men, so that no one would notice them. They were – since it is no longer a secret – first, Liputin, then Virginsky himself, the long-eared Shigalyov, who was Mrs Virginsky's brother, Lyamshin, and lastly, a certain Tolka-chenko – a queer fellow, a man of about forty who was famous for his great knowledge of the common people, mostly rogues and rob-bers. He was fond of visiting low pubs (though not entirely for the study of the common people) and he liked to impress us with his shabby clothes, tarred boots, the cunning look of his screwed-up eyes and colloquial expressions of a rather florid kind. Lyamshin had once or twice brought him to Stepan Verkhovensky's parties, where he did not, however, create any special effect. He used to make an appear-ance in our town only occasionally, mostly when he was out of a job, and he was employed on the railway. Every one of these five public men had formed the first group in the fervent belief that it was only one among hundreds and thousands of similar groups of five men scattered all over Russia, and that they all were connected with some vast and mysterious central organization which was in turn intimately connected with the European world revolutionary movement. But I must regretfully confess that even at that time there were already signs of dissension among them. The trouble was that though they had been waiting since the spring for the arrival of Peter Verkhovensky, first announced to them by Tolkachenko and then by Shigalyov, who had just returned to our town, though they had been expecting great miracles from him, and though they had joined the group at once and without the slightest hesitation at his first summons, all of them felt for some reason let down, and I can't help thinking that it was because of the promptitude with which they had agreed to join the group. They had joined, of course, from a high-minded feeling of shame, so that people should not say afterwards that they had not the courage to join; but, for all that, Peter Verkhovensky ought to have appreciated their valiant and selfless action, and as a reward at least told them some really important piece of news. But Verkhovensky had not the slightest intention of satisfying their legitimate curiosity, and never told them anything that he did not tell everybody else; generally speaking, he treated them with quite extraordinary severity and even casualness. This was absolutely exasperating, and one member of the group, Shigalyov, was already agitating among the rest 'to demand an account' of him, but, naturally, not now at Virginsky's where so many strangers had gathered.

Apropos of these strangers, I have an idea that the above-mentioned members of the group of five were inclined to suspect the presence of members of other unknown groups at Virginsky's party that evening, formed in our town according to the identical methods of the secret organization by the same Verkhovensky, so that in the end everyone in the drawing-room suspected everyone else, and assumed an air of importance, which gave the whole meeting a rather confused and even a slightly romantic character. However, there were people there who were quite above suspicion. Such, for instance, was a serving army Major, a close relation of Virginsky's, a perfectly innocent man, who had not been invited, but had come of his own accord to congratulate Virginsky on his birthday, so that it was quite impossible not to receive him. But Virginsky was not in the least worried because the Major could not possibly 'inform the police', for, though being a stupid man, he had all his life showed a liking for associating with extreme 'liberals'; he did not sympathize with their views himself, but he was very fond of listening to them. What's more, he had even been compromised once. It had happened that when he was a young man thousands of copies of Herzen's periodical *The Bell*, as well as political leaflets, had passed through his hands, and though he had been afraid even to open them, he would have considered it absolutely dishonourable to refuse to distribute them – and there are such Russians even to this day.

The rest of the guests represented either persons whose self-esteem had been crushed and who had become embittered because of it, or those who were still in the first generous flush of youthful ardour. The former included two or three teachers, one of whom, a lame man of forty-five, a master of our local secondary school, was a very spiteful and exceedingly vain man, and two or three army officers. Of the latter one was a very young artillery officer who had arrived straight from his military college only a short time before, a taciturn boy who had not yet had time to make any friends and who now suddenly turned up at Virginsky's. He had a pencil in his hand and, while scarcely taking part in the conversation, kept making notes in his notebook. They all saw him do it, but for some reason they all pretended not to notice it. The idle divinity student who had helped Lyamshin put the indecent photographs into the gospel-woman's pack was there too. He was a big fellow with free-and-easy, but at the same time mistrustful manners, with an eternally sardonic smile, and yet with the calm air of triumphant conviction of his own superiority. There was also present – I don't know why – the nasty-minded and prematurely aged son of our mayor to whom I have already referred in telling the story of the second lieutenant's little wife. Finally, there was a hot-headed and tousled schoolboy of eighteen who sat with the grim look of a young man whose dignity has been wounded and who was suffering visibly because of his eighteen years. This youngster was already the head of an independent small group of conspirators which had been formed in the top class of his school, which fact came to light – to everyone's astonishment – afterwards.

I haven't mentioned Shatov: he was sitting at the farthest end of the table, his chair pushed back a little from the row, his eyes fixed on the ground. He was gloomily silent, refused tea and bread, and kept his cap in his hand all the time, as though wishing to indicate that he was not one of the guests but was there on business, and would get up and go away when he had a mind to. Kirilov took a seat not far from him. He, too, was very silent, but he did not look on the ground; on the contrary, he scrutinized every speaker with a motionless stare of his lustreless eyes and listened to everything without the slightest excitement or surprise. Some of the guests who had never seen him before cast stealthy and inquisitive glances at him.

I don't know whether Mrs Virginsky herself knew anything about the existence of the group of five. I imagine she knew everything and, no doubt, from her husband. The girl student, of course, took no part in anything, but she had a worry of her own: she intended to stay in our town only for a day or two, and then to travel farther and farther afield, visiting every university town 'to take a sympathetic interest in the sufferings of the poor students and to arouse them to protest'. She was taking with her several hundred copies of a lithographed appeal which, I believe, was her own composition. It is remarkable that the schoolboy conceived a deadly hatred for her at the first glance, though it was the first time in his life that he had seen her, and she fully reciprocated his feeling. The Major was an uncle of hers and met her that evening for the first time in ten years. When Stavrogin and Verkhovensky entered the room, her cheeks were as red as cranberries: she had only a minute before had a furious argument with her uncle about his views on the woman question.

2

Verkhovensky sprawled with amazing unconcern in the chair at the head of the table almost without greeting anyone politely, but in spite of the fact that everybody was waiting for them, they all, as though by a word of command, pretended that they had scarcely noticed them. Mrs Virginsky turned severely to Stavrogin as soon as he took his seat.

'Stavrogin, do you want tea?'

'Yes, thank you,' he replied.

'Tea for Stavrogin,' she ordered her sister. 'And,' she turned to Verkhovensky, 'what about you?'

'Thanks, I'll have some tea, of course. What a question to ask your visitors! And let me have some cream too, please. You always give one such horrible stuff instead of tea, and at a name-day party, too.'

'Why, do you recognize name-days?' the girl student laughed suddenly. 'We were just discussing it.'

'Old stuff,' the schoolboy muttered from the other end of the table.

'What is old stuff? To get rid of prejudices, even the most innocent, isn't old-fashioned. On the contrary, it's still quite a new thing, to everyone's disgrace,' the girl student declared promptly darting forward in her chair. 'Besides, there are no innocent prejudices,' she added fiercely.

'I merely wanted to say,' cried the schoolboy, getting terribly excited, 'that prejudices, of course, are old-fashioned and ought to be extirpated, but that so far as name-days are concerned everybody knows already that they are stupid and very old-fashioned, indeed, a sheer waste of time, which is being wasted as it is, so that you could have employed your wits on a more useful subject.'

'You go on and on, but one can't understand a word you are saying,' the girl student cried.

'It seems to me that everyone has the same right to express an opinion as everyone else, and if I wish to express my opinion like anyone else, then –'

'No one deprives you of your right to express an opinion,' Mrs Virginsky herself interrupted sharply. 'You were only asked not to mumble because no one can understand you.'

'I must say you don't seem to treat me with any respect. If I could not finish what I had to say, it is not because I had nothing to say, but because I had too much to say,' the schoolboy muttered almost in despair, becoming completely muddled.

'If you don't know how to talk, you'd better shut up,' the girl student snapped.

The schoolboy jumped up from his chair.

'All I wanted to say,' he cried, his cheeks burning with shame and afraid to look round, 'is that you merely wanted to show how clever you are because Mr Stavrogin has just come in – that's it!'

'That's a filthy and immoral thing to say, and merely shows that you're suffering from arrested mental development. I'll thank you not to address yourself to me again,' the girl student rattled on.

'Stavrogin,' Mrs Virginsky began, 'before you came they'd been having a furious discussion about the rights of the family. This army officer here,' she nodded towards her relation the major, 'and of course I shouldn't dream of bothering you with such old-fashioned rubbish which has long been disposed of. But how could the conception of the rights and duties of the family have arisen in the form of the superstitious nonsense in which they appear to us now? That is the question. What's your opinion?'

'What do you mean by how they could have arisen?'

'What she means is that, for instance, we know that the superstition about God arose from thunder and lightning,' said the girl student, throwing herself again into the fray and staring at Stavrogin with her eyes almost popping out of her head. 'It's a well-known fact that primitive man, terrified by thunder and lightning, deified the invisible enemy, being aware of his own weakness before it. But how did the superstition about the family arise? How did the family itself arise?'

'That's not at all what I meant –' Mrs Virginsky made an attempt to stop her.

'I suppose the answer to such a question would be rather indiscreet,' replied Stavrogin.

'What do you mean?' the girl student asked, darting forward.

But a tittering was heard in the group of the teachers, which was at once echoed by Lyamshin and the schoolboy at the other end of the table, followed by a hoarse chuckle from the Major.

'You should be writing vaudevilles,' Mrs Virginsky observed to Stavrogin.

'A remark like that hardly does you credit, sir – I don't know what your name is,' the girl student rapped out with positive indignation.

'Don't you be too cheeky, madam,' the Major blurted out. 'You're a young lady, and you ought to behave modestly, but you seem to be sitting on needles.'

'Hold your tongue, please, and don't you dare to speak to me in so familiar a tone, sir, with your disgusting comparisons. I've never seen you before, and I don't care whether you're a relative of mine or not.'

'But I'm your uncle. I used to carry you about in my arms when you were a baby.'

'What do I care what you used to carry about? I didn't ask you to carry me about, did I? Which means that you liked carrying me about as a baby. And let me add that I strongly object to your familiar tone unless it's as a fellow citizen. Otherwise I forbid you to talk to me like that once and for all.'

'They're all like that now!' the Major addressed Stavrogin, who was sitting opposite, banging the table with his fist. 'And let me tell you, sir, that I am fond of liberalism and modern ideas and I'm fond of listening to intelligent conversation, but, mind you, only to men's.

As for listening to women, sir, to these modern forward minxes – no, sir, I just can't put up with 'em. They're a pain in the neck, that's what they are, sir. Don't fidget, madam!' he shouted at the girl-student, who was fidgeting on her chair. 'No, sir, I, too, demand to be heard. I've been insulted, sir!'

'You're only interfering with the others,' Mrs Virginsky muttered indignantly. 'You can't say anything yourself.'

'Oh, no, sir, I shall most certainly say what's in my mind,' the Major cried agitatedly, addressing Stavrogin. 'I'm counting on you, Mr Stavrogin, because you have only just come in, though I haven't the honour of knowing you. Without men they'll perish like flies, sir; that's what I think. All their woman question is just lack of originality. I assure you, sir, that all this woman question has been invented for them by men, out of sheer stupidity, as if they hadn't enough trouble in the world. Thank God, I'm not married! No sense of discrimination, sir, none whatever. Can't invent a dress pattern of their own. Even that men invent for them! Take her, sir; take that girl. I used to carry her about in my arms, used to dance the mazurka with her when she was ten years old, and when she arrived to-day I naturally rushed to embrace her, but all she had to say to me – and before I had time to speak a word, mind you – was that there was no God. If she had just waited a little, and not got it out as soon as she opened her mouth! But, you see, she was in such a devil of a hurry! Well, I sup-pose intelligent people don't believe; but if they don't, it's because they're brainy chaps. But you, I said to her, you dumpling, what do you know about God? Why, I said to her, I'm damned if it wasn't some student who taught you all this, and if he had taught you to light the lamp before an icon, you'd jolly well have lighted it.'

'You're always telling stories,' the girl student retorted disdainfully and as though she were ashamed to waste too many words on a man like him. 'You're a very spiteful person, and only a few moments ago I proved to you conclusively that you're quite incapable of conducting a rational argument. In fact, I told you just now that we have all been taught in the Catechism that if you honour your father and your mother, you will live long and be given riches. That's in the ten com-mandments. If God found it necessary to offer rewards for love, then your God must be immoral. That's how I proved it to you, and not at all the moment I opened my mouth. I did it because you asserted your rights. It's not my fault if you're stupid and haven't grasped it yet. You feel hurt and you're angry – that's what's really the matter with your generation.'

'You're a silly goose!' said the Major.

'And you're a silly fool!'

'Call me names!'

'But, look here, sir,' Liputin squeaked from the end of the table, 'didn't you tell me yourself that you don't believe in God?'

'Well, what if I did? I'm quite a different matter! Perhaps I do believe, but not altogether. And though I do not entirely believe, it would never occur to me to say that God ought to be shot. I thought about God while I served in the Hussar regiment. It is the accepted thing in poetry to pretend that hussars only drink and make merry. Well, sir, I might have been drinking; but, believe me, sir, I used to jump out of bed at night in my socks and start crossing myself before the icon so that God should give me faith, because even then I was worried by the question whether there was a God or not. I had a bad time of it, I can tell you! In the morning, of course, you'd amuse yourself and your faith would apparently be gone again. I've noticed that, as a rule, your faith tends to evaporate a little in the mornings.'

'Haven't you any cards?' Verkhovensky asked their hostess, yawning heartily.

'I'm entirely, entirely in sympathy with your question,' the girl student put in quickly, blushing with indignation at the Major's words.

'We're wasting precious time listening to stupid talk,' Mrs Virginsky rapped out with a severe look at her husband.

The girl student pulled herself up.

'I should like to tell the meeting about the sufferings and the protest of the students, but as our time is being wasted in immoral conversations –'

'There's no such thing as moral or immoral,' the schoolboy declared, unable to restrain himself, as soon as the girl student began.

'I knew that long before they taught it to you, Mr Schoolboy,' said the girl student.

'And what I say is,' the schoolboy rasped out in a fury, 'that you are a child who has just arrived from Petersburg to enlighten us all, while we know it all ourselves. As for the commandment "Honour thy father and thy mother", which you misquoted, everyone in Russia knows that it is immoral since Belinsky's days.'

'Will this never end?' Mrs Virginsky addressed her husband in a firm tone of voice.

As the hostess she blushed at the triviality of the conversation, especially as she had noticed that some of the newly invited guests smiled, and even looked bewildered.

'Ladies and gentlemen,' Virginsky suddenly raised his voice, 'if anyone would like to say anything more pertinent to our business, or if anyone has any statement to make, I propose that he does so without wasting more time.'

'I should like, if I may, to ask one question,' the lame teacher who had been sitting very decorously till then, without uttering a word, said quietly. 'I should like to know whether we constitute a meeting here now, or whether we are just a collection of ordinary mortals who have come to a party? I'm asking it just as a matter of form, and because I don't want to remain in ignorance.'

The 'crafty' question created an impression; they all exchanged glances, as though everyone were expecting an answer from everyone else, and suddenly, as though at a word of command, they all turned round to Verkhovensky and Stavrogin.

'I simply propose that we should take a vote on the question whether we are a meeting or not,' Mrs Virginsky said.

'I second it,' Liputin concurred, 'though the proposal is a little vague.'

'I second it, too, and I,' they cried.

'I, too, think that it will be more in order,' Virginsky confirmed.

'Let's take a vote, then,' Mrs Virginsky declared. 'Lyamshin, will you please sit down at the piano? you can vote from there.'

'Not again?' Lyamshin cried. 'Haven't I been thumping it long enough?'

'Go on, please. I beg you to sit down at the piano and play. Don't you want to be useful to the cause?'

'But I assure you, my dear Mrs Virginsky, that no one is eavesdropping on us. It's just your imagination. Besides, your windows are so high, and who would be able to make anything out even if he did eavesdrop?'

'We can't make anything out ourselves,' someone muttered.

'And I'm telling you that precautions are always necessary. I mean, in case there should be spies,' she explained, turning to Verkhovensky, 'let them hear from the street that we are having a birthday party and music.'

'Damnation!' Lyamshin swore, sitting down at the piano and beginning to play a waltz, banging on the keys almost with his fists.

'Those who are in favour of having a meeting, please raise their right hands,' Mrs Virginsky proposed.

Some raised their hands, others did not. Some raised them and put them down, others put them down and raised them again.

'Damn it all, I don't understand a thing,' one army officer cried.

'I don't either,' another one cried.

'Well, I do,' cried a third one. 'If it's *yes*, then up with your hand.'

'But what does *yes* mean?'

'It means a meeting.'

'No, it doesn't mean a meeting.'

'I voted for a meeting,' the schoolboy cried, turning to Mrs Virginsky.

'Then why didn't you raise your hand?'

'I was looking at you: you didn't raise yours, so I didn't raise mine.'

'How silly! I didn't raise mine because I was the proposer. Ladies and gentlemen, I propose we do it the other way round: those who are in favour of a meeting, sit quietly and don't raise your hands, and those who are not in favour of it, raise your right hands.'

'Those not in favour?' the schoolboy repeated the question.

'You're not saying that on purpose, are you?' Mrs Virginsky cried angrily.

'No, please, who is in favour or who is not in favour, because you have to define it more precisely?' two or three voices cried.

'Those not in favour, *not* in favour.'

'Very well, but what have we to do? Must we put up our hands or not if we are *not* in favour?' the officer asked.

'Ah, well,' the Major remarked; 'it seems we haven't got used to a constitution yet.'

'Mr Lyamshin, would you mind not banging away so much?' the lame teacher observed. 'It's impossible to hear anything.'

'But, really, Mrs Virginsky, no one is listening,' Lyamshin cried, jumping up. 'I haven't the slightest wish to play. I've come here as a guest, and not as a piano thumper.'

'Ladies and gentlemen, will you answer verbally – are we or are we not a meeting?' Virginsky proposed.

'We are, we are!'

'Well, if so, there's no need to vote. Are you satisfied, ladies and gentlemen, or do you still wish to vote?'

'No, no! We understood!'

'Is there anyone here who does not want a meeting?'

'No, no, we all want it.'

'But what is a meeting?' someone asked; but he received no reply.

'We must elect a chairman,' people cried from different parts of the room.

'Our host, of course, our host!'

'Ladies and gentlemen,' the elected chairman began, 'if so, I should like to move my first proposal: if there's anyone here who'd like to say anything more pertinent to the business in hand, or if there's any-one who'd like to make a statement, let him do so without wasting any more time.'

No one spoke. Everyone in the room again turned to Verkhoven-sky and Stavrogin.

'Verkhovensky, have you no statement to make?' Mrs Virginsky asked him directly.

'None whatever,' he replied, yawning and stretching on his chair. 'I'd like a glass of cognac, though.'

'Stavrogin, what about you?'

'No, thank you. I don't drink.'

'I mean would you like to speak or not? I didn't mean cognac.'

'Speak? What about? No, I don't want to.'

'They'll bring you your cognac,' she said, addressing Verkhoven-sky.

The girl student got up. She had been jumping up from her chair several times.

'I have come to make a statement about the sufferings of our un-fortunate students and the ways of rousing them everywhere to pro-test. ...'

But she stopped short; at the other end of the table a rival had ap-peared, and everybody's eyes turned to him. Long-eared Shigalyov slowly rose from his seat, looking grim and gloomy, and, with a melancholy expression, put down a thick, closely written note-book on the table. He remained standing in silence. Many people looked in bewilderment at his note-book, but Liputin, Virginsky, and the lame teacher seemed to be pleased about something.

'I ask leave to address the meeting,' Shigalyov said gloomily but firmly.

'Please,' Virginsky gave his permission.

The orator sat down, said nothing for half a minute, then uttered in a solemn voice:

'Ladies and gentlemen!'

'Here's the cognac,' Mrs Virginsky's relation who had been pouring out tea and gone to fetch the brandy snapped distastefully and contemptuously, placing a bottle of brandy and a glass, which she had not put on a tray or a plate, before Verkhovensky.

The interrupted orator waited with a dignified air.

'Never mind, go on, I'm not listening,' Verkhovensky cried, pouring himself out a glass.

'Ladies and gentlemen,' Shigalyov began again, 'in calling for your attention and, as you will see later, in asking for your assistance in a matter of first-class importance, I must first of all say a few words by way of an introduction.'

'Mrs Virginsky, have you any scissors?' Verkhovensky asked suddenly.

'What do you want scissors for?' Mrs Virginsky glared at him.

'I've forgotten to cut my nails – been meaning to for the last three days,' he replied, examining his long and dirty nails imperturbably.

Mrs Virginsky flushed, but Miss Virginsky seemed pleased at something.

'I believe I saw them on the window-sill a short while ago,' she said, getting up from the table.

She went up to the window, found the scissors, and brought them back at once. Verkhovensky did not even glance at her. He took the scissors and began busying himself with them. Mrs Virginsky realized that there was sound method in Verkhovensky's request, and was ashamed of her touchiness. The people exchanged silent glances. The lame teacher was watching Verkhovensky enviously and angrily. Shigalyov went on:

'Having devoted all my energies to the study of the social organization of the society of the future which is to replace our present one, I have come to the conclusion that all the inventors of social systems, from the ancient times to our present year, have been dreamers, story-tellers, fools who contradicted themselves and had no idea of natural science or that strange animal called man. Plato, Rousseau, Fourier, aluminium pillars, all that is only good for sparrows, and not for human society. But as the future form of society is of the utmost importance now that we at last are all ready to act, I am submitting to you my own system of the world organization so as to make any further thinking unnecessary. Here it is!' he exclaimed, tapping the note-book. 'I intended to explain the contents of my book to this meeting in the most abbreviated form possible. I'm afraid, however, that I shall have to add a great many verbal explanations, and that the whole of my exposition will therefore take up at least ten evenings, one evening for each chapter of my book.' (There was laughter in the room.) 'In addition, I should like to state beforehand that my system is not yet complete.' (Again laughter.) 'I'm afraid I got rather muddled up in my own data, and my conclusion is in direct contradiction to the original idea with which I start. Starting from unlimited freedom, I arrived at unlimited despotism. I will add, however, that there can be no other solution of the social formula than mine.'

The laughter in the room grew louder and louder, but it was mostly the young people who laughed and, as it were, the uninitiated visitors. Mrs Virginsky, Liputin, and the lame teacher looked annoyed.

'If you couldn't work out your system yourself, and are in despair about it, what do you expect us to do?' an officer observed cautiously.

'You are right, my dear serving officer,' Shigalyov said, turning to him sharply, 'and most of all because you used the word "despair". Yes, I was in despair. Nevertheless, everything I say in my book is irrefutable, and there is no other solution. No one can invent anything else. And that is why I should like, without wasting any time, to invite you, ladies and gentlemen, to express your opinion after you have heard the contents of my book during the next ten evenings. If, however, the members of our society refuse to listen to me, let us part at the very beginning, the gentlemen to carry on with their official duties and the ladies to go back to their kitchens, for if you reject my solution, you will find no other. None whatever! By missing their opportunity, they'll have only themselves to blame, for they are bound to come back to it again sooner or later.'

The people began to stir. 'What's the matter with him? Is he mad?' voices could be heard asking.

'What it comes to,' Lyamshin concluded, 'is Shigalyov's despair, and the important question seems to be: should he or should he not be in despair?'

'The fact that Shigalyov is so near to despair is a personal question,' the schoolboy declared.

'I move that a vote should be taken how far Shigalyov's despair affects our common cause and, at the same time, whether it is worth listening to him or not,' an officer suggested gaily.

'It's not that at all,' the lame teacher at last intervened, speaking, as was his wont, with rather an ironic smile, so that it was difficult to say whether he was serious or joking. 'This, ladies and gentlemen, isn't the point at issue at all. Mr Shigalyov is too much devoted to his task and, besides, he is too modest. I know his book. He proposes as a final solution of the problem to divide humanity into two unequal parts. One-tenth is to be granted absolute freedom and unrestricted powers over the remaining nine-tenths. Those must give up their individuality and be turned into something like a herd, and by their boundless obedience will by a series of regenerations attain a state of primeval innocence, something like the original paradise. They will have to work, however. The measures the author proposes for depriving the nine-tenths of humanity of their true will and their transformation into a herd by means of the re-education of whole generations, are very remarkable. They are based on the facts of nature and very logical. It is possible not to agree with some of his conclusions, but it is impossible to doubt the author's intelligence or knowledge. It is a pity that his stipulation that we should devote ten evenings to his theory is impracticable, or we might hear a great deal that is interesting.'

'Are you really serious?' Mrs Virginsky turned to the lame teacher in some alarm. 'I mean if that man, not knowing what to do with people, turns nine-tenths of them into slaves? I've suspected him for a long time.'

'Do you mean your brother?' asked the lame teacher.

'Family relationship? Are you laughing at me?'

'And, besides, to work for the aristocrats and obey them as if they

were gods – that's an odious suggestion!' the girl student observed
fiercely.

'What I'm offering you is not odious suggestions, but paradise,
paradise on earth; for there can be no other one on earth,' Shigalyov
concluded peremptorily.

'For my part,' Lyamshin cried, 'instead of putting them into paradise, I'd take these nine-tenths of humanity, if I didn't know what to
do with them, and blow them up, leaving only a small number of
educated people who'd live happily ever after in accordance with
scientific principles.'

'Only a clown could talk like that!' the girl student cried, flushing.

'He is a clown, but he's useful,' Mrs Virginsky whispered to her.

'And very likely that is the best solution of the problem,' Shigalyov
said, addressing Lyamshin heatedly. 'I don't expect you even realize
what a profound thing you've just said, my dear, merry friend. But
as it is practically impossible to carry out your idea, we must, I'm
afraid, be content with the earthly paradise, since that's what it has
been called.'

'What awful rot!' Verkhovensky could not help saying, without
raising his eyes, though he went on cutting his nails unconcernedly.

'But why is it rot?' the lame teacher took it up at once, as though
he had been expecting him to say something in order to attack him.
'Why rot? Mr Shigalyov is rather a fanatic lover of mankind; but remember that Fourier, Cabet, and particularly Proudhon himself have
proposed many more despotic and fantastic solutions of the problem.
Mr Shigalyov's solution is perhaps far more sober. I assure you that,
having read his book, it is almost impossible not to agree with certain
things in it. He is perhaps much nearer to realism than anyone, and his
earthly paradise is almost the real one, the same one, for the loss of
which mankind is sighing, if it ever existed.'

'Well, I knew I'd get it in the neck,' Verkhovensky muttered again.

'Allow me to point out, sir,' the lame teacher went on, getting
more and more excited, 'discussions on the future social organization
of mankind are almost an urgent necessity for all modern thinking
men. Herzen spent his whole life worrying about it. Belinsky – and I
know it for a fact – used to spend whole evenings with his friends debating and solving the smallest, as it were, domestic details of the
future social organization of mankind.'

'Some even go off their heads,' the Major suddenly remarked.

'Anyway, you are more likely to arrive at something by talking than by sitting about without uttering a word as if you were dictators,' Liputin hissed, as though at last plucking up courage to start his attack.

'I didn't mean Shigalyov when I said it was rot,' Verkhovensky mumbled. 'You see, ladies and gentlemen' – he raised his eyes a little – 'in my view all these books, Fourier, Cabet, all this talk about the "right to work", all this Shigalyov business – all are like novels, of which you can write a hundred thousand. An aesthetic pastime. I realize that in this provincial hole of a town you are bored, and so you rush to pick up any piece of paper that has something written on it.'

'If you don't mind my saying so, sir,' said the lame teacher, fidgeting on his chair, 'we may be provincials, and I daresay that we deserve to be pitied on that account alone, but we do know that so far nothing new has happened in the world to make us shed tears because we've missed it. We are urged, for instance, in the various leaflets of foreign make which are distributed among us, to close our ranks and form groups with the sole purpose of bringing about general destruction on the pretext that however much you tried to cure the world, you would never succeed in curing it, while by adopting the radical measure of chopping off a hundred million heads we should ease our burden and be able to jump over the ditch with much less trouble. It's an excellent idea, but one at any rate which is as incompatible with reality as the Shigalyov "theory", which you referred to just now with such contempt.'

'I'm afraid I haven't come here to engage in discussions,' Verkhovensky let drop a significant hint and, as though completely unaware of the slip he had made, drew the candle nearer to him to see better.

'It is a pity, a great pity, that you haven't come here to engage in discussions, and don't you think it's an even greater pity that you should be preoccupied with your toilet now?'

'What's my toilet got to do with you?'

'It's as difficult to cut off a hundred million heads as it is to change the world by propaganda. Much more difficult, perhaps, especially in Russia,' Liputin ventured again.

'It's Russia they pin all their hopes on now,' said an army officer.

'Yes, we've heard about that, too,' the lame teacher put in. 'We know that a mysterious *index* finger is pointing to our fair country as the country most suitable for accomplishing the great task. Except for this: in the event of a gradual solution of the problem by propaganda I, at any rate, might gain something personally. I mean, I might enjoy some pleasant talk at least, and even obtain some reward from the Government for my services to social advancement. But in the event of the second solution by the rapid method of cutting off a hundred million heads, I don't stand to gain anything, do I? If you started propagating that, you might end up by having your tongue cut out.'

'Yours certainly would be,' said Verkhovensky.

'Ah, so there you are, sir. And since it is quite impossible, even in the most favourable circumstances, to complete such a massacre in less than fifty, or at most thirty years, for they are not sheep and they wouldn't allow themselves to be slaughtered, wouldn't it be better to collect your pots and pans and emigrate overseas to some Pacific islands and there close your eyes in peace? Believe me' – he tapped his finger significantly on the table – 'all you're likely to achieve by such propaganda is mass emigration and nothing more!'

He concluded looking very pleased with himself. He was one of the intellectuals of our province. Liputin was smiling craftily. Virginsky listened a little dejectedly, but all the others followed the discussion with great attention, especially the ladies and the officers. They all realized that the upholders of the hundred million heads theory had been pushed against a wall, and they waited to see what would come of it.

'You certainly put it very well,' Verkhovensky mumbled more unconcernedly than ever, looking as though he were bored. 'Emigration is a good idea. And yet if, in spite of the obvious disadvantages you foresee, the number of people who are ready to fight for the common cause grows daily, we shall be able to do without you. For what is happening here, my dear sir, is that a new religion is taking the place of the old one, and that is why we are getting so many new fighters and it is such a big thing. You can emigrate! And, you know, I'd advise you to go to Dresden, and not to the Pacific islands. For, in the first place, it is a city which has never been visited by any epidemics, and as you're an educated man, you're quite certainly afraid of death; secondly, it is near the Russian border, so that you will be able to receive your income from your beloved country more easily; thirdly, it contains what are known as treasures of art, and you're an aesthetic fellow, a former teacher of literature, I believe; and, finally, it is a sort of miniature Switzerland – and that will provide you with poetic inspiration, for I am sure you write verse. In a word, it's a treasure in a snuffbox.'

There was a general stir, especially among the officers. Another second and they would all have begun talking at once. But the lame man rose to the bait irritably.

'No, sir, perhaps I won't run away from the common cause. You must realize, sir, that –'

'Do you really mean that you would agree to join the group of five if I proposed it to you?' Verkhovensky suddenly rapped out, and he put the scissors down on the table.

They all looked startled. The mysterious man had shown his hand too suddenly. He had even spoken openly about 'the group of five'.

'Everyone feels himself to be an honest man and will not shrink from his responsibility for the common cause,' the lame teacher tried to wriggle out of it, 'but –'

'No, sir, this isn't any longer a question of *but*,' Verkhovensky interrupted him sharply and peremptorily. 'Ladies and gentlemen, I demand a straight answer. I realize very well that having come here and having called you together myself, I'm obliged to give you some explanations' (another unexpected disclosure), 'but I can't possibly give you any before I find out what your frame of mind is. Disregarding all this talk – for we can't just go on talking for another thirty years as people have done for the last thirty – let me ask you which you prefer: the slow way consisting of the composition of social novels and the dry, unimaginative planning of the destinies of mankind a thousand years hence, while despotism swallows the morsels of roast meat which would fly into your mouths of themselves, but which you fail to catch; or are you in favour of a quick solution, whatever it may be, which will at last untie your hands and which will give humanity ample scope for ordering its own social affairs in a practical way and not on paper? They shout: a hundred million heads; well, that may be only a metaphor, but why be afraid of it if with the slow paper day-dreams despotism will in a hundred or so years devour not a hundred but five hundred million heads? And please note that a man suffering from an incurable illness will not be cured, whatever prescriptions are written for him on paper; on the contrary, if there is any delay, he will go on festering so much that he will infect us all and corrupt all the healthy forces on which we can count now, so that in the end we shall all come to grief. I entirely agree that to chatter liberally and eloquently is an exceedingly pleasant pastime, and that to act is a little dangerous. Anyway, I'm afraid I'm not very good at talking. I came here with certain communications, and I should, therefore, like to ask all of you, ladies and gentlemen, not to vote, but to tell me frankly and simply which appeals to you more – a snail's pace in a swamp or full steam ahead across it?'

'I'm all for crossing at full steam!' the schoolboy cried enthusiastically.

'Me, too,' said Lyamshin.

'Well, of course,' an officer, followed by another and by someone else, muttered, 'there can be no doubt as to the choice.'

What struck them most was that Verkhovensky had some 'communications' to make and that he had promised to speak at once.

'Ladies and gentlemen, I see that almost all of you have decided to act in the spirit of the leaflets,' he said, scanning everybody in the room.

'All, all,' a majority of voices cried.

'I must confess that I am more in favour of a humane policy,' said the Major, 'but as all are in favour of yours, I am with the rest too.'

'It would seem, therefore, that even you are not against it,' Verkhovensky addressed the lame man.

'I'm not really,' said the cripple, blushing, 'but if I agree with the others now, it's solely because I don't want to upset the –'

'You're all like that! He's ready to argue for six months to show off his liberal eloquence, but he ends up by voting with the rest! Think it over, ladies and gentlemen. Are you really all ready?'

(Ready for what? A vague, but very tempting question.)

'Of course all –' they cried, but not without watching each other.

'But afterwards perhaps you'll be sorry for having agreed so quickly? That's how it almost always happens with you, you know.'

They grew excited for different reasons, very excited. The lame teacher flew at Verkhovensky.

'I should like to point out,' he said, 'that the answers to such questions depend on certain conditions. Even if we have given our decision, the question which was put to us in so strange a fashion, you must realize –'

'In what strange fashion?'

'A fashion such questions are not asked in.'

'Tell me how, please. But, you know, I was sure that you'd be the first to take offence.'

'You've extracted from us an answer about our readiness for immediate action, but what right had you to do so? What authority had you to ask us such questions?'

'You should have thought of asking that question before! Why did you answer my question? First you agree and then you change your mind.'

'If you ask me, I think that the irresponsible frankness of your principal question shows that you've neither the authority nor the right to ask it, but you did so out of personal curiosity.'

'What are you driving at?' Verkhovensky cried, as though he were beginning to be greatly disturbed.

'What I am driving at is that new members are, anyway, recruited with the utmost secrecy, and not in the company of twenty people one doesn't know!' the lame teacher blurted out.

He had put all his cards on the table, but then he was in a state of uncontrollable irritation. Verkhovensky turned quickly to the company with a well-simulated expression of alarm.

'Ladies and gentlemen, I deem it my duty to announce to you all that all this is nonsense and that our conversation has gone too far. I have recruited no members so far, and no one has the right to say of me that I am recruiting members. We were simply discussing our opinions. Isn't that so? But be that as it may' – he turned to the lame man, – 'you, sir, alarm me greatly. I never thought that such innocent things had to be discussed in secrecy here. Or are you afraid that the police may be informed? Do you really think that there is an informer among us?'

They became terribly excited; everybody was talking.

'Ladies and gentlemen, if that is the case,' Verkhovensky went on, 'then I have compromised myself more than anybody, and, therefore, I must ask you to answer one question, if you care to, of course. It's entirely up to you.'

'What question? What question?' they all began to shout.

'A question that will make it absolutely clear whether we are to re-main together or take our hats and go our several ways in silence.'

'The question, the question?'

'If any of us knew of the existence of a proposed political murder, would he inform the police about it, in view of all the consequences, or would he stay at home and wait to see what happened? There can be all sorts of opinions about that. The answer to the question will tell us clearly whether we are to separate or whether we are to remain to-gether, and that not for this evening only. May I ask you for your answer first?' He turned to the lame teacher.

'Why me first?'

'Because you started it all. Please don't try to wriggle out of it. Cleverness won't help you. Still, just as you like. It's entirely up to you.'

'I'm sorry, but such a question is an insult.'

'No, sir, that's not good enough. Please be more explicit.'

'I've never been an agent of the secret police,' the lame teacher said, wriggling more than ever.

'Please be more explicit, and don't keep us waiting.'

The lame man got so angry that he wouldn't even reply. He glared furiously at his tormentor from under his glasses without uttering a word.

'Yes or no? Would you or would you not inform the police?' Verkhovensky cried.

'Of course I would *not*,' the lame teacher shouted twice as loudly.

'No one would inform the police! Of course not!' many voices cried.

'May I ask you, Major, whether you would inform the police or not?' Verkhovensky went on. 'And, mind, I ask you on purpose.'

'No, sir, I would not inform.'

'But if you knew that someone wished to rob and murder a man, an ordinary mortal, you would inform the police, wouldn't you?'

'Yes, sir, but that would be merely a case of civil law, while what we are discussing is a political matter. I've never been an agent of the secret police.'

'No one here has,' voices cried again. 'An unnecessary question. Everyone can give only one answer. There are no informers here!'

'What's that gentleman getting up for?' the girl student cried.

'That's Shatov. Why did you get up, Shatov?' Mrs Virginsky cried.

Shatov had really got up. He held his hat in his hand and was looking at Verkhovensky. It seemed as though he wanted to say something to him, but was hesitating. He looked pale and angry, but he controlled himself and walked to the door without saying a word.

'Shatov, that won't do you any good, you know,' Verkhovensky shouted enigmatically after him.

'But it will do you good, you dirty spy and scoundrel,' Shatov shouted back at him from the doorway and went out.

More cries and exclamations.

'So that's the test, is it?' a voice cried.

'Came in useful!' cried another.

'I hope it isn't too late,' remarked a third.

'Who asked him to come? Who received him? Who is he? Who's Shatov? Will he inform the police or not?' – questions were fired from all over the room.

'If he were an informer, he'd have pretended not to be one, but he had his say and went out,' someone observed.

'Stavrogin, too, is getting up,' the girl student cried. 'Stavrogin hasn't answered the question, either.'

Stavrogin actually got up, and after him Kirilov, too, got up at the other end of the table.

'I'm sorry, Mr Stavrogin,' Mrs Virginsky addressed him sharply, 'but we've all answered the question, but you are leaving without a word.'

'I see no necessity to answer the question which interests you so much,' Stavrogin murmured.

'But we've compromised ourselves and you haven't,' a few voices cried.

'What do I care whether you've compromised yourselves or not?' Stavrogin said with a laugh, but his eyes flashed.

'What do you care? What do you care?' several voices exclaimed. Many people jumped up from their chairs.

'I say, ladies and gentlemen, I say,' the lame teacher cried, 'Mr Verkhovensky hasn't answered the question, either; he's merely asked it.'

His words produced an extraordinary sensation. They all exchanged glances with one another. Stavrogin laughed aloud in the lame man's face and went out, followed by Kirilov. Verkhovensky rushed out into the hall after them.

'What are you doing to me?' he murmured, seizing Stavrogin's hand and squeezing it with all his might.

Stavrogin pulled his hand away without a word.

'Wait for me at Kirilov's. I'll be there. It's absolutely necessary! Absolutely!'

'There's no need for me to be there!' Stavrogin cut him short.

'Stavrogin will be there,' Kirilov observed with an air of finality. 'Stavrogin, it is necessary for you to be there. I'll explain it to you there.'

They went out.

8

Ivan the Crown-Prince

THEY went out. Peter Verkhovensky was about to rush back to the 'meeting' in order to quell the clamour, but apparently coming to the conclusion that it was not worth troubling about, he left everything, and two minutes later was already streaking along the street after the two men. As he ran along, he remembered a short cut to Filippov's house; up to his knees in mud, he ran through a side-street, and actually reached the house at the moment Stavrogin and Kirilov were going through the gates.

'Here already?' Kirilov observed. 'That's good. Come in.'

'Why did you tell me that you lived alone?' Stavrogin asked as he passed a boiling samovar in the passage.

'You'll see presently who I'm living with,' Kirilov muttered. 'Come in.'

As soon as they had gone in, Verkhovensky took out of his pocket the anonymous letter he had been given by Lembke earlier that day, and put it before Stavrogin. The three of them sat down. Stavrogin read the letter in silence.

'Well?' he asked.

'That scoundrel will do as he writes,' Verkhovensky explained. 'Since he is under your control, I'd be glad if you would tell me what to do. I assure you he may go to Lembke to-morrow.'

'Well, let him go.'

'Let him go? But surely it can be arranged.'

'You're mistaken; he doesn't depend on me. And, besides, it's all one to me. He doesn't threaten me. He threatens you.'

'You, too.'

'I don't think so.'

'But others may not spare you. Don't you see? Listen to me, Stavrogin. This is only quibbling. You don't grudge the money, do you?'

'Is it money that is needed?'

'Most certainly, two thousand or at least fifteen hundred. Let me have the money to-morrow or even to-day, and I'll pack him off to Petersburg to-morrow evening. That's all he wants. With his sister Mary, if you like. Make a note of that.'

He seemed to be a little distraught; he spoke, somehow, carelessly and without weighing his words.

Stavrogin watched him with amazement.

'There's no need for me to send Mary away.'

'I daresay you don't even want to, do you?' Verkhovensky smiled ironically.

'Perhaps I don't.'

'In short, are you going to let me have the money or not?' Verkhovensky shouted at Stavrogin with furious impatience and rather imperiously.

Stavrogin looked him up and down gravely.

'There won't be any money.'

'Look here, Stavrogin; you either know something or have done something already. You're pulling my leg!'

Peter's face was distorted, the corners of his mouth twitched, and he suddenly burst out laughing a curiously aimless and meaningless laugh.

'You've just received money from your father for your estate,' Stavrogin observed calmly. 'My mother paid you six or eight thousand for your father. Well, why don't you lay out fifteen hundred of your money? After all, why should I pay for somebody else? And, besides, I've already paid out so much that I can't help feeling annoyed.' He smiled himself at his own words.

'Oh, you're beginning to joke, are you?'

Stavrogin got up from his chair. Verkhovensky, too, was on his feet in a flash and stood with his back against the door as though barring the way. Stavrogin was about to push him away from the door in order to go out, but suddenly stopped dead.

'I won't let you have Shatov,' he said.

Verkhovensky gave a start; both looked at each other.

'I told you this evening why you wanted Shatov's blood,' Stavrogin said with flashing eyes. 'You want to cement your little groups with it. The way you drove out Shatov just now was perfect: you knew very well that he would never say: "I won't inform the police," and he'd think it mean to tell a lie in your presence. But what do you want me for now? Me? You've been pestering me ever since I met you abroad. The explanation you've given me so far is just madness. And yet you suggest that I should give Lebyatkin fifteen hundred roubles and thus provide Fedka with an opportunity for murdering him. I know you think I'd like him to murder my wife, too. By tying me hand and foot with this crime, you hope, of course, to get me in your power. Why do you want to have me in your power? What the hell do you want me for? Once for all, have a good look at me: am I your man? And leave me alone.'

'Has Fedka been to see you himself?' Verkhovensky asked breathlessly.

'Yes, he has. His price is fifteen hundred roubles. He'll confirm it himself. There he is.'

Stavrogin stretched out his hand. Verkhovensky turned round quickly. A new figure emerged out of the darkness on the threshold: Fedka, in a sheepskin but without a cap, stood there as if he were at home. He stood there grinning to himself and showing his even white teeth. His black eyes, with yellowish whites, darted cautiously about the room as he watched the gentlemen. There was something he did not understand; Kirilov must have brought him in just now, and it was on Kirilov that he fixed his questioning glance. He stood in the doorway, but did not seem anxious to enter the room.

'I suppose you got him here to listen to our business transaction, or even to see the money in our hands, didn't you?' Stavrogin asked, and without waiting for a reply, left the house.

Verkhovensky overtook him at the gates almost in a mad frenzy.

'Stop! Not another step!' he cried, catching hold of his elbow.

Stavrogin tried to pull away his arm, but couldn't. He was

overcome with fury: seizing Verkhovensky by the hair with his left hand, he flung him with all his might on the ground and walked out of the gate. But he had not walked thirty paces before Verkhovensky overtook him again.

'Let's make it up, let's make it up,' he implored him in a spasmodic whisper.

Stavrogin shrugged, but he did not stop or turn round.

'Listen, I'll bring you Lisa to-morrow. Do you want me to? No? Why don't you answer? Tell me what you want me to do and I'll do it. Listen, I'll give you Shatov. All right?'

'So it is true that you've decided to murder him?' cried Stavrogin.

'But what do you want Shatov for? What do you want him for?' the frantic man went on, breathlessly and rapidly, running ahead and seizing Stavrogin by the elbow, probably without noticing it himself. 'Listen, I'll give him to you. Let's make it up. You're asking a big price, but – let's make it up!'

Stavrogin glanced at him at last and was shocked. It was not the same voice or the same look as always or as they had been in the room just now. He saw almost another face. The inflexion of the voice was not the same, either. Verkhovensky was begging him, beseeching him. He was a man whose most precious thing was being or had been taken away and who had not yet had time to recover from the shock.

'Good Lord! what's the matter with you?' Stavrogin cried.

Verkhovensky did not reply, but ran after him, looking at him with the same imploring and yet relentless eyes.

'Let's make it up!' he whispered again. 'Listen, like Fedka, I carry a knife in my boot, but I'll make it up with you.'

'But, damn you, what do you want me for?' Stavrogin cried in positive amazement and anger. 'Is it a secret or what? Have you got to have me as a sort of talisman?'

'Listen, we'll create political disturbances,' Verkhovensky muttered rapidly, almost in delirium. 'Don't you believe that we'll create disturbances? We shall create such an upheaval that the foundations of the State will be cracked wide open. Karmazinov is right. We have nothing to hold on to. Another dozen of such small groups in Russia, and I'm safe.'

'All the same sort of fools,' Stavrogin interposed involuntarily.

'Oh, try to be more foolish yourself, Stavrogin! Try to be more foolish yourself! You're not so clever, you know, that such a wish should seem absurd. You're afraid, you lack faith, you're scared by the magnitude of things. And why are they fools? They are not such fools. To-day no one has a mind of his own. There are awfully few people with a mind of their own to-day. Virginsky is a man of the purest heart – ten times purer than ours. But never mind him. Liputin is a scoundrel, but I know his one weak spot. There's not a scoundrel in the world who hasn't a weak spot. Lyamshin alone hasn't any, but he is completely in my hands. A few more groups, and I should have money and passports everywhere, that at least. Isn't that enough? That alone? And hiding-places, too. Let them search. They'll destroy one group and miss another. We'll stir up trouble. Don't you really believe that we two are quite enough?'

'Take Shigalyov and leave me alone.'

'Shigalyov is a genius! Do you realize that he is a genius like Fourier? But bolder than Fourier, and stronger than Fourier. I'll give a lot of my time to him. He's invented "equality"!'

'He's in a fever and he is raving; something peculiar has happened to him,' Stavrogin thought, glancing at him again.

Both walked on without stopping.

'He's got everything perfect in his note-book,' Verkhovensky went on. 'Spying. Every member of the society spies on the others, and he is obliged to inform against them. Everyone belongs to all the others, and all belong to everyone. All are slaves and equals in slavery. In extreme cases slander and murder, but, above all, equality. To begin with, the level of education, science, and accomplishment is lowered. A high level of scientific thought and accomplishment is open only to men of the highest abilities! Men of the highest ability have always seized the power and become autocrats. Such men cannot help being autocrats, and they've always done more harm than good; they are either banished or executed. A Cicero will have his tongue cut out, Copernicus will have his eyes gouged out, a Shakespeare will be stoned – there you have Shigalyov's doctrine! Slaves must be equal: without despotism there has never been any freedom or equality, but in a herd there is bound to be equality – there's the Shigalyov doctrine for you! Ha, ha, ha! You think it strange? I am for the Shigalyov doctrine!'

Stavrogin tried to quicken his pace and get home as soon as possible. 'If the fellow is drunk, where did he manage to get drunk?' he wondered. 'Not the cognac, surely?'

'Listen, Stavrogin: to level the mountains is a good idea, not a ridiculous one. I'm for Shigalyov! We don't want education. We have had enough of science. We have plenty of material without science to last us a thousand years. The thing we want is obedience. The only thing that's wanting in the world is obedience. The desire for education is an aristocratic desire. The moment a man falls in love or has a family, he gets a desire for private property. We will destroy that desire; we'll resort to drunkenness, slander, denunciations; we'll resort to unheard-of depravity; we shall smother every genius in infancy. We shall reduce everything to one common denominator. Full equality. "We've learned a trade and we are honest men – we want nothing more," that was the answer given recently by English workers. Only what is necessary is necessary; that's the motto of the whole world henceforth. But a shock, too, is necessary; we, the rulers, will take care of that. Slaves must have rulers. Complete obedience, complete loss of individuality, but once in thirty years Shigalyov resorts to a shock, and everyone at once starts devouring each other, up to a certain point, just as a measure against boredom. Boredom is an aristocratic sensation; in the Shigalyov system there will be no desires. Desire and suffering are for us; for the slaves – the Shigalyov system.'

'You make an exception of yourself, do you?' Stavrogin could not help asking again.

'And of you. Do you know, I was thinking of delivering the world up to the Pope. Let him go out barefoot and show himself to the mob, saying "See what they have brought me to!" and they will all follow him, even the army. The Pope on top, we all round him, and below us – the Shigalyov order. All we need is that the Internationale should come to an agreement with the Pope; this will come about. The old boy will agree at once. He can't do anything else. Mark my words. Ha, ha, ha! Silly? Tell me, is it silly or not?'

'That's enough,' Stavrogin muttered with annoyance.

'Enough! Listen, I'd give up the Pope! To hell with the Shigalyov order! To hell with the Pope! What we want is something more immediate, something more thrilling. We don't want the Shigalyov order, for that is something too exquisite. That's an ideal. That can only come to pass in the future. Shigalyov is an aesthete, and a fool like every philanthropist. What we want is hard work, manual labour; and Shigalyov despises manual labour. Listen, let the Pope rule in the West, and you shall rule over us, you shall rule over our country!'

'Leave me alone; you're drunk!' Stavrogin muttered, quickening his pace.

'Stavrogin, you're beautiful!' Verkhovensky cried almost in ecstasy. 'Do you know that you are beautiful? What is so fine about you is that sometimes you don't know it. Oh, I've made a thorough study of you! I often watch you without your being aware of it. You're even simple-minded and naïve – do you know that? You are, you are! I suppose you must be suffering, and suffering genuinely, too, because of your simple-mindedness. I love beauty. I am a nihilist, but I love beauty. Don't nihilists love beauty? The only thing they do not love is idols, but I love an idol. You are my idol! You don't insult anyone, and everyone hates you; you look on everyone as your equal, and everyone is afraid of you. That's good. No one will ever come up to you to slap you on the shoulder. You're an awful aristocrat. An aristocrat who goes in for democracy is irresistible. To sacrifice life – yours and another man's – is nothing to you. You're just the sort of man we need. I – I, especially, need a man like you. I don't know of anyone but you. You're my leader, you're my sun, and I am your worm.'

He suddenly kissed his hand. A shiver ran down Stavrogin's spine and he snatched his hand away in dismay. They stopped.

'Mad!' Stavrogin whispered.

'I may be raving, I may be raving,' Verkhovensky agreed, speaking rapidly, 'but it is I who have thought of the first step! Shigalyov would never have thought of the first step. There are hundreds of Shigalyovs. But only one man, only one man in Russia hit on the first step, and only one man knows how to take it. I am that man. Why are you staring at me? It is you I need – you! Without you I am nothing. Without you I am a fly, an idea in a bottle, Columbus without America.'

Stavrogin stood looking intently into his mad eyes.

'Listen,' Verkhovensky spoke rapidly, as though in a great hurry, continually seizing Stavrogin by the left sleeve, 'to begin with, we'll stir up trouble. I've already told you: we'll go to the common people; we'll win them over to our side. Do you realize that we are very

powerful already? Our party consists not only of those who kill and
burn, or fire off pistols in the classical manner or bite their superiors.
Such people are only in our way. Without discipline nothing has any
meaning for me. You see, I'm a rogue, and not a Socialist, ha, ha!
Listen, I've summed them all up: the teacher who laughs with the
children at their God and at their cradle is ours already. The barrister
who defends an educated murderer by pleading that, being more mentally developed than his victims, he could not help murdering for
money, is already one of us. Schoolboys who kill a peasant for the
sake of a thrill are ours. The juries who acquit all criminals without
distinction are ours. A public prosecutor, who trembles in court because he is not sufficiently progressive, is ours, ours. Administrators,
authors – oh, there are lots and lots of us, and they don't know it themselves. On the other hand, the docility of schoolboys and fools has
reached the highest pitch; the schoolmasters are full of bile; everywhere we see vanity reaching inordinate proportions, enormous bestial appetites. ... Do you realize how many converts we shall make by
trite and ready-made ideas? When I went abroad, Littré's theory that
crime is insanity was the vogue; when I returned, crime was no
longer insanity, but just commonsense, indeed, almost a duty and, at
any rate, a noble protest. "How can an educated man be expected to
refrain from killing his victim if he must have money?" But this is
only a beginning. The Russian God has already capitulated to cheap
vodka. The peasants are drunk, the mothers are drunk, the children
are drunk, the churches are empty, and all one hears in the courts is:
"Two hundred strokes of the birch or stand us a gallon of vodka."
Oh, let the present generation only grow up! A pity we can't afford
to wait, or we might have let them get more drunk. Oh, what a pity
there's no proletariat! But there will be, there will be – all points to
that.'

'It is a pity, too, we've grown more stupid,' Stavrogin muttered
and walked on towards home.

'Listen, I once saw a child of six who was taking his drunken mother
home while she swore at him with foul words. You think I'm glad of
it? When she gets into our hands we shall, I daresay, cure her. If it
should be necessary, we'll drive them for forty years into the wilder-
ness. But one or two generations of vice are absolutely essential now.
Monstrous, disgusting vice which turns man into an abject, cowardly,

cruel, and selfish wretch – that's what we want! And, on top of it, a little "fresh blood" to make them get used to it. What are you laughing at? I'm not contradicting myself. I'm only contradicting the philanthropists and Shigalyov, not myself. I'm a rogue, and not a socialist. Ha, ha, ha! A pity we haven't got much time, though. I promised Karmazinov to start in May and finish by the first of October. Too soon? Ha, ha! Do you know what, Stavrogin? Though Russian people use foul language, they have so far shown no trace of cynicism. Do you know that the peasant slave had more self-respect than Karmazinov? He was flogged, but he preserved his gods, while Karmazinov hasn't.'

'My dear Verkhovensky, I've listened to you for the first time, and it is with amazement that I'm listening to you,' said Stavrogin. 'You're not a socialist at all, it seems, but some sort of – ambitious politician, aren't you?'

'A rogue, a rogue. Are you worried about what sort of man I am? I'll tell you presently what I am. That's what I've been leading up to. It wasn't for nothing that I kissed your hand. But it is necessary that the common people, too, should believe that we know what we want and that the others are merely "waving their cudgels about and hitting their own men". Oh, if only we had more time! The trouble is we have no time. We shall proclaim destruction – why? why? – well, because the idea is so fascinating! But – we must get a little exercise. We'll have a few fires – we'll spread a few legends. Every mangy little group will be useful. I shall find you such keen fellows in each one of these groups that they'll be glad to do some shooting and will be grateful for the honour. Very well, then, so an upheaval will start. There's going to be such a to-do as the world has never seen. Russia will become shrouded in a fog, the earth will weep for its old gods. And it will be then that we shall let loose – whom?'

'Whom?'

'Ivan the Crown-prince.'

'Who-om?'

'Ivan the Crown-prince. You! You!'

Stavrogin thought for a moment.

'A pretender?' he asked suddenly, gazing at the madman in sheer amazement. 'Oh, so that's your plan, is it?'

'We shall say that he is "in hiding",' Verkhovensky said quietly, in a sort of amorous whisper, as though he really were drunk. 'Do you know what the expression "in hiding" means? But he will appear. He will appear. We shall spread a legend which will be much better than that of the sect of castrates. He exists, but no one has ever seen him. Oh, what a wonderful legend one could spread! And the main thing is – a new force is coming. And that's what they want. That's what they are weeping for. After all, what does socialism amount to? It has destroyed the old forces, but hasn't put any new ones in their place. But here we have a force, a tremendous force, something unheard of. We need only one lever to lift up the earth. Everything will rise up!'

'So you've been seriously counting on me, have you?' Stavrogin asked, with a malicious laugh.

'Why do you laugh, and so maliciously? Don't frighten me. I'm like a little child now: I can be frightened to death by just one smile like that. Listen, I shan't show you to anyone, not to anyone: it must be so. He exists, but no one has seen him. He is in hiding. And, you know, I daresay one could show you to one man out of ten thousand, for instance. And the news will spread all over the face of the earth: "We've seen him! We've seen him!" The leader of the flagellants, Ivan Filippovich, had been seen, too, ascending into heaven on a chariot in the presence of a multitude of people. They saw him with their "own" eyes. And you are not Ivan Filippovich; you are beautiful, you are proud as a god, you are seeking nothing for yourself, you are "in hiding" with the halo of a victim round your head. The main thing is the legend! You will conquer them. You will have only to look, and you will conquer them. He is bearing a new truth and he is "in hiding". And he'll pass two or three judgements of Solomon. Our small groups, our small groups of five – we don't need newspapers. If we grant only one petition out of ten thousand, all will come to us with petitions. In every country district every peasant will know that there is, as it were, somewhere a hollow tree where he can put his petition. And the whole earth will resound with the cry: "A new and righteous law is coming," and the sea will be in a turmoil and the whole trumpery show will crash to the ground, and then we shall consider how to erect an edifice of stone. For the first time; *We* shall build it, we, we alone!'

'Madness,' said Stavrogin.

'Why, why don't you want to? Are you afraid? But I seized on you just because you're afraid of nothing. Have I been unreasonable? But so far I am only a Columbus without America. Can a Columbus without America be reasonable?'

Stavrogin said nothing. Meanwhile they had arrived at his house and stopped at the front door.

'Listen,' Verkhovensky said, bending down to his ear, 'I'll do it for you without the money. I'll finish with Mary to-morrow – without the money, and I shall bring Lisa to you to-morrow. Do you want Lisa – to-morrow?'

'Has he really gone off his head?' Stavrogin thought, smiling.

The front door was opened.

'Stavrogin, is America ours?' asked Verkhovensky, seizing him by the hand for the last time.

'What for?' Stavrogin asked earnestly and sternly.

'You don't want to – I knew it!' Verkhovensky cried in a fit of furious anger. 'You're lying, you miserable, lecherous, stunted, pampered little aristocrat. I don't believe you. You've a wolf's appetite. Understand that you've run up too big an account, and that I can't give you up now. There's no one like you in the whole world! I invented you abroad; I invented it all while looking at you. If I had not watched you from a corner, nothing of all this would have occurred to me!'

Stavrogin mounted the stairs without answering.

'Stavrogin,' Verkhovensky shouted after him, 'I give you one day – two days – three – I can't give you more than three, and then I shall come for your answer!'

9

Stepan Verkhovensky is Raided

IN the meantime an incident occurred which surprised me and shocked Stepan Verkhovensky. At eight o'clock in the morning Nastasya came running to me from him with the news that her master was 'raided'. At first I could not understand what she was talking about; all I could make out was that officials had 'raided' Mr Verkhovensky's house and had taken away some papers, and that a soldier tied them up in a bundle and 'carried them off in a wheel-barrow'. The news struck me as absurd. I hastened at once to Mr Verkhovensky.

I found him in a most remarkable state of mind: upset and greatly agitated, but at the same time decidedly triumphant. On the table in the middle of the room the samovar was boiling, and a glass of tea was poured out, but untouched and forgotten. Mr Verkhovensky was walking round the table, pacing the room from one corner to another, without realizing what he was doing. He was dressed as usual in his red woollen sweater, but, on catching sight of me, he hastened to put on his coat and waistcoat, which he had never done before when any of his intimate friends caught him wearing his red woollen sweater. He seized me warmly by the hand at once.

'*Enfin un ami!*' he cried, heaving a deep sigh. '*Cher*, I have sent for you only, and no one knows anything. I must tell Nastasya to lock the doors and not let anyone in, except *them*, of course. *Vous comprenez?*'

He looked at me uneasily, as though expecting an answer. I naturally enough began questioning him at once, and with some difficulty found out from his incoherent speech, interspersed with frequent pauses and digressions, that at seven o'clock in the morning an official 'suddenly' came to see him.

'*Pardon, j'ai oublié son nom. Il n'est pas du pays*, but I think Lembke must have brought him, *quelque chose de bête et d'allemand dans la physionomie. Il s'appelle Rosenthal.*'

'You're sure it wasn't Blum?'

'Blum. Yes, that's the name he gave me. *Vous le connaissez? Quelque chose d'hébété et de très content dans la figure, pourtant très sévère, roide et sérieux.* A police type, one of those who carry out orders, *je m'y connais.* I was still asleep, and – just fancy – he asked me if he could "have a look" at my books and manuscripts, *oui, je m'en souviens, il a employé ce mot.* He didn't arrest me, but only the books. ... *Il se tenait à distance,* and when he started explaining to me why he had come, he looked as if I – *enfin il avait l'air de croire que je tomberai sur lui immédiatement et que je commencerai à le battre comme plâtre. Tous ces gens du bas étage sont comme ça,* when they are dealing with a decent fellow. I need hardly say that I understood everything at once. *Voilà vingt ans que je m'y prépare.* I unlocked all my drawers for him and handed him all the keys; gave them to him myself, gave him everything. *J'étais digne et calme.* From my books he took the foreign editions of Herzen's works, the bound volume of *The Bell*, four copies of my poem, *et enfin tout ça*. Then my papers and my letters *et quelques-unes de mes ébauches historiques, critiques et politiques*. They took it all away. Nastasya tells me that a soldier carted it away in a wheel-barrow and that it was covered with an apron; *oui, c'est cela*, an apron.'

The whole thing seemed crazy. Who could make head or tail of it? I began firing questions at him again: did Blum come alone or with somebody else? In whose name? By what right? How had he dared? How did he explain it?

'*Il était seul, bien seul*, but I think there was someone else *dans l'anti-chambre, oui, je m'en souviens, et puis* – yes, there was someone else, too, I believe, and there was a guard in the passage. You'd better ask Nastasya; she knows all about it better than I. *J'étais surexcité, voyez-vous. Il parlait, il parlait – un tas de choses*; however, he said very little, it was I who was talking all the time. I told him the story of my life, from that point of view only, of course. *J'étais surexcité, mais digne, je vous l'assure*. But I'm afraid I cried, I believe. They got the wheel-barrow from the shop next door.'

'Good heavens! how could it all have happened? But for God's sake, sir, let me have some more details. What you tell me sounds like a dream!'

'*Cher*, I feel as if I were in a dream still. *Savez-vous! Il a prononcé le nom de Teliatnikof*, and I'm thinking that it was he who was hiding in the passage. Yes, I remember he suggested calling the public prosecutor and, I think, also Dmitry Mitrych – *qui me doit encore quinze roubles de* whist, *soit dit en passant*. But I got the better of them, and what do I care for Dmitry Mitrych? I think I asked him to keep the whole thing dark. Yes, I begged him very much indeed, I'm afraid I've rather demeaned myself, *comment croyez-vous? Enfin, il a consenti*. Oh, yes, I remember, it was he, as a matter of fact, who asked me to keep it dark because he had merely come "to have a look round" *et rien de plus*, and nothing more, nothing – er – and that if they found nothing, nothing was going to happen. So that we finished it all *en amis, je suis tout-à-fait content*.'

'But, good heavens, sir,' I cried with friendly indignation, 'he only offered you the usual guarantees and the usual procedure in such cases, and you yourself declined to take them.'

'No, it's much better without any guarantees. What do we want a public scandal for? For the time being let it just be *en amis*. In our town, you know, if they get to know of it – *mes ennemis – et puis à quoi bon ce procureur, ce cochon de notre procureur, qui deux fois m'a manqué de politesse et qu'on a rossé à plaisir l'autre année chez cette charmante et belle* Natalya Pavlovna, *quand il ce cacha dans son boudoir. Et puis, mon ami,* don't contradict me and don't please, don't, make me feel bad about it, because there's nothing more unbearable when a man is worried than for a hundred friends to point out to him that he's behaved like a fool. But please sit down and have some tea. I confess, I'm awfully tired – ought I not to lie down and put vinegar on my head – what do you think?'

'Yes, yes, of course,' I cried, 'and some ice, too. You look very upset. You're pale and your hands are trembling. Lie down, have a rest and tell me about it later. I'll sit beside you and wait.'

He did not want to lie down, but I insisted. Nastasya brought a cup of vinegar; I wetted a towel and put it to his head. Then Nastasya stood on a chair and proceeded to light the little lamp in front of the icon in the corner. I noticed it with surprise; there had never been a little lamp there before, but now it had suddenly appeared.

'I told her to put it there this morning after they had gone,' Mr Verkhovensky muttered, giving me a cunning look. '*Quand on a de ces choses dans la chambre et qu'on vient vous arrêter*, it makes an impression and they are bound to report that they have seen it –'

Having finished with the lamp, Nastasya stood in the doorway, put her right hand to her cheek, and began gazing at us with a tearful expression

'*Éloignez-la* on some excuse,' he said, nodding to me from the sofa. 'Can't bear that Russian pity *et puis ça m'embête*.'

But she went away herself. I noticed that he kept looking at the door and listening for any sound in the passage.

'*Il faut être prêt, voyez-vous,*' he said, giving me a meaningful look, '*chaque moment* – they may come, take me away *et fuit* – the man's vanished into thin air.'

'Good Lord! Who will come? Who's going to take you away?'

'*Voyez-vous, mon cher,* I asked him straight as he was going out what they would do with me now.'

'You'd better have asked him where they were going to exile you to,' I cried with the same indignation.

'That's what I had in mind when I asked him the question, but he went away without answering. *Voyez-vous*, so far as underwear and clothes are concerned, warm clothes, especially, that depends entirely on them. If they tell me to take them – all right, but they're quite capable of sending me off in a soldier's greatcoat. But,' he went on, lowering his voice suddenly and glancing at the door through which Nastasya had just gone out, 'I've put thirty roubles quietly away in the lining of my waistcoat pocket – here, feel it, please. I don't think they'll make me take off my waistcoat, and I left seven roubles in my purse for appearance's sake – that's all I possess, as it were. You see, there on the table – some small change and a few coppers, so that it will never enter their heads that I've hidden the money. They'll think that's all I have. For goodness only knows where I shall have to sleep to-night.'

I bowed my head at such madness. It was clear that no man could be arrested or searched as he had described it, and, no doubt, he must have got it all mixed up. It is true it all happened before the latest laws had come into force. It was no less true that, according to his own words, he had been offered the choice of a more correct procedure, but he *got the better of them* and declined it. But, of course, in those days – that is, not so long ago – a governor could in extreme cases – but, again, what sort of an extreme case could this be? That was what baffled me.

'I daresay they must have had a telegram from Petersburg,' Stepan Verkhovensky said suddenly.

'A telegram! About you? You mean, because of Herzen's works and that poetic drama of yours? Have you gone mad? They could never arrest you for that.'

I simply got angry. He pulled a face and was evidently hurt – not because I had shouted at him, but because I had suggested that he might not be arrested.

'Who can tell in these times what he might be arrested for?' he muttered enigmatically.

A wild and preposterous idea flashed through my mind.

'Tell me, sir, as your friend, as your real friend,' I cried, 'I shan't betray you: are you a member of some secret society or not?'

And, to my surprise, he did not seem himself to be sure whether he was or was not a member of some secret society.

'It depends how you look at it, *voyez-vous* –'

'What do you mean by "how you look at it"?'

'Well, if you are wholeheartedly for progress, you – er – you can't possibly tell for certain. You don't think you belong to such a society, but before you know where you are, you seem to belong to something or other.'

'How's that possible? It's either yes or no.'

'*Cela date de Pétersbourg* when she and I intended to found a periodical there, Mrs Stavrogin and I. That's what's at the bottom of it. We gave them the slip then, they forgot all about us, but now they've remembered. *Cher, cher,* don't you know me?' he cried in a pained voice. 'And so they're going to take us, put us in a covered wagon, and march us off to Siberia for the rest of our lives, or they might forget us in some fortress prison.'

And he suddenly burst out crying bitterly. The tears gushed out of his eyes. He covered his face with his red silk handkerchief and sobbed, sobbed convulsively for five minutes. I felt awful. This was the man whom we had looked upon as a prophet for twenty years. A preacher, a teacher, a patriarch. The Kukolnik who had borne himself so grandly and majestically before us all, whom we regarded with such admiration, thinking it an honour to do so – and suddenly this man was sobbing like a naughty little child who is waiting for his teacher's return with the cane. I felt awfully sorry for him. He obviously believed in the 'covered wagon' as firmly as that I was sitting beside him, and he was waiting for it to arrive that very morning, that very minute, and all because of Herzen's works and some poetic drama of his! Such complete, utter ignorance of everyday reality was both touching and somehow repulsive.

He stopped crying at last, got up from the sofa, and started pacing the room again, continuing his conversation with me, and every moment looking out of the window and listening for any sound in the entrance hall. Our talk went on disjointedly. All my assurances and all my efforts to calm him rebounded from him like peas from a wall. He hardly listened to me, but still he wanted me badly to calm him, and he spoke to me without stopping, with that idea at the back of his mind. I saw that he could not do without me now and that he would not let me go for anything in the world. I stayed, and we sat for over two hours together. While talking to me, he remembered that Blum had taken away with him two political leaflets he had found in his place.

'Political leaflets?' I was foolish enough to look frightened. 'Why, have you –'

'Oh,' he replied irritably (one moment he spoke to me irritably and haughtily, and another in a terribly plaintive and humble tone of voice), 'they put ten through my door, but I had got rid of eight. Blum took only two away with him.' And he suddenly got red in the face with indignation. '*Vous me mettez avec ces gens-là!* Do you really think that I like the company of those scoundrels, those secret scatterers of illegal literature, that miserable son of mine, *ces esprits-forts de la lacheté*! Dear Lord!'

'Oh dear, they haven't mistaken you for someone else, have they? However, it's all nonsense. It just can't be true!' I observed.

'*Savez-vous,*' he suddenly burst out, 'I feel at times *que je ferai là-bas quelque esclandre.* Oh, please don't go! *Ma carrière est finie aujourd'hui, je le sens.* You know, I will probably fling myself upon somebody there and bite him, like that second lieutenant.'

He gave me a strange look, a look that was frightened and at the same time one that seemed to be intended to frighten me. He really was getting more and more irritated with someone or something as time passed and the 'covered wagon' did not appear; he was even getting angry. Suddenly Nastasya, who had gone for something to the passage from her kitchen, brushed against the clothes-stand, which fell to the floor. Mr Verkhovensky trembled all over and stood still, rooted to the ground; but when the accident was explained, he almost screamed at Nastasya and, stamping, drove her back to the kitchen. A minute later he said, looking at me in despair:

'I'm done for! *Cher,*' he went on, suddenly sitting down beside me and looking intently and with a miserable expression into my eyes, '*cher,* I'm not afraid of Siberia, I swear to you, oh, *je vous jure*' (tears even started in his eyes), 'I'm afraid of something else. ...'

I guessed from the way he looked that he wanted at last to tell me something of the utmost importance, which he must have kept back till that moment.

'I'm afraid of the disgrace,' he whispered mysteriously.

'What disgrace? Why, it's just the contrary! Believe me, sir, all this will be satisfactorily explained to-day and it will all end in your favour.'

'Are you so sure that they will pardon me?'

'What have they got to "pardon" you for? What a way to talk! What crime have you committed? I assure you, you have done nothing!'

'*Qu'en savez-vous*; all my life has been – *cher* – they'll remember everything, and – and if they find nothing, it'll be all the worse,' he suddenly added, unexpectedly.

'All the worse?'

'Yes.'

'I don't understand.'

'My friend, my friend, let them send me to Siberia or to Archangel – let them deprive me of my civil rights – if I am to perish, let me perish! But – I'm afraid of something else,' he repeated again in a whisper, looking frightened and mysterious.

'What? What are you afraid of?'

'Of being flogged,' he said and looked at me with a worried expression on his face.

'Who's going to flog you? Where? What for?' I cried, afraid that he might be going mad.

'Where? Why, there – where it's done.'

'But where is it done?'

'Oh, *cher*,' he whispered almost in my ear, 'the floor suddenly parts from under you, you drop half through – everybody knows that.'

'Fairy tales,' I cried, guessing what he meant. 'Old fairy tales. Surely you haven't really been believing in them till now?' I burst out laughing.

'Fairy tales? There must be some foundation for these fairy tales. The man who's been flogged won't tell. I've pictured it all in my imagination thousands of times.'

'But why should they do that to you? You've done nothing.'

'All the worse. They'll realize that I've done nothing, and they'll flog me.'

'And you're quite certain that that's why they're going to take you to Petersburg, are you?'

'My friend, I've told you already that I regret nothing, *ma carrière est finie*. Ever since she said good-bye to me at Skvoreshniki life's lost all meaning for me – but the disgrace, the disgrace, *que dira-t-elle* if she finds out?'

He looked at me in despair and, poor fellow, flushed crimson. I, too, lowered my eyes.

'She won't find anything out, because nothing is going to happen to you. I feel as though I were talking to you for the first time in my life, sir, so greatly have you surprised me this morning.'

'My dear friend, it is not fear. Suppose they pardon me, suppose they bring me back here and do nothing to me, I'm still done for. *Elle me soupçonnera toute ma vie* – me, me, the poet, the thinker, the man she worshipped for twenty-two years!'

'It'll never enter her head.'

'It will,' he whispered with utter conviction. 'I've discussed it with her many times in Petersburg, in Lent before we left, when we were both afraid. *Elle me soupçonnera toute ma vie* – and how am I to disabuse her? It'll sound improbable. And, besides, can you think of anyone in this wretched town who will believe me? *C'est invraisemblable. Et puis les femmes*. She'll be glad of it. She will be very sorry, sincerely sorry, like a true friend, but at heart – she will be glad of it. I shall give her a weapon against me for the rest of my life. Oh, my life's ruined! Twenty years of such perfect happiness with her – and now!'

He buried his face in his hands.

'Oughtn't you to let Mrs Stavrogin know of what has happened at once, sir?' I proposed.

'The Lord forbid!' he cried with a start, jumping to his feet. 'Not for anything in the world after what we said to each other when we parted at Skvoreshniki – never, never!'

His eyes flashed.

We went on sitting together for at least an hour, if not more, all the time expecting something to happen – we just could not get rid of that notion. He lay down again, even closed his eyes, and lay for twenty minutes without speaking a word, so that I thought that he was asleep or unconscious. Suddenly he sat up impetuously, tore the towel off his head, jumped up from the sofa, rushed up to the looking-glass, tied his cravat with trembling fingers, and shouted to Nastasya in a voice of thunder for his coat, his new hat and his walking-stick.

'I can't bear it any longer,' he said in a shaking voice. 'I can't, I can't! I'll go myself.'

'Where?' I asked, also jumping up.

'To Lembke. *Cher*, I must; it is my duty. I'm a citizen, a man, and

not a piece of wood. I have rights. I want my rights. For twenty years
I never demanded my rights. All my life I have criminally neglected
them – but now I'm going to demand them. He must tell me everything, everything. He received a telegram. He has no right to torment
me. Let him arrest me, if he likes. Let him arrest me! Let him arrest
me!' he kept screaming with a strange shrill note in his voice and
stamping his feet.

'I think you're quite right,' I said in a deliberately calm tone of
voice, though I was very much afraid for him. 'It certainly is much
better than to sit here in such a state of mental anguish, but I'm sorry
I cannot approve of your present mood. See what you look like and
in what an awful state you're going there. *Il faut être digne et calme
avec* Lembke. You really might fling yourself upon somebody there
and bite him.'

'I'm giving myself up. I'm walking straight into the lion's den.'

'I'll come with you.'

'I didn't expect anything less from you. I accept your sacrifice, the
sacrifice of a true friend. But I shan't let you come farther than the
house, no farther than that: you mustn't, you have no right to compromise yourself by being in my company. O, *croyez moi, je serai
calme!* I feel at this moment *à la hauteur de tout ce qu'il y a de plus
sacré. …*'

'I might even go into the house with you,' I interrupted him. 'I
heard from that stupid committee through Vysotsky yesterday that
they were counting on me and had invited me to act at to-morrow's
fête as one of the stewards, or whatever they're called – I mean one
of the six young men who've been appointed to look after the refreshments, look after the ladies, take the guests to their seats, and wear
a rosette of crimson-and-white ribbon on the left shoulder. I meant to
refuse, but now there's no reason in the world why I should not go
into the house on the excuse of discussing it with Mrs Lembke herself.
So we'll go in together, you see.'

He listened, nodding his head, but I don't think he understood a
word. We were standing in the doorway.

'*Cher*,' he said, stretching out his hand to the lamp before the icon,
'*cher*, I never believed in it but – so be it, so be it!' He crossed himself.
'*Allons!*'

'Well, that's better,' I thought to myself as I went out on the front steps with him. 'The fresh air will do him good; he'll calm down, go back home and – so to bed.'

But I was counting without my host. On the way we became involved in an adventure which shocked Mr Verkhovensky even more and was responsible for his making up his mind finally – so that, I confess, I never expected our friend to show such energy as he suddenly showed that morning. Poor old friend! Good old friend!

10

Filibusters. A Fatal Morning

I

THE incident in which we became involved on the way was very remarkable too. But I must tell everything in order. An hour before Mr Verkhovensky and I went out into the street, a crowd of people marched through the town and was watched by many curious spectators. They were the workers from Spigulin's factory, about seventy of them or more. They marched through the streets very quietly, almost in silence, in a carefully arranged order. It was claimed afterwards that the seventy workers were delegates representing all the workers of the factory, about nine hundred all told, who intended to go to the Governor and, in the absence of the factory owners, ask him to deal with the manager, who had impudently cheated them when he closed the factory and paid off the workers, a fact about which there can be no doubt whatever now. Others still refuse to believe that there was an election of delegates, and they base their claim on the fact that seventy was too large a delegation to choose. They assert that the crowd of workmen simply consisted of those who had been most unfairly treated and that they came to ask the Governor to intercede on their behalf, so there could be no question of a general 'mutiny' of factory workers, the news of which created such a sensation afterwards. Others still passionately maintained that the seventy men were not just mutineers, but positively political agitators – that is to say, that they were not only the unruliest of the lot, but were also stirred up by the revolutionary leaflets left in the factory. In short, it is impossible to say even now whether there had been any incitement or even any outside influence. My personal opinion, however, is that the workers had not read the revolutionary leaflets, and that even if they had read them, they would not have understood a word, if only because the authors of those leaflets wrote them too obscurely, in spite of the crudeness of their style. But as the workers really were in great straits, and the police to whom they had applied for help had refused to have anything to do with their plight, nothing could be more natural than that they should have decided to go in a body to 'the general himself', if possible even with a petition, draw up respectfully before his house and, the moment he appeared, fall down on their knees and cry out to him as if to Providence itself. In my view, that did not require either a mutiny or delegates, for it is an old, historic custom; from days immemorial the Russian people have been fond of having a talk with 'the general himself', for the mere pleasure of it, even if that talk had no other tangible result.

And that is why I am absolutely convinced that though Peter Verkhovensky, Liputin, and perhaps someone else – even Fedka, perhaps – had gone about among the workmen and talked to them (as indeed there is good evidence of this), they must have spoken to no more than two or three, or five at most, just by way of an experiment, and that nothing came of those talks. As for the mutiny, if the factory workers had understood anything of their propaganda, they would have stopped listening to them at once, since they would have considered it an utterly inappropriate and absurd business. Fedka was a different matter: he had apparently much better luck than Peter. It is pretty clear now from the collected evidence that Fedka and two factory workers did indeed take part in causing the fire in the town three days later, and two months after the fire three workers who had been employed at the factory were arrested on charges of robbery and arson. But if Fedka did succeed in inducing them to resort to direct action, it was only those five, for no similar charges were ever brought against the others.

Be that as it may, the workers arrived at last in a crowd at the little square in front of the Governor's residence and drew up there soberly and silently. I am told that as soon as they stopped they took off their hats, that is, half an hour perhaps before the arrival of the Governor, who, as though on purpose, did not happen to be at home at the time. The police appeared immediately, first in small groups and then in full force. They began, of course, by ordering the workers in menacing tones to disperse. But the workers refused to budge, like a flock of sheep at a fence, replying laconically that they had come to see 'the general himself'. There could be no doubt that they were firmly determined to carry out their plan. The unnatural shouting of the police ceased; it was quickly succeeded by quiet deliberations, mysterious orders issued in whispers, and stern, bustling anxiety, which furrowed the brows of the police officers. The Police Commissioner preferred to wait for the arrival of Lembke himself. It is nonsense to say that he came galloping in a *troika* at breakneck speed and started dealing out blows before he even had time to alight. He certainly was fond of driving at breakneck speed through our town in his carriage with a yellow back, and while the trace horses, utterly 'debauched' by the fast driving, were driven more and more frantic, to the great delight of all the shopkeepers of the arcade, he would rise in his carriage, draw himself up to his full height, holding on to the strap which had been fixed for that purpose at the side, and stretching forth his right hand like a figure on a monument, survey the town in that posture. But in the present case he did not start hitting out right and left, and though, as he got out of his carriage, he could not refrain from using strong language, he did it merely not to lose his popularity. It is even greater nonsense to assert that soldiers with fixed bayonets had been drawn up and that a telegram had been sent somewhere demanding the dispatch of artillery and Cossacks: those are fairy tales in which their inventors themselves no longer believe now. The report that firemen had brought their water-barrels from which they had drenched the people with water is also nonsense. All that happened was that the Police Commissioner shouted in his excitement that he would not let one of them get off scot free and that he would let them have a taste of bread and water; that, no doubt, was the origin of the story of the water-barrels which afterwards found its way into the Moscow and Petersburg papers. The most accurate version was that a police cordon was immediately formed round the crowd, and a special messenger – the police inspector of the first district – was sent for Lembke and drove off in the Police Commissioner's open carriage on the road to Skvoreshniki, where he knew von Lembke had gone in his carriage about half an hour before.

But, I must confess, I can't find an answer to the question how an unimportant, that is, an ordinary crowd of petitioners, it is true seventy men strong, was from the very outset transformed into a rebellion which threatened the safety of the State? Why was Lembke himself so quick to accept that idea when he arrived twenty minutes later with the messenger? My theory is (and, again, it is only my private opinion, of course) that our Police Commissioner, who was a great friend of the factory manager's, found it to his advantage to represent the crowd in that light to von Lembke just because he did not want him to start a proper enquiry into the affair; and it was Lembke himself who had given him the idea. During the last two days he had had two special and secret talks with him – very confused talks, it is true, but which suggested the idea to the Police Commissioner that the Governor was firmly of the opinion that the political leaflets were of great significance and that someone or other was inciting the Spigulin workers to stage a socialist rising, and so firmly was he convinced of that, that he would quite possibly have been sorry had the story of the incitement proved to be a mare's nest. 'Wants to earn some recognition in Petersburg,' our cunning Police Commissioner thought as he left Lembke. 'Well, why not? It won't do me any harm.'

But I'm convinced that poor Lembke would never have desired a rebellion even if it had brought him recognition. He was a most conscientious Civil Servant who had remained in a state of innocence up to the time of his marriage. And was he to blame that instead of being put in the innocent job of a buyer of fuel for Government departments and marrying an equally innocent Minchen, a forty-year-old princess had raised him to her social level? I have it from an almost unimpeachable source that it was from that fatal morning that the first unmistakable symptoms of the mental condition began which, it is said, eventually brought poor Lembke to that notorious private nursing home in Switzerland where he is supposed to be recuperating now. But if we admit that the unmistakable symptoms of *something* came to light that morning, then it is also right to assume, in my opinion, that similar symptoms may have been in evidence the day before, though perhaps not so clearly. I happen to know from the most intimate sources (well, assume that Mrs Lembke herself, not in triumph but *almost* in remorse – for a woman is never capable of *complete* remorse – had told me part of that story herself), I happen to know that Mr Lembke had gone to see his wife on the previous night – in the small hours, in fact, at about two o'clock in the morning – had wakened her and had

demanded that she should hear his 'ultimatum'. His demand was so insistent that she was obliged to get out of bed, highly indignant and in
her curling papers, and, sitting down on a settee, had to listen to what
her husband had to say, though with an expression of sardonic contempt. It was only then that she realized for the first time how far gone
her husband was, and she was secretly appalled. She ought to have
come to her senses and relented, but she concealed her horror and became more stubborn than ever. She (like any other married woman, I
suppose) had her own method of dealing with her husband, which she
had tried many times already and which had more than once driven him
into a state of frenzy. Mrs Lembke's method consisted of remaining
contemptuously silent for one hour, two hours, a whole day, and almost for three days; keeping silent at all costs, whatever he said or did,
even if he had attempted to throw himself out of a third-floor window – a method unbearable for a sensitive man! Whether Mrs Lembke
was punishing her husband for his blunders of the last few days and
for his jealousy, as the Governor of a province, of her administrative
abilities; whether she was indignant at his criticism of her behaviour
with the young people and our society as a whole and his utter lack of
understanding of her subtle and far-sighted political aims; or whether
she was angry with him for his stupid and senseless jealousy of Peter
Verkhovensky – whatever the reason, she made up her mind not to
give in even now, notwithstanding the lateness of the hour and the
fact that never before had she seen Mr Lembke in such a state of
agitation.

Pacing up and down and all over the rugs of her boudoir, he told
her everything – everything, incoherently it is true, but everything
that had accumulated in his heart, for it was 'beyond endurance'. He
began by asserting that everybody was laughing at him and that he
was 'being led by the nose'. 'Damn the expression,' he cried shrilly at
once, noticing her smile, 'let it be "by the nose", for it's true! No,
madam, the time has come; please, understand it's not the time for
laughter or female coquetry now. We're not in the boudoir of a
mincing society lady, but, we are, as it were, two abstract creatures in
a balloon who have met to speak the truth.' (He was, of course, getting confused and could not find the right words in which to express
his thoughts, correct though they were.) 'It is you – you, madam –
who were responsible for my giving up my old job. I took up my

present one entirely for your sake, for the sake of your ambition. You smile sarcastically? Don't look so triumphant, and don't be in such a hurry. I want you to know, madam, I want you to know that I could, that I should have been able to cope with this job of mine, and not only with this job alone but with a dozen such jobs, because I've got the ability. But with you, madam, I can't cope with it, for when you are present I have no abilities. Two centres of administration cannot co-exist, and you've created two such centres – one in my office and the other in your boudoir, two centres of power; and I won't allow it, I won't allow it! In the service, as in marriage, there must be only one centre, for two are impossible. How have you repaid me?' he went on shouting. 'Our married life has consisted only in your demonstrating to me all the time, every hour, that I'm a nonentity, that I'm a fool and even a villain, while I have been forced to prove to you all the time, every hour, and in a most humiliating way, that I was not a nonentity, that I was not at all such a fool and that I impress everybody with my honourable character. Well, don't you think it's humiliating for both of us?' At this point he began stamping rapidly with both feet on the carpet, so that Mrs Lembke was obliged to draw herself up with a look of stern dignity. He calmed down quickly, but grew sentimental and began sobbing (yes, sobbing), smiting his breast for almost five minutes, getting more and more beside himself because of Mrs Lembke's profound silence. At length he made a fatal mistake and let out that he was jealous of Peter Verkhovensky. Realizing that he had made an utter fool of himself, he went off the deep end and began shouting that he would not allow anyone to deny God, that he would close down her 'impudent *salon* of unbelievers', that a governor was in duty bound to believe in God and 'hence his wife was, too'; that he would not put up with the young men; that 'you, madam, out of a sense of your own dignity, should have taken your husband's part and have stood up for his intelligence even if he had no abilities (and I'm not at all without abilities), and yet it is you who're really responsible for everyone here despising me, it is you who have put them all up to it!' He shouted that he would put an end to the woman question, that he'd smoke it out, that he'd forbid and break up the idiotic fête in aid of the governesses (to hell with them!) to-morrow, and that the first governess he came across he'd throw out of the province to-morrow morning 'with a Cossack, madam!' 'Just to

spite you, just to spite you,' he screamed. 'Do you know,' he shouted
– 'do you know that your blackguards are inciting the men at the
factory and that I'm aware of it? Do you know that they're scattering
revolutionary leaflets deliberately, de-li-berately, madam! Do you
know that I know the names of four of these blackguards, and that
I'm going off my head, going off my head completely, com-pletely!'
But at this point Mrs Lembke suddenly broke her silence and declared sternly that she herself had long known about the criminal
plans and that the whole thing was absurd, that he had taken too serious a view of it, and that as for the foolish boys, she knew not only
four, but all of them (she told a lie); but that she had no intention
whatever of going off her head because of it, but, on the contrary,
trusted more than ever her own intelligence and had hopes of bringing the whole affair to a peaceful conclusion: to encourage the young
people, bring them back to their senses, prove to them suddenly and
unexpectedly that their plots were known, and then point out new
aims for more reasonable and more beneficial activity to them.

Oh, what a shock that was to Mr Lembke! Learning that Peter
Verkhovensky had again deceived him and again made him look such
a fool, that he had told her much more and much sooner than he had
told him, and, finally, that Peter Verkhovensky was quite likely the
chief instigator of all these criminal plots, he flew into a rage. 'I want
you to know, you fatuous but poisonous woman,' he cried, snapping
his bonds all at once, 'I want you to know that I shall arrest your unworthy lover at once, put him in chains and have him taken to a fortress or – I shall jump out of the window this minute before your very
eyes!' In reply to this tirade Mrs Lembke, turning green with rage, at
once burst into prolonged and ringing laughter, going off into shrill
peals, such as one can hear at a French play when a Parisian actress,
imported at a salary of 100,000 roubles and playing flirts, laughs in
her husband's face for daring to be jealous of her. Von Lembke was
about to rush to the window, but suddenly stopped dead and, folding
his hands on his chest and pale as a corpse, looked at his laughing
spouse with baleful eyes. 'Do you know, do you know, Julia,' he said
in a breathless and imploring voice, 'do you know that I, too, can do
something?' But at the renewed outburst of even louder laughter
which followed his last words, he clenched his teeth, groaned and
rushed, not to the window, but at his wife with his raised fist! He did

not bring it down – no, a hundred times no; but it was the end. Oblivious of everything, he rushed to his study and, dressed as he was, flung himself face downwards on the bed, wrapped himself convulsively in a sheet, pulling it over his head, and lay like that for two hours – without falling asleep, without thinking of anything, with a heavy load on his heart and blank, stark despair in his soul. From time to time a violent, agonizing shudder shook his whole body feverishly. All sorts of incoherent images floated into his mind without any relation to anything: he would think, for instance, of the old clock which used to hang on the wall of his room in Petersburg about fifteen years ago and which had lost its minute-hand; or of the high-spirited Civil Servant Millebois, with whom he had once caught a sparrow in Alexandrovsky Park and had laughed so that they could be heard all over the park, remembering that one of them had already reached the rank of collegiate assessor. I suppose he must have fallen asleep at about seven in the morning and, without being aware of it, slept soundly with pleasant dreams. Waking about ten o'clock, he suddenly jumped wildly out of bed, remembered everything in a flash, and gave himself a resounding slap on the forehead: he had no breakfast and refused to receive Blum, or the Police Commissioner, or the official who came to remind him that the members of a certain committee were expecting him to take the chair that morning; he did not listen to anything and did not want to understand, but rushed like a madman to his wife's rooms. There Sofia Antonovna, an old gentlewoman who had lived with Mrs Lembke for many years, explained to him that his wife had left at ten o'clock with a large company in three carriages to pay a call on Mrs Stavrogin at Skvoreshniki, to inspect the house for the second fête that was planned to take place in a fortnight, and that the visit had been arranged with Mrs Stavrogin three days before. Stunned by the news, Lembke returned to his study and impetuously ordered the carriage. He could hardly wait for it to be brought. His soul was yearning for Julia – to look at her, to be near her for five minutes; perhaps she would glance at him, notice him, smile at him as she used to, forgive him – oh! 'What's the matter with the carriage?' Mechanically he opened a thick book lying on the table (sometimes he liked to try his fortune by the book, opening it at random and reading the first three lines on the top of the right-hand page). What he read was: '*Tout est pour le mieux dans le meilleur des mondes possibles.*' Voltaire, *Candide*. He snorted and ran out to get into his carriage: 'To Skvoreshniki!' The driver said afterwards that his master urged him on to drive faster all the way, but that as soon as they got near the mansion he suddenly told him to turn round and drive back to town: 'Faster, please! Faster!' But before they reached the town ramparts, 'he told me to stop again, got out of the carriage, crossed the road and went into a field; I thought he wanted to relieve himself, but he stopped and started looking at the flowers; stood there for hours, he did; it was queer all right, it was; made me wonder, I can tell you.' That was the driver's testimony. I remember the weather that morning: it was a bright, cold, but windy September day; before Lembke, as he had walked off the road, stretched the harsh landscape of bare fields from which the crops had long been gathered; the howling wind tossed the wretched remnants of some dying yellow flowers. Did he want to compare himself and his fate to those stunted flowers battered by the autumn and the frost? I don't think so. Indeed, I can't help feeling that he did not do anything of the sort, and that he was not even aware of the existence of the flowers, in spite of the evidence of the driver and of the Police Inspector of the first district, who drove up at that moment in the Police Commissioner's carriage and who asserted afterwards that he really did find the Governor standing with a bunch of yellow flowers in his hand. The Police Inspector – an ecstatically administrative figure, Vassily Ivanovich Filibusterov by name – had only been in our town a short time, but had already distinguished himself and became known far and wide as a quite incredibly conscientious officer who was inordinately zealous in the execution of his duties and as an inveterate drunkard. Jumping out of the carriage, and not in the least surprised at the sight of the Governor's occupation, he rapped out his report with the cocksure air of a lunatic that 'disturbances have broken out in the town'.

'What? What was that?' Lembke turned round to him with a stern face, but without the slightest surprise or any recollection of his carriage and his driver, just as though he had been in his own study.

'Police Inspector of the first district, Filibusterov, sir. There's rioting in town.'

'Filibusters?' Lembke repeated thoughtfully.

'Yes, sir. The Spigulin workmen are rioting.'

'The Spigulin men!'

The name 'Spigulin' seemed to remind him of something. He even gave a start and put his finger to his forehead: 'The Spigulin men!' He went silently and without hurrying to his carriage, still deep in thought, took his seat and told the driver to drive to the town. The Police Inspector followed in the open carriage.

I suppose many interesting things must have occurred to him vaguely during that drive, but I doubt whether he had any clear idea or any definite intention as he drove into the square in front of the Governor's residence. But the moment he saw the crowd of 'rioters' drawn up resolutely in orderly ranks, the police cordon, the helpless (and quite likely deliberately helpless) Police Commissioner, and the general expectation directed towards him, all the blood rushed to his heart. He got out of his carriage looking very pale.

'Caps off!' he said in a hardly audible voice, panting for breath. 'On your knees!' he shrieked unexpectedly, unexpectedly for himself, too, and it was perhaps in that very unexpectedness that one must look for an explanation of what followed. It's just the sort of thing that happens on the snow-covered hills at Shrove-tide: is it possible for a sledge to stop in the middle of a hill as it rushes headlong down the slope? To his misfortune, Lembke had all his life been distinguished for the imperturbability of his character, and never shouted at any-one or stamped his feet; and such people are much more dangerous if for some reason their sledge should happen to hurtle down a hillside suddenly. Everything was going round and round before his eyes.

'Filibusters!' he screamed even more shrilly and more absurdly, and his voice broke.

He stood there, still not knowing what he was going to do, but knowing and feeling with all his being that he would most certainly do something at once.

'Lord!' someone cried in the crowd. A young fellow began to cross himself; three or four men were really about to kneel, but the rest moved forward three steps in one mass and, suddenly, all began to yell: 'Sir – we were engaged for the whole time – the manager – you can't say –' and so on. It was impossible to make anything out.

Alas, Lembke was not in a condition to make anything out: the flowers were still in his hands. The riot was as real to him as the 'covered wagons' were to Stepan Verkhovensky a short while ago.

And in the crowd of 'rioters' who were glaring at him he could see
Peter Verkhovensky going from one man to another and 'inciting'
them, Peter Verkhovensky, who had never left his mind for a moment
since the day before, Peter Verkhovensky – the hated Peter Verkhovensky.

'Birch-rods!' he shouted still more unexpectedly.

A dead silence ensued.

That was what happened at the very beginning, according to the
most reliable accounts and my own conjectures. But the accounts of
what happened afterwards are not so exact, and the same is true of my
conjectures. There are some facts, however.

To begin with, the birch-rods materialized somehow too quickly;
they had obviously been got ready beforehand by the Commissioner
of Police, just in case they might be needed. Only two men, or three
at most, were flogged; I am absolutely sure of that. The report that
all the men or, at any rate, half of the men were flogged is sheer invention. The story that some poor gentlewoman who happened to
pass by at the time was seized and for some reason also flogged is pure
nonsense; yet I myself read the report about this gentlewoman in one
of the Petersburg papers a few days later. Many people in the town
talked of a woman called Avdotya Tarapygin, who was an inmate of
the workhouse near the cemetery. She was said to have been on her
way back to the workhouse from a visit and, passing the square, to
have pushed her way through the crowd out of natural curiosity.
Seeing what was going on, she cried out, 'What a shame!' and spat.
For doing that, it is alleged, she had been seized and 'dealt with'.
That incident was not only published in the papers, but even led to a
subscription being raised on her behalf on the spur of the moment. I
subscribed twenty copecks myself. And what do you think? It appears now that no woman by the name of Tarapygin ever lived in the
workhouse. I went to make inquiries at the workhouse near the cemetery myself, and they had never heard of a woman called Tarapygin
there; what's more, they were quite offended when I told them about
the rumour that was going round. But I mention this non-existent
Avdotya Tarapygin because what happened to her (if she really
existed) nearly happened to Mr Verkhovensky; and indeed it is quite
possible that the incident in which Mr Verkhovensky became involved had given rise to the rumour – that is to say, in its passage

from mouth to mouth he was simply transformed into a Mrs Tara-pygin. The thing that puzzles me most was how he had succeeded in giving me the slip the moment we walked into the square. Anticipating some trouble, I meant to take him round the square straight to the entrance of the Governor's residence, but I am afraid my own curiosity was rather aroused and I stopped only for one minute to inquire what was happening from the first person I came across. Suddenly I realized that Mr Verkhovensky was no longer at my side. Instinctively I ran off immediately to look for him in the most dangerous place; for some reason, I had a premonition that his sledge, too, was hurtling down the hill. And, to be sure, I found him in the very centre of things. I remember grasping him by the hand; but he gazed quietly and proudly at me with a look of immense authority?

'Cher,' he said in a voice in which the quivering note of a man in anguish could be perceived, 'if they all settle things so unceremoniously here in the square before us, what could we expect from *that one* – if he should happen to act on his own authority.'

And trembling with indignation and with an irresistible desire to defy them, he pointed his stern, accusing finger at Filibusterov, who was standing and glaring at us only two paces away.

'*That one!*' cried the policeman, blind with rage. 'Which that one? And who are you?' He rushed up to him, clenching his fist. 'Who are you?' he roared furiously, hysterically and desperately (I may add that he knew perfectly well who Stepan Verkhovensky was).

Another moment and he would, of course, have caught Mr Verkhovensky by the scruff of the neck, but, fortunately, Lembke turned his head at his cry. He looked bewilderedly but intently at Mr Verkhovensky, as though wondering who he might be, and then suddenly waved his hand impatiently. Filibusterov stopped short. I dragged Mr Verkhovensky away from the crowd. However, he was probably glad himself to get away.

'Home, home,' I insisted. 'It is no doubt thanks to Lembke that you were not beaten.'

'You go, my friend. I'm to blame for exposing you to danger. You have a future and a career of some sort, but I – *mon heure est sonnée.*'

He firmly mounted the steps of the Governor's residence. The porter knew me, and I told him that we were both going to see Mrs Lembke. In the reception-room we sat down and waited. I did not want to leave my friend, but thought it unnecessary to say anything more to him. He looked like a man who had made up his mind to die for his country. We did not sit down side by side, but in different corners of the room, I nearer to the entrance door; he facing me, in the far end of the room, his head lowered pensively, leaning lightly on his walking-stick. He held his wide-brimmed hat in his left hand. We sat like that for about ten minutes.

2

Lembke suddenly came in hurriedly in the company of the Police Commissioner, looked absent-mindedly at us and, paying no attention to us, was about to enter his study on the right. But Mr Verkhovensky got up and stopped before him, barring the way. The tall figure of Mr Verkhovensky, which was so unlike any other, made an impression; Lembke stopped.

'Who's this?' he muttered, looking bewildered, as though addressing his question to the Police Commissioner, without, however, turning his head towards him, as he went on gazing at Mr Verkhovensky.

'Retired collegiate assessor Stepan Verkhovensky, sir,' Stepan Verkhovensky replied with a dignified inclination of the head.

The Governor went on gazing at him with a very blank expression, though.

'What is it?' he asked laconically, like a man in authority, turning his ear with fastidious impatience towards Mr Verkhovensky, having finally taken him for an ordinary person with a written petition of some sort.

'My house was to-day searched by an official who was acting in your name, sir. I should therefore like to –'

'Name? Name?' Lembke asked impatiently, as though he suddenly remembered something.

Mr Verkhovensky repeated his name with an even more dignified air.

'Oh–h! It's that – er – hotbed. ... You, sir, have shown yourself to be – er – you're a professor? A professor?'

'I once had the honour of delivering some lectures to the young men of a certain university.'

'The young men!' Lembke seemed to give a violent start, though I

am ready to bet that he understood very little of what it was all about
and not even with whom he was talking.

'I shan't permit it, sir!' he shouted, suddenly getting very angry.
'I won't permit young men. It's all these revolutionary leaflets. It's an
attack on society, sir, an attack by pirates filibusters. ... What is it
you want?'

'On the contrary, sir, it is your wife who wants me to read something to-morrow at her fête. I don't want anything. I merely came to
demand my rights.'

'At the fête? There will be no fête. I won't allow your fête, sir!
Lectures? Lectures?' he screamed, beside himself.

'I'd appreciate it, sir, if you would be so good as to talk to me more
civilly, and not stamp and shout at me as if I were a boy.'

'I don't suppose you realize who you're talking to, sir!' cried
Lembke, turning red in the face.

'Perfectly, sir.'

'I'm protecting society, sir, while you're destroying it! Destroying!
You, sir – wait, though, I believe I know something about you. It was
you who were employed as a tutor in Mrs Stavrogin's house, weren't
you?'

'Yes, sir, I was – er – a tutor in – er – Mrs Stavrogin's house.'

'And for twenty years you've been forcing all the ideas that have
now come to a head on people – the fruits of your teaching we're
gathering now. It was you I saw just now in the square. Beware, sir,
beware! The ideas you stand for are well known. You may be sure
that I'm keeping an eye on you. I can't permit your lectures, sir. I
can't, sir. Don't come with such requests to me.'

He was again about to pass on.

'I repeat, sir, that you are mistaken: it was your wife who asked me
to give – not a lecture, but a literary reading of some kind, at to-
morrow's fête. But I decline to do so myself now. My request to you,
sir, is that you should explain to me, if you can, why my house was
searched to-day – what was the reason for the search? Some of my
books and papers, and private letters, which I value for sentimental
reasons, were taken away from me and trundled through the streets
in a wheel-barrow –'

'Who made the search?' said Lembke, recollecting himself completely with a start and suddenly flushing crimson.

He turned quickly to the Police Commissioner. At that moment the tall, stooping, gawky figure of Blum appeared in the doorway.

'That's the official who made it,' said Mr Verkhovensky, pointing to him.

Blum stepped forward with a guilty, but far from contrite, look.

'*Vous ne faites que des bêtises,*' Lembke remarked to him in a vexed and angry tone, and suddenly he was transformed and completely recovered his senses.

'I'm sorry,' he murmured, overwhelmed with confusion and turning red in the face. 'It was all, I suppose, a blunder, a misunderstanding – just a misunderstanding.'

'As a young man, sir,' Mr Verkhovensky observed, 'I happened to be the witness of a very characteristic incident. In the corridor of a theatre one evening, a man went up quickly to another and gave him a resounding slap in the face in the presence of a crowd of people. Noticing immediately, however, that his victim was not at all the person he had intended to slap, but quite a different person who resembled him slightly, he said spitefully and in a hurry, like a man who cannot afford to waste his time, just as you, sir, did just now: "I'm sorry, I've made a mistake; it was a misunderstanding, just a misunderstanding." And when the insulted man quite naturally went on protesting in a loud voice, he observed to him with great annoyance, "But I'm telling you that it was a misunderstanding, so what are you shouting for?"'

'Yes, of course, I see,' Lembke said with a wry smile; 'it's very amusing, I'm sure; but – but can't you see how unhappy I am myself?'

He almost screamed the last words and – and, I believe, he felt like hiding his face in his hands.

This unexpectedly painful exclamation, almost a sob, was unbearable. That was probably the first moment since the previous day of his full and clear realization of all that had happened, and it was followed instantaneously by complete and humiliating despair that could not be concealed – another moment and he would perhaps have burst out sobbing. Mr Verkhovensky looked wildly at him at first, then he suddenly bowed his head.

'Sir,' he said in a deeply sympathetic voice, 'do not trouble yourself with my peevish complaint any longer, and just tell them to return my books and letters. ...'

He was interrupted. For at that very moment Mrs Lembke returned noisily with all the party that had accompanied her. But I should like at this point to describe what occurred in much greater detail.

3

To begin with, all of them, from all the three carriages, entered the reception-room in a crowd. There was a separate entrance to Mrs Lembke's private rooms on the left hand of the entrance hall. This time, however, they all went through the large reception-room, and I think that was because Stepan Verkhovensky was there, and because Mrs Lembke had been told about everything that had happened to him, as well as the incident with the Spigulin men, as soon as she drove into the town. It was Lyamshin who had managed to tell her. He had been left behind for some misdemeanour, and did not take part in the trip to Skvoreshniki, so that he had learnt about it before anyone else. With malicious glee he galloped off on a hired Cossack nag along the road to Skvoreshniki, hoping to meet the returning cavalcade with the glad tidings. I expect Mrs Lembke, in spite of her great determination, must have felt a little embarrassed on hearing such extraordinary news – but only for an instant. The political aspect of the affair, for example, would hardly have worried her, for Peter Verkhovensky had impressed upon her three or four times that it would be a good thing to give the Spigulin rowdies a good flogging, and Peter had certainly for some time been regarded by her as a great authority. 'But,' she must have thought to herself, 'I shall make him pay for it all the same,' the 'him', of course, referring to her husband. I may add in passing that this time Peter, as though on purpose, had not taken part in the expedition, and no one had seen him since early morning. I must also mention, by the way, that after having received her visitors, Mrs Stavrogin returned with them to the town (in the same carriage as Mrs Lembke) to be present at the last meeting of the committee which was arranging the fête next day. She, too, was of course highly interested, and perhaps even agitated by the news Lyamshin brought concerning Mr Verkhovensky.

The settling of accounts with Mr Lembke began at once. Alas, he felt it coming the moment he caught sight of his excellent spouse. Quite openly and with a most charming smile she went quickly up to

Mr Verkhovensky, held out her delightfully gloved hand to him and overwhelmed him with most flattering compliments, as though the only thing in the world she wanted to do that morning was to rush up to Mr Verkhovensky and be extremely kind to him because at last she saw him in her house. Not a single hint of the search that morning, as though she knew nothing about it. Not a word to her husband, not one glance in his direction, as though he had not been there at all. What's more, she at once peremptorily confiscated Mr Verkhovensky and carried him off to the drawing-room, as though she had had no arguments with Lembke and as though she did not think it worth her while to continue them if there had been any. Again let me repeat: it seems to me that notwithstanding her high and mighty tone, Julia Lembke made another bad mistake in this particular instance. Karmazinov was particularly helpful to her at this juncture. (He had taken part in the visit to Mrs Stavrogin's country house at Julia Lembke's special request and in that way had paid his visit, though indirectly, to Mrs Stavrogin, which, low-spirited as she was, greatly delighted her.) On seeing Mr Verkhovensky, he called out to him while still in the doorway (he came in after the rest) and rushed up to embrace him, interrupting even Mrs Lembke.

'Haven't seen you for ages, my dear fellow! At last. ... *Excellent ami.*'

He went through the ceremony of exchanging kisses, offering his cheek. Mr Verkhovensky was so flustered that he could not help imprinting a kiss on it.

'*Cher*,' he said to me that evening, recalling the events of that day, 'I wondered at that moment which of us was more contemptible – he who was embracing me with the idea of humiliating me, or I who despised him and his cheek, but who was kissing it, though I might have turned away – horrible!'

'Well, tell me, my dear fellow, tell me everything,' Karmazinov mumbled in his affected voice, as though Mr Verkhovensky could possibly tell him the story of his life during the last twenty-five years. But that stupid piece of frivolity was considered to be 'good form'.

'Remember, the last time we met was at a dinner in Moscow in honour of Professor Granovsky, twenty-four years ago,' Mr Verkhovensky began quite reasonably (and hence not at all according to 'good form').

'*Ce cher homme,*' Karmazinov interrupted shrilly and familiarly, squeezing his shoulder a little too amicably, 'but, my dear Mrs Lembke, do take us to your drawing-room. He'll sit down there and tell us everything.'

'And yet,' Mr Verkhovensky went on complaining to me that evening, shaking with anger, 'I never was on intimate terms with that bad-tempered old baggage. At the time we were almost boys and I'd begun to hate him even then – just as he had me, of course.'

Mrs Lembke's *salon* filled up quickly. Mrs Stavrogin was particularly excited, though she tried her best to appear indifferent, but I caught her once or twice glancing with hatred at Karmazinov and with anger at Mr Verkhovensky – she was angry with him in anticipation, angry with him out of jealousy, out of love: if Mr Verkhovensky had been guilty of some stupid blunder this time and had allowed himself to be snubbed by Karmazinov in the presence of the whole company, she would, I can't help thinking, have immediately jumped up and thrashed him. I have forgotten to say that Lisa was also there, and I had never seen her more radiant, carelessly gay and happy. Mr Drozdov was there too, of course. In the crowd of young ladies and meretricious young men, who composed Mrs Lembke's usual retinue and among whom this meretriciousness was taken for gaiety and cheap cynicism for wit, I noticed one or two new faces: a very obsequious Pole, who had just arrived in our town, a German doctor, a healthy-looking old man who kept laughing aloud and with enjoyment at his own jokes, and, lastly, a very young princeling from Petersburg who looked like an automaton but had the grand manners of a statesman and wore a terribly high collar. But I could see that Julia Lembke thought greatly of this visitor and was even worried about the impression her *salon* was making on him.

'*Cher M. Karmazinov,*' Mr Verkhovensky began, assuming a very picturesque pose on the sofa and suddenly beginning to talk in a voice which was no less affected than Karmazinov's, '*cher M. Karmazinov,* the life of a man of our time and of well-known convictions must appear very monotonous after an interval of twenty years.'

The German burst out into a loud and abrupt laugh which sounded just as though he had neighed, under the impression that Mr Verkhovensky had said something terribly amusing. Mr Verkhovensky looked at him with studied surprise, without, however, producing the slightest effect. The prince, too, glanced at the German, turning his head and collar to him and putting on his pince-nez without showing the slightest curiosity, though.

'... Must appear monotonous,' Mr Verkhovensky repeated on purpose, drawling each word unblushingly. 'My life, too, has been like that during this quarter of a century, *et comme on trouve partout plus de moines que de raison* and as I'm entirely in agreement with this sentiment, it has turned out that during the whole of this quarter of a century –'

'*C'est charmant, les moines,*' Mrs Lembke whispered, turning to Mrs Stavrogin who was sitting beside her.

Mrs Stavrogin replied by a proud look. But Karmazinov could not bear the success of the French phrase and interrupted Mr Verkhovensky quickly and shrilly.

'For my part, I'm quite satisfied so far as that is concerned, and I've been living in Karlsruhe for the last seven years. And when last year the Town Council decided to lay down a new water-pipe, I felt in my heart that this question of water-pipes in Karlsruhe was much dearer to me than all the questions of my beloved mother-country – during the whole period of these so-called reforms.'

'I can't help sympathizing with you,' Mr Verkhovensky sighed, inclining his head impressively, 'much as it hurts my feelings.'

Mrs Lembke was triumphant: the conversation was becoming both profound and political.

'A sewage pipe?' the doctor inquired loudly.

'A water-pipe, doctor, a water-pipe, and I even helped them to draw up the plan.'

The doctor went off into a peal of laughter. Many people also burst out laughing, this time in the doctor's face, who did not seem to be aware of it, but was very pleased that everyone was laughing.

'I'm afraid I must disagree with you, Karmazinov,' Mrs Lembke hastened to put in. 'Karlsruhe is all very well, but you are fond of mystifications, and this time we shan't believe you. What Russian writer has created so many modern characters, has made us aware of so many modern problems, and has drawn our attention to these highly important modern points which make up the modern type of statesman? You, only you and no one else. You can assure us as much as you like of your indifference to your native country and your frightful interest in the Karlsruhe water-pipes! Ha, ha!'

'Why, I don't deny,' Karmazinov declared in his mincing voice, 'that I have shown up all the faults of the Slavophils in the character of Pogozhev and all the faults of the Westerners in the character of Nikodimov –'

'Not *all*, surely,' Lyamshin whispered softly.

'But I do this just by the way, to kill time which hangs on my hands and – to satisfy the persistent demands of my fellow countrymen.'

'I suppose you know, Mr Verkhovensky,' Mrs Lembke went on ecstatically, 'that to-morrow we shall have the joy of hearing the delightful lines – one of the latest of Mr Karmazinov's most exquisite literary inspirations – it is called *Merci*. He declares in this piece that he will write no more, that nothing in the world will make him, even if an angel from heaven or, better still, our best society were to beg him to change his mind. In a word, he's laying down his pen for good, and this charming *Merci* is addressed to the public as a token of gratitude for the constant enthusiasm with which it has for so many years followed his unremitting services to honest Russian thought.'

Julia Lembke was quite blissfully happy.

'Yes, I'm going to make my farewell. I shall say my *Merci* and depart, and there – in Karlsruhe – I shall close my eyes.' Karmazinov was gradually growing sentimental.

Like many of our great writers (and we have so many great writers), he could not resist flattery and began to weaken at once, notwithstanding his penetrating wit. But I cannot help thinking that this is excusable. I am told that one of our Shakespeares was careless enough to declare in a private conversation that 'we, *great men*, can't do otherwise', etc., and did not even notice it.

'There in Karlsruhe I shall close my eyes. All that is left for us great men after our work's done is to close our eyes as soon as possible without seeking a reward. I, too, shall do so.'

'Let me have your address, sir, and I'll come to Karlsruhe to visit your grave,' said the German, going off into a peal of laughter.

'Nowadays they even transport the dead by train,' one of the insignificant young men said unexpectedly.

Lyamshin squealed with delight. Julia Lembke frowned. Nicholas Stavrogin came in.

'And I was told that you were dragged off to the police-station,' he said loudly, addressing himself first of all to Mr Verkhovensky.

'No, that was only a matter of private *policy*,' Mr Verkhovensky punned.

'But I hope that it will not have the slightest influence on my request,' Mrs Lembke again put in quickly. 'I hope that in spite of that unfortunate incident, which I can't for the life of me understand, you will not disappoint our eager expectations and rob us of the enjoyment of hearing your reading at our literary matinée.'

'I'm afraid I – er – I don't know – now –'

'My dear Mrs Stavrogin, I really am so unlucky – and fancy just when I was so anxious to make the personal acquaintance of one of our most remarkable and independent Russian thinkers, and now Mr Verkhovensky suddenly expresses his intention of deserting us.'

'Your compliment, madam, was uttered in so audible a voice that, of course, I couldn't help hearing it,' Mr Verkhovensky said with a flourish, emphasizing every word, 'but I cannot believe that my humble person is so indispensable at your fête to-morrow. However, I –'

'You're spoiling him!' cried Peter Verkhovensky, bursting into the room. 'I've only just taken him in hand and suddenly – in one morning – a search, an arrest, a police officer seizes him by the collar, and now ladies are saying sweet nothings to him in the drawing-room of the Governor of our town! Why, every bone in his body must be aching with rapture; he never dreamt of such a triumph. Dear me, I expect he'll start denouncing the socialists now!'

'Impossible, Peter! Socialism is too great an idea for Mr Verkhovensky not to realize it' – Mrs Lembke took Mr Verkhovensky's part energetically.

'A great idea, but those who profess it are not always giants, *et brisons-là, mon cher*,' Mr Verkhovensky concluded, addressing his son and rising gracefully from his seat.

But at this moment a most unexpected thing happened. Von Lembke had been in the drawing-room for some time, but no one seemed to have noticed him, though they had all seen him come in. In accordance with her old policy, Mrs Lembke continued to ignore him. He took up his position near the door and listened gloomily and with a stern face to the conversation. Hearing the thinly disguised references to the events of the morning, he began stirring agitatedly; first he stared at the Prince, evidently struck by the protruding corners of his stiffly starched collar; then he seemed to give a sudden start on hearing the voice of Peter Verkhovensky and seeing him rushing in, and as soon as Mr Verkhovensky had finished his sentence about the socialists, he suddenly went up to him, pushing aside Lyamshin, who at once jumped back with an affected gesture of surprise, rubbing his shoulder and pretending to have been terribly hurt.

'That's enough!' said von Lembke, gripping the dismayed Mr Verkhovensky forcefully by the hand and squeezing it with all his might in his. 'Enough! The filibusters of our time have been found out. Not another word. Measures have been taken.'

He spoke in a loud voice which could be heard by all in the room, and concluded energetically. The impression he created was painful. They all felt that something was wrong. I saw Mrs Lembke turn pale. The effect was heightened by a stupid accident. After announcing that measures had been taken, Lembke turned sharply and walked quickly out of the room, but after taking a couple of steps, he tripped over a rug, lurched forward, and almost fell. He stood still for a moment, stared at the spot where he had tripped over, and saying aloud, 'Have it changed!' walked out of the room. Mrs Lembke ran after him. After she was gone, an uproar arose in which it was difficult to make anything out. Some said that he was 'upset', others that he was 'touched'; still others tapped their foreheads; Lyamshin, in the corner, put his two fingers above his forehead. Hints were made at some domestic scenes – all in a whisper, of course. No one thought of leaving, for all were expecting something. I don't know what Mrs Lembke had managed to do, but five minutes later she came back, doing her best to appear calm. She replied evasively that Mr Lembke was a little excited, but that that was nothing, that he had been like that since childhood, that she knew 'much better', and that the fête next day would, of course, cheer him up. She then said a few more flattering words to Mr Verkhovensky, but simply out of politeness, and concluded by a loud invitation to the members of the committee to open their meeting. At this point those who were not members of the committee began to prepare to go home; but the painful incidents of this fatal day were not yet at an end.

The moment Nicholas Stavrogin entered the room I noticed that Lisa threw a quick and penetrating glance at him and did not take her eyes off him for a long time afterwards. She stared at him so long that at last it attracted attention. I saw Mr Drozdov leaning over to her from behind, evidently wishing to whisper something to her, but he apparently changed his mind and drew himself up quickly, looking round at everybody guiltily. Nicholas Stavrogin, too, aroused everybody's curiosity: his face was paler than usual and he looked very absent-minded. Having flung his question at Mr Verkhovensky as soon as he entered the room, he seemed to forget about him at once, and I really think that he even forgot to go up to Mrs Lembke. He did not look once at Lisa, not because he did not want to, but, I maintain, because he did not notice her, either. And suddenly, after a short pause following Mrs Lembke's invitation to open the meeting without wasting any more time – Lisa spoke in a ringing and deliberately loud voice. She called to Nicholas Stavrogin.

'Mr Stavrogin,' she said, 'a certain captain, who calls himself your relation, the brother of your wife, and whose name is Lebyatkin, keeps writing improper letters to me in which he complains of you and promises to tell me some secrets about you. If he really is a relation of yours, I'd be grateful if you would forbid him to insult me and save me from unpleasantness.'

There was a fearful challenge in those words – everyone realized that. The accusation was unmistakable, though perhaps rather unexpected even to her. I got the impression of a man who, screwing up his eyes, is about to throw himself off a roof.

But Stavrogin's answer was even more extraordinary.

To begin with, it was certainly very strange that he was not at all surprised, and listened to Lisa with unruffled attention. Neither confusion nor anger was reflected on his face. He replied to the fatal question simply, firmly, and with an air of absolute readiness.

'Yes, I have the misfortune to be a relation of that man. I have been the husband of his sister, née Lebyatkin, for nearly five years. You may be sure I shall convey your demands to him as soon as possible and I promise you he will never trouble you again.'

I shall never forget the horror on Mrs Stavrogin's face. She got up from her seat with a frenzied look, her right hand raised before her as though she were defending herself against an assailant. Stavrogin looked at her, at Lisa, at the spectators, and suddenly smiled with infinite arrogance; he walked out of the room unhurriedly. Everyone saw how Lisa jumped up from the sofa the moment Stavrogin turned to go and quite plainly made a movement to run after him; but she recollected herself and did not run after him; she left the room quietly, without saying a word to anyone and without looking at anyone, accompanied, of course, by Mr Drozdov, who rushed after her.

I shall say nothing of the uproar and the talks in the town that evening. Mrs Stavrogin shut herself up in her town house and Stavrogin, I was told, drove straight to Skvoreshniki without seeing his mother. Mr Verkhovensky sent me that evening to *cette chère amie* to beg her to permit him to go to see her, but she would not receive me. He was terribly shocked; he wept. 'Such a marriage!' he kept repeating, 'Such a marriage! Such a frightful thing to happen in the family!' However, he remembered Karmazinov, too, and abused him terribly. He was getting himself ready energetically for next day's reading and – the artistic temperament – rehearsed it before a looking-glass, trying to memorize all the puns and jokes he had made in the course of his life and which he had carefully written down in a note-book, so as to insert them into his reading next day.

'My friend,' he said to me, evidently wishing to justify himself, 'I do this for the sake of a great idea. *Cher ami*, for the first time in twenty years I've begun to move and suddenly I'm off – whither I know not – but I'm off. ...'

PART THREE

1

The Fête. Part One

I

THE FÊTE DID TAKE PLACE NOTWITHSTANDING THE PERPLEXI-
ties of the previous 'Spigulin' day. I can't help thinking that even if
Lembke had died that very night, the fête would still have taken place
next morning – so special was the significance Mrs Lembke ascribed
to it. Alas, up to the last minute she remained completely blind and
had no idea of the real state of public opinion. In the end no one believed that the festive day would pass without some distressing incident, without some 'catastrophe', as some people expressed it, rubbing their hands in anticipation. Many people, indeed, tried to assume
a most gloomy and knowing air; but, generally speaking, every public scandal cheers a Russian up no end. It is true that what we felt was
something much more serious than the mere longing for a scandal:
there was a general sense of irritation, something implacably malicious; it seemed as though everyone were thoroughly sick of everything. The prevalent public feeling was one of a vague, strained sort
of cynicism, a forced cynicism, as it were. The ladies alone were not
in the least vague, but that, too, only on one particular point: –
namely, their relentless hatred of Julia Lembke. The ladies of all political opinions were agreed about that. And Mrs Lembke, poor thing,
did not even suspect it; up to the last hour she was convinced that she
had a 'following' and that all of them were still 'fanatically loyal' to
her.

I have already hinted that all sorts of low-class individuals had made
an appearance among us. In troubled times of uncertainty or transition

all sorts of low individuals always appear everywhere. I am not talking about the so-called 'progressives', who are always in a greater hurry than everyone else (that is their chief concern) and whose aims, though mostly absurd, are more or less definite. No, I am speaking only of the rabble. This rabble, which you will find in any society, usually rises to the surface in every period of transition, and is not only without any aim, but also without an inkling of an idea, merely expressing with all its strength unrest and impatience. And yet this rabble, without realizing it itself, almost always finds itself under the command of the small crowd of 'progressives', who act with a definite aim, and it is they who direct this scum where they like, provided they themselves are not composed of utter idiots, which, however, happens, too. It is said, for instance, in our town, now that it is all over, that Peter Verkhovensky was controlled by the *Internationale*, Mrs Lembke by Peter Verkhovensky, while she, in turn, controlled, under his command, every kind of rabble. The most sound intellects among us are now surprised at themselves: how could they have been so stupid at the time? What our troubled times were about or what the transition was we were passing through, I don't know, and I don't suppose anyone knows – except perhaps some of those visitors of ours. And yet the most worthless individuals suddenly gained a predominant influence and began loudly criticizing everything sacred, whereas before they had never dared open their mouths, while the foremost people among us, who had hitherto satisfactorily kept the upper hand, began suddenly listening to them, keeping silent themselves; and some of them most shamelessly tittered their approval. People like Lyamshin, Telyatnikov, landowners like Gogol's Tentyotnikov, snivelling home-bred Radishchevs, wretched little Jews with a mournful but haughty smile, guffawing travellers, poets with political tendencies from the capital, poets who made up for their lack of political tendencies or talent by wearing peasant coats and tarred boots, majors and colonels, who laughed at the senselessness of their profession and who for an extra rouble would be ready to take off their swords and leave the army for a job as railway clerks; generals who had left their posts to become lawyers; educated arbitrators between the peasants and the landowners and little merchants who were still educating themselves, innumerable divinity students, women who were the embodiment of the woman question – all these suddenly gained the upper

hand among us, and over whom? Over the club, over men who occupied high positions in the Civil Service, over generals with wooden
legs, and over the most strict and unapproachable ladies of our society.
If Mrs Stavrogin herself, with her darling son, almost ran errands for
all that rabble, right up to the time of the catastrophe, then our other
local Minervas may to a certain extent be pardoned their temporary
aberration. Now, as I have already mentioned, everything is laid at the
door of the wretched *Internationale*. This idea is now so generally
accepted that it is offered up as an explanation to visitors to our town.
Quite recently Councillor Kubrikov, a man of sixty-two, wearing the
order of St Stanislaus round his neck, came forward of his own accord
and declared in an ecstatic voice that for fully three months he had
been under the influence of the *Internationale*. But when, with due regard to his advanced age and services, he was invited to be a little more
specific, he stuck firmly to his statement, though he could bring no
documentary evidence except that he 'had felt it with every fibre in
his body', so that they did not even think it necessary to continue with
his cross-examination.

Let me repeat again. Even among us there was a small group of
sober-minded people who had held aloof from the very beginning
and who even locked themselves up. But what lock can hold out
against natural law? There are marriageable girls in the most careful
families, and they have to go to dances. And so these young ladies also
ended up by subscribing to the governesses' fund. It was generally believed that the ball was going to be a brilliant social occasion – something, indeed, quite terrific. All sorts of marvellous stories were told
about it. There were rumours of princes with lorgnettes travelling to
the ball; of ten stewards, all of them young bachelors, with ribbons on
their left shoulders; of some Petersburg people who were the prime
movers of the whole affair; of Karmazinov, who had consented to
read *Merci* in the costume of a governess of our province so as to increase the subscriptions; of a 'literary quadrille', also in fancy dress,
each costume representing some literary movement. Finally, some
'honest Russian thought' would also dance in costume, which was by
itself alone a complete novelty. How was it possible not to subscribe?
Everyone subscribed.

2

The programme of the festive day was divided into two parts: a literary matinée, from twelve to four o'clock, and a ball, from ten o'clock
and through the night. But in this arrangement germs of disorder
were concealed. To begin with, from the very start a rumour had
gained ground among the public about a luncheon which was to be
given immediately after the literary matinée, or even while it was going on, during a specially arranged interval. It was to be a free luncheon, of course, which was to be part of the programme, and with
champagne. The high price of the tickets (three roubles) gave substance to the rumour. 'Would I have subscribed for nothing? The
fête is supposed to go on for a whole day, so they jolly well have to
provide food, or the people will be famished,' – that is how people
reasoned. I must confess that Mrs Lembke herself had given rise to
the disastrous rumour by her own thoughtlessness. A month earlier,
under the first spell of her great plan, she discussed her fête with anyone she met, and she even sent a report to one of the Petersburg papers
in which she declared that there would be toasts offered in the course
of it. She seemed to be quite fascinated by those toasts, she meant to
propose them herself, and kept composing them in anticipation. They
had to explain what our main purpose was (what was it? – I bet the
poor woman composed nothing after all), to be published in the form
of reports in the Moscow and Petersburg newspapers, to charm and
impress the highest authorities in the land and then spread all over the
provinces in Russia, arousing surprise and imitation. But for toasts one
had to have champagne, and as it was impossible to drink champagne
on an empty stomach, it followed that a luncheon became indispensable, too. Later on, when, thanks to her efforts, a committee had been
formed and the whole thing had been tackled in a more business-like
manner, it was immediately made clear to her that if they were going
to dream of banquets there would be little left for the governesses,
however much money the subscriptions brought in. The problem
could, therefore, be solved in one of two ways: either Belshazzar's
feast with toasts and about ninety roubles for the governesses, or a considerable amount of money with the fête only, as it were, as a matter
of form. The committee, however, only wanted to frighten her a
little. It naturally devised a third solution, a compromise solution

based on common sense – that is to say, quite a decent fête in every respect, but without champagne, thus leaving quite a respectable sum of money over for the governesses: much more than ninety roubles. But Mrs Lembke would not agree; a paltry compromise was not in her character. She decided there and then that if her first idea could not be realized, they should rush to the opposite extreme – namely, raise so enormous a sum of money that they would be the envy of all the other provinces. 'The public must be made to realize,' she concluded her fiery speech to the committee, 'that the attainment of objects which are of universal human interest is of incomparably greater importance than any transient bodily enjoyments, that the fête is essentially only a proclamation of a great idea, and that therefore people ought to be satisfied with the most economic German ball, merely as a symbol, if, that is, we can't do without this odious ball altogether!' – so much did she suddenly detest it. But they pacified her at last. It was then that the 'literary quadrille' and all the other aesthetic items were invented and proposed as substitutes for the bodily delights. It was then, too, that Karmazinov finally gave his consent to read *Merci* (till then he had only mumbled and kept them on tenterhooks) and so eradicate the very idea of food from the minds of our incontinent public. So the ball was again to become a magnificent public occasion, though of a different sort. But to keep at least one foot firmly on the ground, it was decided that tea with lemon and round biscuits should be served at the beginning of the ball, followed by cold *orgeat* and lemonade, and at the end even ices, and that was all. But for those who are always and everywhere hungry and, above all, thirsty, they might arrange a special buffet in the farthest room on the same floor, which would be under the management of Prokhorych (the club chef), who would – under the strictest supervision of the committee, however – serve anything they might ask for a special charge, a notice to be displayed on the doors of the ballroom to the effect that the buffet was not included in the programme. But next morning it was decided not to open the buffet at all, for it was feared that it might interfere with the reading, in spite of the fact that the buffet was to have been five rooms away from the White Hall in which Karmazinov had agreed to read *Merci*.

It is interesting that the committee, including the most practical of its members, should have attached so much importance to that event –

that is, to the reading of *Merci*. As for the people who were poetically inclined, the wife of the marshal of nobility, for instance, told Karmazinov that after the reading she would at once have a white marble slab put up on the wall of the White Hall with an inscription in gold letters, to the effect that on such and such a date the great Russian and European writer, on laying down his pen, had read his *Merci* there and so had for the first time taken leave of his Russian public, represented by the leading citizens of our town, and that this inscription would be read by those invited to the ball – that is, only five hours after *Merci* had been read. I know for a fact that it was Karmazinov who had demanded that under no circumstances should there be a buffet during his reading in the morning, though some members of the committee had pointed out that this was not at all how we liked to do things in our town.

That was the state of affairs at a time when in the town people still believed in a Belshazzar's feast – that is, in free drinks and refreshments; they believed in it to the last hour. Even the young ladies were dreaming of lots and lots of sweets and preserves and something more wonderful still. Everyone knew that an enormous sum of money had been subscribed, that practically the whole town was anxious to be at the festival, that people were coming from the surrounding country districts, and that all the tickets had been sold. It was also common knowledge that, in addition to the price paid for the tickets, many contributions had been received: Mrs Stavrogin, for example, had paid 300 roubles for her ticket and given all the flowers from her conservatory for the decoration of the ballroom. The Marshal's wife (a committee member) provided the house and the lighting; the club – the music, the attendants, and gave up Prokhorych for the whole day. There were other contributions, though not so big, so that the idea was even mooted of reducing the original price of the tickets from three roubles to two. Indeed, the committee were at first afraid that the young ladies might not come if they had to pay three roubles for a ticket, and suggested issuing special family tickets, so that each family should pay for one girl only, while the other young ladies of the family, even if there were a dozen specimens, should be admitted free. But all their apprehensions proved to be groundless: it was just the young ladies who did turn up. Even the poorest Civil Servants brought their girls with them, and it was all too evident that if they had had no girls, it would never have occurred to them to subscribe. One quite insignificant secretary brought all his seven daughters, not to mention his wife, and his niece too, and every one of these ladies had a ticket in her hand for which three roubles had been paid.

It can be imagined what a commotion it created in the town. Take, for instance, the fact that, the fête being divided into two parts, every lady had to have two different costumes each – a morning dress for the reading and an evening dress for the dances. Many middle-class people, as it became known afterwards, had pawned everything they had for that day, even the family linen and sheets and almost the mattresses, with our local Jews, who, as though on purpose, had been settling in our town in great numbers for the last two years, and whose numbers grew as time went on. Almost all our Civil Servants had asked for their salary in advance, and some of the landowners had even to sell some of their cattle they could not spare, and all because they simply had to bring their daughters dressed like grand ladies, and be able to hold their own with the others. The magnificence of the dresses this time was something quite unheard of in our town, which for a fortnight before the fête was full of comic stories at once conveyed to Mrs Lembke's court by our wits. Caricatures depicting the plight of some families began to pass from hand to hand. I myself have seen some drawings of that sort in Mrs Lembke's album. All this became known to the people who were the material of these jokes. That was why, I think, Mrs Lembke became the object of such hatred among the families in our town. They all abuse her now and, when they think of it, are consumed with rage. But it was obvious even before that if the committee failed to please them in anything, or if something untoward were to happen at the ball, the outburst of indignation would be quite astonishing. That was why everybody was secretly expecting a public scandal; and if they were expecting it so much, it could not possibly fail to come about.

Punctually at twelve o'clock the band struck up. As one of the stewards – that is, one of the twelve 'young gentlemen with a rosette' – I saw with my own eyes how this day of ignominious memory began. It began with an unimaginable crush at the doors. How did it happen that everything went wrong from the very first, beginning with the police? I do not blame the genuine public: the fathers of families did not crowd nor did they push against anybody,

in spite of their social standing. On the contrary, I am told that they
looked embarrassed, even in the street, at the sight of the unprecedented crush of people besieging the entrance, trying to storm it,
and not just going in. Meanwhile the carriages kept driving up, and at
length blocked the whole street. Now, as I write this, I have good
grounds for asserting that some of the lowest rabble in our town were
brought in without tickets by Lyamshin and Liputin, and quite possibly by someone else who was a steward like myself. At any rate,
there were people there nobody knew who had arrived from the
country districts and elsewhere. As soon as these savages entered the
hall, they began asking where the buffet was (as though they had been
put up to it) and, learning that there was no buffet, began swearing
without the least constraint and with an arrogance which was quite
unprecedented in our town till then. It is true, some of them arrived
drunk. Others, like real savages, were struck dumb by the magnificence of the ballroom of the Marshal's wife, never having seen anything like it before, and as they went in they grew silent for a moment,
gazing at it open-mouthed. The great White Hall was indeed magnificent, though the building was badly in need of repair: it was of enormous size, with two rows of windows, with a ceiling painted in the
old style and ornamented with gilt mouldings, with a gallery, with
mirrors on the walls, red and white draperies, marble statues (horrible
ones, but still statues), with heavy, antique furniture of the Napo-
leonic period, white and gold and upholstered in red velvet. At the
moment I am describing, a high platform had been erected at the far
end of the hall for the authors who were to read their works, and the
entire hall was filled with chairs, like the stalls of a theatre, with wide
gangways for the audience. But after the first moments of surprise,
the most senseless questions and exclamations were heard. 'Perhaps
we don't want any reading. ... We've paid our money. ... The public
has been impudently swindled. ... We're the people who count, not
the Lembkes. ...' In a word, it was just as though they had been admitted for this purpose. I particularly remember one clash in which
the princeling with the stiff collar and the face of a wooden doll, who
was present in Mrs Lembke's drawing-room the morning before, distinguished himself. He, too, had, at her urgent request, agreed to pin
a ribbon to his left shoulder and become one of our fellow stewards.
Apparently this dumb wax figure on springs could, if not talk, at least

act in some sort of way of his own. When a huge, pockmarked retired army Captain, supported by a whole crowd of riff-raff at his heels, began pestering him by asking which was the way to the buffet, he gave a wink to a policeman. His injunction was promptly carried out: notwithstanding the drunken Captain's abuse, he was dragged out of the hall. In the meantime the 'genuine' public began to make its appearance at last and stretched in three long files along the three gangways between the chairs. The disorderly element began to quiet down, but the public, even the most 'immaculate' among them, looked dissatisfied and perplexed; some of the ladies, indeed, were simply frightened.

At last they were all in their seats; the music, too, stopped. They began blowing their noses and looking round. They waited with too solemn an air, which is in itself always a bad sign. But the 'Lembkes' had not arrived yet. Silks, velvets, diamonds shimmered and glittered on all sides; the air was full of the fragrance of expensive perfumes. The men were wearing all their decorations, and the old men were even in uniform. The Marshal's wife, accompanied by Lisa, arrived at last. Never before had Lisa been so dazzlingly beautiful as that morning, or in such a gorgeous dress. Her hair was done up in curls, her eyes sparkled, her face was radiant with a smile. She obviously created a sensation; people kept looking at her and whispering about her. I heard some say that she was searching for Stavrogin with her eyes, but neither Stavrogin nor his mother was there. I could not understand the expression on her face at the time: why was there so much happiness, joy, energy, and strength in that face? I recalled the incident of the day before and was at a loss what to think. But still the 'Lembkes' did not arrive. This was undoubtedly a bad mistake. I learned afterwards that Mrs Lembke had been waiting for Peter Verkhovensky till the last moment, for she could not take a step without him, though she never admitted it to herself. Let me add parenthetically that at the last committee meeting on the previous day Peter had refused to be one of the stewards, which distressed her greatly, even to the point of tears. To her surprise, and subsequently to her extreme embarrassment (I say this in anticipation of what happened later), he disappeared during the whole of the morning, and did not make his appearance at the reading at all, so that no one saw him till the evening. At length the audience began to show signs of impatience. No one appeared on the platform, either. In the back rows people began applauding as in a theatre. The old gentlemen and the ladies frowned: 'The Lembkes are evidently giving themselves airs.' Even among the more respectable section of the audience an absurd whisper arose to the effect that perhaps there would be no fête at all, that Lembke himself was perhaps indisposed, and so on. But, thank God, Lembke appeared at last: his wife leaning on his arm. To tell the truth, I myself was beginning to fear that they might not come. But apparently the fairy-tales were false, and truth asserted itself. The audience seemed to breathe freely. Lembke himself seemed to be in excellent health, and that, I remember, was the general opinion of the audience, for it can be imagined how many eyes were turned on him. To give an idea of the state of mind of our society, I may observe that, generally speaking, very few of our people of quality were of the opinion that there was anything wrong with Lembke's state of health; his actions were considered to be perfectly normal, so much so that they even accepted with approval the events in the square the previous morning. 'That's the way he should have treated them from the first,' our higher officials said. 'For if they are philanthropists when they arrive, they are forced to take the same measures in the end, without realizing that such measures are necessary from the point of view of philanthropy itself.' That, at any rate, is what they thought of it at the club. He was only criticized for having lost his temper. 'Such a thing ought to be carried out much more coolly, but, after all, he is only a new man,' the experts said.

All eyes turned with the same eagerness to Mrs Lembke. Of course, no one has a right to expect from me, as the narrator, too exact an account concerning one point: for we are dealing with a mystery here, we are dealing with a woman. But one thing I do know: on the previous evening she had gone into Mr Lembke's study and stayed with him there till long after midnight. Mr Lembke was forgiven and comforted. Husband and wife came to a complete understanding, everything was forgotten, and when towards the end of the interview von Lembke, in spite of everything, went down on his knees, recalling with horror the main and final incident of the previous night, his wife's exquisite little hand, and afterwards her lips, checked the passionate outpourings of penitent speeches of the chivalrously delicate gentleman, rendered powerless with emotion. Everyone could see by her face that she was happy. She walked looking open-hearted and natural and wearing a magnificent dress. It seemed that she had reached the very pinnacle of her ambition: the fête – the goal and the crown of her political aspirations – was an accomplished fact. As they walked to their seats in front of the platform, both Lembkes bowed and acknowledged the greetings of the audience. They were immediately surrounded. The Marshal's wife got up to welcome them. ... But at this point a most regrettable incident occurred: the band, without the slightest excuse, struck up a flourish, not just a march, but simply the sort of flourish that is usually struck up at an official dinner at our club when people drink to someone's health. I know now that it was Lyamshin who was responsible for it as one of the stewards, the flourish being apparently meant in honour of the entrance of the 'Lembkes'. He could, of course, always excuse himself by saying that he had done it from stupidity or from excessive zeal. Alas, at the time I had no idea that they were no longer bothering about any excuses and that they hoped to accomplish all their plans that very day. But the flourish was not the end of the matter: amid the smiles and the annoyed and perplexed looks of the audience cries of 'hurrah' were suddenly raised at the back of the hall and in the gallery, also as though in Lembke's honour. The cheers were few, but, I must confess, they went on for some time. Mrs Lembke blushed crimson and her eyes flashed. Lembke stopped dead at his seat and, turning towards the cheering people, cast a majestic and severe look over the audience. They made him sit down quickly. Again I noticed with apprehension the same dangerous smile on his face which he had worn in his wife's drawing-room the previous evening, when he looked at Mr Verkhovensky before going up to him. It seemed to me that now, too, there was an ominous expression on his face, and, what was worse, a rather comic one, too – the expression of a man who had made up his mind to sacrifice himself in order to humour his wife's higher aims.

Mrs Lembke beckoned to me hurriedly and whispered to me to run to Karmazinov and implore him to begin. But I had scarcely time to turn round when another disgraceful incident, much more disgraceful than the first, occurred.

On the platform – the empty platform on which till that moment the eyes and expectations of the audience were fixed, and where they only saw an empty table, a chair in front of it and a glass of water on a silver tray on it – on this empty platform I suddenly caught sight of the gigantic figure of Captain Lebyatkin in a frock-coat and white tie. I was so astonished that I could not believe my eyes. The Captain apparently felt embarrassed, and he remained standing at the back of the platform. Suddenly a shout was heard in the audience: 'Lebyatkin, is it you?' The Captain's stupid red face (he was dead drunk) expanded in a broad, vacant grin at this cry. He raised his hand, wiped his forehead, shook his shaggy head and, as though making up his mind to go through with it, took two steps forward and – all of a sudden burst out laughing, not loudly, but happily, his stout figure shaking with prolonged, irrepressible laughter and his little eyes screwed up. This spectacle made almost half of the audience burst out laughing and about two dozen people began clapping. The more sedate section of the audience looked at each other gloomily; all this, however, did not last more than half a minute. Liputin, wearing his steward's rosette, and two attendants suddenly rushed out on the platform; they took the Captain carefully by both arms and Liputin whispered something to him. The Captain frowned, muttered, 'All right, if you insist,' waved his hand, turned his huge back on the audience and disappeared with his escort. But a moment later Liputin jumped out on the platform again. His lips were distended in one of his sweetest smiles, which usually suggested vinegar and sugar. He had a sheet of note-paper in his hands. With short but quick steps he walked up to the edge of the platform.

'Ladies and gentlemen,' he said, addressing the audience, 'I'm very sorry for the comical misunderstanding which has occurred through an oversight and which, I'm glad to say, has now been removed. But I have, ladies and gentlemen, promised to convey to you, not without some hope of success, a most humble and respectful request from one of our local poets. Deeply touched by the humane and high purpose – in spite of his appearance – the same purpose which has brought us all together – er – to dry the tears of poor, educated girls of our province – this gentleman – I mean, this local poet – who – er – wishes to remain incognito – would dearly like to have his poem read before the beginning of the ball – sorry, I mean, the literary reading. Though this poem is not in the programme and – er – couldn't have been included in it because it only reached us half an hour ago, *we*' (Who are the *we*? I am quoting this incoherent and confused speech verbatim) 'thought that in view of the remarkably ingenuous feelings expressed in it, combined, too, with quite extraordinary gaiety, the poem ought to be read – I mean, not as something serious, but as something that is appropriate to to-day's great occasion – in a word, the whole idea of it – particularly as it only consists of a few lines – and I'd therefore like to ask for your kind permission to read it to you.'

'Read it!' a voice roared at the back of the hall.

'So I have your permission to read it?'

'Read it! Read it!' many voices cried.

'I will read it, with your permission, ladies and gentlemen,' Liputin said in his affected voice and with the same sugary smile.

He was still apparently undecided, and I could not help feeling that he was rather agitated. These people sometimes come a cropper for all their impudence. Still, a divinity student would not have come a cropper, and Liputin did, after all, belong to the older generation.

'I must warn you, I mean I have the honour of warning you with all due respect, ladies and gentlemen, that the poem I am about to read is not the kind of ode that used to be written in former times on the occasion of some festivity, but is almost a jest, as it were, though it certainly is full of feeling combined with playful gaiety and, as it were, most realistic truth.'

'Read it! Read it!'

He unfolded the paper. No one, of course, had time to stop him. Besides, he appeared with his steward's rosette. He declaimed in a ringing voice:

'To a local Russian governess from a poet at the fête:

> Fair governesses all, good morrow!
> True Blue or true George Sander,
> Triumph now and banish sorrow,
> Now the world will be much kinder!

'But it's Lebyatkin's! It *is* Lebyatkin's!' a few voices cried.

There was some laughter and applause, though not from many people.

> Teaching French to snively children,
> Over your grammar book you'd look
> To give the wink to catch a sexton,
> For him, too, you'd bait your hook.

'Hurrah! Hurrah!'

> But in these days of great reformings
> Not a sexton e'en will marry you.
> Unless, my dear, you have 'the doings' –
> That, you know, is sadly true.

'Quite right! Quite right! That's realism for you! You can't do much without "the doings".'

> But now when, feasting, we've collected
> Gold and dowries for you all,
> You may go with hearts uplifted
> From this ball and festive hall, –
> > True Blue or true George Sander,
> > Triumph now and banish care,
> > Off you go with step much lighter,
> > Damn 'em all and 'scape their snare!

I must confess I could not believe my ears. It was a piece of such unmistakable impudence that it was impossible to excuse Liputin even on the ground of stupidity. Not that Liputin was so stupid, either. His intention was clear, to me, at any rate: it looked as though they were in a hurry to create disorder. Some of the lines of that idiotic poem – the last ones, for instance – were of such a nature that no stupidity could possibly have let them pass. I believe Liputin himself felt that he had gone too far; having accomplished his heroic deed, he was so overcome by his own impudence that he did not even leave the platform, but remained standing there, as though wishing to add something. He must have expected quite a different effect; but even the small crowd of rowdies who had applauded during the disgraceful prank suddenly fell silent, as though they, too, were dumbfounded. The really absurd thing about it was that many of them found the poem very pathetic   that is to say, they did not realize that it was just a lampoon, but took it to be the truth about the governesses, took it to be verses with a political tendency. But the excessive freedom of the verses struck them, too, at last. As for the audience as a whole, they were not only scandalized, but obviously offended. I am certain I'm not mistaken in thus describing the impression. Mrs Lembke said afterwards that another moment and she would have fainted. One of the most respectable old gentlemen helped his old lady on to her feet, and they both walked out of the hall accompanied by the agitated glances of the audience. Who knows but others might have been induced to follow their example had not Karmazinov himself, in a frock-coat, a white tie, and with a manuscript in his hand, appeared on the platform at that moment. Mrs Lembke turned her ecstatic gaze on him as on her deliverer. ... But I was already behind the scenes; I had to get hold of Liputin.

'You did it on purpose!' I said, seizing him indignantly by the arm.

'I really didn't think – honestly, I didn't,' he said, cowering at once and beginning to lie and pretending to be very upset. 'They only just brought the verses, and I thought that since it was such a good joke –'

'You didn't think anything of the sort. Do you really find that stupid rubbish a good joke?'

'Yes, sir, I do.'

'You're simply lying, and it wasn't brought to you just now. You composed it yourself with Lebyatkin, perhaps yesterday, to create a row. The last verse is certainly yours and the line about the sexton, too. Why did he come dressed in a frock-coat? You wanted him to read it, if he had not been drunk, didn't you?'

Liputin gave me a cold and malevolent look.

'What business is it of yours?' he suddenly asked with strange equanimity.

'What do you mean? You, too, are wearing the steward's rosette – where's Peter Verkhovensky?'

'Don't know. Here somewhere, I suppose. Why?'

'Because I see it all now. It's simply a plot against Mrs Lembke, an attempt to discredit the day. ...'

Liputin again looked askance at me.

'What do you care?' he grinned, shrugged and walked away.

I was stunned. All my suspicions had proved true. And I was still hoping that I might be wrong! What was I to do now? I thought of asking Mr Verkhovensky for his advice, but he was standing before the looking-glass, trying on different smiles and constantly consulting a piece of paper on which he had written down some notes. He had to go on immediately after Karmazinov, and he was no longer in a condition to talk to me. Should I run to Mrs Lembke? But it was too soon to talk to her: she had first to be taught a good lesson to cure her of her idea of having a 'following' and of the 'fanatic loyalty' of all her followers. She would not have believed me. She would have thought that I was seeing things. And, besides, what could she have done to help? 'Good Lord,' I thought to myself, 'what business is it of mine? I'll take off my steward's rosette and go home *when it starts.*' I actually did say: 'when it starts,' I remember that clearly.

But I had to go and listen to Karmazinov. Taking a last look round behind the scenes, I noticed that a large number of people who had no business there, among them even women, were walking about, going in and out. 'Behind the scenes' was a rather narrow space, screened off from the audience by a curtain and communicating with the other rooms at the back by means of a corridor. It was here our readers were waiting their turns. But I was particularly struck at that moment by the lecturer who had to follow Mr Verkhovensky. He, too, was some sort of professor (even now I don't know exactly who he was) who had voluntarily retired from an educational establishment after an incident among the students and who had only arrived in our town on business a few days earlier. He, too, had been recommended to Mrs Lembke, and she had received him with reverence. I know now that he had seen her only once during the evening before the reading, that he never uttered a word all that evening, smiling ambiguously at the jokes and the general tone of the company that surrounded Mrs Lembke and leaving an unpleasant impression on everybody by his air of disdain and, at the same time, his timorous susceptibility. It was Mrs Lembke herself who had roped him in as a reader. Now he was walking from one corner to the other and, like Mr Verkhovensky, was whispering to himself, but his eyes were fixed on the ground, and not the looking-glass. He was not trying out any smiles, though he grinned frequently and rapaciously. It was plain to me that it was impossible to talk to him, either. He was a short, bald man of about forty with a greyish beard, and was decently dressed. But the most interesting thing about him was that every time he turned round he raised his right fist aloft, brandished it in the air above his head, and then suddenly brought it down as though reducing an opponent to dust and ashes. He went through this performance every minute. It made me feel ill at ease. I hurried away to listen to Karmazinov.

3

There was a feeling in the hall that something had gone wrong again. Let me say once and for all: I have the greatest admiration for genius, but why do our men of genius at the end of their illustrious careers sometimes behave exactly like little boys? What did it matter if he was Karmazinov and strode on to the platform looking like five Court chamberlains rolled into one? Is it possible to hold the attention of an audience like ours for a whole hour with one paper? In my experience even a super genius could not possibly hope to keep the attention of an audience at a light literary reading for more than twenty minutes with impunity. It is true, the entrance of the great literary genius was received with the utmost respect: even the most severe old gentlemen showed signs of approval and interest, and the ladies even displayed some enthusiasm. The applause, however, did not last long, and it was somehow not unanimous, but ragged. But there was not a single interruption from the back rows up to the very moment when Mr Karmazinov began to speak, and even then nothing particularly bad happened, but just a little misunderstanding. I have mentioned already the fact that he had a rather shrill voice, a somewhat feminine voice even, and, to boot, the affected lisp of a born gentleman. No sooner had he uttered a few words than someone permitted himself a loud laugh, no doubt some stupid little fool who had never come across a real gentleman and who was, besides, a bit of a wag. But there was no question of any hostile demonstration: on the contrary, the fool was hissed down, and he effaced himself completely. But Mr Karmazinov went on to declare, in his affected manner and in mincing tones, that 'at first he would not agree to read' (as though it was really necessary to say that!). 'There are,' he said, 'some things which come so straight from the heart that one hesitates to utter them aloud, so that so sacred a thing cannot be exposed to the public gaze' (so why on earth expose them?); but as he had been asked so much, he was going to expose it, and as, moreover, he was laying down his pen for good and had vowed never to write anything again, he had written this last thing of his; and as he had vowed 'never, not for anything in the world, to read anything in public', and so on and so forth, all in the same vein.

But all that would not have mattered, for who does not know what an author's introduction is like? Though I must say that taking the ignorance of our public and the irritability of the back rows into consideration, all this may have had an influence. Would it not have been much better to have read some little story, one of those very short stories he used to write in the past – that is, a story which, though it was highly polished and affected, was sometimes witty? That would have saved the situation. But no! Not a bit of it! Instead he read us a whole edifying oration! Dear me, what wasn't there in it? I can positively say that it would have reduced even a Petersburg audience to a state of stupor, let alone ours. Imagine over thirty printed pages of the most pretentious and useless chatter; and, besides, this gentleman read it in a sort of mournfully condescending tone of voice, as though he were doing us a favour, so that it sounded rather like an insult to our public. The subject ... But who could make it out – that subject of his? It was a sort of account of certain impressions and reminiscences. But of what? And about what? However much we knit our provincial brows during the first half of the reading, we could not make head or tail of it, and we listened to the second part simply out of politeness. It is true, there was a lot of talk about love – the love of the genius for some lady – but, I confess, it produced rather an awkward impression on the audience. For the great genius to tell us about his first kiss, seemed to my mind somehow inconsistent with his short, fat little figure. ... And, again, it was a pity that those kisses were somehow different from the kisses of ordinary mortals. There were always some gorse-bushes about (it had to be gorse or some other plant which has to be looked up in a botanical dictionary). And there had to be some violet tint in the sky, such as no mortal, of course, had ever observed, or if he had seen it, he would not have taken any notice of it; but, you see, 'I jolly well did see it, and now I'm describing it to damn fools like you as if it were the most ordinary thing.' The tree under which the fascinating couple sat had naturally to be of an orange colour. They were sitting somewhere in Germany. Suddenly they behold Pompey or Cassius on the eve of the battle, and a chill of rapture runs down their backs. Some water-nymph starts squeaking in the bushes. Gluck plays a fiddle in the rushes. The title of the piece he was playing was given in full, but no one seemed to have heard of it, so that it would have to be looked up in a musical dictionary. Meanwhile a mist arises, which is more like a million pillows than a mist.

And suddenly everything vanishes, and the great genius is crossing the
Volga in winter in a thaw. Two and a half pages of the crossing, but
he still manages to fall through a hole in the ice. The genius is drowning – did he get drowned, you think? Good Lord, no! All this is
merely dragged in to show that when he was already on the point of
drowning and yielding up the ghost, he caught sight of a little ice-floe,
a tiny little ice-floe the size of a pea, but pure and transparent 'like a
frozen tear', and in that ice-floe the whole of Germany was reflected,
or, to be more precise, the sky of Germany, and by its iridescent glitter
recalled to his mind the very same tear, which 'you remember rolled
down from your eyes when we sat beneath the emerald tree and you
cried joyfully, "There is no crime!" "No," I said, through my tears,
"but if that is so, there are no saints, either." We burst into sobs and
parted for ever.' She went off somewhere to the sea-coast, and he to
some caves; and then he descends and descends for three years in Moscow beneath the Sukharev Tower, and suddenly in the very bowels of
the earth, in a cave, he finds a lamp burning before an icon, and
before the lamp – a hermit. The hermit is saying his prayers. The
genius puts his face close to the bars of a tiny window and suddenly
hears a sigh. You think it was the hermit who sighed? What does he
care about your hermit! No, this sigh simply reminds him of her first
sigh, thirty-seven years ago, when 'do you remember how we sat
beneath an agate tree in Germany and you said to me, "Why love?
Look, ruddle is growing all round, and I am in love, but when the
ruddle ceases to grow, I shall fall out of love." Here a mist rises again,
Hoffmann appears, the water-nymph whistles a tune from Chopin,
and suddenly out of the mist Ancus Marcius appears over the roofs
of Rome, wearing a laurel wreath. A shiver of rapture ran down our
backs and we parted for ever,' and so on and so forth. In a word,
I may not be reporting it correctly and, indeed, I may not even know
how to report it, but the burden of the chatter was something of that
sort. And, really, how disgraceful is this passion of great intellects for
abstruse epigrams! The great European philosopher, the great scholar,
the inventor, the toiler, the martyr – all these who labour and are
heavy laden are to our great Russian genius just like so many cooks in
his kitchen. He is the master, and they come to him with their tall chef
hats in their hands and wait for his orders. It is true, he sneers contemptuously at Russia, too, and he likes nothing better than to pro-

claim the bankruptcy of Russia in every respect before the great intellects of Europe, but so far as he himself is concerned – no, sir! – he has
risen higher than the great intellects of Europe; they all are merely
material for his epigrams. He takes someone else's idea, tacks its anti-
thesis on to it, and the epigram is ready. There is such a thing as crime,
there are no such things as secrets; there is no truth, there are no such
men as searchers for truth; atheism, Darwinism, Moscow church-
bells. ... But, alas, he no longer believes in the Moscow church-bells;
Rome, laurels. ... But he doesn't believe even in laurels. ... Here you
get a conventional attack of Byronic spleen, a grimace from Heine,
something of Pechorin – and off he goes full steam ahead, with his
engine emitting a shrill whistle. .. 'But do praise me, do praise me,
for I like it awfully; I'm only just saying that I'm laying down my
pen; you wait, I'm going to bore you three hundred times more, you'll
get tired of reading me. ...'

Of course, it did not go off so well. But the trouble was that it was
his own fault. People had for some time been shuffling their feet,
blowing their noses, coughing, and doing everything people do when
a writer, whoever he may be, keeps an audience for more than twenty
minutes at a literary reading. But the genius noticed nothing of all
this. He went on lisping and mumbling, without paying any attention to the audience, so that everybody began to look bewildered.
And then suddenly a solitary voice in the back rows exclaimed
loudly:

'Lord, what nonsense!'

The interjection was quite involuntary and, I am sure, there was
no question of any demonstration. The man was simply worn out.
But Mr Karmazinov stopped, looked ironically at the audience,
and suddenly said in his highly affected voice and with the dignified air of a Court chamberlain whose feelings had been badly
hurt:

'I'm afraid, ladies and gentlemen, I have been boring you awfully,
haven't I?'

His mistake, of course, was that he was the first to speak; for by
provoking a reply in this way, he presented every ruffian with the
opportunity of having his say, too, and quite legitimately, so to speak,
while if he had controlled himself, they would have gone on blowing
their noses, and it would have passed off somehow. Perhaps he

expected applause in reply to his question; but there was no applause; on the contrary, they all seemed to shrink within themselves, to get frightened and fall silent.

'You never saw Ancus Marcius; it's just your way of writing,' an irritated and apparently even hysterical voice cried suddenly.

'That's right,' another voice echoed at once. 'There aren't any ghosts nowadays, only natural phenomena. Look it up in a book on natural sciences.'

'Ladies and gentlemen, I expected such objections least of all,' Karmazinov said, looking terribly surprised. The great genius had completely lost touch with his native country in Karlsruhe.

'In our age it is shameful to say that the world stands on three fishes,' a young girl suddenly burst out. 'You could not possibly have gone down to the hermit's cave, Karmazinov. And, besides, who talks of hermits nowadays?'

'Ladies and gentlemen, what surprises me most of all is that you take it all so seriously. However – however, you're absolutely right. No one respects truth and realism more than I do.'

Although he was smiling ironically, he was greatly startled. His face seemed to say: 'But I'm not at all the sort of person you take me for. Why, I'm on your side; only, please, praise me, praise me more, praise me as much as possible, I like it awfully. ...'

'Ladies and gentlemen,' he cried at last, stung to the quick, 'I can see that my poor poem is out of place here. And I am rather out of place here myself, I'm afraid.'

'You aimed at a crow and hit a cow,' some fool shouted at the top of his voice. He must have been drunk, and, of course, no notice should have been taken of him. It is true, though, that his words evoked some disrespectful laughter.

'A cow, you say?' Karmazinov echoed at once, his voice growing shriller and shriller. 'I'm afraid, ladies and gentlemen, I'd better say nothing about crows and cows. I've too great a respect for any audience to permit myself any comparisons, however innocent. But I thought –'

'If I were you sir, I'd be more careful,' someone from the back rows shouted.

'But I imagined that, as I was laying down my pen and taking leave of my readers, I'd be given a fair hearing.'

'Yes, yes, we want to hear, we want to hear,' a few voices at last plucked up courage to cry from the first row.

'Read! Read!' a few ecstatic female voices echoed the cry, and, at last, there was some applause, thin and feeble, it is true.

Karmazinov smiled wrily and got up from his chair.

'Believe me, Karmazinov, everybody thinks it an honour –' even the Marshal's wife could not refrain from saying.

'Mr Karmazinov,' cried a fresh young voice from the back of the hall suddenly. It was the voice of a very young teacher from the district school, an excellent young man, quiet and honourable, who had only recently come to our town. 'Mr Karmazinov, if I were so lucky as to fall in love as you've described to us, I should never have put my love in a story intended for public reading.'

He even blushed to the roots of his hair.

'Ladies and gentlemen,' Karmazinov cried, 'I have finished. I will leave the end out and go. But let me read the last six lines:

'"Yes, dear reader, farewell!"' he began at once to read from the manuscript without resuming his seat. '"Farewell, reader; I don't even insist on our parting friends: why, indeed, should I trouble you? You may even abuse me. Oh, abuse me as much as you like, if that gives you any pleasure. But much better if we forget each other for ever. And if all of you, readers, were suddenly so kind as to go down on your knees and begin begging me with tears: 'Write, oh, write for us, Karmazinov – for the sake of your country, for the sake of posterity, for the sake of laurel wreaths,' I'd reply to you, after thanking you, of course, very courteously, 'No, my dear fellow-countrymen, we've had quite enough of one another, *merci*! It is time we went our several ways! *Merci, merci, merci!*'"'

Karmazinov bowed ceremoniously and blushed red, as though he had been cooked, and was about to go off behind the scenes.

'No one is going down on their knees – what ridiculous nonsense!'
'Conceited, isn't he?'
'It's only his humour,' someone more sensible corrected.
'May the Lord save me from your humour.'
'But, really, it's damned cheek, ladies and gentlemen.'
'Thank goodness he's finished.'
'Dear me, what a dull programme!'
But all these ignorant exclamations in the back rows (not only in

the back rows, incidentally) were drowned in the applause from the other section of the audience. There were calls for Karmazinov. A number of ladies, headed by Mrs Lembke and the Marshal's wife, crowded round the platform. In Mrs Lembke's hands was a gorgeous laurel wreath, on a white velvet cushion, surrounding another wreath of roses.

'Laurels!' said Karmazinov with a faint and somewhat caustic smile. 'I'm touched, of course, and I accept this wreath which has been prepared beforehand and which has not yet had time to wither, with deep emotion; but I assure you, my dear ladies, that I have suddenly become so great a realist that I think laurels are in this age more appropriate in the hands of a skilful cook than in mine.'

'Yes, a cook is more useful,' the divinity student who had been at the 'meeting' in Virginsky's house cried.

There was some disorder. In many rows people jumped up to watch the presentation of the laurel wreath.

'I'd give another three roubles for a cook this instant,' another voice echoed loudly – too loudly, indeed: so loudly as to be insistent.

'Me, too.'

'Me, too.'

'Is there really no buffet here?'

'Why, this is simply a swindle!'

However, it must be admitted that these unruly fellows were still very much afraid of our high officials and the police inspector who was present in the hall. Ten minutes later they all, somehow or other, resumed their seats, but there was not the same good order as before. And it was this seething chaos that poor Mr Verkhovensky had to face.

4

Still, I again ran out to see him behind the scenes, and I had just time to warn him excitedly that in my opinion the whole thing had fallen through and that he had better not come out, but go home at once on the excuse of a sudden attack of his gastric catarrh, and that I would take off my badge and go with him.

He was just about to walk on to the platform, but he stopped suddenly and, looking me up and down haughtily, said solemnly:

'And why, sir, do you think me capable of such baseness?'

I let him alone. I was absolutely convinced that before he came back something terrible was bound to happen. While I was standing there feeling utterly depressed, I again caught sight of the figure of the unknown professor, whose turn it was to appear after Mr Verkhovensky, and who kept raising his fist and bringing it down with all his might. He was still walking up and down as before, absorbed in himself and muttering something under his breath with a malicious but triumphant grin. I walked up to him somehow almost unintentionally.

'I wonder if you realize, sir,' I said, 'that, judging from many examples, if a lecturer keeps his audience for more than twenty minutes, it will stop listening to him. Not even a celebrity can hold the attention of an audience for half an hour.'

He stopped short suddenly, and seemed almost to shake with resentment.

'Don't worry,' he muttered contemptuously and walked past me.

At that moment I heard Mr Verkhovensky's voice in the hall.

'Oh, to blazes with you all!' I thought and rushed into the hall.

Mr Verkhovensky sat down in his arm-chair even before the disorder had died down. He was greeted by the first rows with none too friendly looks. (People, somehow, had stopped liking him at the club recently and treated him with much less respect than before.) However, thank goodness, they did not boo him. I had had a queer idea in my head ever since the previous day: I could not help feeling that he would be booed the moment he appeared. And yet because of the disorder in the hall he was not even noticed at first. But what could that man hope for if they had treated Karmazinov in that way? He was pale; he had not faced an audience for ten years. Judging by his agitation and everything I knew so well about him, it was clear to me that he himself regarded his present appearance on the platform as the most decisive moment of his life, or something like that. That was just what I was afraid of. The man was dear to me. And I can't tell you what I felt when he opened his lips and I heard his first phrase!

'Ladies and gentlemen,' he said suddenly, as though determined to go through with it, and in an almost shaking voice, too – 'Ladies and gentlemen, only this morning there lay before me one of the illegal leaflets that have been scattered lately in our town, and I asked myself for the hundredth time, "Wherein lies its secret?"'

The entire hall fell silent suddenly, all eyes were turned on him, some looking at him with alarm. He certainly knew how to hold their interest from the very first word! Even from behind the scenes heads were thrust out: Liputin and Lyamshin were listening avidly. Mrs Lembke again waved to me.

'Stop him, stop him, for goodness sake!' she whispered in alarm.

I merely shrugged; how was one to stop a man who *was determined to go through with it*? Alas, I understood Mr Verkhovensky.

'Oho, he's talking about the leaflets,' people whispered to one another in the audience.

The entire hall was stirred.

'Ladies and gentlemen, I have solved the whole mystery. The whole secret of their effect lies in their stupidity!' (His eyes flashed.) 'Yes, ladies and gentlemen, if this stupidity had been intentional, if it had been a calculated stupidity – oh, that would have been a stroke of genius! But we must do them justice: they did not calculate anything. It is the most bare, the most ingenuous, the most silly little stupidity – *c'est la bêtise dans son essence la plus pure, quelque chose comme un simple chimique*. If they had put it just a little more cleverly, everyone would see at once the whole paltriness of this silly little stupidity. But now everyone looks perplexed; no one can believe that it could be such elementary stupidity. "It's impossible that there's nothing more in it," everyone says to himself, and tries to discover the secret of it, sees a mystery in it, tries to read between the lines – the effect has been achieved! Oh, never before has stupidity been so triumphantly rewarded, in spite of the fact that it so often deserved it. For, *en parenthèse*, stupidity, like the greatest genius, is equally useful in shaping human destiny.'

'Epigrams of the late forties,' a voice cried, though rather modestly, but it was followed by an uproar: people began shouting and yelling.

'Ladies and gentlemen, hurrah! I propose a toast to stupidity!' Mr Verkhovensky shouted, defying his audience in an absolute frenzy.

I rushed up to him under the pretext of pouring out some water for him.

'Please leave it alone, sir. Mrs Lembke begs you –'

'No, you leave me alone, idle young man,' he turned on me, shouting at the top of his voice.

I fled.

'Ladies and gentlemen,' he went on, 'why all this excitement, why all these outcries of indignation I hear? I have come to you with an olive branch. I have brought you my last word – for in this business I have the last word   and we shall part friends.'

'Down with him!' some shouted.

'Order, order! Let him speak. Let him say what he wants to say!' others yelled.

The young teacher was particularly excited, for, having once plucked up courage to speak, he could no longer stop himself.

'Ladies and gentlemen, my last word in this business is universal forgiveness. I, an old man who expects nothing more from life, I solemnly declare that the spirit of life still breathes in us, and that the younger generation has not yet lost its living strength. The enthusiasm of our modern youth is as bright and pure as it was in our time. Only one thing has happened: a shift of aims, the substitution of one beauty for another! The whole misunderstanding has arisen only round the question what is more beautiful: Shakespeare or a pair of boots, Raphael or petroleum!'

'Informer!' cried some.

'Compromising questions!'

'*Agent provocateur!*'

'And I maintain,' Mr Verkhovensky squealed, beside himself with excitement, 'and I maintain that Shakespeare and Raphael are higher than the emancipation of the serfs, higher than nationalism, higher than socialism, higher than the younger generation, higher than chemistry, higher even than almost all humanity, for they are the fruit of all mankind, and perhaps the highest fruition that can possibly exist. A form of beauty already attained, but for the attaining of which I should perhaps not consent to live. Oh, Lord,' he cried, throwing up his hands, 'ten years ago I said the same thing from the platform in Petersburg, in exactly the same words, and they did not understand it in exactly the same way, they laughed and booed as now; you little men, what is it you lack still, that you don't understand? Why, do you realize, do you realize that mankind can get along without the Englishman, without Germany, too, and most certainly without the Russians – it can get on without science, without bread, but without beauty it cannot carry on, for then there will be nothing more to do in the world! The whole mystery is there, the whole of history is there! Even science could not exist a moment without beauty – do you know that, you who are laughing at me? It will sink into dark ignorance – you won't invent a nail even! I shan't give in!' he shouted idiotically in conclusion, and banged his fist on the table with all his might.

But while he was screaming senselessly and incoherently the disorder in the hall increased. Many people jumped up from their seats, and some of them dashed forward, nearer to the platform. It all happened much more quickly than I describe it, and there was no time to take adequate measures. Quite likely they did not wish to, either.

'It's all very well for you who have everything you want, you spoilt darlings!' the same divinity student bellowed at the foot of the platform, grinning with relish at Mr Verkhovensky, who noticed it and rushed up to the very edge of the platform.

'Have I not just this minute declared that the enthusiasm of our younger generation is as pure and bright as it was, and that it was coming to grief because it was mistaken only in the forms of the beautiful? Isn't that enough for you? And if you take into consideration the fact that the man who says this is a crushed and insulted father, then surely – oh, you little men – surely, one can't rise higher than that in impartiality and fair play! Ungrateful ones – unjust ones – why, oh why don't you want to be friends?'

And he suddenly burst into hysterical sobs. He wiped his streaming tears with his fingers. His shoulders and breast shook with sobbing. He was oblivious of everything in the world.

The audience was in a real panic, and almost everyone got up from their seats. Mrs Lembke, too, jumped up quickly, seized her husband by the arm and pulled him up. ... The whole affair had degenerated into a veritable public scandal.

'Mr Verkhovensky,' the divinity student bellowed gleefully, 'Fedka, the convict, an escaped prisoner, is now roaming about the town and its outskirts. He robs people and has recently committed another murder. Let me put this question to you: If you had not sold him into the army fifteen years ago in payment of a debt you had incurred at cards – if, that is, you had not lost him at cards – would he have been sentenced to penal servitude? Tell me, please. Would he have been murdering people now in his struggle for existence? What have you got to say to this, Mr Aesthete?'

I cannot possibly describe the scene that followed. To begin with, there was a furious outburst of applause. Not everybody was applauding – only one-fifth of the audience, perhaps – but they applauded madly. The rest of the audience rushed to the exit, but as the applauding section of the audience kept pressing forward, a general mêlée ensued. The ladies screamed, a few girls began crying and asking to be taken home. Lembke, standing by his seat, kept gazing wildly about him. Mrs Lembke completely lost her head – for the first time during her career among us. As for Mr Verkhovensky, he seemed at first to be literally crushed by the divinity student's words; but suddenly he raised his arms, as though spreading them over the audience, and yelled:

'I shake the dust from off my feet and I curse you – it's the end, the end. ...'

And, turning round, he ran behind the scenes, waving his hands menacingly.

'He has insulted the audience! ... Verkhovensky!' the furious members of the audience roared. They even wanted to run in pursuit after him. It was impossible to pacify them – not at the moment, at any rate – and suddenly the final catastrophe burst over the meeting like a bomb: the third reader, the maniac who had kept brandishing his fist behind the scenes, suddenly rushed out on to the platform.

He looked quite mad. He gazed at the excited hall with a broad, triumphant smile, full of boundless self-confidence, and seemed to be glad at the disorder. He was not in the least perturbed at having to speak in such an uproar; on the contrary, he was quite obviously delighted. This was so obvious that it attracted attention at once.

'What's this now?' people could be heard asking each other. 'Who on earth is this? What has he got to say?'

'Ladies and gentlemen,' the maniac shouted at the top of his voice, standing at the very edge of the platform and in almost the same shrill feminine voice as Karmazinov's, though without the latter's affected tones of the born gentleman – 'Ladies and gentlemen, twenty years ago, on the eve of the war against half of Europe, Russia was looked upon as an ideal country by all State and Privy Councillors. Literature was the handmaiden of the censorship; in the universities they taught military drill; the army was turned into a ballet, and the peasants paid their taxes and kept silent under the whip of serfdom. Patriotism meant the extortion of bribes from the living and the dead. Those who refused to take bribes were looked upon as rebels, for they disturbed the harmony of the existing order. Birch-woods were destroyed to uphold law and order. Europe trembled ... But never in the thousand years of her senseless existence had Russia sunk to such infamy. ...'

He raised his fist and, brandishing it menacingly over his head, suddenly brought it down as though crushing his opponent into dust. A furious roar arose from every side, followed by ear-splitting applause. Now almost half of the audience was applauding; the most innocent people were carried away: Russia was being abused in public and before the whole people, so how were they not to roar with delight?

'That's the stuff! That's the real stuff to give 'em! Hurrah! Yes, sir, that's none of your aesthetics!'

The maniac went on enthusiastically: 'Twenty years have passed since then. The universities have been opened and multiplied. Military drill has turned into a legend; thousands of officers are wanted to complement the army. The railways have eaten up all the capital and have covered Russia like a spider's web, so that in about fifteen years one will perhaps be able to get somewhere. Bridges are set on fire only occasionally, but the towns are burnt down regularly, according to a well-established order, each one in turn, during the fire season. In our courts we get King Solomon's judgements, and jurymen only take bribes because of the struggle for existence, for otherwise they would be doomed to starvation. The serfs have been liberated, and belabour one another with staves, instead of being flogged by their former landowners. Seas and oceans of vodka are consumed to support the budget, and in Novgorod, opposite the ancient and useless St Sofia Cathedral, an enormous bronze globe has been put up as a memorial to the thousand years of disorder and confusion. Europe frowns and begins to be uneasy again. Fifteen years of reforms! And yet even in the most grotesque epoch of her confused history Russian has never sunk –'

His last words could not be heard in the roar of the crowd. He could be seen raising his hand once more and bringing it down triumphantly. The enthusiasm of the crowd was unimaginable: they yelled, they clapped their hands, and some of the ladies even shouted: 'Enough! You won't say anything better!' They were like drunkards. The orator looked at them all and seemed to melt with delight at his own triumph. I caught sight of Lembke, who was pointing something out to someone in indescribable agitation. Mrs Lembke, pale as a sheet, was saying something hurriedly to the Prince, who had run up to her. But at that moment about six men, some sort of officials, rushed from behind the scenes on to the platform, grabbed the orator, and dragged him away behind the scenes. I can't understand how he could manage to tear himself away from them, but he did, and rushing up to the edge of the platform again, he just had time to shout with all his might, brandishing his fist:

'But never has Russia sunk so –'

But he was finally dragged away again. I saw about fifteen men, perhaps, rush off behind the scenes to set him free, not across the platform, but from the side, breaking down the light partition so that it finally collapsed. Then, hardly believing my own eyes, I saw the girl student (Virginsky's relative) jump up on the platform with the same roll of paper under her arm, wearing the same dress, and looking as red and as plump as ever, surrounded by two or three other women and two or three other men and accompanied by her mortal enemy, the schoolboy. I even had time to make out the phrase:

'Ladies and gentlemen, I have come here to tell you of the sufferings of the unhappy students and arouse them everywhere to protest.'

But I fled. I hid my badge in my pocket and by devious ways known only to myself got out of the house into the street. First of all, I ran, of course, to Mr Verkhovensky.

2

The End of the Fête

I

HE would not see me. He had locked himself up and was writing. At my repeated knocks and calls, he replied through the door:

'My friend, I've finished with everything. Who can ask anything more of me?'

'You haven't finished with anything, but have merely helped to make a mess of everything. For God's sake, no more epigrams, Mr Verkhovensky. Open the door. We must take steps. They may still come and insult you.'

I considered myself entitled to be particularly severe, and even exacting. I was afraid that he might do something still more crazy. But, to my surprise, I met with unusual firmness.

'Don't you be the first to insult me, then. Thank you for all you've done; but, I repeat, I have finished with people, good and bad. I'm writing a letter to Miss Shatov, whom I have so unpardonably been overlooking till now. You can take it to her to-morrow if you wish, but now *merci*.'

'I assure you, sir, that the affair is much more serious than you think. You believe you knocked someone on the head there, don't you? Well, you didn't.' (Oh, I was rude and discourteous, and I recall it now with regret!) 'There's no reason in the world why you should write to Miss Shatov. And – and what will become of you without me now? What do you know of practical life? You're hatching out some plan, aren't you? If you are, you'll only find yourself in trouble again.'

He got up and came up close to the door.

'You haven't been long with them, but you've got infected with their tone and language, *Dieu vous pardonne, mon ami, et Dieu vous garde*. I've always noticed the rudiments of decency in you, and, I dare-say, you'll change your mind, *après le temps*, of course, like all of us Russians. As for your remarks about my being impractical, let me re-mind you of an old idea of mine, namely that we have thousands and thousands of people in Russia whose only occupation in life is to attack other people for being impractical, with special fury and with the quite unbearable persistence of flies in summer, hurling accusations at all and sundry except themselves. *Cher*, please remember that I'm agitated, and don't torture me. Once again *merci* for everything, and let us part as Karmazinov parted from his public – that is to say, let us forget each other as generously as possible. He was talking with his tongue in his cheek when he begged his former readers to forget him; *quant à moi*, I am not so conceited, and I pin my hopes most of all on the youth of your inexperienced heart: why should you waste your time in remembering a useless old man? "Live on," my friend, as Nastasya wished me at my last name-day (*ces pauvres gens ont quelque fois des mots charmants et pleins de philosophie*). I do not wish you much happiness – you'll get tired of it; I do not wish you trouble, either; and, following the precept of the popular philosophy, I'll simply re-peat: "Live on" and try somehow or other not to be bored too much;

this vain wish I add from myself. Well, farewell, and farewell in all seriousness. And don't stand there at my door. I shan't open it.'

He went away, and I got nothing more out of him. In spite of his 'agitation' he spoke smoothly, unhurriedly, with weight and obviously trying to impress me. No doubt, he was a little vexed with me and was avenging himself indirectly on me, perhaps for yesterday's 'covered wagons' and 'trap-doors'. His public tears this morning, in spite of his having achieved a victory of sorts, had put him, he knew, in a somewhat absurd position, and there was no one who cared more about the beauty and severity of form in his relations with friends than Mr Verkhovensky. Oh, I don't blame him! But it was this fastidiousness and sarcasm, which still clung to him in spite of all shocks, that put my mind at rest at the time: a man who had apparently changed so little compared with what he had been, was most certainly not disposed at that moment to do anything tragic or untoward. That was how I reasoned at the time and, goodness me, how wrong I was! I did not take enough into consideration. ...

Anticipating things, I shall quote the first few lines of his letter to Miss Shatov, which she really did receive the next morning.

'*Mon enfant*, my hand is shaking, but I have done with everything. You were not present at my last encounter with the people, you did not come to that "reading" and you did well. But you will be told that in our Russia, which is so poor in men of character, one plucky man got up and, in spite of the dire threats hurled at him on every side, told those little fools the truth, that is, that they are little fools. *O, ce sont – des pauvres petits vauriens et rien de plus, des petits* fools – *voilà le mot!* The die is cast; I am going from this town for good, and I don't know whither I'm going. Everyone I loved has turned away from me. But you – you who are a pure and naïve creature; you who are so gentle, you whose destiny was nearly linked with mine at the bidding of a capricious and despotic heart; you who perhaps looked at me with contempt when I shed cowardly tears on the eve of our abortive marriage; you who cannot, however good you may be, look on me except as a comic figure – oh, for you, for you is the last cry of my heart, for you my last duty, for you alone! For I cannot leave you for ever with the thought that I am an ungrateful fool, a boor and an egoist, as, no doubt, a cruel and ungrateful heart, whom, alas, I cannot forget, assures you daily that I am. ...'

And so on and so forth, four closely written pages of large size.

Having knocked three times with my fist on the door in reply to his 'I shan't open', and having shouted after him that I was sure he would send his Nastasya to me three times that day, but that I would not come, I left him and ran off to Mrs Lembke.

2

There I was the witness of an outrageous scene: the poor woman was being cheated to her face, and I could do nothing. And, indeed, what could I have told her? I had had time to come to my senses a little and to realize that all I had to go upon were some vague feelings, some suspicious premonitions, and nothing more. I found her in tears, almost in hysterics, dabbing her forehead with eau-de-Cologne and sipping cold water. Peter Verkhovensky stood before her, talking without stopping, and the Prince, who kept silent as though his lips had been sealed. She was reproaching Peter, in a shrill voice and with tears, for his 'apostasy'. I was at once struck by the fact that she ascribed the whole failure, the whole disgrace of that morning – indeed, everything – to Peter's absence.

I noticed one important change in him: he looked as though he were a little too much worried about something; he was almost serious. As a rule, he never seemed serious; he was always laughing, even when he was angry – and he was often angry. Oh, he was angry even now; he spoke coarsely, carelessly, with vexation and impatience. He swore that he had been taken ill with a sick headache at Gaganov's lodgings, where he had happened to go early in the morning. Alas, the poor woman wanted so badly to be deceived again! The main question which I found under discussion was whether the ball – that is, the second half of the fête – should take place or not. Mrs Lembke would not hear of appearing at the ball after 'the insults she had suffered in the morning', in other words, she simply longed to be compelled to go, and by him, by Peter Verkhovensky, most of all. She looked on him as an oracle, and I really believe that if he had gone away at once she would have taken to her bed. But he never thought of going away; so far as he was concerned, it was absolutely essential that the ball should take place that evening and that Mrs Lembke should be there.

'Good heavens, why cry? Must you make a scene? Vent your spite on somebody? All right, vent it on me. Only hurry up, for goodness sake, because time's passing and you must make a decision. If the reading was a failure, the ball will make up for it. The Prince, too, is of the same opinion. A jolly good thing the Prince was there, or I don't know how it would have ended.'

The Prince had been against the ball at first (that is, against Mrs Lembke's appearance at the ball, for the ball had to take place, anyway), but after two or three such references to his opinion he began gradually to grunt in sign of agreement.

I was also surprised by the rather extraordinary discourtesy of Peter's tone. Oh, I indignantly reject the base story spread afterwards about some sort of liaison between Peter Verkhovensky and Mrs Lembke. There was no such thing, nor could there be. He got the upper hand of her merely by supporting her with all his might from the very start in her dreams of exerting an influence on society and the Ministry. He entered into all her plans, made them up for her himself, worked on her with the grossest flattery, entangled her from head to foot, and became as indispensable to her as the air she breathed. Catching sight of me, she uttered a cry, her eyes flashing.

'You'd better ask him,' she exclaimed. 'He never left me for a moment, just like the Prince. Tell me,' she addressed me, 'isn't it clear that it was a plot, a base, cunning plot to do as much harm as possible to me and Mr Lembke? Oh, they had it all arranged! It's a political movement, a regular movement!'

'You're going a bit too far as always. A whole romantic poem in your head, as usual. But I'm glad to see Mr – er –' (he pretended to have forgotten my name). 'He'll tell us what he thinks.'

'I'm entirely in agreement with Mrs Lembke,' I hastened to declare. 'It's quite obviously a plot. I've brought you back these badges, Mrs Lembke. Whether the ball is going to take place or not, is not my business, of course, because it's not in my power to decide; but my role as steward is at an end. Forgive my excitement, but I can't act against the dictates of common sense and my own convictions.'

'You hear? You hear?' she cried agitatedly.

'I hear, ma'am, and let me tell you this, sir,' he turned to me. 'I can only presume that you must have all eaten something that has turned you into raving lunatics. So far as I can see, nothing has happened, absolutely nothing, that has not happened before and that could not have happened at any time in this town. What plot? What happened was not nice; indeed, the whole thing was disgracefully stupid; but where's the plot? Is it a plot against Mrs Lembke who has spoiled them, protected them, and foolishly forgiven them all their childish pranks? Mrs Lembke, what have I been telling you constantly for the last month? What have I been warning you against? What on earth do you want all those people for? Why did you have to get mixed up with such a crew? Why? Whatever for? To unite society? But will they ever be united, for goodness sake?'

'When did you warn me? Quite the contrary, you approved, you even demanded. ... I must say I'm so astonished – why, you brought many strange people to see me yourself.'

'On the contrary, I argued with you and I did not approve what you did. As for bringing them to see you, it's quite true I did, but only after they'd come to you themselves by the dozen, and that, too, only quite recently to form that "literary quadrille", for you could not have done it without those blockheads. But I bet you anything you like that to-day they let in a dozen or more such blockheads without tickets!'

'I'm sure they did,' I confirmed.

'Well, you see, you're agreeing already. Just try to remember the tone that has been prevalent here recently – I mean in this rotten little town. Why, it was just pure insolence and shameless impertinence; it's been a crying shame all the time. And who's been encouraging it? Who covered it all up with her authority? Who's got them all confused? Who's made all that small fry angry? Why, all their family secrets can be found in your album. Didn't you pat your poets and artists on the head? Didn't you let Lyamshin kiss your hand? Wasn't it in your presence that a divinity student called a Regular State Councillor names and ruined his daughter's dresses with his tarred boots? Why, then, are you so surprised that the public is incensed against you?'

'But it was all your doing, yours and no one else's! Oh, my God!'

'No, madam, I kept warning you. We quarrelled about it. Do you hear? We quarrelled!'

'Goodness, you're lying to my face!'

'Well, naturally, you would say that. You must have a victim on whom you could vent your spite. Very well, vent it on me, as I've said already. I'd better ask you, Mr – er –' (He still could not remember my name.) 'Let's count on our fingers: I maintain that, with the exception of Liputin, there was no plot, no plot at all! I'll prove it, but first let us analyse Liputin. He came out with that fool Lebyatkin's verses – well, do you really believe that that was a plot? Has it never occurred to you that all Liputin was after was to show how clever he was? Seriously, seriously. He simply came out on to the platform with the aim of making everyone laugh and cheering them up, his patroness Mrs Lembke first of all. You don't believe me? But isn't that in keeping with all that has been going on here for the last month? And shall I tell you the whole truth? I'm sure that under other circumstances everything might have gone off without a hitch! It was a crude sort of a joke, and, I admit, a bit strong perhaps, but it was funny, wasn't it?'

'What? You think what Liputin did was witty?' Mrs Lembke cried in intense indignation. 'Such a stupid thing! Such a tactless thing! So mean, so contemptible – why, it was done intentionally! Oh, you're saying this on purpose! You must be in the plot with them!'

'To be sure. I was sitting behind them, hiding myself, setting the whole machinery going. But, good Lord, don't you see, if I had had anything to do with the plot – it would not have ended with Liputin alone! Or do you think that I had also arranged with my dear father that he should cause such a scene on purpose? Well, who is responsible for letting Father address the meeting? Who tried to stop you yesterday, only yesterday?'

'*Oh, hier il avait tant d'esprit,* I was counting so much on him; and, besides, he has such fine manners: I thought that he and Karmazinov – and then!'

'Yes, madam, and then! But in spite of his *tant d'esprit* my dear father has let you down, and if I had known beforehand that he would let you down so badly, then, being in the plot against your fête, I should certainly not have tried to persuade you yesterday not to let the goat into the kitchen garden, shouldn't I? And yet I did my best to dissuade you yesterday, and I did so because I had a feeling that this would happen. But, no doubt, I could not have foreseen everything: I daresay he did not know himself a minute before what he was going to blurt out. These neurotic old gentlemen aren't like other people. But the situation can still be saved: to satisfy the public, send two doctors to him to-morrow by administrative order and with all the honours due to such a solemn occasion to find out what's wrong with him. You could do it even to-day, and get him off straight to the hospital for a cold-water cure. It will at least make everyone laugh, and they'll realize that there was nothing to take offence at. I could make a public announcement about it this very evening at the ball, as I am his son. Karmazinov is a different matter. He showed himself to be a perfect ass, and dragged out his address for a whole hour – he must without any doubt have been in the plot with me! "Why shouldn't I make an unholy mess of it, too, to injure Mrs Lembke?" was what he probably said to himself – or did he?'

'Oh, Karmazinov, *quelle honte!* I nearly died with shame for our audience!'

'Well, I shouldn't have died, but I'd have grilled him instead. The audience was absolutely right. And who, again, is to blame for Karmazinov? Did I thrust him on you or not? Did I take any part in worshipping him or not? Well, to hell with him! But what about the third maniac, the political one? That's quite a different matter. Here we all made a bad slip. That wasn't only my plot.'

'Oh, don't speak of it. It was dreadful, dreadful! I alone am to blame for that!'

'Of course you are; but there I'll acquit you of all blame. Good Lord, who can keep an eye on them, those open-hearted ones! You can't guard against them even in Petersburg. He was recommended to you, wasn't he? Excellent recommendations he had, too! So you'll admit that you simply have to appear at the ball now. For that's a serious matter, since it was you who put him on the platform. Now it is your duty to declare publicly that you have nothing to do with that man, that the fellow is already in the hands of the police, and that you were deceived in a most inexplicable manner. You must state indignantly that you were the victim of a madman. For he is, of course, a madman and nothing else. That's what you have to tell the authorities about him. I can't stand fellows who bite. I say worse things, perhaps, but not from a public platform. And they are raising a clamour about a senator now.'

'What senator? Who's raising a clamour?'

'Well, you see, I don't understand it myself. You don't know anything about a senator, do you, Mrs Lembke?'

'A senator?'

'You see, they're all convinced that a senator has been appointed to be governor here and that you're being replaced from Petersburg. I've heard it from lots of people.'

'I've heard it, too,' I confirmed.

'Who said so?' cried Mrs Lembke, flushing all over.

'You mean, who said it first? I'm sure I don't know. But, there you are, people are talking. They were talking about it yesterday especially. They all seem to be very serious about it, though it's difficult to make anything out. Of course, those who're more intelligent and competent don't talk; but some of them, too, listen.'

'How despicable and – and how stupid!'

'That's why you simply must appear at the ball now, to show these fools.'

'I admit I feel myself that it is my duty to be there, but – what if another disgrace awaits us there? What if they don't turn up? No one will come, no one!'

'What excitement! They won't come? And what about the new clothes they have made, and the girls' dresses? I simply refuse to regard you as a woman after that. What a judge of character!'

'The marshal's wife won't be there! She won't be there!'

'But, after all, what has happened? Why shouldn't they come?' he cried at last with angry impatience.

'Dishonour, disgrace – that's what's happened. I can't tell you how frightful it was, and after that I simply can't go in there.'

'Why not? For goodness sake, you're not to blame for whatever has happened, are you? Why, then, do you take the blame on yourself? Don't you think that it's the audience rather that is to blame? Those venerable elderly gentlemen of yours, those heads of families of yours? They should have kept those blackguards and good-for-nothings in their place, for it's only a matter of blackguards and good-for-nothings and nothing serious. You can't rely on the police alone in any society anywhere. Here everyone seems to ask for a special policeman to protect him wherever he goes. They don't seem to understand that society must protect itself. And what do our high officials, our heads of families and their wives and daughters do in such circumstances? They hold their tongues and sulk. There is not enough social sense to control the mischief-makers.'

'Oh, that's quite true. They hold their tongues, sulk and – look about them.'

'And if it's true, then you have to tell them about it aloud, proudly, sternly. Indeed, you must show them that you're not beaten. Show those doddering old men and mothers of families. Oh, you can do it. You have the gift when your head is clear. You'll gather them round you and say it aloud, aloud. And afterwards a report to the *Voice* and *Stock Exchange News*. You wait, I'll do it myself. I'll arrange it all for you. And, of course, pay more attention to things, the buffet must be looked after; you must ask the Prince, you must ask this gentleman. ... You can't possibly leave us in the lurch, sir, when we have to start everything all over again. Well, and finally, Mr Lembke and you – arm in arm. How is Mr Lembke?'

'Oh, how unjustly, how wrongly, how cruelly you've always judged that angelic man!' Mrs Lembke suddenly cried with quite unexpected impulsiveness and almost with tears, putting her handkerchief to her eyes.

At that moment Peter Verkhovensky was almost speechless with astonishment.

'Why, good Lord, I – but what have I – I've always ...'

'You never, never! You have never done him justice!'

'You never can understand a woman!' Peter muttered with a wry smile.

'He's the most truthful, the most considerate, the most angelic person! He's kindness itself!'

'But, good Lord, did I ever say he wasn't kind? Why, I always – er – always said he was – er –'

'Never! But let's drop it. I'm afraid I haven't stuck up for him as I should. This morning that little Jesuit, the Marshal's wife, also dropped a few sarcastic hints about what happened yesterday.'

'Oh, she has other fish to fry now – she has to-day's affair to worry about. And why are you so upset about her not coming to the ball? Of course, she won't come, if she's got herself mixed up in such a scandal. Perhaps she had nothing to do with it, but still her reputation is at stake – her hands are soiled.'

'What are you talking about? I don't understand. Why are her hands soiled?' Mrs Lembke asked, looking bewildered.

'I mean to say I – I don't know anything really, but the town is

already ringing with the news that it was she who brought them
together.'

'What are you talking about? Brought who together?'

'Good Lord, don't you really know?' he cried with well-simulated
astonishment. 'Stavrogin and Lisa, of course!'

'What did you say?' we all cried together.

'Do you really mean to tell me that you don't know? Dear me!
Why, all sorts of tragic love affairs have been happening here: Lisa
slipped out of the carriage of the Marshal's wife and got straight into
Stavrogin's carriage and ran off with "the latter gentleman" to
Skvoreshniki in broad daylight. Just an hour ago, hardly an hour.'

We were dumbfounded. We, of course, began firing questions at
him; but, to our surprise, though he 'accidentally' witnessed the scene
himself, he was not able to give us a circumstantial account of it. The
whole thing apparently happened this way: when the Marshal's wife
was driving Lisa and Mr Drozdov from the 'reading' to the house of
Lisa's mother (who was still confined to bed with bad legs), they saw
a carriage waiting not far from the entrance, about twenty-five paces
away, just round the corner. When Lisa jumped out, she ran straight
to that carriage, the door was opened and quickly shut again; Lisa
shouted to Drozdov: 'Spare me!' – and the carriage drove off at full
speed to Skvoreshniki. To our hurried question whether it had been
all previously arranged and who was in the carriage, Peter replied
that he knew nothing about it; no doubt the whole thing must have
been arranged, but that he did not catch sight of Stavrogin in the carriage; possibly the old butler Alexey Yegorych was there. When
asked how he happened to be there and how he was so certain that
Lisa had gone to Skvoreshniki, he replied that he was there because he
had just happened to be passing and that, having caught sight of Lisa,
he had rushed up to the carriage (and yet, for all his curiosity, he could
not make out who was in it!), and that Mr Drozdov did not attempt
to give chase, and did not even try to stop Lisa and, indeed, kept back
the Marshal's wife, who was shouting at the top of her voice: 'She's
going to Stavrogin! She's going to Stavrogin!' But at this point I
could no longer restrain myself, and shouted furiously at Peter Verkhovensky:

'It's you who arranged it all, you blackguard! That's what kept
you so busy this morning. You helped Stavrogin, you came in the

carriage, you helped her into it – you, you, you! Mrs Lembke, he's
your enemy! He'll ruin you, too! Take care!'

And I ran headlong out of the house.

To this day I can't understand how I could have brought myself to
hurl those words at him. I can't help wondering at it myself. But I was
right: everything, as appeared afterwards, happened almost exactly as
I had said it would. Above all, the equivocal way in which he broke
the news was too obvious. He had not told us about it immediately on
his arrival as a sensational piece of news, but pretended that we already knew it without his telling us – which was quite impossible in
so short a time. And if we had known it, we shouldn't have been able
to keep it to ourselves till he mentioned it. Nor could he have heard
that the town was 'ringing' with the story about the marshal's wife in
so short a time. Besides, while telling us the story he allowed himself
a rather contemptible and self-satisfied smirk once or twice, no doubt
considering that we were fools whom he had taken in completely.

But I had other worries now. I was convinced of the truth of the
main fact, and I rushed out of Mrs Lembke's drawing-room beside
myself. The catastrophe had struck me to the very heart. I felt so upset
that I could have cried, and perhaps I did cry. I did not know what to
do. My first impulse was to go and see Mr Verkhovensky, but the disagreeable fellow again refused to open the door. Nastasya assured me
in a deferential whisper that he had gone to bed, but I did not believe
it. At Lisa's house I succeeded in questioning the servants; they confirmed the report about her elopement, but knew nothing themselves.
The house was in a turmoil; Mrs Drozdov was having fainting fits and
Maurice Drozdov was with her. I did not think it possible to ask for
Drozdov. I asked them about Peter Verkhovensky, and they told me
that he had been in and out of the house continually during the past
few days, sometimes twice in one day. The servants looked sad, and
spoke of Lisa with a special sort of respect; they were fond of her.
That she was ruined, utterly ruined, I had no doubt, but I simply could
not understand the psychological aspect of the affair, especially after
her scene with Stavrogin the previous day. I did not relish the idea of
running about the town and making inquiries in the houses of our
malicious acquaintances, who, of course, already knew the news; for,
apart from anything else, it was so humiliating for Lisa. But it was
certainly strange that I should have run to see Miss Shatov. But I was

not admitted (no one had been admitted to Mrs Stavrogin's house since the previous day); I don't know what I could have said to her and why I was so anxious to see her. From there I went to see her brother. Shatov listened gloomily and in silence. I may add that I found him looking quite unusually depressed; he seemed extraordinarily self-absorbed, and apparently listened to me with an effort. He said practically nothing and began pacing his cubby-hole from one corner to the other, stamping more loudly than usual. But as I was descending the stairs he shouted after me that I should go and see Liputin: 'You'll learn everything there.' But I did not go to see Liputin. Instead, I retraced my steps, though I had already gone a good way, and went back to Shatov's. I half opened the door of his room, and without going in asked him laconically and without any preliminaries whether he intended to go and see Mary that day. Shatov just swore at me, and I went away. I note here, so as not to forget, that he went specially to the other end of the town that very evening to see Mary, whom he had not seen for some time. He found her in excellent health and spirits, and Lebyatkin dead drunk, asleep on the sofa in the front room. That was exactly at nine o'clock. He told me so himself the following day when we met for a moment in the street. Before ten o'clock I made up my mind to go to the ball, no longer as 'a young steward' (I had left my badge at Mrs Lembke's, anyway), but because I was very curious to hear (without asking any questions) what the townspeople were saying about all those happenings in general. And, besides, I was rather anxious to have a look at Mrs Lembke, too, if only from a distance. I reproached myself a great deal for having rushed out of her house like that in the afternoon.

3

The whole of that night, with its almost grotesque happenings and the terrible *dénouement* in the morning, still haunts me like some horrible nightmare, and forms (for me, at any rate) the most distressing part of my chronicle. Though I was too late for the ball, I did arrive towards its end – so rapidly was it destined to end. It was past ten o'clock when I reached the entrance of the Marshal's house, where the same White Hall, in which the reading had taken place, had, in spite of the short interval of time, been cleared and made ready as the chief ballroom for (as was supposed) the whole town. But however much I had been against the ball in the morning, I had even then no idea of the whole truth; not one family of quality appeared; even the Civil Servants who occupied positions of any consequence were not there – and this was certainly a most striking fact. As for the ladies and girls, Peter Verkhovensky's conjectures (the insidious nature of which was all too plain now) turned out to be utterly wrong: only a few people had come to the ball; there was scarcely one lady to four men, and what ladies! Some "nondescript" wives of regimental officers, post office clerks and low-grade Civil Servants, and other small fry, three doctors' wives with their daughters, two or three poor country gentlewomen, the seven daughters and the niece of the secretary I believe I have mentioned earlier, shopkeepers' wives – was this what Mrs Lembke expected? Half of the merchants of our town even had kept away. As for the men, there were great numbers of them, even though all the people of quality were conspicuously absent, but they made an ambiguous and suspicious impression. There were, of course, some very quiet and respectable army officers with their wives, a few very docile fathers, like that secretary, for instance, the father of seven daughters. All these humble, insignificant people had come because it was 'inevitable', as one of these gentlemen expressed it. On the other hand, the large number of 'smart' individuals and, besides, the large number of persons whom Peter Verkhovensky and myself had suspected of having been admitted without tickets, seemed even bigger than in the morning. For the time being they were all sitting in the refreshment bar, and had gone straight there as soon as they had arrived, as though it were a prearranged meeting-place. So, at least, it seemed to me. The refreshment bar was in a large room at the end of a long succession of rooms. It was there Prokhorych installed himself with all the attractions of the club kitchen and with a tempting display of snacks and drinks. I noticed several individuals whose coats were almost in tatters and whose rig-out was certainly highly unsuited for a ball. It was clear that someone must have taken a great deal of trouble to bring them there in a state of sobriety which would not last long; goodness only knows where they had come from, they were certainly not residents of our town. I knew, of course, that it was Mrs Lembke's idea that the ball should bear a democratic character, and that 'even artisans should not be refused admission if one of them should happen to pay for his ticket'. She could boldly utter those words at her committee meeting, for she knew perfectly well that it would never have occurred to any of our artisans, who were all extremely poor, to buy a ticket. But still I doubted very much whether the fellows in the shabby and almost tattered clothes should have been admitted, in spite of the democratic sentiments of the committee. But who let them in and with what object? Liputin and Lyamshin had been deprived of their steward's badges (though they were present at the ball, as they were taking part in the 'literary quadrille'); but, to my surprise, Liputin's place was taken by the divinity student who had done more than anybody else to discredit the 'matinée' by his brush with Mr Verkhovensky, and Lyamshin's place by Peter; what was one therefore to expect in such circumstances? I tried to listen to the conversations. Some of the opinions I heard expressed struck me by their utter grotesqueness. In one group, for instance, it was maintained that Lisa's elopement with Stavrogin had been arranged by Mrs Lembke, who had been paid for it by Stavrogin. Even the amount of money was mentioned. It was asserted that she had organised the fête with that aim in view, that that was the reason why half of the townspeople, having got wind of what was on foot, had not come to the ball, and that Lembke himself was so shocked that he 'had gone off his head', and she was now 'leading a madman on a string'. There was a great deal of laughter in the ballroom – hoarse, wild, and cunning. Everyone, too, was violently criticizing the ball and abusing Mrs Lembke without ceremony. Taken as a whole, it was a disorderly, incoherent, drunken, and agitated babble, so that it was difficult to make head or tail of it or draw any conclusions from it. In the refreshment bar there were people, too, who were simply enjoying themselves, as well as a number of highly obliging and gay ladies of the sort who were not surprised at, or frightened of, anything – mostly regimental ladies and their husbands. They formed gay tea-parties at the little tables. The refreshment bar became the cosy refuge for almost half the guests. And yet in a little time all this mass of people would rush into the ballroom; it was a horrifying thought.

Meanwhile three meagre quadrilles were formed in the White Hall with the help of the Prince. The young ladies were dancing, while their parents were fondly watching them. But many of the more respectable guests were beginning to wonder how they could, after providing a little amusement for their girls, get away in good time before 'the trouble starts'. For absolutely everyone was convinced that the trouble would certainly start. I should have found it difficult to describe Mrs Lembke's state of mind. I did not attempt to speak to her, though I did go close up to her. She did not reply to my bow as I entered, for she did not notice me (she really did not notice). She had a worried look and a haughty and contemptuous, though restless and troubled, expression in her eyes. She controlled herself, though the whole thing was obviously an ordeal to her – who and what was she doing it for? She ought to have left and, above all, taken her husband away, but she remained! I could see from her face that her eyes were 'fully opened' and that she had nothing more to expect. She did not even ask Peter to come and talk to her (he seemed to avoid her himself; I saw him in the refreshment bar, and he looked extremely cheerful). But she remained at the ball nevertheless, and did not let Mr Lembke leave her side for a moment. Oh, up to the last moment she would have repudiated any hint about his health with genuine indignation, even that morning. But now her eyes were to be opened about that, too. For my part, I could not help thinking from the first glance that Mr Lembke looked worse than he had done in the morning. It seemed to me as though he were in a sort of coma and did not realize where he was. Sometimes he would suddenly look round him with unexpected severity; he did so, for instance, twice at me. Once he tried to say something. He began in a loud, resonant voice but did not finish the sentence, throwing a humble old Civil Servant who happened to be near him almost into a panic. But even this humble section of the public in the White Hall tried to get out of Mrs Lembke's way gloomily and fearfully, at the same time throwing rather strange glances at her husband, glances that were too penetrating and frank to be in keeping with the timidity of these people.

'It was that fact that sent a chill through my heart,' Mrs Lembke admitted later to me, 'and I suddenly began to suspect what was wrong with Mr Lembke.'

Yes, she was to blame again! Probably when she decided with Peter Verkhovensky that the ball should take place and that she should be present, she must have gone again to the study of Mr Lembke, who had been completely 'shaken' at the 'reading', and had again used all her seductive arts and made him go with her. But how she must have suffered just now! And yet she did not leave! Whether it was her pride that tormented her or whether she simply lost her head – I don't know. In spite of her haughtiness, she tried to say a few words to some of the ladies with humiliation and smiles, but they looked embarrassed, tried to shake her off with mistrustful monosyllabic 'Yes, ma'am,' and 'No, ma'am,' and quite obviously avoided her.

The only one of all the persons of high rank in our town to be present at the ball was the pompous General whom I have already had occasion to describe before, and who at the party of the Marshal's wife after Stavrogin's duel with Gaganov 'opened the door to public impatience'. He walked importantly about the room, watched and listened, trying to imply by his demeanour that he had come more for the sake of observing the proceedings than for his own indubitable pleasure. He finished up by attaching himself to Mrs Lembke and not moving away from her a step, obviously trying to cheer her up and reassure her. He undoubtedly was a most kind-hearted man, very dignified, and so old that one could even put up with his compassion. But to admit to herself that this old windbag had the impudence to pity and almost to patronize her, knowing that he was honouring her by his presence, was extremely galling. The General, however, would not leave her and kept chattering without stopping.

'They say a town cannot exist without seven righteous men – seven, I believe, it is – can't remember the exact number. I don't know how many of these seven – er – unquestionably righteous men of our town – er – have had the honour of coming to your ball, ma'am, but in spite of their presence I'm beginning to feel rather – er – in danger. *Vous me pardonnez, charmante dame, n'est-ce pas?* I speak allegorically, but I've just been to the – er – refreshment bar and I'm glad to be back safe and sound. Our priceless Prokhorych, I'm afraid, ma'am, isn't quite in his element there and I shouldn't be surprised if – er – his tent disappeared from over his head by the morning. I'm joking though. I'm only waiting to see what the "literary quadrille" is going to be like, then I'm off to bed. You must excuse a gouty old fellow, ma'am, but as a rule I go early to bed and you, too, ma'am, I'd advise you to go bye-bye, as they say *aux enfants*. Dammе, ma'am, I've come here to have a look at some pretty girls whom – er – I can never hope to see in such rich variety as in this place. They're all from the other side of the river, and I'm afraid I never drive down there. There's the wife of

an officer, ma'am, of the regiment of chasseurs, I believe – er – not at
all bad looking, ma'am, not bad looking at all and – er – knows it herself, she does, too. I've had a few words with the little rogue – a forward filly – and – er – the girls, too, are fresh, ma'am, fresh. Pity,
though, there's nothing else but their freshness to – er – commend
them. However, one mustn't grumble, what? Some of 'em are real
peaches, except that their lips are a little too thick. As a rule, ma'am,
the beauty of Russian women's faces hasn't got that regularity and –
er – I'm afraid they're more like pancakes than anything else. *Vous me
pardonnez, n'est-ce pas* – their eyes, though, are pretty – laughing eyes.
These peaches are very charming during the first two years of their
youth – three years even, I daresay – but after that I'm sorry to say,
ma'am, they tend to – er – spread incontinently – er – producing in
their husbands that sad indifferentism which – er – I'm afraid rather
contributes to the development of the woman question – if I understand it correctly. H'm! The hall's nice; the rooms aren't badly decorated. Could be worse, I suppose. The music, too, could have been
worse – I don't say should have been. It's the scarcity of ladies that
makes such a bad effect. Afraid the clothes aren't worth mentioning.
Disgusting the way that chap in the grey trousers is dancing the can-
can. No sense of decency. I shouldn't have minded if he did it because
he was a bit merry, since he's our local chemist, but – er – it's a bit too
early at eleven o'clock even for a chemist. Two fellows in the refreshment bar had a fight, but they weren't thrown out. Fellows who start
a fight at eleven o'clock should be thrown out whatever the customs of the public. It's different at three o'clock. One has to make
allowances for public opinion then, if, that is, the ball lasts as long as
that. I see, ma'am, Mrs Stavrogin hasn't kept her word and hasn't sent
flowers. Well, I suppose, *pauvre mère*, she's something else to worry
about now besides flowers. And what about poor Lisa, eh? You've
heard, haven't you? I'm told the whole thing's rather mysterious and
– er – and that chap Stavrogin's again mixed up in it … Well, well.
I really ought to go home to bed – afraid can't keep my eyes open.
But what about that "literary quadrille"? When's that coming on?'

At last the 'literary quadrille' began. Whenever during the past few
days the forthcoming ball was being discussed in our town, the conversation was invariably and immediately switched over to the 'literary quadrille', and as no one had the faintest idea what it was all about,

it always aroused immense curiosity. There could be nothing more dangerous for its success – and what a terrible disappointment it turned out to be!

The hitherto locked side-doors of the White Hall were suddenly thrown open and a few masked figures appeared. The public surrounded them eagerly. All the people in the refreshment bar flocked to the last man into the ballroom. The masks took their places for the dance. I succeeded in squeezing my way through to the front, and I took up a position immediately behind Mrs Lembke, von Lembke, and the General. At that moment Peter Verkhovensky, who was not to be seen till then, hurried up to Mrs Lembke.

'I've been in the refreshment room all the time keeping an eye on things,' he whispered with the expression of a guilty schoolboy, which he assumed on purpose to provoke her even more.

She flushed with anger.

'I wish you'd stop deceiving me now at least, you insolent man!' she blurted out almost aloud, so that it was distinctly heard by several people.

Peter rushed off, looking extremely satisfied with himself.

It would be difficult to imagine a more wretched, vulgar, tasteless, and insipid allegory than that 'literary quadrille'. Nothing less suitable for our public could have been devised; and yet, I am told, it was Karmazinov who had devised it. It is true it was Liputin who had arranged it in consultation with the lame teacher who had been at Virginsky's party. But, all the same, it was Karmazinov who had thought of the idea and, it was rumoured, even meant to dress up and take a special and principal part in it. The quadrille was made up of six miserable pairs of masks – not really masks even, for they all wore the same clothes as everyone else. Thus, for instance, one short, elderly gentleman in a frock-coat – in fact, dressed like everyone else – and a venerable grey beard (tied on – this constituted the whole of his fancy dress) was bobbing up and down on the same spot as he danced with a stolid expression on his face, working away as fast as he could with his feet without moving an inch. He emitted curious sorts of sounds in a soft but husky bass, and it was that huskiness of his voice that was meant to suggest one of the well-known newspapers. Opposite this mask danced two giants X and Z, and these letters were pinned on their frock-coats, but what the X and Z meant remained a mystery.

The 'honest Russian thought' was represented by a middle-aged gentleman wearing spectacles, a frock-coat, gloves and – manacles (real manacles). Under the arm of this 'thought' was a brief-case containing documents referring to some 'case'. An opened letter from abroad to convince the sceptics of the honesty of the 'honest Russian thought' peeped out of his pocket. All this the stewards explained by word of mouth, since it was impossible to read the letter which protruded from his pocket. In his raised right hand 'the honest Russian thought' held a wine-glass, as though he were about to propose a toast. Close at each side of him two short-haired nihilist girls capered and *vis-à-vis* danced another elderly gentleman in a frock-coat, but with a heavy cudgel in his hand, apparently representing a very redoubtable periodical, though not a Petersburg one: 'I'll wipe you off the face of the earth!' But though armed with a cudgel, he just could not bear the spectacles of 'the honest Russian thought' fixed intently upon him and tried to look away, and when he did his *pas de deux*, he twisted and turned and did not know what to do with himself, so much, apparently, did his conscience prick him. ... However, I am afraid I cannot recall all those rather absurd inventions of theirs; it was all of the same kind, so that in the end I felt thoroughly ashamed. And it was the same feeling of shame that could be read on the faces of the audience, even on the most morose countenances of those who had come from the refreshment bar. When a man feels ashamed, he generally begins to get angry and is inclined to become cynical. Gradually, our audience, too, began to murmur.

'What's all this about?' a man in one group who came from the refreshment bar muttered.

'Some stupid nonsense.'

'Some sort of literature. They're criticizing *The Voice.*'

'What do I care?'

From another group:

'Donkeys!'

'No, they're not donkeys; it's we who are the donkeys.'

'Why are you a donkey?'

'I'm not a donkey.'

'Very well, if you're not a donkey, then I'm certainly not.'

From a third group:

'Kick them all in the behind and to hell with them!'

'Pull the hall down!'

From a fourth group:

'I wonder the Lembkes aren't ashamed to look on!'

'Why should they be ashamed? You aren't, are you?'

'Of course I'm ashamed, but he's the Governor.'

'And you're a pig!'

'Never in my life have I seen such a dull and uninteresting ball,' a lady next to Mrs Lembke remarked viciously, quite obviously with the intention of being overheard.

The lady was about forty, plump and painted, wearing a bright-coloured silk dress; almost everyone in town knew her, but no one received her. She was the widow of a State Councillor, who had left her a wooden house and a meagre pension, but she lived well and kept a carriage and horses. She had been the first to pay a visit to Mrs Lembke about two months before, but the Governor's wife had not received her.

'I could have foretold that,' she added, looking insolently into Mrs Lembke's face.

'If you could have foretold it, why did you come?' Mrs Lembke could not refrain from asking.

'Because, madam, I was too simple,' the quick-witted lady snapped back in a flash in great agitation (she was spoiling for a fight); but the General placed himself between them.

'*Chère dame*,' he said, bending over Mrs Lembke, 'I honestly think you ought to be going. We're only in their way, and they're sure to have a thoroughly good time without us. You've done your part, you've opened the ball for them, and now – er – you can leave them in peace. And – er – I don't think, ma'am, Mr Lembke is quite at his best just now, is he? I only hope there won't be any trouble.'

But it was too late.

During the quadrille Mr Lembke was watching the dancers with a sort of wrathful perplexity, and when comments began to be made in the audience, he began to cast agitated glances round him. Then for the first time he caught sight of some of the individuals who had come from the refreshment-room; an expression of extreme surprise appeared on his face. Suddenly there was loud laughter at some horse-play in the quadrille: the editor of 'redoubtable periodical not published in Petersburg', who was dancing with the cudgel in his hands, feeling that he could no longer endure the staring spectacles of 'honest Russian thought', and not knowing how to escape it, suddenly, in the last figure, walked upside down towards the spectacles, which, by the way, was meant to signify the continual upside-down distortion of common-sense in 'the redoubtable periodical not published in Petersburg'. As Lyamshin was the only one who could walk upside down, it was he who had volunteered to represent the editor with the cudgel. Mrs Lembke had no idea that anyone would be walking upside down. 'They concealed it from me,' she kept repeating to me afterwards in indignation and despair. The loud laughter of the crowd greeted not the allegory, of course, for nobody cared anything about it, but simply the spectacle of a man walking upside down in a dress-suit with tails. Lembke flew into a rage and trembled all over.

'Blackguard!' he cried, pointing to Lyamshin. 'Seize the villain and turn him over – turn his legs – his head – with his head up – up!'

Lyamshin jumped to his feet. The laughter grew louder.

'Turn out all the villains who're laughing!' Lembke suddenly ordered.

The crowd began to mutter and roar with laughter.

'You can't do that, sir!'

'You mustn't abuse the public, sir!'

'You're a fool yourself!' a voice cried from a corner.

'Filibusters!' someone cried from another corner.

Lembke turned round quickly at the cry and turned pale. A blank smile appeared on his face, as though he suddenly remembered and understood something.

'Ladies and gentlemen,' Mrs Lembke addressed the crowd, which was pressing forward, drawing her husband after her at the same time – 'Ladies and gentlemen, please excuse Mr Lembke. Mr Lembke is not feeling well – excuse – forgive him, ladies and gentlemen!'

I heard her distinctly say 'forgive'. The whole thing happened very quickly. But I distinctly remember that a section of the public, as though in alarm, made for the door just at that moment, immediately after those words of hers. I also remember a woman's hysterical, tearful cry:

'Oh, the same thing again!'

And suddenly another bombshell burst in the midst of the crush that had started at the door, exactly 'the same thing again':

'Fire! The suburb across the river is on fire!'

The only thing I cannot remember is where this cry first arose: whether it was uttered by someone in one of the rooms or, as it seems likely, by someone who came running in from the stairs leading to the entrance hall, but it was followed by such an uproar that I can't possibly describe it. More than half of the guests at the ball came from across the river – owners or occupiers of wooden houses in the suburb. They rushed to the windows, pulled back the curtains at once and tore down the blinds. The fire, it is true, had only just started, but it was burning fiercely in three separate places, and that was what had frightened them.

'Arson! The Spigulin men!' people in the crowd yelled.

I remember a few highly characteristic exclamations:

'I had a feeling that they'd set fire to the town – I've had a premonition that they'd do it for these last few days!'

'The Spigulin men, the Spigulin men! No one else!'

'They got us all here on purpose so that they could set fire to the suburb!'

This last most amazing cry came from a woman; it was an unintentional and involuntary cry of some hard-fisted woman whose worldly goods were all on fire. They all now rushed to the exit. I shall not attempt to describe the crush in the entrance hall over the sorting out of fur coats, shawls, and cloaks, the shrieks of frightened women, and the crying of girls. I don't think there was any theft, but it would not surprise me if in such disorder some people went away without their warm clothes because they were unable to find them, which gave rise to all sorts of legends, appropriately embellished, long afterwards. Mr and Mrs Lembke were almost crushed to death by the crowd in the doorway.

'Stop 'em all! Don't let anyone out!' Lembke shouted, stretching out his arms menacingly towards the people who pressed round him on all sides. 'Search everyone – everyone without exception – at once!'

There was an outburst of loud and violent swearing in the ball-room.

'Andrey! Andrey!' Mrs Lembke cried in utter despair.

'Arrest her first!' Mr Lembke shouted, pointing a menacing finger at his wife. 'Search her first! The ball was arranged with the object of setting fire to the town!'

She uttered a cry and fainted (oh, this time it was a real faint, of course!). The Prince, the General and I rushed to her aid; there were others who came to our help at that difficult moment, including some women. We carried the unhappy woman out of that hell to her carriage; but she only recovered consciousness as she reached her house, and her first cry was again about her husband. With the destruction of all her illusions, only her husband remained to her. A doctor was sent for. I stayed at her place for a whole hour, and so did the Prince; the General, in a fit of generosity (though he had been very frightened himself), expressed the wish to remain 'at the bedside of the unhappy woman' all night, but ten minutes later he fell asleep in an arm-chair in the drawing-room while waiting for the doctor, and there we left him.

The Police Commissioner, who had hastened from the ball to the fire, had succeeded in bringing Mr Lembke out of the hall after us. He tried to get him to join his wife in the carriage, doing his best to persuade His Excellency 'to rest'. I cannot understand why he did not succeed. Of course, Mr Lembke refused to hear of a rest, and was anxious to rush to the fire; but that was no excuse. It ended in his taking him to the fire in his open carriage. He told us afterwards that Lembke was gesticulating all the way and 'gave expression to ideas which were impossible to carry out because they were so extraordinary'. It was officially stated later that His Excellency had at that time been in a delirious condition owing to 'sudden shock'.

There is no need to describe how the ball ended. A few dozen revellers, and with them some ladies, remained. There were no police. The band was forced to stay behind, and the musicians who attempted to leave were beaten black and blue. By the morning 'Prokhorych's tent' was pulled down, they drank and danced with complete abandon, made a mess of the rooms, and only at daybreak some of the gang, drunk as lords, arrived at the fire in time for new disorders. The rest fell asleep in the rooms dead drunk on the velvet sofas and the floor. In the morning they were dragged out by their legs into the street. So ended the fête in aid of the governesses of our province.

4

The fire alarmed those guests at the ball who lived in the suburb across the river because it was a clear case of arson. It is remarkable that the first cry of 'Fire!' was immediately followed by another shout: 'The Spigulin men have set fire to the suburb.' Now it is, indeed, well known that three Spigulin men did in fact take part in setting fire to the suburb, but – that was all; the rest of the workmen of the factory were entirely exonerated both by public opinion and officially. Besides those three blackguards (one of whom has been caught and confessed, and the other two are still at large), there can be no doubt that Fedka the convict also took part in the incendiarism. That is all that is so far known for certain about the origin of the fire; the theories of the fire are quite a different matter. What was the motive of the three blackguards? Were they or were they not acting on instructions? It is difficult to give an answer to all these questions even now.

The fire, owing to the strong wind, the fact that practically all the houses of the suburb were wooden, and, finally, that they had been set alight from three sides, spread rapidly, and a whole quarter of the suburb was soon blazing fiercely (the suburb was actually set alight at two ends: the third fire was dealt with in time and extinguished almost as soon as it began, of which later). The Petersburg and Moscow papers, however, exaggerated our calamity: no more (and perhaps even less) than a quarter of the entire suburb, roughly speaking, was burnt down. Our fire brigade, though rather inadequate to the size and population of the town, acted, however, very efficiently and with great devotion. But it would not have been able to do much, even with the vigorous assistance of the inhabitants, if the wind, which suddenly abated at dawn, had not changed. When I reached the suburb, only one hour after our flight from the ball, the fire was already at its height. A whole street which ran parallel to the river was blazing. It was as light as day. I shall not attempt to describe the scene of the fire: who in Russia does not know what it is like? The side-streets close to the burning street were teeming with bustling people. Expecting the fire to spread any moment, the inhabitants were dragging out their belongings, but still refused to leave their dwellings and were sitting, in expectation, on the trunks and feather beds they had dragged out, each under his own windows. Part of the male population were hard at work ruthlessly chopping down fences, and even taking to pieces whole hovels which were nearest the fire and on the windward side. Only the children who had been wakened were crying, and the women who had already dragged out their chattels were howling and

wailing. Those who had not managed to save their belongings got on
with their work in silence and were busily hauling them out into the
street. Sparks and embers were flying in all directions, and people put
them out as best they could. At the scene of the fire itself there were
crowds of spectators who had come running from all over the town.
Some of them helped to put out the flames, others stood gazing,
fascinated by the sight. A big fire at night always produces an exciting
and exhilarating effect; this explains the attraction of fireworks; but
in the case of fireworks, the graceful and regular shape of the flames
and the complete immunity from danger produce a light and playful
effect comparable to the effect of a glass of champagne. A real fire is
quite another matter: there the horror and a certain sense of personal
danger, combined with the well-known exhilarating effect of a fire at
night, produce in the spectator (not, of course, in one whose house
has burnt down) a certain shock to the brain and, as it were, a challenge to his own destructive instincts, which, alas, lie buried in the
soul of even the meekest and most domesticated official of the lowest
grade. This grim sensation is almost always delightful. 'I really don't
know if it is possible to watch a fire without some enjoyment!' This
is word for word what Mr Verkhovensky said to me one night on
returning from a fire, at which he happened to be present by accident,
and under the first impression of the scene. Doubtless, the man who
enjoys watching a fire at night will not hesitate to rush into the flames
himself to save a child or an old woman; but that is an entirely different matter.

Following close behind the crowd of curious onlookers, I eventually
came, without making any enquiries, to the main and most dangerous
spot, where I at last caught sight of Lembke, whom I was looking for
at the request of Mrs Lembke herself. His position was amazing and
extraordinary. He was standing on the ruins of a fence; to the left,
about thirty paces away, rose the blackened skeleton of a wooden
two-storied house which had almost completely burnt down, with
holes instead of windows in each story, with its roof fallen in, and
with flames still creeping here and there among the charred beams. At
the back of the courtyard, about twenty paces from the burnt house,
a small cottage, also two stories high, was just beginning to blaze, and
the firemen were doing their utmost to save it. To the right the firemen and a crowd of people were concentrating on a large wooden

building which was not burning, but which had caught fire several times already and which was quite certain to burn down presently. Lembke shouted and gesticulated, standing with his face to the cottage, giving orders which nobody carried out. At first I thought that he had been left standing there on purpose and that no one bothered about him any more. At least, though the large mixed crowd, which surrounded him and among which were some gentlemen and even the cathedral priest, was listening to him with curiosity and astonishment, no one attempted to speak to him or tried to get him away. Pale and with glittering eyes, Lembke was delivering himself of the most amazing things; and, to crown it all, he was bareheaded, having lost his hat long ago.

'It's all incendiarism! It's nihilism! Whatever is burning, is nihilism!' I heard almost with horror, and though there was nothing to be surprised at any longer, reality always has something shocking about it.

'Your Excellency,' a policeman, who rushed up to him suddenly, said, 'hadn't you better go home and have a rest? It's dangerous for Your Excellency even to stand here.'

This policeman, as I found out later, had been detailed by the Police Commissioner to watch over Lembke and to do his utmost to get him home, and in case of danger even to use force – a task evidently beyond his power.

'They'll dry the tears of the victims of the fire, but they'll burn down the town. It's all those four blackguards, four and a half. Arrest the rascal! He insinuates himself into the honour of families. They used governesses to set fire to the houses. That's disgraceful, disgraceful. Good Lord! what is he doing there?' he shouted, suddenly noticing a fireman on the top of the blazing cottage, under whom the roof had almost burnt away and round whom flames were flaring up. 'Pull him down! Pull him down! He'll fall through! He'll catch fire! Put him out! What is he doing there?'

'He's putting out the fire, sir.'

'Not likely. The fire's in the minds of people, and not on the roofs of houses. Pull him down and give it up! Better give it up! Better give it up! Let it put itself out! Good heavens, who's crying there? An old woman! An old woman is screaming! Why have you forgotten the old woman?'

To be sure, on the ground floor of the blazing cottage an old woman was screaming, an eighty-year-old relative of the merchant who owned the burning house. But she had not been forgotten. She had gone back to the burning house herself, while it was still possible, with the insane idea of dragging out her feather-bed from a corner which was still untouched by the flames. Choking in the smoke and screaming with the heat, for the room had in the meantime caught fire, she was trying with all her might to push her feather-bed through a broken window-pane with her feeble hands. Lembke rushed to her assistance. They all saw him run up to the window, catch hold of one end of the feather-bed and pull it with all his strength through the window. As ill luck would have it, a rafter from the roof fell at that moment and hit the unhappy man; it did not kill him, merely grazing his neck as it fell, but Mr Lembke's career came to an end, in our province, at any rate; the blow knocked him off his feet and he fell down on the ground unconscious.

Daybreak came at last, bleak and dismal. The fire abated; a calm descended suddenly after the wind, and then a drizzling rain fell slowly, as though through a sieve. By that time I was already in a different part of the suburb, far from the place where Lembke had collapsed, and there I heard strange things being said in the crowd. A very curious fact had come to light: at the very edge of the suburb, on a piece of waste land behind the kitchen gardens, not less than fifty yards from any other buildings, stood a small, newly built wooden house, and this solitary house caught fire at the very beginning, almost before any other house. If it had burnt down, it could not have set any other building on fire because it was so far from any other house, and vice versa, if the whole of the suburb had burnt down, that house would have escaped even if a gale had been blowing. It therefore followed that it had caught fire quite independently and separately, and hence that there was something wrong about it. But the important thing was that it had not burnt down, and at daybreak astonishing things were discovered in it. The owner of the new house, an artisan who lived in a nearby suburb, rushed to his house as soon as he saw it on fire, and with the help of his neighbours he succeeded in saving it by scattering the heap of logs which had been set on fire at one of the side walls. But there were lodgers in the house – a captain who was well known in the town, his sister, and an elderly maid, and the three of them, the captain, his sister and their maid, had been murdered during the night, and apparently robbed. (It was there that the Police Commissioner had gone when Lembke had been trying to salvage the feather-bed.) In the morning the news had spread, and a huge crowd of all sorts of people, including even victims of the fire, had rushed to the waste land and the new house. It was difficult to pass through so dense a crowd. I was at once told that the Captain had been found lying dressed on a bench with his throat cut, and that he had apparently been dead drunk when murdered, so that he was not aware of anything, and that he had bled 'like a bull'; that his sister, Maria Timofeyevna, had been 'pierced through and through' with a knife and was lying on the floor near the door, so that she must have been awake and had resisted and struggled with the murderer. The maid, who had also probably been awake, had her skull broken. According to the landlord, the Captain had been to see him the previous morning. He was drunk and boasted about his money, showing the landlord about 200 roubles. The Captain's old green wallet was found empty on the floor; but his sister's trunk had not been touched, and the silver setting of the icon had not been touched either. The Captain's wardrobe, too, had not been tampered with. It was obvious that the robber had been in a hurry, that it was a man who was familiar with the Captain's private affairs, who had come only for the money, and that he knew where it was kept. If the landlord had not been in time, the burning logs would have set fire to the house and it would have been difficult to find out the truth from the charred bodies.

This is how the story was related to me. Another piece of information was added: the house had been taken for the Captain and his sister by Stavrogin, the son of the General's widow, and he had come himself to arrange about the rent; that he had had a great deal of trouble in persuading the landlord to let it, because the latter had intended to use it as a public-house; but Stavrogin was ready to pay any rent the landlord asked and had paid for six months in advance.

'The fire was no accident,' people were saying to each other in the crowd.

But the majority were silent. Their faces were sullen, but I did not notice any signs of great anger. They went on talking about Stavrogin, pointing out that the murdered woman was his wife and that on the previous day he had 'dishonourably' abducted the daughter of Mrs

Drozdov, a General's widow, a girl who belonged to one of the best families in the town, and that a complaint was to be lodged against him with the authorities in Petersburg. As for the motive of his wife's murder, it was clear enough that she had been killed to make it possible for him to marry Miss Lisa Tushin.

Skvoreshniki was only about two miles away, and I remember wondering whether I ought not to let them know about it. However, I did not notice that anybody was trying to incite the crowd, though in it, to be quite honest, I did catch sight of two or three of the ruffians I had seen in the refreshment room at the ball, whom I recognized at once. But I particularly remember one thin, tall lad of the artisan class – a confirmed drunkard, by the look of him – and, as I found out later, a locksmith by trade, with a curly head and a face so grimy that it seemed to be covered with soot. He was not drunk, but seemed, in contrast to the sullen and motionless crowd, to be in a frenzy of excitement. He kept addressing the people, though I do not remember the exact words he used. He did not say anything coherent that was longer than: 'I say, fellows, this is terrible! We can't just stand about and do nothing, can we?' and, as he spoke, he kept waving his arms about.

3

The End of a Love Affair

I

FROM the large drawing-room at Skvoreshniki (the same in which the last interview between Mrs Stavrogin and Mr Verkhovensky had taken place) the fire could be plainly seen. At daybreak, at about six o'clock in the morning, Lisa was standing at the farthest window on the right and watching the dying red glow in the sky. She was alone in the room. She was wearing the party dress she had worn at the reading the day before – light green, gorgeous, covered with lace, but already crumpled and put on carelessly and in haste. Noticing suddenly that her corsage was undone, she blushed, quickly put her dress to rights, snatched up the red shawl she had thrown down on an armchair when she came in the day before, and put it round her neck. Her luxuriant hair fell in a disorderly disarray of curls on her right shoul-

der from under the shawl. Her face looked tired and worried, but her
eyes glowed under her knit brows. She went up to the window again
and pressed her burning forehead against the cold pane. The door
opened and Stavrogin came in.

'I've sent a messenger on horseback,' he said. 'In ten minutes we
shall know everything. Meanwhile all I could find out from the servants was that part of the suburb across the river has been burnt down,
near the embankment on the right side of the bridge. The fire started
about midnight. It is dying down now.'

He did not go up to the window, but stopped three paces behind
her; she did not turn round to him.

'By the calendar it should have been daylight an hour ago, but it's
still almost dark,' she said irritably.

'All calendars tell lies,' he observed with a polite smile, but, feeling
ashamed, he hastened to add: 'It's boring to live by the calendar,
Lisa.'

And he fell silent, annoyed with himself for the platitude he had
uttered. Lisa smiled wrily.

'You are in such a melancholy mood that you can't even find words
to speak to me. But don't worry: you were quite right: I do live by
the calendar. Every step I take is according to the calendar. Does that
surprise you?'

She turned away from the window quickly and sat down in an
arm-chair.

'Won't you, too, sit down, please? We shall be only a short time
together, and I want to speak my mind. Why shouldn't you do the
same?'

Stavrogin sat down beside her and took her hand quietly, almost
timidly.

'What does this tone mean, Lisa? Where did you suddenly get it
from? What do you mean – we shall be only a short time together?
This is the second enigmatic phrase you have used, darling, since you
woke up half an hour ago.'

'Are you beginning to count my enigmatic phrases?' she said,
laughing. 'Do you remember I spoke of myself as a dead woman as I
came in yesterday? You thought it necessary to forget that. To forget
or not to notice.'

'I don't remember, Lisa. Why a dead woman? We must live. ...'

'And is that all? You've lost your eloquence completely. I've had my hour, and that's enough. Do you remember Christophor Ivanovich?'

'No, I don't,' he said, frowning.

'Christophor Ivanovich at Lausanne? You got awfully tired of him. He always used to open the door and say, "I've just dropped in for a minute," but he stayed the whole day. I don't want to be like Christophor Ivanovich and stay the whole day.'

A pained look came into his face.

'Lisa, I can't bear this morbid talk. This affectation must hurt you too. What do you want it for? What for?' His eyes glowed. 'Lisa,' he cried, 'I swear to you I love you now more than I did yesterday when you came to me!'

'What a strange confession! Why to-day and yesterday? Why these two comparisons?'

'You won't leave me, will you?' he went on almost in despair. 'We'll go away together – to-day – won't we? Won't we?'

'Ugh, don't squeeze my hand so! It hurts. Where are we to go away together to? To-day, too? Somewhere where we should "rise from the dead" again? No, I've had enough of experiments and, besides, it takes too long for me. And I'm not fit for it, either. It's much too lofty for me. If we are to go anywhere, it is to Moscow. To pay visits there and receive visitors. That's my ideal, you know. I haven't concealed the sort of person I am from you, even in Switzerland. But as it is quite impossible for us to go to Moscow and pay visits because you are a married man, it's no use talking about it.'

'Lisa! Then what happened yesterday?'

'What happened, just happened.'

'That's impossible! That's cruel!'

'What if it is cruel? You just have to put up with it, cruel as it is.'

'You're avenging yourself on me for yesterday's whim,' he muttered, grinning maliciously.

Lisa flushed.

'What a mean thought!'

'In that case why did you make me a present of – "so much happiness"? Have I the right to know?'

'No, I'm afraid you'll have to do without rights. Don't make the meanness of your supposition worse by stupidity. You're not your usual self to-day. You're not by any chance afraid of public opinion or that you'll be blamed for "so much happiness"? If that is so, then for goodness sake don't worry. You're not responsible for whatever happened, and you haven't got to answer to anyone for it. When I opened your door yesterday, you did not even know who was coming in. Yes, it was just a whim of mine, as you expressed it just now, and nothing more. You can look everyone boldly and triumphantly in the face!'

'Darling, your words, this laugh of yours, have been making me turn cold with horror for the last hour. This "happiness" of which you talk with such frenzied fury means – everything to me. How can I give you up now? I swear to you I loved you less yesterday. Why do you rob me of everything to-day? Do you know what it has cost me – this new hope? I've paid for it with life.'

'Your life or somebody else's?'

He got up quickly.

'What do you mean?' he said, staring at her fixedly.

'Have you paid for it with your life or mine – that's what I wanted to ask you. Or have you ceased to understand me altogether now?' Lisa flushed. 'Why did you jump up so suddenly? What are you looking at me like that for? You frighten me. What are you afraid of? I've noticed for some time that you are afraid – that you are afraid at this very moment – yes, at this very moment. Goodness, how pale you are!'

'If you know something, Lisa, then I swear that I don't and – and that I wasn't talking of *that* at all when I said that I had paid with life.'

'I – I don't understand you at all,' she faltered timidly.

At last a slow, wistful smile appeared on his lips. He sat down slowly, put his elbows on his knees, and buried his face in his hands.

'A bad dream – a nightmare. We were talking of two different things.'

'I don't know what you were talking about. Didn't you know yesterday that I'd leave you to-day? Did you or didn't you? Don't lie. Did you or didn't you?'

'I did,' he said softly.

'Well, then, what more do you want? You knew, and you reserved that "moment" for yourself. What else is there left for us to settle?'

'Tell me the whole truth,' he cried in great agony. 'When you opened the door of my room yesterday, did you know that you were opening it only for one hour?'

She looked at him with hatred.

'Really, the most serious person can ask the most extraordinary questions. And what are you so worried about? Is it because your vanity is hurt because a woman should be the first to throw you over and not you her? You know, Mr Stavrogin, since I've been here I've happened to find out that you're awfully generous to me, and it's just that I can't put up with from you.'

He got up and took a few steps round the room.

'All right, suppose it had to end like that. But how can it all have happened?'

'What do you care? The main thing is that you know it perfectly well yourself and that you understand it better than anyone in the world, and that you were counting on it yourself. I am a young lady, and my heart has been brought up on the opera. That's how it all started. That's the whole explanation.'

'No.'

'There's nothing here to hurt your vanity, and it's all absolutely true. It all began with a beautiful moment which was too much for me to bear. The day before yesterday when I "insulted" you in public and you replied to me like a real gentleman, I came home and realized at once that you were drawing away from me because you were married and not at all because you despised me, which, being a society girl, I dreaded most of all. I realized that by running away from me you were merely trying to save me, fool that I was. You see how greatly I value your generosity. Just then Peter turned up and explained it all to me at once. He revealed to me that you couldn't make up your mind about a great idea, before which he and I were as nothing, but that I was in your way, all the same. He said he, too, was in it; he was determined that the three of us should keep together, and he talked the most fantastic things, about a boat and maple oars from some Russian song. I complimented him and told him that he was a poet, and he swallowed it all just as if I had meant it. And as I knew perfectly well anyhow that I should have the courage only for one moment, I made up my mind to go through with it. Well, that's all there is to it, and please no more explanations. We might end up by quarrelling. Don't be afraid of anyone. I take the whole blame upon myself. I'm a bad, capricious girl. I was tempted by that operatic boat. I am a young lady. But, you know, I still thought that you were awfully in love with me. Don't despise a foolish girl and don't laugh at this tear which just rolled down my cheek. I'm awfully fond of crying because I'm "sorry for myself". Well, all right. All right. I'm no good for anything, and you're no good for anything; my vanity has been hurt as well as yours; let that be our comfort. At least, it makes it easier for our vanity.'

'A mad dream!' Stavrogin cried, wringing his hands and pacing the room. 'Lisa, my poor darling, what have you done to yourself?'

'I've burnt my fingers, that's all. You're not crying, too, are you? Please behave more as becomes a gentleman; be more indifferent ...'

'Why, why did you come to me?'

'But, really, I don't think you realize in what a ridiculous position you put yourself in the eyes of the world by such questions.'

'Why did you have to ruin yourself so horribly and so stupidly? And what's to be done now?'

'And is this Stavrogin, the "vampire Stavrogin", as a lady who is in love with you calls you? Look, I've told you already: I've exchanged my whole life for one hour, and I'm content. Do the same with yours – still, there's no reason why you should: you'll have plenty more "hours" and "moments".'

'As many as you: I give you my solemn word. Not one hour more than you.'

He was still pacing the room, and did not see her quick, penetrating glance, which seemed suddenly like a ray of hope. But the light went out instantly.

'If you knew what my present *impossible* sincerity costs me, Lisa, if only I could reveal to you –'

'Reveal? You want to reveal something to me? May the Lord preserve me from your revelations!' she interrupted him almost in terror.

He stopped and waited uneasily.

'I must tell you frankly that ever since those days in Switzerland I have been sure that there was something horrible, something loathsome on your conscience, some blood – and – and at the same time something which makes you look awfully ridiculous. Beware of revealing it to me, if it's true: I shall make a laughing-stock of you. I shall laugh at you all your life. Oh dear, so you've turned pale again? I won't, I won't, I'm going at once!' She jumped up from her chair with a disdainful and contemptuous movement.

'Torture me, kill me, work off your spite on me,' he cried in despair. 'You've the right to do so! I knew I did not love you, and I ruined you. Yes, "I've kept the moment for myself". I had a hope – I've had it a long time – my last hope ... I could not resist the bright light that flooded my heart when you came to me yesterday of your own accord, alone, first. I suddenly believed that I loved you. Perhaps I believe it even now.'

'Let me return such noble frankness by being as frank myself. I don't want to be a compassionate hospital nurse for you. Perhaps I will really end up as a hospital nurse if I don't find a way of dying conveniently this very day; but even if I do become a nurse, I won't be your nurse; though, of course, you need one more than any legless or armless man. I always imagined that you would take me to some place where there was a huge, wicked spider as big as a man, and we should spend the rest of our lives looking at it and being afraid of it. That's what our love would be wasted on. You'd better go to Dasha: she will go with you anywhere you like.'

'You would think of her even now, wouldn't you?'

'The poor little lapdog! Give her my regards. Does she know that even in Switzerland you'd decided to have her for your old age? What solicitude! What foresight! Oh dear, who's that?'

At the far end of the room a door was opened; a head was thrust in and quickly disappeared.

'Is that you, Alexey Yegorych?' Stavrogin asked.

'No, it's only me.' Peter Verkhovensky thrust himself half in again. 'How do you do, Miss Tushin? Anyway, good morning. I knew I'd find you both in the drawing-room. I've just come in for a moment. I'm sorry, Mr Stavrogin, but I simply must have a few words with you – just a few words!'

Stavrogin went towards the door, but after taking three steps he returned to Lisa.

'If you hear anything presently, Lisa, I want you to know that it's all my fault!'

She gave a start and looked timidly at him; but he went out of the room hurriedly.

2

The room from which Peter Verkhovensky had looked in was a large oval ante-room. The butler had been sitting there before he came in, but he sent him out. Stavrogin closed the drawing-room door behind him and stood waiting expectantly. Peter Verkhovensky gave him a quick and searching look.

'Well?'

'I mean, if you know already,' Peter began hurriedly, as though wishing to dive into Stavrogin's soul with his eyes, 'then none of us, of course, is to blame for anything, and you least of all, for it's – er – it's such a conjunction of – I mean, such a coincidence – I mean, legally there's no case against you, and I rushed here to tell you so beforehand.'

'Burnt? Murdered?'

'Murdered, but not burnt, worse luck; but I give you my word of honour that I had nothing to do with that, either, however much you may suspect me, because – er – you do suspect me, don't you? Want me to tell you the whole truth? You see, the idea really did cross my mind – you suggested it to me yourself, not seriously, but just to tease me (for you would never have suggested anything like that seriously), but I could not make up my mind, and I should never have done so for anything in the world, not for a hundred roubles; and besides there was nothing to be gained by it, for me, I mean, for me ...' He was in a terrific hurry and was rattling away. 'But there's a coincidence for you: I gave this drunken idiot Lebyatkin two hundred and thirty roubles out of my own pocket (you see, it was my money, there was not a rouble of yours and, the main thing is, you know that yourself). That was the day before yesterday, in the evening – you see, the day before yesterday, and not yesterday after the reading – note that: it is an extremely important coincidence, for at that time I did not know for certain whether Miss Tushin would come to you or not; I gave him my own money solely because you excelled yourself the day before yesterday by taking it into your head to reveal your secret to everybody. Well, of course, I don't want to go into that – it's your business – very chivalrous and so on – but I must confess that I was surprised. It was just as if you had hit me over the head with a cudgel. But as I was sick and tired of all these tragedies – and I'm

quite serious, mind, though I may be using a colloquialism, since after
all it was interfering with my plans – I vowed to get rid of the Lebyatkins at all costs by sending them off to Petersburg without your knowledge, more particularly as he was very anxious to go there himself.
I made one mistake, though: I gave the money in your name. Was it
a mistake or not? Perhaps it wasn't, eh? Now, listen to me – please,
listen how it all turned out –'

In the excitement of his talk he walked close up to Stavrogin and
was about to take hold of the lapel of his coat (quite likely deliberately). Stavrogin struck him violently on the arm.

'What on earth – I mean, really – you'll break my arm, you know.
The important thing is how it all turned out,' he rattled on, without
apparently being in the least surprised at the blow. 'I gave him the
money in the evening so that he and his sister should set off as early
next morning as possible. I entrusted this little business to that scoundrel Liputin. I instructed him to see them safely on the train himself.
But that swine Liputin took it into his head to play a prank on the
public at the reading – you've heard of it, I suppose, haven't you? At
the reading? Now, listen, listen: both of them had a few drinks, composed verses, half of which are Liputin's; Liputin got Lebyatkin into
a dress suit, while he told me that he had sent him off in the morning.
But he kept him hidden in a little room at the back with the intention
of pushing him out on to the platform. Lebyatkin, however, got
quickly and unexpectedly drunk. That was followed by the scandalous scene. The Captain was then taken home more dead than alive,
while Liputin took the two hundred roubles quietly out of his pocket,
leaving some change there. But unfortunately it appears that the Captain had already taken the two hundred roubles out of his pocket that
very morning to boast about them and show them where he shouldn't.
And as that was what Fedka was waiting for and had overheard something at Kirilov's (remember, your hint?), he decided to take advantage of it. That's the whole truth. I'm glad Fedka at least did not find
the money, for the scoundrel was counting on a thousand! He was in
a great hurry and seems to have got frightened by the fire. Believe
me, that fire was a real blow to me. No, really, it's simply abominable. It's mob-law. Now, you see, I expect so much of you that I
wouldn't dream of concealing anything: I admit frankly that this
idea of a fire has been maturing at the back of my mind for a long

time, for it has a strong popular appeal; but I was keeping it for a critical hour, for that precious moment when we shall all rise up and – But they suddenly took it into their heads to do it now on their own authority and without any orders, at a moment when we ought to be lying low and be as quiet as mice. I must say that is just mob-law! In a word, I don't know anything for certain so far. I've heard people mention two Spigulin workmen – but if *ours*, too, are mixed up in it, if only one of them is in any way implicated – he'd better look out! You see what it means to let them get even a little bit out of hand! No, this democratic riff-raff with their groups of five is a poor support. What we want is one magnificent and despotic will, an idol of the people, resting on something solid and standing outside everything. Then the groups of five, too, will cringe obediently and obsequiously and be useful whenever the occasion should arise. But, anyway, though they may be trumpeting abroad that Stavrogin had to burn his wife and that's why the town was set on fire –'

'Are they already trumpeting that abroad?'

'I mean, they are not doing anything of the kind and, I must confess, I haven't heard anything at all; but what can you do with people, especially if their houses have been burnt down: *vox populi, vox Dei?* Would it take long for the most idiotic rumour to be spread abroad? But, as a matter of fact, you have nothing at all to fear. Legally you are absolutely clear, and your conscience, too, is quite clear – you did not want it to happen, did you? Did you? No evidence whatever, just a coincidence. ... Unless of course Fedka should remember your careless words at Kirilov's that night (and why did you have to say them?), but that does not prove anything. As for Fedka, we shall stop his mouth. I shall deal with him to-day. ...'

'And weren't the bodies burnt at all?'

'Not a bit. That rascal could not manage anything properly. But I'm glad that you, at any rate, are so calm – because though you had nothing whatever to do with it, not even in thought, all the same, you know. And you must admit that all this does solve your problem beautifully: you suddenly become a free widower and you can at once marry a lovely girl with a lot of money, who is already yours as it is. That's the sort of thing that a simple, crude coincidence can do – eh?'

'Are you threatening me, you fool?'

'Well, well, really, fool indeed; and what a tone to use! Another one in your place would be glad, but you – I rushed here on purpose to let you know in good time. And, besides, how could I threaten you? What good would you be to me if I could only get you by threats? What I want is your good will. I don't want you to join me just because you're afraid of me. You're the light and the sun. It is I who am terrified of you, and not you of me. I'm not Drozdov. And – can you imagine it? – as I came flying here in a chaise I saw Drozdov standing by the fence at the back of your garden – in his greatcoat, drenched through, must have spent the whole night there! Wonder of wonders! It's extraordinary how mad people can be!'

'Drozdov? Is it true?'

'It's true all right. Sitting there by the fence. Oh, I should think not more than three hundred yards from here. I hurried past him, but he saw me. Didn't you know? In that case I'm very glad I didn't forget to tell you. A fellow like that can be really dangerous if he should happen to have a gun on him, and then there is the night, the slush, natural exasperation – for, after all, think of his position, ha, ha! Why do you think he is sitting there?'

'Waiting for Lisa, naturally.'

'Oh, I see! But why on earth should she go out to him? And – in such rain – what a damned fool he must be!'

'She is going out to him presently.'

'Oho! That's news! So that – But look here, her position has radically changed now: what does she want Drozdov for now? Why, you're free, a widower, and you can marry her to-morrow. She doesn't know yet, but leave it to me and I'll arrange everything in a jiffy. Where is she? We must tell her the good news, too.'

'The good news?'

'Rather! Let's go.'

'And do you really think she won't put two and two together about those dead bodies?' Stavrogin asked, screwing up his eyes in a peculiar way.

'Of course she won't put two and two together,' said Peter quickly, just as if he were a real fool, 'because, you see, legally – Oh, you! What if she did guess? Women are so good at ignoring such things. I can see that you don't understand women at all! Don't you realize that it's in her own interest to marry you now because, say what you like, she has compromised herself, and, besides, I talked to her nineteen to the dozen about the "boat": for I could see that it was by the "boat" that I could make an effect on her, because that is the sort of a girl she is. Don't worry, she'll step over those dead bodies without hesitating for a moment, particularly as you are absolutely innocent, aren't you? She'll just keep them in cold storage to use them against you, say, after you've been married two or, perhaps, three years. Every woman saves up something of the kind from her husband's past as she is walking down the aisle with him to the altar, but by that time – what may not happen in a year? Ha, ha, ha!'

'If you've come in a chaise, take her to Drozdov now. She just told me that she couldn't stand me and that she was going to leave me, and I don't think she'll accept my carriage.'

'Not really? Is she actually leaving? How did that happen?' Peter asked, staring stupidly at him.

'She has realized somehow during the night that I don't love her – which, of course, she has known all along.'

'But don't you love her?' Peter asked with a look of great surprise. 'But if that is so, then why did you let her stay when she came to you yesterday? Why didn't you tell her, like an honourable man, that you were not in love with her? That was awfully mean of you. And how mean you make me appear in her eyes.'

Stavrogin suddenly laughed.

'I'm laughing at my monkey,' he explained at once.

'Oh, I see, you realized that I was playing the fool,' Peter cried, laughing very gaily. 'I did it to make you laugh! Do you know, I guessed at once from your face as you came in here that you'd been "unlucky". A complete fiasco, perhaps. Eh? I bet,' he cried, almost breathless with delight, 'that you've been sitting side by side in the drawing-room all night, wasting your precious time in discussing some high and noble subject. Sorry! Awfully sorry. I don't care. I was quite sure yesterday that the whole thing would end stupidly. I brought her to you simply to amuse you and to show you that you'll never be bored with me; you'll find me useful in that way a hundred times; I, generally speaking, like to please people. But if you don't want her now, which was what I was expecting when I came here just now, then –'

'So you brought her just for my amusement, did you?'

'What else?'

'And not to make me kill my wife?'

'Good Lord! have you killed her? What a tragic chap you are!'

'It makes no difference. You killed her.'

'I killed her? But didn't I tell you that I had nothing whatever to do with it? I'm afraid you're beginning to worry me –'

'Go on. You said that "if you don't want her" –'

'Then let me deal with her, of course. I shall marry her off in a most excellent fashion to Drozdov, whom, by the way, I have not put in your garden – don't you go imagining that! You see, I'm scared of him now. You say: take her in your chaise, but I just dashed by him – what if he really has a gun? It's a good thing I've got mine on me. Here it is.' He took a revolver out of his pocket, showed it to Stavrogin, and put it back again. 'Took it with me as it was such a long way. However, I'll put it right for you in a jiffy: I expect her little heart must be aching for Maurice just now – it should be, at any rate, and, you know, I – I'm really a little sorry for her. If I take her to Maurice, she'll start thinking of you at once – saying nice things about you to him and abusing him to his face – a woman's heart! Laughing again, are you? I'm awfully glad you're so cheerful now. Well, let's go. I'll start with Maurice at once. As for those – those who've been murdered – don't you think it will be wiser to – er – say nothing about them now? She's quite sure to find it out later.'

'Find out what? Who's been murdered? What did you say just now about Mr Drozdov?' Lisa asked, opening the door suddenly.

'Oh! You've been eavesdropping?'

'What did you say just now about Mr Drozdov? Has he been murdered?'

'Oh, so you didn't hear! Calm yourself. Mr Drozdov is alive and well, and you can ascertain that for yourself this minute; for he's just outside here, by the garden fence and – er – I believe he's been sitting there all night. He's drenched to the skin in his greatcoat. He saw me as I drove past.'

'That's not true. You said "murdered". Who's been murdered?' she insisted with poignant mistrust.

'The only people who have been murdered are my wife, her brother Lebyatkin, and their maid,' Stavrogin declared firmly.

Lisa gave a start and went terribly pale.

'It's a brutal, strange case, Miss Tushin – a most stupid case of robbery: just robbery under cover of the fire,' Peter at once rattled off. 'It was that robber Fedka the convict who did it, and that fool Lebyatkin, too, was to blame, for he showed his money to everybody. I rushed down here to tell you about it – it was a terrible blow to me. Stavrogin was greatly shocked when I told him. We were just discussing whether to let you know at once or not.'

'Nicholas, is he telling the truth?' Lisa just managed to ask.

'No, he isn't.'

'Not telling the truth?' Peter said with a start. 'What on earth do you mean?'

'My God, I shall go mad!' Lisa cried.

'But please understand he's not in his right mind now!' Peter shouted at the top of his voice. 'After all, it is his wife who's been murdered. You can see how pale he is. Why, he has been the whole night with you. He hasn't left you for a minute, has he? Well, so how can you suspect him?'

'Nicholas, tell me as before God are you guilty or not, and I swear to you I'll believe your word as if it were the word of God, and I'll follow you to the end of the earth. Oh, yes, I will follow you like a dog. ...'

'Why are you tormenting her, you fantastic fellow?' Peter cried furiously. 'Miss Lisa, do anything you like to me, but I tell you he's innocent. On the contrary, he is, as you see, terribly upset himself. He isn't guilty of anything, not of anything in the world. Not even in thought. The murder has been committed by some robbers who will most certainly be caught within a week and flogged. It's Fedka the convict and the Spigulin men. The whole town is talking about it. That's why I'm convinced of it, too.'

'Is it true? Is it true?' Lisa asked, trembling all over, as though waiting for her final sentence.

'I did not kill them and I was against it, but I knew that they were going to be killed and I did not stop the murderers. Leave me, Lisa,' Stavrogin said, and he walked into the drawing-room.

Lisa covered her face with her hands and walked out of the house. Peter was about to run after her, but he changed his mind and went back into the drawing-room.

'So that's your game! That's what you're doing! You're not afraid of anything, are you?' He flew at Stavrogin in an absolute frenzy, muttering incoherently, almost unable to find the right words and foaming at the mouth.

Stavrogin stood in the middle of the room without uttering a word in reply. He grasped a strand of his hair in his left hand and smiled forlornly. Peter pulled him violently by the sleeve.

'Do you think you're done for? So that's your game? Inform the police on us all, and go to a monastery yourself or go to the devil. ... But I shall kill you, though you may not be afraid of me!'

'Oh, it's you chattering, is it?' said Stavrogin, becoming aware of his presence in the room at last. 'Run,' he said, recovering his senses suddenly, 'run after her, order the carriage; don't leave her. Run, run! See her home so that no one should know, and so that she shouldn't go there – to the dead bodies – to the dead bodies. Force her to get into the carriage. Alexey Yegorych! Alexey Yegorych!'

'Wait; don't shout! She's already in Drozdov's arms now. Drozdov won't get into your carriage. Wait! Something much more important than your carriage is at stake!'

He snatched out his revolver again; Stavrogin looked at him gravely.

'You can kill me, if you like,' he said quietly, almost resignedly.

'Damn it all, the lie a man will saddle himself with!' Peter cried, shaking with fury. 'By God, I ought to kill you! She ought really to have spat on you! What sort of "boat" are you? You're just a leaky, wooden, useless old hulk. Why, you ought to come to your senses, if only out of spite! Oh-h! What difference does it make to you? You don't seem to care if I put a bullet through your head.'

Stavrogin gave a strange laugh.

'If you weren't such a clown, I might have said yes now. If only you had just a little more sense ...'

'I may be a clown; but I don't want you, my better half, to be a clown! Do you understand me?'

Stavrogin understood. Perhaps he was the only one to understand. Wasn't Shatov surprised when Stavrogin told him that Peter Verkhovensky had enthusiasm?

'Go to blazes now! I may think of something to-morrow. Come to-morrow.'

'You will? You will?'

'How do I know? To blazes with you!'

And he walked out of the drawing-room.

'Well, perhaps it's all for the best,' Peter muttered to himself, putting away his gun.

3

He rushed off to overtake Lisa. She had not gone far, only a few yards from the house. The butler had detained her. He followed close behind her, in his frock-coat and without a hat, his head bowed respectfully. He kept begging her to wait for the carriage; the old man was scared and he almost cried.

'Go back; your master is asking for tea and there's no one to give it to him,' said Peter Verkhovensky, pushing him away and taking Lisa's arm.

Lisa did not snatch her arm away, but she seemed not to know what she was doing, as she had not recovered from her shock.

'In the first place, you're not going the right way,' Peter began, talking fast as usual. 'We have to go in that direction, and not past the garden; and, secondly, we can't possibly walk, for it's about three miles to your place and you're not even dressed for walking. Please wait a minute. I have my chaise here in the yard. I'll fetch it in a jiffy, put you in and drive you home so that no one will see us.'

'How kind you are!' Lisa said sweetly.

'Good Lord! in a case like that every humane man in my place would also –'

Lisa glanced at him and was surprised.

'My goodness, and I thought it was still that old man here.'

'Listen, I'm awfully glad that you take it like this, for the whole thing is just stupid prejudice, and come to think of it, wouldn't it be better if I told the old man to get the carriage ready? It'll only take ten minutes, and in the meantime we could go back and wait for it in the porch. Don't you think so?'

'First I want – where are those murdered people?'

'Good Lord! what an idiotic notion is this? I was afraid of that. No, we'd better leave those wretches alone. Besides, there's nothing there for you to see.'

'I know where they are. I know that house.'

'Well, what if you do know it? Good Lord! it's raining and it's foggy. (What a damned nuisance this sacred duty is that I've taken on myself!) Listen, Miss Tushin, one of two things: either you come along with me in my chaise, in which case you'd better wait here and don't go a step further, for another twenty yards and Mr Drozdov is sure to see us.'

'Mr Drozdov? Where? Where?'

'Well, if you want to go with him, I shall take you a little further, if you like, and show you where he is sitting, and then bid you good-bye. I don't care to go near him now.'

'He's waiting for me! Oh, God!' she cried, suddenly stopping, her face suffused with colour.

'But, good heavens, he's a man without prejudices! Look here, Miss Tushin, this is none of my business. I've nothing to do with it at all, and you know that yourself. But, still, I wish you well ... If our "boat" has proved a failure, if it turned out to be only a rotten old hulk –'

'Oh, that's wonderful!'

'Wonderful, and yet tears are streaming down your face. What you want is courage. You must be as good as any man in everything. In our age, when women – oh, hell!' (Peter was almost on the point of spitting.) 'You see, the important thing is that there's nothing to regret; perhaps it's turned out for the best. Mr Drozdov is – er – I mean, he's a man of sentiment, though he doesn't like to talk a lot, which, as a matter of fact, is a good thing, too, provided of course that he has no prejudices. ...'

'Wonderful, wonderful!' Lisa laughed hysterically.

'Oh, damn it all – Miss Tushin,' said Peter suddenly, feeling exasperated, 'I'm really here just for your sake – it makes no difference to me. I did you a favour yesterday when you wanted it yourself, but to-day – Well, you can see Mr Drozdov from here. There he is – he doesn't see us. I wonder, Miss Tushin, if you've ever read *Polinka Sachs*?'

'What's that?'

'There's a novel of that name – *Polinka Sachs*. I read it when I was a student. In it a Civil Servant by the name of Sachs – a very rich man – arrested his wife at his country house for infidelity. But damn it, it doesn't matter! You'll see that Mr Drozdov will make you a proposal of marriage before you reach your house. He hasn't caught sight of us yet.'

'Oh, don't let him see us!' Lisa suddenly cried like a crazed woman. 'Let's go away, let's go away! Into the woods! Into the fields!'

And she ran back.

'Miss Tushin,' Peter cried, running after her, 'this is sheer cowardice! And why don't you want him to see you? On the contrary, you must look him straight in the face – proudly. ... If you're worried about *that* – I mean that you're no longer a virgin – then it's such a stupid prejudice, such an out-of-date convention. ... But where are you going? Where are you going? Oh dear, she's running! We'd better go back to Stavrogin – let's take my chaise. Where are you going? That's the way to the fields. Now she's fallen down ...'

He stopped. Lisa was flying like a bird without any idea where she was going, and Peter was already fifty yards behind her. She stumbled over a mound and fell down. At that moment a heart-rending cry was heard from somewhere behind. It was Drozdov who had seen her flight and fall and was running to her across the field. Peter at once retreated through the gates of the Stavrogin mansion to get into his chaise as quickly as possible.

Meanwhile Drozdov was already standing in great alarm beside Lisa, who had sat up, bending over her and holding her hand in his. The wholly incredible circumstance of that meeting had given him a terrible shock, and tears were streaming down his cheeks. He saw the girl he worshipped running madly across a field at such an hour and in such weather, wearing only her dress, the gorgeous party dress she had worn the day before, now crumpled and covered with mud from her fall. He could not utter a word. He took off his greatcoat and with trembling hands put it round her shoulders. Suddenly he uttered a cry: he felt that she had touched his hand with her lips.

'Lisa,' he cried, 'I am not good for anything, but, please, don't drive me away from you!'

'Oh, let's go away from here quickly,' she said, clutching him by the hand and dragging him after her. 'Don't leave me, Maurice,' she said, suddenly lowering her voice timidly. 'All the time I tried to be brave there, but now I'm afraid to die. I shall die, I shall die very soon, but I'm afraid, I'm afraid to die,' she whispered, squeezing his hand.

'Oh, if only there was someone here!' he cried in despair, looking round. 'Some passer-by! You'll get your feet wet, you – you will lose your reason!'

'I'm all right, I'm all right,' she comforted him. 'With you I'm not so much afraid. Hold my hand, lead me. Where are we going now? Home? No, I want first to see the people who have been murdered. They say his wife has been murdered, and he says he has killed her himself. It's not true, is it? I want to see the people who've been killed myself – for me – it's because of them that he stopped loving me last night. I shall see and find out everything. Quick, quick. I know the house – there's a fire there. ... Maurice, my dear friend, don't forgive me who have dishonoured myself! Why forgive me? Slap my face and kill me here in this field like a dog!'

'No one is your judge now,' Drozdov said firmly. 'May the Lord forgive you. I am your judge least of all!'

Their conversation would sound strange if I tried to describe it. Meantime both walked arm in arm, quickly, hurrying along madly. They were going straight towards the fire.

Drozdov still hoped to get a lift on a cart at least, but no one came their way. A fine drizzle of rain enveloped the whole countryside, swallowing up every ray of light and every shade of colour and turning everything into one smoky, leaden, indistinguishable mass. It had long been daylight, but it seemed as though it were still dark. And suddenly a figure loomed out of this foggy, cold haze, a strange and absurd figure which was walking towards them. I can't help thinking now that I shouldn't have believed my eyes if I had been in Lisa's place, and yet she uttered a joyful cry and at once recognized the approaching man. It was Stepan Verkhovensky. How he had gone off and how the crazy idea of his flight could have come to pass – of that later. I shall merely mention the fact that he was in a fever that morning, but his illness did not stop him; he was walking firmly on the wet ground; it was clear that he had thought out the enterprise as carefully as he could, without any help and lacking practical experience. He was dressed 'for travel' – that is, in a greatcoat with a wide patent-leather belt, fastened with a buckle, and a pair of new topboots pulled over his trousers. He must have for some time past imagined a traveller to look like that and a few days earlier he had got himself the belt and the high boots with shining tops like those of a hussar's, in which he could hardly walk. A broad-brimmed hat, a worsted yarn scarf, wrapped tightly round his neck, a walking-stick in his right hand and a very small but extremely tightly packed travelling bag in his left completed his get-up. He had, besides, an open umbrella in his right hand. These three things – the umbrella, the walking-stick, and the travelling-bag – had been very awkward to carry for the first mile and rather heavy for the second.

'Is it really you?' Lisa cried, looking at him with grief-stricken surprise which followed on her first transport of unconscious joy.

'Lise!' Mr Verkhovensky, too, cried, rushing to her almost deliriously. 'Chère, chère, is it you – in such a fog? I can see, I can see, don't tell me, but don't ask me any questions, either. Nous sommes tous malheureux, mais il faut les pardonner tous. Pardonnons, Lise, and let us be free for ever and ever. To be rid of the world and be completely free – il faut pardonner, pardonner, et pardonner!'

'But why are you kneeling?'

'Because in bidding a last farewell to the world, I'd like to take leave of all my past, too, in your person,' he replied, weeping and raising both his hands to his tear-stained eyes. 'I kneel to everything that was beautiful in my life. I kiss and offer up thanks! Now I've torn myself in half: there is the madman who dreamed of soaring into the clouds, vingt-deux ans! Here is a broken-down and shivering old man – a tutor – chez ce marchand, s'il existe pourtant ce marchand. ... But how drenched you are, Lise!' he cried, jumping to his feet, feeling that his knees, too, had got drenched on the wet ground. 'And how is it possible – you are in such a dress? – and on foot, and in this field? You are crying? Vous êtes malheureuse? Why, I did hear something ... But where have you come from now?' He fired his questions at her, uneasily gazing in great bewilderment at Drozdov. 'Mais savez-vous l'heure qu'il est?'

'Mr Verkhovensky, have you heard anything about people who have been murdered there? Is it true? It is, isn't it?'

'Oh, these people! I watched the glow of their evil deeds in the sky all night long. They couldn't end up otherwise. ...' His eyes flashed again. 'I'm running away from a nightmare, from a delirious dream. I'm running away to find Russia, existe-t-elle la Russie? Bah, c'est vous, cher capitaine! I never doubted that I would come across you one day engaged on some high adventure. ... But take my umbrella and – why must you walk on foot? For God's sake, at least take my umbrella; I shall hire a carriage somewhere, anyway. You see, I am on foot because *Stasie* (I mean Nastasya) would have screamed the street down if she'd found out that I was going away for good; that is why I slipped away as far as possible incognito. I don't know, in the *Voice* they print reports of robberies everywhere; but, surely, I thought to myself, I couldn't possibly meet a robber the moment I came out on the road. *Chère Lise*, I believe you said that someone had murdered someone, didn't you? *Oh, mon Dieu*, you are ill!'

'Come along, come along!' Lisa cried almost in hysterics, again dragging Drozdov after her. 'Wait a minute, Mr Verkhovensky,' she shouted, returning to him suddenly, 'wait, you poor darling; let me make the sign of the cross over you. Perhaps it would be better to tie you up, but I'd rather make the sign of the cross over you. Please, you, too, pray for your "poor" Lisa – just a little; don't trouble yourself too much. Mr Drozdov, give that baby back his umbrella. Please give it back to him! So … Now, come along! Come along!'

They arrived at the fatal house at the very moment when the large crowd which had gathered round it had already heard a great deal about Stavrogin and about how much it was to his advantage to murder his wife. But, I repeat, the vast majority of the people continued to listen in silence and apathetically. The only people who lost control of themselves were the yelling drunkards and 'mentally unbalanced' people like the artisan who was waving his arms about. Everybody knew him to be a quiet man, but if anything struck him forcibly in a certain way, he was liable to lose control of himself and break out. I did not see Lisa and Drozdov arrive. I first noticed Lisa, to my amazement and utter stupefaction, when she was some considerable distance away from me in the crowd, and I did not catch sight of Drozdov at all at first. He seemed to have lagged a step or two behind her for a moment because of the crush or because he had been pushed back. Lisa, who was forcing her way through the crowd without seeing anything or noticing anything around her, like one in a delirium, or like a patient escaped from a hospital, naturally very soon attracted everybody's attention: they began talking in loud voices and, suddenly, a clamour arose. Someone shouted: 'That's Stavrogin's girl!' And on the other side: 'They're not satisfied with murdering people, they come to look at them!' Suddenly I saw a hand rise and fall over her head from behind; Lisa fell to the ground. Drozdov uttered a terrible cry as he rushed forward to her assistance and struck with all his strength the man who stood between him and Lisa. But at that very moment the artisan seized him with both arms from behind. For some time it was impossible to see what was happening in the rough-and-tumble of the fight. I believe Lisa got up, but was knocked down by another blow. Suddenly the crowd parted and a small circle was formed round Lisa, who lay prostrate on the ground, while Drozdov, covered with blood and beside himself with grief, stood over her, wringing his hands, screaming and weeping. I can't remember exactly what happened afterwards; all I remember is seeing Lisa being carried away. I ran after her; she was still alive and, perhaps, even conscious. The artisan and three other men from the crowd were seized. These three men still deny having had any part in the murder, maintaining stubbornly that they were seized by mistake; perhaps they are right. The artisan, though caught in the act, but being feeble-minded, is still unable to give a detailed account of what happened. I, too, had to give evidence at the inquest, as one who was a witness of the crime, though from a distance. I declared that it had all happened entirely by accident through the action of people who, though perhaps evilly disposed, were hardly conscious of what they were doing, being drunk and not in the full possession of their senses. I am still of that opinion.

4

The Last Decision

I

THAT morning many people saw Peter Verkhovensky: those who saw him remembered that he was in a highly excited state. At two o'clock in the afternoon he went to see Gaganov, who had arrived from the country the day before and whose house was full of visitors hotly discussing the recent events. Peter talked more than anybody, and made people listen to him. He was always considered in our town to be 'a talkative student with a screw loose', but now he was discussing Mrs Lembke and in the general excitement the subject was of absorbing interest. As one who had recently been her intimate and confidential friend, he disclosed many new and unexpected details about her, incidentally (and, of course, thoughtlessly), he disclosed several of her personal opinions of all the important personages in town and, by doing so, hurt their vanity. Whatever he said was not very clear and rather incoherent, like a man who was not very clever, but who found himself in the painful position of clearing up a whole mountain of misunderstandings and who, simple-minded and rather clumsy as he was, did not know himself how to begin and how to end his story. Quite indiscreetly, too, he let slip out the information that Mrs Lembke had known the whole of Stavrogin's secret and that it was she who had engineered the whole intrigue. She had taken him in, too, because he was in love with the unhappy Lisa himself, and yet he was so cleverly 'taken in' that he had *almost* led her to Stavrogin in the carriage. 'Yes, yes, it's all very well for you to laugh, gentlemen, but if I had only known, if I'd only known how it would all end!' he concluded. In reply to several anxious inquiries about Stavrogin, he declared frankly that in his opinion the catastrophe with Lebyatkin was a pure coincidence and that it was all Lebyatkin's fault for having shown his money. He explained this particularly well. One of his listeners remarked that it was no good his 'pretending', that he had eaten, drunk, and almost slept in Mrs Lembke's house, yet he was the first now to blacken her reputation, and that all this was not as nice as he seemed to think. But Peter immediately defended himself:

'I ate and drank there not because I had no money and it is not my fault if I was invited there. Let me judge for myself, sir, how much I have to be grateful to her for.'

On the whole the impression was in his favour. 'Granted he is an absurd and, of course, an empty-headed fellow, but why should he be blamed for Mrs Lembke's stupidities? It seems, on the contrary, that he was trying to stop her. ...'

At about two o'clock the news suddenly came that Stavrogin, about whom there was so much talk, had suddenly left for Petersburg by the midday train. This interested people very much; many of them frowned. Peter Verkhovensky was so astonished that it is said that he went pale and exclaimed strangely: 'But who could have let him out?' He at once hurried away from Gaganov's. However, he was seen in two or three other houses.

Towards dusk he found an opportunity of going in to see Mrs Lembke, though with the greatest difficulty, for she absolutely refused to receive him. I learnt about his visit three weeks later from Mrs Lembke herself before her departure for Petersburg. She did not tell me all the details, but observed with a shudder that he had astonished her on that occasion beyond all belief. I expect he must have simply frightened her by the threat of claiming her as his accomplice if she took it into her head 'to talk'. The necessity of frightening her was closely connected with his plans at the time, which she, of course, knew nothing about; and only afterwards, five days later, she realized why he was not so sure about her keeping silent and why he was so afraid of her outbursts of indignation.

At about eight o'clock in the evening, when it was already quite dark, all the five members of *our* group gathered at the lodgings of the second lieutenant Erkel in a crooked little house in Fomin Lane at the end of the town. The meeting had been arranged by Peter Verkhovensky himself, but he was inexcusably late and the members waited an hour for him. The second lieutenant, Erkel, was the young officer, a stranger in our town, who had sat all the time at Virginsky's birthday party with a pencil in his hand and a notebook in front of him. He had arrived in our town only recently, rented a room in a lonely lane from two old ladies sisters, of the artisan class – and was due to leave the town soon; a meeting at his room was least likely to attract attention. This strange boy was distinguished by unusual taciturnity: he could spend a dozen evenings in succession in a noisy company, with the most exciting conversations going on around him, without uttering a word himself, and yet watching the speakers with his child-like eyes and listening to them with the greatest attention. He was very handsome, and even gave the impression of being clever. He was not a member of the group of five; he was supposed to have instructions from somewhere of an executive character. It is known now that he had been entrusted with no mission at all, and it is doubtful if he himself realized his position. He had merely fallen under the spell of Peter Verkhovensky, having met him only a short time before. If he had met some prematurely depraved monster and had been persuaded by him on some socially romantic pretext to found a band of bandits and, as a test, had been ordered to rob and murder the first peasant he came across, he would most certainly have gone and done it. He had an invalid mother to whom he sent half of his precarious pay, and how she must have kissed that poor fair head of his! How she must have trembled and prayed over it! I speak so much about him because I am very sorry for him.

The members of the group were very excited. The events of the previous night had taken them by surprise and, I expect, they had become scared. An ordinary, though systematically contrived, public scandal in which they had hitherto so zealously taken part had quite an unexpected ending for them. The fire of the previous night, the murder of the Lebyatkins, the lynching of Lisa by the mob – had been surprises they had not taken into account in their programme. They hotly accused the hand that had guided them of despotism and lack of frankness. In a word, while waiting for Peter Verkhovensky, they had worked themselves up into such a state that they decided again to demand a final and categoric explanation from him, and if, as had happened before, he once more declined to give it, to dissolve the group of five and to found in its place a new secret society for the 'propagation of ideas', and on their own initiative and in accordance with the principles of democracy and equal rights. Liputin, Shigalyov, and the authority on the peasants supported this plan; Lyamshin would not express an opinion, though he seemed to agree with it. Virginsky could not make up his mind, and wanted to hear what Peter Verkhovensky had to say first. They decided to hear Peter Verkhovensky, but he still did not show up, and such perfunctoriness added fuel to the flames. Erkel said nothing at all, and merely ordered tea, which he brought from his landladies in glasses on a tray, without bringing in the samovar or letting the maid into the room.

Peter Verkhovensky came only at half-past eight. With rapid steps he went up to the round table in front of the sofa, at which the company was sitting, keeping his hat in his hands and refusing tea. He looked angry, stern, and overbearing. He must have at once noticed from the expression on their faces that they were 'rebellious'.

'Before I open my mouth, you'd better tell me everything, for I can see that you've got something on your minds,' he observed, gazing at each of them in turn with a malicious grin.

Liputin began 'in the name of all those present', and declared in a voice shaking with resentment that 'if we go on like this, we might break our own necks'. Not that they were afraid to break their necks. Indeed, they were quite ready to, but only for the good of the common cause (a general movement of approbation). And therefore they demanded that he should be frank with them, that he should let them know beforehand, 'or else what's going to happen?' (Again a general stir and a few guttural sounds.) To behave like this was humiliating and dangerous. 'We are not demanding it because we are afraid, but if one acts and the rest are only pawns, then one may make a slip and all will be caught.' (Exclamations: 'Hear, hear!' and general approval.)

'Damn it all, what *do* you want?'

'And what relation to our common cause have Stavrogin's silly little intrigues?' Liputin asked furiously. 'Even if he does in some mysterious way belong to the centre, if, that is, that fantastic centre really exists, but we have not the slightest wish to know anything about it. Meantime a murder has been committed, the police have been roused; by following one clue, they'll eventually get to us.'

'If they catch you and Stavrogin, they'll catch us too,' the authority on the peasants added.

'And it's of no use whatever to the common cause,' Virginsky concluded despondently.

'What nonsense is this! The murder was just an accident. It was committed by Fedka from motives of robbery.'

'I see! A strange coincidence, though,' Liputin remarked, writhing.

'And if you really want to know, it's all through you.'

'Through us? How do you mean?'

'First of all, you, Liputin, took part in this intrigue yourself, and, secondly – and that is the main point – you were ordered to pack Lebyatkin off and you were given the money; but what did you do? If you had packed him off, nothing would have happened.'

'But wasn't it you yourself who suggested that it would be a good thing if he were to be let out to read his verses?'

'An idea is not an order. Your orders were to pack him off.'

'Orders! Rather a curious word, don't you think? On the contrary, your orders were to stop his departure.'

'You made a mistake and showed how foolish and self-willed you are. As for the murder, it is Fedka's doing. He acted on his own, and his motive was robbery. You have heard the stories they are spreading all over the town, and you believe them. You are scared. Stavrogin isn't so stupid, and the proof is that he left town at twelve o'clock today after an interview with the vice-governor; if there were anything in it, they wouldn't have let him go to Petersburg in broad day-light.'

'But we never asserted that Mr Stavrogin had committed the mur-der himself,' Liputin put in maliciously and unceremoniously. 'He need not even have known about it, just like me. And you know perfectly well that I did not know anything, though I seem to have asked for trouble.'

'Whom are you accusing, then?' Peter asked, looking grimly at him.

'Those who find it necessary to burn down towns, sir.'

'You make things worse by trying to wriggle out of it. However, won't you read this and show it to the others? It's for your informa-tion only.'

He took out of his pocket Lebyatkin's anonymous letter to Lembke and gave it to Liputin. The latter read it, was evidently surprised, and handed it thoughtfully to his neighbour. The letter quickly went the round.

'Is that really Lebyatkin's handwriting?' Shigalyov asked.

'It is,' declared Liputin and Tolkachenko (that is, the authority on the peasants).

'I've shown it to you only for your information and because I know how sentimental you feel about Lebyatkin,' Peter repeated, taking the letter back. 'So it seems, gentlemen, that Fedka quite accidentally got rid of a dangerous person for us. That's what an accident does for you sometimes! Instructive, isn't it?'

The members of the group exchanged glances.

'And now, gentlemen, it's my turn to ask questions,' Peter said, assuming a dignified air. 'Will you please tell me what on earth made you set fire to the town without permission?'

'What are you talking about? *We* set fire to the town? Are you in your right mind?' they all exclaimed.

'I realize that you've gone too far,' Peter went on stubbornly, 'but that's not the same thing as playing some silly prank on Mrs Lembke. I've called you together, gentlemen, to explain to you how great the danger is in which you've so stupidly involved yourselves and which threatens much besides yourselves.'

'But, if you don't mind my saying so, it is we who were about to point out the degree of despotism and lack of equality with which such a serious and strange step was taken without the knowledge of the members,' Virginsky, who had been silent till then, declared almost with indignation.

'So you deny any complicity in it, do you? But I maintain that you set fire to the town, you and no one else. Gentlemen, don't lie to me. My information is unimpeachable. By your self-will and by your action you put our common cause in jeopardy. You're only one link in the endless links of the chain, and you owe implicit obedience to the centre. And yet three of you suborned the Spigulin workmen to set fire to the town without receiving any orders, and the fire has taken place.'

'What three? Which of us are they?'

'The day before yesterday at about three o'clock in the morning you, Tolkachenko, were instigating Fomka Zavyalov at the "Forget-me-not".'

'Good Lord!' Tolkachenko cried, jumping to his feet, 'I hardly uttered a word, and that, too, without intention, simply because he had been flogged that morning, and I gave it up almost at once because I could see that he was dead drunk. If you had not reminded me of it, I shouldn't have remembered it at all. A word could not have set the town on fire.'

'You remind me of a man who is surprised that one spark could blow up a gunpowder magazine.'

'I spoke in a whisper in his ear, in a corner of the pub, so how could you have got to know about it?' Tolkachenko said, looking surprised.

'I was sitting there under the table. Don't worry, gentlemen, every step of yours is known to me. You smile spitefully, Mr Liputin? Well, I know, for instance, that four days ago you pinched your wife black and blue at midnight in your bedroom as you were going to bed.'

Liputin gaped in astonishment and turned pale.

(It became known afterwards that he learnt about Liputin's gallant act from Agafya, Liputin's maid, whom he had paid from the very beginning to act as his spy, a fact which came to light only later.)

'May I state a fact?' Shigalyov asked, getting up suddenly.

'Yes, do.'

Shigalyov sat down and drew himself up.

'As far as I can make out – and I can hardly be wrong – you yourself, at the beginning and on another occasion later on, drew with great eloquence – though perhaps rather theoretically – a picture of Russia covered with an endless network of small groups. Each of these active groups, while enrolling new members and branching out endlessly, aims by systematic propaganda to expose the local authorities and to undermine their prestige, to throw the village population into confusion, to promote cynicism and public scandals, utter disbelief in everything under the sun, a desire for better things and, finally, by means of fires, as a measure likely to have the greatest possible effect on the common people, to throw the country at a given moment, if necessary, into a mood of despair. Aren't those your very words which I have tried to remember verbatim? Isn't that the programme of action you communicated to us as one authorized by the central committee, about which we know nothing at all and which we have every right to regard as entirely mythical?'

'Quite true; only you're taking a long time to say it.'

'Every man has a right to express himself as he likes. In giving us to understand that there are at present several hundred separate knots of the network already covering the whole of Russia, and in propounding the theory that if everyone does his work successfully, the whole of Russia at a certain date and at a given signal –'

'Hell, I've plenty to do without this!' cried Peter, turning in his chair.

'Very well, I'll cut it short and I'll end by putting just one more question to you: we've witnessed the public scandals, we've seen the discontent of the people, we have been present at, and taken part in, the downfall of the local administration and, finally, we've seen with our own eyes the town on fire. Why are you dissatisfied? Isn't that your programme? What can you accuse us of?'

'Of self-will!' Peter cried furiously. 'While I'm here, you had no right to act without my permission. Enough. The man who is going to inform the police has everything ready, and to-morrow or perhaps even to-night you will all be arrested. So there you are. My information is absolutely correct.'

This time all of them gaped with astonishment.

'You will be arrested not only as the instigators of the fire, but as members of the group of five. The man knows all the secrets of the network. That's the sort of mess you've made of it!'

'It is Stavrogin, isn't it?' Liputin cried.

'What – why Stavrogin?' Peter stopped short suddenly. 'Oh, hell,' he cried, recollecting himself at once, 'it's Shatov! I believe you all know now that at one time Shatov was an active member of the organization. I must disclose to you that, watching him through persons he does not suspect, I discovered, to my amazement, that the organization of the network is no secret to him and that, in short, he knows everything. To save himself from being charged with active participation in it, he's going to inform the authorities against us all. Till now he still could not make up his mind, and I have spared him. But now you've made up his mind for him by this fire: he is deeply shocked and will hesitate no longer. To-morrow we shall be arrested as incendiaries and political criminals.'

'Is it true? How does Shatov know?'

'It's absolutely true. I have no right to disclose my sources of information and how I found it out, but this is what I can do for you meanwhile: I can influence Shatov through a certain person so that, without suspecting anything, he will put off sending his written denunciation to the police, but only for twenty-four hours. I can't delay it any longer. So that you can consider yourselves safe till the day after to-morrow.'

They were all silent.

'Oh, let's send him to the devil!' Tolkachenko was the first to cry.

'We should have done it long ago!' Lyamshin put in spitefully, striking the table with his fist.

'But how are we to do it?' Liputin murmured.

Peter at once took up the question and explained his plan. He proposed that at nightfall on the following day Shatov should be lured to a lonely spot to hand over the illegal printing press which had been in his keeping and which was buried there and – 'deal with him there'. He went into many necessary details, which we will omit here, and explained circumstantially Shatov's present ambiguous relations with the central society, which are already known to the reader.

'Seems all right,' Liputin observed doubtfully, 'but since it will be another – er – adventure of the same kind, it might – er – create too big a sensation.'

'No doubt,' Peter agreed, 'but that has been foreseen, too. There is a way of averting suspicion completely.'

And he told them about Kirilov with the same minute attention to detail, of his intention to shoot himself, of how he had promised to wait for the signal, and before he died, to leave a note behind taking on himself anything they dictated to him. (In a word, all that the reader knows already.)

'His firm intention to take his life, a philosophic and, in my opinion, quite crazy decision, has become known *there*,' Peter went on to explain. 'Not a hair, not a speck of dust is overlooked. Everything *there* is done for the good of the common cause. Realizing the advantage of such a decision, and convinced that he was quite determined to carry it out, they had offered him the means to come to Russia (for some reason he had expressed his firm intention to die in Russia), given him his instructions which he undertook to carry out (and he has carried them out), and, in addition, made him promise, as you know already, to take his life only when he was told to. Please note that he joined our organization for special reasons, and that he wants to be useful. More than that I cannot tell you. To-morrow, *after we have dealt with Shatov*, I shall dictate the note to him, in which I shall declare that he is responsible for Shatov's death. That will seem very plausible: they were friends and travelled together to America, they quarrelled there, and it will all be explained in the note and – and I daresay, if necessary, I could dictate something else to Kirilov – oh, something about the leaflets, for instance, and even perhaps something about the fire. I shall think it over, though. Don't worry, he has no prejudices; he'll sign anything.'

Doubts were voiced. The story seemed fantastic. They had all, however, heard something or other about Kirilov; Liputin more than the others.

'What if he should suddenly change his mind and refuse?' said Shigalyov. 'After all, he is a madman, so that our hopes might be falsified.'

'Don't worry, gentlemen; he will not refuse,' Peter snapped. 'According to our agreement, I have to warn him the day before – that is, to-day. I invite Liputin to go with me at once to his place to make quite sure, and he will let you know to-day, if necessary, whether I've told you the truth or not. However,' he broke off suddenly with intense exasperation, as though feeling suddenly that he was doing people like them too great an honour by wasting his time in persuading them, 'do as you like. If you decide not to go on with it, then our union is broken up, but solely because of your insubordination and treachery. In that case, we shall from this moment go our separate ways. But I want you to know that, if that happens, you will, in addition to the unpleasantness of Shatov's denunciation and its consequences, incur another little unpleasantness, of which you were clearly apprised at the time of the formation of the union. So far as I'm concerned, gentlemen, I'm not very much afraid of you. Don't imagine that I'm in any way tied to you. ... However, that makes no difference.'

'All right, we'll do it,' declared Lyamshin.

'There's no other solution,' Tolkachenko murmured. 'And provided Liputin confirms the story about Kirilov, we –'

'I'm against it,' Virginsky declared, getting up. 'I protest with all the power at my command against such a dastardly decision!'

'But?' asked Peter.

'*But* what?'

'You said *but* – and I'm waiting.'

'I don't think I said *but*. I only wanted to say that if such a decision is taken, then –'

'Then?'

Virginsky said nothing.

'I think one can disregard the danger to one's own life,' Erkel said, suddenly opening his mouth, 'but if our common cause is at stake, then I think we have no right to disregard the danger to our own lives.'

He got confused and blushed. However much each of them was preoccupied with his own thoughts, they could not help glancing at him with surprise, so little did they expect that he, too, would speak.

'I am for the common cause,' Virginsky said suddenly.

They all got up. It was decided to communicate again and make final arrangements at noon the next day. The place where the printing press was buried was disclosed, and each was given his part and assigned his post. Liputin and Peter at once set off to see Kirilov.

2

All of them believed that Shatov was going to inform the police; but they also believed that Peter Verkhovensky was playing with them like pawns – and yet they also knew that they would all be at the appointed place next day in spite of everything, and that Shatov's fate was sealed. They suddenly felt like flies caught in the web of a huge spider; they were furious, but they shook with fear.

Peter had undoubtedly behaved unfairly to them; everything could have been arranged far more harmoniously and *easily* if he had cared to make the facts look a little more pleasant. Instead of presenting the facts in a more becoming light and putting them on the same footing as citizens of ancient Rome, or something of the sort, he merely appealed to their animal fears and emphasized the danger to their own skins, which was simply not nice. No doubt everything had to be considered from the point of view of the struggle for existence and there was no other principle, they all knew that, but all the same –

But Peter had no time to bring up the Romans; he was dumbfounded. Stavrogin's flight shocked and crushed him. He had lied when he said that Stavrogin had seen the vice-governor; the trouble was that he had gone off without seeing anyone, even his mother, and it really was strange that he had not even been questioned by the police. (Afterwards the authorities were called to account for it.) Peter had spent a whole day making inquiries, but so far he had discovered nothing, and had never been so worried. And how could he be expected to give up Stavrogin all at once like that? That was why he could not be very tender with the members of the group of five. Besides, they had forced him to act quickly: he had already decided to run after Stavrogin, but Shatov kept him back. He had to make absolutely sure of the loyalty of the group of five, in case anything happened. 'Can't give it up; it may come in useful one day.' So, I suppose, he must have argued.

As for Shatov, he was absolutely convinced that he would inform the police. He had told them a lie about having actually seen Shatov's letter of denunciation to the police: he had never seen it or heard of it, but he was as sure of it as that twice two makes four. It seemed to him that what had happened – the death of Lisa, the death of Mary – was bound to influence Shatov, and that he would make up his mind now. Who knows? Perhaps he had a good reason for thinking like that. It is also known that he hated Shatov personally; they had had some quarrel, and Peter never forgave an insult. Indeed, I am convinced that that was his main reason.

We have narrow brick pavements in our town, and in some streets they are made of wooden planks. Peter was striding along in the middle of the pavement, occupying it entirely and paying no attention to Liputin, who had no room to walk beside him and had either to run a step behind him or, if he wanted to speak to him, run off into the muddy road. Peter suddenly recalled that he, too, had had to splash through the mud the other day to keep pace with Stavrogin, who had walked, as he was doing now, in the middle of the pavement, occupying the whole of it. He remembered the whole scene, and nearly choked with rage.

But Liputin, too, was choking with resentment. Peter might treat the others as he liked, but how dare he treat him like that? Didn't he *know* more than all the rest? Wasn't he in closer touch with the affairs of the organization? More intimately connected with it and continuously active on its behalf, though perhaps only indirectly? Oh, he knew that even now Peter Verkhovensky could ruin him *if matters came to a head*. But he had long hated Peter, and not because he was afraid of him, but because he had treated him with such utter contempt. Now that he had to make up his mind to do such a thing, he was more furious than all the rest put together. Alas, he knew that, 'like a slave', he would be the first next day at the appointed place and that he would bring the rest with him, and if he could have killed Peter before to-morrow without in some way implicating himself, he would most certainly have killed him.

Brooding over his sensations, he kept silent and hurried along after his tormentor. Peter seemed to have forgotten about him; only from time to time he pushed him aside rudely and carelessly with his elbow. Suddenly Peter stopped in one of our principal streets and went into a restaurant.

'Where on earth are you going?' Liputin cried, boiling over with rage. 'This is a restaurant.'

'I want a beefsteak.'

'But, good Lord, this restaurant is always full of people.'

'What about it?'

'But – we shall be late. It's ten o'clock.'

'We can't be too late there.'

'But I shall be late. They are expecting me back.'

'Let them. Only you'd be stupid to go back to them. With all this business of yours, I've had no dinner. And the later we go to Kirilov's, the surer we are to find him.'

Peter took a private room. Liputin sat down in an easy-chair away from the table, looking angry and resentful, and watched him eating. Half an hour and more passed. Peter was in no hurry, ate with an appetite, rang for the waiter, asked for a different kind of mustard, then for beer, and still never uttered a word. He was absorbed in thought. He could do two things at once – eat with relish and ponder deeply. Liputin began to loathe him so much that he could not take his eyes off him. It was like an attack of madness. He counted every morsel of beefsteak Peter put into his mouth, he loathed him for the way he opened it, for the way he chewed, for the way he smacked his lips over the fatter morsels, he loathed the steak itself. At last, everything began to swim before his eyes, he felt a little giddy, hot and cold flushes ran up and down his spine.

'As you're not doing anything, read that,' Peter said, throwing him a piece of paper suddenly.

Liputin went nearer to the candle. The paper was closely covered with bad handwriting and corrections in every line. By the time he had made out the writing, Peter had paid his bill and was ready to go. On the pavement Liputin handed him back the piece of paper.

'Keep it. I'll tell you about it later. Still, what do you think of it?' Liputin shuddered all over.

'In my opinion – such a leaflet is – er – just absurd nonsense.'

His resentment broke though. He felt as though he had been caught up and carried along.

'If we decide to distribute such leaflets,' he said, shaking as though in a palsy, 'we shall make people despise us for our stupidity and incompetence.'

'I see,' Peter said, striding firmly along. 'I'm afraid I don't think so.'

'I don't think so, either. You didn't write it yourself, did you?'

'That's not your affair.'

'I think, too, that silly poem "A Noble Character" is utter trash, and could never have been written by Herzen.'

'You're wrong. It's an excellent poem.'

'I am also surprised,' Liputin went on breathlessly, his words bounding and leaping along uncontrollably, 'that we are told to act in a way that can only end in disaster. It is natural that in Europe they should wish everything to end in disaster, because they have a proletariat there, while we're just amateurs here and, in my opinion, merely throwing dust in people's eyes.'

'I thought you were a follower of Fourier.'

'You will find nothing of the kind in Fourier, nothing of the kind.'

'I know it's nonsense.'

'No, Fourier is not nonsense. ... I'm sorry, but I just can't believe that a rising is possible in May.'

Liputin even unbuttoned his coat, he was so hot.

'All right, that's enough; and now, so as not to forget,' Peter changed the subject with quite amazing coolness, 'this leaflet you'll have to set up and print with your own hands. We shall dig up Shatov's printing press and you'll take it to-morrow. You must print as many copies as you can as quickly as possible and then distribute them all the winter. You'll be provided with the necessary funds. We must have as many copies as possible, for you'll get orders for them from other places.'

'I'm sorry, but I'm afraid I cannot undertake such a – I refuse.'

'You'll do it, all the same. I'm acting on the instructions of the central committee, and you must obey.'

'And I consider that our centres abroad have forgotten what Russia is like and have broken all connexions with her, and that's why they talk such nonsense. I even think that instead of many hundred groups of five in Russia, we're the only one in existence and that there is no network at all,' Liputin said, panting for breath.

'All the more contemptible of you to have embraced a cause without believing in it and – you are running after me now like a mean little cur.'

'No, sir, I am not running. We have a perfect right to leave you and form a new society.'

'You damn fool!' Peter suddenly thundered menacingly, with flashing eyes.

Both stood facing each other for some time. Peter turned and continued on his way confidently.

The thought flashed through Liputin's mind: 'I'll turn and go back – if I don't turn now I shall never go back.' He thought like that for exactly ten yards, but at the eleventh a new and desperate idea flashed into his mind: he did not turn and did not go back.

They came to Filippov's house, but before reaching it they went down a little lane, or rather along a hardly discernible path by the side of a fence, so that for some time they had to make their way along a steep bank of a ditch and had to hold on to the fence to avoid slipping into it. In the darkest corner of the leaning fence, Peter removed a plank and crawled through the opening. Liputin looked surprised, but he, too, crawled through the gap in the fence; the plank was then replaced. This was the secret entrance by which Fedka used to visit Kirilov.

'Shatov must not know that we are here,' Peter whispered sternly to Liputin.

3

As usual at that hour of the night, Kirilov was sitting on his leather sofa and having tea. He did not get up to welcome them, but winced violently and looked at his visitors anxiously.

'You're not mistaken,' said Peter Verkhovensky; 'that's what I've come about.'

'To-day?'

'No, no, to-morrow – about this time.'

And he quickly sat down at the table, watching Kirilov's agitation with some disquiet. Kirilov, however, had composed himself and looked as usual.

'You see, these people still refuse to believe. You're not angry with me for bringing Liputin, are you?'

'To-day I'm not angry, but to-morrow I want to be alone.'

'But not before I come, and therefore in my presence.'

'I'd rather not in your presence.'

'You remember you promised to write and sign everything I dictated.'

'Makes no difference to me. Are you going to be long here now?'

'I must see a certain person and stay here for half an hour, so I'm afraid I'll stay here for half an hour whatever you say.'

Kirilov said nothing. Meanwhile Liputin found a seat near the portrait of the bishop. The desperate idea that had occurred to him a few moments before took more and more possession of him. Kirilov hardly noticed him. Liputin had heard about Kirilov's theory before, and always laughed at him; but now he was silent and looked gloomily around him.

'I'd like some tea, if you don't mind.' Peter moved closer to the table. 'I've just had a beefsteak, and I counted on being in time for tea at your place.'

'Help yourself to some.'

'You used to offer it to me yourself before,' Peter remarked sourly.

'Makes no difference. Liputin can have some, too.'

'No, thanks. I – I can't.'

'You can't or don't want to – which is it?' Peter asked, turning to him.

'I'm not going to drink tea here,' Liputin said emphatically.

Peter frowned.

'Smells of mysticism. I'm damned if I can make out what sort of people you all are!'

No one answered; they were silent for a whole minute.

'But one thing I do know,' he suddenly added sharply: 'that no prejudices will stop each of us from doing his duty.'

'Has Stavrogin gone?' asked Kirilov.

'Yes.'

'He's done well.'

Peter's eyes flashed, but he restrained himself.

'I don't care what you think so long as every one of you keeps his word.'

'I shall keep mine.'

'As a matter of fact, I always knew that you would do your duty like an independent and progressive man.'

'You're funny.'

'May be; I'm very glad if I amuse you. I'm always glad to please people.'

'You're very anxious I should shoot myself, and you're afraid I might suddenly decide not to.'

'Well, you see, it was your idea to carry out your plan when it should suit us. Counting on your plan, we've already done something, so that you couldn't possibly refuse now because otherwise you would let us down.'

'You've no claim whatever.'

'I understand, I understand; you're free to do as you like and we can't force you; but all we want is that you should carry out what you'd finally decided to do.'

'And will I have to take upon myself all the disgusting things you've done?'

'Look here, Kirilov; you're not afraid, are you? If you want to go back on your promise, you'd better say so at once.'

'I'm not afraid.'

'I'm merely saying this because you're asking too many questions.'

'Are you going soon?'

'Another question?'

Kirilov looked at him with contempt.

'You see,' Peter went on, getting angrier and angrier, feeling more and more worried, and unable to find the right tone, 'you want me to go so that you should be left alone and be able to concentrate, but all that is a dangerous sign in you – in you above all. You want to think a lot. In my opinion, it would be much better not to think at all, but just carry on. You really worry me.'

'The only thing I don't like is that at that moment a reptile like you should be beside me.'

'Well, that shouldn't make much difference. I could go out of the house at the time and wait on the front steps. You see, if you're so concerned about things when you're about to die – then it is a very dangerous sign. I'll go out on the front steps, and you can think that I understand nothing, and that I am a man infinitely beneath you.'

'No, not infinitely. You're a man of ability, but you don't understand many things because you're a mean fellow.'

'Very much obliged indeed. I've already told you that I'm very glad to provide entertainment – at such a moment.'

'You don't understand anything.'

'I mean I – I listen with respect, at any rate.'

'You can't do anything; even now you cannot conceal your petty spite, though it doesn't pay you to show it. You may make me angry, and then I may want another six months.'

Peter looked at his watch.

'I never did understand anything about your theory, but I know that you didn't invent it for our sake, and that you will therefore carry it out without us. I know, too, that you haven't swallowed the idea, but that the idea has swallowed you and that, therefore, you won't put it off.'

'What? The idea has swallowed me?'

'Yes.'

'And it is not I who have swallowed the idea? That's capital. You have some sense. Only you tease me, and I'm proud.'

'That's good, very good. That's what you need – to be proud.'

'All right. You've had your tea, now go.'

'Damn it, I suppose I'll have to,' said Peter, getting up. 'But it's still too soon. Listen, Kirilov, shall I find the man I want at Myasnichikha's? You know whom I mean, don't you? Or has she been telling me lies?'

'You won't find him there, because he's here.'

'Here? Damnation – where?'

'In the kitchen, eating and drinking.'

'But how did he dare come here?' Peter cried, reddening angrily. 'He had to wait – what nonsense! He has neither money nor a passport.'

'Don't know. He came to say good-bye. He's dressed and ready. He's going away and won't come back. He said you were a scoundrel and that he did not want to wait for your money.'

'Oh! He's afraid that I – well, I suppose I could even now, if – where is he? In the kitchen?'

Kirilov opened the side door into a tiny dark room; from this room three steps led down straight into the partitioned-off little room in the kitchen where the cook's bed usually stood. It was there that Fedka was now sitting in a corner under the icons before a plain deal table. On the table before him stood a pint bottle of vodka, a plate with bread, and some cold beef with potatoes in an earthenware dish. He was eating apathetically and was already half tipsy, but he sat in his sheepskin, and was apparently ready to leave on his journey at any moment. Behind the partition the samovar was beginning to boil, but it was not for Fedka, who had every night for about a week or more blown up the coals in it for Kirilov, 'for Mr Kirilov is very partial to tea at night, that he is.' I am strongly of the opinion that, as he had no cook, Kirilov himself had cooked the beef and potatoes for Fedka that morning.

'What do you mean by being here?' Peter cried, sweeping into the room. 'Why didn't you wait where you were told?'

And raising his fist he brought it down with a thud on the table.

Fedka sat up with an air of dignity.

'Wait a bit, sir, wait a bit,' he said, rolling out each word smartly. 'You ought to realize first of all that you're a-visiting Mr Kirilov, whose boots you don't deserve to clean, for compared with you he's a man of eddication, he is, and as for you, sir, why, you're jest this –'

And, turning his head, he pretended to spit smartly. There was unmistakable haughtiness and determination in his manner and a certain very dangerous assumed desire for engaging in a calm argument before the explosion. But Peter was in no mood to notice the danger, and, besides, this did not suit his way of looking at things. The incidents and disasters of the day had completely turned his head. Liputin was watching the scene with curiosity from the little dark room, at the top of the three steps.

'Do you or don't you want to have a real passport and good money to take you where you've been told to go? Yes or no?'

'Now, look here, sir, seeing as how you've been deceiving me from the very beginning, all I have to say is that you've treated me like a regular scoundrel. You're just a filthy human louse – that is what I thinks of you. You promised me piles of money for shedding innocent blood and you swore it was for Mr Stavrogin, though as it turned out it was just your bad manners. I ain't got a brass farthing out of it, let alone fifteen hundred, and Mr Stavrogin punched you on the nose good and proper, he did, and I heard of it all right. Now you're threatening me again and promising money, but you ain't mentioned what for. But I have a good notion that you're sending me to Petersburg to get your own back on Mr Stavrogin, you're that spiteful, thinking to take advantage of my trusting nature. And that proves that you are the real murderer. And do you know what you deserves to get for not believing in the iniquity of your heart in God himself, the true Creator? You're nothing but an idol worshipper, that's what you are, and you're the same as a Tartar or a Mordva. Mr Kirilov, what is a real philosopher, has many times explained the true God and the true Creator to you, and he told you about the creation of the world, and what's to be our fate in future and the transformation of every creature and every beast from the book of Revelation.

But, like a senseless idol, you've persisted in your deafness and your dumbness, and you've brought Lieutenant Erkel to the same, just like that villainous seducer, called the atheist ...'

'Oh, you drunken rascal! Robs icons himself and then preaches about God!'

'Now, you see, sir, I never made any bones about robbing them icons; but I jest took out the pearls, and how do you know, maybe my tear, too, was at that moment turned into a pearl in the furnace of the Most High for the trials I've suffered in this world, seeing as how I'm just an orphan child what has no proper place or refuge. You must know from the books that in the old days a merchant with just the same tearful lamentations and prayers stole a pearl from the halo of the Blessèd Virgin and then laid the whole price at her feet, falling on his knees before all the people, and that the Holy Mother of God protected him with her cloak before all the people, so that even then it was proclaimed a miracle, and the Government ordered it to be written down in the official books exactly as it happened. And you let a mouse in, so you insulted the very hand of God. And if you was not my natural master, whom I carried in my arms when I was only a lad, I'd have killed you this minute without budging from my place!'

'Tell me, have you seen Stavrogin to-day?' Peter asked, flying into a rage.

'This you ain't got no right to ask me. Mr Stavrogin, I'll warrant, is surprised at you, and he had no hand in it at all. He ain't wished it to happen, nor ordered it, nor given no money for it. It's you what dared me do it.'

'You'll get your money, and you'll get another two thousand in Petersburg, when you get there, the whole lot, and more.'

'You're lying, my good man. I can't help laughing when I see how gullible you are. Why, put beside you, Mr Stavrogin stands on the very top of the ladder, and you bark at him from the ground like a silly little cur, and he'd think he was doing you a great honour even to spit at you from above.'

'You don't seem to realize that I won't let a blackguard like you take a step out of here and that I'll hand you straight over to the police,' Peter cried in a rage.

Fedka leapt to his feet, his eyes flashing furiously. Peter pulled out his gun. There followed a rapid and horrible scene: before Peter could take aim, Fedka swung round and struck him across the face with all his might. The first blow was followed immediately by another terrible blow, then a third and a fourth, all across the face. Peter was dazed, his eyes started out of his head; he muttered something and suddenly crashed full length to the ground.

'There you are – take him!' Fedka cried, with a triumphant twist of the body, and, snatching up his cap and his bundle from under the bench, was gone.

Peter was unconscious and breathing heavily. Liputin even thought that he had been murdered. Kirilov rushed headlong into the kitchen.

'Water!' he cried, and filling an iron jug from a bucket, he poured the water on his head.

Peter stirred, raised his head, sat up and stared senselessly before him.

'Well, how do you feel?' asked Kirilov.

Peter stared at him, still without recognizing him; but catching sight of Liputin, who was leaning forward from the kitchen, he smiled his ugly smile and suddenly jumped to his feet, snatching up the revolver from the floor.

'If you try to run away to-morrow like that scoundrel Stavrogin,' he cried, pouncing furiously on Kirilov, pale and stammering as though he could not enunciate the words, 'I'll get you on the other side of the world – hang you – swat you like a fly – understand?'

And he put his revolver to Kirilov's head; but almost at the same moment, recollecting himself, he put the revolver in his pocket and, without uttering another word, rushed out of the house. Liputin ran out after him. They crawled through the same gap in the fence and again walked along the slope, holding on to the fence. Peter strode rapidly along the lane, so that Liputin could scarcely keep pace with him. At the first crossroads he suddenly stopped.

'Well?' He turned challengingly to Liputin.

Liputin remembered the revolver and was still trembling after the scene in the kitchen; but his answer slipped off his tongue somehow suddenly and irresistibly:

'I don't think – I don't think they're waiting for the "student" with such impatience "from Smolensk to far Tashkent".'

'And did you see what Fedka was drinking in the kitchen?'

'What he was drinking? He was drinking vodka.'

'Well, let me tell you that it was the last time in his life that he will be drinking vodka. I suggest you keep that in mind. And now go to hell. You're not wanted till to-morrow. But look out: don't do anything foolish!'

Liputin ran home as fast as his legs would carry him.

4

He had long before procured himself a passport made out in a false name. It seems absurd that this punctilious little man, this petty family tyrant, who clung to his job in the Civil Service (though a Fourierist), and who was, above all, a capitalist and moneylender, should long before have conceived the fantastic idea of getting that passport ready in case of emergency so as to be able to escape abroad *if* – he therefore must have entertained the possibility of this *if*, though, of course, he himself would have found it very difficult to formulate what this *if* might mean. ...

But now it suddenly formulated itself, and in a most unexpected manner. That desperate idea with which he had gone to Kirilov's after Peter Verkhovensky had called him a 'fool' in the street was that he would abandon everything early next morning and emigrate abroad! Those who do not believe that such fantastic things are happening every day in Russia, should consult the biographies of all our real *émigrés*. Not one of them ran off for a more intelligent and realistic reason. It has always been the same unrestrained kingdom of phantoms and nothing more.

On his arrival home, Liputin began by locking himself in, getting out his suitcase, and beginning to pack. His main preoccupation was money and how much of it he would have time to raise. Yes, to raise, for according to his ideas he had not an hour to spare, because as soon as it got light he would have to be on his way. Nor did he know how he would manage to get into the train; he vaguely decided to take it at the second or third big station from our town and make his way there on foot if necessary. It was thus that he busied himself instinctively and mechanically with his suitcase, his head in a whirl of ideas, when – suddenly he stopped short, relinquished everything, and with a deep groan stretched himself on the sofa.

He perceived clearly and in a flash that he might run away all right, but that he was absolutely incapable of deciding now whether he should run away *before* or *after* Shatov had been disposed of; that now he was just a gross, impassive body, an inert mass; that he was entirely in the power of a terrible external force; and that though he had a passport and though he could run away from Shatov (otherwise what was his hurry?), he would run away not before Shatov had been disposed of and not from Shatov, but most certainly *after* Shatov, and that all that had already been decided, signed, and sealed. In unbearable anguish, trembling every moment, and surprised at himself, groaning and holding his breath in turn, he somehow managed to carry on, locked up in his room, and lying on the sofa, till eleven o'clock the following morning. It was then that the shock came which he was expecting and which steeled him for what was to happen that day. No sooner had he unlocked his room and gone out to his household at eleven o'clock than he was told that the escaped convict Fedka, who was terrorizing the town, the robber of churches, who had only the day before committed murder and arson and whom our police were looking for but could not catch, had been found murdered early that morning seven miles from the town at the spot where the highroad turned towards the village of Zakharyino, and that the whole town was talking of it already. He at once rushed out of the house to find out the particulars of the murder. He learnt first of all that Fedka, who was found with his skull smashed in, had apparently been robbed and, secondly, that the police had good reason to suspect, and even good grounds for believing, that his murderer was the Spigulin workman Fomka, the same man who had been his accomplice in killing the Lebyatkins and setting fire to their house, and that they had apparently quarrelled on the road about a large sum of money Fedka had stolen from Lebyatkin and was supposed to have hidden. ... Liputin rushed to Peter's lodgings and succeeded in learning at the back door, in secret, that though Peter had not returned home before one o'clock in the morning, he had been peacefully asleep up to eight o'clock. There could be no doubt whatever that there was nothing unusual in Fedka's death and that people of Fedka's occupation quite often came to such an end; but the coincidence of the fatal words uttered by Peter, namely that 'it was the last time Fedka would be drinking vodka' with the prompt fulfilment of the prophecy was so significant that Liputin suddenly gave up hesitating. The shock had been administered; it was as though a huge boulder had fallen on him and crushed him for ever. Returning home, he silently pushed his suitcase back under the bed with his foot, and at the appointed hour in the evening he was the first to arrive at the place fixed for the meeting with Shatov, still with his passport in his pocket, it is true. ...

5

The Globe Trotter

I

THE catastrophe with Lisa and Mary's death made an overwhelming impression on Shatov. I have already mentioned the fact that I had met him for a moment that morning and that he looked to me like a man who was not in his right mind. He told me, incidentally, that on the previous evening at about nine o'clock (that is, about three hours before the fire) he had called on Maria Timofeyevna. In the morning he went to have a look at the bodies but, as far as I know, he made no statement to the police that morning. Meanwhile towards the end of the day a veritable storm arose in his mind and – and I think I can say with some certainty that there was a moment at dusk when he felt like getting up and – telling everything. What that *everything* was, he could not say himself. He would, of course, have achieved nothing, but would have simply betrayed himself. He had no proof of any kind that might have brought about the conviction of the criminals. Besides, his own theories about it were of the vaguest nature and carried full conviction only for himself. But he was prepared to ruin himself if only he could 'crush the blackguards' – his own words. Peter Verkhovensky had guessed fairly correctly this impulse of his and he realized himself that he was running a great risk in postponing the execution of his terrible new plan till next day. What made him do it was, as usual, his great self-confidence and contempt for all these 'wretches', and for Shatov in particular. He had long despised Shatov for his 'whining idiocy', as he had expressed himself concerning him when both of them were still abroad, and he was quite confident of being able to deal with such a simple-minded man, that is to say, by not letting him out of his sight all that day and by intercepting him at the first sign of danger. What saved 'the blackguards' for a short time, however, was quite an unexpected circumstance, which none of them had foreseen.

At about eight o'clock in the evening (just at the time when the group of five had gathered at Erkel's and were waiting in indignation and excitement for Peter Verkhovensky), Shatov was lying stretched out on his bed in the darkness, without a candle. He had a headache and was slightly feverish; he was tormented by uncertainty, he was angry, kept making up his mind but was unable to make it up finally, and, cursing himself, felt that nothing would come of it, anyway. Gradually, he fell for a short time into a light slumber and had something like a nightmare. He dreamt that he was lying on his bed tied up with ropes and could not move, while someone was knocking furiously at the fence, at the gates, at his own door, at Kirilov's cottage, so that the whole house was shaking, and some faint and familiar voice that awoke poignant memories was calling to him piteously. He suddenly woke up and raised himself on his bed. To his surprise, the knocking at the gates went on, though not nearly so violently as in his dream. The knocks followed upon each other without interruption and the strange voice that brought back those 'poignant' memories could be heard, though not at all piteously, but, on the contrary, impatiently and irritably, calling to him from downstairs at the gates, interrupted now and again by a more restrained and ordinary voice. He jumped up from his bed, opened the little ventilation window, and put out his head.

'Who's there?' he shouted, literally petrified with terror.

'If you are Shatov,' someone answered him from below in a firm and harsh voice, 'then please would you mind telling me frankly and honestly whether you want to let me in or not?'

He was right: he recognized the voice.

'Marie! Is that you?'

'Yes, I am Mary Shatov, and I assure you I can't keep the driver waiting a minute longer.'

'One moment – let me light a candle,' Shatov cried faintly.

Then he dashed off to look for matches. The matches, as usually happens on such occasions, could not be found. He dropped the candlestick and the candle on the floor, and as soon as the impatient voice was heard again downstairs, he left everything and rushed headlong down the steep stairs to open the gate.

'Would you mind holding my bag till I get rid of this blockhead?' Mrs Shatov welcomed him downstairs, thrusting into his hand a rather light, cheap canvas bag studded with brass nails, made in Dresden. Meanwhile she pounced on the cabby with exasperation.

'May I point out to you that you're charging me too much. If you've dragged me for an extra hour all through these filthy streets, that's your own fault, for it shows that you did not know yourself where to find this idiotic street and this silly house. Please be so good as to accept your thirty copecks and be sure you won't get any more.'

'But, madam, you kept telling me yourself Voznesenskaya Street, and this here street is Bogoyavlenskaya: Voznesensky lane is miles from here. Look at my poor gelding, madam. It's steaming!'

'Voznesenskaya, Bogoyavlenskaya, you ought to know all those silly names better than I do, for you're one of the local inhabitants. Besides, you're unfair: the first thing I told you was Filippov's house, and you said you knew it. Anyway, you can issue a summons against me to-morrow, if you like, and now I'd thank you not to bother me.'

'Here, take another five copecks,' Shatov said, impetuously pulling a five-copeck piece out of his pocket and giving it to the cabby.

'I beg you not to do it!' Mrs Shatov cried, flaring up, but the cabby had started his 'gelding' and driven off, while Shatov, grasping her hand, drew her through the gate.

'Quick, Mary, quick – all this doesn't matter and you're wet through. Mind, we have to go up here – pity there's no light – the staircase is steep, hold tight, hold tight – well, here's my little room. I'm sorry, I have no light. One moment!'

He picked up the candlestick, but he could not find the matches for a long time. Mrs Shatov stood waiting in the middle of the room without uttering a word and without moving.

'Thank goodness, at last!' he cried joyfully, lighting up the room.

Mary made a cursory inspection of the room.

'I was told you lived atrociously, but I didn't expect it to be like this,' she said querulously, going towards the bed.

'Oh, I'm fagged out!' she said, sitting down with an exhausted air on the hard bed. 'Please put down my bag and sit down on the chair yourself. But, of course, just as you like. It worries me to see you standing there. I shall only spend a short time here, till I can find some work, for I don't know anything of this town and I have no money.

But if I'm in your way, please tell me at once, I beg you, as indeed you're obliged to do if you're an honest man. I've still got something I could sell to-morrow to pay for a room at an hotel, but you'll have to take me to the hotel yourself. Oh, I'm so tired!'

Shatov trembled all over.

'You mustn't go to an hotel, Mary, you mustn't! What hotel? Why? Why?'

He clasped his hands imploringly.

'Well, if I needn't go to an hotel, I have still to explain the position. You remember, Shatov, how we lived in Geneva as man and wife for just over a fortnight and how it's now almost three years since we parted, without any particular quarrel, though. But don't run away with the idea that I've come back to start all that silly business over again. I've come back to look for work, and if I've come straight to this town, it's only because it makes no difference to me. I haven't come to say that I'm sorry for anything. Please don't go imagining anything as silly as that.'

'Oh, Mary! You shouldn't have said that! You shouldn't have said that!'

'Very well, if you're so civilized as to be able to understand that, I don't mind confessing that if I have turned to you now and have come to your lodgings, it's partly because I've always thought you were not really a scoundrel and that you were perhaps much better than other – blackguards!'

Her eyes flashed. She must have suffered a great deal at the hands of some 'blackguard' or other.

'And please understand that I never dreamed of laughing at you just now when I said that you were good. I spoke plainly, without fine phrases, which I can't stand. However, that's all nonsense. I always hoped that you would have sense enough not to be a nuisance. Well, that's all, I think. Oh, I'm so tired!'

And she gazed at him with harassed and weary eyes. Shatov was standing about five paces away from her at the other end of the room and listened to her timidly, but looking just as if he had been reborn, and with an unwonted radiance on his face. This strong and uncouth man, all bristles on the surface, suddenly became all softened and trans-figured. Something extraordinary, something entirely unexpected stirred in his soul. Three years of separation, three years of the broken marriage had not banished anything from his heart. And perhaps every day during these three years he had dreamed of her, of that being who was so dear to him, who had once said to him: 'I love you.' Knowing Shatov, I can say with certainty that he could never have allowed himself even to dream that a woman might say to him: 'I love you.' He was quite absurdly modest and chaste, he regarded himself as a veritable monster, he hated his own face and his character, comparing himself to some freak only fit to be exhibited at a fair. Because of this he valued honesty above everything in the world and was fanatically devoted to his convictions. He was gloomy, proud, prone to anger, and taciturn. But now this single human being who had loved him for a fortnight (he always, always believed that) – a being he always regarded as immeasurably above him in spite of his perfectly sober estimation of her mistakes; a being whom he could forgive everything, absolutely *everything* (there could be no question of that, and indeed it should have been the other way round, so that it followed that he held himself entirely responsible for everything) – this woman, this Maria Shatov, was all of a sudden again in his house, again there in front of him – oh, that was almost inconceivable! He was so overcome. this event meant something so terrifying to him and at the same time so much happiness, that he could not, of course, and perhaps would not, perhaps he was afraid to, take a sensible view of the situation. It was a dream. But when she looked at him with those harassed eyes of hers, he suddenly realized that the woman he loved so much was suffering and perhaps had been wronged. His heart froze. He gazed at her features with pain: the first bloom of youth had long vanished from this exhausted face. It is true she was still good-looking – in his eyes she was as beautiful as ever. (In reality she was a woman of twenty-five, rather strongly built, above medium height, taller than Shatov, with luxuriant dark brown hair, a pale oval face, and large dark eyes which now glittered with feverish brilliance.) But the light-hearted, naïve, and good-natured energy so familiar to him in the past was replaced now by sullen irritability, disappointment, a sort of cynicism to which she had not yet got used and which she herself resented. But the chief thing was that she was ill – that he clearly perceived. In spite of all his fear of her, he suddenly went up to her and grasped her by both hands.

'Mary – you know – I think you must be very tired – for God's sake, don't be angry. Won't you have some tea – eh? Tea is very strengthening – eh? Oh, if only you'd have some tea!'

'Why ask me if I'll have some tea? Of course I will. What a child you are! You haven't changed a bit. If you can get me some tea, please let me have it. How tiny your room is! How cold!'

'Oh, I'll get some logs at once – some logs – I've got logs!' Shatov began pacing the room excitedly. 'Logs – I mean – but – however, I'll get the tea at once,' he said with a wave of his hand, as though with desperate determination, and grabbed his cap.

'Where are you going? So you haven't any tea in the house, have you?'

'Yes, yes, yes, I'll get everything at once – I –'

He snatched up his revolver from the shelf.

'I shall sell this revolver at once – or pawn it –'

'Don't be silly, and, besides, it'll take such a long time! Here, take my money if you have nothing. There's eighty copecks here, I think. That's all I have. It's like a madhouse here.'

'I don't want your money, don't want it. I'll be back directly. I can get it without the revolver.'

And he rushed off straight to Kirilov's. This must probably have been two hours before the visit of Peter Verkhovensky and Liputin to Kirilov. Shatov and Kirilov, who lived in the same yard, hardly ever saw each other, and when they did meet, they did not speak or greet each other; they had been 'lying side by side' too long in America.

'Kirilov, you always have tea. Have you got tea and a *samovar*?'

Kirilov who was pacing the room (as he was wont to do all night from one corner to the other), suddenly stopped and looked intently at Shatov, who had rushed into his room, without, however, betraying any particular surprise.

'I have tea and sugar, and I've also got a *samovar*. But you don't want a *samovar*. The tea's hot. Sit down and just drink it.'

'Kirilov, we lay side by side in America. My wife's come back to me. I – let me have the tea. I must have the *samovar*.'

'If it's for your wife, then you need the *samovar*. But the *samovar* will wait. Now take the teapot from the table. It's hot – boiling hot. Take everything. Take the sugar – all of it. Bread. I've got lots of bread. Take it all. I've got some veal. I've a rouble.'

'Give it me, friend; I'll pay it back to-morrow. Oh, Kirilov!'

'Is it the same wife who was in Switzerland? That's good. And your running in like that, that's good too.'

'Kirilov,' cried Shatov, taking the teapot under his arm and carrying the sugar and bread in both hands, 'Kirilov, if only – if only you'd give up your dreadful delusions and get rid of your atheistic madness – oh, what a man you'd be, Kirilov!'

'I can see that you love your wife after Switzerland. That's good, if it's after Switzerland. When you want more tea, come again. Come all night; I don't sleep at all. There'll be a *samovar*. Take the rouble, here! Go to your wife; I'll stay here and think about you and your wife.'

Maria Shatov was obviously pleased at his haste and fell upon the tea almost greedily, but there was no need to run for the *samovar*; she drank only half a cup and swallowed a tiny morsel of bread. The veal she refused irritably and with disgust.

'You're ill, Marie; all this is just a sign that you are,' Shatov observed timidly, as he waited, timidly, on her.

'Of course I'm ill. Please sit down. Where did you get the tea, if you haven't any?'

Shatov told her about Kirilov in a few brief sentences. She had heard something about him.

'I know he's mad. Don't tell me any more. There are lots of fools in the world. So you've been in America? I heard, you wrote.'

'Yes, I – I wrote to you in Paris.'

'Enough, and please talk of something else. Are you a Slavophil by conviction?'

'I'm – I'm not really – since I cannot be a Russian, I became a Slavophil,' he said, with a wry smile, with the effort of a man who feels that his joke is strained and inappropriate.

'Aren't you a Russian?'

'No, I'm not a Russian.'

'Oh, well, that's all nonsense. Please sit down, will you? Why are you rushing about all over the room? You think I'm delirious? Well, perhaps I soon shall be delirious. You say there are only two of you in the house?'

'Two – downstairs –'

'And both of them so clever. What's there downstairs? You said downstairs?'

'Oh, nothing.'

'What nothing? I want to know.'

'I only wanted to say that there are only the two of us in the house, but that before the Lebyatkins lived downstairs.'

'You mean the woman who was murdered last night?' she suddenly asked excitedly. 'I heard of it. I heard of it as soon as I arrived. There was a fire here, wasn't there?'

'Yes, Marie, and I daresay I'm behaving like a scoundrel just now in forgiving the swine,' he declared, getting up suddenly and beginning to pace the room, throwing up his arms as though in a frenzy.

But Marie had not quite understood him. She listened to his replies absent-mindedly. She asked questions, but did not listen.

'Fine things are happening here, I must say! Oh, how disgusting it all is! What disgusting people they all are! But do sit down, for goodness sake! Oh, how you exasperate me!' and, so saying, she fell back exhausted on the pillow.

'Marie, I won't – perhaps you'll lie down, Marie?'

She did not reply and closed her eyes, feeling utterly exhausted. Her pale face looked death-like. She fell asleep almost immediately. Shatov looked round, snuffed the candle, looked uneasily at her face again, clasped his hands tightly in front of him and tiptoed out of the room into the passage. On the landing he pressed his face against the wall in the corner and stood like that for ten minutes without uttering a sound or making a movement. He would have stood there longer, but he suddenly became aware of the sound of soft, cautious steps downstairs. Someone was coming up the stairs. Shatov remembered that he had forgotten to lock the gate.

'Who's there?' he asked in a whisper.

The unknown visitor went on mounting the steps without haste and without answering. On reaching the top landing, he stopped; it was impossible to see him in the dark. Suddenly Shatov heard his cautious question:

'Ivan Shatov?'

Shatov gave his name, and at once stretched out his hand to stop him; but the visitor himself grasped his hand and – Shatov shuddered as though he had touched some horrible snake.

'Stay here,' he whispered quickly. 'Don't go in; I can't receive you now. My wife has come back. I'll fetch a candle.'

When he returned with the candle, he saw a very young army officer standing there; he did not know his name, but he had seen him somewhere before.

'Erkel,' the officer introduced himself. 'You've seen me at Virginsky's.'

'I remember. You sat there taking notes. Look here,' Shatov said, flying suddenly into a rage and walking angrily up to him, but still speaking in a whisper, 'you gave me a sign with your hand when you took mine. But I want you to know that I don't care a damn for your signs! I don't acknowledge them – don't want to. I can throw you downstairs this minute – do you know that?'

'No, I know nothing about that and I don't know what you are so angry about,' the visitor replied without resentment and almost good-naturedly. 'I've only come to give you a message, being very anxious not to lose time. You have a printing press that does not belong to you and that you're obliged to account for, as you know yourself. I've been instructed to ask you to hand it over to Liputin to-morrow at seven o'clock sharp in the evening. I've further been instructed to tell you that nothing more will be required of you.'

'Nothing?'

'Absolutely nothing. Your request has been granted, and you're no longer a member of the society. I was instructed to tell you that definitely.'

'Who instructed you to tell me?'

'Those who told me the sign.'

'Have you come from abroad?'

'I don't think that has anything to do with you.'

'Oh, hell! And why didn't you come before if you were instructed to?'

'I followed certain instructions, and was not alone.'

'I understand, I understand that you were not alone. Oh – hell! But why didn't Liputin come himself?'

'So I'll come for you to-morrow evening at exactly six o'clock and we shall go there on foot. There'll only be the three of us there.'

'Won't Verkhovensky be there?'

'No, he won't. Verkhovensky is leaving the town at eleven o'clock to-morrow morning.'

'I thought so,' Shatov whispered furiously and he smote his hip with his fist. 'He's run off, the swine!'

He was thinking it over agitatedly. Erkel looked intently at him, saying nothing and waiting.

'How will you carry it? You can't possibly pick it up in your hands and carry it away.'

'We won't have to. You'll just point out the place, and we'll make sure it really is buried there. We only know the whereabouts of the place. We don't know the exact spot. Have you shown it to anyone else?'

Shatov looked at him.

'You, too, a young fellow like you, a silly boy like you – you, too, are up to your neck in it? But, good Lord, it's just young blood like you they want! Well, go along! Oh, dear, that scoundrel has cheated you all and run away.'

Erkel looked at him serenely and calmly, but did not seem to understand.

'Verkhovensky ran away, Verkhovensky!' Shatov cried, grinding his teeth furiously.

'But he's still here,' Erkel observed softly and persuasively. 'He hasn't left yet. He's not going till to-morrow. I particularly asked him to be present as a witness. My instructions all concerned him,' he confided frankly like a very young and inexperienced boy. 'But I'm sorry to say he did not agree on the ground that he was leaving to-morrow. I must say he is in rather a hurry.'

Shatov glanced pityingly at the simpleton again, but suddenly gave it up with an impatient wave of the hand, as though he thought that he was not worth pitying.

'All right, I'll come,' he put an end to their conversation suddenly. 'And now get out!'

'So I'll be here at six o'clock precisely,' Erkel said, bowing politely, and without hurrying walked downstairs.

'Little fool!' Shatov could not restrain himself from shouting after him from the landing.

'What did you say, sir?' Erkel asked from below.

'Nothing; you can go.'

'I thought you said something.'

2

Erkel belonged to that type of 'little fools' who lack only the higher forms of reasoning powers; but he had plenty of the other, the lesser, reasoning powers, even to the point of cunning. Fanatically, childishly devoted to 'the common cause', but really to Peter Verkhovensky, he acted on the instructions he had received at the meeting of the group of five when the parts each of them had to play next day had been arranged and distributed. When Peter gave Erkel the part of messenger, he had managed to take him aside and talk to him for ten minutes. To carry out orders was an absolute necessity for his petty, unreasoning nature, which always yearned to submit itself to someone else's will – oh, of course, only for the sake of the 'common' or 'great' cause. But even that would not have mattered greatly, for little fanatics like Erkel cannot understand the service to an idea unless they identify it in their minds with the person who gives expression to it. The sensitive, tender-hearted, and good-natured Erkel was perhaps the most callous of murderers who planned to kill Shatov and was quite ready to be present at his killing without a trace of any personal hatred and without batting an eyelid. He was told, for instance, to have a good look at Shatov's surroundings while carrying out his instructions, and when Shatov incautiously let slip the information (probably without being aware of it himself) that his wife had come back to him, Erkel was sufficiently cunning not to show any curiosity, in spite of the fact that the thought flashed through his mind that the fact of the return of Shatov's wife was of great importance to the success of their enterprise.

And so it really was: it was that fact alone that saved 'the blackguards' and prevented Shatov from carrying out his intention and, at the same time, helped them to 'get rid of him'. To begin with, it flustered Shatov, put him off his stride, deprived him of his habitual foresight and caution. Any thought for his own safety would be the last thing to enter his head now that he was preoccupied with something else. On the contrary, he was only too eager to believe that Peter Verkhovensky was going to run away next day: that seemed to prove that he was right in his suspicions! Returning to his room, he sat down in a corner again, put his elbows on his knees and covered his face with his hands. Bitter thoughts tormented him. ...

Presently he raised his head again, got up and went on tiptoe to
have a look at her: 'Oh, God, she will be in a fever to-morrow morning – she may be running a high temperature already! She must have
caught a cold. She is not used to this terrible climate, and she had to
travel third class in her thin coat and without any warm clothes at all.
And to leave her here, abandon her without any help at all! Her bag –
such a tiny little bag, so flimsy, so crumpled – must weigh no more
than ten pounds! Poor thing, she is so fagged out! How she must have
suffered! She is proud. That's why she doesn't complain. It's her illness. Even an angel would be irritable in illness. How dry and hot her
forehead must be – what dark circles under her eyes and – and yet how
beautiful the oval of her face is, and that luxuriant hair – how –'

And he quickly turned his eyes away. He made haste to walk away,
as though afraid of the very idea that he might see in her something
different from an unhappy, exhausted creature who had to be helped.
'What sort of *hope* could he have! Oh, how mean, how contemptible
a man is!'

'Oh, I'm so tired, so tired!' He recalled her cries, her weak, broken
voice. 'Good God! to abandon her now, when she has only eighty
copecks left – she had offered him her purse; such a tiny, old purse!
She came to look for a job – what does she know about jobs? – what
do they know about Russia? Why, they are all just silly children; all
they have are their fantastic ideas made up by themselves. And she is
angry, poor thing, that Russia is not like their foreign dreams! Oh, the
unhappy, the innocent creatures! But – it's really freezing cold in
here!'

He remembered that she had complained of the cold and that he had
promised to heat the stove. 'There are logs in the house; I can fetch
them, but I must not wake her. However, I'll chance it. But what am
I to do about the veal? She may be hungry when she gets up. Well,
that can wait. Kirilov does not go to bed all night. What could I cover
her with? She's fast asleep, but she must be cold – oh, she must be
cold!'

And he went up to have another look at her; her dress was a little
turned up and her right leg was half uncovered to the knee. He turned
away suddenly, almost in dismay, took off his warm overcoat, and
remaining in his threadbare old coat, covered her bare leg, trying not
to look at it.

The lighting of the logs, the walking about on tiptoe, the examination of his sleeping wife, the dreams in his corner, then another look at the sleeping young woman took up a lot of time. Two or three hours passed. During that time Verkhovensky and Liputin had managed to pay a visit to Kirilov. At last he, too, dozed off in the corner. He heard her groan; she had wakened and was calling for him. He jumped to his feet like a criminal.

'Marie, I'm afraid I fell asleep. Oh, what a scoundrel I am, Marie!'

She raised herself a little, looking round the room in surprise, as though she did not know where she was, and suddenly she became very agitated. She was angry and indignant with herself.

'I've taken your bed – I fell asleep dead with exhaustion. Why didn't you wake me? What made you think that I meant to be a burden to you?'

'But I could not possibly waken you, Marie, could I?'

'You could – you should have done it! You have no other bed here, and I've taken yours. You shouldn't have put me in a false position. Or do you think I came here to take advantage of your charity? Get into your bed at once, please, and I'll lie down on some chairs in the corner.'

'But, Marie, I haven't so many chairs and, besides, I have nothing to put on them.'

'Well, in that case I'll lie on the floor. Otherwise you'll have to lie on the floor – now – now!'

She got up and tried to take a step, but suddenly a spasm of agonizing pain deprived her of all strength and resolution and she fell back on the bed again with a loud groan. Shatov ran up, but Marie, hiding her face in the pillows, grabbed his hand and started squeezing it with all her might. This went on for a minute.

'Marie, darling, there's a doctor Frenzel – a friend of mine – if you think I ought to call him in – I could run out and fetch him.'

'Nonsense!'

'Nonsense? Not at all. Tell me, Marie, what is hurting you? We could try fomentations – on your stomach, for instance. I could do that without the doctor. Or a mustard plaster –'

'What is this?' she asked strangely, raising her head and looking at him in dismay.

'What is what, Marie?' Shatov asked, not understanding. 'What are you asking about? Oh dear, I'm quite at a loss, Marie. I'm sorry, I don't understand anything.'

'Oh, leave me alone. It's not your business to understand. And it would have been funny if you had,' she added, with a bitter laugh. 'Speak to me about something. Just walk up and down the room and talk. Don't stand beside me and don't look at me. I ask you particularly not to do it, please.'

Shatov started pacing the room, looking at the floor and doing his utmost not to glance at her.

'Don't be angry with me, Marie, please don't; but there's some veal I can get you – and there's tea not far off. You had so little before. ...'

She waved him away spitefully and with disgust. Shatov held his tongue in despair.

'Listen, I intend to open a bookbinding business on rational competitive principles. Since you live here, what's your opinion: would it be successful or not?'

'Good heavens, Marie, people don't read books here, and there aren't any at all. Why should they start binding them?'

'Who are "they"?'

'The local reader and the local inhabitant, in general, Marie.'

'Why don't you speak more clearly, then? They – and who they are one doesn't know. You don't know grammar.'

'It's in the spirit of the language, Marie,' Shatov murmured.

'Oh, leave me alone, with your spirit. I'm sick and tired of you. Why shouldn't the local reader or inhabitants have his books bound?'

'Because to read a book and have it bound are two stages in development, and enormously different stages too. At first he gets slowly used to reading. That takes him ages, of course, but he doesn't take care of his book and throws it about. Doesn't take it seriously. To have a book bound, on the other hand, implies a respect for the book; it implies that they not only like to read it, but regard it as something essential. Russia has not yet reached that period. Europe has been binding books for a long time.'

'Well, that may be expressed pedantically, but at least it is not silly. It reminds me of you three years ago: you were sometimes quite witty three years ago.'

She said this in the same disdainful voice as all her other capricious remarks.

'Marie, Marie,' Shatov addressed her, deeply moved, 'oh, Marie, if only you knew how much I have been through during the last three years. I heard afterwards that you seemed to despise me for the change in my opinions. But who are the people I gave up? They are the enemies of life, old-fashioned liberals, who are afraid of their own independence, flunkeys of thought, enemies of individuality and freedom, flabby preachers of dead and rotten ideas. What is it they have to offer? Senility, the golden mean, horrible middle-class mediocrity, envious equality, equality without self-esteem, equality such as a flunkey understands it, or as the Frenchman of 1793 understood it. And the worst of it is that everywhere there are scoundrels, scoundrels, scoundrels!'

'Yes, there are lots of scoundrels,' she said, abruptly and painfully.

She lay stretched out on the bed, without moving and as though afraid to move, her head thrown back on the pillow a little on one side, gazing at the ceiling with tired but feverish eyes. Her face was pale, her lips dry and parched.

'You realize it, Marie, you realize it!' Shatov cried.

She wanted to shake her head in sign of disagreement, but suddenly she was again writhing with pain. She buried her face in the pillow again, and again for a whole minute she gripped with all her might the hand of Shatov, who had rushed up to her, beside himself with fear.

'Marie, Marie, but this may be very serious! Marie!'

'Shut up. I won't have it, I won't have it, I won't have it,' she cried, almost in a frenzy, turning her face upwards again. 'Don't you dare look at me like that! I can't bear your pity! Walk about the room – talk about something – talk– '

Shatov, like one distraught, started muttering something again.

'What exactly are you doing here?' she asked, interrupting him with disdainful impatience.

'I've got a job at a merchant's office. I could earn a good wage, Marie, if I really put my mind to it.'

'So much the better for you.'

'Oh, don't misunderstand me, Marie, I merely said it as –'

'And what do you do besides? What are you preaching? You can't help preaching, can you? That's your character.'

'I'm preaching God, Marie.'

'In whom you don't believe yourself. That idea I never could understand.'

'Let's drop it, Marie. We'll discuss it later.'

'What sort of person was that Miss Mary Lebyatkin?'

'That, too, we'll discuss later, Marie.'

'Don't keep on saying such things to me! Is it true that her death was caused by – the wickedness – of those men?'

'There's no doubt about it,' Shatov replied, grinding his teeth.

Marie suddenly raised her head and cried hysterically: 'Don't speak to me of that again – never – never!'

And she fell back on the bed again, in the throes of the same writhing pain. This was the third time, and this time her groans had become louder and rose to screams.

'Oh, you insufferable man! Oh, you loathsome man!' she cried, tossing about and no longer sparing herself, and pushing away Shatov, who bent over her.

'Marie, I'll do anything you like – I'll walk about, I'll talk –'

'But can't you see that it's begun?'

'What has begun, Marie?'

'How do I know? Do I know anything about it? Oh, damn! Damn it all from the beginning!'

'Marie, if you'd just tell me what is beginning – otherwise how am I to know?'

'You're a useless, chattering theoretician! Oh, damn, damn everything in the world!'

'Marie! Marie!' He seriously thought that she was beginning to go mad.

'But, goodness, can't you see that I'm in labour?' she said, raising herself a little and looking at him with a terrible, hysterical bitterness which distorted her whole face. 'May he be damned beforehand – this child!'

'Marie,' Shatov cried, having at last realized what was the matter with her. 'Marie! But why didn't you tell me before?' He suddenly pulled himself together and grabbed his cap with purposeful determination.

'How was I to know when I came in here? Would I have come to you? I was told it would be in another ten days! Where are you going? Where are you going? Don't!'

'I'm going for a midwife! I'll sell my revolver. We must get money before everything else now!'

'Don't dare to do anything of the sort! Don't dare to fetch a midwife! Get some peasant woman, an old woman – I have eighty copecks in my purse. Peasant women have babies without midwives, don't they? And if I die, so much the better!'

'I'll fetch a midwife and an old woman – only how am I to leave you alone, Marie?'

But realizing that it was better to leave her alone now in spite of her frantic state than leave her without help later, he refused to listen to her groans or angry screams and ran downstairs as fast as he could.

3

First of all he went to Kirilov. It was about one o'clock in the morning. Kirilov was standing in the middle of the room.

'Kirilov, my wife's having a baby!'

'What do you mean?'

'She's giving birth to a baby – a baby!'

'Are you sure?'

'Of course I am sure! She's in agony. I want a woman, any old woman, at once – I must have her. Do you think I could get one now? You used to have lots of women in the house.'

'What a pity I don't know how to give birth to a baby,' Kirilov replied thoughtfully. 'I mean, it isn't I who could give birth to a baby, but that I don't know what to do to give birth to a baby – oh, dear, I don't know how to say it.'

'You mean you can't deliver a baby. But it wasn't that I was thinking of. I want an old woman, a peasant woman, a nurse, a servant.'

'I'll find you an old woman, but not immediately, perhaps. If you like, I'll come instead –'

'No, no, that's quite impossible. I'll go and fetch Mrs Virginsky, the midwife, now.'

'That horrible woman!'

'Oh yes, Kirilov, that's true, but she is the best midwife of them all. Oh, I know, it will be all without reverence, with disdain, with abuse, with blasphemy – at such a great mystery, at the birth of a new human being! Oh, she is already cursing it!'

'If you like, I'll –'

'No, no, but while I'm running about (oh, I shall fetch that Virgin-sky woman!), I'd be glad if you would go up my staircase and listen quietly. Only don't for goodness sake go in. You'll frighten her. Don't go in on any account – just listen, in case of emergency. If anything happens, then go in.'

'I understand. I've another rouble. Here. I was thinking of getting a chicken to-morrow, but I don't want it now. Run quickly – run as fast as you can! There's a *samovar* all the night.'

Kirilov knew nothing about the decision to murder Shatov, nor had he any idea of the great danger that threatened him. All he knew was that he had some accounts to settle with 'those fellows', and though he was partly implicated in the business himself by the instruc-tions he had received from abroad (they were of a general nature, however, for he had never taken any active part in anything), he had given it all up lately – all the instructions, having completely disso-ciated himself from everything, indeed, from the entire 'common cause', devoting himself wholly to a life of contemplation. Although at the meeting Verkhovensky had invited Liputin to go with him to Kirilov's to make sure that the engineer would take upon himself the responsibility for the 'Shatov business', he never said a word in his talk with Kirilov about Shatov, nor alluded to him, probably because he did not think it politic to do so and because he did not think Kirilov sufficiently reliable. He put it off till next day, when it would be all over and, therefore, would make no difference to Kirilov. That at least was what Verkhovensky thought of Kirilov. Nor did it escape Liputin's notice that, in spite of Peter's promise, not a word had been said about Shatov, but Liputin was too agitated to protest.

Shatov rushed off to Virginsky's house, cursing the distance and seeing no end to it. He had to knock a long time at Virginsky's: they had all been sound asleep for hours. But Shatov started banging on the shutter unceremoniously and with all his might. The dog on a chain in the yard was dashing about and barking furiously. The dogs in the street caught it up and a veritable bedlam of barking arose.

'Why are you knocking and what do you want?' Virginsky him-self asked at last from a window in a very gentle voice which was not at all what one would have expected in the circumstances.

The shutter was pushed back a little and the ventilating window was opened.

'Who's there? What scoundrel is this?' the old maid, Virginsky's relative, shrieked angrily in a voice that was more like what one would have expected.

'I'm Shatov. My wife's come back and she is just going to have a baby. ....'

'Well, let her. Go away!'

'I've come for Mrs Virginsky, and I won't go without her!'

'She can't attend any confinement, especially at such short notice. Go to Maksheyeva's, and stop making a row!' the angry female voice rattled on.

Shatov could hear how Virginsky was trying to stop her, but she pushed him aside and would not give in.

'I shan't go away!' Shatov cried again.

'Wait, wait a little!' Virginsky cried at last, overpowering the old maid. 'I beg you to wait five minutes, Shatov, I'll wake Mrs Virginsky. Please don't knock and don't shout ... Oh, this is terrible!'

After five minutes which lasted an eternity Mrs Virginsky appeared.

'Your wife has come back to you?' he heard her voice through the small ventilating window.

To Shatov's surprise her voice did not sound angry at all, but just peremptory as usual. But, then, Mrs Virginsky could not speak otherwise.

'Yes, and she's having a baby.'

'Marie?'

'Yes, Marie. Of course it's Marie!'

A pause followed. Shatov waited. They were whispering to each other inside.

'How long has she been with you?' Mrs Virginsky asked again.

'Since this evening. She arrived at eight o'clock. Please make haste.' They whispered again. They seemed to be consulting each other.

'Look here, you're not making a mistake, are you? She has sent you for me herself?'

'No, she hasn't sent me for you. She wants a peasant woman because she doesn't want to burden me with the expense, but don't worry, I'll pay you.'

'All right, I'll come whether you pay me or not. I have always had a high opinion of Marie's independent principles, though I don't think she remembers me. Have you got the most necessary things?'

'I have got nothing, but shall get them. I shall – I shall.'

'So these people possess some generosity after all,' Shatov thought as he set off to Lyamshin's. 'A man and his convictions are two different things. Perhaps I haven't been fair to them! We are all to blame, we are all to blame and – if only we were all convinced of that!'

He did not have to knock long at Lyamshin's; to his surprise, Lyamshin opened the little ventilating window at once, having jumped out of bed barefoot and in his night-clothes at the risk of catching cold. He was very concerned about his health, and was continually worried about it. But there was a special reason for such alertness and precipitancy: Lyamshin had been in a state of nerves all the evening, and had not been able to sleep for excitement as a result of the meeting of the group of five. He was all the time haunted by the fear of a visit of uninvited and unwished-for guests. The news that Shatov was an informer worried him most of all. And, as ill-luck would have it, somebody was suddenly knocking so dreadfully loudly at the window.

He was so frightened at the sight of Shatov that he immediately slammed the window and rushed back to bed. Shatov began shouting and knocking furiously.

'What do you mean by knocking like that in the middle of the night?' Lyamshin shouted menacingly, but almost dead with fear, having at last, two minutes later, made up his mind to open the window again to satisfy himself that Shatov had come alone.

'Here's your revolver – take it back and give me fifteen roubles.'

'What's the matter with you? Are you drunk? I'm going to catch a cold. Wait a minute; I'll throw a blanket over me.'

'Let me have the fifteen roubles at once. If you won't give it me, I'll knock and shout till daybreak. I'll break your window for you.'

'I'll shout for help and they'll take you off to the lock-up.'

'Well, I'm not drunk, either. I'll start shouting for help, too! Which of us has more reason to be afraid of the police – you or I?'

'And to think that you can hold such rotten opinions! I know what you're hinting at. Wait, wait. Don't knock, for goodness sake! Good heavens! who can raise money at night? Well, what do you want money for if you're not drunk?'

'My wife has come back. I'm letting you have it back for ten roubles less than what I paid for it, and I haven't fired it once. Take your revolver – take it at once.'

Lyamshin put his hand mechanically out of the window and took the revolver. He waited a little, and then he thrust his head quickly out of the window and said as though beside himself with a shiver running down his spine:

'You're lying. Your wife hasn't come back to you at all. You – you simply want to run away.'

'You're a fool. Where am I to run away to? Let your Verkhovensky run away – not I. I've just come from the midwife, Mrs Virginsky, and she has agreed to come to me at once. Ask them. My wife's in agony. I must have money. Give me the money.'

A regular firework of ideas burst in Lyamshin's shifty mind. Everything suddenly appeared in quite a different light, but his panic still prevented him from thinking clearly.

'But how is this possible? You don't live with your wife, do you?'

'I'll knock your head off for asking me such questions.'

'Oh, dear, I'm sorry. I understand – I'm afraid I was taken by surprise. But I understand – I understand. But – but will Mrs Virginsky really come to you? You said just now that she was already on the way. You know, I don't believe you. You see, you see, you see you're telling fibs, fibs, fibs! ...'

'She is probably with my wife by now – don't keep me waiting. It's not my fault that you're a fool.'

'That's not true. I'm not a fool. I'm sorry, but I just can't –'

And, completely at a loss, he began closing the little window for a third time, but Shatov raised such a clamour that he at once thrust his head out again.

'But that's a damned infringement of my rights as a citizen! What are you demanding of me? What? Just try to formulate your demands. And in the middle of the night, too!'

'I'm demanding fifteen roubles, you fathead!'

'But for all you know I may not want my revolver back. You have no right to make any demands on me. You bought the thing, and that's the end of it – you have no right to demand it. Besides, I can't possibly raise such a sum at night. Where can I get it?'

'You've always got money. I've taken off ten roubles, and you're known to be a damned miser!'

'Come the day after to-morrow – you hear? – the day after to-morrow at twelve o'clock and I'll give you the lot – that's fair, isn't it?'

Shatov knocked furiously at the window for the third time.

'Give me ten roubles, and early to-morrow another five.'

'No, the day after to-morrow the other five. I swear I shan't have it to-morrow. You'd better not come – you'd better not come.'

'All right, let me have the ten. Oh, you swine!'

'Why call me names? Wait a minute, I must light a candle. You've broken the window. Good Lord, nobody swears like that at night. Here!' He held out a note to him through the window.

Shatov grabbed it: it was a five-rouble note.

'I tell you I can't give you more. I just haven't got it. I shall be able to let you have it all the day after to-morrow, but I can do nothing more now.'

'I shan't go!' Shatov roared.

'Oh, all right, here's something more for you. You see, here's some more. But I won't give you any more. You can scream the street down, but I won't give any more. Do what you damned well like, you won't get more. I won't give it you, I won't.'

He was in a frenzy, in despair, in a cold sweat. The two notes he had given him were one rouble notes. Shatov had seven roubles altogether now.

'Oh, to hell with you! I'll come to-morrow. I'll break every bone in your body, Lyamshin, if you haven't the eight roubles ready for me.'

'And I shan't be at home, you fool,' Lyamshin thought quickly to himself.

'Wait, wait!' Lyamshin shouted frantically after Shatov, who was already running off. 'Wait, come back. Tell me, please, is it true that your wife has come back?'

'Damn fool!' Shatov spat and ran home as fast as his legs would carry him.

4

I may mention that Mrs Virginsky knew nothing of the decision taken at the meeting of the group of five the day before. Virginsky, who came back home feeling weak and stunned, did not dare to tell her of the decision that had been taken, but he could not restrain himself, and told her half – that is to say, the news Verkhovensky confided to them about Shatov's unmistakable intention to inform the police. But he added at once that he was not quite sure that it was true. Mrs Virginsky was terribly frightened. That is why she decided to go at once when Shatov came to fetch her, in spite of the fact that she was very tired, having spent the whole of the previous night at a difficult confinement. She had always been of the opinion that 'such trash as Shatov are capable of any mean political trick'; but the arrival of Mrs Shatov put things in a different light. Shatov's panic, the desperate tone of his entreaties, the whole manner in which he implored help, showed a change of heart in the traitor: a man who had decided to betray himself merely for the sake of ruining others would, she could not help thinking, have looked and spoken differently. In short, Mrs Virginsky decided to look into the matter herself. Virginsky remained satisfied with her decision – he felt as if a heavy load had been taken off his mind! He even began to feel more hopeful: the way Shatov behaved seemed to him incompatible with Verkhovensky's theory.

Shatov had not been mistaken; when he came back, he found Mrs Virginsky already with Marie. She had only just arrived, had scornfully dismissed Kirilov, who was keeping watch at the bottom of the stairs, had hastily introduced herself to Marie, who had not recognized her as an old acquaintance. She had found Marie in 'a very bad way', that is, distraught, spiteful, and 'in a state of the most abject despair', and in about five minutes overcame all her protests.

'Why do you go on saying that you don't want an expensive midwife?' she was saying at the moment when Shatov came in. 'Absolute nonsense! It's just the sort of thing you would say in your abnormal condition. It's a fifty-fifty chance that you would end up badly if you had got just any old woman, some peasant midwife. That would cost you much more than an expensive midwife – not to mention the trouble you might let yourself in for. How do you know I am an expensive midwife? You can pay me afterwards, and I won't charge you more than necessary, and I answer for my success. With me here, you won't die. I've seen worse cases. And I'll place your baby in a found-ling home to-morrow, if you like, and then send him to be brought up in the country, and that'll be the end of that. Meantime you'll get well again, you'll take up some rational work, and in less than no time you'll have paid Shatov for the room and expenses, which won't be so great at all.'

'I don't mean that. I have no right to be a burden —'

'Your enlightened civic feelings do you credit, but believe me, Shatov will spend scarcely anything if only he is willing to transform himself from an eccentric into a man whose ideas are even just a little bit normal. All he has to do is to refrain from making a fool of him-self, beating the drum, and rushing about the town gasping for breath. If we don't keep him under control, he'll rouse all the doctors in town before morning — he roused all the dogs in our street. But we don't want any doctors. I've said already that I'll answer for every-thing. I daresay you could hire an old woman as a help, it won't cost you anything. But I think he'll be of some use himself, and not only for doing all sorts of silly things. He's got hands and feet, he can run to the chemist's without offending your feelings by his charity. Charity indeed! Wasn't he responsible for bringing you into this position? Didn't he make mischief between you and the family in which you were a governess with the selfish object of marrying you? We've heard about it, you know. However, he just came running to me like a madman and raised din enough to wake the whole street. I am not forcing myself on anyone and have come only for your sake, on principle, for we are all bound to stand up for each other. I told him so before I left the house. If you think I'm not wanted here, then good-bye. I only hope there won't be any trouble that can't be easily averted.'

And she even got up from her chair.

Marie was so helpless, she was in such pain, and, to tell the truth, she was so frightened of what might happen to her, that she did not have the heart to let her go. But that woman suddenly became hateful to her: she'd got it all wrong; it was not at all what Marie had in mind. Yet the prediction that she might die in the hands of an in-competent midwife overcame her repugnance. But then she became more exacting and more ruthless to Shatov from that moment. In the end she forbade him not only to look at her, but even to stand facing her. Her pains became fiercer. Her cursing and even blaspheming grew more frantic.

'Oh, I think we'd better send him out of the room,' Mrs Virginsky rapped out. 'He looks ghastly. He's only frightening you. White as a sheet. Why, you funny man, what is it to you? What a comedy!'

Shatov made no answer. He had made up his mind to say nothing.

'I've seen many a foolish father in such cases. They, too, go off their heads. But they at least –'

'Stop it or leave me alone to die! Don't say another word! I won't have it! I can't stand it!'

'It's quite impossible not to say another word, unless you're out of your mind. That's what I think you are in your condition. We have to talk of the things you want. Tell me, have you got anything ready? You'd better answer, Shatov. She's not in a position to.'

'Tell me what is needed.'

'Which means that you've nothing ready?'

She told him the things she had to have, those which were necessary, and, to do her justice, she asked only for those that were absolutely indispensable, the necessities. Shatov had some of them. Marie took out her key and held it out to him, for him to look in her bag. As his hands shook, he took a little longer than was necessary to open the unfamiliar lock. Marie flew into a rage, but when Mrs Virginsky went up to take the key from him, she would not let her look into her bag and insisted, screaming and weeping like one demented, that Shatov alone should open her bag.

For some things he had to run down to Kirilov. But no sooner had Shatov turned to go than she began calling him back furiously, and only calmed down when Shatov, who rushed back headlong from the stairs, told her that he was going away only for a minute to fetch the most necessary things and that he would be back at once.

'Well, it seems it is difficult to please your ladyship,' Mrs Virginsky said with a laugh. 'One minute it is, "Stand with your face to the wall and don't dare to look at me", and another, "Don't dare to leave me for a minute or I shall start crying." You'll only give him all sorts of ideas if you go on like this. All right, all right, don't be silly and don't frown; I'm only joking.'

'He won't dare to get any ideas.'

'Dear, dear, I daresay he wouldn't if he were not head over heels in love with you, if he did not run about the streets with his tongue out and if he did not rouse all the dogs in the town. He broke one of my windows.'

5

Shatov found Kirilov still pacing up and down his room and so pre-occupied with his own thoughts that he had even forgotten about the arrival of Shatov's wife, and listened without understanding.

'Oh yes,' he suddenly remembered, as though tearing himself away with an effort and only for a minute from some absorbing idea. 'Yes – an old woman. A married woman or just any old woman? Wait, an old married woman – is it? I remember – I've been – the old woman will come, but not just now. Take the pillow. What else? Oh, yes. Wait a minute. Have you ever had moments of eternal harmony, Shatov?'

'You know, Kirilov, you must get some sleep at night.'

Kirilov came out of his dream and – strange to say – spoke more coherently than he usually did. It was evident that he had formulated it all in his head long ago and had, perhaps, written it down, too.

'There are seconds – they come five or six at a time – when you suddenly feel the presence of eternal harmony in all its fullness. It is nothing earthly. I don't mean that it is heavenly, but a man in his earthly semblance can't endure it. He has to undergo a physical change or die. This feeling is clear and unmistakable. It is as though you suddenly apprehended all nature and suddenly said: "Yes, it is true – it is good." God, when He created the world, said at the end of each day of creation: "Yes, it is true, it is good." It is not rapture, but just glad-ness. You forgive nothing because there is nothing to forgive. Nor do you really love anything – oh, it is much higher than love! What is so terrifying about it is that it is so terribly clear and such gladness. If it went on for more than five seconds, the soul could not endure it and must perish. In those five seconds I live through a lifetime, and I am ready to give my life for them, for it's worth it. To be able to endure it for ten seconds, you would have to undergo a physical change. I think man ought to stop begetting children. What do you want chil-dren for, what do you want mental development, if your goal has been attained? It is said in the gospel that in the resurrection they neither marry nor are given in marriage, but are as the angels of God in heaven. It's a hint. Is your wife giving birth to a baby?'

'Kirilov, does this often happen?'

'Once in three days, once a week.'

'You're not an epileptic?'

'No.'

'You will be one. Take care, Kirilov. I've heard that's just how an epileptic fit begins. An epileptic described to me exactly that preliminary sensation before a fit, exactly as you've done. He, too, said it lasted five seconds and that it was impossible to endure it longer than that. Remember Mohammed's pitcher from which no drop of water was spilt while he flew round paradise on his horse. The pitcher – that's your five seconds. It's too much like your eternal harmony, and Mohammed was an epileptic. Be careful, Kirilov – it's epilepsy!'

'There won't be time,' Kirilov laughed softly.

6

The night was passing. Shatov was sent on errands, he was abused, he was called back. Marie was reduced to the extremity of fear for her life. She cried that she wanted to live, that she must, must live, and was afraid to die. 'I don't want to, I don't want to!' she kept repeating. But for Mrs Virginsky things would have gone badly. Gradually she gained complete control over her patient. Marie began obeying every word she uttered, every order from her, like a child. Mrs Virginsky got her way by sternness, not by kindness, but she worked wonders. It was beginning to get light. Mrs Virginsky suddenly imagined that Shatov had run out on to the stairs to say his prayers, and she started laughing. Marie also began to laugh, spitefully, venomously, as though that laughter made her feel better. At last, Shatov was driven out altogether. It was a damp, cold morning. He pressed his face against the wall, just as he had done on the previous evening when Erkel had come. He was shaking like a leaf, was afraid to think, but his mind was already clinging to every image that came into his head, as it does in dreams. He was incessantly caught up by his fancies which incessantly snapped off short like a rotten thread. At last the groans that were coming from the room turned into dreadful animal cries, unbearable, incredible. He wanted to stop his ears but couldn't, and he fell on his knees, repeating unconsciously, 'Marie, Marie!' Then, at last, there came the sound of a cry, a new cry, which made Shatov shudder and jump up from his knees – the cry of an infant child, weak and discordant. He crossed himself and rushed into the room. A tiny, red, crumpled human being screamed and moved its tiny arms and legs in Mrs Virginsky's hands. It was dreadfully help-less and, like a speck of dust, was at the mercy of the slightest puff of wind, but it was screaming and asserting itself as though it also had every right to live.

Marie lay as though she were unconscious, but a minute later she opened her eyes and gave Shatov a strange look: it was quite a new kind of look, though he was still quite unable to understand what it meant, but never before had he known or remembered her looking at him like that.

'A boy? A boy?' she asked Mrs Virginsky in a feeble voice.

'A boy!' Mrs Virginsky shouted in reply, as she swaddled the baby.

After she had swaddled it and before she laid it across the bed be-tween two pillows, she gave it to Shatov to hold for a moment. Marie, as though afraid of Mrs Virginsky, signed to him on the sly. He understood at once and brought the baby to show her.

'He's so – pretty!' she whispered weakly with a smile.

'Look at him!' the triumphant Mrs Virginsky laughed gaily as she glanced at Shatov's face. 'What a silly face he has!'

'Rejoice, Mrs Virginsky,' Shatov, radiant at the few words Marie had uttered about the child, murmured with an idiotically blissful expression. 'It's a great joy!'

'What great joy are you babbling about?' Mrs Virginsky said merrily, bustling about, clearing away and working like a Trojan.

'The mystery of the coming of a new human being is a great and incomprehensible mystery, Mrs. Virginsky, and what a pity it is you don't understand it!'

Shatov muttered incoherently, dazed and entranced. It was as though something were swaying about in his head and pouring out of his soul involuntarily, in spite of himself.

'There were two, and now there's a third human being, a new spirit, whole and complete, which no human hands can fashion – a new thought and a new love – it makes me feel frightened. And there's nothing bigger in the world!'

'The things the man says! It's simply a further development of the organism, and there's no mystery whatever here,' Mrs Virginsky said with a sincere and merry laugh. 'If you were right, every fly would be a mystery. But let me tell you this: superfluous people ought not to be born. First change everything so that there shouldn't be any superfluous people and then bring them into the world. As it is, we shall have to take him to the home for foundlings to-morrow. Still, I suppose that can't be helped.'

'I'll never let him go to a home,' Shatov declared firmly, staring at the floor.

'You're going to adopt him as your son?'

'He is my son.'

'Of course, he's a Shatov, legally he is a Shatov; you needn't pretend to be a benefactor of the human race. You don't seem to be able to get on without fine phrases. There, there, it's all right; only I'm afraid, ladies and gentlemen,' she said, having at last finished tidying up, 'I must go now, I'll look in again this morning, and in the evening, if necessary; but now, since everything has gone off so well, I have to go and see my other patients. They've been waiting for me for a long time. You've got an old woman somewhere, Shatov, I believe. Well, the old woman's all right; only don't you leave her for long. Don't forget you're her husband, and sit beside her, perhaps you may be of some use. I don't think Marie will drive you away – there, there, I was only laughing. ...'

At the gate, to which Shatov had seen her off, she added to him alone:

'You've given me something to laugh at for the rest of my life. I shan't charge you anything. I shall be laughing at you in my sleep. I've never seen anything funnier than you last night in all my life.'

She went away completely satisfied. From Shatov's appearance and his talk it was as clear as daylight that the man was 'getting ready to be a father and was an absolute nincompoop'. She ran back home on purpose to tell Virginsky about it, although it would have been much quicker to go straight to her patient.

'Marie,' Shatov began timidly, 'she told you not to go to sleep for

a little time, though I can see how hard it is for you. I'll sit down by
the window and take care of you, shall I?'

And he sat down by the window behind the sofa where she could
not see him. But a minute later she called him and asked him querulously to adjust the pillow.

'No, that's not right – oh dear – what clumsy hands you've got!'

Shatov did it again.

'Bend over to me,' she suddenly said wildly, doing her best not to
look at him.

He gave a start, but bent over.

'A little more – not like that – nearer,' and suddenly she put her left
arm round his neck and he felt on his forehead her ardent, moist
kiss.

'Marie!'

Her lips twitched, she was trying to restrain herself, but suddenly
she raised herself a little and said with flashing eyes:

'Nicholas Stavrogin is a cad!'

And she fell back on the bed helplessly, as though she had been
struck down, with her face buried in the pillow, sobbing hysterically
and squeezing Shatov's hand in hers.

From that moment she would not let him leave her side. She insisted that he should sit by her bedside. She could only talk a little, but
she gazed at him and smiled happily at him. She seemed suddenly to
have been transformed into a silly girl. Everything seemed to be different. Shatov kept crying like a little boy or talking goodness knows
what, in a wild, entranced, and inspired way. He kissed her hands. She
listened to him enraptured, perhaps not understanding him, but strok-
ing his hair caressingly with her weak hand, smoothing it and admiring it. He spoke to her of Kirilov, of how they would now begin a
'new life' and 'for ever'; and of the existence of God, of how good
everybody was. ... In their excitement they took out the child again
to have a look at it.

'Marie,' he cried, holding the child in his arms, 'the old nightmare
is over – the disgrace and all that dead stuff! Let us work hard and begin a new life, the three of us – yes, yes! Oh, yes, and what shall we
call him, Marie?'

'Him? What shall we call him?' she repeated with surprise, and a
look of terrible grief came suddenly into her face.

She clasped her hands, looked reproachfully at Shatov and buried her face in the pillow.

'Marie, what's the matter?' he cried with grief-stricken dismay.

'And you – you could – oh, you ungrateful man!'

'Marie, forgive me, Marie. I only asked what we should call him. I don't know –'

'Ivan, Ivan,' she said, raising her flushed, tear-stained face. 'Surely you didn't think we could call him any other horrible name?'

'Marie, calm yourself. Oh, how upset you are!'

'It's silly of you to think that I'm upset because of that. I bet if I'd proposed to call him by that – horrible name, you would have agreed at once. You wouldn't have noticed it even. Oh, you're all so ungrateful, so mean – all of you, all!'

A minute later, of course, they made it up. Shatov persuaded her to go to sleep. She fell asleep, but still kept his hands in hers. She woke frequently and looked at him as though afraid he would go away, and went to sleep again.

Kirilov sent up the old woman with his 'congratulations' and, in addition, fried cutlets and made some soup with white bread for Mrs Shatov. The patient drank the soup greedily. The old woman swaddled the baby again. Marie made Shatov have the cutlets.

Time was passing. Shatov, worn out, fell asleep in the chair, with his head on Marie's pillow. So they were found by Mrs Virginsky, who kept her word. She wakened them gaily, had a chat with Marie about her condition, examined the baby, and again told Shatov not to leave his wife. Then, after a few bantering remarks about 'the happy couple', which were not without a shade of contempt and superciliousness, she went away as well satisfied as before.

When Shatov awoke it was already quite dark. He hastened to light a candle and rushed to fetch the old woman. But as soon as he had gone downstairs, he was struck by the sound of the soft, unhurried steps of a man who was coming to meet him. Erkel came in.

'Don't come in,' Shatov whispered and, seizing his hand impetuously, he dragged him back to the gate. 'Wait for me here. I'll be back directly. I'd completely forgotten about you! Oh, how you brought it all back to me!'

He was in such a hurry that he did not even run in to see Kirilov, but only called the old woman. Marie was indignant and in despair that he could dream of 'leaving her alone'.

'But,' he cried rapturously, 'this is the very last step! And then a new life and we'll never, never think of the old horrors again!'

He succeeded in appeasing her somehow and promised to be back punctually at nine. He kissed her affectionately, kissed the baby, and ran down quickly to Erkel.

Both set off to Stavrogin's park at Skvoreshniki, where eighteen months before he had buried the printing press, which had been entrusted to him, in a secluded place at the very edge of the park adjoining the pine-wood. It was a wild and deserted spot, quite hidden and at some distance from the Skvoreshniki mansion. They had to walk two or perhaps three miles from Filippov's house.

'Are we going to walk there? I'll take a cab.'

'Please don't,' Erkel replied. 'They insisted on that. A cabman could be a witness.'

'Oh – damn! All right, all I want is to make an end of it!'

They walked very fast.

'Erkel, you darling little boy!' Shatov cried. 'Have you ever been happy?'

'You seem to be very happy now,' Erkel observed with curiosity.

6

A Very Busy Night

I

VIRGINSKY spent two hours during that day in running round to see all the members of the group of five to tell them that Shatov would not inform the police because his wife had come back and given birth to a child. Anyone who 'had any knowledge of the human heart', he declared, could not possibly suppose that he could be dangerous at this moment. But, to his embarrassment, he found no one at home except Erkel and Lyamshin. Erkel listened to him in silence, looking placidly into his eyes, and in answer to Virginsky's question whether he would go at six o'clock or not, replied with a very candid smile that, of course, he would go.

Lyamshin was in bed, apparently seriously ill, with his head covered with a blanket. He got frightened at the sight of Virginsky, and the moment the latter opened his mouth, he waved him away frantically, imploring him to leave him alone. Still, he listened to all Virginsky had to say about Shatov, and seemed to be for some reason surprised at the news that Virginsky had found no one at home. It seemed that he knew already (through Liputin) of Fedka's death, and told Virginsky about it hurriedly and incoherently, which, in turn, greatly surprised the latter. In answer to Virginsky's straight question whether they ought to go or not, he suddenly began brandishing his arms about and begging Virginsky to remember that he (Lyamshin) had nothing to do with it, that he knew nothing about it, and that he wished to be left alone.

Virginsky came back home feeling depressed and greatly perturbed. What made things worse for him was that he had to conceal it from his family. He was accustomed to disclosing all his secrets to his wife, and but for the fact that a new idea took hold of his feverish brain at that moment – some new plan of action which might reconcile him to whatever happened in future – he would have taken to his bed like Lyamshin. But the new idea gave him courage and, what was more, he began waiting impatiently for the appointed time, and set off for the meeting-place earlier than was necessary.

It was a very gloomy spot at the end of the huge Stavrogin park. Afterwards I went purposely to look at it. How forlorn it must have appeared on that grim autumn evening. The old Crown pine-forest began just there. Huge, century-old pines were silhouetted in the darkness as vague and sombre shapes. It was so dark that they could hardly see each other two feet away, but Peter Verkhovensky, Liputin, and later Erkel brought lanterns with them. For some unknown reason and at some unknown time long ago, a rather absurd-looking grotto had been built there of rough hewn stones. The tables and benches inside the grotto had long decayed and crumbled into dust. About a hundred feet to the right was the third pond of the park. These three ponds, starting from the very house, stretched, one after the other, for about a mile to the very end of the park. It was hard to believe that any noise, shout, or even shot could reach the inhabitants of the deserted Stavrogin mansion. With the departure of Nicholas on the previous day and the butler's absence in town, there remained only five or six people, most of them old servants. In any case, it was quite safe to assume that even if some of the retired servants had heard shouts or cries for help, they would only have aroused a feeling of panic and that none of them would have stirred from the warm stoves or cosy benches to offer assistance.

By twenty past six almost all of them except Erkel, who had been sent to fetch Shatov, were there. This time Peter was not late; he came with Tolkachenko, who looked worried and was frowning. All his assumed arrogance and boastful determination had disappeared. He scarcely left Peter's side and, it would seem, had suddenly become greatly devoted to him. He frequently rushed up to whisper something to him fussily, but Peter hardly even bothered to answer him, or muttered something irritably just to get rid of him.

Shigalyov and Virginsky had arrived even before Peter, and as he came they withdrew a little in profound and obviously deliberate silence. Peter raised his lantern and examined them with unceremonious and insulting care. 'They want to talk,' flashed through his mind.

'Isn't Lyamshin here?' he asked Virginsky. 'Who said he was ill?'

'I'm here,' Lyamshin replied, appearing suddenly from behind a tree.

He wore a warm overcoat and was closely wrapped in a rug, so that it was difficult to make out his face even with a lantern.

'So Liputin is the only one not here?'

Liputin, too, silently came out of the grotto. Peter raised his lantern again.

'Why did you hide there? Why didn't you come out?'

'I suppose we all still keep the right of the freedom – of our movements,' Liputin murmured, without apparently knowing himself what he really meant by that.

'Gentlemen,' Peter said, raising his voice for the first time above a whisper, which produced an effect, 'I think you realize full well that now is not the time for discussions. We have said and thoroughly discussed everything yesterday, frankly and explicitly. But – as I see from your faces – maybe someone would like to make some statement. In that case, let him hurry up. Damn it, we have very little time. Erkel may bring him any moment.'

'He's quite sure to bring him,' Tolkachenko for some reason thought it necessary to add.

'If I am not mistaken, the printing press will be handed over in the

first place, won't it?' Liputin inquired, again without really understanding why he asked the question.

'Naturally, we're not going to lose the thing,' said Peter, raising the
lantern to his face. 'But I believe we all agreed yesterday that it was
not necessary actually to take it. Let him only show us the spot where
it's buried. We shall dig it up afterwards ourselves. I know that it is
somewhere within ten feet of one of the corners of this grotto. But,
damn it, Liputin, how could you have forgotten it? We agreed that
you should meet him alone and that we'd only come out afterwards.
It's strange that you should be asking all the questions – or are you just
doing it to while away the time?'

Liputin remained gloomily silent. All were silent. The wind stirred
the tops of the pine-trees.

'I hope, though, gentlemen, that every one of us will do his duty,'
Peter snapped impatiently.

'I know that Shatov's wife came back to him and gave birth to a
child,' Virginsky suddenly spoke up, agitatedly and hurriedly, bringing out the words with difficulty and gesticulating. 'Knowing what
the human heart is like, I think we could all safely assume that – er –
that he won't inform the police because – because he's so happy. As I
went to see everyone this morning and found no one at home – I – er –
suggest that perhaps we needn't do anything now ...'

He stopped short: his breath failed him.

'If you suddenly became happy, Mr Virginsky,' Peter said, taking
a step towards him, 'would you have put off – not informing the
police, there could be no question of that – but some risky public
action requiring a certain amount of pluck which you had planned
before you were happy and which you would have considered it your
sacred duty to carry out in spite of the risk and loss of happiness?'

'No, I shouldn't have put it off! I shouldn't have just put it off for
anything in the world,' Virginsky said with a sort of terribly absurd
warmth, gesticulating violently.

'You'd rather become unhappy again than be a scoundrel?'

'Yes, yes – I'd rather be an absolute – er – I mean, I'd be willing to
be an absolute scoundrel – I'm sorry, I didn't mean that – not really a
scoundrel, but, on the contrary, absolutely unhappy than be a scoundrel.'

'Well, in that case you'd better know that Shatov considers it his public duty to inform the police, that he regards it as a matter of the highest principle, and the proof of it is that to a certain extent he runs a risk himself, though the Government would forgive him a lot for the information. Such a man as he will never give up the idea. No happiness will deflect him from doing what he thinks is his duty. In another day he will reproach himself for forgetting it and go to the police and do it. Besides, I can't for the life of me see why he should be so happy that his wife had come back to him after three years to give birth to Stavrogin's child.'

'But no one has seen Shatov's written statement to the police,' Shigalyov suddenly said emphatically.

'I've seen it,' Peter cried. 'It does exist, and all this is awfully stupid, gentlemen.'

'And I,' Virginsky suddenly flew into a rage, 'I protest – I protest with all the force at my command. I want – this is what I want: I want that when he arrives we should all come out and ask him whether it is true. If it is, we ought to make him repent, and if he gives us his word of honour, we ought to let him go. At all events, there ought to be a trial, and we ought to act accordingly, but not hide ourselves and then fall upon him.'

'To put our whole cause in jeopardy on a word of honour would be the height of folly! Damn it all, how stupid it all is now, gentlemen! And what sort of a part do you choose to play in the hour of danger?'

'I protest, I protest,' Virginsky kept repeating.

'Don't yell, anyway, or we shan't hear the signal. Shatov, gentlemen – (Damn it, how stupid it all is now!) – I've told you already that Shatov is a Slavophil – that is, one of the stupidest of people. But, damn it, this is neither here nor there. It's of no importance whatever. You're only confusing me. Shatov, gentlemen, is a man with a grudge against the world; since he, willy-nilly, belonged to the society, I had hoped till the last minute that he might be of some use to the common cause and that I might use him as a man with a grudge. I watched over him and spared him in spite of the most exact instructions. ... I spared him a hundred times more than he deserved! But he ended up by informing the police. However, damn it, I don't care! And I shouldn't advise any one of you to try to do a bunk now! Not one of you has any right to leave our cause in the lurch! You can embrace him, if you like, but you have no right to stake our common cause on his word of honour! Only swine and people in the pay of the Government would do such a thing!'

'Who's in the pay of the Government here?' Liputin brought out slowly.

'You, perhaps. You'd better hold your tongue, Liputin. You go on talking like that just from habit. Traitors, gentlemen, are all those who take fright in the hour of danger. There'll always be some fool who'll run to the police at the last minute because he's frightened and shout: "Oh, please, forgive me and I'll betray them all!" But you may as well know, gentlemen, that they'll never pardon you now, whatever you may choose to tell them. Even if they acquit you on two counts, it'll still mean Siberia for every one of you, and you won't escape nemesis of a different kind. And that sword is sharper than the Government's!'

Peter was furious, and said more than he should. Shigalyov took three steps towards him resolutely.

'Since yesterday evening I've thought it all over carefully,' he began confidently and methodically (and I can't help feeling that if the ground were to have given way under him, he would even then not have raised his voice or changed a single note of his methodical exposition), 'having thought it all over, I have come to the conclusion that the projected murder is not only a waste of precious time, which could have been employed in a more suitable and more pressing business, but presents, besides, that pernicious deviation from the normal method which has always been most harmful to our cause and has delayed its success for scores of years by subjecting it to the influence of shallow-minded and mostly political men, instead of convinced and unadulterated socialists. I've come here for the sole purpose of protesting against the projected enterprise so that it should be a lesson to you all, and then shall have nothing whatever to do with this actual moment which, I don't know for what reason, I regard as a moment of peril to you. I am going – not because I am afraid of this peril or because I am sorry for Shatov, whom I certainly do not intend to kiss, but solely because the whole of this business – from beginning to end – is literally a contradiction of my programme. As for my informing the police or being in the pay of the Government, you can set your minds completely at rest: I shall not inform the police.'

He turned and walked away.

'Damn it, he'll meet them and warn Shatov!' cried Peter, pulling out his revolver.

They heard him raise the cock of his gun.

'You may be sure,' Shigalyov said, turning round, 'that if I meet Shatov on the way, I may exchange greetings with him, but I shall not warn him.'

'And do you know that you may have to pay dearly for this, Mr Fourier?'

'I should like to point out to you that I am not Fourier. By mixing me up with that sentimental, theoretical mumbler, you merely show that though my manuscript has been in your hands, you have no idea what it is about. As for your threat of revenge, let me tell you that you've cocked your gun for no reason at all. At this moment it is entirely against your interests to shoot. But even if you threaten to shoot me to-morrow or the day after, you won't gain anything by it except unnecessary trouble: you may kill me, but sooner or later you'll come to my system all the same. Good-bye.'

At that moment a whistle was heard about a hundred yards away from the direction of the pond. Liputin at once answered by another whistle, as had been arranged the evening before (as he practically had no teeth in his head and was not sure that he could manage to whistle, he had bought a cheap child's clay whistle in the market that morning). Erkel had warned Shatov on the way that they had arranged to whistle as a signal, so as not to arouse any suspicion in his mind.

'Don't worry, I'll go the other way round, and they won't notice me at all,' Shigalyov said in an impressive whisper, and then walked home through the dark park without hurrying and without showing the slightest concern.

Now everything, to the last detail, is known of this dreadful affair. At first Liputin met Erkel and Shatov at the entrance to the grotto. Shatov neither bowed to him nor offered him his hand, but at once declared hastily and in a low voice:

'Well, where's your spade, and haven't you got another lantern? And don't be afraid, there's no one here, and they'll never hear you in Skvoreshniki even if you fired a cannon here! This is the place, just here, on this very spot. ...'

And he stamped with his foot nearly ten paces from the back corner of the grotto towards the wood. At that very moment Tolkachenko, who was hiding behind a tree, sprang upon him, and Erkel seized him from behind by the elbows. Liputin attacked him from the front. The three of them at once knocked him down and pinned him to the ground. It was then that Peter rushed up with his revolver. It is said that Shatov had time to turn his head and was able to recognize him. Three lanterns lighted up the scene. Shatov suddenly gave a short and desperate yell. But Peter did not let him go on yelling: he put his revolver firmly and accurately to Shatov's forehead, pressed it hard, and – pulled the trigger. The report did not seem to be very loud, at least they heard nothing in Skvoreshniki. Shigalyov of course heard it, for he had scarcely had time to walk three hundred paces – he heard the shout and the shot, but, according to his own testimony after-wards, he did not turn round or even stop. Death was almost instan-taneous. Peter alone kept his head – I don't think he kept quite cool. Squatting down, he went through the pockets of the murdered man with a quick but firm hand. He found no money (Shatov's purse re-mained under Marie's pillow). He did find two or three scraps of paper, though, but nothing of importance: a note from the office, the title of some book, and an old bill from a restaurant from abroad, which, goodness only knows why, he had kept in his pocket for two years. Peter transferred the scraps of paper to his own pocket and, suddenly noticing that they had all crowded round him and were looking at the corpse, he started cursing them angrily and discourt-eously and telling them to get on with their work. Tolkachenko and Erkel, recollecting themselves, ran off and instantly brought from the grotto two stones, weighing twenty pounds each, which they had got ready in the morning. These stones had already been prepared – that is, they were securely tied with ropes. As they intended to take the body to the nearest (the third) pond and dump it there, they began tying the stones to the legs and the neck. Peter fastened the stones, Tol-kachenko and Erkel holding them and passing them one after the other. Erkel was the first to pass his stone, and while Peter, grumbling and cursing, tied it to the legs of the body with the rope, Tolka-chenko stood holding up the other stone in his hands for a consider-able time, his whole body bending forward, as it were, reverentially, to hand it over without delay as soon as he was told to, and it never occurred to him to put it down on the ground in the meantime.

When the two stones were at last tied on and Peter got up from the ground and looked at the faces of his companions, something rather strange happened suddenly, something quite unexpected that took everyone by surprise.

As I have said already, all except Tolkachenko and Erkel were standing round doing nothing. Though Virginsky had rushed up to Shatov with the others, he had not got hold of him or helped to hold him. Lyamshin, on the other hand, had only joined the others after the shot. Then, while the stones were being tied to the body – which took perhaps ten minutes – all of them seemed to have lost control of their mental faculties. They crowded round, and at first seemed to have felt surprised rather than upset or alarmed. Liputin was standing in front of the group close to the dead body. Virginsky, who stood behind him, peeped over his shoulder with a kind of special and, as it were, detached curiosity, even standing on tiptoe to get a better view. Lyamshin hid behind Virginsky, only from time to time giving an apprehensive glance at the body, and at once disappearing behind him.

But when the stones had been tied on and Peter stood up, Virginsky suddenly began trembling nervously and, throwing up his hands in grief and despair, shouted at the top of his voice:

'That's wrong, wrong! That's all wrong!'

He would have perhaps added something more to his belated exclamation, but Lyamshin did not let him finish. He suddenly seized him from behind, squeezed him with all his might and let out an inhuman scream. There are moments of violent panic when a man, for instance, suddenly utters an unnatural scream, unlike anything that could have been expected from him before, and this sometimes sounds very terrifying. Lyamshin uttered not a human, but a sort of animal scream. Squeezing Virginsky from behind more and more tightly and convulsively, he went on screaming without stopping and without a pause, his eyes popping out of his head and his mouth wide open, stamping rapidly, as though beating a tattoo with his feet. Virginsky was so frightened that he, too, began screaming like a madman, and with a ferocity so vindictive that one could never have expected it from him. He tried to free himself from Lyamshin's grip, scratching and punching him with his hand behind him. Erkel at last helped him to drag Lyamshin away. But when Virginsky jumped in dismay ten paces away from him, Lyamshin, catching sight of Peter Verkhovensky, suddenly started yelling again, and was about to spring at him. Tripping over the body, he fell across it on Peter and gripped him so tightly in his arms, pressing his head against Peter's breast, that Peter, Tolkachenko, and Liputin could do nothing at first. Peter shouted, swore, hit him over the head with his fists; at last he managed to tear himself away, and pulling out his revolver, he put it straight in the open mouth of Lyamshin, who was still screaming, though he was by now tightly held by Tolkachenko, Erkel, and Liputin; but Lyamshin went on screaming in spite of the revolver. At last Erkel, crumpling his lawn handkerchief, succeeded in gagging him deftly, and he stopped screaming. Meanwhile Tolkachenko tied his hands with the remaining length of rope.

'It's very strange,' observed Peter, looking at the madman with uneasy astonishment.

He was obviously taken aback.

'I had quite a different idea of him,' he added reflectively.

For the time being they left Erkel to keep an eye on him. They had to hurry up with the disposal of the body: there had been so much shouting that someone might have heard. Tolkachenko and Peter picked up the lanterns and lifted the body by the hands, while Liputin and Virginsky took the feet, and so they carried it away. The two stones added greatly to its weight and the distance was more than 200 feet. Tolkachenko was the strongest of them all. He advised them to keep in step, but no one answered him, and they walked just anyhow. Peter walked on the right, and, bending double, carried the head of the corpse on his shoulder, holding up the stone with his left hand. As it never occurred to Tolkachenko to help him with the stone till they had covered half the distance to the pond, Peter, at last, swore at him. It was a sudden, solitary cry. They all continued carrying the body in silence, and only when they reached the pond did Virginsky, bent under the heavy load and apparently tired of carrying it, suddenly cry again in the same loud and plaintive voice:

'It's wrong, wrong! It's all wrong!'

The place where the third and rather large Skvoreshniki pond came to an end, and to which they carried the murdered man, was one of the most deserted and least-frequented spots in the park, especially at that late season of the year. The pond, at that end, was overgrown with reeds near the bank. They put down the lantern, swung the corpse, and threw it into the water. There was a big, sharp splash. Peter raised the lantern, and they all peered after him curiously, anxious to see how the dead body would sink, but there was nothing to be seen any more: the body with the two stones sank at once. The big ripples, which spread over the surface of the water, quickly disappeared. It was all over.

'Gentlemen,' Peter said, addressing them, 'now we can disperse. I have no doubt that you must all now be full of that unconstrained feeling of pride which is inseparable from the fulfilment of a duty undertaken without compulsion. If, however, you are unhappily too upset for such feelings, you will, I have no doubt, feel them to-morrow, when you would be ashamed not to feel them. I am quite willing to regard Lyamshin's disgraceful outburst as an attack of nerves, particularly as I am told he has been really ill all day. As for you, Virginsky, I believe that a moment of quiet reflection will show you that in view of the interests of our common cause we could not rely on a word of honour, but had to act as we did. Subsequent events will convince you, I'm sure, that he was an informer. I agree to overlook your exclamations. As for danger, I cannot foresee any. It would never occur to anyone to suspect any of you, particularly if you don't do anything silly. The main thing therefore depends on you alone and on the conviction in which, I hope, you will be fully confirmed to-morrow. The main reason, by the way, why you all joined an independent organization of free men who think alike was to share your common action together at any given moment and, if necessary, to watch and observe each other. Every one of you is bound to give a full account of your actions. You're called upon to bring new life into the organization which has grown decrepit and stinking from stagnation. Keep it always in mind to give you courage. At present all your actions must be animated by one aim – namely, to bring everything down with a crash: the State as well as its moral standards. We alone will be left, we who have prepared ourselves beforehand to take over the government: the intelligent we shall bring over to our side, and the fools we shall use to carry us on their shoulders. You must not be shy of that. We must re-educate a generation to make it worthy of freedom. We shall have many thousand Shatovs to deal with. We shall organize ourselves to become the leaders of our movement. It would be shameful not to take what lies idle and is gaping at us. I'm going at once to Kirilov, and by the morning there ought to be a document ready in which he will take it all on himself before dying by way of an explanation to the Government. Nothing can be more probable than such a combination of murder and suicide. To begin with, he was on bad terms with Shatov; they had lived together in America, so that they had time to quarrel. It was well known that Shatov had changed his views, which means that their hostility was caused by their differences of opinion and their fear that one of them might turn informer – a most implacable hostility. All this will be stated in writing. Finally, it will be mentioned that Fedka lodged in his flat in Filippov's house. All this will completely remove all suspicion from you, because it will throw those fatheads into utter confusion. To-morrow we shall not meet, gentlemen; I shall go into the country for a short time. But you will hear from me the day after to-morrow. I'd advise you to spend to-morrow at home. Now we will all go home by different routes, two at a time. You, Tolkachenko, had better look after Lyamshin and take him home. You may be able to influence him and, above all, make it quite clear to him that he will be the first to suffer if he lets his cowardice get the better of him. I have no more wish to doubt your relative Shigalyov, Mr Virginsky, than I have you; he won't inform the police. I can only regret his action, but as he has not yet tendered his resignation from the society, it is too soon to bury him. Well, hurry up, gentlemen. The police may be fatheads, but there's no harm in being careful.'

Virginsky went off with Erkel. Before handing over Lyamshin to Tolkachenko, Erkel had time to take him to Peter and tell him that Lyamshin had recovered his senses, that he was sorry, and wanted to be forgiven, and that he didn't even remember what had happened to him. Peter went off alone, making a detour, skirting the park on the other side of the ponds. It was the longest way. To his surprise, he was overtaken by Liputin when he was already half-way home.

'I say, Verkhovensky, Lyamshin is sure to inform the police.'

'No, he'll come to his senses and realize that he'll be the first to go to Siberia if he does. No one will inform the police now. You won't, either.'

'And you?'

'I shall most certainly get you all put out of the way the moment you make a move to betray me, and you know it. But you won't turn traitors. Did you run two miles after me to tell me that?'

'But, my dear Verkhovensky, we may never meet again!'

'Why do you say that?'

'Tell me one thing, please.'

'What is it? I must say, though, I wish you'd clear off.'

'One thing; only tell me the truth. Is there only one group of five in the world, or is it true that there are several hundreds of them? I ask you this because I consider it of the utmost importance.'

'I can see that from your excitement. But do you know who is more dangerous than Lyamshin, Liputin?'

'I know – I know; but the answer, please, your answer!'

'You're a fool, Liputin. What difference could it make to you now whether there's only one or a thousand?'

'Which means that there is only one. I knew it!' Liputin exclaimed. 'I knew all the time that there was only one. I knew it all along!'

And without waiting for another reply, he turned and quickly vanished in the darkness.

Peter reflected a little.

'No, no one will inform the police,' he said firmly. 'But the group must remain a group and do what they are told, or else – What trash they are, though!'

2

He first went home and packed his trunk, carefully and without haste. An express train was leaving at six o'clock in the morning. This early express train ran only once a week and had been put on quite recently as an experiment. Although Peter warned the members of the group that he would be going away to the country for a while, his intentions, as appeared afterwards, were quite different. Having finished packing, he settled with his landlady, whom he had told of his departure earlier, and drove in a cab to Erkel's lodgings, which were near the station. And then, about one o'clock in the morning, he went to Kirilov's, entering again by Fedka's secret way.

Peter was in an awful state of mind. Apart from other very grave reasons for feeling dissatisfied (he still could find out nothing about Stavrogin), he, it would seem – for I can't say for certain – received in the course of the day some secret information from somewhere (most probably from Petersburg) of a danger that was threatening him in the near future. There are, no doubt, many legends going round our town relating to that particular time; but if anything were known for certain, it was only to those directly concerned. For my part, I can only express my own opinion that Peter Verkhovensky may have been involved in all sorts of affairs somewhere else, and not only in our town, so that he really could have received such a warning. I am also convinced, in spite of Liputin's cynical and despairing doubts, that he may have had two or three groups of five in addition to ours – in Moscow and Petersburg, for instance. And if not such groups, then all sorts of connexions and friends, and quite possibly very curious ones, too. Not more than three days after he had left we received an order from Petersburg to arrest him immediately, but whether it was for the things he had done in our town or elsewhere, I don't know. This order arrived just in time to strengthen the shattering impression of the almost mystical panic which suddenly took hold of our authorities and our hitherto so persistently frivolous society after the discovery of the mysterious and highly significant murder of the student Shatov – a murder which was the culmination of all the senseless happenings in our town – and the most enigmatic circumstances that accompanied it. But the order came too late: Peter Verkhovensky was already in Petersburg, living under a false name, and having got wind of what was going on, he at once slipped away abroad. However, I am rather anticipating events, I'm afraid.

He went to Kirilov, looking angry and defiant. Apart from his chief business, he seemed bent on getting his own back on him personally for something, to revenge himself on him for something. Kirilov seemed to be glad to see him; it was evident that he had been expecting him a long time with painful impatience. His face was paler than usual and his black eyes had a fixed and dull look.

'I thought you were not coming,' he said in a dull voice from the corner of the sofa, from which he had not, however, stirred to greet him.

Peter stood before him and, before uttering a word, looked fixedly at his face.

'So everything's in order and we shan't go back on our promise – good chap!' he said, smiling with an offensively patronizing air.

'Well,' he added with odious jocularity, 'after all, if I am late, you've nothing to complain about: I made you a present of three hours.'

'I don't want any presents of extra hours from you, and you can't give me any presents – you fool!'

'What?' Peter gave a start, but at once controlled himself. 'Touchy, aren't you? Oh, I see, we are furious, are we?' he added with slow deliberation and with the same offensively supercilious air. 'At such a time it is composure you need most of all. It is best of all that you should consider yourself a Columbus and look on me as a mouse, and not take offence at anything I say. I gave you that advice yesterday.'

'I don't want to look on you as a mouse.'

'Why not? Is it a compliment? Oh dear, your tea's cold, too, and that means that everything is upside down. I fear something funny is going on here. Good Lord! what's that on a plate on the window-sill?' He walked up to the window. 'Aha, boiled chicken with rice! But why haven't you had any of it yet? I see, we are in such a state of mind that even chicken –'

'I've had a meal, and it's not your business. Shut up!'

'Oh, of course; and, besides, it doesn't make any difference, does it? But it does make a difference so far as I'm concerned. Fancy, I had scarcely any dinner, and so if, as I suppose, this chicken is no longer wanted – eh?'

'Eat if you can.'

'Thank you very much, and then I'll have tea, if I may.'

He at once settled himself at the table at the other end of the sofa and fell on the food with extraordinary greediness; but at the same time he never let his victim out of his sight for a moment. Kirilov looked at him fixedly and with angry aversion, as though unable to tear himself away.

'By the way,' Peter suddenly burst out, while going on eating, 'what about our business? We're not going to back out, are we? And the document?'

'I've decided to-night that it's all one to me. I'll write it. About the leaflets?'

'Yes, about the leaflets, too. I'll dictate it, though. It's all one to you, isn't it? Surely you're not going to bother your head about what's in it, are you?'

'That's not your business.'

'It isn't mine, of course. However, it'll only be a few lines: that you and Shatov distributed the leaflets with, incidentally, the help of Fedka, who hid in your flat. This last point about Fedka and your flat is very important — the most important of all, in fact. You see, I'm very frank with you.'

'Shatov? Why Shatov? Not for anything in the world about Shatov.'

'Good heavens, what do you care? You can't do him any harm now.'

'His wife came back to him. She has woken up and has sent to ask me where he is.'

'She has sent to ask you where he is? I see. That's not so good. She may send again. No one must know that I'm here.'

Peter looked worried.

'She won't find out. She's asleep again. The midwife is with her – Mrs Virginsky.'

'I see – so she won't hear anything, I suppose? You know, you'd better lock the front door.'

'She won't hear anything. And if Shatov comes, I'll hide you in the other room.'

'Shatov won't come. And you must write that you quarrelled with him because he had turned traitor and informer – this evening – and caused his death.'

'He's dead!' Kirilov cried, jumping up from the sofa.

'He died shortly after seven o'clock this evening, or rather yesterday after seven o'clock in the evening, for it's one o'clock in the morning already.'

'You have killed him! And I foresaw it yesterday!'

'I should think you did! Here, with this revolver.' He took out his revolver as though to show it, but he did not put it back, but kept it in his right hand as though in readiness. 'You're a funny blighter, Kirilov, though you knew yourself that the stupid fellow was bound to come to such an end. What was there to foresee? And, besides, you, too, had instructions to keep him under observation. You told me so yourself three weeks ago.'

'Shut up! You've done this to him because he spat in your face in Geneva!'

'For that and for something else, too. For lots of things. Without any hard feelings, though. What are you jumping up for? Why pull such faces? Oho, so that's it, is it?'

He leapt to his feet and raised his revolver. What happened was that Kirilov suddenly snatched up from the window his revolver which had been loaded and ready since the morning. Peter took up his position and aimed his weapon at Kirilov. The latter laughed harshly.

'Confess, you swine, that you took your revolver with you because I might shoot you. But I won't shoot you – though – though –'

And he again aimed his revolver at Peter, as though trying it on, as though he could not resist the temptation of denying himself the pleasure of imagining how he would shoot him. Peter, still taking up his position, waited – waited till the last moment, without pulling the trigger, at the risk of being the first to get a bullet in the head: he could expect anything from that 'maniac'. But the 'maniac' at last dropped his hand, gasping for breath and trembling, and unable to speak.

'You've had your little bit of fun and that's enough,' Peter said, putting down his weapon. 'I knew that you were just having me on. Only, you know, you ran a risk: I might have pulled the trigger.'

And he quite calmly sat down on the sofa and poured himself out some tea, though his hand trembled a little. Kirilov put his revolver on the table and began pacing the room.

'I won't write that I killed Shatov and – I won't write anything now. There won't be any document!'

'No?'

'No.'

'How mean and how stupid!' Peter said, going green with resentment. 'I had a feeling you wouldn't, though. I want you to know that you've not taken me by surprise. However, do as you please. If I could have forced you to do it, I would. But you are a scoundrel,' Peter declared, less and less able to restrain himself. 'You asked us for money that time and promised all sorts of things. I won't go away with nothing, however. I want at least to see how you will blow your brains out.'

'You will clear out of here at once,' Kirilov said, standing resolutely before him.

'No, sir, I won't do that,' Peter said, snatching up his revolver again. 'I shouldn't be surprised if out of malice and cowardice you'd decided to put it all off and go to the police to-morrow to get some more money. They'll pay you for that, you know. To hell with you! Only don't be afraid, I've foreseen everything, and I shan't go before I've blown your brains out with this revolver, as I did that swine Shatov's, if you get frightened and decide to put it off, damn you!'

'So you have to see my blood, too, have you?'

'I'm not doing it out of malice – understand that. I'm doing it to be certain that our cause won't suffer. It's impossible to rely on a man. You can see that for yourself. I don't understand what gave you the fantastic idea of doing away with yourself. I never suggested it to you. It was you yourself who thought of it long before, and you told the members of the committee abroad about it before you said anything to me. And don't forget that they did not extort it from you; they did not even know of your existence. You came to them yourself and told them all about it out of a feeling of sentimentality. Well, what's to be done if a certain plan of action, which cannot possibly be altered now, was founded upon that with your consent and at your own suggestion (your suggestion, mind you!)? You've put yourself in a position in which you knew too much. If you should happen to say something stupid and go to the police to-morrow, it might not be to our advantage. What do you think? No, sir. You can't do that. You've pledged yourself, you've given your word, you've taken money. That you can't possibly deny.'

Peter got very excited, but Kirilov had long stopped listening to him. He was again pacing the room, lost in thought.

'I'm sorry for Shatov,' he said, stopping before Peter again.

'I suppose I am sorry for him, too, but surely –'

'Shut up, you swine!' Kirilov roared, making a terrible and unambiguous movement. 'I'll kill you!'

'All right, all right! I told a lie. I'm not sorry for him at all. There, enough of this!' Peter jumped up apprehensively, putting out his hand.

Kirilov suddenly quieted down and began pacing the room again.

'I won't put it off. It is now that I want to kill myself: they are all scoundrels!'

'Well, that's an idea! Of course they are all scoundrels, and since to a decent fellow life's a loathsome business –'

'Fool, I'm as big a scoundrel as you, as all, and not a decent fellow. There's never been a decent fellow anywhere.'

'So you've got it at last. How could you, Kirilov, with your intelligence, have failed to realize till now that all men are alike, that there aren't any better or worse, but that some men are more intelligent and others more stupid, and that if all are scoundrels (which, incidentally, is nonsense) there can be no people who are not scoundrels?'

'Oh, so you really mean it?' Kirilov said, looking at him with some surprise. 'You speak with heat and simply ... Can fellows like you have convictions?'

'Kirilov, I never could understand why you wanted to kill yourself. All I know is that you do it from conviction – firm conviction. But if you feel the need of, as it were, pouring out your heart, I'm at your service. Only you must think of the time.'

'What's the time?'

'Good Lord! two o'clock precisely,' Peter said, looking at his watch and lighting a cigarette.

'It seems we can still come to an arrangement,' he thought to himself.

'I have nothing to say to you,' Kirilov muttered.

'I remember there was something about God there – you explained to me once, even twice. If you shoot yourself, you'll become a god – that's it, isn't it?'

'Yes, I'll become a god.'

Peter did not even smile; he waited. Kirilov looked shrewdly at him.

'You're a political humbug and intriguer. You want me to start a philosophical discussion and become carried away with enthusiasm, don't you? You want to bring about a reconciliation so as to allay my anger and, when I'm reconciled with you, get me to write a note to say that I killed Shatov.'

Peter replied with almost natural good-humour:

'All right, suppose I am such a scoundrel, what difference does it make to you in your last moments, Kirilov? What are we quarrelling about, for goodness sake? You're this sort of a man and I'm that sort of a man – what about it? And, moreover, both of us are –'

'Scoundrels.'

'Yes, scoundrels, if you like. You know perfectly well that that's only words.'

'All my life I didn't want it to be only words. I went on living just because I didn't want it so. Now, too, I want it every day not to be words.'

'Well, every one of us tries to find a place where it will be best for him. A fish – I mean, every one seeks his own kind of comfort. That's all. That's been known for ages.'

'Did you say comfort?'

'Don't let's quarrel over words.'

'No, you said well. Let it be comfort. God is necessary, and so must exist.'

'Well, that's all right, then.'

'But I know that He doesn't exist and can't exist.'

'That's more likely.'

'But don't you understand that a man with two such ideas cannot go on living?'

'Has to shoot himself, you mean?'

'Don't you understand that he might shoot himself for that alone? You don't understand that there may be such a man, one man out of your thousands of millions, one who won't put up with it and who will not want to?'

'All I understand is that you seem to be in two minds about it. That's very bad.'

'Stavrogin, too, was eaten up by an idea,' Kirilov said, pacing the room gloomily and without noticing Peter's remark.

'What?' Peter pricked up his ears. 'What idea? Did he tell you anything yourself?'

'No, I guessed it myself. If Stavrogin believes in God, then he doesn't believe that he believes. And if he doesn't believe, then he doesn't believe that he doesn't believe.'

'Well, Stavrogin has something else much wiser than that,' Peter muttered peevishly, following uneasily the new turn the conversation had taken and watching Kirilov's pale face.

'Damn it, he won't shoot himself,' he thought. 'I always knew it. A kink in his brain and nothing more. What a rabble!'

'You're the last man to be with me: I shouldn't like to part on bad terms with you.' Kirilov suddenly made him a present.

Peter did not reply at once. 'Damn it, what now?' he thought again.

'Believe me, Kirilov, I have nothing against you personally as a man, and I always –'

'You're a scoundrel and a sophist. But I'm just as bad as you, and I shall shoot myself, but you will remain alive.'

'You mean to say that I'm so mean that I want to go on being alive.'

He could not yet make up his mind whether or not it would pay him to continue such a conversation at such a moment, and decided to 'be guided by circumstances'. But Kirilov's superior tone and his undisguised contempt for him had always irritated him, and now for some reason irritated him more than ever. That was perhaps because Kirilov, who was going to die in about an hour (Peter still counted on it), seemed to him, as it were, something like half a man, a sort of man who could not possibly be allowed to be arrogant.

'You seem to be boasting to me because you are going to shoot yourself.'

'It always surprises me that everybody goes on living,' Kirilov said, not hearing his remark.

'Well, I suppose, it is an idea, but –'

'You ape, you agreed with me because you want to get the better of me. Shut up! you won't understand anything. If there is no god, then I am a god.'

'I could never understand that particular point of yours: why are you a god?'

'If there is a God, then it is always His will, and I can do nothing against His will. If there isn't, then it is my will, and I am bound to express my self-will.'

'Self-will? And why are you bound?'

'Because all will has become mine. Is there no man on this planet who, having finished with God and believing in his own will, will have enough courage to express his self-will in its most important point? It's like a beggar who has inherited a fortune and is afraid of it and does not dare to go near his bag of gold, thinking himself too weak to own it. I want to express my self-will. I may be the only one, but I'm going to do it.'

'Do it!'

'I'm bound to shoot myself, because the most important point of my self-will is to kill myself.'

'But you're not the only one to kill yourself. There are lots of suicides.'

'Those have a motive. I'm the only one to do it without any motive, but simply of my own free will.'

'He won't shoot himself,' the thought flashed through Peter's mind again.

'You know what,' he observed irritably, 'to show my self-will, I should in your place have killed somebody else, and not myself. You'd be very useful to us then. I could tell you whom, if you're not afraid. Then you needn't shoot yourself to-day. We could come to terms.'

'To kill someone else would be the least important point of my self-will. Such a suggestion could only have come from a man like you. I am not you: I want the most important point, and I will kill myself.'

'Got there at last without prompting,' Peter muttered spitefully.

'I am bound to express my unbelief,' Kirilov went on, pacing the room. 'No higher idea than that there is no god exists for me. Mankind's history is for me. All man did was to invent God so as to live without killing himself. That's the essence of universal history till now. I am the only man in universal history who for the first time refused to invent God. Let them know it once for all.'

'He won't shoot himself,' Peter thought uneasily.

'Who's going to know it?' he egged him on. 'There are only you and me here. Is it Liputin?'

'Let them all know; all will know. There is no secret that will not be made known. He said so.'

And he pointed with feverish excitement at the icon of the Redeemer, before which a lamp was burning. Peter got angry in good earnest.

'So you still believe in Him, and you've even lighted the lamp. Not "in case" by any chance?'

Kirilov made no answer.

'You know what? I think that you believe perhaps more than any priest.'

'In whom? In Him? Listen,' Kirilov went on, standing still and gazing before him with a motionless and frenzied look. 'Listen to a great idea: there was a day on earth, and in the middle of the earth were three crosses. One on the cross has such faith that He said to

another, "To-day thou shalt be with me in paradise." The day came
to an end, both died, and they went, but found neither paradise nor
resurrection. The saying did not come true. Listen: that man was the
highest of all on earth, He was that for which it was created. The
whole planet, with all that is on it, is sheer madness without that man.
There has never been anyone like Him before or since, and never will
be, not even by a miracle. For that is the miracle that there never was
and never will be such a man as He. And if that is so, if the laws of
nature did not spare even *Him*, if they did not spare their own miracle,
and made even Him live in the midst of lies and die for a lie, then the
whole planet is a lie and is based on a lie and a stupid mockery. So the
very laws of the planet are a lie and a farce of the devil. What, then, is
there to live for? Reply, if you're a man.'

'That's a different matter. I can't help thinking that you've mixed
up two different causes, and that's a dangerous thing to do. But, look
here, what if you are god? If the lie is no more, and you realized that
the lie was merely because of your belief in that former god.'

'So at last you understand!' Kirilov cried rapturously. 'So it can be
understood if a man like you understands! You understand now –
don't you? – that the only salvation for all is to prove this idea to
everyone. Who will prove it? I! I cannot understand how an atheist
could know that there is no god and not kill himself at once! To realize that there is no god and not to realize at the same instant that you
have become god yourself – is an absurdity, for else you would certainly kill yourself. If you do realize it, you are a king and you will
never kill yourself, but will live in the greatest glory. But he who is
the first to realize it is bound to kill himself, for otherwise who will
begin and prove it? It is I who will most certainly kill myself to begin
with and prove it. I am still only a god against my own will, and I am
unhappy because I am *bound* to express my self-will. All are unhappy,
because all are afraid to express their self-will. The reason why man
has hitherto been so unhappy and poor is because he was afraid to express the main point of his self-will, but has expressed it only in little
things, like a schoolboy. I am terribly unhappy because I'm terribly
afraid. Fear is the curse of mankind. But I shall proclaim my self-will.
I am bound to believe that I do not believe. I shall begin and end, and
open the door. And I shall save. Only this will save mankind and will
transform it physically in the next generation. For in his present

physical condition man cannot – as far as I can see – get along without his former God. For three years I've been searching for the attribute of my divinity, and I've found it: the attribute of my divinity is – Self-Will! That's all I can do to prove in the main point my defiance and my new terrible freedom. For it is very terrible. I am killing myself to show my defiance and my new terrible freedom.'

His face was unnaturally pale and his look unendurably melancholy. He was like a man in a high fever. For a moment Peter thought that he would collapse.

'Give me the pen!' Kirilov cried unexpectedly in a sudden onrush of inspiration. 'Dictate! I'll sign everything. I'll sign that I killed Shatov, too. Dictate while I'm amused. I'm not afraid of the thoughts of supercilious slaves! You'll see for yourself that all that is secret will be made plain. And you'll be crushed. I believe! I believe!'

Peter jumped up from his seat, in a trice put ink and paper before him, and began to dictate, seizing the right moment and trembling for the success of his plan.

'I, Alexey Kirilov, declare –'

'Wait! Don't want to. Who am I declaring to?' Kirilov shook as though he were in a fever. This declaration and some special, sudden idea about it seemed suddenly to have absorbed him entirely, as though it were some outlet which his tormented spirit had impetuously sought, if only for a moment.

'Who am I declaring to? I want to know to whom?'

'To no one, to everyone, the first man who reads it. Why be definite about it? To the whole world!'

'To the whole world? Bravo! And I don't want any repentance. I don't want to repent. And I don't want it for the authorities.'

'Of course not. That's not necessary. To hell with the authorities! But go on, write, if you're in earnest!' Peter cried hysterically.

'Wait! I want a face with the tongue out on the top.'

'Oh, what nonsense!' Peter cried angrily. 'You can express it all without a picture by the tone alone.'

'By the tone? That's good. Yes, by the tone. By the tone! Dictate with the tone!'

'I, Alexey Kirilov,' Peter dictated in a firm and imperious voice, bending over Kirilov's shoulder and following every letter which he formed with a hand trembling with excitement, 'I, Kirilov, declare that to-day, the -th October, at about seven o'clock in the evening, I killed the student Shatov in the park for turning traitor and giving information about the political leaflets and Fedka, who has been lodging with us for ten days in Filippov's house, where he also spent the night. I am shooting myself to-day with my revolver, not because I repent and am afraid of you, but because I made up my mind abroad to take my life.'

'Is that all?' Kirilov cried, with surprise and indignation.

'Not another word!' Peter declared, with a wave of the hand, trying to snatch the document from him.

'Wait!' Kirilov cried, putting his hand firmly on the paper. 'Wait. This is nonsense! I want to say with whom I killed him. Why Fedka? And what about the fire? I want everything, and I want to tell them off properly with the tone, the tone!'

'It's quite enough, Kirilov,' Peter almost implored him, trembling that he might tear the paper. 'I assure you that it is quite enough. To make them believe you, you must put it obscurely, just like that, just by hints. You must only give them the faintest hint of the truth, just enough to whet their appetite. They will always tell a much taller story than ours, and they will of course believe themselves more than they would us. And that's much better. Much better! Come on, let's have it. It's excellent as it is. Give it to me! Give it to me!'

And he kept trying to snatch away the paper. Kirilov listened with his eyes starting out of his head and apparently trying to make some sense out of Peter's words, but he seemed incapable of understanding anything.

'Oh, damn it!' Peter suddenly cried angrily. 'He hasn't signed it yet! What are you staring at me for? Sign!'

'I want to tell them off!' Kirilov muttered, taking the pen, however, and signing. 'I want to tell them off.'

'Write "*Vive la république*". That will be enough.'

'Bravo!' Kirilov almost roared with delight. '"*Vive la république démocratique, sociale et universelle ou la mort!*" No, no, that's wrong. "*Liberté, égalité, fraternité ou la mort!*" That's better, that's better!' He wrote it with pleasure under his signature.

'Enough, enough,' Peter repeated.

'Wait, a little more. I'll sign again in French, you know. "*de Kiriloff, gentilhomme russe et citoyen du monde.*" Ha, ha, ha!' He burst out laughing. 'No, no, no. Wait! I've found something better. Eureka! "*Gentilhomme séminariste russe et citoyen du monde civilisé!*" That's better than any –'

He jumped up quickly from the sofa and suddenly snatched up his revolver from the window with a quick gesture, ran out with it to the other room and shut the door tightly behind him. Peter stood still thoughtfully looking at the door.

'If he does it now, he will shoot himself, but if he starts thinking, nothing will come of it.'

Meanwhile he picked up the paper, sat down, and read it over again. The wording of the confession pleased him again.

'What is it I want now? I want to throw them into utter confusion for the time, and so divert their attention. The park? There is no park in the town, so they'll soon guess it's Skvoreshniki. Till they get as far as that, time will pass, till they look for the body – more time will pass, and when they find it, it will mean that the story is true, and that, of course, means that everything is true and that it's true about Fedka, too. And what does Fedka stand for? Why, Fedka stands for the fire, the Lebyatkins. This means that everything originated here, at Filippov's house, and they knew nothing about it, they overlooked it all – that will throw them off the scent altogether! It will never occur to them to look for the group of five – Shatov and Kirilov, and Fedka, and Lebyatkin – and why they killed each other: that's another little mystery for them. Oh, damn, I don't hear the shot!'

Though he had been reading and admiring the wording, he had been listening every moment with excruciating anxiety and – suddenly he flew into a rage. He glanced at his watch uneasily. It was getting rather late, and that fellow had been gone for ten minutes. Seizing the candle, he went to the door of the room in which Kirilov had shut himself up. As he reached the door, it suddenly occurred to him that the candle had practically burnt out and that it would go out in twenty minutes, and that there was no other candle in the room. He took hold of the door-handle and listened cautiously, but there was not a sound to be heard. He suddenly opened the door and raised the candle: something uttered a roar and rushed at him. He slammed the door with all his might and put his shoulder against it, but everything was quiet – dead silence again.

He stood for a long time with the candle in his hand, wondering what to do. In the second that he held the door open, he had been able to see very little. He had, however, caught a glimpse of the face of Kirilov, who stood by the window at the back of the room, and he remembered the savage fury with which Kirilov had suddenly rushed at him. Peter started, hastily put down the candle on the table, got his revolver ready, and went on tiptoe to the farthest corner of the room, so that if Kirilov opened the door and rushed up to the table with the revolver, he would have time to take aim and pull the trigger before Kirilov.

By now Peter no longer believed that Kirilov would commit suicide. 'Standing in the middle of the room, thinking,' it flashed like a whirlwind through Peter's mind. 'The room, besides, was so dark and terrifying. ... He roared and rushed at me. There are two possibilities: either I interfered with him at the moment when he was about to pull the trigger or – or he was standing there planning how to kill me. Yes, that's so. He was planning it. He knows that I won't go away before killing him, if he is too cowardly to do it himself, which means that he must kill me before I kill him. And again – again there is silence there! I feel really frightened: what if he should suddenly open the door? What is so beastly is that he believes in God more than a priest. He won't shoot himself for anything! There are hundreds of people like him "who have come to it by their own reason". The swine! Damnation! The candle, the candle! It will most certainly go out in a quarter of an hour. I must finish it! Must finish it at all costs. Well, I suppose he could be killed now. With that document no one will think that I killed him. I can put him in such a position on the floor with the unloaded revolver in his hand that they will most certainly think that he did it himself. Damn it, how am I to kill him? If I open the door, he'll rush at me again and fire first. Hell, he's sure to miss!'

So he thought, tormenting himself and trembling at the inevitability of his plan and at his own indecision. At last he took the candle and once more went up to the door, raising and getting ready his revolver. With his left hand, in which he held the candle, he pressed on the handle. But he did it clumsily: the handle clicked, there was a noise and a creak. 'He'll fire straight away!' flashed through Peter's head. He flung the door open with his foot, raised the candle, and held out the revolver. But there was no shot, nor cry. There was no one in the room.

He gave a start. There was no other door in the room, no way of escape. He raised the candle higher and examined the room more carefully: there was no one there. He called Kirilov softly, then louder, but there was no reply.

'Has he escaped through the window?'

And, to be sure, the little ventilating window was open. 'It's ridiculous! He couldn't have escaped through the little window.' Peter walked across the room straight to the window. 'He couldn't possibly!' Suddenly he turned round quickly, and something extraordinary froze the blood in his veins.

A cupboard stood against the wall opposite the windows to the right of the door. On the right of the cupboard, in the corner formed by the wall and the cupboard, stood Kirilov, and he was standing in a very curious attitude – rigid, erect, with his arms held stiffly at his sides, his head raised and pressed hard against the wall in the very corner, as though he wanted to hide and efface himself. Everything seemed to show that he was hiding, but, somehow, it was difficult to believe it! Peter was standing a little sideways to the corner, and he could see only the protruding parts of the figure. He still could not make up his mind to move a little to the left to get a full view of Kirilov and solve the mystery. His head began throbbing violently. And suddenly he was overcome by a blind rage: he made a sudden dash and, shouting and stamping his feet, he rushed furiously to the horrible place.

But before he reached it, he again stopped short, rooted to the ground, still more frozen with horror. What struck him most was that the figure never moved, in spite of his shout and mad rush. It never stirred a single limb, as though it were of stone or of wax. The pallor of its face was unnatural, its black eyes were quite motionless, staring fixedly at some point in the distance. Peter moved his candle up and down and up again, lighting the figure from every point and scrutinizing its face. Suddenly he noticed that though Kirilov was looking straight before him, he saw him out of the corner of his eyes and was perhaps even watching him. It then occurred to him to hold the candle right up to the face of 'the blackguard', to burn it and see what he would do. Suddenly he fancied that Kirilov's chin twitched and that a mocking smile passed across his lips – as though he had guessed his thought. He shuddered and, beside himself gripped Kirilov by the shoulder.

Then something so horrible happened, and so quickly, too, that Peter could never afterwards get a coherent picture of it. As soon as he touched Kirilov, the latter quickly lowered his head and knocked the candle out of Peter's hands. The candlestick fell on the floor with a clang and the candle went out. At the same moment he felt a terrible pain in the little finger of his left hand. He screamed, and all he could remember was that in his fury he had struck three resounding blows with his revolver on the head of Kirilov, who had bent down and bitten his finger. At last he tore his finger away and rushed headlong out of the house, groping his way in the dark. He was pursued by terrible shouts from the room:

'Now, now, now, now! ...'

Ten times. But he was still running, and as he ran into the entrance hall, he suddenly heard a loud shot. He stopped there in the darkness and stood thinking for five minutes; at last he went back into the room. But he had to get a candle. All he had to do was to look on the floor on the right of the cupboard for the candlestick which had been knocked out of his hand. But what was he going to light the candle-end with? Then suddenly a vague recollection flashed through his mind: he remembered that when he had run down into the kitchen to attack Fedka the day before, he had caught sight of a large red matchbox. He groped his way to the kitchen door on the left, went through the passage and down the steps. On the shelf, in the very place where he had just remembered seeing it, he felt in the dark a full, unopened box of matches. Without striking a light, he hurriedly went up the steps, and it was only when he reached the cupboard, at the spot where he had struck Kirilov with the revolver and had been bitten by him, that he suddenly remembered his bitten finger and at the same moment felt that it hurt terribly. Clenching his teeth, he managed to light the candle-end, put it back in the candlestick, and look round; Kirilov's body lay with its feet towards the right-hand corner of the room, near the open ventilation window. The shot had been fired at the right temple, and the bullet had come out at the top on the left side, piercing the skull. He saw splashes of blood and brains. The revolver was still in the suicide's hand on the floor. Death must have been instantaneous. Having examined everything with great care, Peter got up and went out on tiptoe, closed the door, put the candle on the table in the front room, thought it over, and decided not to put it out, reflecting that it could not set the place on fire. Glancing once more at the document on the table, he grinned mechanically, and only then left the house, still for some reason walking on tiptoe. He crept through Fedka's passage again and carefully covered it up behind him.

3

Exactly at ten minutes to six Peter Verkhovensky and Erkel walked up and down the platform of the railway station beside a rather long train. Peter was leaving, and Erkel was seeing him off. The luggage had been given in, his suit-case was taken to a second-class compartment and placed on his reserved seat. The first bell had rung already, and they were waiting for the second. Peter was looking round quite unabashed, watching the passengers getting into the train. There were no people he knew well among them; only twice did he have to nod a greeting, to a merchant he knew slightly and to a young country clergyman who was going back to his parish two stations away. Erkel evidently wanted to discuss a rather important matter with him during the few remaining minutes, though perhaps he did not know himself what it was exactly; but he did not have the courage to begin. He felt all the time that Peter Verkhovensky was finding his company rather wearisome and was waiting impatiently for the last two bells.

'You look at everyone so unabashed,' Erkel remarked a little timidly, as though wishing to warn him.

'Why shouldn't I? The time hasn't come for me to go into hiding. Too soon. Don't worry. The only thing I'm afraid of is that the devil should bring Liputin here. If he finds out, he'll be here in no time.'

'None of them is reliable, sir,' Erkel declared firmly.

'Liputin?'

'None of them.'

'Nonsense! They are all bound by what happened yesterday. Not one of them would betray us. Who will run the risk of utter ruin unless he's lost his reason?'

'But they will lose their reason, sir.'

The idea had evidently already occurred to Peter, too, and that was why Erkel's remark angered him the more.

'You're not getting cold feet, too, Erkel, are you? I rely on you more than on any of them. I've seen now what each of them is worth. Give them my instructions by word of mouth to-day. I leave them all in your charge. Make a point of seeing them this morning. You can read my written instructions to them to-morrow or the day after when you meet and when they are capable of listening – but, believe me, they will be quite amenable by to-morrow because they'll be in a terrible funk and become malleable as wax. Above all, don't you lose courage.'

'Oh, if only you weren't going away, sir!'

'But I'm only going away for a few days. I shall be back in no time.'

'I wouldn't mind,' Erkel said cautiously but resolutely, 'if you were going to Petersburg. For, of course, I know that you are only doing what is necessary for the common cause.'

'I didn't expect anything less from you, Erkel. If you've guessed that I'm going to Petersburg, you can understand that I couldn't possibly have told them yesterday, at that moment, that I was going so far for fear of frightening them. But you understand that I'm going for the cause, for a good and highly important reason, for our common cause, and not to do a bunk, as a fellow like Liputin may imagine.'

'Why, even if you went abroad, I'd understand, sir. I should understand that you have to take good care of yourself, because you're everything and we are nothing. I should understand, sir.'

The poor boy's voice trembled.

'Thank you, Erkel. Oh, you've touched my bad finger.' (Erkel had pressed his hand clumsily; the bad finger was conspicuously tied round with black silk.) 'But I'm telling you positively that I'm going to Petersburg only to spy out the lay of the land, and that I shall probably be there only one day, after which I shall come back here at once. For the sake of appearances, I shall stay at Gaganov's country house. If they think that there is any danger, I shall be the first to share it with them. If, however, I have to stay longer in Petersburg, I shall let you know at once – in the way you know, and you'll tell them.'

The second bell rang.

'Oh, that means there's only five minutes left before the train starts. I shouldn't like your local group to break up, you know. Not that I'm afraid of anything. You needn't worry about me. I've lots of such links in the chain, and I don't regard it as of any importance. But an additional link can do no harm. However, I'm not worrying about you, though I'm leaving you almost alone with those horrors. Don't be afraid. They won't go to the police. They won't dare. Hullo, you're going away, too, to-day?' he cried suddenly in quite a different, cheerful voice to a very young man who came up gaily to greet him. 'I didn't know you were going by the express, too. Where? To your mother?'

The mother of the young man was a very wealthy landowner in a neighbouring province, and the young man was a distant relative of Julia Lembke's who had been staying about a fortnight in our town.

'No, I'm going farther than that. I'm off to R—. I shall have to spend eight hours in the train. Off to Petersburg?' the young man asked with a laugh.

'What made you think that I was going to Petersburg of all places?' Peter asked, laughing even more openly.

The young man wagged a gloved finger at him.

'Well, yes, you've guessed right,' Peter whispered to him mysteriously. 'I've got letters from Mrs Lembke, and I shall have to call on three or four influential gentlemen – you know whom I mean – damn 'em, to be quite frank. A devilish job!'

'But why, tell me, is she in such a blue funk?' the young man whispered too. 'She wouldn't see me yesterday. I don't think she need worry about her husband. On the contrary, he collapsed so conspicuously at the fire, as it were, ready to sacrifice his own life.'

'Well, there it is,' Peter said with a laugh. 'You see, she's afraid that some people may have written from here already – I mean, certain gentlemen. In short, Stavrogin is at the bottom of it, or rather Prince K. Oh, it's a long story. I may be able to tell you something about it on the journey – as far as my chivalrous feelings will allow, at least. This is a relative of mine, Second-Lieutenant Erkel, who is stationed in the country not far from here.'

The young man, who had been squinting at Erkel, touched his hat. Erkel bowed.

'But, really, Verkhovensky, eight hours in the train is an awful bore, you know. Colonel Berestov, an awfully amusing chap, owns the place next to ours, is travelling with me in the first class. Married a Garin (*née de Garine*), and, you know, he is an awfully decent fellow. Got ideas, too. Been here only a couple of days. A terrible whist addict. We could get up a game, couldn't we? I've already got a fourth. Pripukhlov, our merchant from T—, big beard and all, a millionaire. I mean, a real millionaire. Take my word for it. I'll introduce him to you – a most interesting money-bag. We shall have a good laugh.'

'With the greatest of pleasure. I'm very fond of a game of cards in the train, but I'm afraid I'm travelling second-class.'

'That's easily arranged, my dear chap. Get in with us. I'll tell them to take your things to the first class. The chief guard eats out of my hand. What have you got? A suit-case? A rug?'

'Excellent, let's go.'

Peter took his suit-case, his rug, and his book, and moved into the first-class compartment at once with the utmost enthusiasm. Erkel helped him. The third bell rang.

'Well, Erkel,' Peter said, holding out his hand to him from the window for the last time, 'I'm sorry, but I have to sit down to cards with them.'

'Why bother to explain it to me, sir? I understand. I understand everything, sir.'

'Well, in that case, so long,' Peter said, turning away suddenly on hearing himself addressed by the young man, who wanted to introduce him to his partners.

And Erkel never saw his Peter Verkhovensky again.

He returned home very sad. Not that he was alarmed at being left so suddenly by Peter, but – but he had turned away from him so quickly when that young dandy had called him, and – and he could have said something different to him, and not just 'so long' or – he could at least have pressed his hand more cordially.

It was the last thing that rankled. Something else was beginning to gnaw at his poor heart – something he could not yet understand himself, something that was connected with the evening before.

7

Stepan Verkhovensky's Last Pilgrimage

I

I AM convinced that Stepan Verkhovensky was very much afraid when he realized that the time he had fixed for his mad enterprise was approaching. I am convinced that he suffered greatly from fear, especially on the night before he had set off – that terrible night. Nastasya mentioned to me afterwards that he had gone to bed late and that he had slept. But that does not prove anything; people sentenced to death, it is said, sleep very soundly even on the eve of their execution. Though he had left his house in daylight, when a nervous man is always more courageous (and the Major, Virginsky's relative, stopped believing in God as soon as the night was over), I am convinced that he could never have imagined himself alone on the highway without horror, and in such a condition, too. No doubt a certain feeling of desperation at first softened the blow of that terrible sensation of solitude in which he suddenly found himself as soon as he had left Stasie and the comfortable home in which he had spent twenty years. But that made no difference: however clearly he realized the horrors awaiting him, he would have gone out and taken to the road! There was a feeling of pride in what he had undertaken that fascinated him in spite of everything. Oh, he could have accepted Mrs Stavrogin's magnificent conditions and have remained dependent on her charity 'comme un ordinary hanger-on!' But he had not accepted her charity and had not remained. And now he left her himself and raised 'the banner of the great idea', and was going to die for it on the highway! That is what he must have been feeling; that was how his action must have appeared to him.

Another question presented itself to me more than once: why did he have to run away – that is, literally run away on foot, and not simply drive away in a carriage? At first I explained it by the impracticability of fifty years and by the fantastic bent of his mind under the influence of strong emotion. I could not help feeling that the idea of ordering fresh post-horses and carriages (even if they had harness-bells) would have appeared too simple and prosaic to him; a pilgrimage, on the other hand, albeit with an umbrella, was much more

picturesque and much more expressive of love and revenge. But now
that everything is at an end, I can only suppose that it all happened
much more simply. To begin with, he was afraid to hire horses because Mrs Stavrogin might have got wind of it and kept him back by
force, which she would most certainly have done, and he would have
certainly complied and then – farewell the great idea for ever! Again,
to give an order for post-horses one has at least to know where one is
going. But the thing that worried him most at that moment was that
he had not the faintest idea where he was going. For if he had made up
his mind to go to a certain city, his enterprise would have appeared
both absurd and impossible in his eyes. He had a strong feeling that it
would be so. For what on earth would he do in that particular city,
and why not another? To look for *ce marchand*? But what *marchand*?
Here again the second and most terrible question cropped up. For, as
a matter of fact, there was nothing he dreaded more than *ce marchand*,
whom he set off to find so suddenly and in such haste and whom he
was in reality very terrified of finding. No, the highway was much
better. Simply walk along it without thinking of anything for as long
as he could refrain from thinking. The highway is something that goes
on for miles and miles and miles, stretching endlessly ahead, like a
man's life, like a man's dream. There is an idea in the open road; but
what sort of idea is there in an order for post-horses? An order for
post-horses is the end of an idea. *Vive la grande route*, and what happens
then is in the lap of the gods.

After the sudden and unexpected meeting with Lisa which I have
described, he walked on in greater self-oblivion than ever. The road
passed within half a mile of Skvoreshniki, and – strange to say – at first
he did not even notice how he had got on it. At that moment he
could not bear to think rationally or to give himself a full account of
his actions. A fine rain kept falling, stopping, and falling again; but he
did not even notice the rain. Nor did he notice how he threw his bag
over his shoulder, and how much easier it was to walk like that. After
walking a mile or so, he suddenly stopped and looked round. The old
road, black and full of deep ruts left by wheels and planted with wil-
lows on each side, stretched before him like an endless thread; on the
right were bare fields covered with stubble after the harvest, on the
left there were bushes, and beyond them a wood. And in the distance
– in the distance was the scarcely perceptible line of the railway run-

ning slantwise, and on it the smoke of a train, but no sound was heard. Mr Verkhovensky felt a little afraid, but only for a moment. He sighed vaguely, put down his bag beside a willow, and sat down to rest. As he was sitting down, he felt shivery and wrapped himself in his rug; becoming aware of the rain, he put up his umbrella. He sat like that for some time, occasionally muttering to himself, and grasping the handle of the umbrella firmly in his hand. Various images passed in a feverish file before him, quickly succeeding each other in his mind. 'Lise, Lise,' he thought, 'and with her *ce Maurice*. ... Strange people. ... But what was that strange fire there, and what were they talking about, and who were murdered? I expect *Stasie* has not yet had time to find out and is still waiting for me with my coffee. ... At cards? Did I really lose men at cards? Well – in Russia during the so-called period of serfdom. ... Dear me, and Fedka?'

He gave a violent start with terror and looked round him: 'What if that Fedka is crouching somewhere behind those bushes? They say he has a whole band of robbers on the highway. Oh dear, I shall then – I shall then tell him the whole truth – I shall tell him that I was to blame and – and that I was greatly distressed for *ten years* on his account, much more than he was as a soldier and – and I shall give him my purse. H'm! *j'ai en tout quarante roubles; il prendra les roubles et il me tuera tout de même.*'

In his panic he shut his umbrella for some unknown reason and put it down beside him. A cart appeared in the distance on the road from the town; he began watching it in dismay.

'*Grâce à Dieu*, it's a cart, and it's coming slowly. That can't be dangerous. Those are local foundered horses. I always said that breed – It was Peter Ilyich, though, who talked at the club about horse-breeding and I mulcted him, *et puis*, but there is something behind that cart and – yes – I believe there's a peasant woman in it. A peasant woman and a peasant – *cela commence à être rassurant*. The woman behind and the peasant in front, *c'est rassurant au plus haut degré*.'

The cart came alongside; it was a fairly well-built and decent-looking peasant cart. The woman was sitting on a well-stuffed sack, and the peasant on the seat in front of the cart with his feet hanging down sideways towards Mr Verkhovensky. A red cow was indeed jogging along behind, tied by the horns to the cart. The peasant and the woman stared at Mr Verkhovensky, and Mr Verkhovensky stared back at them, but after they had gone on twenty paces, he suddenly got up hurriedly and tried to overtake them.

It looked safer to him in the proximity of the cart, but having overtaken it, he again forgot all about it and became once more absorbed in the fragments of thoughts and images which floated through his mind. He walked on without suspecting, of course, that to the two people in the cart he presented at that moment as mysterious and interesting an object as one could meet on the road.

'Who might you be, sir, if you don't mind my asking?' the woman could not resist saying at last, when Mr Verkhovensky suddenly looked up at her absent-mindedly.

The peasant woman was about twenty-seven, black-browed and red-cheeked, with a friendly smile on her red lips, between which gleamed two rows of white even teeth.

'Are you – are you addressing me?' Mr Verkhovensky murmured with mournful surprise.

'A merchant, I daresay,' the peasant remarked confidently.

He was a tall, well-built man of forty, with a broad and intelligent face and with a large reddish beard.

'No, I'm not really a merchant – I – I – *moi c'est d'autre chose*,' Mr Verkhovensky parried the question somehow, and, to be on the safe side, lagged behind a little to the back of the cart so that he was walking alongside the cow.

'Must be a gentleman, then,' the peasant decided, hearing words in a foreign language, and gave a tug at the horse.

'No wonder we was looking at you, sir. Are you out for a walk?' the young peasant woman asked, unable to suppress her curiosity.

'Are you – are you asking me?'

'Foreigners sometimes come here by train, and your boots, sir, don't seem to be from our local shops.'

'Army boots those be,' the peasant put in complacently and gravely.

'No, not really army boots, I'm –'

'What an inquisitive female,' Mr Verkhovensky reflected irritably. 'And how they stare at me – *mais enfin*. In a word, it is strange that I should feel as if I'd done something wrong to them, while I've done them no harm.'

The woman began whispering something to the man.

'Excuse me, sir, but if you'd like we'd give you a lift.'

Mr Verkhovensky suddenly recollected himself.

'Thank you, thank you, my friend. I'd be very glad of a lift because I am very tired, but how am I to get in?'

'How strange it is,' he thought to himself, 'that I've been walking so long beside that cow and it never occurred to me to ask them for a lift. This "real life" has something very characteristic about it.'

The peasant, however, did not pull up the horse at once.

'And where are you going to, sir?' he asked, a little mistrustfully.

Mr Verkhovensky did not get his meaning at once.

'To Khatovo, I suppose?'

'To Khatov? No, not really to Khatov. I don't think I know him very well, though I have heard of him.'

'The village of Khatovo, sir. Seven miles from here.'

'A village? *C'est charmant.* Yes, I've heard of it, of course.'

Mr Verkhovensky was still walking, and they still did not put him on the cart. A wonderful idea flashed through his mind.

'You don't think I am – er – I've got a passport and I'm a professor – I mean, a teacher, if you like. A head teacher. *Oui, c'est comme ça qu'on peut traduire.* I'd be very glad of a lift and – er – I'll buy you – I'll buy you a pint of vodka for it.'

'It'll be fifty copecks, sir. It's a bad road.'

'Or it wouldn't be fair to ourselves, would it, sir?' the woman put in.

'Fifty copecks? Oh, all right, fifty copecks. *C'est encore mieux, j'ai en tout quarante roubles, mais –*'

The peasant pulled up, and Mr Verkhovensky was dragged into the cart by their joint efforts and seated on a sack beside the young woman. His head was still in a whirl. At times he felt himself that he was terribly absent-minded and was not thinking of what he ought to be thinking, and he was amazed at it. This consciousness of the morbid weakness of his mind became very painful to him and even hurt his feelings.

'What – what's this behind? A cow?' he suddenly asked the young woman.

'Why, sir, haven't you ever seen one?' laughed the woman.

'Bought it in the town,' the peasant interposed. 'Our own cattle died in the spring, you see, sir. The plague. All of 'em went down with it. Not half of them left. Enough to make you cry, sir.'

And he whipped the horse, which got stuck in a rut again.

'Yes, that's the sort of thing that happens in Russia – and, generally, we Russians – well, yes, that's what happens,' Mr Verkhovensky broke off.

'If you're a teacher, sir, then what are you going to Khatovo for? Or are you thinking of going farther?'

'I – I mean, I'm not particularly anxious to go any farther – *c'est à dire* – I'm going to a merchant's.'

'To Spasov, is it?'

'Yes, yes, that's right. To Spasov. But it doesn't matter, really.'

'If you're going to Spasov, sir, and on foot, too, it would take you a week in them boots of yours,' laughed the young woman.

'That's right, and it doesn't really matter, *mes amis*, it doesn't matter,' Mr Verkhovensky broke off impatiently.

'Frightfully inquisitive people!' he thought. 'The young woman, though, speaks better than he does, and I notice that since their emancipation of February 19th their language has changed a little and – and what does it matter to me whether I'm in Spasov or not in Spasov? However, I'll pay them, so why do they pester me?'

'If it's Spasov, sir, you want, you'll have to go by the steamer,' the peasant persisted.

'That's quite true, sir,' the young woman put in animatedly. 'If you go by carriage along the bank, it's twenty-five miles more.'

'Forty more likely.'

'You'll just be in time to catch the steamer in Ustyevo at two o'clock to-morrow,' the young woman clinched the matter.

But Mr Verkhovensky fell silent obstinately. His questioners fell silent, too. The peasant tugged at the horse; the woman exchanged short remarks with him from time to time. Mr Verkhovensky dozed off. He was very surprised when the young woman, laughing, woke him by shaking him vigorously and he found himself in a rather large village at the entrance of a cottage with three windows.

'Have you had a nap, sir?'

'What's that? Where am I? Oh well, never mind,' sighed Mr Verkhovensky and got off the cart.

He gazed round him sorrowfully. The village looked strange and terribly outlandish to him.

'I've quite forgotten the fifty copecks,' he addressed the peasant with a sort of incongruously hurried gesture; he was evidently afraid of parting from them.

'We'll settle indoors, sir. Come in, please,' the peasant invited him.

'It's nice inside,' the young woman encouraged him.

Mr. Verkhovensky walked up the rickety steps.

'But how is it possible?' he whispered in great and apprehensive perplexity, going into the cottage, however. '*Elle l'a voulu.*' Something seemed to stab at his heart, and he again suddenly forgot everything, even the fact that he had gone into the cottage.

It was a light and fairly clean peasant's cottage, with three windows and two rooms. It was not an inn, but just a cottage at which people familiar with the place stopped when passing through the village. Mr Verkhovensky went straight to the corner of the room reserved for visitors without showing any embarrassment. He forgot to greet the people, sat down and fell into a reverie. Meanwhile an extremely pleasant sensation of warmth after spending three hours in the damp air suddenly spread all over his body. Even the feverish chill which ran in shivery spasms down his spine, as always happens in a fever, especially with nervous people, suddenly became agreeable to him as he came into a warm room from the cold. He raised his head, and the delicious smell of hot pancakes with which the woman of the house was busy at the stove tickled his nostrils. He smiled a child-like smile and leaned over to the woman.

'What's that?' he suddenly murmured. 'It is pancakes? *Mais – c'est charmant.*'

'Would you like some, sir?' the woman politely offered him some at once.

'I would, indeed I would,' Mr Verkhovensky said, brightening up. 'And – and I'd like some tea, too, if I may.'

'Shall I put on the *samovar*, sir? With pleasure, sir.'

The pancakes were served on a large plate with a big blue pattern – the famous country pancakes, thin, made half of wheat-flour, covered with fresh hot butter – most delicious pancakes! Mr Verkhovensky tasted them with relish.

'How rich and how nice they are! And if only I could have *un doigt d'eau de vie.*'

'I beg your pardon, sir? Is it vodka you'd like?'

'Yes, yes, just a drop. *Un tout petit rien.*'

'Five copecks' worth, sir?'

'Yes, just five, five, five, *un tout petit rien*,' Mr Verkhovensky assented with a blissful little smile.

Ask a man of the lower classes to do something for you, and, if he can only do so, he will do it conscientiously and with great cordiality; but ask him to fetch some vodka, and his customary serene cordiality is suddenly transformed into a sort of hurried and joyful desire to oblige you, almost into a warm-hearted solicitude for you. The man who goes to fetch your vodka – though it is only you who are going to drink it and not he, and he knows it beforehand – seems to feel as though he were to share in your gratification. In less than three or four minutes (the pub was only a few yards away) a half-pint bottle with a large greenish glass stood before Mr Verkhovensky.

'Is all that for me?' he cried in great surprise. 'I've always had vodka, but I never knew that you could get such a lot for five copecks.'

He filled his glass, got up and with a certain solemnity, crossed the room to the other corner where his companion on the sack, the black-browed peasant woman, whose questions had annoyed him so much, had seated herself. The young woman looked embarrassed and would not accept it at first, but having said all that was required of her by custom, she stood up and drank it decorously in three sips, as women do, and gave back the glass and bowed to Mr Verkhovensky with an expression of extreme suffering on her face. He returned the bow solemnly and went back to the table looking very proud.

All this took place on the spur of the moment; a second before he did not know himself that he would go and treat the young peasant woman to a glass of vodka.

'I have a real genius for dealing with the common people, and I've always told them so,' he thought complacently, pouring out the vodka that was left in the bottle; though there was less than a glass, the vodka revived and warmed him and even went to his head a little.

'*Je suis malade tout à fait, mais ce n'est pas trop mauvais d'être malade.*'

'Would you care to buy, sir?' a gentle woman's voice asked beside him.

He raised his eyes, and to his surprise saw a lady standing before him – *une dame et elle en avait l'air* – a lady of over thirty, very modest in appearance, dressed like a townswoman in a darkish gown with a large grey shawl on her shoulders. There was something very friendly in her face which at once appealed to Mr Verkhovensky. She had only just this minute come back to the cottage, in which she had left her things on a bench close by the place where Mr Verkhovensky was sitting. Among them was a brief-case, at which, he recalled, he had glanced curiously, and a not very large bag of American cloth. From this bag she took out two beautifully bound books with a cross engraved on the covers and offered them to Mr Verkhovensky.

'Eh – mais je crois que c'est l'Evangile – with the greatest of pleasure. ... Oh, I understand now. Vous êtes ce qu'on appelle a gospel woman. I've read about it more than once. Fifty copecks?'

'Thirty-five copecks,' replied the gospel woman.

'With the greatest of pleasure. Je n'ai rien contre l'Evangile et – I've been wanting to read it again for a long time.'

The thought flashed through his mind at that moment that he had not read the gospel for thirty years at least and that perhaps only seven years before he had recalled a little from it when reading Renan's Vie de Jésus. As he had no small change on him, he pulled out his four ten-rouble notes – all that he had. The landlady undertook to get change, and it was only then that he noticed, as he looked round the room, that a good many people had come into the cottage and that all of them had been watching him for some time and, he thought, talking about him. They were also discussing the fire in the town, most of all the owner of the cow, for he had only just returned from there. They were talking of arson and the Spigulin workmen.

'He never said a word to me about the fire when he was bringing me here, and yet he talked of everything,' it occurred to Mr Verkhovensky for some reason.

'Stepan Trofimovich, sir, is it you I see? I'd never have expected to meet you here! Don't you know me, sir?' cried an elderly man, who looked like an old serf servant, with a shaven beard and wearing a greatcoat with a long reversible collar.

Mr Verkhovensky got frightened when he heard his name.

'I'm sorry,' he murmured, 'I'm afraid I don't quite remember you.'

'You must have forgotten, sir. Why, I'm Anisim – Anisim Ivanov. I used to be in the service of the late Mr Gaganov, and I've seen you, sir, and Mrs Stavrogin many times at the late Mrs Gaganov's. I used to go to you with books from her and I brought Petersburg sweets twice from her to you, sir.'

'Oh, yes, I remember you, Anisim,' smiled Mr Verkhovensky. 'Do you live here?'

'I live near Spasov, sir, in the village close to the V— monastery. I'm in the service of the late Mrs Gaganov's sister, Marfa Sergeyevna. Perhaps you remember her, sir. She broke a leg jumping out of her carriage on the way to a ball. Now she lives near the monastery, and I'm in her service. And I'm on my way to the town now, you see, sir, to visit my relations.'

'Oh, yes, yes.'

'I was very pleased to see you, sir. You were always so kind to me,' Anisim declared, smiling happily. 'And where are you going to, sir, like that all by yourself, it seems? I don't think you've ever gone on a journey alone before, have you, sir?'

Mr Verkhovensky looked at him timidly.

'Not to us by any chance, sir? To Spasov?'

'Yes, I'm going to Spasov. *Il me semble que tout le monde va à Spasof. ...*'

'Not to Fyodor Matveyevich's, sir? He will be pleased to see you. He used to respect you very much in the old days, sir. Often speaks of you now, he does.'

'Yes, yes, to Fyodor Matveyevich's.'

'I see, sir. So that's why the peasants here are wondering about you, sir. They seem to think they saw you walking on the road. A stupid lot they are, sir.'

'You see, Anisim, I – I wagered, like the Englishmen do, that I would walk on foot and I –'

Beads of perspiration stood out on his forehead.

'I see, sir, I see.' Anisim listened to him with pitiless curiosity.

But Mr Verkhovensky could bear it no longer. He was so embarrassed that he felt like getting up and walking out of the cottage. But they brought the *samovar*, and at that moment the gospel woman, who had gone out for something, came back. Anisim gave in and walked away.

The peasants were indeed greatly puzzled: 'What sort of person is he? Found walking on the highway, says he is a teacher, dresses like a foreigner, and has no more sense than a little child, gives funny answers, as though he has run away from someone, and he has got money!' They were even proposing to inform the police, particularly as things were not very quiet in the town. But Anisim put things right in a moment. He went into the passage and told everyone who cared to listen that Mr Verkhovensky was not just a teacher but 'a great scholar engaged in learned studies, and he used to be a local landowner himself, and has been living for the last twenty-two years in the house of Mrs Stavrogin, the wife of an army general, and was the most important person there, and greatly respected by everybody in the town. He used to lose fifty- and hundred-rouble notes at the Gentlemen's Club in one evening, and he was a Councillor by rank, which is the same as a lieutenant-colonel in the army, only one rank lower than a full colonel. As for his having money, he gets lots of money through Mrs Stavrogin,' etc., etc.

'*Mais c'est une dame et très comme il faut*,' Mr Verkhovensky thought, resting after Anisim's attack and watching with agreeable curiosity the gospel woman, who was, however, drinking her tea in not quite a lady-like fashion from a saucer and with a lump of sugar in her mouth. '*Ce petit morceau du sucre, ce n'est rien*. There is something noble and independent and, at the same time, gentle about her. *Le comme il faut tout pur*, but rather of a different sort.'

He soon found out from her that her name was Sophia Matveyevna Ulitin and that she really lived at K—, where she had a sister, a widow, who had been married to an artisan; she was a widow too, and her husband, a second-lieutenant who had been a sergeant before he received his commission, had been killed at Sebastopol.

'But you're still so young, *vous n'avez pas trente ans*.'

'Thirty-four,' Mrs Ulitin said with a smile.

'Do you understand French?'

'A little. After my husband's death I lived for four years in a gentleman's house and picked it up from the children.'

She told him that she was only eighteen when her husband was killed, that she was for some time in Sebastopol as a nurse, and that after that she lived in different places, and was now travelling about selling the gospel.

'*Mais mon Dieu*, wasn't it with you that that queer, that very queer story happened in our town?'

She blushed; it turned out that it was she.

'*Ces vauriens, ces malhereux!*' he began in a voice trembling with indignation; the painful and hateful recollection sent a pang through his heart. For a moment he seemed lost in thought.

'Good Lord! she's gone away again,' he thought, recollecting himself with a start and noticing that she was no longer sitting beside him. 'She keeps going in and out, and seems to be busy with something. I can see that she seems to be worried, too. *Bah, je deviens égoiste!*'

He raised his eyes and saw Anisim, but this time in most threatening surroundings. The cottage was full of peasants, and it was evidently Anisim who had brought them there. The owner of the cottage was there, too, and the peasant who owned the cow, two other peasants (they turned out to be coachmen), another little man, half drunk, and dressed like a peasant, though clean-shaven, who looked like an artisan ruined by drink and who talked more than any of them. And all of them were talking about him, Stepan Verkhovensky. The peasant with the cow persisted that to go by road would mean a journey of more than thirty-five miles, and that he most certainly must go by steamer. The half-drunk artisan and the master of the house contested his point warmly.

''Cause, you see, if the gentleman goes by steamer across the lake, it'll be nearer all right. There ain't nobody saying nothing against it. But the trouble is the steamer don't go there, not at this time of the year – see?'

'It does, it does, it does go there for another week,' cried Anisim, who seemed to be more excited than any of them.

'Aye, so it does. But it don't come punctual like, seeing as how it is so late in the season. It has to wait three days in Ustyevo sometimes.'

'It will be here to-morrow, at two o'clock sharp. You'll be in Spasov before evening, sir,' Anisim raged.

'*Mais qu'est ce qu'il a, cet homme?*' Mr Verkhovensky cried in trepidation, waiting in terror for what they were going to do with him.

It was now the coachmen's turn to join in the argument. They began to bargain with him. They demanded three roubles to Ustyevo. The others shouted that that was the right fare, and that they had been driving to Ustyevo all summer for that price.

'But – er – it's nice here, too,' Mr Verkhovensky mumbled. 'And I don't want to –'

'Aye, sir, you're quite right. It's very nice in Spasov, and Fyodor Matveyevich will be pleased to see you.'

'*Mon Dieu, mes amis*, this is such a surprise to me.'

At last Mrs Ulitin came back. But she sat down on the bench looking sad and dejected.

'I will never get to Spasov,' she said to the woman of the house.

'Why, are you going to Spasov, too?' Mr Verkhovensky asked with a start.

It turned out that a lady had told her the day before to wait for her in Khatovo, promising to drive her to Spasov, but she had not come.

'What am I going to do now?' Mrs Ulitin kept repeating.

'*Mais, ma chère et nouvelle amie*, I can take you there just as well as that lady of yours, to that village, whatever it is, to which I've hired a carriage, and to-morrow – why, to-morrow we'll go on to Spasov together.'

'Are you going to Spasov too?'

'*Mais, que faire, et je suis enchanté!* I shall be delighted to take you there. They want to take me, and I have already hired them. Which of you have I hired?' Mr Verkhovensky asked, suddenly overcome by an intense desire to go to Spasov.

A quarter of an hour later they got into a covered cart; he very lively and completely satisfied, she with her pack and a grateful smile beside him. Anisim helped them in.

'A good journey to you, sir,' he said, bustling round the cart. 'It's been a great pleasure to see you, sir.'

'Good-bye, my friend, good-bye, good-bye!'

'You'll see Fyodor Matveyevich, sir.'

'Yes, my friend, yes – Fyodor Matveyevich – good-bye now.'

2

'You see, my friend – you will let me call you my friend, *n'est-ce pas?*' Mr Verkhovensky began hurriedly the moment the cart started. 'You see, I – *J'aime le peuple, c'est indispensable, mais il me semble que je ne l'avais jamais vu de près. Stasie – cela va sans dire qu'elle est aussi le peuple – mais le vrai peuple*, the true ones, I mean, the ones you meet on the road, it seems to me that all they are interested in is where exactly I am going. But let's drop all this unpleasant business. I believe I'm talking nonsense, but that's only because I'm talking so fast.'

'You seem to be ill, sir,' Mrs Ulitin said, watching him narrowly but respectfully.

'No, no. I must only wrap myself up, and, besides, there's a fresh wind blowing, a very fresh wind; but never mind that. That's not what I meant to say really. *Chère et incomparable amie*, I think I'm almost happy, and you're the cause of it. Happiness doesn't pay me, because I start at once forgiving all my enemies. ...'

'Why, that's very good, sir.'

'Not always, *chère innocente*. *L'Evangile* – *Vous voyez, desormais nous le prêcherons ensemble*, and I shall gladly sell your beautiful little books. Yes, I must say it is rather an idea, *quelque chose de très nouveau dans ce genre*. The common people are religious, *c'est admis*, but they don't yet know the gospel. I will expound it to them. By expounding it to them verbally it is possible to correct the errors of that remarkable book, which, of course, I shall treat with the utmost respect. I will be useful to you even on the road. I've always been useful. I always told *them* that *et à cette chère ingrate*. Oh, let us forgive, let us forgive; first of all let us forgive all and always. Let us hope that we, too, shall be forgiven. Yes, because all, every one of us, have wronged one another. We are all guilty!'

'That, I think, you said that very well, sir.'

'Yes, yes. I feel that I'm speaking well. I shall speak to them very well, but – what was it I was going to say? It was something important. I keep losing the thread and I cannot remember. You won't let me part from you, will you? I feel that the way you look at me and – and I can't help being surprised at your manners: you're so simple-hearted, you call me "sir", and you pour your tea from the cup into the saucer, and – and that horrid lump of sugar. But there is something delightful about you, and I can see from your features — Oh, don't blush, and don't be afraid of me as a man. *Chère et incomparable, pour moi une femme c'est tout*. I can't live without a woman at my side, but only at my side. ... Oh, I'm afraid, I'm awfully confused. I can't remember what I was going to say. Oh, blessed is he to whom God always sends a woman and – and, I think, indeed, that I am a little too excited. And there's a great idea in the open road, too! That's – that's what I was going to say – about the idea. I've remembered it now, but

I kept losing it. And why have they taken us farther? It was very nice there too, but here – *cela devient trop froid. A propos, j'ai en tout quarante roubles et voilà cet argent.* Take it. Please, take it. I don't know how to take care of it. I'm sure to lose it. It will be taken away from me and – I think I'm going to fall asleep. My head's swimming. It's going round and round and round. Oh, how kind you are! What is it you're wrapping me up with?'

'I'm afraid, sir, you're feverish, and I've covered you with my blanket. Only about the money, sir, I'd rather –'

'Oh, for heaven's sake, *n'en parlons plus, parce que cela me fait mal.* Oh, how kind you are!'

He stopped talking rather abruptly and very soon fell into a feverish, shivery sleep. The country road by which they travelled the twelve miles was far from smooth, and the carriage jolted terribly. Mr Verkhovensky woke up frequently, raised his head quickly from the little pillow which Mrs Ulitin had slipped under it, and asked, 'Are you here?' as though he were afraid that she would leave him. He also told her that he dreamt of gaping jaws full of teeth and that it made him feel very horrid. Mrs Ulitin was greatly worried about him.

The coachmen brought them straight to a large cottage with four windows and other small cottages in the courtyard. Mr Verkhovensky woke up and went straight into the second room, the best and most spacious room of the house. His sleepy face assumed a most fussy expression. He at once explained to the woman of the house, a tall and thick-set woman of forty with very black hair and almost with a moustache, that he required the whole room for himself.

'Shut the door, please,' he ordered, 'and don't let anyone in, *parce que nous avons à parler. Oui, j'ai beaucoup à vous dire, chère amie.* I'll pay you, I'll pay you!' He waved his arms at the woman.

Though he was in a hurry, he seemed to speak with difficulty. The woman listened with an ungracious air, but was silent to signify assent, but there was a feeling of something menacing in her silence. He did not notice anything, however, and demanded hurriedly (he seemed to be in an awful hurry) that she should leave them and get some dinner ready for them, 'without a moment's delay'.

At that point the woman with the moustache could restrain herself no longer.

'This isn't an inn, sir, and we don't serve dinners for travellers. I could boil some crayfish for you or put on the *samovar*, but we have nothing else. There won't be fresh fish till to-morrow.'

But Mr Verkhovensky waved his hands, repeating with angry impatience, 'I'll pay you; only be quick, be quick!' They settled on fish soup and roast chicken. The woman declared that there was not a chicken to be had in the whole village, but she agreed to go and see if she could find one, though with an air as if she were doing him a great favour.

As soon as she had gone, Mr Verkhovensky sat down on the sofa and made Mrs Ulitin sit down beside him. There were arm-chairs and a sofa in the room, but they were in a most dreadful condition. The whole room, which was rather large (it had a partition with a bed behind it) and covered with old, tattered yellow paper, and horrible lithographs of mythological subjects on the walls, and a long row of icons and sets of copper ones in the nearest corner, presented, with its strange assortment of furniture, an unsightly mixture of urban and traditional peasant life. But he did not even look at it. He didn't even look through the window at the huge lake, the shore of which was only about twenty yards from the cottage.

'At last we are alone, and we shan't let anyone in! I want to tell you everything from the very beginning.'

Mrs Ulitin stopped him with a look of great uneasiness.

'Do you realize, Mr Verkhovensky –'

'*Comment, vous savez déjà mon nom?*' he asked with a happy smile.

'I heard it this morning from Anisim when you were talking to him. What I'd like to tell you is –' and she began whispering to him rapidly, looking nervously at the closed door, for fear that anyone might overhear her, '– that the village isn't safe, sir. All the local peasants, though they are fishermen, make their living chiefly by charging visitors every summer what they think fit. The village is not on the highway, but is miles from anywhere, and people only come here because steamers stop here, and when the steamer does not call – for if the weather is bad it never does – lots of travellers are stranded here for several days and all the cottages are full, and this is just what the villagers are waiting for. They charge three times its value for everything, and the landlord here is very proud and high-handed because he is rich, according to the local ideas of wealth. His net alone is worth a thousand roubles.'

Mr Verkhovensky looked almost reproachfully at Mrs Ulitin's extremely animated face and tried to stop her several times. But she persisted and said all she had to say. According to her, she had been there once before in the summer with 'a very genteel lady' from the town. They had had to spend two days there waiting for the arrival of the steamer, and he could not imagine what they had to put up with. 'You, sir, have asked for this room for yourself. I only mention it to warn you. They already have travellers in the other room — an elderly gentleman, and a young gentleman, and a lady with children — and to-morrow the house will be full of people who will be staying here till two o'clock; for the steamer hasn't called for two days and is quite certain to call to-morrow. So for a special room and for ordering dinner and for keeping other travellers out they will charge you much more than they would dream of charging anyone in Petersburg or Moscow.'

But he was suffering. He was truly suffering.

'*Assez, mon enfant*, I beg you, *nous avons notre argent et après — et après e bon Dieu*. And I'm really surprised that a person like you, a person with your high ideals — *assez, assez, vous me tourmentez*,' he cried hysterically. 'We have all our future before us, and you — you are trying to frighten me by what might happen to-morrow.'

He at once began to tell her the story of his life in such a hurry that at first it was difficult to understand. It went on for a long time. The fish soup was served, followed by the chicken, and at last the *samovar* was brought in, but he was still talking. It all sounded rather strange and neurotic, but, then, he was ill. It was a sudden exertion of all his mental faculties which, of course — and Mrs Ulitin foresaw it anxiously all the time he was talking — in the present state of his health was bound to result immediately afterwards in extreme exhaustion. He began almost with his childhood days, when 'with a high heart he raced through the fields'; only an hour later did he reach the story of his two marriages and his life in Berlin. I should not dream of laughing at him, however. There was really some high spiritual significance in it for him and, in modern parlance, almost a question of the struggle for existence. He saw before him the woman he had chosen to share his future life and he was, as it were, in a hurry to initiate her. The fact that he was a genius must no longer remain a secret to her. Maybe he formed a rather exaggerated opinion of Mrs Ulitin, but he had already chosen her. He could not live without a woman. He could see clearly from her face that she scarcely understood him, and that she could not even grasp the essential point of his story.

'*Ce n'est rien, nous attendrons*, and meanwhile her intuition will tell her what I mean.'

'My friend, all I want is your heart!' he exclaimed, interrupting the story of his life, 'and this charming, this entrancing look with which you're gazing at me now. Oh, don't blush, I've told you already –'

Poor, trapped Mrs Ulitin found it particularly hard to follow Mr Verkhovensky when his story developed almost into a whole dissertation on how no one ever had been able to understand him and how 'men of genius go to rack and ruin in Russia'. It was all 'much too clever', she used to say afterwards dejectedly. She listened to him with undisguised distress, a little open-eyed. When Mr Verkhovensky plunged into humour and began delivering himself of witty pin-pricks at the expense of 'our progressive and governing classes', she made two desperate attempts to laugh in response to his laughter. But the effect she produced was worse than if she had burst into tears, so that Mr Verkhovensky was at last embarrassed himself and launched out into a passionate and spiteful attack on the nihilists and the 'new' men. At this point he simply frightened her, and she only breathed more freely, though not for long, when he embarked on the story of the great romance of his life. A woman is always a woman, even if she is a nun. She smiled, shook her head, and then blushed and lowered her eyes, which threw Mr Verkhovensky into a state of absolute rapture and inspiration, so that he even told a few lies. Mrs Stavrogin appeared in his story as a ravishing brunette ('who was the admiration of Petersburg and many more European capitals'), and her husband had died, 'struck down by a bullet at Sebastopol', simply because he did not deem himself worthy of her love and yielded her to his rival, that is, to Mr Verkhovensky, of course. 'Do not be shocked, my gentle one, my Christian!' he exclaimed to Mrs Ulitin, almost himself believing in the story he was telling her; 'it was something spiritual, something so fine that we never spoke of it to one another all our lives.' The cause of this extraordinary state of affairs appeared to be a blonde (if not Miss Shatov, then I don't know whom Mr Verkhovensky was thinking of). This blonde owed everything to the brunette, in whose house she grew up as a distant relative. The brunette, having become aware at last that the blonde was in love with Mr Verkhovensky, locked her secret up in her breast. The blonde, for her part, becoming aware that the brunette was in love with Mr Verkhovensky, also locked her secret up in her breast. And so the three of them, pining away with magnanimity towards each other, kept silent for twenty years, locking their secrets in their breasts. 'Oh, what a passion that was! What a passion that was!' he exclaimed, whimpering with genuine emotion. 'I saw the full bloom of the brunette's beauty, watched her passing by me heart-brokenly every day, as though ashamed of her beauty.' (Once he said, 'ashamed of her stoutness'.) At last he had run away, abandoning all this feverish dream of twenty years – *vingt ans!* – and now he had taken to the open road. Then, in a sort of overwrought condition of his brain, he began to explain to Mrs Ulitin the real meaning of their 'so accidental and yet so fateful meeting' that day, a meeting that had joined their lives 'for ever and aye'. Mrs Ulitin, looking terribly embarrassed, got up from the sofa at last. He even made an attempt to go down on his knees before her, which made her cry.

It was getting dark: they had spent a few hours locked up in the room. 'You'd better let me go to the other room, sir,' she murmured, 'or what will people say?'

She tore herself away at last; he let her go, promising her to go to bed at once. As he bade her good night, he complained that he had a bad headache. Mrs Utilin had left her pack and her things in the front room, intending to spend the night with the people of the house; but she got no rest.

At night Mr Verkhovensky had an attack of his gastric catarrh, so familiar to me and to all his friends – the inevitable result of all his nervous and spiritual shocks. Poor Mrs Ulitin did not sleep all night. While nursing the invalid, she had to go in and out of the cottage through the landlady's room several times during the night, which made the landlady and the travellers who were sleeping there grumble and even swear at her when she started getting the *samovar* ready early in the morning. Mr Verkhovensky was in a state of semi-consciousness during the whole of his attack; sometimes he was dimly aware that the *samovar* was brought in, that he was given something to drink (raspberry tea), and that hot fomentations were being applied to his stomach and chest. But every moment he felt that *she* was there beside him; that it was she who was going in and out of the room, lifting him off the bed and laying him down again. At about three o'clock in the morning he felt better; he sat up, put his legs out of the bed and, without warning, fell on the floor before her. This was no longer a question of kneeling before her; he simply fell at her feet and kissed the hem of her dress.

'Please don't do it, sir. I'm not worthy of it,' she murmured, trying to lift him on to the bed.

'My saviour,' he cried, folding his hands reverently before her. '*Vous êtes noble comme une marquise!* I – I am a blackguard! Oh, all my life I've been dishonest!'

'Please calm yourself!' Mrs Ulitin implored him.

'I told you awful lies last evening – just for the sake of self-glorification, self-indulgence, and self-conceit. All, all, every word of it – oh, what a blackguard, what a blackguard!'

His gastric attack thus passed into another attack – an attack of hysterical self-reproach. I mentioned these attacks when I spoke of his letters to Mrs Stavrogin.

He suddenly remembered *Lise* and his meeting with her the previous morning. 'It was so awful, and I'm sure something terrible must have happened, and I never asked her – I never found out! I was only thinking of myself! Oh, I wonder what happened to her. Do you know what happened to her?' he besought Mrs Ulitin.

Then he vowed that he would never 'betray' her, that he would return to *her* (he meant Mrs Stavrogin). 'We shall walk up to her house every morning' (he and Mrs Ulitin, that is), 'when she is getting into her carriage for her morning drive, and will watch her very quietly. ... Oh, I'd like her to strike me on the other cheek! I long for her to do it. I will turn my other cheek to her *comme dans votre livre*! Only now I understand for the first time what is meant by turning the other cheek. I never understood it before.'

The following two days were the most dreadful days in Mrs Ulitin's life. She remembers them with a shudder to this day. Mr Verkhovensky became so seriously ill that he could not go on board the steamer, which this time arrived punctually at two o'clock in the afternoon. She, for her part, could not bring herself to leave him alone, and she did not leave for Spasov, either. According to her, he was very pleased when the steamer had sailed.

'Well, that's fine, that's excellent!' he murmured in his bed. 'And I was all the time afraid that we would have to go. It's so nice here. Better than anywhere else. You won't leave me, will you? Oh, you haven't left me!'

It was not so 'nice', however. He did not want to know anything of her difficulties. His head was full of all sorts of fancies. He did not take his illness seriously at all, thinking that it would soon pass. He did not worry about it at all. He only thought of how they would go and sell 'those books'. He asked her to read him the gospel.

'I haven't read it for a long time – in the original. Someone might ask me about it, and I shall make a mistake. I must after all prepare myself.'

She sat down beside him and opened the book.

'You read beautifully,' he interrupted her after the first sentence. 'I can see, I can see that I was not mistaken!' he added vaguely, but rapturously.

He was, generally, in a continuous state of great excitement. She read the Sermon on the Mount.

'Assez, assez, mon enfant, enough. Don't you think that is enough?'

And he felt so exhausted that he closed his eyes. He was very weak, but he did not lose consciousness. Mrs Ulitin got up, thinking that he wanted to sleep. But he stopped her.

'My friend, all my life I've been lying. Even when I spoke the truth. I never spoke for the sake of the truth, but for my own sake. I knew it before, but it is only now that I see it. Oh, where are my friends whom I have insulted with my friendship all my life? And all, all! Savez-vous, perhaps I'm lying even now. The trouble is that I believe myself when I am lying. The hardest thing in life is to live and not to lie, and – and not believe your own lie. Yes, yes, that's it! But wait a little; I'll tell you about it later. We're together, we're together!' he added with enthusiasm.

'Don't you think, Mr Verkhovensky,' she asked timidly, 'we ought to send to the town for a doctor?'

He was taken aback greatly.

'Whatever for? Est-ce que je suis si malade? Mais rien de sérieux. And what do we want strangers for? They might find out – and what's going to happen then? No, no. We don't want any stranger. We're together, we're together!'

'You know,' he said after a short pause, 'read me something more. Anything you like. Anything that strikes your eye.'

She opened the book again and began to read.

'He that openeth, and no man shutteth; and shutteth, and no man openeth,' he repeated.

'And unto the angel of the church of the Laodiceans write –'

'What's that? What? Where is it from?'

'It is from Revelation.'

'*Oh, je m'en souviens, oui, l'Apocalypse. Lisez, lisez!* I am trying to tell our future by the book. I want to know what has turned up. Read on from the angel, the angel …'

'And unto the angel of the church of the Laodiceans write: These things saith the Amen, the faithful and true witness, the beginning of the creation of God. I know thy works, that thou art neither cold nor hot: I would thou wert cold or hot. So then because thou art lukewarm, and neither cold nor hot, I will spue thee out of my mouth. Because thou sayest, I am rich, and increased with goods, and have need of nothing; and knowest not that thou art wretched and miserable, and poor, and blind, and naked.'

'This – and this is in your book!' he cried, flashing his eyes and raising his head from the pillow. 'I never knew that grand passage! You hear, better be cold than lukewarm, than *only* lukewarm! Oh, I'll prove it. Only don't leave me, don't leave me alone! We shall prove it! We shall prove it!'

'But I won't leave you, Mr Verkhovensky; I won't ever leave you!' she cried, seizing his hand and, pressing it in hers, put it to her heart, looking at him with tears in her eyes. ('I was terribly sorry for him at that moment,' she told me, describing this scene.)

His lips twitched, as though spasmodically.

'But, Mr Verkhovensky, what are we to do? Ought we not to let your friends, or your relations, perhaps, know?'

But he grew so alarmed at her suggestion that she was sorry she had mentioned it again. Shaking and trembling, he besought her not to fetch anyone and not to do anything. He made her give him her word. 'No one, no one!' he urged her. 'Just we two, we two, *nous partirons ensemble.*'

What made things worse was that the people of the house, too, were beginning to be uneasy; they grumbled and kept pestering Mrs

Ulitin. She paid them and did her best to let them see that they had money. That quieted them for a time. But the landlord demanded to see Mr Verkhovensky's 'papers'. The sick man motioned to his bag with a disdainful smile. Mrs Ulitin found in it the certificate of his resignation from the university, which had served him as a passport all his life. The landlord was not satisfied and said that 'he'd better be taken away somewhere, because this isn't a hospital, and if he dies, we shall as likely as not get into trouble'. Mrs Ulitin spoke to him about getting a doctor, but it seemed that if they were to send to the town for one, it would cost so much that the whole idea had to be given up as impractical. She went back in anguish to her patient. Mr Verkhovensky was getting weaker and weaker.

'Now read me another passage – about the swine,' he said suddenly.

'What did you say, sir?' she asked in great alarm.

'About the swine – it's also there – *ces cochons*. I remember the devil entered the swine and they were all drowned. You must read it to me. I'll tell you why afterwards. I want to remember it literally – word for word.'

Mrs Ulitin knew the gospel well, and at once found the passage in St Luke, which I used for an epigraph to my chronicle. I'll quote it here again.

'And there was there an herd of many swine feeding on the mountain: and they besought him that he would suffer them to enter into them. And he suffered them. Then went the devils out of the man, and entered into the swine: and the herd ran violently down a steep place into the lake, and were choked. When they that fed them saw what was done, they fled, and went and told it in the city and in the country. Then they went out to see what was done; and came to Jesus, and found the man, out of whom the devils were departed, sitting at the feet of Jesus, clothed, and in his right mind: and they were afraid. They also which saw it told them by what means he that was possessed of the devils was healed.'

'My friend,' said Mr Verkhovensky in great excitement, '*savez-vous*, this wonderful and – extraordinary passage has been a stumbling-block to me all my life – *dans ce livre* – so that I remembered that passage from childhood. But now an idea has occurred to me; *une comparaison*. An awful lot of ideas keep occurring to me now. You see, that's just like our Russia. These devils who go out of the sick man and enter the swine – those are all the sores, all the poisonous exhalations, all the impurities, all the big and little devils, that have accumulated in our great and beloved invalid, in our Russia, for centuries, for centuries! *Oui, cette Russie, que j'aimais toujours.* But a great idea and a great Will shield her from on high, as with that madman possessed of the devils, and all those devils, all those impurities, all those abominations that were festering on the surface – all of them will themselves ask to enter into swine. And, indeed, they may have entered into them already! They are we, we and them, and Peter – *et les autres avec lui,* and perhaps I at the head of them all, and we shall cast ourselves down, the raving and the possessed, from the cliff into the sea and shall all be drowned, and serves us right, for that is all we are good for. But the sick man will be healed, and "will sit at the feet of Jesus", and all will look at him and be amazed. My dear, *vous comprendrez après. Nous comprendrons ensemble.'*

He became delirious, and at last lost consciousness. So it went on for the whole of the next day. Mrs Ulitin sat beside him and wept. She had had practically no sleep for three nights, and avoided meeting the people of the house, who, she felt, were beginning to take some steps. Deliverance only came on the third day. In the morning Mr Verkhovensky recovered consciousness, recognized her, and held out his hand to her. He wanted to look out of the window: '*Tiens, un lac,*' he said. 'Good Lord, I hadn't seen it till now.' At that moment a carriage rumbled along the road and stopped at the door of the cottage. A hubbub arose in the house.

3

It was Mrs Stavrogin herself. She arrived in a four-seater carriage drawn by four horses, with two servants and Dasha. The miracle had happened very simply: Anisim, full of his meeting with Mr Verkhovensky, arrived in the town, and on the following day went to Mrs Stavrogin's and told the servants that he had met Mr Verkhovensky in a village, that he had been seen by some peasants walking on the highway alone, and that he had gone to Spasov by way of Ustyevo together with Sophia Ulitin. As Mrs Stavrogin, for her part, was greatly worried and had done her best to find her runaway friend, she was at once told of Anisim. When she had heard his story, and above all, the details of his departure to Ustyevo, together with a certain Sophia Ulitin in the same carriage, she immediately got ready for the journey and, following the hot trail, arrived in Ustyevo herself.

Her stern and imperious voice resounded throughout the house; even the landlord and his wife quailed. She had only stopped to make inquiries, being convinced that Mr Verkhovensky had reached Spasov long before. Having learnt, however, that he was in the cottage and ill, she went into the cottage in a state of great agitation.

'But where is he? Where is he?' she cried, seeing Mrs Ulitin, who at that moment appeared in the doorway of the next room. 'I can see from your shameless face that you're the woman. Get out, you slut! Don't let me see you in the house again! Turn her out, or else, my good woman, I'll have you locked up in jail for the rest of your life. See that she is kept in one of your cottages in the yard, landlord. She's been in jail once before in the town, and she'll go there again. And see to it, landlord, that while I'm here no one is allowed to stay in your house. I'm Mrs Stavrogin, the widow of a general, and I'll take the whole house. As for you, my good woman, you'll have to give me a full account of everything.'

The familiar voice horrified Mr Verkhovensky. He began to tremble. But she had already stepped behind the partition. With flashing eyes she drew up a chair with her foot, and leaning against the back, shouted to Dasha:

'You'd better leave the room. Stay with the landlady for a while. Why this curiosity? And close the door behind you properly!'

She looked at his frightened face in silence for some time with a sort of predatory gaze.

'Well, how are you, Mr Verkhovensky? Did you have a nice time?' The words escaped her suddenly with furious irony.

'*Chère*,' he cried, beside himself, 'I have found out what real Russian life is like. *Et je prêcherai l'Evangile. ...*'

'Oh, you shameless, ungrateful man!' she cried suddenly in a loud voice, throwing up her hands. 'Haven't you disgraced me enough already, and now you've got yourself attached to – Oh, you shameless old roué!'

'*Chère* –'

His voice failed him and he could not utter a word, but just stared at her in terror.

'Who is *she*?'

'*C'est un ange. C'était plus qu'un ange pour moi.* Oh, don't shout at her! Don't frighten her, please! *Chère, chère.* ...'

Mrs Stavrogin suddenly jumped up from her chair with a loud noise. 'Water! water!' she cried in a frightened voice. And though he had come to, she was still shaking with terror and, turning white as a sheet, looked at his distorted face. It was at this point that she realized for the first time how gravely ill he was.

'Dasha,' she suddenly whispered to the girl, 'send for the doctor at once, for Salzfisch. Let Yegorych go at once. Let him hire horses here and get another carriage in town. Tell him he must be here before it's dark.'

Dasha rushed out to carry out her order. Mr Verkhovensky still looked at her with the same wide-opened, frightened eyes. His lips had gone white and quivered.

'Wait, my dear, wait!' she said, coaxing him like a child. 'There, there, wait a little. Dasha will be back presently and – Heavens, landlady, landlady, come here, my good woman!'

In her impatience she ran to the landlady herself.

'Bring *that* woman back at once! Bring her back! Bring her back!'

Luckily, Sophia Ulitin had not yet had time to leave the house, and was only just going out of the gate with her pack and her bundle. She was brought back. She was so frightened that her hands and legs were shaking. Mrs Stavrogin seized her by the hand, as a vulture seizes a chick, and dragged her impetuously to Mr Verkhovensky.

'Well, here she is. I haven't eaten her up. You thought I had eaten her, didn't you?'

Mr Verkhovensky seized Mrs Stavrogin's hand and put it to his lips, and burst into tears, sobbing loudly, hysterically, convulsively.

'There, calm yourself, my dear, calm yourself. There, there. Goodness me, calm yourself, won't you?' she shouted furiously. 'Oh, you torturer! You torturer! All my life you've tortured me!'

'My dear,' Mr Verkhovensky murmured at last, addressing Mrs Ulitin, 'won't you go to the other room, my dear? I have something to say here.'

Mrs Ulitin hurried out of the room at once.

'*Chérie, chérie,*' he gasped.

'Wait a little. Don't talk before you've had a rest. Here's some water. Wait a little, won't you?'

She sat down on the chair again. Mr Verkhovensky clasped her hand firmly. She would not let him speak for a long time. He raised her hand to his lips and began kissing it. She clenched her teeth and looked away into the corner of the room.

'*Je vous aimais!*' escaped him at last.

She had never heard such an avowal from him, uttered in such a voice.

'H'm,' she growled in reply.

'*Je vous aimais toute ma vie   vingt ans!*'

She still said nothing – two minutes – three.

'But when you came wooing Dasha, you sprinkled yourself with scent,' she said suddenly in a terrible whisper.

Mr Verkhovensky gazed speechlessly at her in utter amazement.

'Put on a new cravat –'

Again silence for two minutes.

'Remember the cigar?'

'My friend,' he mumbled, horrified.

'Your cigar – in the evening – by the window – the moon was shining – after the summer-house – in Skvoreshniki? Do you remember it? Do you remember it?' she cried, jumping up from her chair, seizing his pillow by the two corners and shaking it together with his head. 'Do you remember, you futile man, you futile, disgraceful, cowardly, always, always futile man?' she hissed in her ferocious whisper, barely restraining herself from screaming. At last she let him go and sank in the chair, covering her face in her hands. 'Enough!' she snapped out, drawing herself up. 'The twenty years have gone. We can't bring them back. I, too, was a fool.'

'*Je vous aimais,*' he cried, folding his hands again.

'*Aimais, aimais, aimais!* You keep on repeating it, don't you? Enough!' She jumped up again. 'If you don't go to sleep at once, I'll – You must rest. Go to sleep! Go to sleep at once! Shut your eyes! Oh dear, he probably wants his lunch. What do you have? What does he have? Oh dear, where's that woman? Where is she?'

She would have started a commotion, but Mr Verkhovensky murmured in a weak voice that he would really like to go to sleep for *une heure*, and then *un bouillon, un thé – énfin il était si heureux.*

He lay down and really seemed to go to sleep (he probably pretended to). Mrs Stavrogin waited a little, and then she went out on tiptoe from behind the partition.

She settled herself in the landlady's room, turned out the landlady and her husband, and told Dasha to fetch *that* woman. A serious cross-examination began.

'Tell me, my dear, everything in detail. Sit down beside me – so. Well?'

'I met Mr Verkhovensky –'

'Wait a moment. Be quiet. I warn you that if you conceal anything from me or tell me a lie, I shall get you from the other end of the earth. Well?'

'Mr Verkhovensky and I – As soon as I arrived in Khatovo, ma'am —' Mrs Ulitin was almost breathless.

'One moment. Be quiet. Wait a little. What are you gabbling away like that for? First of all, what sort of person are you?'

She told her something about herself, as briefly as possible, beginning with Sebastopol. Mrs Stavrogin listened to her in silence, sitting erect in her chair and looking sternly straight into the woman's eyes.

'Why are you so frightened? Why do you lower your eyes? I like people to look straight at me and to answer me back. Go on.'

She told of their meeting, of her books, and of how Mr Verkhovensky treated the peasant woman to vodka.

'That's right. Don't leave out the smallest detail,' Mrs Stavrogin encouraged her.

At last she told her how they had left in the cart and how Mr Verkhovensky kept on talking, though he was 'quite ill', and how he had told her the whole story of his life from the very beginning, talking for several hours.

'Tell me about his life.'

Mrs Ulitin suddenly stopped, completely at a loss.

'I can't tell you anything about that, ma'am,' she said, almost crying. 'And, besides, I hardly understood a word of it.'

'You're lying! You must have understood something.'

'He told me about a lady of high rank with black hair,' Mrs Ulitin said, blushing crimson, noticing, however, Mrs Stavrogin's fair hair and that she was quite unlike the 'brunette'.

'Black hair? What did he say? Come on, speak!'

'How this lady was deeply in love with him, all her life, for twenty years, but never dared to tell him about it, and how she was ashamed before him because she was fat.'

'The fool!' Mrs Stavrogin said reflectively, but resolutely.

Mrs Ulitin had burst into tears by then.

'I'm sorry, ma'am, but I don't know how to tell you about it properly because I myself was so terrified for him and I couldn't really understand him, as he is such an intellectual person.'

'It isn't for a ninny like you to judge of his intellect. Did he offer you his hand in marriage?'

The poor woman trembled.

'Did he fall in love with you? Go on, tell me! Did he offer you his hand?' Mrs Stavrogin shouted at her.

'It was almost like that, ma'am,' she whimpered. 'Only I did not take it seriously because I could see how ill he was,' she added firmly, raising her eyes.

'What's your name? Your Christian name and patronymic?'

'Sophia Matveyevna, ma'am.'

'Well, Sophia Matveyevna, I want you to know that he is a most worthless and a most wretched little man. Good Lord! who do you take me for? A wicked old woman?'

Sophia stared at her open-eyed.

'A wicked old woman? A tyrant? A woman who has ruined his life?'

'How can that be, ma'am, when you're crying yourself?'

Mrs Stavrogin really had tears in her eyes.

'All right, sit down. Sit down. Don't be afraid. Look at me again. Straight in the eyes. What are you blushing for? Dasha, come here. Have a look at her. What do you think? Her heart is pure. ...'

And to Mrs Ulitin's surprise and perhaps also to her great consternation, Mrs Stavrogin suddenly patted her on the cheek.

'A pity you're a fool, though. Too great a fool for your age. All right, my dear, I'll look after you. I can see that it's all nonsense. Stay near here for the time being. I'll see that a room is provided for you and you'll get food and everything from me, till I ask for you.'

Mrs Ulitin murmured fearfully that she was rather anxious to go.

'There's no hurry. I'll buy all your books, and you can stay here.

Hold your tongue, and no excuses, please. If I had not come, you wouldn't have left him, would you?'

'I wouldn't have left him for anything in the world,' Mrs Ulitin said quietly and firmly, drying her tears.

Dr Salzfisch was brought late at night. He was a very respectable old man and a fairly experienced medical practitioner, who had recently lost his post in the service because of some quarrel with his superiors over some imagined slight. Mrs Stavrogin at once took him under her wing. He subjected the patient to a painstaking examination, questioned him, and cautiously informed Mrs Stavrogin that the condition of 'the sufferer' was extremely dubious in consequence of complications and that she had better prepare herself for 'the worst'. Mrs Stavrogin, who had become accustomed during twenty years to expect nothing serious or decisive from Mr Verkhovensky personally, was profoundly shocked and even turned pale.

'Is there no hope at all?'

'It is quite impossible to say that there is no hope at all, but –'

She did not go to bed all night, and could scarcely wait for the morning to come. As soon as the patient opened his eyes and regained consciousness (so far he had remained conscious, though he was losing strength every hour), she approached him with a most resolute air.

'Mr Verkhovensky, we have to be prepared for everything. I've sent for a priest. You must do your duty. ....'

Knowing his convictions, she was very much afraid of a refusal. He looked at her in surprise.

'Nonsense, nonsense!' she cried, thinking that he was already refusing. 'There's no time for any of your whimsies now. You've played the fool long enough.'

'But – am I really so very ill?'

He agreed thoughtfully. And indeed I was very surprised to learn from Mrs Stavrogin afterwards, that he was not afraid of death at all. Perhaps he simply did not believe her, and still regarded his illness as a trifling one.

He confessed and took the sacrament very readily. All of them, even Mrs Ulitin and the servants, came to congratulate him on receiving the sacrament. All of them wept softly as they looked at his thin and haggard face and his twitching lips.

'*Oui, mes amis,* I'm surprised that you – take so much trouble. To-morrow I shall most probably get up and we'll set off. *Toute cette cérémonie* – to which of course I pay due respect – was –'

'Please, Father, I want you to stay with the invalid,' Mrs Stavrogin said, quickly stopping the priest, who was about to take off his surplice. 'As soon as tea is served, I want you to talk to him about some religious subject to sustain his faith.'

The priest began to speak; all of them were standing or sitting round the sick-bed.

Mr Verkhovensky seemed to come to life suddenly; a sly smile passed over his lips.

'*Mon père, je vous remercie, et vous êtes bien bon, mais –*'

'There's no *mais* about it, no *mais* at all!' Mrs Stavrogin cried, jumping up from her chair. 'Father,' she addressed the priest, 'he's such a man – such a man that in an hour you'd have to give him absolution again! That's the sort of man he is!'

Mr Verkhovensky smiled quietly.

'My friends,' he said, 'God is necessary to me if only because he is the only being whom one can love eternally.'

And indeed he was converted, perhaps because of the majestic ceremony of the administration of the sacrament which moved him deeply and awoke the artistic sensibilities of his nature, but, I am told, he uttered with great feeling some words which were in direct contradiction to his former convictions.

'My immortality is necessary if only because God would not do anything unjust to extinguish completely the flame of love for him once kindled in my heart. And what is more precious than love? Love is higher than existence. Love is the crown of existence. And how is it possible that existence should not be subjected to it? If I have come to love Him and rejoice in my love – is it possible that He should extinguish both me and my joy and turn us into nothingness? If God exists, then I, too, am immortal! *Voilà ma profession de foi!*'

'There is a God, Mr Verkhovensky, I assure you, there is a God,' Mrs Stavrogin implored him. 'Renounce your beliefs, give up your foolishness for once in your life.' (I don't think she quite understood his *profession de foi.*)

'My friend,' he murmured, growing more and more inspired, though his voice broke frequently, 'my friend, when I grasped the meaning of that – turning of the cheek, I – at once understood something else. *J'ai menti toute ma vie*, all, all my life! I'd have liked – however, to-morrow – to-morrow we shall all set off –'

Mrs Stavrogin burst into tears. He was looking for someone with his eyes.

'Here she is – she is here!' Mrs Stavrogin took Sophia by the hand and led her to him.

He smiled tenderly.

'Oh, I'd like to live my life again!' he cried in a great access of energy. 'Every minute, every second of life ought to be a blessing to man – they ought to be – they must be! It is the duty of every man to make it so. This is the law that is hidden deep down in his nature, a law that most certainly exists. Oh, I wish I could see my son Peter – and all of them – Shatov!'

I may add that no one as yet knew of Shatov's death, neither Mrs Stavrogin, nor Dr Salzfisch, who was the last to arrive from the town.

Mr Verkhovensky was growing more and more agitated, morbidly so, beyond his strength.

'The mere presence of the everlasting idea of the existence of something infinitely more just and happy than I, already fills me with abiding tenderness and – glory – oh, whoever I may be and whatever I may have done! To know every moment, and to believe that somewhere there exists perfect peace and happiness for everyone and for everything, is much more important to a man than his own happiness. The whole law of human existence consists merely of making it possible for every man to bow down before what is infinitely great. If man were to be deprived of the infinitely great, he would refuse to go on living, and die of despair. The infinite and the immeasurable is as necessary to man as the little planet which he inhabits. My friends – all, all my friends: long live the Great Idea! The eternal, immeasurable Idea! Every man, whosoever he may be, must bow down before what is the Great Idea. Even the most stupid man must have something great. Peter, my boy – Oh, how I wish I could see them all again! They do not know – they do not know that the same eternal Great Idea dwells in them too!'

Dr Salzfisch was not present at the ceremony. Coming in suddenly, he was horrified, and ordered them all out of the sick-room, insisting that his patient must not be excited.

Mr Verkhovensky died three days later, but by then he was completely unconscious. He seemed to have passed away quietly, like a candle that is burnt out. Mrs Stavrogin, after having the funeral service performed at the cottage, took the body of her poor friend to Skvoreshniki. The grave in the churchyard is already covered with a marble slab. The inscription and the railing have been left till the autumn.

Mrs Stavrogin had been away from the town for eight days. Sophia Ulitin arrived with her in her carriage, and seems to have settled with her for good. I may add that as soon as Mr Verkhovensky lost consciousness (the same morning), Mrs Stavrogin had Mrs Ulitin removed from the cottage again and nursed the sick man herself to the end; but the moment he had breathed his last, she sent for her at once. She refused to listen to any objections to her proposal (or rather command) to settle at Skvoreshniki for good. Mrs Ulitin was terribly frightened by it.

'That's all nonsense! I'll go with you myself to sell gospels. I have no one left in the world.'

'But you have a son,' Dr Salzfisch observed.

'I have no son!' Mrs Stavrogin cut him short – and it was almost as though she had uttered a prophecy.

8

Conclusion

ALL the knaveries and crimes that had been perpetrated came to light with extraordinary rapidity, much more quickly than Peter Verkhovensky had anticipated. To begin with, the unhappy Marie Shatov awoke before daybreak on the night of her husband's murder, missed him, and became greatly agitated when she did not see him beside her. A woman hired by Mrs Virginsky had spent the night with her. Unable to calm her, she ran to Mrs Virginsky's as soon as it was light, having told Mrs Shatov that the midwife knew where her husband was and when he would return. Meanwhile, Mrs Virginsky, too, was beginning to be worried: she had already found out from her husband about the gallant deed at Skvoreshniki. He had returned home about eleven o'clock in a terrible state, wringing his hands; he flung himself

on the bed face downwards, and kept repeating, shaking with con-
vulsive sobs: 'That wasn't right! That wasn't right! That wasn't right
at all!' It goes without saying that he ended by confessing everything
to his wife, though to her alone in the house. She left him lying on the
bed, having sternly impressed on him that if he wanted to whine, he'd
better do it in his pillow, so that no one should hear, and that he'd be
a fool if he showed any traces of it next day. She became rather
thoughtful, however, and began at once clearing away things, just in
case anything happened: she succeeded in hiding or completely destroying all suspicious papers, books, and perhaps even political leaflets. At the same time she realized that she, her sister, her aunt, the
girl student, and her lop-eared brother had nothing much to be afraid
of. When the nurse came for her in the morning, she went to Mrs
Shatov's without giving it another thought. She was very anxious,
too, to find out whether it was true what her husband had told her
in a frightened and frenzied whisper that night – namely, whether
Peter Verkhovensky was right in thinking that Kirilov would shoot
himself for their general benefit.

But she arrived at Mrs Shatov's too late: having sent off the maid
and having remained alone in the house, Marie could not bear the suspense any longer. She got out of bed and, throwing the first piece of
clothing she could find – something very light and unsuitable for the
weather – round her, went down herself to Kirilov's cottage, thinking
that he would be the most likely person to tell her something about
the whereabouts of her husband. One can easily imagine the effect on
the woman who had been so recently confined of what she saw there.
It is remarkable that she did not read Kirilov's note, which lay conspicuously on the table, having, no doubt, overlooked it in her panic.
She rushed back to her room, snatched up the baby, and walked out
of the house with it into the street. It was a damp, misty morning. She
met no passers-by in such a deserted street. She kept running breathlessly through the cold, wet mud, and at last began knocking at the
doors of houses. In one house they would not open the door, in another house they were so long in opening it that she gave it up impatiently and began knocking at a third door. That was the house of
our merchant Titov. Here she raised a terrible din, wailing and declaring incoherently that her husband was murdered. Something was
known of Shatov and his story in the Titov household: they were

horror-stricken that, having been confined the day before, as she her-self had told them, she should be running about the streets so scantily dressed and in such cold, with her baby scarcely covered in her arms. At first they thought that she might be delirious, particularly as they could not make out whether it was Kirilov or her husband who was murdered. Realizing that they did not believe her, she was about to run out of the house, but she was restrained by force and, I am told, she screamed and struggled terribly. They went to Filippov's, and two hours later Kirilov's suicide, and the note he had left before his death, were known to the whole town. The police questioned Marie Shatov, who was still conscious. It was then discovered that she had not read Kirilov's note. But they could not find out from her why she should have jumped to the conclusion that her husband, too, had been mur-dered. She just kept screaming that if Kirilov had been murdered, then her husband was murdered, because they were together! By midday she sank into unconsciousness, from which she never recovered, and she died three days later. The baby had caught cold and died before her.

Not finding Marie and her baby in her room, and realizing that things had come to a head, Mrs Virginsky was about to run home. But she stopped at the gate and sent the nurse to ask the gentleman in the cottage whether Mrs Shatov was not there and whether he knew any-thing about her. The woman returned screaming at the top of her voice. Having persuaded her not to scream and not to breathe a word about what she had seen to anyone by the famous argument that she would 'get into trouble', Mrs Virginsky stole out of the yard.

Needless to say, the police came to question her that morning, as Mrs Shatov's midwife. But they did not get much out of her. She told them very coolly and in a most business-like manner everything she had seen and heard at Shatov's, but as to what had happened, she said that she knew nothing whatever and could not make head or tail of it.

One can imagine the uproar that arose in the town. A new 'sensa-tion', another murder! But there was something else, too: it became clear that there really was a secret society of assassins, revolutionary in-cendiaries, and rebels. Lisa's terrible death, the murder of Stavrogin's wife, Stavrogin himself, the fire, the ball for the governesses, the dis-soluteness of the people round Mrs Lembke. ... People insisted on see-ing a mystery even in Stepan Verkhovensky's disappearance. All sorts

of stories were going around about Nicholas Stavrogin. Towards the
evening Peter Verkhovensky's absence, too, became known. But,
strange to say, he was talked about least of all. What people were discussing most was the 'senator'. There was a crowd almost all morning
at Filippov's house. The police were, in fact, led astray by Kirilov's
note. They believed that Kirilov had murdered Shatov and then committed suicide. However, though the police were at a loss, they were
not altogether deceived. The word 'park', for instance, so vaguely inserted in Kirilov's note, did not baffle them, as Peter had expected it
would. They rushed off at once to Skvoreshniki, and that not only because there was no other park within miles of our town, but also by a
sort of instinct. For all the horrors of the last few days were directly
or indirectly connected with Skvoreshniki. That, at any rate, is my
theory. (I may add that Mrs Stavrogin had left early that morning in
pursuit of Mr Verkhovensky without any knowledge of what had
happened in the town.)

The body was found in the pond towards the evening of the same
day as a result of certain clues left by the murderers. On the scene of
the murder the police found Shatov's cap, which the murderers had
very carelessly forgotten to pick up. The police investigation and the
post-mortem evidence and certain deductions made from it at once
aroused the suspicion that Kirilov must have had accomplices. It became clear that a secret society, of which Kirilov and Shatov were
members, did exist, and that it was connected with the political leaflets.
But who were these accomplices? No one had the slightest suspicion
of the group of five that day. It was discovered that Kirilov lived like
a hermit and led so solitary a life that, as was explained in the note,
Fedka had found it possible to live with him for so many days while
the police were looking for him everywhere. What puzzled everybody was that not a single fact in all that confusing mass of evidence
pointed to anything that might lead to a satisfactory solution of the
mystery. It is hard to say what conclusions and absurdities our panic-
stricken society would have reached if the whole mystery had not
been suddenly solved next day, thanks to Lyamshin.

He broke down completely. What happened to him was what
Peter Verkhovensky had in the end begun to suspect would happen.
Left in the charge of Tolkachenko, and later of Erkel, he spent the
whole of the next day in bed, apparently calm, with his face turned

to the wall, almost refusing to say anything when spoken to. He therefore knew nothing of what was happening in the town that day. But Tolkachenko, who knew very well what was going on, took it into his head by the evening to throw up the role of Lyamshin's guard with which Peter Verkhovensky had entrusted him, and left the town for the country – that is, simply ran away. In fact, he lost his head, as Erkel had suspected that they all would. I may add, incidentally, that Liputin, too, disappeared from the town before noon on the same day. But it so happened that the police discovered his disappearance only in the evening of the following day, when they came to question the members of his family, who had been thrown into a panic by his absence, and were too frightened to say anything. But to continue about Lyamshin. As soon as he was left alone (relying on Tolkachenko, Erkel had gone home earlier), Lyamshin at once rushed out of his house and, of course, very soon learnt the position of affairs. Without even going back home, he, too, attempted to escape. But the night was so dark, and what he had to do was so terrible and so difficult to carry out, that after walking through two or three streets, he went back home and locked himself up in his room, where he stayed all night. In the morning he seemed to have attempted to commit suicide, but had not succeeded. He stayed locked up in his room till almost twelve o'clock, and then, suddenly, rushed off to the police. I am told he crawled on his knees, sobbed and shrieked, kissed the floor, crying that he was not worthy to kiss the boots of the high officials who stood before him. They calmed him and spoke nicely to him. His examination is said to have lasted three hours. He told them everything – absolutely everything: all the facts, all he knew, anticipating their questions, giving them information about things they were not interested in and they would never have thought of asking him. It turned out that he knew enough, and gave quite a satisfactory explanation of the whole affair; the tragedy of Shatov and Kirilov, the fire, the death of the Lebyatkins, and so on, all receded to the background. The first place was taken by Peter Verkhovensky, the secret society, the organization, and the network. Asked why so many murders, scandals, and villainies had been perpetrated, he replied with feverish haste that it was all done 'for the systematic destruction of society and the principles on which it was based, with the object of throwing everybody into a state of hopeless despair and of bringing about a state of general confusion: so that when society – sick, depressed, cynical, and godless, though with an intense yearning for some guiding idea and for self-preservation – had been brought to a point of collapse, they could suddenly seize power, raising the banner of revolt and supported by a whole network of groups of five, which were in the meantime recruiting new members and discovering the best methods of attacking the weak spots. He concluded by declaring that in our town Peter had made the first attempt to bring about such a systematic disorder, which was to serve as the programme for further activities and for all the groups of five. That, he added, was his own idea, his own theory, and he hoped that they would remember it and bear in mind how frankly and satisfactorily he had explained everything, for he might be of great service to the authorities in future. When he was asked to say definitely how many groups of five there were, he replied that there were thousands of them, and that all Russia was covered with a network of them, and though he could give no proof of his statement, I believe his answer was perfectly sincere. He produced only the programme of the society, printed abroad, and the plan for the development of a system of further activities, a draft document written in Peter Verkhovensky's hand. It appeared that Lyamshin had quoted the sentence about the 'undermining of the foundations' word for word from this document, without leaving out a single stop or comma, though he insisted that it was only a conjecture of his. So far as Mrs Lembke was concerned, he expressed himself very amusingly and even without being asked, and in anticipation of any further questions, to the effect that 'she is innocent' and that 'she has been made a fool of'. But the remarkable thing was that he exonerated Nicholas Stavrogin from every share in the secret society and from every collaboration with Peter Verkhovensky. (Lyamshin knew nothing about the secret and rather absurd hopes which Peter Verkhovensky reposed in Stavrogin.) The murder of the Lebyatkins, according to his evidence, had been planned only by Peter Verkhovensky, with the astute aim of involving Stavrogin, who had nothing to do with it, in the crime, and thus obtain a hold over him; but instead of the gratitude on which he had so rashly and so confidently counted, he had aroused only indignation and even despair in the 'noble-minded' Nicholas Stavrogin. He concluded his evidence about Stavrogin by declaring – again hurriedly and without being asked, though evidently as an intentional hint –

that he was a very important personage, but that there seemed to be some mystery about his real position; that he had been living in our town, as it were, incognito, that he had been entrusted with some mission or other, and that it was highly probable that he would come back to us from Petersburg (Lyamshin was convinced that Stavrogin was in Petersburg), but in quite a different capacity and in quite different surroundings and attended by persons of whom perhaps we, too, should soon hear, and that all this he had heard from Peter Verkhovensky, 'the secret enemy of Stavrogin'.

I'd better explain here that two months later Lyamshin confessed that he had exonerated Stavrogin on purpose, hoping that he would help him and would obtain a mitigation of his sentence in Petersburg and secure his acquittal on two counts and supply him with money and letters of introduction in Siberia. It can be gathered from his confession that he really had an exaggerated idea of Stavrogin's social position.

Virginsky was, of course, arrested on the same day and, in their excitement, the police arrested his whole family as well. (Mrs Virginsky, her sister, her aunt, and even the girl student were released long ago: I am told that Shigalyov, too, will most certainly be released in the near future because, unlike the other prisoners, he cannot be charged under any of the articles of the legal code; but all that is just talk so far.) Virginsky at once pleaded guilty; he was lying ill in bed with a high temperature when arrested. I am told that he seemed almost glad. 'It's a weight off my mind,' he is reported to have remarked. It is rumoured about him that he is giving his evidence without demur, but with a certain dignity, and that he has not given up a single one of his 'bright hopes', though at the same time cursing the political method (as opposed to the Socialist one) which he had been led so unwittingly and so stupidly to follow by 'the whirlwind of combined circumstances'. It seems that a favourable view is taken of his conduct at the time of the murder and that he can expect a mitigation of his sentence. So, at least, it is asserted in our town.

But I think it is extremely unlikely that anything can be done to mitigate Erkel's sentence. Ever since his arrest he has persisted in his refusal to give evidence and has misrepresented the truth as much as he could. So far not one word of regret could be got out of him. And yet he has aroused the pity of the severest judges – by his youth, by his helplessness, and by the obvious fact that he was only a fanatical victim of a political seducer, and, most of all, by his conduct to his mother, to whom he sent almost half of his scanty pay. His mother is now in our town; she is a delicate and ailing woman, prematurely aged; she weeps and literally grovels, imploring mercy for her son. But whatever happens, many people in our town are sorry for Erkel.

Liputin was arrested in Petersburg, where he had been living for a fortnight. A most extraordinary thing happened to him – something that is difficult to explain. It is said that he had a passport in a false name, that he could have very easily escaped abroad, and that he had a considerable sum of money on him, and yet he remained in Petersburg and did not attempt to go anywhere. He spent some time trying to find Stavrogin and Peter Verkhovensky, and then he suddenly took to drinking and began leading a life of wild dissipation, like a man who had lost all common sense and understanding of his position. He was arrested drunk in a Petersburg brothel. It is rumoured that he does not look down-hearted at all, that he tells lies in his evidence, and that he is getting ready for his approaching trial with a certain solemnity and hope(?). He even intends to make a speech at the trial. Tolkachenko, who was arrested in the country within ten days of his flight, conducts himself with incomparably more decorum. He does not lie or prevaricate, tells all he knows, does not try to justify himself, puts the blame on himself with all modesty, but is also inclined to become rhetorical; he speaks readily and a great deal, and when the subject of the peasants and their revolutionary(?) elements is touched upon, he even starts showing off and striking attitudes, eager to produce an effect. He, too, I understand, intends to make a speech at the trial. On the whole, neither he nor Liputin seem to be very much afraid, which is strange.

I repeat, the case is not by any means over. Now, three months afterwards, our local society has had time to rest, to recover, to rally, to formulate its own opinions, so much so that some even regard Peter Verkhovensky almost as a genius, or 'at least' as a man 'with the abilities of a genius'. 'Organization, sir!' they say at the club, raising a finger aloft. However, all this is very innocent, and there are not many people who talk like that. Others, on the other hand, do not deny that he possesses a certain acuteness of perception, but they claim that he is totally ignorant of life and is inclined to be terribly abstract

in his judgements, grotesquely and obtusely one-sided, and, as a result, extremely wrong-headed. About his moral qualities all are
agreed; about that there are no two opinions.

I really don't know whom to mention so as not to forget anyone.
Maurice Drozdov has gone away somewhere for good. Old Mrs Drozdov has sunk into senility. However, there still remains some very
sombre story to tell. I will confine myself to the bare facts.

On her return to the town, Mrs Stavrogin stayed in her town house.
All the accumulated news broke on her at once and gave her a terrible
shock. She shut herself up in her room. It was evening; they were all
tired, and went to bed early.

In the morning a maid handed Dasha a letter with a mysterious air.
The letter, according to her, arrived the night before when everyone
had gone to bed, and she dared not waken her. It did not come by
post, but by an unknown man who had given it to Alexey Yegorovich in Skvoreshniki. The butler had at once taken it to town and put
it into her hands, and immediately gone back to Skvoreshniki.

Dasha looked at the letter for a long time with a beating heart, not
daring to open it. She knew who it was from: it had been written by
Nicholas Stavrogin. She read the address on the envelope: 'To Alexey
Yegorovich, to be handed to Miss Shatov secretly.'

Here is the letter, word for word, without the correction of a single
mistake, in the style of a Russian landed gentleman who has never
mastered Russian grammar in spite of his European education:

'DEAR DASHA,

'At one time you wanted to come to me as my nurse and made me
promise to send for you when necessary. I am going away in two
days and I am not coming back. Last year, like Herzen, I took out
naturalization papers in the canton of Uri, and no one knows about it.
I have bought a little house there. I have still got twelve thousand
roubles; we shall go and live there. I do not want to go anywhere else
ever.

'The place is very dull, a narrow valley, the mountains constrict both
vision and thought. It is very gloomy. I chose it because there was a
little house for sale. If you don't like it, I shall sell it and buy another
house in some other place.

'I am not well, but I hope to get rid of my hallucinations with the
help of that air. This is the physical aspect; as for the moral one, you
know all about it, don't you?

'I have told you a great deal of my life. But not everything. I didn't tell everything even to you! By the way, I admit that in my conscience I regard myself as guilty of the death of my wife. I have not seen you since then, and that is why I make this admission. I am to blame for Lisa, too. But that you know; you predicted almost all that.

'Perhaps you'd better not come. It is awfully mean of me to ask you to come. And why, indeed, should you bury your life with mine? You are dear to me, and when I was depressed, I felt all right beside you; to you alone I could speak of myself aloud. That proves nothing. It was you who offered yourself as my "nurse" – it is your own expression. But why sacrifice so much? Also understand that I am not sorry for you, since I call you, and I do not respect you, since I expect you to come. And yet I do call you and I do expect you. In any case, I need your answer, because I shall have to go very soon. In that case, I shall go alone.

'I don't hope for anything in Uri; I am simply going there. I have not chosen a gloomy place on purpose. I have nothing to keep me in Russia – everything is as foreign to me there as anywhere else. It is true I disliked life there more than anywhere else; but even there I can't hate anything!

'I've tried my strength everywhere. You advised me to do that so as to learn "to know myself". When I tried it for my own sake and for the sake of self-display, it seemed infinite, as it has before in my life. Before your eyes I put up with a blow in the face from your brother; I acknowledged my marriage in public. But what to apply my strength to – that's what I've never seen and don't see now in spite of your words of approval in Switzerland which I believed. I can still wish to do something good, as I always could, and that gives me a feeling of pleasure. But the one and the other feelings are, as before, too petty, and strong they never are. My desires are never strong enough. They cannot guide me. You can cross a river on a tree-trunk, but not on a chip. I say this that you may not think that I am going to Uri with any sort of hopes.

'As always, I do not blame anyone. I tried wild debauchery and wasted my strength in it: but I do not like debauchery and I had no desire for it. You have been watching me lately. Do you know that I looked even upon our iconoclasts with envy and spite because I was jealous of their hopes? But you need not have been afraid. I could not possibly be their comrade, for I shared nothing with them. And I could not do it for fear or from spite, and not because I was afraid of the ridiculous – I cannot possibly be afraid of the ridiculous – but because I have, after all, the habits of a decent man, and it nauseated me. But if I had felt more envious or spiteful towards them, I might perhaps have gone with them. You judge for yourself how easy it has been for me and how I have been tossed about.

'Dear friend, tender and generous soul which I have divined! Perhaps you dream of giving me so much love and lavishing upon me so much that is beautiful in your beautiful soul that you hope at last to set up some aim for me by it? No – you'd better be more careful: my love will be as petty as I am myself, and you will be unhappy. Your brother told me that he who loses his ties with his native soil, loses his gods – that is, all his aims. One can go on arguing about anything for ever, but from me nothing has come but negation, with no magnanimity and no force. Even negation has not come from me. Everything has always been petty and lifeless. Kirilov, in his magnanimity, could not compromise with an idea and – shot himself. But I can see that he was so magnanimous because he was insane. I can never lose my reason and I can never believe in an idea to the same extent as he did. I cannot even be interested in an idea to the same extent. I can never, never shoot myself!

'I know that I ought to kill myself, to brush myself off the earth, like some loathsome insect; but I am afraid of suicide, because I am afraid of showing magnanimity.

'I know that it will be another delusion again, a delusion in an infinite sequence of delusions. What is the use of deluding oneself merely in order to play at magnanimity? Indignation and shame I can never feel, therefore not despair, either.

'Forgive me for writing so much. I have come to my senses now, and this has happened by accident. A hundred pages would be too little and ten lines are enough. Ten lines would be enough to ask you to be my "nurse".

'Since I left Skvoreshniki I have been living at the stationmaster's at the sixth station from the town. I met him at a drinking party in Petersburg five years ago. No one knows I am living here. Write to me in his name. I am enclosing the address.

'NICHOLAS STAVROGIN.'

Dasha immediately went to Mrs Stavrogin and showed her the letter. She read it and asked Dasha to go out of the room so that she might read it again; but she called her back very quickly.

'Will you go?' she asked almost timidly.

'I will,' Dasha replied.

'Get ready. We'll go together.'

Dasha looked questioningly at her.

'What is there left for me to do here? What difference does it make?

I, too, will become a citizen of Uri and end my days in a narrow valley. Don't worry, I won't be in your way.'

They began packing quickly to catch the midday train. But about half an hour later Alexey Yegorovich arrived from Skvoreshniki. He announced that Stavrogin had come back in the morning 'suddenly' by the early train and was at present in Skvoreshniki 'in such a state that he did not answer any questions; he walked through all the rooms and shut himself up in his own part of the house'.

'I decided to come and tell you about it, ma'am, without asking master's permission,' the butler added, with a very significant look.

Mrs Stavrogin gave him a piercing look and did not put any questions to him. The carriage was got ready immediately. She took Dasha with her. I am told that all the way to Skvoreshniki she kept crossing herself.

In Stavrogin's 'part of the house' all the doors were open and he was nowhere to be found.

'He isn't in the attic, is he?' Foma ventured to suggest cautiously.

It was remarkable that several servants followed Mrs Stavrogin to her son's rooms, while the others all waited in the large drawing-room. Never before would they have dared to permit themselves such a breach of etiquette. Mrs Stavrogin saw it and said nothing.

They went up to the attic. There were three rooms there: but he was not in any of them.

'Would Master have gone up there?' a servant asked, pointing at the door of the little room in the loft.

Indeed, the door of the loft, which was always closed, was wide open. The little room, practically under the roof, was reached by a long, terribly steep, and very narrow wooden staircase.

'I won't go there,' Mrs Stavrogin said, looking at the servants and turning terribly pale. 'Why should he go up there?'

The servants looked at her and said nothing. Dasha was trembling.

Mrs Stavrogin dashed up the narrow staircase; Dasha after her. But the moment she entered the little room, she uttered a scream and collapsed on the floor in a faint.

The citizen of the canton of Uri was hanging there behind the door. On the table lay a scrap of paper with the words: 'No one is to blame, I did it myself.' Beside it on the table lay a hammer, a piece of soap, and a large nail, evidently prepared in case of need. The strong silk cord with which Stavrogin had hanged himself had evidently also been prepared and chosen beforehand. It was thickly smeared with soap. All this was evidence of premeditation and consciousness to the last minute.

The verdict of our doctors after the post-mortem was that it was most definitely not a case of insanity.

Appendix

STAVROGIN'S CONFESSION

At Tikhon's*

I

STAVROGIN did not sleep all that night. He sat on the sofa, his eyes fixed on one point in the corner by the chest of drawers. All night long the lamp burnt in his room. At about seven o'clock in the morning he fell asleep where he sat and when his valet Alexey Yegorovich, according to the once and for all established routine, entered his room at exactly half past nine with his morning cup of coffee, he opened his eyes and seemed unpleasantly surprised that he should have been asleep so long and that it was so late. He hastily drank his coffee, hastily dressed himself and hurriedly left the house. To his valet's timid question, 'Any orders, sir?' he made no reply. He walked along the street, his eyes fixed on the ground, deep in thought, and only when he occasionally raised his head did he suddenly show a certain vague but intense anxiety. At one crossing not far from his house a crowd of peasants, about fifty or more, crossed the road; they walked sedately, almost in silence, with calm deliberation. At a little shop, where he had to wait a moment, he heard someone say that they were 'Shpigulin's workmen'. He hardly paid any attention to them. At last, at about half past ten, he reached the gates of our St Yefimyev Monastery of Our Lady, on the outskirts of the town, by the river. It was only there that he seemed to remember something that troubled and worried him. He stopped, hastily felt

---

*This chapter should have followed Chapter Eight of the Second Part (*Ivan the Crown-Prince*). The Editor of the *Russian Messenger* refused to publish it when the novel was being serialized in his journal. Dostoyevsky later tried to revise it, but finally decided to omit it from the first edition of the novel in 1873. It was discovered in 1921 among the papers left by Dostoyevsky's wife and first published separately in 1922.

something in his side pocket and – smiled. On entering the enclosure, he asked the first novice who happened to cross his path where he could find Bishop Tikhon, who was living in retirement in the monastery. The novice began bowing and immediately took him to see the bishop. Near the front steps at the end of the long two-storied monastery building a fat, greyhaired monk took him over authoritatively and promptly from the novice and led him along a long, narrow corridor, also bowing all the time, although because of his corpulence he could not bend low, but merely jerked his head frequently and abruptly. He went on begging him to follow, though Stavrogin was following him anyhow. The monk kept asking all sorts of questions and speaking of the Father Archimandrite, but, receiving no answer, became more and more deferential. Stavrogin could not help noticing that he was known here, although so far as he could remember he had only been there as a child. When they reached the door at the very end of the corridor, the monk opened it as though he were fully authorized to do so, inquired familiarly of the monk who looked after the bishop's rooms and who had rushed up to him whether they could go in, and without bothering to wait for a reply, flung the door wide open and, bending down, let the 'dear' visitor pass. On receiving a gratuity, he quickly disappeared, as though in flight. Stavrogin entered a small room and almost at that very moment a tall, lean man appeared at the door of the adjoining room. He was about fifty-five, was wearing a simple indoor cassock and looked a little ill. He smiled rather vaguely and had a strange, somewhat shy expression. This was Tikhon himself, the same Tikhon of whom Stavrogin had heard for the first time from Shatov and about whom he had since managed to pick up certain bits of information.

The information he had picked up was contradictory and of a rather varied nature, but it also seemed to have something in common, to wit, that those who liked and those who disliked Tikhon (and there were quite a few of those) were somehow not too keen to talk about him, those who disliked him probably because they did not think much of him, and those who were his supporters and even admirers out of a kind of considerateness, as though they were anxious to conceal something about him, some kind of weakness or even aberration. Stavrogin had found out that Tikhon had been living in the monastery for about six years and that the people who came to see him were ordinary peasants as well as persons of high social standing. Indeed, even in faraway Petersburg he had ardent admirers, though mostly among women. On the other hand, a portly elderly member of our club, a very pious one at that, expressed an opinion to the effect that 'that Tikhon was practically insane and quite certainly fond of the bottle'. Let me add here, although in anticipation, that the last statement was utter nonsense, but that the bishop did suffer from a chronic rheumatic affliction in the legs and was at times subject to some nervous spasms. Stavrogin also learnt that Tikhon had not been able to inspire any particular respect in the monastery itself either through weakness of character or 'because of his absent-mindedness which was unforgivable and quite unnatural in a person of his rank'.

It was said that the Father Archimandrite, a stern man who was very strict in regard to carrying out his duties as Father Superior and who was, besides, a well-known scholar, even seemed to feel a sort of hostility towards Tikhon and condemned him (not to his face, but indirectly) for his casual mode of life, and almost accused him of heresy. The attitude of the monks towards the saintly bishop was also, if not a little too casual, then at least, as it were, familiar. The two rooms which composed Tikhon's cell were also rather strangely furnished. Side by side with the heavy old bits of furniture, covered in worn leather, were three or four quite elegant pieces: a most expensive armchair, a large writing desk of excellent craftsmanship, an elegant carved bookcase, little tables, bookstands, all of which of course he had received as presents. There was a magnificent Bokhara carpet and next to it straw mats. There were engravings depicting scenes of 'fashionable society' and mythological subjects, and near them, in the corner, a large icon case, glittering with silver and gold icons, one of which was of a very ancient date and contained relics. His library, too, it was said, was of too contradictory and diverse a character: next to the works of the great Christian saints and martyrs were 'works of the stage and of fiction and, perhaps, even something much worse'.

After the first greetings, exchanged for some reason with undisguised awkwardness on both sides, as well as hurriedly and even mumblingly, Tikhon led his visitor to his study and, still as it were in a hurry, made him sit on the sofa in front of the table, while sitting down himself nearby in a wicker armchair. At that moment Stavrogin, to his own surprise, got completely flustered. It looked as though he were trying with all his might to do something extraordinary and unavoidable and, at the same time, something that he found almost impossible to do. For a moment or two he looked round the study quite obviously unaware of anything he was looking at; he fell into thought, but perhaps he hardly knew what he was thinking about. It was the stillness in the room that roused him from his stupor and it seemed to him suddenly that Tikhon cast down his eyes shyly and with a smile that was quite out of place. This at once aroused in him a feeling of disgust and revolt; he felt like getting up and going away; in his view, Tikhon was quite decidedly drunk. But at that moment Tikhon raised his eyes and looked at him with a gaze so firm and full of thought and, at the same time, with so unexpected and enigmatic an expression, that he nearly gave a start. Then all of a sudden something quite different occurred to him: he felt that Tikhon already knew why he had come, that he had already been forewarned about it (though no one in the whole world could have known the reason) and, if he did not speak first, it was because he was sorry for him and fearful of his humiliation.

'Do you know who I am?' he suddenly asked abruptly. 'Did I introduce myself when I came in or not? I'm sorry, I am so absent-minded . . .'

'You did not introduce yourself, but I had the pleasure of seeing you once four years ago, here in the monastery – by chance.'

Tikhon spoke very slowly and evenly, in a soft voice, enunciating his words clearly and distinctly.

'I wasn't in this monastery four years ago,' Stavrogin replied with what seemed like unnecessary discourtesy. 'I was here only as a child long before you were here.'

'Are you sure you haven't forgotten?' Tikhon asked guardedly and without insisting.

'No, I haven't forgotten,' Stavrogin insisted for his part rather obstinately. 'Why, it would be ridiculous not to remember. You must have just heard about me and formed some idea and that's why you imagined that you had seen me.'

Tikhon said nothing. It was just then that Stavrogin noticed that Tikhon's face sometimes twitched nervously, a reminder of his breakdown some years before. 'But I can see,' he said, 'that you are not well today. Perhaps it would be better if I went.'

He was even about to get up from his chair.

'Yes, I had violent pains in my legs yesterday and today and I slept little during the night.'

Tikhon stopped short. His visitor had suddenly sunk into a kind of strange reverie. The silence lasted for quite a long time, for two whole minutes.

'Why are you staring at me?' Stavrogin asked suddenly in alarm and suspiciously.

'I was looking at you and remembering what your mother looked like. You don't resemble one another, but there is a great deal of inner spiritual resemblance.'

'No resemblance at all, certainly no spiritual – none whatever!' Stavrogin declared, looking worried and insisting again without reason and without knowing himself why. 'You're just saying it out of – out of pity for my state of mind,' he suddenly blurted out. 'Good Lord, it must be my mother who visits you!'

'She does.'

'I didn't know. She never said anything about it to me. Often?'

'Nearly every month. More often sometimes.'

'She never, never told me. Never told me,' he repeated, looking for some reason terribly alarmed by that fact. 'I suppose you must have heard from her that I am insane,' he blurted out again.

'No, not that you are insane. Still, I have heard that said, but by others.'

'You must have an excellent memory if you can remember such trifles. Did you hear about that slap in the face too?'

'I did hear something about it.'

'You've heard everything then. You must have had plenty of time to listen to all that. About the duel too?'

'About the duel too.'

'You don't need newspapers here, do you? Did Shatov warn you about me?'

'No. I do know Mr Shatov, though, but I haven't seen him for a long time.'

'I see ... What's that map you've got there? Ah, a map of the last war! What on earth do you want that for?'

'I was looking it up while reading this book. A most interesting description.'

'Show me. Yes, not at all bad. A curious kind of reading for you, though.'

He pulled the book towards him and cast a perfunctory glance at it. It was a lengthy and talented account of the circumstances of the last war, not so much from the military as from the literary point of view. After turning over a few pages, he suddenly threw the book down impatiently.

'I simply don't know what I've come here for,' he said with an expression of disgust on his face, looking straight into Tikhon's eyes as though expecting an answer from him.

'You don't seem to be very well, either.'

'Yes, I daresay.'

And suddenly he told him, although rather briefly and abruptly, so that some of what he was saying was difficult to understand, that he was subject, especially at nights, to some kind of hallucinations, that he sometimes said or felt beside him the presence of some kind of malignant creature, mocking and 'rational', 'in all sorts of guises and in different characters, but it is the same, and it always makes me angry'.

These revelations were wild and confused and really seemed to come from a madman. But at the same time Stavrogin spoke with such strange frankness, never seen in him before, with such simple-heartedness, which was so out of character as far as he was concerned, that one could not help feeling that his former self had suddenly and quite unaccountably completely disappeared. He was not at all ashamed of revealing the fear with which he talked about his apparition. But it was all a matter of a moment and it was gone as suddenly as it had come.

'It's all a lot of nonsense,' he said quickly and with an awkward feeling of vexation, recollecting himself. 'I must go and see a doctor.'

'You certainly must,' Tikhon agreed.

'You speak with such conviction. Have you met anyone like me with the same kind of apparitions?'

'I have, but very rarely. I remember only one man like that in my life. He was an army officer. I met him after he had lost his wife whom he badly missed. I've only heard of one other case like it. Both of them afterwards went abroad for medical treatment. How long have you suffered from this?'

'For about a year, but it's all a lot of nonsense. I shall go and see a doctor. It's all nonsense, utter nonsense. It's myself, different aspects of myself. Nothing more. You don't think, do you, that because I've just added that – er – phrase I'm still doubtful and not sure that it's me and not in fact the devil.'

Tikhon looked up questioningly.

'Do you – do you really see him?' he asked in a tone of voice that implied that he did not doubt for a moment that it was nothing but an imagined, morbid hallucination. 'Do you actually see some kind of image?'

'It's funny you should harp on it after I've already told you that I see it,' Stavrogin said, growing more and more irritated with every word he uttered. 'Of course I see it. I see it as plainly as I see you. Sometimes, though, I see it and yet I'm not sure that I see it, and sometimes I don't know which of us is real – me or him. It's all a lot of nonsense. Surely, you couldn't possibly have imagined that it really was the devil, could you?' he asked, laughing and passing a little too abruptly into a derisive tone of voice. 'Well, I suppose it would be more in keeping with your profession, wouldn't it?'

'Most probably it is an illness, although . . .'

'Although what?'

'Devils most certainly exist, but one's idea of them may vary considerably.'

'You lowered your eyes just now,' Stavrogin interjected with an irritable laugh, 'because you feel ashamed that while believing in the devil I should pretend not to believe in him and cunningly confront you with the question: does he or does he not really exist?'

Tikhon smiled vaguely.

'Well, I want you to know that I am not at all ashamed, and to make amends for my rudeness to you I'll tell you seriously and unashamedly: I do believe in the devil, I believe canonically, in a personal devil, not an allegory, and I have not the slightest desire to try to elicit an answer from anyone. That's all I want to make clear to you.'

He gave an unnatural, nervous laugh. Tikhon looked at him with curiosity, but also, as it were, rather timidly and gently.

'Do you believe in God?' Stavrogin suddenly blurted out.

'I do.'

'It is said, isn't it, that if you have faith and tell a mountain to move, it will move. . . . However, forgive me for all this nonsense. All the same I'm rather curious to know: will you or will you not move a mountain?'

'If God commands, I will,' Tikhon said quietly and calmly, again dropping his eyes.

'Oh well, that's just the same as saying that God himself will move it. No, no. What about you, you yourself? As a reward for your belief in God.'

'Perhaps I won't move it.'

'Perhaps? Well, that's not bad, either. However, you're still doubtful, aren't you?'

'I'm doubtful because of the imperfection of my belief.'

'Good Lord, so you, too, don't believe absolutely?'

'Well, no. Perhaps I do not altogether believe absolutely,' replied Tikhon.

'That I would never have suspected, looking at you,' Stavrogin declared, glancing at him suddenly with some surprise, quite genuine surprise, which did not at all harmonize with the sarcastic tone of his preceding questions.

'Still, you at least believe that with God's assistance you will move, which is something. At any rate, you wish to believe. And you take the mountain literally too. It's an excellent principle. I have observed that the most advanced of our Levites show a strong inclination towards Lutheranism. All the same, this is better than the *très peu* of one of our archbishops, under the threat of the sword, it is true. I assume, of course, that you are also a Christian.'

Stavrogin spoke rapidly, his words pouring out uninterruptedly, now seriously, now derisively.

'Of thy Cross, O Lord, may I not be ashamed,' Tikhon almost whispered with a kind of passionate intensity, bowing his head still lower.

'But can one believe in the devil without believing in God?' Stavrogin said with a laugh.

'Oh, very much so,' said Tikhon, raising his eyes and smiling. 'You come across it everywhere.'

'I'm sure you find such a belief more acceptable than complete disbelief,' Stavrogin said, laughing loudly.

'On the contrary,' Tikhon replied with unconcealed gaiety and good humour, 'complete atheism is much more acceptable than worldly indifference.'

'Oh, I see, so that's what you really think!'

'The absolute atheist stands on the last rung but one before most absolute faith (whether he steps higher or not), while an indifferent man has no faith at all, nothing but dismal fear, and that, too, only occasionally, if he is a sensitive man.'

'I see . . . Have you read the Apocalypse?'

'I have.'

'Do you remember: "Write to the Angel of the Laodicean Church"?'

'I do.'

'Where's the book?' Stavrogin asked, thrown into a strange hurry and anxiety and searching with his eyes for the book on the table. 'I'd like to read you . . . You have a Russian translation, haven't you?'

'I know the passage, I remember it,' said Tikhon.

'You know it by heart? Let me hear it.'

He lowered his eyes quickly, rested both his hands on his knees and impatiently prepared to listen. Tikhon recited it word for word.

'And unto the angel of the church of the Laodiceans write: Those things saith the Amen, the faithful and true Witness, the beginning of the creation of God. I know thy works, that thou art neither cold nor hot: I would thou wert cold or hot. So that because thou art lukewarm, and neither cold nor hot, I will spue thee out of my mouth. Because thou sayest, I am rich and increased with goods, and have need of nothing; and knowest not that thou art wretched, and miserable and poor, and blind and naked . . .'

'Enough,' Stavrogin cut him short. 'I love you very much, you know.'

'I love you too,' Tikhon replied in a low voice.

Stavrogin fell silent and suddenly lapsed again into his old reverie. The same thing had happened fitfully before. This was the third time. He said 'I love' to Tikhon as though in a trance. At least he never expected it himself. Over a minute passed.

'Don't be angry with me,' whispered Tikhon, touching his elbow lightly with a finger and as though not really daring to do it.

Stavrogin started and frowned angrily.

'How did you know that I was angry?' he said quickly.

Tikhon was about to say something, but Stavrogin suddenly interrupted him in inexplicable alarm.

'Why did you assume that I simply had to be angry? Yes, I was furious. You are quite right. Just because I had said to you "I love". You are right, but you're a coarse cynic, you have a very low opinion of human nature. I might not have been furious, if I had not been myself but someone else. However, it is not a question of anyone else, but of me. All the same, you're an eccentric and quite crazy.'

He was getting more and more irritated and, strangely, did not seem to care what he said.

'Listen, I don't like spies and psychologists, at least not those who creep into my soul. I don't invite anyone into my soul. I have no need of anyone. I can look after myself. You think I'm afraid of you,' he went on, raising his voice and looking up defiantly. 'You're quite convinced that I came to tell you some "terrible secret", and you are waiting for it with the monkish curiosity you are capable of. Well, then, I want you to know that I shall not reveal anything to you, no secret, for I can perfectly well do without you.'

Tikhon looked at him firmly.

'You were surprised that the Lamb should love a cold man more than a merely lukewarm one,' he said. 'You don't want to be merely lukewarm. I can't help feeling that you are about to take an extreme, perhaps even a terrible, decision. I beg you not to torture yourself and to tell me everything.'

'So you are quite sure that I have come with something.'

'I . . . I guessed it,' said Tikhon, lowering his eyes.

Stavrogin was rather pale, his hands trembled a little. For a few seconds he stared fixedly and in silence, as though on the point of taking a final decision. At last he took some printed sheets out of his side pocket and put them on the table.

'These are the sheets which are meant to be distributed,' he said in a faltering voice. 'I want you to know that if one man reads them I shall not conceal them any longer and they will be read by everyone. That's settled. I don't need you at all because my mind is made up. But do read them. Don't say anything while you're reading them. Tell me everything after you've read them.'

'Shall I read?' Tikhon asked hesitantly.

'Yes, read. I don't mind.'

'I'm afraid I shall not be able to read without my glasses. The print is very small. Foreign.'

'Here are your glasses,' Stavrogin said, handing him the glasses from the table and leaning against the back of the sofa. Tikhon did not look at him and became absorbed in the reading.

2

The print really was foreign: three sheets of ordinary notepaper printed and stitched together. It must have been printed secretly on some foreign press abroad. At the first glance the sheets of paper looked like some political pamphlet. The heading read: From Stavrogin.

I insert this document verbatim in my chronicle. I have allowed myself to correct some numerous spelling mistakes which rather surprised me, for the author was after all an educated and even well-read man (relatively speaking, of course). I made no alterations in the style in spite of its irregularities. It is in any case clear that the writer was, above all, not a literary man.

I shall allow myself one more remark, though I am anticipating. In my opinion, this document is a morbid work, the work of the devil who took possession of that man. It reminds me of a man who is suffering from an acute pain and is tossing about in bed trying to find a position to relieve his pain even for a moment. And not even to relieve his pain, but to change it, if only for a moment, for another kind of suffering. In a situation like that there can be, of course, no question of the position being either beautiful or rational. The basic idea of the document is an undisguised, terrible need for retribution, the need for the cross, for a public execution. And yet this need for the cross in a man who does not believe in the cross is in itself an 'idea', as Stepan Trofimovich put it once, though on a different occasion. On the other hand, the whole of this document is something wild and reckless, though apparently written with a different intention. The author declares that he could not help writing it, that he was 'forced' to write it, and that seems quite likely to have been the case. He would have been glad to have that cup pass from him, if only he could, but it seems he really could not do so and jumped at the first favourable opportunity for indulging in a new act of violence. Yes, indeed, a sick man tosses about in bed and wishes to change one kind of suffering for another, and now the fight against society seems to him to be the easiest position and he throws out a challenge to it.

Indeed, the very fact of such a document presupposes the existence of a new and unpardonable challenge to society.

But who knows, perhaps all this, that is to say, all these sheets of paper and their intended publication, is again nothing but the governor's bitten ear, only in a different form. Why this should even occur to me now when so many things have already been explained is something I can't understand. I adduce no proof and I certainly do not maintain that the document is false, that is to say, that it has been completely made up and invented. More likely, the truth ought to be sought somewhere midway. However, I've already run on too far ahead: I'd better turn to the document itself. This is what Tikhon read:

From Stavrogin.

I, Nikolai Stavrogin, a retired army officer, lived in Petersburg in 186 . . ., leading a life of dissipation in which I found no pleasure. At that time I had three lodgings during a certain period. In one of them I lived myself, in furnished rooms with board and service. Maria Lebyatkin, my lawful wife, also lived there at the time. My other two lodgings I rented by the month to accommodate my two mistresses: in one I received a high society woman who was in love with me and in the other her maid, and for some time I toyed with the idea of bringing the two of them together, so that the society woman and her servant girl should meet each other in my rooms. Knowing the character of both, I anticipated a great deal of fun from that amusing encounter.

While secretly making all the necessary arrangements for that meeting, I had to visit more often one of the two lodgings in a large house in Gorokhovaya Street, for that was the place where I and the maid used to meet. I had only one room there on the fourth floor, which I rented from some Russian working class people. They themselves lived in the next room, which was much smaller, so much so that the door dividing the two rooms was always open, which was what I wanted. The husband, who was working at some office, was away from morning till night. His wife, a woman of about forty, used to cut up old clothes and refashion them into new, and she used to leave the house quite often to deliver her sewing. I remained alone with her daughter, quite a child in appearance. Her name was Matryosha. Her mother loved her, but often chastised her and, as is customary with these people, shouted at her a lot. This little girl waited on me and made up my bed behind the screen. I declare that I have forgotten the number of the house. Having made some inquiries recently, I now know that the old house was pulled down and a new and very large house built on the site of two or three houses. I have also forgotten the name of my landlord (I may never have known it even at the time). I remember that the woman was called Stepanida and I believe her patronymic was Mikhailovna. I do not remember him. I suppose if one were seriously to make some inquiries at the Petersburg police stations, one might be able to trace them. Their flat was in the courtyard, in the corner. It all happened in June. The house was painted a light blue colour.

One day I missed my penknife from the table. I did not want it at all. It was just lying about there. I told my landlady about it without thinking that she would thrash her daughter for it. But she had been screaming at her daughter for the loss of some rag and had even pulled her hair. But when that rag was found under the tablecloth, the little girl did not utter a word of complaint but just looked on in silence. I noticed that and it was then that I saw for the first time the little girl's face, which until that moment I had not particularly noticed. She had flaxen hair and a freckled face, quite an ordinary face, but it had a great deal of childishness in it, and it was very gentle, quite extraordinarily gentle. Her mother resented the fact that her daughter did not complain for having been beaten for nothing and she made as if to strike her with her fist, but stopped herself in time. It was just then that the subject of my penknife came up. There was no one in the flat besides the three of us. The little girl was the only one to go behind the screen in my room. The woman flew into a rage for having the first time punished the girl unjustly, rushed up to the besom, pulled some twigs out of it, and gave the girl a thrashing in front of me until her body was covered in weals, and that in spite of the fact that the girl was already in her twelfth year. Matryosha did not scream while she was being flogged, probably because I was there, but she gave a funny sort of sob at each blow. Afterwards she sobbed bitterly for a whole hour.

But before that happened something else caught my eye: at the very moment my landlady was rushing up to the besom to pull out the twigs, I saw my penknife on my bed where it must have fallen from the table. It occurred to me at once not to tell them about it so that she should be thrashed. I made my decision instantly; at such moments I always begin to breathe heavily. But I am determined to tell everything without flinching so that nothing should remain concealed any longer.

Every extraordinarily disgraceful, infinitely humiliating, vile and, above all, ridiculous situation in which I happened to find myself in my life, invariably aroused in me not only intense anger, but also a feeling of intense pleasure. It was the same in moments when I was committing a crime and in moments when my life was in danger. If I were to steal something, I should at the time of committing the theft have felt like dancing with pleasure at the thought of the depth of my villainy. It was not the villainy that I loved (here my mind was absolutely clear). What I liked was the feeling of rapture caused by the agonizing consciousness of my baseness. I felt just the same when, standing at the barrier, I waited for my opponent to fire: I experienced the same shameful and frenzied feeling, and on one occasion I did so with quite extraordinary force. I admit that I often sought it myself, for to me it was the strongest of any sensation of that kind. Whenever I received a slap in the face (and I received two in my life), it was there, too, in spite of my terrible anger. But I controlled my anger at the time, my feeling of pleasure exceeding anything that could be imagined. I never spoke to anyone about it, not even hinted at it, concealing it as something shameful and disgraceful. I did not experience that sensation but merely intense anger when I was once beaten up in a pub in Petersburg and dragged by the hair. Not being drunk, I merely put up a fight. But if I had been seized by the hair and forced down by the French vicomte who, when I was abroad, slapped me on the cheek and whose lower jaw I shot off for it, I should have experienced the same feeling of ecstasy and most likely have felt no anger at all. So it seemed to me then.

I am saying all this so that everyone should know that that feeling never got hold of me entirely, but that I always remained in control of my mental faculties (indeed, everything depends on that). Although it would take possession of me to a point of madness, to a point when it became an obsession, it would never be to a point when I lost control of myself entirely. When I was about to explode, I was able to overcome it entirely before it reached its climax. But I never wanted to stop it myself. I'm convinced that I could have lived all my life like a monk in spite of the brutish voluptuousness with which I have been endowed and which I always evoked. I am always master of myself when I want to be. And so I should like it to be known that I do not want to plead irresponsibility for my crimes either on the ground of my background or on the ground of illness.

The thrashing over, I put the penknife in my waistcoat pocket and, without uttering a word, left the house and threw it away in the street, having first walked a long way so that no one should ever find out. Then I waited two days. Having had a good cry, the little girl became even more taciturn; but I am sure she felt no resentment against me. I cannot help feeling, though, that she must have felt somewhat ashamed to have been punished in such a way in front of me. But I am sure that she blamed only herself for feeling ashamed, as any child would.

It was during those two days that I put to myself the question whether I should not go away and give up the plan I had devised. I felt immediately that I could, that I could give it up any time and at any moment. About that time I contemplated killing myself, for I was suffering from the disease of indifference, though I am not sure that that was the real reason. But during those two or three days (for I had to wait till the little girl had forgotten all about it) I committed a theft probably as a diversion from my obsession or maybe just for the fun of it. That was the only theft in my life.

A large number of people lived in those rooms. Among them was a civil servant with his family, who lived in two furnished rooms.

He was about forty, not altogether a fool, of decent appearance, but poor. I did not become friends with him and he was afraid of the company that surrounded me there. He had only just drawn his salary of thirty-five roubles. What chiefly made me think of it was that at that particular moment I really needed money (though four days later I received money by post), so that I seemingly stole out of want and not for fun. It was done impudently and without any attempt at concealment. I simply entered his flat when he and his wife and children were having their dinner in the other little room. His folded uniform lay on a chair near the door. The idea occurred to me suddenly when I was still in the corridor. I put my hand into the pocket of his uniform and took out the purse. But the civil servant must have heard a slight movement, for he looked out of his room. I believe he did see at least something, but as he did not see it all, he did not, of course, believe his eyes. I said that I was passing down the corridor and had come to see the time by his clock. 'I'm afraid it has stopped,' he said, I went out.

I was drinking a great deal at the time and I always had a crowd of people in my rooms, Lebyatkin among them. I threw away the purse with the small change and kept the notes. There were thirty-two roubles, three red notes and two yellow. I changed the red note at once and sent out for champagne; then I sent the second red note and the third. Four hours later, in the evening, the civil servant was waiting for me in the corridor.

'You did not accidentally throw my uniform from the chair when you came in a few hours ago?' he asked. 'I found it lying on the floor.'

'I'm sorry I don't remember. Was your uniform there?'

'Yes, sir, it was.'

'On the floor?'

'First on the chair, then on the floor.'

'Did you pick it up?'

'I did.'

'Well, so what more do you want?'

'Well, sir, in that case it's all right.'

He dared not speak out and he dared not say anything to anybody in the house, so timid are these people. Anyhow, they were all terribly afraid of me in that house and respected me. Later I enjoyed exchanging glances with him in the corridor once or twice. Soon I got bored with it.

Three days later I returned to Gorokhovaya Street. The mother was going out somewhere with a bundle; her husband, of course, was not at home. Matryosha and I were alone in the flat. The windows were open. The house was full of workmen and all day long the sound of hammers and singing could be heard from all the floors. We had already been there for an hour. Matryosha sat in her small room on a little bench with her back to me and was busy with her needle. At last she suddenly began to sing softly, as she often did. I took out my watch and saw that it was two o'clock. My heart began to pound. I got up and began stealing towards her. On their window-sill were many pots of geranium and the sun was shining very brightly. I sat down quietly on the floor beside her. She gave a start and at first looked terribly frightened and jumped up. I took her hand and kissed it quietly, forced her down on the bench again and began looking into her eyes. The fact that I kissed her hand suddenly amused her like a child, but only for one second, for she jumped up precipitately the next moment, this time looking so frightened that a spasm passed across her face. Her eyes were motionless with terror and her lips began to quiver as though she were on the verge of tears, but she did not scream all the same. I kissed her hand again and put her on my knee. Then she suddenly drew back and smiled as if ashamed, but with a kind of wry smile. Her face flushed with shame. I was whispering to her all the time, as though drunk. At last a most strange thing happened, something I shall never forget, something that quite amazed me: the little girl flung her arms round my neck and all of a sudden began to kiss me frenziedly. Her face expressed complete rapture. I nearly got up and went away, so shocked was I to find this sort of thing in a little creature for whom I suddenly felt pity.

When all was over, she looked embarrassed. I did not try to reassure her and no longer caressed her. She looked at me, smiling timidly. Her face suddenly appeared stupid to me. She was getting more and more embarrassed with every minute that passed. At last she covered her face with her hands and stood motionless in a corner with her face to the wall. I was afraid she might be frightened again as she had been a short while earlier, and silently left the house.

I can only imagine that all that had happened to her must have seemed utterly hideous, a deathlike horror. In spite of the Russian swearwords which she must have heard from her very cradle and all sorts of strange conversations, I am quite convinced that she did not yet understand anything. I am sure that in the end it must have seemed to her that she had committed a terrible crime and was guilty of a mortal sin. 'She had killed God.'

That night I had that punch up in the pub which I have mentioned in passing. But I woke up in my rooms in the morning: Lebyatkin had taken me home. On awakening my first thought was: had she told them or not? It was a moment of real fear, though as yet not very intense. I was very gay that morning and terribly kind to everybody, and the whole gang was very pleased with me. But I left them all and went to Gorokhovaya Street. I met her downstairs in the entrance hall. She was coming from the shop where she had been sent for chicory. On catching sight of me, she looked terribly frightened and ran off upstairs. When I entered, her mother had already bashed her for rushing in like mad, which helped to conceal the real reason for her fright. So far then everything was all right. She seemed to have hidden herself away somewhere and did not come in while I was there. I stayed there for an hour and then went away.

Towards evening I was again overcome by fear, this time incomparably more intense. No doubt I could have denied it all, but I might be found out and I could already see myself as a convict in a Siberian prison. I had never felt fear and, except for this incident in my life, I never before or after was afraid of anything. Certainly not of Siberia, though I might have been sent there more than once. But this time I was frightened and really felt fear, I don't know why, for the first time in my life – a very painful feeling. Besides, I conceived such a hatred for her that evening in my room that I decided to kill her. The recollection of her smile was the chief reason for my hatred. I began to feel contempt and intense loathing for her because after it was all over she had rushed off to a corner of the room and covered her face with her hands. I was seized with an inexplicable rage, then I became feverish, and when towards morning I began to feel that I had a temperature, I was again overcome by panic which became so intense that I never experienced a torment more violent. But I no longer hated the little girl, at least my hatred did not reach such a paroxysm as on the previous evening. I perceived that intense fear completely ousts hatred and the feeling of revenge.

I woke about mid-day feeling well and was surprised at the force of yesterday's sensations. However, I was in a bad mood and again felt compelled to go to Gorokhovaya Street in spite of all my aversion. I remember that I wanted terribly to have a quarrel with someone on the way, a real violent quarrel. But on arriving at Gorokhovaya Street I unexpectedly found there Nina Savelyevna, the maid, who had been waiting for me for an hour. I did not love that girl at all and she was afraid that I might be angry with her for coming unasked. But I suddenly felt very glad to see her. She was not bad-looking, modest and with the manners the lower middle classes set such store by, so that my landlady had been telling me for a long time what a nice girl she was. I found them both having coffee together and my landlady highly pleased with their pleasant conversation. In the corner of their small room I caught sight of Matryosha. She stood gazing motionless at her mother and the visitor. When I came in she did not hide herself as before and did not run away. I could not help observing that she had grown very thin and that she had a temperature. I was nice to Nina and locked the door leading into the landlady's room, which I had not done for a long time, so that Nina left looking very happy. I saw her off myself and did not return to Gorokhovaya Street for two days. I was bored with the whole business. I decided to put an end to it all by giving up my rooms and leaving Petersburg.

But when I came to give notice I found my landlady greatly worried and upset: Matryosha had been ill for three days, she had a high temperature and was delirious at night. I asked of course what she said in her delirium (we were talking in whispers in my room), and she whispered that her daughter was saying 'terrible things', such as 'I killed God'. I offered to call a doctor at my own expense, but she would not hear of it. 'God willing, it will pass, she isn't in bed all the time, she goes out during the day, she has just run round to the shop.' I made up my mind to see Matryosha alone and, as the landlady informed me in passing that she had to go to the Petersburg suburb about five o'clock, I decided to come back in the evening.

I had lunch in a pub. Exactly at a quarter past five I returned. I always let myself in with my key. There was no one there except

Matryosha. She was lying in the small room on her mother's bed behind the screen and I saw her looking out. But I pretended not to have noticed. All the windows were open. The air was warm, even hot. I paced the room for a while and then sat down on the sofa. I remember everything to the last moment. It positively gave me pleasure not to talk to Matryosha but to keep her in suspense. I don't know why. I waited for a whole hour when she suddenly rushed out from behind the screen herself. I heard both her feet hit the floor when she jumped out of bed, then her fairly quick steps, and presently she stood on the threshold of my room. She stood and gazed in silence. I was so mean that my heart missed a beat with joy: I was so glad that I had not given in and waited for her to come out first. During the days that I had not seen her even once so close since our last meeting, she really had grown very thin. Her face had shrunk and her head, I was quite certain, was hot.

Her eyes had grown large and she gazed at me without blinking with a dull curiosity, as I thought at first. I sat still, looked and did not move. Then suddenly I again felt that I hated her. But very soon I realized that she was not a bit afraid of me, though she was perhaps still delirious. But she was not delirious at all. She suddenly began shaking her head at me, as ingenuous and unmannered people do when they disapprove of someone. Then suddenly she raised her tiny fist and began shaking it at me from where she stood. At first this gesture seemed ridiculous to me, but soon I could stand it no longer. Her face was full of such despair which was quite unbearable to see on the face of a child. She was still shaking her fist at me threateningly and shaking her head reproachfully. I got up, took a few steps towards her in fear, and began speaking cautiously to her, quietly and kindly, but I realized that she wouldn't understand. Then suddenly she covered her face impulsively with both hands as she had done at that time, moved off and stood at the window with her back to me. I went back to my room and also sat down at the window. I simply cannot understand why I did not leave then, but remained as though waiting for something. Soon I again heard her quick steps. She went out through the door on to the wooden landing at the top of the stairs. I ran up to my door at once, opened it a little and was just in time to see Matryosha go into the tiny box-room, which was like a hen-coop, next to the lavatory. A very curious thought flashed through my mind. To this day I cannot understand why it should have come into my head so suddenly. So it would seem that it was at the back of my mind all the time. I left the door ajar and again sat down by the window. Of course it was still impossible to believe in the thought that had flashed through my mind, 'but still . . .' (I remember everything, and my heart beat violently).

A minute later I looked at my watch and made a note of the time with absolute accuracy. Why I had to know the time so exactly I can't tell, but I seem to have been able to do so and, anyway, at that moment I wanted to make a note of everything. So that I remember now what I observed and I can see it as if it were happening at this moment. The evening was drawing in. A fly was buzzing over my head and kept settling on my face. I caught it, held it in my fingers, and put it out of the window. Very loudly a cart drove into the yard. Very loudly (and for some time before) a tailor, sitting at a window in the corner of the yard, sang a song. He sat at his work and I could see him. It occurred to me that since no one had seen me when I walked through the gates and went upstairs, it was quite unnecessary for anyone to see me when I should be going downstairs. I moved my chair quietly from the window so that I could not be seen by the lodgers. I picked up a book, but put it down again and began looking at a tiny red spider on the leaf of a geranium and lost count of the time. I remember everything to the very last moment.

Suddenly I whipped out my watch. Twenty minutes had passed since she went out of the room. My guess was assuming the aspect of reality. But I decided to wait for exactly another quarter of an hour. It had also crossed my mind that she might have returned and that I might have failed to hear her. But that was impossible: there was dead silence and I could hear the whirr of every midge. Suddenly my heart started pounding again. I took out my watch: there were three minutes to go; I sat them out, though my heart was pounding painfully. Then I got up, put on my hat, buttoned my overcoat and looked round the room to make sure that I had left no trace of my presence there. I moved the chair nearer to the window just as it had stood there before. At last I opened the door quietly, locked it with my key and went up to the little box-room. It was closed, but not bolted. I knew that it was never bolted, but I did not want to open it.

I stood on tiptoe and began looking through the chink. At that very moment, just as I raised myself on my toes, I recalled that when I sat at the window and looked at the little red spider and then lost count of the time, I had been thinking how I should stand on tiptoe and look through this chink. In putting in this trifling detail I want to prove without a shadow of doubt to what an extent I was quite clearly in the full possession of my mental faculties and how much I am responsible for everything. I looked through the chink a long time, for it was very dark there, but not so dark as to prevent me at last from seeing what I wanted. . . .

At last I decided to leave. I came across no one on the stairs. Three hours later we were all drinking tea in our shirtsleeves in our rooms and playing with a pack of old cards. Lebyatkin recited poems. We were telling lots of stories, all of them, as it happened, clever and amusing and not as foolish as usual. No one was drunk, though there was a bottle of rum on the table, Lebyatkin alone helping himself to it.

Prokhor Malov once observed that 'when Stavrogin is contented and not depressed, all our lads are cheerful and talk cleverly'. I remembered it at that time which shows that I was cheerful and contented and not depressed. This was what it looked like from the outside. But I remember that I was conscious of being a low and despicable coward simply because I was glad of having escaped and that I should never again be an honourable man (neither here, nor after death, nor ever). And something else happened to me at the time: it seems that the Jewish saying: 'The thing you do may be bad, but it doesn't smell', just fitted me. For although I felt that I was a scoundrel, I was not ashamed of it and not in the least upset. When sitting at the tea table and chattering away with them, I formulated for the first time in my life what appeared to be the rule of my life, namely, that I neither know nor feel good or evil and that I have not only lost any sense of it, but that there is neither good nor evil (which pleased me), and that it is just a prejudice: that I can be free from any prejudice, but that once I attain that degree of freedom I am done for. This I formulated for the first time at that very moment when we were all having tea, when I laughed so much and talked such a lot of nonsense with them. But that is also why I remember it all. Old ideas which everyone knows often suddenly appear as if they were quite new, sometimes even after one has lived for fifty years.

But all the time I was waiting for something. So it came about that at eleven o'clock the houseporter's little daughter came running from my landlady in Gorokhovaya Street with the news that Matryosha had hanged herself. I went with the little girl and saw that the landlady herself did not know why she had sent for me. She wailed and screamed hysterically, there were lots of people and policemen. I remained there for a while and then went away.

The police scarcely troubled me, though I had to answer the usual questions. But except that the girl was ill and at times delirious and that I had offered to call a doctor at my expense, I said nothing that might have been taken down in evidence. They did question me about myself and the penknife. I told them that my landlady had given the girl a beating, but that that was nothing. No one knew of my having been there that evening.

For about a week I did not call round there. I went there long after the funeral to give notice. The landlady was still crying, although she was already busying herself as usual with her rags and her sewing. 'You see, sir,' she said to me, 'I hurt her feelings because of your pen knife.' But she did not seem to blame me particularly. I settled my account and gave as my excuse for leaving that I could not possibly receive Nina Savelyevna after what had happened in the house. She said again a few nice things about Nina Savelyevna at parting. Before leaving, I gave her five roubles over and above what I owed her.

The main thing was that I was bored with life, sick and tired to death of it. I should have completely forgotten the incident in Gorokhovaya Street after the danger had passed just as I had forgotten everything else that happened at the time, if I had not kept remembering angrily what a coward I had been.

I vented my anger on anyone I could. It was at that time, but not for any particular reason, that I took it into my head to ruin my life somehow or other, but only in as disgusting a way as possible. A year earlier I had been thinking of shooting myself: however, something better turned up.

One day, looking at Maria Lebyatkin, who occasionally did some charring in my rooms and who in those days had not yet gone mad but was just an ecstatic idiot who was madly in love with me in secret (which my friends had found out), I suddenly decided to marry her. The idea of the marriage of Stavrogin to a low creature like that excited my nerves. One could not imagine anything more outrageous. At all events I did not marry her merely because of 'a bet for a bottle of wine after a drunken dinner'. Kirilov and Peter Verkhovensky, who happened to be in Petersburg at the time, as well as Lebyatkin and Prokhor Malov (now dead) acted as witnesses. No one else ever knew anything about it, and they gave me their word to say nothing about it. The silence always seemed to me rather disgusting, but it has not been broken till now, though I did intend to make it public. I do so now together with the rest.

After the wedding I left for the country to stay with my mother. I left because I wanted some distraction. In our town I left behind me the idea that I was mad, an idea that still persists and that undoubtedly does me harm, as I shall explain later. Then I went abroad and spent four years there.

I went to the East, to Mount Athos, where I stood through midnight masses which went on for eight hours, I went to Egypt, lived in Switzerland, went even to Iceland; I spent a whole year in Goettingen University. During the last year I struck up an acquaintance with an aristocratic Russian family in Paris and two young Russian girls in Switzerland. About two years ago, passing a stationer's shop in Frankfort, I noticed among the photographs for sale a portrait of a little girl, wearing an elegant dress but looking very like Matryosha. I bought the photograph at once and, on returning to my hotel room, I placed it on the mantelpiece. There it lay untouched for a whole week. I never once looked at it and when I left Frankfort I forgot to take it with me.

I mention it only to show to what an extent I could get the better of my memories and how indifferent I had become to them. I repudiated them all *en masse* and the whole pile of them obediently disappeared every time I wanted it to disappear. I always found my memories of the past boring and I never could discuss the past as almost everybody does, particularly as it was so hateful to me, like everything else that concerned me. As for Matryosha, I even forgot her photograph on the mantelpiece. One spring, travelling through Germany a year ago, I absentmindedly went on past the station where I had to change trains and found myself on the wrong line. I got out at the next station. It was past two o'clock in the afternoon, a bright, lovely day. It was a tiny German town. I was shown to a hotel. I had to wait, for the next train was not due before eleven o'clock at night. I was quite glad of my adventure, for I was not in any particular hurry to go anywhere. The hotel was very small and rather shabby, but it was all covered in greenery and surrounded with flower-beds. I was given a very small room. I had an excellent meal and as I had been travelling all night I soon fell sound asleep at four o'clock in the afternoon.

I had quite an extraordinary dream. I had never had one like it before. In the Dresden gallery there is a picture by Claude Lorraine, called, I think, 'Acis and Galatea' in the catalogue. I always called it The Golden Age. I don't know why. I had seen it before, but now, three days before, as I passed through Dresden, I saw it again. I went specially to the gallery to have a look at it and for all I know I must have stopped at Dresden for the sole purpose of seeing it again. It was that picture that I saw in my dream, not as a painting, but as a fact.

A corner of the Greek archipelago; blue, caressing waves, islands and rocks, a foreshore covered in lush vegetation, a magic vista in the distance, a spell-binding sunset – it is impossible to describe it in words. Here was the cradle of European civilization, here were the first scenes from mythology, man's paradise on earth. Here a beautiful race of men had lived. They rose and went to sleep happy and innocent; the woods were filled with their joyous songs, the great overflow of their untapped energies passed into love and unsophisticated gaiety. The sun shed its rays on these islands and that sea, rejoicing in its beautiful children. A wonderful dream, a sublime illusion! The most incredible dream that has ever been dreamed, but to which all mankind has devoted all its powers during the whole of its existence, for which it has sacrificed everything, for which it has died on the cross and for which its prophets have been killed, without which nations will not live and cannot even die. I seem to have lived through all these sensations in my dream; I do not know what exactly I dreamed about, but the rocks and the sea and the slanting rays of the setting sun – I still seemed to see them all when I woke and opened my eyes, which were literally wet with tears for the first time in my life. A sensation of happiness that I had never experienced before went right through my heart till it hurt. It was already evening; through the window of my little room, through the green leaves of the flowers on the windowsill, a whole bunch of bright slanting rays of the setting sun poured upon me and bathed me in light. I shut my eyes quickly once more as though panting to bring back the vanished dream, but suddenly in the centre of that bright, bright light I beheld a tiny point. Suddenly the point began to take on a kind of shape, and all at once I could clearly see a tiny red spider. I immediately remembered the red spider on the leaf of the geranium which was also bathed in the rays of the setting sun. I felt as if something had gone right through me. I raised myself and sat on my bed. . . .

(That is all how it happened then!)

I saw before me (Oh, not really! Oh, if it had only been a real phantom!) Matryosha, emaciated and with feverish eyes, exactly as she was when she stood on the threshold of my room and, shaking her head, shook her tiny fist at me. Nothing has ever been so distressing to me! The pathetic despair of a helpless creature with an unformed mind threatening me (with what? what could she do to me, O Lord?), but blaming of course only herself! Nothing like that has ever happened to me. I sat there till nightfall without moving and forgetful of the time. I do not know and I cannot tell to this day whether this is what is called remorse or repentance. But what I find so unbearable is the image of her standing on the threshold and threatening me with her small raised fist, just the way she looked at me then, just that shaking of her head. It is this that I cannot stand, for since then it has appeared to me almost every day. It doesn't come itself. I myself summon it up and I cannot help summoning it up though I cannot live with it. Oh, if only I could ever see her real self, even if it were were a hallucination!

Why then does not any memory of my life arouse in me anything like this? Have I not had many memories, some of them perhaps much worse in the judgment of men? Why only one hatred and that one, too, stirred up by my present state, for before I forgot it cold-bloodedly and dismissed it out of hand?

I wandered about after that for almost a whole year and tried to find some occupation. I know that I can dismiss Matryosha from my mind any time I wish. I am as much in command of my will as ever.

But the whole point is that I never wanted to do so, I do not want to myself and never shall want to. It will go on like that till I lapse into madness.

Two months later in Switzerland I had an outburst of the same kind of passion accompanied by the same kind of uncontrollable impulses as I used to have in the past before. I felt a terrible temptation to commit a new crime, namely to enter into a bigamous marriage (for I was already married); but I fled on the advice of another girl whom I told almost everything, even that I was not at all in love with the girl whom I desired so much and that I could never love anyone. Besides, that new crime would not have rid me of Matryosha.

I therefore decided to have these pages printed and take three hundred copies of them to Russia; when the time comes I shall send some of them to the police and the local authorities; simultaneously I shall send them to the editors of all the newspapers with a request to publish them, and to many persons in Petersburg and in Russia who know me. It will also be published abroad in translation. I realize that legally I have nothing to fear, not to any considerable extent at any rate. It is I alone who am informing against myself, for I have no accuser; besides, there is no evidence against me, or what there is is extremely slight. There is, finally, the prevailing idea that I am not in my right mind, an idea which I am quite sure my family will make use of in their efforts to quash any legal prosecution that might be dangerous to me. I make this statement, incidentally, in order to prove that I am in full possession of my mental faculties and realize my position. So far as I am concerned, there will remain those who will know everything and they will look at me and I at them. I want everyone to look at me. Whether it will make things easier for me I do not know. I fall back on it as my last resource.

Once more: if a thorough search were made in the records of the Petersburg police something might perhaps be discovered. Matryosha's parents may still be living in Petersburg. The house, of course, will be remembered. It was painted a light blue colour. As for me, I shall not go anywhere and for some time (for a year or two) I shall always be found at Skvoreshniki, my mother's estate. If summoned, I will appear anywhere.

NIKOLAI STAVROGIN.

3

The reading went on for about an hour. Tikhon read slowly and, perhaps, read some passages twice over. All that time Stavrogin sat silent and motionless. Strangely enough, the trace of impatience, absentmindedness and even delirium that had been on his face all the morning, had almost disappeared, being replaced by calmness and a kind of sincerity that gave him an air almost of dignity. Tikhon took off his glasses and began to speak, at first rather guardedly.

'Don't you think certain corrections could be made in this document?'

'Why?' asked Stavrogin. 'I wrote sincerely.'

'In the style perhaps a little?'

'I forgot to warn you,' Stavrogin said quickly and sharply with a forward thrust of his body, 'that all you say would be useless. I shall not give up my intention. Don't try to dissuade me. I shall publish it.'

'You did not forget to warn me about it before I began to read.'

'Never mind,' Stavrogin interrupted harshly. 'Let me repeat again: however strong your objections may be, I shall not give up my intention. Please note that by this happy or unhappy phrase – think of it what you like – I am not at all trying to suggest you should start at once objecting or attempt to persuade me.'

'I could hardly raise any objections or try to persuade you to give up your intentions. The idea of yours is a great idea, nor could a Christian idea be expressed more perfectly. Further than the wonderful act of heroism you have conceived repentance cannot go unless . . .'

'Unless what?'

'Unless it was in fact repentance and in fact a Christian idea.'

'I wrote sincerely.'

'You seem to wish to make yourself out to be worse than your heart would desire,' said Tikhon, gradually growing bolder: the 'document' had evidently made a strong impression on him.

'Make myself out to be? I repeat: I did not "make myself out to be" and I certainly did not try to "show off".'

Tikhon quickly cast his eyes down.

'This document comes straight from a heart which has been

mortally wounded – do I understand you right?' he said emphatically and with extraordinary warmth. 'Yes, this is repentance and the natural need for it that has got the better of you, and you have taken the great road, a miraculous road. But you seem already to hate and despise beforehand all those who will read what you have described here and to challenge them to battle. You were not ashamed to confess your crime, why are you ashamed of repentance?'

'Ashamed?'

'Yes, ashamed and afraid.'

'Afraid?'

'Terribly. Let them look at me, you say. But what about you? How will you look at them? Some passages in your statement are overstressed. You seem to be admiring your psychology and clutching at every detail merely with the intention of surprising your reader by a callousness which is not in you. What else is this but a proud challenge by an accused to the judge?'

'Where's the challenge? I eliminated all personal discussions.'

Tikhon made no answer. His pale cheeks flushed.

'Let's drop it,' Stavrogin dismissed it sharply. 'Let me now ask you a question. We've been talking for five minutes since you read that (he nodded in the direction of the sheets of paper) and I cannot detect any expression of shame or aversion in you. You're not very squeamish, are you?'

He did not finish.

'I shall conceal nothing from you: what horrified me was the vast unused energy that was deliberately spent on some abomination. As for the crime itself, many people sin like that, but they live in peace and quiet with their conscience, even considering it the unavoidable misdemeanours of youth. There are also old men who sin the same way, not taking it seriously and regarding it as innocent amusement. The whole world is full of these horrors. But you felt the whole depth of your degradation which is extremely rare.'

'You haven't begun respecting me after what you've been reading, have you?' Stavrogin said with a wry smile.

'I'm not going to give you a straight answer to this. But there certainly is not, nor can there be, any greater or more terrible crime than what you did to that girl.'

'Let's stop judging people by our own yardstick. Perhaps I do not suffer as much as I've written and perhaps I really have told a lot of lies about myself,' he added unexpectedly.

Tikhon again made no comment.

'And what about the girl with whom you broke off in Switzerland?' Tikhon began again. 'Where, may I ask, is she at this moment?'

'She's here.'

Again there was silence.

'Perhaps I did tell you a lot of lies about myself,' Stavrogin repeated insistently. 'Still, what does it matter if I do challenge them by the coarseness of my confession, seeing that you have noticed the challenge? I shall make them hate me even more, that's all. That ought to make things easier for me.'

'You mean spite in you will rouse spite in others and, hating them, you will feel happier than if you had accepted their pity.'

'You're right. You know,' he laughed suddenly, 'they may perhaps call me a jesuit and a sanctimonious hypocrite after the document. Ha, ha, ha! Don't you think so?'

'Why, of course, there's sure to be such an opinion. And how soon do you hope to carry out your intention?'

'Today, tomorrow, the day after tomorrow, how do I know? Very soon, though. You're right. I think it will indeed happen like that: I shall make it public suddenly and indeed in some revengeful and hateful moment when I hate them most.'

'Answer me one question, but sincerely, me alone, only me,' Tikhon said in quite a different tone of voice. 'If anyone forgave you for this [Tikhon pointed at the sheets of paper] not anyone whom you respect or fear, but a complete stranger, someone you will never know, who, reading your terrible confession, forgave you inwardly, in silence, would that make you feel better or would it make no difference to you?'

'Better,' replied Stavrogin in an undertone. 'If you forgave me,' he added, lowering his eyes, 'I'd feel much better too.'

'On condition that you forgave me also,' Tikhon said in a voice full of emotion.

'False humility! These monastic formulas, you know, are not at all elegant. Let me tell you the whole truth: I want you to forgive me and one, two or three others with you, but not everybody else – I'd

rather everybody else hated me. I want this so that I should be able
to bear it with humility. . . .'

'And what about universal pity for you? Would you not be able
to bear that with the same kind of humility?'

'Perhaps I could not. But why do you . . .'

'I feel the extent of your sincerity and I am, of course, much to
blame for not being able to approach people. I've always felt it to
be a great fault in myself,' Tikhon said with great sincerity, looking
straight into Stavrogin's eyes. 'I'm saying this only because I'm
terribly afraid for you,' he added. 'There's almost an impassable abyss
before you.'

'You don't think I shall be able to stand it? That I shan't be able to
bear their hatred?' Stavrogin said with a start.

'Not only hatred.'

'What else?'

'Their laughter,' Tikhon almost forced himself to say in a very
soft whisper.

Stavrogin looked embarrassed; his face expressed alarm.

'I knew you'd say that,' he said. 'So you thought me a very
comical person after reading my "document", did you? Don't
worry and don't look so disconcerted. I expected it.'

'The horror will be general and, needless to say, more false than
sincere. People fear only what directly threatens their interests. I'm
not talking of pure souls: they will be horrified inwardly and accuse
themselves, but they will not be noticed, for they will be silent.
But the laughter will be universal.'

'I'm surprised what a low opinion you have of people, how loath-
somely you regard them,' Stavrogin said with some bitterness.

'I know you won't believe me,' cried Tikhon, 'but I judged more
by myself than by other people.'

'Did you? Is there also something deep inside you that makes you
amused at my misfortune?'

'Who knows? Perhaps there is. Oh, perhaps there is!'

'Enough. Show me what it is exactly that strikes you as ridiculous
in my manuscript? I know what it is myself, but I want you to put
your finger on it. And say it as cynically as possible. Indeed, say it
with all the sincerity of which you are capable. And let me tell you
again that you are a terrible eccentric.'

'Why, even in the form of this great penance there is something ridiculous. Oh, don't try to persuade yourself that you won't emerge victorious from it,' he cried suddenly, almost beside himself. 'Even this form [he pointed to the manuscript] will triumph provided you sincerely accept the contumely and the vituperation. It always ended in the most ignominious cross becoming a great glory and a great force, if the humility of the great deed was sincere. It is quite possible that you will be comforted even in your lifetime.'

'So you think there's something ridiculous perhaps in the form alone, do you?' Stavrogin insisted.

'And in the substance. The ugliness will kill it,' Tikhon whispered, lowering his eyes.

'Ugliness? What ugliness?'

'Of the crimes. There are crimes that are truly ugly. Crimes, whatever their nature, are more impressive, more, as it were, picturesque, the more blood and the more horror. But there are crimes that are shameful and disgraceful quite apart from the horror, crimes that are, as it were, a little too inelegant. . . .'

Tikhon stopped short.

'You mean,' Stavrogin broke in excitedly, 'you find that I cut a rather ridiculous figure when I kissed the hand of a dirty little girl. I understand you very well. You despair of me just because it is so ugly, so loathsome. No, I don't mean that it is loathsome, but that it is shameful and ridiculous. You think it is this that I shall be able to bear least of all.'

Tikhon was silent.

'Now I understand why you asked me about the girl from Switzerland. I mean, whether she was here.'

'You're not prepared, not hardened,' Tikhon whispered timidly. 'You're uprooted, you do not believe.'

'Listen, Father Tikhon: I want to forgive myself. That is my chief purpose, my only purpose!' Stavrogin said suddenly, with gloomy rapture in his eyes. 'I know that only then will the apparition vanish. That is why I seek boundless suffering. Seek it myself. Don't try to frighten me or spite will kill me.'

The sincerity of his outburst was so unexpected that Tikhon got up.

'If you believe,' Tikhon exclaimed rapturously, 'that you can forgive yourself and obtain that forgiveness for yourself in this world through suffering, if you set that purpose before you with faith, then you believe in everything already. Why, then, did you say that you did not believe in God?'

Stavrogin made no answer.

'God will forgive you for your unbelief, for you respect the Holy Spirit without knowing him.'

'By the way, Christ will forgive, won't He?' asked Stavrogin with a wry smile, quickly changing his tone, and there was an unmistakable touch of irony in the tone of his question.

'It says in the Book, "And whosoever shall offend one of these little ones" – remember. According to the Gospel, there is no greater crime.'

'You simply don't want a good old row and you're laying a trap for me, dear old Father Tikhon,' Stavrogin mumbled casually and with annoyance, trying to get up. 'In short, what you want is that I should settle down, get married and end my days as a member of our club, visiting your monastery on every church festival. Real to goodness church penance! Isn't that so? Still, as an expert in the human heart you foresee, no doubt, that it will certainly be so and that all that remains to be done now is to ask me nicely, just as a matter of form, for I am only waiting to be asked, isn't that so?'

He chuckled affectedly.

'No, it isn't that kind of penance,' Tikhon cried warmly, without taking any notice of Stavrogin's laugh and remark. 'I'm getting quite another one ready for you. I know an elder, not here, but not far from here, a hermit and an ascetic, a man of such great Christian wisdom as is beyond your or my understanding. He will listen to my entreaties. I'll tell him everything about you. Go to him, share his retreat as a novice, stay under his guidance for five or seven years, for as long as you may find necessary yourself. Take a vow and by this great sacrifice you will acquire everything you crave for and even what you do not expect, for you cannot possible conceive now what you will obtain.'

Stavrogin heard him out gravely.

'You propose that I enter that monastery as a monk.'

'You need not live in the monastery, you need not take your vows as a monk, you can be just a novice, a secret, not an open one. It can be arranged for you to go on living in society. . . .'

'Leave me alone, Father Tikhon,' Stavrogin interrupted him, looking disgusted and getting up. Tikhon also got up.

'What's the matter with you?' Stavrogin suddenly cried, looking intently at Tikhon almost in fear.

Tikhon stood before him, his hands clasped in front of him, a painful spasm passing for a moment across his face as though from a terrible fright.

'What's the matter with you? What's the matter?' Stavrogin kept repeating, rushing forward to support him. He thought that Tikhon was going to fall.

'I see, I see, just as if it were happening in front of me now,' Tikhon cried in a voice that penetrated the soul and with an expression of great sadness, 'that you, poor, lost youth, have never been so near another and still greater crime as you are at this moment.'

'Calm yourself,' pleaded Stavrogin, who was really alarmed for him. 'Perhaps I shall still postpone it . . . You're quite right. . . .'

'No, not after the publication, but before it. A day, an hour perhaps before the great step, you will commit a new crime as a way out, and you will commit it solely in order to avoid the publication of these pages.'

Stavrogin was shaking with anger and almost with fear.

'You damned psychologist!' he cut him short suddenly in a rage and, without looking back, left the cell.